Lord of Lies

Voyager

Lord of Lies

Book Two of the Ea Cycle

DAVID ZINDELL

HarperCollins*Publishers*

HarperCollins*Publishers*
77–85 Fulham Palace Road,
Hammersmith, London W6 8JB

www.voyager-books.com

Published by HarperCollins*Publishers* 2003
1 3 5 7 9 8 6 4 2

A catalogue record for this book
is available from the British Library

hb ISBN 0 00 224757 7
tpb ISBN 0 00 224758 5

Typeset in Giovanni by Palimpsest Book Production Limited
Polmont, Stirlingshire

Printed and bound in Great Britain by
Clays Ltd, St Ives plc

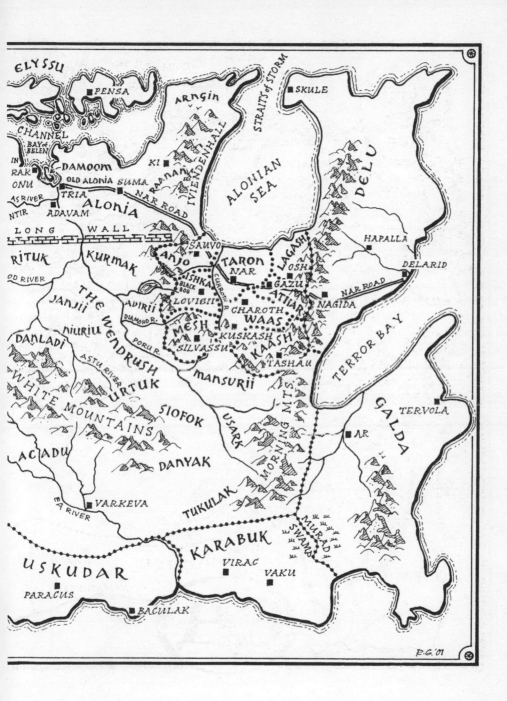

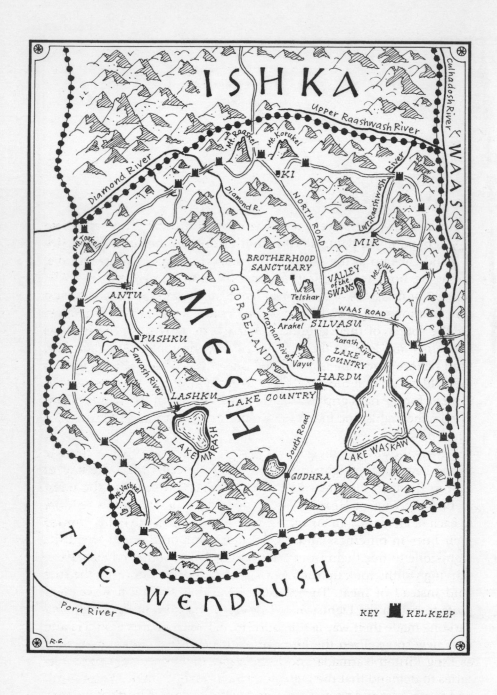

1

A man's fate, the scryers say, is written in the stars. Beneath these fiery points of light, we come forth from our mother earth to live and gaze up at the sky in wonder, to dance and dream and die. Some are born to be tillers of the soil or huntsmen; others to be weavers or minstrels or kings. Murderers might find the bright Dragon constellation pulling at their souls while saints seek in the Seven Sisters for the source of their goodness. A few turn away from the heavens altogether and look to the fire of their own hearts to forge their fate. But I believe that there is one – and one only – who is chosen to bear the golden cup that the angels sent to earth long ago. Even as a sword is made for the hard grip of a warrior, only the Shining One was meant to take the Lightstone in his hands and bring forth its secret light for all to behold.

Others, however, believe other things. In the year 2813 of the Age of the Dragon, the Lightstone having been wrested from the hall of Morjin the Liar, the Great Red Dragon himself, word that the quest to find the Cup of Heaven had been fulfilled spread like a wildfire to each of Ea's lands. In far-off Hesperu, the slaves in the fields gripped their hoes in bitterness and prayed that some hero might wield the Lightstone to free them from their bondage; in conquered Surrapam, starving youths took up their bows and dreamed of hunting the true gold instead of meat. The priests of Morjin's Kallimun wove their plots to regain the Lightstone while minstrels from fallen Galda and Yarkona made their way across burning plains to sing its wonders and hear new songs. Even the kings of realms still free – great men such as King Kiritan Narmada and King Waray of Taron – sent out emissaries to demand that the Lightstone be brought to them. From north and south, east and west, they joined a whole army of lordless knights, exiles, scryers, seekers and rogues who journeyed to Mesh. To the castle of my father, Shavashar Elahad, they came to view the wonder

1

of the Lightstone. For there, behind the castle's white granite walls, my friends and I had brought it to be guarded against the world's evil and greed.

On a warm Sunday afternoon in late spring, with the cherry trees in the foothills in full bloom, I joined Master Juwain Zadoran and Sar Maram Marshayk at the top of the castle's great Adami tower. It was our first gathering in nearly half a year – and our first in Master Juwain's guest chamber since we had set out on the great Quest half a year before that. Master Juwain had recently returned from Taron in great haste, and had called this meeting to discuss matters pertaining to the Lightstone – and other things.

The room in which he resided when visiting my father's castle was large and well-lit. Four arched windows looked out upon the white-capped peaks of Arakel and Telshar and the other mountains to the west. Four more windows gave a good view of the rest of the castle below us: the round and graceful Swan Tower and the Tower of the Stars; the courtyards full of wagons and knights on panting horses arriving for the evening's feast; the great shield wall cut with crenels along its top like a giant's teeth. Largest of all the castle's structures was the massive keep, a huge cube of granite, and the adjoining great hall where the Lightstone was displayed for all to see. I might rather that it had been brought into the fastness of Master Juwain's chamber, with its comforts of thick Galdan carpets, bright tapestries and many cases full of books, but I reminded myself that the golden cup was not meant to be kept in private by Master Juwain or Maram – or even me.

As I closed the door behind me and crossed the chamber's tiled floor, Master Juwain of the Great White Brotherhood called out to me with a disquieting formality: 'Greetings, Lord Valashu Elahad, Knight of the Swan, Guardian of the Lightstone, Prince of Mesh.'

He stood with my best friend, Maram, by the chamber's west windows, looking at me strangely as if trying to peer beneath the mantle of these newly-won titles to apprehend a deeper thing inside me. His silver-gray eyes, large and luminous as moons, were full of wisdom and his great regard for me. Although some called him an ugly man, with his brown, squashlike nose and head as bald and lumpy as walnut, the light of kindness seemed to burn through these surface features and show only a being of great beauty.

'Sir,' I called back to him. I had addressed him thus for ten years, since the day that I had begun my studies at the age of eleven at the Brotherhood's sanctuary in the mountains nearby. Although that happier time had long passed and we had been companions on the great Quest, he was still a Master Healer and Ea's greatest scholar, and he deserved no less. 'It's good to see you!'

I rushed forward to embrace him. Despite being well into his middle years, his short, stocky body was still hard from the various disciplines to which he subjected it. A long, brown tunic of homespun wool covered him from neck to knee. From a chain, over his heart, dangled a gold medallion showing a sunburst and plain cup in relief. Seven rays streaked out of this cup to fall upon the medallion's rim. King Kiritan had bestowed such gifts upon all who had vowed to make the quest to find the Lightstone. Maram and I wore our medallions as did Master Juwain: in bittersweet memory and pride.

'It's good to see you, Val,' Master Juwain said, smiling at me. 'Thank you for coming.'

Maram, dressed in a bright scarlet tunic emblazoned with two gold lions facing each other, did not like being left out of the greetings. He stepped up to me and threw his arms around me, a feat made difficult by his big, hard belly, which pushed out ahead of him like a boulder. He was a big man with a great, blazing heart of fire, and he drummed his hamlike hands against my back with such force that they threatened to stave-in my ribs.

'Val, my brother,' he said in his booming voice.

When he had finished pummeling me, we stood apart regarding each other. We *were* true brothers, I thought, and yet our lineages were as different as the river country of gentler climes and the highlands of Mesh. We were different, too. Although he was tall, for an outlander, I looked down upon him. He had his people's curly chestnut hair, while mine was that of my father and mother: long, straight and black, more like a horse's mane than the hair that covered the heads of most human beings. His face was of mounds of earth and rounded knolls, soft, pliable as red river clay; mine was all clefts and crags, cut as with walls of rock: too stark, too hard. He had a big, bear's nose while mine was that of an eagle. And where his eyes were brown and sweet like alfalfa honey, my eyes, it was said, were black and bright as the night-time sky above the winter mountains.

'Ah, Val,' he said, 'it's good to see *you* again, too.'

I smiled because we had taken breakfast together that very morning. Although Maram had been born a prince of Delu, he had resided in my father's kingdom for half a dozen years. Once a novice of the Brotherhood under Master Juwain, he had renounced his vows and was now a sort of permanent guest in the castle. I looked at the jeweled rings on the fingers of his left hand and the single silver ring encircling the second finger of his right hand. It was set with two large diamonds: the ring of a Valari knight. Thus my father had honored him upon the fulfillment of the quest, declaring that Maram, in spirit at least, now belonged to my people.

Master Juwain invited us to sit at his tea table, inlaid with mother of pearl and precious woods, and years ago imported from Galda at great cost. He bent over one of the chamber's fireplaces and retrieved a black iron pot. After heaping some green leaves into it, he brought it to the table and set it down on a square tile, along with three blue cups.

'Ah, I think I'd rather have a bit of beer,' Maram said, eyeing his empty cup. 'I don't suppose –'

'I'm afraid it's time for tea, Brother Maram,' Master Juwain said. He, at least, remained true to his vows to renounce wine, women and war. 'We've need for clear heads today – and tonight.'

Maram regarded the tea pot as he sat pulling at his thick, curly beard. I looked at Master Juwain and said, 'What is troubling you, sir? It's said that you nearly killed your horse returning from Taron.'

'My poor horse,' Master Juwain murmured, shaking his head. 'But I had heard that King Kiritan's emissaries were on the road toward Mesh, and I wanted to be here when they arrived. Have they?'

'Only an hour after yourself,' I told him. 'Count Dario Narmada and a small army of knights. It will be hard to find rooms for so many.'

'And the emissaries from Sakai? I had heard that the Red Dragon has sent seven of his priests to treat with your father.'

'That is true,' I said. 'They've remained sequestered in their chamber since their arrival three days ago.'

I listened to the distant echoes and sounds that seemed to emanate from the stone walls around me. A wrongness pervaded the castle, like a child's scream, and a sense of dread clawed at my insides. I thought of the five Kallimun priests and the cowled yellow robes that hid their faces; I prayed that none of them had been among the priests that had tortured my friends in Morjin's throne room in Argattha.

'They should never have been allowed into Mesh,' Master Juwain said. He touched the enlarged opening of his ear that one of Morjin's priests had torn with a heated iron. 'That's almost as dangerous as allowing the Red Dragon's poisonous dreams into our minds.'

'Dangerous, yes,' I agreed. 'But my father wishes to hear what they have to say. And he wishes it to be known that all are welcome in Mesh to view the Lightstone.'

I looked out the east windows where the city of Silvassu was spread out beneath the castle. It was a small city, whose winding streets and sturdy stone houses gave way after about a mile to the farmland and forest of the Valley of the Swans. And every inn and stable, I thought, was full with pilgrims who hoped to stand before the Lightstone. Even the fields at Silvassu's edge were dotted with the brightly colored pavilions of nobles and knights who could not find rooms in the castle, and who disdained sleeping in a common inn with exiles, adventurers, soothsayers and all the others who had flocked to Mesh.

'We can guess what the Red Priests will say: lies and more lies,' Master Juwain told us. 'But what of King Kiritan's emissaries? Could he have agreed to the conclave?'

My father, King Shamesh, upon the deliverance of the Lightstone to Mesh, had sent emissaries of his own to Alonia and Delu, to the Elyssu and Thalu at the edge of the world. And to Eanna and Nedu, too, and of course, to the Nine Kingdoms of the Valari: to all of Ea's Free Kingdoms my father had sent a call for a conclave to be held in Mesh, that an alliance might be made to oppose Morjin and his rampaging armies.

'Ah, now that the Lightstone has been found,' Maram said, 'King Kiritan will *have* to agree to the conclave. And everyone else will follow Alonia's lead – won't they, Val?'

In truth, it had been I who had asked my father to call the conclave. For it had been I – and my friends – who had seen with our own eyes the great evil that Morjin was working upon the world.

'The Valari kings,' I said, 'will never follow the lead of an outland king, not even Kiritan. We'll have to find other means of persuading them.'

'Indeed, but persuading them toward what end?' Master Juwain asked. 'Merely meeting in conclave? Making an alliance? Or making war?'

This word, dreadful and dark, stabbed into my heart like the long sword I wore at my side. It was as heavy and burdensome as the steel rings of the mail that encased my limbs and pulled me down toward the earth. Once, in my father's castle, in my home, I had dressed otherwise, in simple tunics or even in my hunting greens. But now that I was Lord Guardian of the Lightstone, I went about armored at all times – especially with the Red Dragon's priests waiting to get close to a small golden cup.

'If we make an alliance,' I told Master Juwain, 'then perhaps we won't have to make war.'

It was my deepest dream, I told myself, to end war – forever.

'An alliance,' Master Juwain said, shaking his head. 'I'm afraid that the Red Dragon will never be defeated this way.'

'It is not necessary to defeat him,' I said. 'At least not outright, in battle. It will be enough if we secure the Free Kingdoms. Then, with

5

the Brotherhoods working at the Dragon Kingdoms from within, and the Alliance doing the same from without, the realms Morjin has conquered can be won back one by one.'

'I see how your thinking has progressed since I went away.'

'It is not just my thinking, sir. It's that of my father and brothers.'

'But what of the Lightstone, then?'

'It is the Lightstone,' I said, 'that makes all this possible.'

'But what of the one for whom the Lightstone was meant? Have you given thought, as I've asked, to this Shining One?'

Master Juwain poured our tea then. Through the steaming liquid, I watched the little bits of leaves swirl about and then settle into my cup.

'There's been thought of little else,' I told him. 'But the Free Kingdoms should be strengthened so that the Shining One can come forth without fear. *Then* Morjin will have much to fear.'

'Indeed, he would,' Master Juwain said. 'But will the Red Dragon be content while you make alliance against him? Your way, I'm afraid, is that of the sword.'

'Perhaps,' I said, letting my hand rest on the seven diamonds set into the swan-carved hilt of my sword.

'We've all seen enough evil for one lifetime, Val.'

I drew my sword then, and held it so that it caught the sunlight streaming in through the western window. Its long blade, wrought of silustria, shimmered like a silver mirror. Its edges were keen enough to cut steel even as the power of the silustria cut through darkness and gave me to see, sometimes, the truth of things. The sword's maker had named it Alkaladur. In all the history of Ea, no greater work of gelstei had ever been accomplished, and none more beautiful.

'This sword,' I said to Master Juwain, 'is not evil.'

'No, perhaps not. But it can do evil things.'

Maram took a sip of his tea and grimaced at its bitterness. Then he said, 'There can't be enough evil for Morjin and all his kind.'

'Do not speak so,' Master Juwain said, holding up his hand. 'Please, Brother Maram, I ask you to –'

'*Sar* Maram, I'm called now,' Maram said, patting the sword that he wore sheathed at his side. It was a Valari kalama, like unto length and symmetry as my sword, only forged of the finest Godhran steel.

'Sar Maram, then,' Master Juwain murmured, bowing his bald head. 'You mustn't wish evil upon anyone – not even the Red Dragon himself.'

'*You* say that? After he blinded Atara with his own hands? After what he did to you?'

'I have another ear,' Master Juwain told him, tapping his large, knotty

6

finger against the side of his head. 'And if I could, I'd wish to hear no talk of revenge.'

'And *that*,' Maram said, 'is why you're a master of the Brotherhood and I am, ah, what I am. Evil deserves evil, I say. Evil should be opposed by any means.'

'By any means *virtuous*.'

'But surely virtue is to be seen in the end to be accomplished. And what could be a greater good than the end of Morjin?'

'The Red Dragon, I'm afraid, would agree with the first part of your argument. And that is why, Brother Maram, I must tell you that —'

'Please, sir, call me Maram.'

'All right,' Master Juwain said with a troubled smile. Then he looked deep into Maram's eyes and said, 'To use evil, even in the battle against evil, is to become utterly consumed by it.'

I held my sword pointing north toward the castle's great hall where the Lightstone was kept. Alkaladur's silver gelstei flared white in resonance with the greater gold gelstei of which the cup was wrought. Its bright light drove back the hate that threatened to annihilate me whenever I thought of Morjin and how he had torn out the eyes of the woman I loved.

'It is . . . not evil to guard the Lightstone for the Maitreya,' I forced out, speaking the ancient name for the Shining One. In Ardik, Maitreya meant Lord of Light. 'Can we not agree that this is our best means of fighting Morjin?'

I sheathed my sword and took a sip of tea. It was indeed bitter, but it cleared my head and cooled the wrath poisoning my heart.

'Very well,' Master Juwain said, 'but I'm afraid we've little time for making alliances or battles. We must find the Maitreya before Morjin does. We must seek him out in whatever land has given him birth.'

At this, Maram took another sip of tea and smiled to try to hide the dread building inside him. 'Ah, sir, it almost sounds as if you're proposing another quest to find this Maitreya. Please tell me that you're thinking of no such thing?'

'A moment ago,' Master Juwain reminded him, 'you were ready to oppose Morjin in any way you could.'

'I? I? No, no – you misunderstand me,' Maram said. 'I have already done my part in fighting Morjin. More than my part. We all have.'

I said nothing as I took a long sip of tea and gazed into Maram's eyes.

'Don't look at me that way, Val!' he said. He drained his cup in a sudden gulp, and banged it down upon the table. Then he stood up and began pacing about the room. 'I don't have your courage and devotion to truth. Ah, your faith in these great dreams of yours. *I* am just a man. And a rather delicate one at that. I've been bludgeoned by one of Morjin's assassins, and nearly eaten by bears. And in the Vardaloon, I *was* eaten by every mosquito, leech and verminous thing in that accursed forest. I've been frozen, burnt, starved and nearly drained of blood. And the Stonefaces, ah, I don't even want to speak of them! I've been shot with arrows . . .'

Here he paused to rub his fat rump, each half of which had been transfixed by a feathered shaft during the siege of Khaisham. To this day, he claimed, it pained him to sit on top of a horse – or on chairs.

'Isn't all this enough?' he asked us. 'No, no, my friends, if there's another quest to be made, let someone else make it.'

I felt the ache in my side where one of Morjin's assassins had run me through with a sword. In my veins stilled burned, and always would burn, the kirax poison that he had fired into me with an evil arrow shot out of the darkness of the woods. 'We've all suffered, Maram,' I said softly. 'No one should ask that you suffer more.'

'Ah, but you ask when you speak to me like that. When you look at me with those damn Valari eyes of yours.'

'My apologies,' I said, glancing down at the floor.

'I just want to drink a little beer and write a few poems for Behira – what's wrong with that?'

In truth, Maram liked to consume much more than a 'little' beer. Ever since we had returned to Mesh with the Lightstone, he had devoted his considerable passions toward savoring life. My brother, Asaru, often accused him of sloth, but he really worked very hard in his pursuit of pleasure, filling up each day of the week. Sunday nights, for instance, were for drinking, and sacred Oneday brought more beer and brandy. Moonday was equally holy, and Arday was needed to recover from so much holiness. Then came Eaday, which he reserved for walks in the mountains and rides through the forest – usually with his betrothed, Behira, or another beautiful young woman – so that he could worship the glories of the earth. Valday nights were for singing and stargazing in similar company, while on Asturday he wrote love poems, and on Sunday he rested yet again in preparation for the evening's drinkfest.

I smiled at Maram's peccadilloes, and so did Master Juwain, with curiosity as much as concern. Then he asked Maram, 'And what of Behira, then? Have you set a date for the wedding?'

'Ah, I've set at least *three* dates.'

He explained that he had kept postponing the wedding, offering one excuse or another. Most recently, he had argued that he and Behira should have news of the conclave before deciding anything so private and permanent as a wedding.

'I did not think Lord Harsha,' Master Juwain said, 'could be put off so easily in matters concerning his daughter's happiness.'

'Did I say there was anything *easy* about all this? You should have seen Lord Harsha's face when I told him I couldn't possibly make vows in Ashte because the auguries were unfavorable.'

Master Juwain pushed back his chair, stood and went over to Maram. He rested his hand on his arm and asked, 'What's wrong? I thought you loved Behira?'

'Ah, I *do* love her – I'm certain I do. More than I've ever loved any woman. In fact, I'm nearly certain that she's the one I've been seeking all my life. It's just that . . .'

His voice trailed off as he reached into a deep pocket of his tunic and removed a red crystal nearly a foot in length. It was six-sided and pointed at either end; a large crack ran down its center, and a webwork of smaller ones radiated out from it so that no part of the crystal remained untouched. With this great gelstei, Maram had wounded the dragon, Angraboda, in the deeps of Argattha. But the great blast of fire had broken the crystal so that it would unleash fire no more.

'My poor firestone,' he lamented, squeezing the red crystal. 'I had hoped to find, in the Cup of Heaven, the secret of how it might be mended or forged anew. But I've failed.'

'I'm afraid I don't understand,' Master Juwain said.

Maram gazed at the crystal and said, 'As with this firestone, so with my heart. There's a crack there, you see. Some fundamental flaw in my being. Every time I look at Behira, love flows into me like fire. But I can't quite hold it. I had hoped to find in the Lightstone a way that I could. The way to make love last: *that's* the secret of the universe.'

Maram, I thought, was no different to anyone else. Everyone who stood before the Lightstone sought the realization of his deepest desire. But no one, it seemed, knew how to unlock the secrets of this blessed, golden vessel.

'I see, I see,' Master Juwain said. Then he reached into the pocket of *his* tunic. He brought out an emerald crystal, much smaller than Maram's, and stood looking at it. He said, 'Don't give up hope just yet.'

'Why, do you propose to heal my heart with *that*?'

Master Juwain studied the green gelstei that he had gained on our quest. With it, he had healed Atara of a mortal wound, as he had more minor ones torn into Maram's and my flesh. But too often the gelstei failed him. I knew that he dreamed the Lightstone might infinitely magnify the power of his healing crystal.

9

'I wish I could,' Master Juwain told Maram. 'But you see, I've little more knowledge of how the Lightstone might be used than you do.'

'Then your journey was unsuccessful?'

'No, I wouldn't quite say that. In fact, I discovered several things of great interest in Nar.'

'What sort of *things*?'

'Well, to begin with, it's becoming ever clearer that only the Maitreya will show what the Lightstone is really *for*.'

Here he turned toward me, and his large eyes filled with a soft, silver radiance. 'And you, Val – what have *you* found in the Lightstone?'

'More than I ever dreamed,' I said. 'But less than I hoped.'

Maram had said that love is the secret of the universe. But why did the One, in love, give us life only to take it away in the bitterness of death?

'I have looked for the secret of life,' I admitted.

'And what have you found?'

'That it's a mystery no man will ever solve.'

'Nothing else?'

I stood up and walked over to look out the window. Above Silvassu – above all the world – Telshar's white diamond peak was gleaming in the light of the late sun.

'There have been moments,' I said at last. 'Once or twice, while I stood looking at the Lightstone, meditating – these bright moments. When the gold of the cup turns clear as diamond. And inside it, there is . . . everything. All the stars in the universe. I can't tell you how bright is their light. It fell upon me like the stroke of a shining sword that brought joy instead of death. I was alive as I've never been alive before, and every particle of my being seemed to blaze like the sun. And then, for a moment, the light, myself – there was no difference. It was all as one.'

As Maram pulled at his beard, Master Juwain listened quietly and waited for me to say more. Then he spoke with a strange gravity: 'You should mark well the miracle of these moments. We all should.'

'Why, sir? Others have experienced similar things. I'm no different to anyone else.'

'Aren't you?'

He stepped closer to me and studied the scar cut into my forehead. It was shaped like a lightning bolt, the result of a wound to my flesh during the violence of my birth.

'It was you,' he said, 'who found the Lightstone in the darkness of Argattha when it was invisible to everyone else. As it had remained invisible for all of an age.'

'Please, sir – we shouldn't speak of this again.'

'No, I'm afraid we *must* speak of it, before it's too late. You see, Master Sebastian–'

'He's a great astrologer,' I admitted. I hated interrupting Master Juwain, or anyone, but I had gone too far to stop. 'His knowledge is very great, but a man's fate can't be set by the stars.'

'No, perhaps not set, as a chisel's mark in stone,' Master Juwain said. 'It is more like a jeweled tapestry. All that is, or ever will be, is part of it. And each golden thread, each diamond woven into it, reflects the light of all the others. There is only one pattern, one master pattern, as I've said a hundred times. As above, so below. The stars, from where we came, mark the place we will return to. And mark it in patterns within the one pattern resonant with the patterns of our lives. *Your* life, Val, has already been marked out from all others. Everyone has seen this, in who you are, in what you've done. But Master Sebastian has seen it in the stars.'

He motioned for Maram and me to follow him across the room to where a large desk stood facing the wall. Many old books were heaped on top of it. One was a genealogy of the noble Valari families, another was entitled, simply: *The Lesser Gelstei*. The largest book was Master Juwain's prized copy of the *Saganom Elu*, bound in ancient leather. He had placed it, and other books, so that they weighted down the corners of a scroll of parchment. Inked onto its yellow-white surface was a great wheel of a circle, divided by lines like slices of a pie. Other lines formed squares within the circle, and there was a single, equal-sided triangle, too. Around the circle's edge were written various arcane symbols which I took to represent other worlds or the greatest of the heavens' constellations.

'Before I left for Nar,' Master Juwain said to me, 'I asked Master Sebastian to work up this horoscope from the reported hour of your birth.' Here he stabbed his finger at a cluster of symbols at the top of the circle. 'Do you see how your sun is at the midheaven in the constellation of the Archer? This is the sign of a soul that streaks out like an arrow of light to touch the stars. At the midheaven also is Aos, and this is an indication of a great spiritual teacher. And there also, Niran, which portends a spiritual master or great king. Their conjunction is striking and very strong.'

As the afternoon deepened toward evening, and Maram bent over the desk with me, breathing in my ear, Master Juwain went on to point out other features of my horoscope: the grand trine formed by Elad, Tyra and my moon; my moon, itself, in the Crab Constellation, indicating deep and powerful passions for life that I kept hidden inside

11

to protect myself and avoid hurting others; my Siraj in the castle of service in the sign of the Ram, which marked me out as a man who blazed new paths for others to follow. Directly across the circle from it was to be found my Shahar, planet of vision and transcendence. Its opposition with Siraj, according to Master Juwain, told of the great war that I waged inside myself – and with the world.

'We see here the paradox of your life, Val. That you, who love others so deeply, have been forced to slay so many.'

The sword I wore at my side suddenly felt unbearably heavy. The silustria of its blade was so hard and smooth that blood would not cling to it or stain it. I wished the same were true of my soul.

'And this conflict runs even deeper,' Master Juwain continued. 'It would be as if your soul is pulled in two directions, between the glories of the earth and the still light at the center of all things. In a sense, between life and death.'

As Master Juwain paused to take a deep breath, I felt my heart beating hard and painfully inside me. And then he said, 'For one born beneath stars such as yours, it is necessary to die in order to be reborn – as the Silver Swan emerges with wings of light from the flames of its own funeral pyre. Such a one is rare, indeed. A master astrologer, and many men, might call him the Shining One.'

Sweat was now running down my sides in hot streams beneath my armor. I could scarcely breathe, so I pushed back from the desk and moved over to the window for some fresh air. I fairly drank in the wind pouring down from the mountains. Then I turned to Master Juwain and said, 'What did you mean he *might* be called the Shining One?'

'You see, your horoscope is certainly that of a great man, and almost that of a Maitreya.'

'Almost? Then –'

Before I could say more, the faint fall of footsteps sounded in the hall outside the door, punctuated by the sound of wood striking stone. Master Juwain, who had a mind like the gears of a clock, smiled as if satisfied by the result of some secret calculation.

'You see,' he said by way of explanation, 'I've asked for help in deciding this matter.'

There came a soft rapping at the door. Master Juwain crossed the room and opened it. Then he invited inside a small, old woman who stepped carefully as she tapped a wooden cane ahead of her.

'Nona!' I cried out. It was my grandmother, Ayasha Elahad. I rushed across the room to embrace her frail body. Then I placed her arm around mine, and led her over to one of the chairs at the tea table. 'Where is Chaya? You shouldn't go walking about by yourself.'

12

I spoke the name of the maidservant who had volunteered to help my grandmother negotiate the castle's numerous corridors and treacherous stone stairs. For during the half year of my journey, my grandmother had lost her sight almost overnight: now the white frost of cataracts iced over both her eyes. But strangely, although the cataracts kept out the light of the world, they could not quite keep within a deeper and sweeter light. Her essential goodness set my heart to hurting with the sweetest of pains, as it always did. I had often thought of her as the source of love in my family – as the sun is the source of life on earth.

While Maram and I sat at the table on either side of her, Master Juwain made her tea, peppermint with honey, as she requested. He set a new pot and cup before her and made sure that she could reach it easily. I knew that he lamented being unable to heal her of her affliction.

My grandmother held herself with great dignity as she carefully moved her hand from the edge of the table toward her cup. Then she said to me, 'I sent Chaya away. There is no reason to burden her, and I must learn to get about by myself. Sixty-two years I've lived here, ever since your grandfather captured my heart and asked me to marry him. I think I know this castle as well as anyone. Now if you please, may we speak of more important things?'

She slowly turned her head as if looking for Master Juwain. Then, to Maram and me, Master Juwain said, 'I've asked the Queen Mother to come here so that she might tell of Val's birth.'

As far as I knew, three woman had attended my entrance to the world: my grandmother and the midwife, Amorah – and, of course, my mother, who had nearly died giving me life.

My grandmother breathed on the hot tea before taking a long sip of it. Then she said, 'Six sons Queen Elianora had already borne for *my* son, the king. Val was the last, and so he should have been the easiest, but he was the hardest. The biggest, too. Amorah, may she abide with the One, said that he'd baked too long in the oven. She finally had to use the tongs to pull Val out. They cut his forehead, as you can see.'

Although *she* could no longer see, she tilted her head as if listening for the sound of my breath. Then, with only slight hesitation, she leaned forward, and her hand found the top of my head. Her palm moved slowly down my forehead as she found the scar there, then she traced the cold zags with her warm and trembling finger.

'But what can you tell us,' Master Juwain said, 'about the *hour* of Val's birth?'

13

My grandmother hesitated a little longer this time before touching my cheek, then withdrawing her hand to pull at the soft folds of skin around her neck. 'He was born with the sun high in the sky, at the noon hour, as was recorded.'

Both Master Juwain and I turned to glance at the parchment still spread across the nearby desk. Then the heat of Master Juwain's gaze fell upon my grandmother as he asked her, 'Then it was at this hour that Val drew his first breath?'

Master Juwain's eyes gleamed as if he were about to solve an ancient puzzle. He watched my grandmother, who sat in silence as my heart beat ten times. Finally, she said, 'No, Val drew his first breath an hour before that. You see, the birth was so hard, he had trouble breathing at all. He was so cold and blue it made me weep. For an hour, Amorah and I thought that he would go over to the other world. At last, though, at noon, his little life quickened. When we knew the fire wouldn't go out, we announced his birth.'

In the sudden quiet of Master Juwain's chamber, twenty-one years after the day that my grandmother had told of, my breathing had stopped yet again. Master Juwain and Maram were staring me. My grandmother seemed to be staring at me, too.

'The Morning Star burned brightly that day,' she continued. 'It shone almost like a second sun from before dawn all through the morning, as it does once every hundred years. And so my grandson was named Valashu, after that beautiful star.'

Master Juwain stood up and marched over to the desk. He gathered up the parchment and a similar one that had lain concealed beneath it. After tucking a large, musty book beneath his arm, he marched back toward us.

'Maram,' he called, 'please clear the table for me.'

I helped Maram clear the pots and cups from the tea table. Then Master Juwain spread both parchments on top of it, side by side. He stepped back over to the desk and returned with a few more books to hold them down.

'Look,' he said, pointing at the first horoscope that we had already studied. Then he traced his finger around the circle and symbols of the second parchment. As we could see, the array was nearly the same. 'I confess that I guessed what the Queen Mother has just disclosed today. And so before I left for Nar, I asked Master Sebastian to work up this second horoscope.'

Now his finger trembled with excitement as he touched two small symbols written at the edge of the circle described upon the second parchment. 'Here, of course, is the Morning Star, as on the first horoscope. But

14

here, too – look closely – the stars of the Swan are rising in the east at Val's earlier and true hour of birth.'

Master Juwain straightened and stood like a warrior who has vanquished a foe. He said, 'There are other changes to the horoscope, but this is the critical one. Master Sebastian has advised me that the effect of the Swan rising would be to exalt and raise the purity of Val's entire horoscope. He has said that *these* are certainly the stars of a Maitreya.'

I couldn't help staring at the two parchments. The late sun through the windows glared off their whitish surface and stabbed into my eyes.

'It's possible, isn't it,' I said, 'that many men, at many times, would have a similar horoscope?'

'No, not *many* men, Val.'

Master Juwain now brought forth the book from beneath his arm. As he opened it and began turning its yellow pages with great care, I noticed the title, written in ancient Ardik: *The Coming Of The Shining One*. At last, he reached the page he had been seeking. He smiled as he set down the book next to the second parchment.

'I found this in the library of the Brotherhood's sanctuary at Nar. It was always a rare book, and with the burning of Khaisham's Library, it might be the last copy remaining in the world.' He tapped his finger against the symbol-written circle inscribed on the book's open page. 'This is the horoscope of Godavanni the Glorious. Look, Val, look!'

Godavanni had been the greatest of Ea's Maitreyas, born at the end of the great Age of Law three thousand years before. He had also been, as I remembered, a great King of Kings. I gasped in wonder because the two horoscopes, Godavanni's and mine, were exactly the same.

'No,' I murmured, 'it cannot be.'

For my grandmother's sake, Master Juwain explained again the features of my horoscope – and Godavanni's. Then he turned to Maram and said, 'You see, our quest to find the new Maitreya might already be completed.'

'Ah, Val,' Maram said as he pulled at his beard and gazed at me. 'Ah, Val, Val.'

My grandmother reached out her hand and squeezed mine. Then she set it on top of the parchments, fumbling to feel the lines of the symbols written on them.

'Here,' I said, gently pressing her fingertip against the rays denoting the Morning Star. 'Is this what you wanted?'

There was both joy and sadness in her smile as she turned to face me. Her ivory skin was so worn and old that it seemed almost transparent. The smell of lilacs emanated from her wispy white hair. The cataracts over her eyes clouded their deep sable color, but could not conceal the bright thing inside her, almost too bright to bear. Her breath poured like a warm wind from her lips, and I could feel the way that she had breathed it into me at my birth, pressing her lips over mine. I could feel the beating of her heart. There was a sharp pain there. It hurt me to feel her hurting so, with sorrow because she was blind and could not look upon me in what seemed my hour of glory. My eyes filled with water and burning salt a moment before hers did, too. And then, as if she knew well enough what had passed between us, she reached out her hand to touch away the tears on my cheek that she could not see.

'It was this way with your grandfather, too,' she said. 'You have his gift.'

She gave voice to a thing that we had never spoken of before. For many years it had remained our secret. During the quest, however, Master Juwain and Maram – and my other companions – had discovered what my grandmother called my gift: that what others feel, I feel as well. If I let myself, their joy became my joy, their love flowed into me like the warm, onstreaming rays of the sun. But I was open to darker passions as well: hatred, pain, fury, fear. For my gift was also a curse. How many times on the journey to Argattha, I wondered, had Master Juwain and Maram watched me nearly die with every enemy I had sent on to the otherworld in the screaming agony of death?

My grandmother, as if explaining to Master Juwain and Maram something that she thought it was time for them to know, smiled sadly and said, 'It was this way with Valashu from his first breath: it was as if he were breathing in all the pain in the world. It was why, at first, he failed to quicken and almost died.'

For what seemed an hour, I sat next to her in silence holding her hand in mine. And then, to Master Juwain and Maram, to me – to the whole world – she cried out: 'He's my grandson and has the heart of an angel – shouldn't this be enough?'

My gift, this mysterious soul force within me, had a name, an ancient name, and that was *valarda*. I remembered that this meant 'the heart of the stars'.

As Master Juwain looked down at the two parchments, and Maram's soft, brown eyes searched in mine, I kissed my grandmother's forehead, then excused myself. I stood up and moved over to the open window. The warm wind brought the smell of pine trees and earth into the room. It called me to remember who I really was. And that could *not* be, I thought, the Maitreya. Was I a great healer? No, I was a knight of the sword, a great slayer of men. Who knew as well as I did the realm of death where I had sent so many? In the last moment of life, each of my enemies had grasped at me and pulled me down toward that lightless land. I remembered lines of the poem that had tormented me since the day I had killed Morjin's assassin in the woods below the castle:

> *The stealing of the gold,*
> *The evil knife, the cold –*
> *The cold that freezes breath,*
> *The nothingness of death.*
>
> *And down into the dark,*
> *No eyes, no lips, no spark.*
> *The dying of the light,*
> *The neverness of night.*

Even now, in the warmth of a fine spring day, I felt this everlasting cold chilling my limbs and filling me with dread. The night that knows no end called to me, even as the voices of the dead carried along the wind. They spoke to me in grave tones, telling me that I waited to be one of them and that I could not be the Shining One, for he was of the sun and earth and all the things of life. A deeper voice, like the fire of the far-off stars, whispered this inside me, too. I did not listen. For just then, with my quick breath burning my lips and Telshar's diamond peak so beautiful against the sky, I recalled the words to another poem, about the Maitreya:

> *To mortal men on planets bound*
> *Who dream and die on darkened ground,*
> *To bold and bright Valari knights*
> *Who cross the starry heavens' heights,*
> *To all: immortal Elijin*
> *As well the quenchless Galadin,*
> *He brings the light that slays the Lie:*
> *The light of love makes death to die.*

'"It is said that the Maitreya shall have eternal life",' I whispered, quoting from the *Book of Ages* of the *Saganom Elu*.

It was also said that he would show this way to others. How else, I wondered, did men gain the long lives of the Star People and learn to sail the glittering heavens? And how did the Star People advance to the order of the immortal Elijin, and the Elijin become the great

17

Galadin, they who could not be killed or harmed in any way? Men called these beings angels, but they were of flesh and blood – and perhaps something more. Once, in the depths of the black mountain called Skartaru, I had seen a great Elijin lord unveiled in all his glory. Had the hand of a Maitreya once touched him and passed on the inextinguishable flame?

Master Juwain stood up and came over to me, laying his hand on my arm. I turned to him and asked, 'If I were the Maitreya, wouldn't I know this?'

He smiled as he hefted his copy of the *Saganom Elu* and began thumbing through its pages. Whether by chance or intuition, he came upon words that were close to the questioning of my heart:

> *The Shining One*
> *In innocence sleeps*
> *Inside his heart*
> *Angel fire sleeps*
> *And when he wakes*
> *The fire leaps*
>
> *About the Maitreya*
> *One thing is known:*
> *That to himself*
> *He always is known*
> *When the moment comes*
> *To claim the Lightstone.*

'But that's just it, sir,' I said to him. 'I *don't* know this.'

He closed his book and looked deep into my eyes. He said, 'In you, Val, there is such a fire. And such an innocence that you've never seen it.'

'But, sir, I –'

'I think we *do* know,' he told me. 'The evidence is overwhelming. First, there is your horoscope, the Swan rising, which purifies – wasn't it only by purifying yourself that you were able to find the Lightstone? And you are the seventh son of a king of the most noble and ancient line. And there is the mark.' He paused to touch the lightning bolt scar above my eye. 'The mark of Valoreth – the mark of the Galadin.'

Just then a swirl of little, twinkling lights fell out of the air as of a storm of shooting stars. In its spiraling patterns were colors of silver, cerulean and scarlet. It hovered near my forehead as if studying the scar there. Joy and faith and other fiery emotions seemed to pour from its center in bursts of radiance. This strange being was one of the Timpum, and Maram had named him Flick. He had attached himself to me in a magical wood deep in the wild forest of Alonia. It was said that once, many ages ago, the bright Galadin had walked there, perhaps looking for the greatest and last of Ea's Maitreyas: the Cosmic Maitreya who might lead all the worlds across the stars into the Age of Light. It was also said that the Galadin had left part of their essence shimmering among the wood's flowers and great trees. Whatever the origins of the Timpum truly were, they did indeed seem to possess the fire of the angels.

'And of course,' Master Juwain said, pointing at the space above my forehead, 'there is Flick. Of all the Timpum, only he has ever made such friends with a man. And only he left the Lokilani's wood – to follow you.'

I looked over toward the tea table, where Maram sat squeezing my grandmother's hand. Then I turned back to Master Juwain and said, 'There is evidence, yes, but it's not *known* . . . how the Maitreya will be known.'

'I believe,' Master Juwain said, 'that the Maitreya, alone of all those on earth, will have a true resonance with the Lightstone.'

'But how is this resonance to be accomplished?'

'That is one mystery I am trying to solve. As you must, too.'

'But *when* will I solve it?'

In answer, he pointed out the window at the clouds glowing with colors in the slanting rays of the sun. 'Soon, you will. This is the time, Valashu. The Golden Band grows stronger.'

As men such as he and I lived out our lives on far-flung worlds like Ea, the Star People built their great, glittering cities on other worlds closer to the center of the universe. And the Elijin walked on worlds closer still, while the Galadin – Ashtoreth and Valoreth and others – dwelled nearest the stellar heart, on Agathad, which they called Star Home. It was said that they made their abode by an ancient lake, the source of the great river, Ar. The lake was a perfect silver, like liquid silustria, and it reflected the image of the ageless astor tree, Irdrasil, that grew above it. Irdrasil's golden leaves never fell, and they shone even through the night.

For beyond Agathad, at the center of all things, lay Ninsun, a black and utter emptiness out of which eternally poured a brilliant and beautiful light. It was the light of the Ieldra, beings of pure light who dwelled there. This numinous radiance streamed out like the rays of the sun toward all of creation. The Golden Band, it was called, and it fell most strongly on Agathad, there to touch all living things with a glory that never failed.

19

But other worlds around other stars, on their slow turn through the universe, moved into its splendor more rarely: with Ea, only once every three thousand years, at the end of old ages or the beginning of new ones. The Brotherhood's astrologers had divined that, some twenty years before, Ea had entered the Golden Band. And it was waxing ever stronger, like the wind before a storm, like a river in late spring gathering waters to nourish the land. Now men and women, if they listened, might hear the voices of the Ieldra calling them closer to their source, even as they called to the Star People on their worlds and to the Elijin on theirs – and called eternally to the angels on Agathad to free the light of their beings and return home as newly created Ieldra themselves.

'The Golden Band,' Master Juwain explained, 'is like a river of light that men do not usually see. It shimmers, the scryers say. There are eddies and currents, and a place where it swells and flows most deeply.'

He gazed out the window for a moment, then shook his head as if all that *he* could see was the blazing sun and the drifting clouds – and two golden eagles that soared among them.

'The constellations,' he said to me, 'somehow affect the Band's strength – and direct it, too. It's known that the Band flared with great intensity on the ninth of Triolet, at the time of your birth.'

I, too, looked out the window for this angel fire that remained invisible to me.

'I believe,' Master Juwain said, 'that a Maitreya is chosen. By the One's grace, through the light of the Ieldra where it falls most brightly.'

I looked back to the tea table to see that Maram and my grandmother were attending his every word.

'The Maitreya is made, Val. Made to come forth and take his place in the world. And he must come *soon*, don't you see?'

Soon, he said, the Golden Band would begin to weaken, and a great chance might be lost. For men's hearts, now open to the light that the Maitreya would bring, would soon close and harden their wills yet again toward evil and war.

'You see,' he said, 'all the other Maitreyas failed. Of those of the Lost Ages, of course, we know almost nothing. But at the end of the Age of the Mother, it's said that Alesar Tal entered the Brotherhood and grew old and died without ever setting eyes upon the Lightstone. And at the end of the Age of Swords, Issayu was enslaved by Morjin and the Lightstone kept from him. Godavanni was murdered at the moment that the Lightstone was placed into his hands. Now we are in the last years of the Age of the Dragon. This terrible time, the darkest of ages. How will it end, Val? In even greater darkness or in light?'

Out of the window I saw cloud shadows dappling the courtyard below and darkening the white stone walls of the castle. The foothills rising above them were marked with indentations and undulations, their northern slopes invisible to the eye, lost in shadow and perhaps concealing eagles' aeries and bears' caves and the secret powers of the earth. I marveled at the way the sunlight caught the rocky faces of these hills: half standing out clearly in the strong Soldru light, half darkened into the deeper shades of green and gray and black. I saw that there was always a vivid line between the dark and the light, but strangely this line shifted and moved across the naked rock even as the sun moved slowly on its arc across the sky from east to west.

'Val? Are you all right?'

Master Juwain's voice brought me back to his comfortable room high in the Adami tower. I bowed my head to him, then asked if I could borrow his copy of the *Saganom Elu*. It took me only a moment to flip through its pages and find the passage I was seeking. I read it aloud word by word, even though I knew it by heart:

'"If men look upon the stars and see only cinders, if the sun should be seen to set in the east – if a man comes forth in falseness as the Shining One concealing darkness in his heart, if he claims the Lightstone for his own, then he shall become a new Red Dragon, only mightier and more terrible. Then red will burn black and all colors die; the heavens' lights will be veiled as if by smoke, and the sun will rise no more."'

I closed the book and gave it back to him. I said, 'I must know, sir. If I am truly this one who shines, I must know.'

We returned to the table to rejoin Maram and my grandmother. Master Juwain made us more tea, which we sat drinking as the sun fell behind the mountains and twilight stole across the world. Master Juwain reasserted his wish that I might come forth as Maitreya in sight of the emissaries who had assembled in my father's castle; it was why, he said, he had hurried home to Mesh. As much as I might need to know if I were really the Lord of Light foreseen in the prophecies, the world needed to be told of this miracle even more.

At last, as it grew dark and the hour deepened into full night, I went over to the window one last time. The sky was now almost clear. The dying of the sun had revealed the stars that always blazed there, against the immense black vault of the heavens. The constellations that my grandfather had first named for me many years before shimmered like ancient signposts: the Great Bear, the Archer, the Dragon, with its sinuous form and two great, red stars for eyes. I searched a long time in these glittering arrays for any certainty that I was the one whom

Master Juwain hoped me to be. I did not find it. There was only light and stars, infinite in number and nearly as old as time.

Then Maram came up to me and clapped me on the shoulder. 'It's time for the feast, my friend. You *might* very well be this Maitreya, but you're a man first, and you have to eat.'

We walked back across the room, where I helped my grandmother out of her chair and took her arm in mine. Then we all went down to the great hall to take food and wine with many others and view the wonder of the Lightstone.

2

The great hall adjoined the castle's keep where my father and most of his guests resided. By the time we had gone outside and made our way through the dark middle ward, past the Tower of the Moon and the Tower of the Earth, and entered the hall through its great southern doors, it was almost full of people. Brothers from the sanctuary near Silvassu stood wearing their brown robes and drinking apple cider in place of wine or beer; nobles from Alonia gathered in a group next to their table. I immediately recognized Count Dario Narmada, King Kiritan's cousin and the chief of his emissaries. With his flaming red hair and bright blue tunic emblazoned with the gold caduceus of the House Narmada, he was hard to miss. In this large room, opening out beneath its vaulted ceiling of stone, were many Valari: simple warriors and knights as well as great princes and even kings. Lord Issur, son of King Hadaru of Ishka, seemed to be discussing something of great importance with a tall man who displayed many battle ribbons in his long, gray hair and great longing on his much-scarred face. This was King Kurshan of Lagash, whose ferocious countenance hid a kind and faithful heart. I knew that he had journeyed to Mesh to make a marriage for his daughter, Chandria – and to stand before the Lightstone like everyone else.

On a long dais at the north end of the room, beneath a wall hung with a black banner showing the swan and stars of the House of Elahad, was an ancient white granite pedestal. On top of it sat a plain, golden cup. It was small enough to fit the palm of a man's hand; indeed, it had been my hand that had placed it there some months before. At first glance, it did not seem an impressive thing. No gem adorned it. No handles were welded onto its sides, nor did it rest upon a long and gracefully shaped base, as with a chalice. It did not, except at rare moments, even radiate much light. But its beauty stole away the breath, and in its golden shimmer was something lovely that drew the eye and called to the soul. Not a few of those gathered in the hall were staring at it with tears streaming down their cheeks. Even the oldest and hardest of warriors seemed to melt in its presence, like winter's ice beneath the warm spring sun.

Standing to either side of the pedestal were fifteen knights, each of whom wore a long sword at his side, even as did I. They wore as well suits of mail like my own; to the various blazons on their surcoats had been added a unique mark of cadence: a small, golden cup. For these were thirty of the Guardians of the Lightstone who had sworn to die in its defense. I had chosen them – and seventy others not presently on duty – from among the finest knights of Mesh. They, too, seemed in awe of that which they protected. Their noble faces, I thought, had been touched by the Lightstone's splendor, and their bright, black eyes remained ever watchful, ever awake, ever aware.

Before we had crossed ten paces into the hall, a stout, handsome woman wearing a black gown came up to us, with her dark eyes fixed on Maram. He presented her as Dasha Ambar, Lord Ambar's widow. After bowing to my grandmother, she smiled at Maram and asked, 'Will we go riding tomorrow, Sar Maram?'

'Tomorrow?' Maram said, glancing about the hall as he began to sweat. 'Ah, tomorrow is Moonday, my lady. Why don't we wait until Eaday, when we've recovered from the feast?'

'Very well,' Dasha said. 'In the morning or the afternoon?'

'Ah, I must tell you that the morning, for me, quite often *begins* in the afternoon.'

Dasha smiled at this, as did my grandmother and I. Then Dasha excused herself and moved off toward the throng of knights who had gathered around Lord Tomavar's table.

'You're playing a dangerous game,' I told Maram as his eyes drank in Dasha's voluptuous form.

'What am I to do?' Maram said, turning toward me. 'Your Valari women are so beautiful, so bold. The widows especially. And there are so many of them.'

'Just be careful that Lord Harsha doesn't make Behira a widow before you even have the chance to marry her.'

'All right, all right,' Maram muttered. He gazed across the hall toward the Lightstone as if hoping its radiance might bestow upon him fidelity and other virtues. Then he seemed to forget his resolve as he looked away and said, 'But *someone* must console these poor women!'

Again, my grandmother smiled, and she told Maram, 'When the Ishkans made *me* a widow, it was not possible for me to marry again.

But had it been, it would have been my wish to marry for love, not just for my husband's renown.'

'Then you are different from your countrywomen, my lady.'

'No, not so different, Sar Maram.' My grandmother turned her sightless eyes toward his face. Her smile radiated warmth. 'Perhaps in you they hope to find both.'

'Do you see?' Maram said to me as he held his hands toward the ceiling. 'Even in your own grandmother, this damn Valari boldness!'

We all had a good laugh at this, my grandmother especially. She let go of my arm and took Maram's as if grateful for his strength. And strong he truly was, growing more so by the day. Now that he wore in his silver ring the two diamonds of a Valari knight, he was obliged to practise with his sword at least once each day. His body, I thought, was a sort of compromise between this fierce discipline and self-indulgence: the layers of fat, which fooled the undiscerning, covered great mounds of muscle and battle-tempered bone. There was about him a growing certainty of his prowess and physical splendor, and this attracted women like flowers to the sun.

Just then Jasmina Ashur, who had lost her husband in the war against Waas, espied Maram and hurried over to him. She was graceful and slender as a stem, barely eighteen, and her adoring eyes fell upon Maram with an almost smothering desire. After greeting us, she began discussing with Maram the poetry-writing session he had promised her.

'Someone,' she told Maram, 'must put the account of your quest to verse. Since you are too modest to hoist your own banner.'

'Ah,' Maram said, the blood rushing to his face, 'I *am* too modest, aren't I?'

'Yes, you are. Even so, the world needs to be told of your feats, before others make free with your story.'

'What do you mean?'

'Well, I overheard Count Dario claiming that you are really Alonian.'

'Why, that's not true! My grandmother was the daughter of the old Baron Monteer of Iviendenhall before King Kiritan's father conquered it and added it to his realm. Does that make me Alonian?'

'They're saying other things, too. About the Maitreya.'

Maram fell silent as my grandmother squeezed his arm and Master Juwain looked at me. Then Master Juwain rubbed the back of his bald head and asked Jasmina, 'And what are they saying about the Shining One?'

'That he has almost certainly been found. In a village near Adavam. They say that he's the son of a blacksmith and has made miracles: healing the blind and turning lead into gold.'

Adavam, I remembered, lay only fifty miles from Tria, and was clearly within the bounds of Old Alonia.

'But have these miracles been verified?' Master Juwain asked. 'In Galda, before it fell, came stories of a shepherd removing growths from people's bodies with his bare hands. We sent Brother Alexander to investigate. It turned out that the shepherd was showing his poor patients sheep offal through sleight of hand.'

Jasmina grimaced as if such trickery disgusted her. Then she said, 'Who can trust the Galdans? Or the Alonians? It seems to me more likely that the Maitreya would be one of those who found the Lightstone.'

Here she smiled at Maram, and again his face flushed bright red. He coughed out, 'No, no – I'm no Maitreya! Do diamonds bleed? Can you make a silk purse out of a sow's ear?'

'Only in Alonia,' Jasmina said with a little laugh. Then she bowed her head to me and laid her hand on my arm. 'But if not Sar Maram, then perhaps you, Lord Valashu. Many are saying this, that you were the first to touch the golden cup, and much of its light passed into you.'

Maram removed Jasmina's hand from my arm and stood holding her questing fingers in his. 'Val, the Maitreya? No, no – he can't be!'

'But why not?'

'Why, ah, because he just *can't.*' Maram paused to take a deep breath as he looked at me. 'The one you speak of, my lady, would be more like the wind than the mountains and rivers over which it blows. He would have fire in his veins, not blood. And it would be a cold fire, I think, like that of the stars. Too pure, too . . . evanescent. How could such a one ever bring himself to slay his enemies or love a woman? I've *seen* Val's blood, you know, too many times, too bad. It's as red and hot as mine.'

At that moment, Maram's face fell rigid, and he dropped Jasmina's hand as if it were a hot coal. I turned to see Lord Harsha and Behira enter the hall. They made their way straight toward us with surprising speed, considering the lameness of Lord Harsha's smashed leg, which caused him to limp badly. Despite his age, he was still straight and sturdy, and as hard as the rocks in the fields he still plowed with his own hands. A black eye patch stood out against the long white hair that flowed from his square head; his single eye, like a black diamond, gleamed at Maram, upon whom he advanced with his hand gripping the hilt of his kalama.

'Oh, no!' Maram muttered. And then, as Lord Harsha and his daughter drew up to us, Maram called out, 'Good evening, my lord. Behira, I've never seen you look so beautiful.'

Behira, who was as plump and pretty as a well-fed swan, was dressed in a white silk gown that failed to conceal her large breasts and even larger hips. Her raven-black hair spilled over her shoulders nearly down to her waist. Her oval face, usually quite pleasant to look at, was now marred by some of the darker passions. I knew her to be generous of heart and sweet as the honey that Maram loved, but she was also quite spirited, and there was within her more than a little of her father's steel, sharpened to a razor edge.

'Jasmina,' she said, 'has Maram invited you yet to our *wedding*? We were considering making vows at the end of Soal – what do you think?'

Valari women wield weapons only at times of life and death, but at that moment Behira's black eyes were daggers that tore Jasmina open. Jasmina allowed that Soal would indeed be a good month for marriage. Then she excused herself and moved off toward a table of young knights.

'Ah, Behira,' Maram said as she turned her cutting gaze on him. 'We were just discussing the Maitreya.' He coughed into his hand, twice, and then extended it toward Behira as if to present her to me. Then he said, 'Do you see, Val? Why should one look to the stars when there is such beauty on earth? Do you want heaven? Then *I* say you'd be more likely to find it in a woman's kiss – at least a woman such as my beloved.'

'Here now,' Lord Harsha said, moving forward between his daughter and Maram. 'We'll not speak of *that* until we've spoken of a date. What about Soal, Sar Maram?'

'Ah, Soal *is* a good month,' Maram said, wiping the sweat from his forehead. 'Of course, Ioj might be even better, with the aspen leaves going gold, or even Valte after the harvest is –'

'The question must be asked,' Lord Harsha said, '*are* you looking for a better match than my daughter?'

'No, no – of course not!'

'Then why all these flirtations of yours?'

'*My* flirtations? Ah, Lord Harsha, you don't understand – it is they who flirt with me.'

'Well it must stop.' Lord Harsha was as blunt as a river stone. 'Do you wish to wound my daughter's heart beyond all repair?'

Maram turned to look at Behira, whose bright eyes were fixed upon him. 'I would rather,' he said, 'that my own heart were torn out.'

'*That* can be accomplished,' Lord Harsha said, his fist tightening around the hilt of his sword.

Seeing this, Maram blanched and blurted out, 'I love Behira!'

'Perhaps – but how is *she* to know that?'

27

'But Lord Harsha, don't you see? It is the very extravagance of the attentions of the widows of your realm that is the measure of my love and devotion to your daughter. It is that way with women, isn't it? That the more a man loves one woman, the more others will see seducing him as a challenge?'

Lord Harsha, who was steady and true of mind, was not especially quick or clever. He stuck to his main point, saying, 'Then the sooner you are wed, the better. Today is the sixth of Soldru. The sixth of Marud will not be too soon for the wedding. One month, Sar Maram.'

The look in Maram's eyes just then was that of an animal caught in a trap. He pulled at the collar of his red tunic as if struggling to breathe, then gasped out, 'One month! But Lord Harsha, with the news I've just had and all my duties, that is far too little –'

'What duties? Trying to outdrink any man in Mesh? And what news are you speaking of?'

Maram's eyes fell upon me and brightened as if seeing a way out of such sudden – and final – matrimony. He said, 'Why, the news about Val. Master Juwain believes that he is likely the Maitreya.'

Lord Harsha had a great respect for authority, and great regard for the Brotherhood and Master Juwain. He listened quietly as Master Juwain recounted the evidence cited earlier in the Adami tower. Master Juwain admitted that his hope for me was not yet proven beyond doubt, and he asked Lord Harsha not to speak of my horoscope to anyone. Like a warrior receiving battle orders from his king, Lord Harsha agreed to this. Then he nodded his hoary head toward me, saying, 'It's always been clear that there is something remarkable about Val.'

'Yes, there is,' Maram said, laying his hand on my shoulder. 'And that is why, my lord, we should not be too quick to set a date. You see, I've allegiance to Val, and who knows where fate might take us if he truly *is* the Maitreya?'

In his relief in possibly postponing his wedding yet again, and in his pride for me, his big voice boomed out into the hall a little too loudly. It drew the attention of two off-duty Guardians: my friends, Sunjay Naviru and Baltasar Raasharu. They smiled and walked toward us, followed by a tall, dignified man whose long face and white teeth reminded me of a warhorse. This was Lord Lansar Raasharu, Baltasar's father – and *my* father's trusted seneschal. I knew of no warrior braver in battle or more loyal to my family than he. Although the deepest of passions sometimes gloomed his heart, he had resolved to carry himself at all times as if his essentially melancholic nature would never master him.

'Lord Raasharu!' I said as he came up to me. 'Sunjay! Baltasar!'

Lansar Raasharu bowed his head to me, but Sunjay and Baltasar took turns in embracing me. Sunjay was bright of manner and expression, like a shooting star; from his well-formed mouth poured forth a steady stream of friendly words and smiles. Baltasar was a more difficult man. His lively, black eyes spoke of intelligence and restlessness of the soul; his ruddy cheeks gave evidence of his fiery blood. He was quick to take insult and even quicker to forgive – as quick as he was to love and be loved. All my life, it seemed, he had been like a seventh brother to me. He had all of Asaru's grace and Karshur's strength of purpose; while his quicksilver laughter reminded me of Jonathay, his pride burned hotter than did even Yarashan's.

After Maram had blurted out the topic of conversation, Baltasar flashed a bright smile at me and said, 'It was hard enough to get used to calling you "Lord Valashu" – and now it seems you're to be called "Lord of Light" as well?'

'Please,' I told him, 'it will be enough if you call me "friend".'

Baltasar's hand darted out to clasp mine. For a moment, our eyes locked together, and in the light of recognition that passed between us, I relived the Battle of Red Mountain against Waas. On that broken and bloody field, Baltasar had recklessly attacked three knights trying to impale me with their lances – and had taken a grievous wound to his neck in driving them off. His valor had saved my life. After the battle, my father had honored him with the double-diamond ring of a full knight. And *his* father, the noble Lord Raasharu, had looked upon him as if Baltasar was the great joy of his life. Even as he looked upon him now.

'All right, friend,' Baltasar said to me in the warm glow of his father's countenance. 'But can it really be true that you're this Maitreya that everyone is talking about?'

His hand gripped mine more tightly as if trying to squeeze the answer to this question out of me. I squeezed back, not in affirmation, but only to keep him from breaking my finger bones.

'It's said,' Baltasar continued, gazing at me, 'that the Maitreya will be a bringer of peace. But how can there ever be peace in this world?'

'There *must* be peace,' I told him. 'Godavanni the Glorious –'

'Godavanni was High King in an age when people thought that war had ended forever. It's said that he never lifted his sword against any man. But in the end, Morjin murdered him, and war began again.'

As Baltasar formed the sounds of the Red Dragon's name, he let go of my hand to touch the gem he wore over his heart. Dangling from a steel chain around his neck was a small stone, blood-red in color like a carnelian. It was called a warder, and it bore the power to deflect poisonous thoughts or curses directed at its wearer. It also rendered one invisible to scryers and mindspeakers; most especially, it was proof against the illusions that the Lord of Lies sent to madden his enemies. As one of the lesser gelstei, it was both powerful and rare, but even so, all of the Guardians wore one.

'If war can begin,' I told Baltasar, 'it can end.'

'Never,' he said. 'Never so long as Morjin is left undefeated – all his evil, all his lies.'

'But evil can't be vanquished with a sword, Baltasar.'

'*You* say that, who have vanquished so many with *your* sword?'

My hand fell down upon my sword's hilt, with its diamond pommel and swan-carved hilt of black jade. I swallowed against the pain in my throat as I said, 'Darkness can't be defeated in battle but only by shining a bright enough light.'

'Are these the words of the Lord of Light, then?'

They were, in fact, words that Master Juwain had spoken to me on the night when I had vowed to recover the Lightstone. Now he stood near me beaming his approval that I had taken to heart the deepest of his lessons. Maram, Behira, Lord Harsha and Lord Raasharu – and others – pressed in close to hear what we might say next.

'You should know, Val,' Baltasar confided to me, 'that many are saying the Maitreya would be a great warlord. Like Aramesh. That he would unite the Valari and lead us to victory over the Red Dragon. *Then* this Age of Light of which you dream might begin.'

Red flames seemed to dance in his eyes as he glanced at the knights and warriors gathered around us. I remembered the words from the *Trian Prophecies*: 'He shall be the greatest warrior in the world.'

I said to him, 'You love war too much, Baltasar.'

'As I love life itself, dear friend. What else calls to life so deeply as the duty to surrender it in protecting family and friends?'

I might have agreed with him – with the qualification that the Valari were meant to be warriors of the spirit only. But just then, to the sound of trumpets announcing the beginning of the feast, my father, mother and brothers entered the hall from its western portal.

Lord Harsha cried out, 'The King!' as hundreds of people turned to watch Shavashar Elahad make his way toward the front of the room where my family's table was set. My father was a tall man whose black tunic, showing the swan and stars of our house, draped in clean lines about his large and powerful frame. Despite his years, he moved with a flowing grace that even a young knight might envy; his black eyes seemed filled with starlight and blazed with that fearlessness to which all Valari aspired. Many there were who could not bear the brilliance of his gaze and said that he was too hard on men: whether they be his enemies or those who had sworn him allegiance. But many more loved him precisely because he called them to find the best part of themselves and polish their souls until they sparkled like diamonds.

As he and my mother, with my brothers, took their places at table, ten warriors escorting a group of yellow-robed men appeared in the western portal. A silence befell the hall. All eyes turned toward these men, for they were Morjin's emissaries: the hated Red Priests of the Kallimun. I, and many others, struggled to get a good look at these seven priests who had been locked in their rooms in the keep for the last three days. But the great cowls of their robes hid their faces. The warriors led them to the table next to that of the Alonians. There, scarcely twenty feet from my father's withering gaze, they were seated.

And then the silence was suddenly broken as one of the knights near me cried out, 'Must we take meat with *them*? Send them back to Sakai!'

And then Vikadar of Godhra, one of the fiercest knights in Mesh, shouted, 'Send them back to the stars!'

His call for the priests to be executed out of hand gained the immediate approval of the more bloodthirsty in the hall. Next to me, Baltasar stood staring at the priests, and I could almost feel the heat of his ire beating through his veins. Many others burned for vengeance as well. But my father cooled the passions running through the hall with a sudden lifting of his hand. His bright eyes caught up Vikadar in reproach to remind him of one of Mesh's most sacred laws: that anyone who willfully killed an emissary should himself be put to death.

'It is said,' my father called out in his strong, clear voice, 'that these emissaries have been sent by Morjin to sue for peace. Very well – we shall hear what they have to say. But only after we've *all* taken meat.'

This was a signal that everyone still standing should take their seats. While Maram went off to join Lord Harsha and Behira at their table with Lord Tanu and Lord Tomavar, Master Juwain made his way toward his fellows of the Brotherhood. Sunjay and Baltasar sat with the other off-duty Guardians in the second tier of tables from the front of the hall. Upon taking my grandmother's arm in mine, I walked with her to our family's table where I pulled out her chair next to my father. I sat at the right end of the table next to my brother, Ravar. He had the face of a fox, and his dark, quick eyes flickered from my father to the cowled faces of the Red Priests at their table before us. His sharp and secretive smile reminded me that our father would not be moved by fear of Morjin's men, which would be the same as admitting to fear of the Red Dragon himself.

It was strange eating our supper beneath the dais on which stood the Lightstone, guarded by thirty Knights of the Swan. Nevertheless, eat we all did: fishes and fowls, joints of mutton and whole suckling pigs roasted brown and sheeny with fat. There were loaves of black barley bread, too, and pies and puddings – and much else. The feast began with talk of war on the Wendrush. A minstrel from Eanna brought rumor that Yarkona had finally fallen, conquered in Morjin's name by Count Ulanu the Cruel, who had been made that tormented realm's new king. From the various tables lined up through the hall came the buzz of many voices. Although it was impossible to follow so many streams of conversation, I heard more than one person speak of the Maitreya. Some feared that unless the Shining One came forth soon to lay hands upon the Lightstone, its radiance would fade and it might even turn invisible again. Others, citing verses from the *Saganom Elu*, gave voice to forebodings of some great disaster that would befall Ea if the Maitreya wasn't found and united with the golden cup. Too many of those present, I thought, cast quick, longing looks toward me before turning back to their neighbors to speak in hushed tones or taking up knives again to cut their meat.

Finally, after the last bit of gravy had been mopped up with the last crust of bread and every belly was full, brandy and beer were poured, and it came time for the many rounds of toasting. I watched Maram, sitting between Behira and the dour, old Lord Tanu, down glass after glass of thick, black beer. At our table, my family drank with less abandon. Next to me, Ravar nursed his single brandy, while next to him, the dashing Yarashan, who had once boasted that he could outdrink any man in Mesh, contented himself with two slow beers. Karshur, Jonathay and Mandru did likewise. Asaru, his fine and noble face alert for the verbal sparring with the emissaries that soon must come, drank only a single glass. And my father joined Nona and my mother, the beautiful Elianora wi Solaru, in taking only one small sip of beer with each toast.

After all honors and compliments had been made, it came time for that part of the feast that was less a gathering in good company than it was like battle and war. And so my father again held up his hand for silence. Then he called out into the hall: 'We will now hear from the emissaries and all who wish to voice their concerns.'

32

The first to speak that night would be Prince Issur. As he pushed back his chair and stood to address my father, everyone turned toward the Ishkan table to hear what he would say.

3

Prince Issur was a rather homely-looking man with a narrow forehead and a nose too big for his face. But he was spirited and prudent, and I knew him to be capable of a sort of harsh justice, and even kindness. His long hair, tied with five battle ribbons, hung down over his bright red surcoat showing the great white bear of the Ishkan royal house.

'King Shamesh,' he said to my father, 'King Hadaru bids me to remind you of your promise made on the field of the Raaswash: that the Lightstone is to be shared among all the Valari. More than half a year now the Cup of Heaven has resided here in Silvassu. King Hadaru bids me to ask you when it might be brought to Ishka?'

Despite the reasonableness of the man's voice, some of King Hadaru's arrogance and demanding ways shaded the words of his emissary. A murmur of discontent rumbled from the warriors and knights in the hall. Almost all of them had stood upon the field of the Raaswash when the delicate peace between Ishka and Mesh had been made. They must have recalled, as I did, how King Hadaru's eldest son, Salmelu, had been exposed there as a betrayer of all the Valari and had been driven off forever from the Nine Kingdoms. If Prince Issur, however, suffered from the shame of his brother's treason, he gave no sign of it.

Finally, my father nodded at Prince Issur and said, 'The Lightstone shall be brought into Ishka, and the other kingdoms, soon.'

'Soon,' Prince Issur repeated as if the word had a sour taste. 'Do you mean within a month, King Shamesh? Another half a year? Or might "soon" mean another century or even an age lasting three *thousand* years?'

Once, at the end of the Age of Swords, the great Aramesh had wrested the Lightstone from Morjin and had brought it back to this very castle, where my ancestors had kept it all during the long Age of Law.

'Soon means soon,' my father said to Prince Issur with a soft smile. 'Arrangements are being made for that which you desire. May a little more patience be asked of King Hadaru?'

My father, I thought, was a wise man and deep. He knew very well, as did I, that the Ishkans had come to Mesh seeking to set a date for the Lightstone to be brought to King Hadaru's palace in Loviisa. He knew, too, that the Ishkans expected to be put off with all the forcefulness for which my father was famed. Thus his gentle manner disarmed Prince Issur.

'Perhaps a *little* more patience, then,' Prince Issur said, flushing from the intensity of my father's gaze. 'Shall we say before autumn's first snow?'

'Autumn is less than half a year away,' my father said. 'With the Red Dragon on the march again and kingdoms going up in flames, it will come soon enough – all too soon.'

He motioned for Prince Issur to take his seat; despite himself, Prince Issur did so. Although he must have been aware that my father had made no real commitment, he would take back to Ishka the impression that my father desired the same thing as did King Hadaru. And, truly, my father did. The duties of kingship might demand that he remain flexible in his strategies, but he would never stoop to deception or outright lies.

Even so, I knew that he hated having to make such oblique responses, that it went against his honest nature. He turned toward me then, and flashed me a quick look as if to say, 'Do you think it is hard being King? What must it be like, then, to be the Maitreya?'

As I sat pondering this mystery, I became aware of the many people covertly watching me, as they had all through the feast. I felt as well a smoldering malevolence directed at me; it stirred me to memory of another night just before the quest when Prince Issur's brother, Salmelu, had sat with the Ishkans silently beating me to death with his hateful heart. I hadn't known then that he had gone over to Morjin, that *he* was the assassin who had fired a kirax-tipped arrow at me in a dark wood. Despite the sensitivity of my gift, I hadn't been able to determine which of the hundreds of faces concealed the wish to make me dead.

My father's eyes now fell upon the Alonian table, and he called out, 'Count Dario – will you speak for Alonia?'

Count Dario, a small, dapper man, stood up quickly as his fingers smoothed the red hairs of his moustache and goatee. Then he bowed his head to my father. 'King Shamesh, you have sent emissaries to all the Free Kingdoms to call for a conclave here in Silvassu that we might

35

make alliance to oppose Morjin. But King Kiritan bids me to inform you that this cannot be. The conclave must be held in Tria. King Kiritan has sent word to each of the Free Kingdoms that the conclave will commence on the twenty-eighth of Marud. What do you say to this?'

I felt anger surge through my father's chest as he said, 'That your king must have a great grievance against me that he would insult me so.'

Lord Harsha and Lord Tanu – and many others across the hall – angrily nodded their heads in support of my father's outrage.

Count Dario now shot me a quick, sharp look. Then he stabbed his short finger toward the Lightstone as he turned back to my father and said, 'Last year, on the seventh of Soldru in Tria, on the night that King Kiritan called the Quest, all the knights who would recover the Lightstone vowed to seek it for all of Ea and not themselves. The Cup of Heaven was to be brought into Tria, from where the questers went forth. King Kiritan would ask King Shamesh why this has not been done?'

While Count Dario awaited my father's answer, Maram suddenly arose and wobbled on his beer-weakened legs. He was drunk enough to forget all protocol – but not so drunk that he was willing to let Count Dario's words stand unchallenged.

'King Shamesh!' he called out, 'may I speak?' Without waiting for permission, he turned toward Count Dario and continued, '*I* stood with the knights who made vows at your king's birthday party; I stood with Master Juwain Zadoran and Lord Valashu Elahad, who are here this night. I remember vowing that our quest to find the Lightstone would not end unless illness, wounds or death struck us down first. Well, illness of the soul anyone will suffer if they go into Argattha. Of wounds we had many, and death struck down the fairest of us in the Kul Moroth. Even so, our quest didn't end, as all can see. We *did* vow to seek the Lightstone for all of Ea. But we never said that we would deliver it to King Kiritan, who remained safe behind his kingdom's walls.'

Maram, puffing and sweating from his little speech, suddenly dropped back into his chair. I thought that he was rather pleased that he had slurred only a few of his words.

Count Dario seemed to be fighting back a smile as he bowed his head toward Maram. 'All the questers must be honored, especially those who went into Argattha and returned. I would not presume to gainsay Prince Maram. But I must strongly declare that it was understood the Lightstone was to be brought to Tria. This was the spirit of the questers' vows.'

From the dais above our table, where the thirty Guardians stood glaring at Count Dario, the Lightstone's radiance poured down upon my father's black and silver hair. He calmly regarded Count Dario, and there was steel in his voice as he said, 'Surely those who made vows are best able to interpret their spirit. Even so, we are all agreed that the Lightstone is for all of Ea, even as you have heard. Soon it will brought to Ishka – soon.'

'Then are we also agreed that it will be brought to Tria soon after?'

'That may be.'

'King Kiritan would ask you to agree that the Lightstone should be kept in Tria, where it will be safest.'

My father's face was grave as he said, 'Where is safety to be found in this world? Wasn't it only last year, at King Kiritan's birthday celebration, that one of his own barons nearly assassinated him?'

'Baron Narcavage, as you must know,' Count Dario said, glancing at the priests at table next to him, 'had gone over to Morjin. The plot was crushed – you can be sure that my king's other nobles remain loyal to him.'

'That is good. There's little enough of surety in this world, either.'

Count Dario's cool blue eyes tried to hold the brilliance of my father's gaze as he said, 'Come, King Shamesh, what do you say as to my king's request?'

'That it is not mine, alone, to grant.'

'No? Whose is it, then?'

My father shifted about in his chair to regard the Lightstone for a long few moments. He bowed his head to the Guardians who protected it. Then he turned back to Count Dario. 'You speak of a permanent residence for that which was meant to reside in one place, and one place only.'

'In this hall, do you mean?'

Count Dario stood bristling with insult while Prince Issur seemed ready to leap out of his chair to speak again.

And then my father said, 'The Lightstone was meant to reside in the hands of the Maitreya. Only he can decide its home – and its fate.'

Count Dario's face brightened as if he had been given the keenest of weapons to wield. 'You will be glad to know then that it is almost certain that the Maitreya has been found: in a village near Adavam. His name is Joakim.'

'Is this the blacksmith of which we have heard?'

'Yes – but he has been taken to Tria to prepare for a higher calling.'

Count Dario went on to say that Joakim now resided at the King's palace where Ea's greatest scholars, healers and alchemists were refining his talents and preparing him to take his place in history.

Here Master Juwain stood clutching the much-worn traveling volume of the *Saganom Elu* that he always carried. He called out, 'King Shamesh, may I speak?'

'Please do, Master Juwain.'

After flipping through the pages of his book, Master Juwain called out even more strongly as he read a passage from *Beginnings*: '"Grace cannot be gained like diamonds or gold. By the hand of the One, and not the knowledge of men, the Maitreya is made."' He closed his book and held it out toward Count Dario as if challenging him to read it, too.

'Those are curious words for a master of the Brotherhood to give us,' Count Dario said. 'Who reveres knowledge more than Master Juwain?'

'Perhaps one who knows the limits of knowledge.'

'Excuse me, but doesn't the Brotherhood teach that men must use all possible knowledge to perfect themselves? That, ultimately, it is their destiny to gain the glory of the Elijin and the Galadin?'

Just then Flick appeared in the space near my head and soared out into the hall in a spiral of silver lights. He swept past the table of the Red Priests, who appeared not to see him. It was strange, I thought, that perhaps only one person out of ten was able to apprehend his fiery form.

'What you say is true,' Master Juwain told Count Dario. 'But I'm afraid that one cannot become the Maitreya this way.'

'Do you deny then the wisdom of King Kiritan's decision to instruct the blacksmith's boy?'

'No – only that he wasn't brought to the Brotherhood to be taught.'

It was plain that Count Dario and Master Juwain might continue such an argument for hours. And so my father finally held up his hand for silence. He regarded Count Dario and said, 'If King Kiritan truly believes this Joakim to be the Maitreya, then why wasn't he brought here with you, that he might stand before the Lightstone? That we all might see if he can hold its radiance and give it back to us, in his eyes, hands and heart?'

Count Dario gazed up at the golden bowl upon its stand. Then he looked at my father and said, 'You have your treasure, King Shamesh, and we Alonians have ours, which we must keep safe behind Tria's walls.'

He went on to tell of the great passions that Joakim had aroused throughout his land. Many of Alonia's greatest barons, he said, were demanding of King Kiritan that the Lightstone be delivered into Joakim's hands. He hinted that they were actually calling for a war to liberate the golden cup from Mesh. Only King Kiritan stood between them and what would be the greatest of tragedies. If Count Dario could be believed, King Kiritan was a noble figure trying to control his bellicose barons for the sake of Mesh – and all of Ea.

After he had finished speaking, my father stared at him as he said, 'You must thank your king for his forbearance on our behalf.'

'That I shall do, but it is not your thanks he requires.'

As my father's stare grew cold and clear as diamonds in deep winter, Count Dario pulled at his goatee and said, 'King Kiritan knows what a sacrifice it would be to send the Lightstone to a distant land. Therefore he offers a gift, a very great gift, in return.'

Here he turned toward me and said, 'On the night the Quest was called, almost every noble in Alonia heard Lord Valashu Elahad ask for Princess Atara's hand in marriage. If the Lightstone is brought to Tria, King Kiritan would bless this marriage. And our two kingdoms might unite in strength against Morjin.'

A thrill of excitement shot through me as if I had been struck by a lightning bolt. Count Dario had spoken of King Kiritan's approval of the one thing I most desired. King Kiritan, who had once denigrated Mesh as a savage little kingdom and me as a ragged adventurer, must have thought that he was granting both the greatest of boons.

I stood up then, and to Count Dario I said, 'King Kiritan's generosity is famous, but even he cannot give away Atara's heart.'

It was the greatest torment I had ever known that Atara could not look at me in love – and would never consent to marry me so long as she couldn't.

'If my king can rule the greatest of Ea's kingdoms,' Count Dario said to me, 'then surely he can rule his own daughter.'

As I recalled the deep and lovely light that had once filled Atara's eyes before Morjin had torn them out, a terrible pain lanced through my head. I gasped out, 'Can one rule starfire?'

'*You* ask that, Lord Valashu? You, whom it's said would be Lord of Light itself?'

And with this rebuke he sat back down in his chair. So did I. Many people were looking at me. As before, I felt the red-hot nails of someone's hate pounding through me. It was not Count Dario, however, who drove this deadly emotion into me. I was as sure of this as I was the direction of my mother's loving gaze or the compassion in my father's eyes. For my gift of valarda had quickened since the gaining of the Lightstone, and it flared stronger in its presence. Now, as I sat looking out at the hundreds of men and women in the hall, my heart beat most quickly when I turned toward the table next to

39

that of the Alonians. There sat the seven Red Priests of the Kallimun. I could not make out any of their faces, for they sat with their heads hung low and their yellow cowls concealing them. I dreaded discovering that one of them might have been among the priests who had tortured Master Juwain – and Atara – in Argattha.

My father nodded at Count Dario, and said, 'You must thank King Kiritan for the offer of his daughter in marriage. It must be difficult to trade so great a treasure for a little gold bowl.'

A donkey, eyeing an apple dangling in front of his nose, might be impelled in its direction, especially if whipped in its hindquarters by a stick. But my father was no donkey. He would not be tempted by a marriage alliance with Alonia, much less moved by King Kiritan's badly veiled threat of war.

'Surely,' my father added, staring at Count Dario, 'King Kiritan will succeed in controlling his barons, whether or not the Lightstone is brought into Tria. As you have said, they *will* remain loyal to him, won't they?'

Having rather neatly finessed Count Dario and his king's demand for the Lightstone, my father said, 'As for the conclave being held in Tria, it will be difficult to persuade the Valari kings to meet there.'

And with that, he turned toward one of these kings. This was King Kurshan of Lagash, who now stood on his long legs to address my father and all gathered in the hall. His blue tunic, embroidered with the white Tree of Life, fell about his long form as he turned his much-scarred visage toward my father and said, 'Tria is far from the Nine Kingdoms, as is Sakai. We Valari need not fear invasions from outland kings, be they the Lord of Lies or those who should be allies against him. No, our worst enemy will remain ourselves.'

King Kurshan, I thought, had the good grace not to publicly reveal his desire to make a marriage for *his* daughter: to Asaru or me. I waited for him to say more.

'For far too long,' he continued, 'we Valari have made war against other Valari . . . because we have forgotten who we really are.'

He stared up at the Lightstone, and for a moment he seemed transported to another world. As he looked back at my father and resumed his speech, his words, too, seemed those of another world: 'It is said that once we Valari sailed the heavens from star to star. Why can't we do so again? In two weeks, lords and kings from Lagash to Mesh will meet in Nar at the great Tournament. Why can't we agree there, as one people, to build a fleet of ships such has never been seen in Ea? For it is said, too, that the waters of all worlds in the universe flow together. If we were to sail across the Alonian sea and into the ocean, we might find at last the Northern Passage to the worlds where the angels walk. The Lightstone will show the way. It was meant for the hands of the Maitreya, yes – but surely not *only* for his hands.'

So saying, he sat back down in his chair. The hall was so quiet that I could almost hear the quick burn of his breath. No one seemed to know if he were more than a little mad – or touched with great dreams.

For once my father seemed at a loss for words. Finally, he smiled at King Kurshan and forced out, 'That . . . is a beautiful idea. Perhaps we *will* build ships to sail the heavens' starry sea. You are a man of vision.'

The ferocious-seeming King Kurshan returned his smile like a little boy praised for a painting he has made. Then my father's gaze swept out into the hall. His eyes fixed upon a table near its far end where three women dressed in white robes sat with other outlanders and exiles. And my father called out, 'It seems that it is time that we heard of *other* visions, as well. Kasandra of Ar would speak to us tonight.'

Kasandra was a tiny woman who seemed as ancient as the cracked stone of the walls. As she struggled to rise out of her chair, Lord Tanu stood up at his table and called out, 'Sire, it might be best if this scryer were made to hold her tongue. We should not have to hear the words of distant oracles, most of which are corrupt.'

His hand swept out toward Kasandra and the two women who accompanied her. 'More to the point, these scryers are from *Galda*, and so who knows if they are Morjin's agents or spies?'

Lord Tanu, I thought, was a crabby and suspicious man. He would mistrust the sun itself because it rose first over the mountains of another land. I sensed that his words wounded Kasandra. There she stood, old and nearly bent double with the weight of some prophecy that she had traveled many miles to deliver – and her shame at Lord Tanu's loathing of scryers burned through her, as it did me.

And so *I* stood up and tried to make light of his insult. I, who had too often listened uncomprehending as Atara spoke of her visions, called out to Lord Tanu and the others in the hall: 'The real difficulty is in understanding the words of *any* scryer. It's like trying to grasp fish bare-handed in the middle of a rushing stream.'

But if I had hoped to cool Kasandra's rising anger, I hoped in vain. Kasandra looked across the hall toward me, and her sharp, old voice cracked out like thunder: 'I must tell you, Valashu Elahad, I have brought words that *you* will want to hold onto with all the strength you can summon.'

From the pocket of her robe, she took out a small, clear scryer's

41

crystal that sparkled in the sudden radiance pouring from the Lightstone.

'This is the vision that I and my sisters have seen: that you, Valashu Elahad, will find the Maitreya in the darkest of places; that the blood of the innocent will stain your hands; that a ghul will undo your dreams; that a man with no face will show you your own.'

She stared at me as my heart beat three times, hard, behind the bones of my chest. And then, without waiting for Lord Tanu or others to question her, she gathered up her sister scryers and stormed past the rows of tables and out through the western portal.

A dreadful silence fell upon the hall. No one moved; no one said anything. Her words seemed to hang in the air like black clouds. I knew, with a shiver that chilled my soul, that she had spoken truly. I wanted to leap up and follow her, to ask her the meaning of her prophecy. But just then a blast of hatred drove into my belly and left me gasping for breath.

While my father and family sat nearly frozen in their chairs, I struggled to turn toward the table of the Red Priests. The red dragons emblazoned on their yellow robes seemed to burn my eyes like fire. These seven men, I thought, were the descendants in spirit of others who had once crucified a thousand Valari warriors along the road to Argattha and had drunk their blood. And now one of them, I thought, perhaps incited by Kasandra's words, was crucifying me with his eyes and sucking at my soul. I looked for his face beneath the drooping cowls, but all I could see were shadows. And then I looked with a different sense.

All men and women burn with passions such as hatred and love, exuberance, envy and fear. These flames of their beings gather inside each person in a unique pattern that blazes with various colors: the red twists of rage, the yellow tint of cowardice, the bright blue bands of impossible dreams. And now the flames of one of these priests – the tall one hunched over his glass of brandy – came roaring out of the black cavern of memory and burned me with their fiery signature. With a sudden certainty that made my hand close around the hilt of my sword, I knew that I knew this man all too well.

And he knew it, too. For he raised up his head in a pride beyond mere arrogance and threw back his robe's yellow cowl. As he stood up to face me, one of the warriors called out, 'It's the traitor! It's Salmelu Aradar!'

'He's been banished from Mesh!' someone else shouted. 'On pain of death, he's been banished!'

'Send him back to the stars!' a familiar voice cried out.

I looked across the hall to see Baltasar standing with his sword half-drawn as he trembled to advance upon Salmelu.

'Hold!' my father called to him. To Salmelu, he said, '*You* have been denied fire, bread and salt while on Meshian soil. Yet here you stand, having taken much more than bread with us tonight!'

'It is true that Salmelu of Ishka has been banished,' Salmelu said. He was an ugly man, with a great bear-snout of a nose and a scar that seamed his face from his low hairline to his weak chin. His small eyes, black as pools of pitch, smoldered with spite for my father and me. 'But you should know, I am Salmelu no longer, for he is dead. You may call me Igasho, which is the new name Lord Morjin has given me.'

On the middle of his forehead was tattooed Morjin's mark: a coiled, red dragon. Some months before, by the banks of the Raaswash, I had exposed this mark for all to behold – and exposed Salmelu as a traitor and aspiring priest of the Kallimun. In the time since then, Salmelu must have travelled to Sakai to be confirmed in Morjin's evil priesthood. And returned here as the chief of Morjin's emissaries.

'It doesn't matter if he's called Igasho or Salmelu . . . or the Dark One himself!' Baltasar cried out, sliding out his sword another inch. 'A corpse by any other name would smell as foul. Let us put this one in the ground!'

'No, hold!' my father commanded. 'Whatever this Igasho is, he *is* Morjin's lawful emissary and may not be harmed. On pain of death, Baltasar – on pain of death.'

It cost my father much to deliver these words, especially in sight of Lansar Raasharu, who was not only his seneschal, but his oldest friend. Lord Raasharu sat at his table frozen to his seat; he stared at Baltasar and silently implored his son to put away his sword. As Baltasar's kalama slid back into its sheath with a loud click, Lord Raasharu breathed a heavy sigh of thanks.

'You,' my father said to Salmelu, 'defile the sacred calling of the emissary. But an emissary you still are, and you have come here to speak for Morjin. So then, speak.'

Salmelu – or Igasho – lifted up his head in triumph. He moved toward the center of the room so that he stood directly in front of the Lightstone, and he fairly whipped out these words: 'Tonight you have heard one scryer's prophecy. I bring you another, from Sakai: that the Day of the Dragon is at hand. For it has been foretold that Lord Morjin will regain the Cup of Heaven that was stolen from him.'

Here his hand pointed like a sword straight past my father's head at the Lightstone. 'Your son, King Shamesh, stole this from Lord Morjin's throne room, and *my* king demands that it be returned!'

'That's a lie!' Maram roared out, rising from his chair. 'How can Morjin claim as stolen that which *he* himself stole long ago?'

Salmelu cast Maram a look of scorn as if to ask why he – or anyone – should listen to the words of a drunkard. Then he turned and pointed his finger at me.

'*You* broke into the sacred city of Argattha – and broke into Lord Morjin's private rooms themselves. You are a thief who took gelstei from my lord: a bloodstone and the very Lightstone that now shines above you. You are a liar who has told false as to how you came by these things. And you are a murderer: how many, Valashu Elahad, did you put to the sword in making your escape? You even butchered a poor beast, the dragon, Angraboda, who was only trying to guard her eggs from you.'

Salmelu paced back and forth in front of my family's table, here pausing to stab his finger at me as he made a point, there sneering at me as he spat out his filthy accusations. He was all of Morjin's rage and hate, which bubbled up in his blood like poison and transformed him from a once-proud Valari warrior into a snarling, vengeful mockery of a man.

Once before, in King Hadaru's palace, Salmelu's lies had nearly driven me mad. And so I had challenged him to a duel that left him with terrible wounds – and had nearly killed me. Now, in the heart of *my* father's castle, I placed my hands flat upon the cool wood of the table before me where I could see them. I commanded them not to move.

'*You*,' Samelu said, pointing at me again, 'are also an assassin who tried to murder Lord Morjin. Is any crime so great as regicide?'

Once, in a dark wood not far from this place, Salmelu had fired into my body an arrow tipped with kirax in which Morjin had set his spite. The poison would always burn through my veins and connect me heart to heart with Morjin. His Red Priest, Salmelu who was now Igasho, continued firing poison into me in the form of his hateful words.

'And now *you*,' he continued, 'pose as the Lord of Light when you know that it is Lord Morjin who has been called to lead Ea into the new age.'

My hands, welded to the table by the stickiness of some spilt beer, no less my will, remained motionless. But I could not keep my lips from forming these words: 'If the Maitreya is Morjin, then light is dark, love is hate, and good has become evil.'

'*You* speak of evil, Lord Valashu? You speak that of one who is famed for his forgivingness?'

So saying, he removed from his pocket a small, gilded box. He stepped forward and laid it on the table just beyond the tips of my fingers.

'What is this?' I asked.

'A gift from Lord Morjin.'

'I want nothing from him!' I said, staring at the box. 'It cannot be accepted.'

'But it belongs to you. Or, I should say, to one of your friends.'

I looked across the hall to see Maram craning his neck to get a glimpse of what the box might hold. Baltasar, too, had half risen out of his seat

'Don't open it, Val!' Master Juwain called from his table. 'Give it back to him!'

At last, as if my hands had a life and will of their own, they moved to grasp the box and open it. I threw back its lid and gasped to see inside two small spheres that looked like chunks of charred meat. They stank of hemlock and sumac and acids used to tan flesh. I coughed and choked and swallowed hard against the bile rising up from my belly. For I knew with a sudden and great bitterness what these two spheres were: Atara's eyes that Morjin had clawed out with his own fingers and cast into a brazier full of red-hot coals.

Every abomination, I thought. *Every degradation of the human spirit.*

'Do you *see*?' Samelu said to me. His mocking voice beat at me like a war drum. 'Lord Morjin would return this treasure to your woman by your hand. And now the Cup of Heaven must be returned to *him*.'

Despite myself, I moved my fingers to touch these blackened orbs that I had once touched with my lips; it was as if I had touched the blackness at the very center of Morjin's heart. I felt myself falling into a bottomless abyss. I leapt up as I whipped out my sword and pointed it at Salmelu.

'I'll return *you* to the stars!' I shouted at him.

'Hold!' my father called out. 'Hold him, Ravar!'

Quick as an arrow, Ravar flew out of his chair and grabbed hold of me. So did Asaru and Karshur, who came up behind me and locked their arms around me as they clasped me close to their strong bodies.

'Do you see?' Salmelu cried out again as he backed away from my table. 'Do you see what a murderer this Elahad is?'

Truly, I thought, I *was* a murderer of men. And now I struggled like a madman against my brothers in a rage to stab my sword through Salmelu's vile mouth. I almost broke free. For my rage was like a poison that my brothers absorbed through their skin and which weakened their will to keep me from slaying Salmelu.

45

'Val!' Asaru gasped in my ear as his hand closed like an iron manacle around my arm. 'Be still!'

But I could not be still. For something bright and terrible was moving inside me. Once, in the lightless depths of Argattha, Morjin had told me that my gift of valarda was like a double-edged sword: as well as being opened by others' emotions, I might wield mine against men to cut and control. Master Juwain had taught me that I must learn to use the valarda, for good, as I might my hands or eyes. But my hands trembled to grasp the hilt of my sword and make murder; my eyes were as blind and blackened with hate as Atara's.

'Val!' a familiar voice cried out from across the hall. 'Oh, Val!'

A black, blazing hatred for Salmelu and Morjin built hotter and hotter inside me. As the valarda opened me to the men and women in the hall, and them to me, they felt this, too. They looked at me in loathing and awe. But a hundred feet away, Baltasar Raasharu arose from his chair and looked toward me as if awaiting my command.

'Do you see?' Salmelu cried out again as he began walking down the rows of tables toward Baltasar. He was that curious type of coward who must continually prove his bravery by goading others. 'Valashu Elahad would even have his friends murder for him. And so he would throw their lives away – as he did with the minstrel in the Kul Moroth.'

At last, I could hold the agony no longer. My eyes found Baltasar's, and the burning steel of my fury for Salmelu struck straight into my young friend's heart. His sword flashed forth as he cried out and leapt toward Salmelu. Probably Salmelu had calculated that the knights at the nearby tables would grab hold of him. But Baltasar moved too quickly to be so easily stopped.

It was the Lightstone that saved Salmelu's life – and Baltasar's. (And perhaps my own.) As I twisted and turned against my brothers' frantic hands, the little cup began shining more brightly from its stand behind me. In its sudden, clear radiance, I saw many things: that Baltasar *would* truly die for me, not because I wished it, but because he loved me even more than he hated Salmelu or his dreadful lord. And so he would not let me be the one to slay Salmelu. The Lightstone cast its splendor on his noble face, and I saw in him the finest flower of Valari knighthood about to cut down Salmelu – and thus be cut down by the failing of my heart.

Baltasar.

The One's creations, I saw, were so beautiful. The promise of life was so sweet and good and great. And yet, in the world, so much evil, so much pain. I couldn't understand it; I knew I never would. And yet I would give anything, tear out my own heart, to keep the promise for

Baltasar, and for everyone: to see them become the great beings we were born to be.

'Baltasar!' I cried out.

The Lightstone blazed with a sudden brilliance like a star. As it burned brighter and brighter, its radiance worked in me a miracle much greater than the transmutation of lead into gold. For, in one magical moment, it turned my hatred of Salmelu and Morjin into an overpowering love for Baltasar. How could I hold such a beautiful thing? And how could my brothers now hold me? My whole being filled with a force that gave me the strength of ten men. It poured through me like a golden fire. As I broke free from Asaru's grasp, I raised up my silver sword and pointed it at Baltasar. He had finally closed with Salmelu, and *his* sword lifted high above his head to cut him in two.

'Baltasar!' I cried out again.

But this was no sound from my throat nor name made by my lips, but only the peal of the bright and beautiful thing inside me. Like a lightning bolt directed by my sword, it suddenly flashed forth from me and streaked across the room. I felt it break open Baltasar's heart. Everyone in the hall, my father and brothers, my mother and grand-mother – even Salmelu himself – felt this, too. Baltasar felt it most deeply of all. The steel mask of fury melted from him. He hesitated as he turned toward me, and his face was all golden in the Lightstone's overpowering radiance. We regarded each other in wonder, and some-thing more.

'The Sword of Light!' a woman called out, pointing toward me.

I looked down to see that the silustria of my sword was flaring brightly – almost as brightly as the sword of valarda inside me. But soon, even as the wildly gleaming Lightstone began to fade, so did both swords, in my hand and heart.

'The Sword of Love!'

I lowered my sword called Alkaladur and sheathed it at the same moment that Baltasar put away his. His smile fell upon me like the rising of the sun.

'Oh, Val!' he whispered.

Everyone in the hall was staring at me. From Lord Harsha's table, Maram and Behira regarded me proudly, and even old Lord Tanu seemed to have forgotten his mistrust of all things. Master Juwain quietly bowed his head to me, and so did Asaru, Karshur and my father. My mother's gaze held only adoration for me, while Count Dario looked at me in fear. The faces of too many knights and nobles were full of awe – as was Salmelu's. For a moment, his whole being

47

seemed wiped clean of the spite that poisoned him. He stared at me as if he couldn't quite believe what had happened. But then, as the Lightstone faded back to its appearance as a small, golden cup, Salmelu returned to his hateful self. His ugly face took on its familiar lines of envy, arrogance and malice.

'*You*,' he said to me with a shame that burned his face, 'have drawn on one who no longer bears a sword of his own. But perhaps some day I will again, and then we'll see whose sword is quicker.'

He marched through the hall straight up to my table. From another pocket in his yellow robes, he removed a sealed letter and slammed it down on the table before me. '*This* is for you! From Lord Morjin!'

And with that, he gathered together his fellow priests and stormed out of the hall.

In that great room, with its many great personages, there was a silence that lasted many long moments. And then Lansar Raasharu, the foremost lord in Mesh, stood up.

'You have saved my son from a terrible dishonor,' he said as he bowed his head to me. Then he glanced at my father's stern face and added, 'And death.'

He went on to say that what he had witnessed, and felt, that night was nothing less than a miracle.

'Baltasar has always been too wild, too quick with his sword – and you have stayed his hand.' Lord Raasharu now turned away from me so that his words might carry out into the hall. 'Has it not been told in the ancient prophecies that the Maitreya will be known by just such miracles? What could be greater than the healing of the hatred in a man's heart?'

Not hating at all, I thought as I recalled the sword that I had put into Baltasar's hand.

Lord Raasharu's strong voice called out to the hundreds in the hall who listened raptly: 'Only a short while ago, we have had another prophecy, from the Galdan scryer: that Valashu would find the Maitreya in the darkest of places. What could be darker than finding this Lord of Light inside the dark cavern of one's own heart?'

He turned back to me, and bowed his head again, this time more deeply. 'Lord Valashu – Lord of Light. You are he. You must be. The way the Lightstone flared when you called to it, so bright, almost impossible.'

He looked up at the Lightstone shimmering on its stand and I heard him whisper, 'I never knew, I never knew.'

Awe colored the faces of many men and women turned toward me. I heard Lord Tanu's wife, Dashira, call out, 'Lord of Light!' while three of the Guardians standing near the Lightstone on the dais above me spoke as one, saying, 'Maitreya!' Others took up this call, too, and through the hall rang shouts of, 'Maitreya! Maitreya! Maitreya!'

This single name, repeated again and again, was sweeter than honey and more intoxicating than whole barrels of brandy.

'Lord Valashu, claim the Lightstone!' Lord Raasharu said to me. Many loud voices, and Lord Raasharu's the loudest of all, began urging me on toward what seemed my fate. They almost drowned out a much quieter voice whispering inside me. How could *I* be the Maitreya, I asked myself? I, who had trembled with murderous wrath only moments before? My father, his bright eyes fixed on me, seemed to be asking me this same question.

And then Master Juwain smiled at me with the happiness of hope fulfilled even as Baltasar came forward and stood at the end of my table. He pulled me up from my chair and embraced me; he kissed my forehead and said, 'My life is yours – thank you, friend.'

'Thank *you*,' I said to him. If not for his wild charge toward Salmelu, I might have charged instead. And my father would have had to order *my* death. 'My life is yours, again. How can it be repaid?'

He smiled and didn't hesitate as he said, 'Claim the Lightstone.'

I smiled, too, as I slowly nodded my head. Then I clasped his hand in mine. To the acclaim of Lord Raasharu and Lord Tomavar – and many others – I turned and mounted the dais behind me. The Guardians in their gleaming suits of mail made two rows on either side of the Lightstone. I stepped straight toward the stand holding up the golden bowl. I felt Alkaladur, at my side, resonating with it. I felt inside for a like resonance of my heart, which it was said was the endowment of the Maitreya – and the Maitreya alone.

All my life, I whispered to myself.

All my life I had longed for one thing above all else. But it was the greatest of ironies that I, whose heart was so open to others, was forced by fate to stand apart from them. For if I did not, their lusts and passions would burn through me and annihilate me utterly. And so I had to climb through a stark and terrible inner landscape to the top of the highest mountain in the world. There the air was cold and thin and bitter. There I breathed the pain of being ever alone. All my life I had known that there must be a cure for the gift that afflicted me, if only I had the courage to find it.

And now, as I stood upon the hard stone dais in my father's hall, I gazed at a little bowl that seemed to hold within its golden hollows all the secrets of life. I knew that it might be used to touch into life the infinite seeds of brotherhood waiting to burst forth inside all men

– and so to touch that infinite tree that shone with the light of the One. And then the pain of being would vanish in a deeper flame, and the promise of life would at last be fulfilled. And no man or woman would ever stand alone again.

'Lord of Light!' someone called out as if from far away. Another voice joined his, and then two, ten and a hundred more. In the rawness of their throats was an aching to come together as a great and beautiful force. 'Lord of Light! Lord of Light! Lord of Light!'

To want to see men and women standing tall as oaks, the sun rising warm upon their faces, whole, happy and unafraid; to see them healed of suffering in the light of that deep joy which pours itself out through their hearts and unites them in glory with all things; to want this for myself and all those I loved, and for everyone – was this so wrong?

'Claim it, Valashu!' someone else called to me. 'Claim the Lightstone!'

Five feet in front of me, on its white granite stand, the little cup of gold gelstei was waiting for me to lay my hands upon it. The thirty Guardians to either side of me were waiting with their eyes grown bright as stars; in the hall behind me, my father and friends and hundreds of others were gazing at me in silent expectation. Even the portraits of my ancestors along the cold stone walls seemed to be looking down at me and demanding that I fulfill my fate.

About the Maitreya one thing is known, I suddenly remembered. *That to himself, the Maitreya always is known.*

'I *must* be he,' I whispered to myself. 'I must be.'

And then fear struck me to the core as my hands began to sweat and I remembered other words from the *Saganom Elu*: *If a man comes forth in falseness as the Shining One concealing darkness in his heart, if he claims the Lightstone for his own, then he shall become a new Red Dragon, only mightier and more terrible.*

'So much evil in the world,' I whispered. 'So much pain.'

At last, I stepped forward and placed my hands around the curve of the bowl. Its cool golden surface seemed instantly to sear my flesh. It was like trying to grasp the fiery substance of a star. The pain was so great I could hardly hold it. But beneath the pain, a deeper and more beautiful thing.

I turned as I lifted the Lightstone high for all to see. And then I called out into the hall: 'It is not yet determined who the Maitreya really is. There are tests still to be made. As far as I know, I am only the Lightstone's Guardian, a Knight of the Swan.'

So saying, I set the Lightstone back on its stand. I looked down at my hands to see if they had been charred black. But the flesh of my

50

palms and fingers showed only its familiar ivory tones and remained untouched.

'Lord of Light!' someone below me cried out. 'Lord of Light!'

Sounds of disappointment and protest now rumbled through the hall. It came to me then that the more I denied that I was the Maitreya, the more that others might interpret this as humility and so be even more inclined to acclaim me as the Shining One.

'Lord of Light! Lord of Light! Lord of Light!'

I was keenly aware, however, that while I hadn't claimed to be the Maitreya, I hadn't denied it, either. It tormented me to remember that Morjin had struck a similar pose before his evil priests in Argattha.

After that, my father announced that the feast had come to an end. The various knights, ladies and lords began standing up from their tables and exited the hall to repair to their chambers. The thirty Guardians remained at their post, the steel rings of their mail reflecting the Lightstone's abiding radiance. Their bright, black eyes remained ever watchful, ever awake, ever aware – and now aware of me in a way that they hadn't been before.

So it was with Lansar Raasharu, who was one of last to say goodnight. He seemed not to want to leave my side. The wonder with which he now regarded me filled me with a gnawing disquiet.

I returned to my family's table, where I retrieved the box that Salmelu had set before me. I resolved to bury its contents deep within the earth. Morjin's letter I picked up with fevered hands and tucked down inside my armor. I didn't know how I would find the courage to open it.

I stood for a long time staring up at the Lightstone as the words of Kasandra's prophecy burned themselves deeper and deeper into my mind: that I would find the Maitreya in the darkest of places; that the blood of an innocent would stain my hands; that a ghul would undo my dreams; that a man with no face would show me my own.

4

y father, before he left the hall, informed me that there was to be a gathering in his rooms. While he walked on ahead with Asaru, Nona and my mother, I proceeded more slowly with Master Juwain and Maram, who had also been invited to this unusual midnight meeting. Maram was in his cups, and in no condition to hurry. I offered my arm around his back to steady him, but he shook me off, saying, 'Thank you my friend, but I'm not *that* drunk – not yet. Of course, your father *has* promised me some of his best brandy. Otherwise, I would have been tempted to find Dasha and recite a few lines that I composed during the feast.'

'Dasha?' I said, shaking my head. 'You mean Behira, don't you?'

'Ah, Behira – yes, yes, Behira.'

We made our way down the short corridor connecting the hall to the castle's keep. There we found another corridor leading straight to my father's rooms. Most of his guests had already retired for the night, but from the deeps of this great building came sounds of low voices and heavy oak doors creaking and closing. We passed by the infirmary, which was quiet enough, though a stench of medicines and bitter herbs emanated from it, as well as a more ancient odor of anguish of all the sick and dying who had ever lain inside. To me, carrying Salmelu's wooden box, brooding upon Kasandra's warning, it seemed to be the very essence of the castle itself, and it overlay other odors of burnt flesh from the kitchens and the centuries of candle smoke that darkened the stone ceiling and walls. I was glad to pass by the empty library and the servants' quarters and so to come to the great door to my parents' rooms. For inside, there had always been happier scents: of soap and wax from the well-scrubbed floors; of flowers that my mother arranged in vases and the honey-cakes that she liked to serve with tea and cream; and most of all, the air of safety and steadfastness with which my father ordered all things within his realm.

Asaru opened the door for us and invited us inside. There we removed our boots and joined my father, mother and grandmother, who were sitting around the edge of a fine Galdan carpet. My father disdained chairs, claiming that they weakened one's back and encouraged poor posture; to suit convention, he filled his hall with many tables and chairs but would allow none in his rooms. I looked around this large chamber as I drank in its familiar contents: the two fireplaces filled with fresh white logs and the six braziers heaped with the coals of fragrant woods that helped drive away the castle's omnipresent chill; a cherrywood chest that had once belonged to my grandfather and a painting of him, hung on the west wall, that my grandmother had once made; another carpet on which rested a chess board with its gleaming ivory and ebony pieces; a loom where my mother wove colored threads into tapestries. And at the room's north end, framed by a massive, carved headboard, stood my parents' bed where twenty-one years before I had come into the world on a warm winter day, with the sun at the midheaven in that bright and fiery constellation of stars that called me ever on toward my fate.

I sat straight across from my father, who poured me a glass of brandy. Maram and Master Juwain sat to my right, while Asaru took his place next to my mother and grandmother on my left. Asaru, it was said, favored my mother, his face cut with the same clean and symmetrical lines in which many found a great beauty. His faithfulness to her, and to all those he honored, could make one cry. He was that rarest of beings: a very intelligent man who saw things simply without ever being simple-minded. His love for me was simple, too – and as strong and bright as a diamond.

'That was a close thing that happened tonight,' he said to me as my father passed him a glass of brandy. 'That traitor nearly got you killed.'

Everyone turned toward my father, who held his face stern. No one seemed to have the courage to ask him if he really would have ordered my death, should I have murdered Salmelu.

'We'll speak of the emissary in a moment,' my father said. 'But we've other things to discuss first.'

'But what of Karshur and Yarashan?' I asked. 'And Jonathay, Ravar and Mandru? Shouldn't we wait for them?'

'No, let them sleep. It will be best if we keep this council small.'

'Ah, sleep,' Maram said as he yawned, then took a sip of his brandy. 'Don't you think we'd all do better, King Shamesh, with a little sleep before discussing anything of importance?'

'Certainly, we would do better, Sar Maram,' my father said. 'But the world won't always wait while we retreat into sleep, will it?'

I shifted on top of the carpet, with its thick and clean-smelling wool. Sitting on it in my steel armor was almost a comfort. I looked at my father and said, 'What is troubling you, sir?'

He looked straight back at me, and his eyes fell dark with a terrible sadness. I knew that *had* he been forced to order my death, he might as well have ordered his own.

'Many . . . things are on my mind,' he said to me. 'Which is why my family has been called to council at such a late hour – and those who are like unto family.'

He smiled at Master Juwain and Maram, then continued: 'We'll begin with the demands of the Alonian emissary. Asaru, what do you think?'

Asaru, sitting straight as the mast of a ship, nodded at my father and said, 'Like it or not, King Kiritan has finessed us. It seems that the conclave will have to be held in Tria, if anywhere.'

'Yes, it does.'

'But the Valari kings will never agree to journey there.'

'No, not as things stand now,' my father said.

'And there would be great trouble in the Nine Kingdoms if the Lightstone were brought into Tria, as King Kiritan has asked.'

'That is true,' my father said. 'Especially if the Lightstone were given into the hands of the blacksmith boy. The Ishkans would make war against us immediately for such a betrayal.'

I again shifted about as I thought of the young Alonian healer named Joakim. And I heard Asaru say to my father, 'Count Dario hinted that King Kiritan's barons are calling for war against us – does this concern you?'

'Do you think it should?'

'That's hard to say. It seems impossible that the Alonians would march against us across such a distance. Not over a little piece of gold.'

Although the Lightstone remained on its stand in the great hall, it seemed that its shimmering presence filled the room and added to the soft radiance of its many flickering candles.

'No, you're right, we need fear no such invasion,' my father said. 'But that Count Dario spoke freely of King Kiritan's problems with his barons – that *does* concern me.'

He went on to say that such strife could weaken any kingdom, even Alonia. And with Morjin gathering armies to his bloody red banner, it would not do for any of the Free Kingdoms to fall into disorder – especially Alonia.

'It would seem,' my father said to Asaru, 'that strengthening his realm is the real reason that King Kiritan has demanded your "little piece of gold". It is probably why he called the Quest in the first place.'

54

'To strengthen Alonia or to strengthen himself?'

'He would think there is no difference,' my father said.

My mother, sitting next to him, brushed the long, black hair away from her face as she said, 'King Kiritan's offer of his daughter's hand must be considered in this light. And like it or not, it must be *considered*.'

Her voice was as clear and sweet as the music of a flute, and it seemed to carry out straight toward me. As she smiled at me, I couldn't help remembering how she had taught me to play that most magical of instruments and had sung me songs of Ramsun and Asha, and the other great lovers who had died for each other in ages past.

'It's said that Atara Ars Narmada is very beautiful,' my mother told me. 'With hair as gold as your cup. With eyes as blue as stars.'

'Once they were,' I said bitterly, squeezing the box that I had set by my side. In barely three heartbeats' worth of time, Morjin had utterly transformed Atara's face from one that was open, bright and alive into something other. For now shadows gathered in the dark hollows beneath her brows, and her lips would have frozen the breath of any man who dared try to kiss her.

It might have been thought that my mother, who was the kindest of women, would have done anything to avoid a topic that caused me so much pain. Compassion, I thought, should be like a soft, warm blanket wrapped around those we love to comfort them, and hers usually was. But sometimes, it was like a steel needle that plunges straight into the heart of a boil to relieve the pressure there. My mother seemed always to know what I needed most.

'You should remember her as she was when you first saw her,' my mother told me. 'Don't you think that is what she would want?'

'Yes . . . she would,' I forced out. And then I added, 'And as she might be again.'

My mother's face softened as she searched for something in mine. 'You've never said much about her, you know.'

'What is there to say, then?'

'Well, nothing, really – nothing that your eyes haven't shouted a hundred times.'

I turned to wipe at my eyes as I remembered the way that Atara had once looked at me. Not so long ago, in the flash of her smile, in beholding the boldness of her gaze, my eyes must have filled with the light of that faraway star that fed the fire of our souls.

My mother's smile reminded me of Atara's in its promise that she would only ever wish all good things for me. She said to me, 'You'd never marry another, would you?'

55

'Never,' I said, shaking my head.

She turned to regard my father a moment, and a silent understanding passed between them. My father sighed and said, 'Then King Kurshan will have to look elsewhere if he wants a match for *his* daughter.'

He spoke of this fierce king from Lagash who would sail the stars – after first marrying off his daughter, Chandria. Then Asaru nodded at my father and asked him, 'Do you wish me to make marriage with her, sir?'

'Possibly,' my father said to him. 'Do you think you might ever come to love her?'

'Possibly,' Asaru said, smiling at him. 'By the grace of the One.'

We Valari do not, as a rule, marry for love. But my grandfather had chosen out my grandmother, a simple woodcutter's daughter, for no other reason. And my father had always said that his love for my mother, and hers for him, was proof of life's essential goodness. For until the moment of his betrothal to Elianora wi Solaru, daughter of King Talanu of Kaash, my father had never set eyes upon her. And now, thirty years later, his heart still leaped with fire whenever he looked her way.

'Well,' he said, taking a sip of brandy, 'we can speak of marriage another time. We have other kings to worry about now.'

He glanced at Master Juwain and said, 'There's an ugly rumor going around that you quarreled with King Waray on your journey to Taron.'

'I'm afraid that is true,' Master Juwain said. His lumpy face pulled into a frown as he rubbed the back of his bald head. 'I'm afraid I have bad news: King Waray has closed our school outside Nar.'

The story that Master Juwain now told, as the logs in the fireplaces burnt down and we all sipped our brandy, was rather long, for Master Juwain strived for completeness in all things. But its essence was this: Master Juwain had indeed gone to Nar to make researches into the horoscope of an ancient Maitreya, as I had discovered earlier that evening. He had also wanted to retrieve relics that the Brothers kept in their collection in the Nar sanctuary. These were thought stones, he said, and therefore lesser gelstei – but still of great value.

'King Waray allowed me to remove a book about the Shining One from the library, as Val will tell,' Master Juwain said. 'But he forbade the removal of any thought stone or gelstei.'

'A king's forbiddance does not make a quarrel,' my father said.

'No, it does not,' Master Juwain agreed. 'But when a certain master of the Brotherhoods very testily reminds that king that his realm ends at the door of the Brotherhood sanctuary, *that* is the beginning of a quarrel.'

'Indeed it is, Master Juwain.'

'And when that king orders all the Brothers to leave the sanctuary and the doors to be locked, some would say that is only the quarrel's natural development and should have been anticipated.'

'Some would say that very thing,' my father said, smiling. 'And they would be surprised that such an otherwise reasonable and non-quarrelsome master would risk such a disaster over some old gelstei.'

'Over a principle, you mean, King Shamesh.'

'Very well, then, but to lose one's temper and court the failure of one's mission over the continuation of what is really an ancient quarrel cannot be counted as the act of a wise man.'

'Did I say I failed?' Master Juwain asked. Now he smiled as he drew out of his pocket a stone the size of a walnut. Its colors of ruby, turquoise and auramine swirled about in the most beguiling of patterns. 'Well, I didn't fail *completely*. I managed to spirit this away before King Waray locked the doors.'

'Spirit it away!' Maram called out, leaning over to examine the thought stone. 'You mean, *stole* it, don't you?'

'Can one steal from one's own house?'

'King Waray,' my father said, 'might feel that since it was his ancestors who built the sanctuary and his knights who defend it still, that the house is his – or at least the treasures gathered inside.'

'You do not feel that way, King Shamesh. You have always honored the ancient laws.'

This was true. My father would never have thought to act as tyrannically as had King Waray. In truth, he honored the Brotherhood even as he did old laws that others had long since repudiated. And so half a year before, when Master Juwain had returned with me bearing the Lightstone, my father had ordered a new building to be raised up at the Brotherhood's sanctuary in the mountains outside our castle. Master Juwain – and the other masters – were to gather gelstei from across Ea that they might be studied. Master Juwain must have seen that King Waray's envy of Mesh and the much greater treasure in my father's hall was the deeper reason that he had closed the sanctuary in Nar.

'Knowledge must be honored before pride of possession,' my father said. His bright eyes fixed on the thought stone. 'Let us hope that this gelstei holds knowledge that justifies incurring King Waray's ill will.'

'I believe it to hold knowledge about the Lightstone,' Master Juwain said. 'And possibly about the Maitreya.'

My father's eyes grew even brighter – and so, I imagine, did mine.

Everyone except my grandmother now turned toward Master Juwain to regard the little stone in his hand.

'You *believe* it to hold this knowledge?' my father said. 'Then you haven't – what is the right word – *opened* it?'

'Not yet,' Master Juwain said. 'You see, there are difficulties.'

What I knew about the thought stones was little: they belonged to the same family of gelstei as did the song stones and the touch stones. It was said that a thought stone, upon the closing of a man's hand, could absorb and hold the contents of his mind as a sponge does water. It was also said that in ages past, the stones could be opened and 'read' by anyone trained in their use. But few now possessed this art.

'One would have thought that a master of the Brotherhood would have overcome any difficulties,' my father said to Master Juwain.

'One would have thought so,' Master Juwain agreed with a sigh. 'But you see, this is not just *any* thought stone.'

He went on to say that in the Age of Law, the ancients had used the Lightstone to fill certain thought stones with a rarefied knowledge: that of the secrets of the Lightstone itself.

'If this stone contains such knowledge,' Master Juwain said to my father, holding up his opalescent little marble, 'it may be that the only way to open it would be with the aid of the Lightstone.'

'Do you wish my permission to use the Lightstone this way?'

Master Juwain's face tightened with dismay. 'I'm afraid I don't know how. Perhaps no one now living does.'

My father swirled the brandy around in his glass and watched the little waves of the amber liquor break against the clear crystal. Then he looked at Master Juwain and said, 'Then you need the Lightstone to open the thought stone, and the thought stone to understand the secrets of how the Lightstone might be used. How are we to solve this conundrum?'

'I had hoped,' Master Juwain said, 'that if I stood before the Lightstone, the answer might come to me.'

He turned toward me and added, 'I had hoped, too, that the thought stone might tell us more about the Maitreya. About how he is to be recognized and how he might use the Lightstone.'

Now I, too, looked down at the swirls of brandy in my glass. For a long few moments, I said nothing – and neither did anyone else.

And then my father said to Master Juwain, 'You may certainly make your trial whenever you wish. It's too bad that you brought back only one such stone. But you say that others remain in Nar?'

'Hundreds of others, King Shamesh.'

My father smiled at him reassuringly and then nodded at Asaru. He said to him, 'Do you still plan to journey to the tournament?'

'If that is still your wish, sir,' Asaru said. 'Yarashan will accompany me to Nar next week.'

'Very good. Then perhaps you can prevail upon King Waray to reopen the Brotherhood's school.'

'Can one prevail upon the sun to shine at night?'

'Does the task daunt you?'

'No more than Master Juwain's conundrum must daunt him,' Asaru said, shrugging his shoulders. 'In either case, there must be a solution.'

'Good,' my father said, smiling at him. 'Problems we'll always have many, and solutions too few. But there's always a way.'

His gaze now fell upon me, and I couldn't help feeling that he regarded me as both a puzzle to be solved *and* its solution.

'Always a way,' I said to him, thinking of my own conundrum. 'Sometimes that is hard to believe, sir.'

My father's gaze grew brighter and harder to bear as he said, 'But we *must* believe it. For believing in a thing, we make it be. As you, of all men, must believe this now.'

Strangely, what had happened earlier in the hall with Baltasar had so far gone unremarked, like some family secret or crime, instead of the miracle that Lansar Raasharu proclaimed it to be. But my family and friends knew me too well. Master Juwain and Maram, on our quest, had seen me sweat and weep and bleed. When I was a child, my mother had wiped the milk from my chin, and once, my father had pulled me off Yarashan when I had tried to bite off his ear in one of our brotherly scuffles. They might or might not believe that I was the Maitreya of ancient legend and prophecy – but it was clear that they did not intend to speak of me in hushed tones or to forget that whatever mantle I might claim, I would always remain Valashu Elahad.

'It is not upon me,' my father said, 'to determine if you are this Shining One that many hope you to be. But you *are* my son, and that *is* my concern. The brightest flower is the one that is most often picked; the elk with the greatest rack of antlers draws the most arrows. You are a target now, Valashu. Even before this thing passed between you and Baltasar, it was so. Consider the way that the traitor nearly brought about your doom – and my own.'

The quiet of the room was broken only by the hissing from the fireplace and my father's measured words. We all listened to him tell of what a great tragedy it would have been for Mesh if I *had* murdered Salmelu. For then my father would have been faced with an excruci-

59

ating choice: either for the king himself to break the law of the land in sparing my life or to order the death of that which gave *his* life purpose – and the death of one who might possibly be the Maitreya.

'The Red Dragon,' he said, 'set a terrible trap for us. By the grace of the One, we found a way out. You did, Valashu. A way – there's always a way.'

'I . . . hated Salmelu as I've only hated one other,' I said. I picked up the box containing the two broken windows to Atara's soul, and gripped it so hard that it hurt my hand. 'And when he gave me this, the hate, like fire in my eyes, like madness . . . *this* is what Morjin must have calculated would make me kill Salmelu. But how could Morjin have been *sure*?'

'Go on,' my father said as everyone looked at me.

'This trap of Morjin's – it wouldn't have caught another. And it shouldn't have caught me.'

'No, it shouldn't have,' my father agreed. 'And from this, what do you conclude?'

'That there will be other traps that we haven't yet seen.'

Across the circle from me, my mother's breath seemed to have been choked-off as if by an invisible hand. I heard Maram muttering in his brandy, even as my father nodded his head and said, 'Yes, just so. This is why we've all been kept from our beds tonight, that we might see these other traps before it's too late.'

Asaru, it seemed, had been making calculations of his own. He eyed the familiar chess set for a moment before turning to my father. 'The Red Dragon was willing to throw away Salmelu's life, like a pawn.'

'No, rather like a knight that must be sacrificed to checkmate an opponent,' my father said.

'Very well, a knight, then. But did Salmelu *know* that he was to be sacrificed?'

My father smiled grimly and shook his head. 'Few men have such devotion for their king.'

'Morjin is no king,' I said, thinking of the whips I had heard cracking in the darkened tunnels of Argattha. 'Men do not follow him out of love.'

'Then shouldn't we consider the Galdan scryer's prophecy?' Asaru asked. 'She spoke of a ghul, didn't she?'

Could Salmelu truly be a ghul, I wondered? Had he given up his soul to Morjin so that Morjin breathed his fell words into Salmelu's mouth and moved his lips and limbs from afar like a puppeteer pulling on strings? The living-dead, ghuls were called: they who were as corpses inside and were forced to think the very thoughts of their masters.

'No,' I said at last, 'Salmelu is no ghul.'

'But, Val, how can you be sure?'

Because the flames of his being burn with different colors than do Morjin's.

I stared off at the candles in their stands as I said, 'In Salmelu and Morjin, so much malice, so much hate. But the fire that eats away at Salmelu is different from that which consumes Morjin. Its source is different. I . . . can *feel* Salmelu's will to destroy me. It's as unique to him as a knight's emblem or a man's face.'

Asaru thought about this for a moment as a sudden dread came over him. 'But, Val, if Salmelu isn't this ghul, who is?'

Master Juwain, now sitting utterly still, cleared his throat and said, 'A scryer's prophecies are famously difficult to interpret, even those that prove true. But we should all give much thought to this one.'

His large, gray eyes fell upon me with the weight of worlds as he continued, 'We see at least one of the Red Dragon's traps within the trap: if Salmelu had failed to goad you into murder, what he brought here out of Argattha could *not* have failed to make you want to murder him.'

'Many wish to murder Morjin,' I said. 'And his priests.'

'But do they wish it as *you* do, Val? A fire, you spoke of, a raging fire that blinded you – like one of his illusions.'

'In Argattha,' I said, 'the Lord of Lies lost the power to make me behold his illusions.'

'Yes, but it seems he still has the power to make you hate.'

The brandy in my glass burned my tongue as I sipped it. 'Are you saying, then, that Morjin is trying to make *me* into a ghul?'

'Trying, yes, with all his might. But your heart is free. And your soul is the gift of the One. It can never be taken, only surrendered.'

'That,' I said, 'will never happen.'

'No, the Lord of Lies has no power to seize your will directly. But how much of your will do you think will remain if you destroy yourself with this terrible hate?'

I had no answer for him. I knew that he was right. For a few moments, I tried to practise one of the light meditations that he had once taught me. But the two blackened orbs inside the box that Salmelu had given me darkened my eyes; and the letter that I had placed down inside my armor was like a crushing weight upon my heart.

I finally brought forth this thick square of folded paper. I held it up toward the candles in their stand. No ray of light pierced the bone-white envelope to show what words Morjin might have written to me. It was sealed with red wax bearing the stamp of the Dragon.

'Is this, then,' I asked, 'another of Morjin's traps?'

'I'm afraid it is,' Master Juwain said.

'Then the trap must be sprung.'

I drew my knife to open it, but Master Juwain held out his hand and shook his head. 'No, do not – burn it instead.'

'But the letter must be read. If Morjin has set traps for me, then his words might betray what these are.'

'I'm afraid his words *are* the trap. Like the kirax, Val. Only this poison will work at your mind.'

'My father,' I said, looking across the circle at the great man who had sired me, 'taught me that an enemy's mind must be studied and known.'

'Not *this* enemy,' Master Juwain said. 'Liljana merged minds with the Dragon in Argattha. It nearly destroyed her.'

I thought of this brave woman with her round, pleasant face and her will of steel. Atara had once warned her that the day she looked into Morjin's mind would be the last day she ever smiled. And yet, if she hadn't dared this dreadful feat, none of us would have escaped from Argattha and the Lightstone would remain in Morjin's possession.

I squeezed the letter between my fingers, and said to Master Juwain, '"Lord of Light," everyone called me. If this is true, how, then, should this Dark Lord called Morjin have power over me with his words?'

'Is this the pride of a prince?'

'It might seem like pride, sir. But I don't think it really is. You see, after being forced to watch what Morjin did to Atara, no help for it and nothing I could do, nothing . . . after that, there wasn't very much to be proud of, ever again. No, it is something else.'

Master Juwain's Juwain's eyes grew bright and sad as he finally understood. 'No, Val – don't do this.'

'Earlier tonight, you made a test of things with your horoscopes. But there are other tests to be made.'

'No, not this way.'

'I must know, sir.'

Master Juwain pointed his gnarled finger at the letter and said, 'I think this is an evil thing.'

I nodded my head to him. 'But didn't you once tell me that light would always defeat the darkness? Either one has faith in this or one does not, yes?'

Master Juwain sighed as he rubbed his eyes. He rubbed the back of his head. He sighed, his troubled eyes on the letter. Then he turned toward my father and asked, 'And what, King Shamesh, do you advise your son to do?'

My father's eyes were like coals as he said simply, 'Open the letter.'

'And you, Queen Elianora?' Master Juwain asked my mother.

Her concern for me hurt my heart as she said, 'Burn it, please.'

Master Juwain asked everyone's counsel. Nona joined my mother and Master Juwain in their desire to see the letter destroyed, while Asaru and Maram agreed with my father that it should be opened and read. And so Master Juwain looked at me and said, 'You must decide, Val.'

I nodded my head, then moved my knife toward the letter.

'Wait!' Master Juwain called out. 'If you don't fear the poison of the Lord of Lies' words, then at least consider that he might have written this letter with a poisoned ink. Do not touch it with your bare hands!'

Again, I nodded toward him. I laid down both the letter and the knife, then removed the riding gloves folded around my belt. I put these on. Then I picked up the knife again and used its sharp steel tip to break the seal of the letter.

'Do you have enough light?' my mother said to me. 'Shall I bring you a candle?'

I shook my head as I drew out the sheets of paper and unfolded them. It was awkward working this way, with my fingers covered in slips of leather. But the gloves kept my sweat from the paper, and the ink from my flesh, even as the small, neat lettering of Morjin's hand leaped like fire into my eyes:

My Dearest Valashu,

I trust this letter finds you in good health, which my friends in your little kingdom assure me has never been better. You will want to know that I have made what could be called a miraculous recovery from the wound to my neck that you must have hoped was mortal. The wound to my heart, however, remains more grievous. For you have taken from me that which is dearer than life itself.

'Well?' Maram called out from next to me. 'What does it say? Read it out loud.'

I nodded my head and took another sip of brandy. I began reading again from the letter's beginning, for Maram's sake and everyone else's. As I intoned the words that Morjin had set to paper, I had to fight to keep my voice from becoming his voice: smooth, suasive, seductive and strong. An image of Morjin as I had first seen him came into my mind: his fine, intelligent face that was radiant with an almost unearthly beauty; his hair like spun gold and his golden eyes. They were the eyes of an angel, and they seemed to know all things. They looked at me out of the black ink of his words as I continued to read:

I know that you keep the Cup of Heaven locked and guarded in your castle as in ancient times. It is a beautiful thing, is it not? The most beautiful in all the world. And so I know that you will see in its golden depths the most beautiful of all temptations: to believe that you are its master, the Lord of Light – the Maitreya. How could it be otherwise? For you, Valashu Elahad, who feels so keenly the suffering of others, must long quite terribly for the suffering to end. This is a noble impulse. But it is misguided, and for the sake of the world, and your own, I must try to make you understand why.

All beings yearn for one thing above all else: the light and love of the One. For this is our source and substance, and we long to return there. But this ecstasy of completion and deep peace is denied to us, and the proof of this is our suffering. Men suffer many things: dread of death and wounds and dashed dreams, but nothing so terrible as the desire that burns our beings to feel ourselves at one with our source. We suffer most of all because we do not understand why we must suffer: why the One, which is said to be all goodness itself, would wish all the agonies of the body and soul upon us. Have you not, Valashu, as you listened to the cries of the children being torn apart at Khaisham, as you cursed life itself, asked yourself the simple question, 'Why?'

The answer, I must tell you, is as simple as it is terrible: because of the One's nature, which is the nature of all things. Can you not yet see that good and evil are the two sides of the One's face, and his two hands, right and left? In one hand he holds the golden gelstei and makes the cosmos and all its creatures from the substance of his own being; with the other he casts them from the light and torments them. He builds walls of flesh around our souls to separate us from our source and from each other; he makes us rot with age, and crucifies us to the cross of life in the most hideous of anguish. He makes us to die. And so, at the end of all things, we must suffer the greatest ignominy: that of being erased. And then, forever, there is only nothingness and the darkness of night.

Who has not raged that the One should make things so? Do you think that I, Valashu, have not wept bitter tears like any other man? Have not known love and loss? To fear that the beautiful light that is my soul will simply die like a candle flame snuffed out by cold wind – do you think I haven't, ten thousand times, shaken my fist at the heavens over the cruelty of such a fate? Should I not, then, hate the One and all the works of his hand? Shouldn't we all?

Indeed, we should, for this too is the nature and design of the One.

Hate, Valashu, is that singular force that separates. We are born as separate selves, and it is our right and duty to strengthen ourselves so that we might live our lives. But since life lives off life, whether beasts or men, we must strengthen ourselves against others, even as they would strengthen themselves against us. Hate gives us great courage in this war of all against all; it breathes fire into our will to become greater beings, and so to succeed in the quest for greater life itself. And so, like dragons, we might stride the earth in our power and pride, rather than cowering behind a rock and wailing at the injustice of life. And it is indeed cruel, as it must always be: for if you do not have the courage to become a predator, you must have the resignation to be prey. As night will follow day, the strong will devour the weak, on and on through all of eternity.

It is just this success that gives us joy. It is measured by the degree of our dominion over others. In many individuals seeking their advantage, the world gains its greatest advantage as the hidden hand of the One raises up the strongest and bestows upon them the only true wealth. Then the accumulation of the riches of power gained, if invested in our bodies and beings, leads to ever greater riches. Thus does a man, training at arms, become a knight; thus do knights go on to become lords and kings. And the greatest kings of men use the great gelstei to turn their sight to the heavens for new conquests, and so learn to walk the stars. Then comes the greatest conquest of all as mortal men strengthen the flame of life so that it cannot be blown out. And so are born the immortal Elijin, and the strongest of these angels gain the power of the quenchless Galadin: they who can not be harmed in any way.

And yet, still they do suffer: terribly, terribly, terribly. For our journey toward the ultimate becomes more, not less, painful at every step. Man is a very small vessel that contains only a small amount of life's bitter poison; the great Galadin hold inside entire oceans. And as their suffering increases without measure, so must their means to bear it.

You know in your heart, Valashu, what this must be: that one's own pain can only be ended by inflicting equal pain upon another. For the power of life and death over the weak is ultimately the power of life over death itself. Can you deny that this is so? Doesn't the scream of another make you give thanks that you are healthy and whole? Doesn't the flesh of animals quicken your own? Do you not feel, like a lion, exalted at the moment when you kill?

This is the secret of the valarda, the secret of life itself. The deepest part of the Law of the One is this: that there is an affinity of opposites. We hate most those we love most deeply. We love: terribly, terribly, terribly. In our love and longing for the One, we feel too keenly the longing of others. If we are not to be overwhelmed by it, what are we to do? Strike

65

fire into their souls! Rend them with our claws! Devour their entrails and take joy in the agony of their eyes! Then they will cry out to be relieved of their suffering. But since it is our hand, the One acting through us, which creates this torment, it is to us they cry for relief. And so, for a moment, we are reminded of our divine nature and why we were created. We touch upon the One's true purpose, and the One itself, and in that light of ecstasy, how should any suffering remain?

Do you not see the terrible beauty of the One's design? As the One is infinite, so is the One's pain – and so must be the means to end it. In the torment of innocents, infinite in number, the One realizes his invulnerability. And the tormented innocents, the strongest of them, raise themselves up as angels to grasp the divine light itself. And so the true magnificence of the One is revealed: for the One's two faces are also love and hate. Our hate of the One for making us suffer leads, in the end, to love of the One for impelling us back to our source. And so the One uses evil to work the greatest possible good. And isn't this, Valashu, true compassion?

I paused for a moment in reading Morjin's letter. Because my mouth was dry, I took a drink of brandy. My hands were sweating inside their casings of slick leather. My eyes burned. The whoosh of Maram breathing heavily beside me merged with the other sounds of the room: the crackle of the fire, the rustle of paper, the grinding of my brother's jaws. Asaru's anger was no greater than mine. True compassion, Morjin had spoken of! *But it was a twisted compassion.* Another image of Morjin, the true image that he did not wish men to see, appeared in my mind: The once-lovely Elijin lord whose very body had rotted as if from the inside out. His ghoulish-gray flesh hung in folds from the sharp bones of his face. His gray hair, stringy and limp, grew in patches as if he had once suffered terrible burns. His eyes, his ancient eyes, were as cold and cruel as iron, rusted red and filled with blood. In them raged a terrible will to suck the life out of others. And they cried out with a terrible hunger. For he spent much of his vital force trying to maintain the illusion of his beauty in order to deceive men – and perhaps himself.

'Read on!' Maram called out beside me. 'Let's finish this, Val!'

I noticed my father studying my face, as my grandmother turned toward me and my mother watched me intently. Even Master Juwain, now caught in his curiosity to hear what Morjin had written next, nodded for me to continue. And so I read on:

The Maitreya is called the Compassionate One. He is said to be a healer of the world's suffering and the anguish that all men know. If this be true, then how could you be he? You, who have killed and maimed so many and caused so much agony? Do you truly wish the ending of war and the forgiving of your foes? Then ask yourself this question, Valashu: if you were this Shining One who bears the light of the divine, would you hold out your healing hand to me?

The Maitreya, it is also said, will show man the world just as it is. For man, faced with the horror of existence, is liable to long for a world without evil that can never be. And to give up under the crushing burden of life and its torment of fire. And so the One, in mercy, in true compassion, sends into the world the Lightstone, all the One's power, so that the Maitreya might seize it and show men the truth. And so the Maitreya eases their suffering, for all then know their place in the natural order and the path of returning to their source. But can you, Valashu, show the world this terrible truth? Can you bear to show it to yourself? No, we both know that you do not have the heart for this. And so you cannot be this Maitreya, either.

But if you aren't he, who are you? You are a Valari of an ancient line of adventurers who are never Maitreyas. You are a warrior who professes to hate war. A murderer of men who justifies his crimes by castigating his foes as evil. A prince . . . of thieves. You are he who steals the light of truth from the world so that darkness will prevail. You are he who opposes the establishment of a natural order where the strong might rise without the waste of war. You are a Lord of Lies, for you tell yourself that you will somehow be redeemed from your dreadful deeds in your suffering of others' pain.

You believe that you have experienced the most bitter of suffering, but I promise you that you have known only the barest twinge of its beginning. You think, too, that what I have done to you is evil. It is just the opposite. Consider this: would you have ever developed the strength to steal the Lightstone if I hadn't opposed you at every step of your journey? What is evil? All that weakens and diminishes a man. What is good? All that strengthens him and drives him toward divinity. Can you deny that you – and the woman you think you love – are now both greater beings as a result of the torments that I have visited upon you? Lord Valashu, Knight Swan, Guardian of the Lightstone – can you deny that it is I who has made you?

And so you are in my debt. And doubly and triply so since you have wounded me and taken the Cup of Heaven. And yet, upon you I wish no vengeance. I must believe that you did what you did out of error and not malice. You are young and full of fanciful dreams, as I was once. Inside you there blazes a truly beautiful light. Who has seen this as I have, Valashu? Open your eyes, and you might see it yourself.

The debt must be repaid. One day, I hope, you will swear allegiance to me. You will serve me – in life or in death. The Lightstone, however, must be returned immediately. If it is, I shall reward you with a million-weight of gold and a kingdom of your own to rule. If it is not, I shall so reward any man who delivers the Lightstone into my hands. And the kingdom of Mesh shall be taken away from you, and you and your family destroyed. My ally, King Angand of Sunguru, stands ready to march by my side that the crime you have committed might be redressed. And the kings of Uskudar, Karabuk, Hesperu and Galda, who owe me allegiance, will march as well. And King Ulanu of Yarkona, whose acquaintance you have already made. Upon this sacred crusade, I pledge my kingdom, my honor and my life.

Faithfully, Morjin, King of Sakai and Lord of Ea

P.S. I have returned with this letter the personal belongings of Atara Ars Narmada. I can only hope that you, or she, might find some use for them. Of course, Atara might find it more useful if she were given new eyes with which to behold you. Return the Lightstone to me, and I shall make it so. It would give me great pleasure.

P.P.S. One day, if you live long enough, you will use the valarda to strike death into another – as you tried to strike it into me. And on that day, I shall be there by your side, smiling upon you as I would my own son.

My parents' room was deathly quiet as I finished reading. My family and friends were all staring at me. Without a word, I crushed the pages of the letter inside my fist. I stood up and walked over to the far fireplace. There I cast the letter into the flames. It took only a moment for these writhing orange tendrils to begin blackening the white paper and consuming the letter. As I watched the pages curl into char, I thought of all the millions of books that Count Ulanu had burned at Khaisham. But *Morjin's* words, I knew, would not be lost, for they were now burned into my brain.

'The gloves, too, Valashu!' Master Juwain called to me. 'Cast them into the fire!'

I did as he advised, and then walked back to the carpet to rejoin those who would give me counsel.

'Lies, such terrible lies,' Master Juwain said.

'Yes – and even more terrible truths,' I said. 'But which is which?'

'How could you hope to sort the truth from the lies of the Lord of Lies?'

'But I must. I must learn to. Everything depends upon it.'

Asaru refilled my glass and pressed it into my hand. He said, 'Morjin feeds you poisoned meat and you still seek to take sustenance from it? You did the right thing burning it. Now forget about the letter.'

'How can I? He said –'

'He said many evil things. Predators and prey, indeed.' He nodded at our father, and continued, 'We Valari are taught to protect the weak, not eat them.'

I smiled at this, and so did everyone else. It was one of the rare moments when my serious brother made a joke. But too much had happened that night for us to sustain a mood of levity.

'It may be,' my father told me, 'that the real purpose in Morjin's writing this letter was to confuse you.'

'Then it seems he has succeeded.'

My grandmother, who knew me very well, turned her cataract-clouded eyes toward me and said, 'You are not as confused as he.'

'Thank you for saying that, Nona. If only it were true.'

'It *is* true!' she said. Her back stiffened as she sat up very straight. I knew that if Morjin had managed to invade this very room, she would have thrown her frail, old body upon him to defend me. 'This Red Dragon speaks of love and power. Well, he may know everything about the love *of* power. But he'll never understand anything about the power of love.'

Her smile as she nodded at me warmed my heart.

'There's only one love that Morjin could be capable of,' my mother added, looking at me. 'And that is that he loves *to* hate. And how he hates you, my son!'

'Even as I hate him.'

'And such passion has always been your greatest vulnerability,' she went on. Her soft, graceful face fell heavy with concern. 'You've always loved others too ardently – and so you hate Morjin too fiercely. But your hatred for each other binds you together more surely than marriage vows.'

My mother's soft, dark eyes melted into mine and then she said an astonishing thing: 'Morjin uses hate to try to compel your love, Valashu. He hates all things but himself most of all. He wishes that you were the Maitreya so that you might heal him of this terrible hate.'

My confusion grew only deeper and murkier, like a mining pit filled with sediments and sludge. 'But he has said that I cannot be the Maitreya!'

'Yes, but this must be only another of his lies.'

Master Juwain nodded his head as he sighed out: 'There's a certain logic to his letter. It indicates that he believes becoming the Maitreya is open to superior beings who wield the Lightstone with power. Certainly he fears Val wielding it this way. It seems that he has written his whole letter toward the end of convincing Val that he *cannot* be the Maitreya.'

I touched Master Juwain's arm and said, 'But what if I cannot?'

'No, Val, you mustn't believe this. I'm afraid that the Lord of Lies is only trying to discourage you from your fate.'

As the candles burned lower, we talked far into the night. Each of us had our own fears and dreams, and so we each felt drawn by different conclusions as to what my fate might truly be. Asaru, I thought, was proud merely to see me become a lord at such a young age and would have been happy if my title remained only Guardian of the Lightstone. My father looked at me as if to ask whether I was one of those rare men who *made* their own fate. Nona, her voice reaching out like a gentle hand to shake me awake, asked me the most poignant of questions: 'If you weren't born to be the Maitreya, who were you born to be?'

It was Maram who made the keenest comment about Morjin and his letter. Although not as deep as my father, he was perhaps more cunning. And it seemed that his two slow glasses of brandy had done little to cloud his wits.

'Ah, Val, my friend,' he said to me as he lay his arm around my shoulders. The heavy bouquet of brandy fell over my face. 'What if Morjin is playing a deep game? The "Lord of Lies", he's called – and so everyone expects him to manipulate others with lies. But what if, this one time, he's telling you the truth?'

'Do *you* think he is?'

'Do *I* think he is? Does it matter what I think? Ah, well, we're best friends, so I suppose it does. All right, then, what I think is that Morjin could use the truth as readily as a lie to poison your mind. Do you see what I mean? The truth denied acts as a lie.'

'Go on,' I said, looking at him.

'All right – Morjin has said that you cannot be the Maitreya. Perhaps he knows that you could never accept such a truth, even if it *is* the truth, and so you'd think it must be a lie. And so you'd be tempted to believe just the opposite. Therefore, isn't it possible that Morjin is trying to lead you into *falsely* believing that you're the Maitreya?'

'But why would he do that?'

'Ah, well, *that* is simple. If you believe yourself to be the Maitreya – never mind the prophecies – you would neglect to find and protect the *true* Maitreya. And then Morjin might more easily murder him.'

70

What Maram had said disturbed me deeply. That he might have great insight into Morjin's twisted mind disturbed me even more. It came to then that I would never find the answers I sought in trying parse Morjin's words and motives – or anyone else's. And so, at last, I drew my sword from its sheath. I held it pointing upwards, and sat looking at its mirrored surface. The Sword of Truth, men called it. In Alkaladur's silver gelstei, I should have been able to perceive patterns and true purposes. But the light of the candles was too little, and I couldn't even see myself – only the shadowed face of a troubled man.

'Valashu,' my grandmother called to me.

I looked away from the sword to see her smiling at me. Her desire to ease my torment was itself a torment that I could hardly bear.

'Valashu,' she said again, with great gentleness. 'You must remember that it is one thing to take on the mantle of the Maitreya. But it is quite another *being* this man. You'll always be just who you are. And that will be as it should.'

'Thank you, Nona,' I said, bowing my head to her.

My father had always looked to her for her wisdom, without shame, as he was looking at her now. And then he turned to me and said, 'Nona is right. But soon enough, you will have to either claim this mantle or not. If you *are* the Maitreya and fail to take the Lightstone, then, as has been prophesied, as has happened before, a Bringer of Darkness will.'

My hands were sweating as I squeezed the black jade hilt of my sword. I felt trapped as if in a deep and lightless crevasse, with immense black boulders rolling down upon me from either end.

I looked at my father and said, 'Morjin spoke of great consequences if the Lightstone is not returned to him. Do you think he *could* mount an invasion of Mesh?'

'No, not in full force, not this month or even this summer. He would have to gather armies from one end of Ea to the other and then march them across the Wendrush, fighting five tribes of the Sarni along the way. We have time, Valashu. Not much, but we have time.'

'Time to unite the Valari,' I said. 'Time even to journey to Tria and meet in conclave with the kings of the Free Kingdoms.'

Asaru shook his head at this. 'Who but Aramesh ever united the Valari? Who ever could?'

My father's bright eyes found mine as he said, 'The Maitreya could.'

Because I could not bear to look at him just then, I stared at my two hands, right and left, wrapped around my sword. I said, 'No one really knows, sir, *what* the Maitreya is.'

71

'Many believe that he would be the greatest warlord the Valari has ever known.'

'No one knows *who* he is,' I said.

'Many believe him to be you.'

A single flicker of light fell off from my sword like a shard of silver. It stabbed into my eyes; it pierced cold and clean straight down to my heart. There, it seemed, in the silence between its quick and violent beats, I heard someone whispering to me.

'I must know,' I suddenly called out. I slipped my sword back into its sheath and picked up the box that Morjin had sent to me. I bowed my head to my father and said, 'Sir, may I be excused?'

Even as he nodded and gave his consent, I pushed myself to stand up.

'It *is* very late,' he said. 'It seems we'll accomplish little more tonight. But where are you going?'

'To the scryers' room,' I said.

'At *this* hour? Kasandra is an old woman, Val.'

'She . . . is not sleeping, sir. She is waiting for me.'

She is calling to me, I thought as my heart pounded against the bones of my chest. *She wants to tell me something.*

I said to my father, to my mother and to Maram and everyone, 'Kasandra said that I would find the Maitreya in the darkest of places. If Morjin has set traps for me, she might have seen them. I must know before it's too late.'

And with that, I tucked the box beneath my arm and moved off toward the door.

5

Maram and Master Juwain hastened to catch up to me as I made my way out into the quiet hallway. They had begun this long night's quest for knowledge with me, they said, and they would end it by my side as well. I was glad for their company, for the long hallway seemed too empty and too dark. Only a few oily torches remained burning. The sound of our boots striking cold stone echoed off the walls. We passed between the servants' quarters and the kitchens, as we had come; when we reached the infirmary, we turned down another hallway. There, the pungent smell of medicines mingled with a deeper odor of sickness, sweat and blood. As we moved past the classroom and Nona's empty room, this odor grew only stronger. It seemed not to emanate from the sanctuary to the right, or the guest quarters to the left where King Kurshan and his daughter had taken up residence. I was afraid to discover its source, even as I pushed my way through a moat of fear and pain that chilled my limbs like icy water.

At last, we came to the stairwell at the keep's southwest corner. We entered, one by one, this dark tube of stone that twisted up toward the higher floors. My father had told me that the scryers had been given rooms on the third floor. We climbed up and up into the dark silence, turning always toward the left as the narrow steps spiraled upward. It was cold and close in that dim space; the smell of Maram's sweat and brandy-sweetened breath fairly nauseated me. He was puffing and grunting behind me, moving as quickly as he could. But he was not quite quick enough, for the fear now pierced through to my heart and drove me up the stairs two and then three at a time.

'Slow down!' he gasped out. 'You're killing me! Ah, have mercy, my friend!'

I did not slow down. We passed by the exit to the second floor, where the Alonians and the Ishkans had taken quarters. We climbed ever higher. We finally reached the arched doorway that gave out onto the third floor. As I pushed out into the quiet hallway, the mortared stones along the walls seemed to be screaming at me. A sharp pain, with the savagery of cold steel, ripped into my belly. I drew my sword and began running past the closed doors of my father's guests.

'Come!' I gasped. Maram and Master Juwain were close behind me, and began running, too. 'It's this door – it must be!'

At the end of the hallway, we came to a door darkened with torch-smoke and reinforced with bands of black iron. I rapped the diamond pommel of my sword against the dense wood and waited. My heart beat ten times, quick as a frightened bird's, before I knocked at the door again, this time louder. I waited another few moments, and then tried turning the doorknob, but it was locked.

'Come!' I said to Maram. I rammed my shoulder against the door with such force that the hard wood drove the rings of my mail armor into my flesh almost down to the bone. 'Help me break this open!'

'But, Val – they're old women!' Maram said.

'They might have taken a draught to help them sleep,' Master Juwain added.

'Come!' I said again. 'They're not sleeping! Help me!'

Maram finally sighed his consent, and added his great bulk in battering at the door. On our second attempt, it burst inward in a scream of splinters and tormented iron. It was nothing against the scream in my eyes, in my belly and lungs. For the hall's dim torch-light showed a small, simple room filled with carnage. The iron-sick smell of blood drove like a hammer against my head. Sprays of blood moistened one wall; the red imprints of boots darkened the floor-stones. On one of the beds sprawled two of the scryers, whose names I had not learned. Their throats had been cut, and rivers of blood had flowed out over their white robes and white wool blankets. On the other bed was Kasandra. Someone had cut open her belly. She lay on her back with her eyes staring up at the ceiling, and it seemed that she was dead.

Master Juwain hurried to her side and placed his rough old fingers against her throat to feel for a pulse.

'Ah, too bad,' Maram gasped out. He held his hands over his *own* belly as if to protect this massive, food-filled outswelling – or to keep from vomiting. 'Ah, I'd thought we were through with this kind of thing, too bad, too bad.'

My heart throbbed inside me as I gripped my sword and cast my eyes about the room's sparse furnishings, looking for any sign of the men who had worked such an evil deed.

'These poor women!' Maram said. 'Ah, but what kind of *scryers* could they have been if they let themselves be murdered in their sleep?'

'They're not all murdered,' Master Juwain said, touching Kasandra's withered face. 'Not yet. This one is still alive.'

I knew that she was. I could feel her faint breathing as a whisper deep inside my throat.

'Can you help her, sir?'

Master Juwain gently prodded the wound to her belly. Someone, like a ravening wolf, had ripped out most of its contents, which lay strewn upon the blankets beneath her like bloody white snakes. 'Help her live through *this*, Val?'

'No, help her live . . . a while longer. I must speak with her.'

Master Juwain nodded his head grimly and said, 'I'll try.'

He wiped his hands on the hem of Kasandra's robes. From his pocket, he removed the green gelstei crystal that looked so much like a long and bright emerald. With its magic, he had once healed Atara of a mortal arrow wound to her lungs. But he had never been able mend such terrible mutilations as one that would soon kill Kasandra.

While Master Juwain positioned the varistei over Kasandra's heart, I knelt by the other side of the bed and took Kasandra's hand in mine. Her skin was as soft as fine leather and still warm.

'Maram!' I called out softly. 'Guard the door! Whoever did this might return.'

With a grumble, Maram drew his sword and positioned himself by the door. But he turned his gaze toward the crystal in Master Juwain's skilled hands. So he must have perceived the clean light that streamed out of the crystal and fell upon Kasandra's chest like a shower of tiny, shimmering emeralds.

'Ah,' Maram said. 'Ah, poor, poor woman.'

A terrible shiver tore through Kasandra's body, and she coughed, once, as her breath rattled in her throat. A faint light filled her eyes. She had no strength to turn her head, nor even to cry out against the agony that I had called her back from the door of death to suffer. But I knew that she could see me, even so. She had been looking for me to come to her rooms, watching and waiting.

'Valashu Elahad,' she gasped out.

I leaned closer to her and asked, 'Who did this to you?'

'The one . . . called Salmelu.'

'But why? You said that a ghul would undo my dreams. Who is this ghul? Did Salmelu kill you to keep you from telling me?'

'Because . . . he is . . . he killed my sisters and . . .'

Her voice died off into a burning exhalation as her frail old body shuddered with another wave of anguish. And Master Juwain said to me, 'Too much, Val. For mercy's sake, ask her one question at a time!'

I swallowed hard against the anguish in my throat. I asked, 'Who is this ghul, then?'

'His name . . . I don't know,' Kasandra said. 'His face, though, is as noble as yours.'

'But what about the last part of your prophecy? You said that a man with no face would show me my own. Who is this man?'

'Who is anyone?'

'Does he have a name?'

'He is no man . . . I know . . .'

Although her voice died off into nothingness, it seemed that she was trying to scream something at me. I asked, 'Will this man show me the face of the Maitreya?'

'No, the slave girl will show you the Maitreya.'

'What slave girl? What is her name?'

'Estrella.'

This strange name seemed to hang in the air like a star in the midst of blackness. I gripped Kasandra's hand in mine as tightly as I dared. And then I asked her, 'But am *I* the Maitreya?'

Kasandra's lips did not move, nor did breath warm her lips. I knew that she was ready to walk through the door to that lightless land even the bravest of warriors feared to tread. I gripped the hilt of my sword in my right hand. And then Kasandra drew in a long breath as if gathering the last of her strength. And she gasped out, 'You are . . .'

These words, too, seemed to hang in the air. *You are*, I thought. *I am.* I looked down at Kasandra to ask her to finish her sentence, if indeed she already hadn't. But the light in her tormented eyes suddenly died, and she would speak no more, ever again. Where, I wondered, did the light go when the light went out?

Master Juwain shook his head at me, and put away his green crystal. He reached out and closed Kasandra's eyes.

'Val,' he said, 'there's nothing –'

'No,' I said softly. 'No, no, no.'

Because Kasandra was pulling me down into death with her, I let go her hand. I retreated inside the walls of the castle of aloneness that had protected me for so long. I stood away from the bed, and held out my sword. Its dark silver flashed with a sudden light.

He killed my sisters, Kasandra had said to me. *His face is as noble as your own. He is no man . . .*

On the floor beneath me were the bloody bootprints of a man, or men. The pattern of these red defilements seemed burned into the stone.

76

I know that you keep the Cup of Heaven locked and guarded in your castle as in ancient times, Morjin had written me. *It is a beautiful thing, is it not? The most beautiful in all the world.*

My sword flared again, this time more brightly. I held it pointing down toward the east in the direction of the great hall where the Guardians stood protecting the Lightstone. Alkaladur blazed with a wild radiance that burned deep into my eyes.

'Master Juwain!' I cried out. 'Go back to my father's room! Ask the King – Asaru, too, my brothers – to come to the great hall!'

'Val, what is it?' Master Juwain asked me.

But I was already running for the door. I paused there only a moment to call out to Maram, 'Go to the Guardians' barracks! Rouse Baltasar! Tell him that a ghul has been sent to steal the Lightstone!'

I had no breath to say more. I sprinted out into the hallway. Our noise of broken doors and shouts must have roused this floor's guests. Two of them – old Lord Garvar's widow and a minstrel from Thalu – had opened their doors halfway to see if the castle might be under attack. I told them to lock themselves inside their rooms. And then, sword in hand, I ran past them toward the stairwell.

I fairly bounced down the twisting stairs like a suddenly released stone. It was a miracle that I negotiated the worn granite slabs without stumbling and breaking my neck. Only seconds, it seemed, sufficed for me to reach the archway into the first floor's hallway. I ran down this deserted corridor as quickly as I could. At the kitchens, I turned right, and sprinted down the shorter corridor connecting the keep to the great hall. Its doors were open, and so I had no trouble passing inside.

There, in this vast, dim space still smelling of beer and roasted meat, I saw an astonishing thing: the thirty Guardians lay in various positions about the dais at the front of the room. Their faces were peaceful, and they all appeared to be sleeping. The Lightstone remained on its stand above them. Its shimmering presence seemed to call forth a new surge of radiance from my sword.

The debt must be repaid, Morjin had written me. *You will serve me – in life or in death.*

'Adamar! Viku! Skyshan!' I called out to three of the Guardians, to no effect. I ran toward the dais and then bounded up its steps. I picked my way around the splayed arms and legs of the downed Guardians. The hand of the Guardian nearest the Lightstone seemed to beckon me – or someone – closer.

'Skyshan!' I called out again as I knelt and tried to shake this large, young man awake. 'Skyshan!'

77

After a few moments, I gave up and rose to my feet. I stood with my sword held ready as I steeled myself to guard the Lightstone – in life or in death.

I waited for the faint sound of boots along the corridor or the creak of doors being opened. Hot sweat trickled down my sides beneath my armor. My breath came in quick bursts, and my heart beat like a war drum. I looked out into the hall at the rows of tables and empty chairs. I glanced up at the portraits of my ancestors along the walls; their grave faces looked down at me as if to take my measure. My grandfather, Elkasar Elahad and *his* father, Aradam, and his grandfather – all the kings of Mesh going back many generations seemed to be waiting with me in the hall. One of the oldest of the portraits was of Julamar Elahad, who had been King of Mesh when last the Lightstone had resided on this stand three thousand years before. His ancient eyes, brilliant as stars, seemed to fix upon me and to ask me if I would give the Lightstone into the Maitreya's hands, even as he had. He asked me if I would die trying to wrest the Lightstone back from Morjin and his murderous priests, even as he had, too.

As my heart beat out the moments of my life in quick, hot surges that tore through my veins, the whole world seemed to wait with me there in the quiet hall. I felt someone watching me. It seemed that he was far away – or perhaps very near. In all that large space, with its smooth walls of stone, there were few places to hide: behind the pillars holding up the ceiling or in the darkened recesses of the south doors. I listened for the rustle of clothing or mail armor from these places; I felt for the beating of another's heart or the quiet steaming of his breath.

All at once, an overpowering desire to sleep flooded into me. My arms felt unbelievably heavy, as if they were encased not in steel but in lead. I had to fight to keep my eyes open. My head was like a great weight that kept falling toward my chest.

I must not, I may not, I silently prayed. *Please don't let me fall asleep.*

A glint of silver sliced the air above me. Flick appeared in a shower of sparks. This mysterious being began looping through the air, around and around both me and the Lightstone, as if weaving a fence of light. Or trying to paint a beguiling pattern of scarlet and silver streaks that might keep me awake.

I raised high my long and brilliant sword and cried out. 'Alkaladur!' The Awakener, men called it. Through its silver gelstei ran a secret pulse that beat in rhythm to my own true pulse. It reminded me that the deepest part of myself remained always awake and always aware, and would remain standing even when I died.

At last, from faroff in the depths of the castle, came the sound of footsteps that I had been dreading. I turned toward the open doorway by which I had entered the hall. My eyes burned as I waited to see who would appear in the rectangular darkness there. My hands seemed fused with the hilt of my sword.

'Valashu!' a strong voice called to me. 'Valashu Elahad!'

My heart surged with joy to see my father charge into the room. He had his shining kalama in hand. Asaru, Karshur and my other brothers, with Lansar Raasharu, followed closely behind him. A few moments later, even as my father hurried up the steps of the dais to join me, Master Juwain appeared in the doorway, too.

'What is this?' Master Juwain cried out when he saw the forms of the sleeping Guardians. 'What poison? What potion?'

'What sorcery, you mean?' Asaru said as he gained the dais and tried to rouse his friends.

Just then came a much louder sound of pounding boots and jangling steel from outside the hall to the east. Suddenly, with a crash of wood, the doors were thrown open, and Baltasar and Maram led seventy mail-clad knights into the room. I smiled to see the grim faces of Shivathar and Artanu of Godhra and others who were like brothers to me. They started straight for the dais. But then I held out my hand and shouted, 'Stay, Baltasar! Guard the doors and stand your distance until we discover the nature of this sorcery!'

While Master Juwain knelt among the fallen Guardians looking for sign of what might have stricken them, Karshur stood like a mountain above him. He yawned and said, 'Perhaps Master Juwain is right – it's some sleeping potion.'

'No,' I said, 'it cannot be.'

I explained that it was one of my rules that the Guardians on duty should never all eat of the same food together nor take the same drink.

Ravar, my cleverest brother, rubbed his fox-like face as he said, 'Then it must be something else. Let us search the hall.'

And so it was done. My brothers and the Guardians still on their feet spread out through the hall as if beating through grass to flush a rabbit. They picked through the rows of tables but paid closest attention to the dais itself. In the end, it was Ravar who discovered the source of what had stricken the Guardians. With a flick of his knife, he wedged out a piece of loose mortar between two of the dais' floor-stones. And in the recess between them, his quick fingers found a small, glassy sphere like an agate or a child's marble.

'I see, I see,' Master Juwain said as Ravar gave it to him. He rolled it between his rough old hands as his gray eyes came alive with a new light. 'This is surely a sleep stone. One of the lesser gelstei, and quite rare. Whoever hid it here must have remained close by, or else it could not have been used to so great an effect.'

His hand swept out and down toward the sleeping Guardians.

'The traitor,' Asaru said. 'Salmelu – it must have been he.'

'Damn him!' Lord Raasharu cried out as he came up upon the dais. 'We had word that he and the other priests left the castle only half an hour ago. In the middle of the night! We thought that he was fleeing only out of shame.'

My father stepped forward and shook his head. He pointed his sword at the Lightstone. 'Why flee at all before gaining that which he had come to steal?'

I traded glances with Maram and Master Juwain, and then told my father and everyone else what had happened in the scryers' chamber. 'He fled to avoid your justice, sir.'

My father's eyes flashed with a dark fire as the flames of wrath built inside him.

'Ah, well,' Maram said, 'it seems that Salmelu couldn't count on his position to shield him from punishment.'

'An emissary who murders old women is no emissary,' my father said. I felt him willing his heart to cool down. 'But what was Salmelu, then? A priest who has defiled my house? A thief? *Was* it he who used the sleep stone?'

'No, it was not,' I said. 'The scryer spoke of a ghul with a noble face. That cannot have been Salmelu.'

I looked at my father as he traded glances with Asaru, and Lansar Raasharu nodded at Ravar. And then suddenly everyone gathered there was regarding everyone else with questioning eyes. Who, I wondered, had more noble faces than did my friends and family?

'No, none of us is this ghul,' I said. I had gazed upon the flames of being of each man in the hall, and I was as sure of this as I was that the sun would rise in the east in a couple more hours. 'It must be another.'

'But who, then?' Ravar asked. He pointed down at the crack in the dais. '*Someone* hid the sleep stone here. Was it a groom bringing drink to the Guardians? Or a knight friendly to them whom they allowed to approach too close?'

I shook my head. Neither I nor anyone else had answers to his questions. 'It's not to be believed that any Meshian could ever so betray his people.'

'No, it is not,' Lord Raasharu agreed. His long face seemed to darken with a sudden shadow. 'And yet Salmelu betrayed *his* people – and of his own free will.'

80

My father, standing above the sleeping Guardians with his sword in hand, suddenly swept it in broad arc from east to west. 'We'll search the castle, then. Let us see if anyone is where he shouldn't be, or if an intruder hides close to the hall.'

As he commanded, so it was done. My father summoned his private guard, and they joined his knights in searching not only the castle's keep, but the Swan Tower and the other towers, too, as well as north, middle and west wards. The sleep stone was given into the charge of three Guardians, who removed it for safekeeping to Master Juwain's rooms in the Adami Tower. The remaining Guardians joined my father and me – and all the rest of us – in watching as Master Juwain tried to rouse the thirty knights who remained sleeping.

After perhaps a half hour had elapsed, one of my father's men entered the hall bearing more dreadful news. This sad-faced squire, whose name was Amadu Sankar, hurried up to my father and gasped out, 'The servants of the Red Priests – they've all been murdered! They lie dead in Lord Salmelu's rooms!'

'More defilement!' my father called out. 'Is there no end to this man's crimes?'

Karshur, the thickest of my brothers in body as well as mind, rubbed his solid jaw and cried out, 'But why would he do such a thing?'

My father, who had already sent knights in pursuit of Salmelu and the other priests, said to him, 'His servants would have slowed him. If my knights ride him down before he escapes from Mesh . . .'

My father did not finish his sentence. There was death in his dark eyes as he slowly shook his head.

I suddenly remembered Kasandra's last words to me: *The slave girl will show you the Maitreya.* Could she have meant, I wondered, one of Salmelu's slaves?

I turned to Amadu Sankar and asked, 'Are you sure all the servants were dead?'

'They . . . *must* have been, Lord Valashu,' Amadu said. His young face was full of horror. 'They were all gutted like rabbits.'

A dreadful hope surged inside me. I stepped over to Master Juwain and said, 'It may be with the servants as it was with Kasandra. Will you come with me to their rooms, sir?'

'If I must,' Master Juwain agreed, nodding his head.

'And you, Maram?' I said, turning to my best friend.

'Must I?' he said as he looked at me. And then, upon perceiving the fire in my eyes, he grumbled, 'Ah, well, then – I suppose I *must.*'

I took my leave of my father, and led Master Juwain and Maram back into the keep. Salmelu and his party had been given rooms on the fifth floor. We hurried as quickly as we could back up the stairs to this great height. Maram complained that his heart hurt from such an exertion, while Master Juwain saved his breath and worked at the spiral of steps in quiet determination.

Two doors down from the large room at the fifth floor's northwest corner and the smaller one adjoining it, where Salmelu and the six other priests had taken residence, we found the room of their servants. There were eight of them, all girls, ranging in age from about nine to thirteen. And, even as Amadu had told us, they were all dead. It looked as if they had been roused off their straw pallets and driven into the corner of the room, and there slaughtered. They lay almost in a heap, some of them on top of others, their arms stretched this way and that, their long hair – black and brown and blonde – soaked in the blood that had been torn from their young bodies. Screams had been torn from their throats, too, and this desperate sound of the dying still hung in the air.

While Master Juwain went among the girls' bodies with his green crystal, Maram stood by the door questioning the guards posted there. I walked about the room, careful not to step in the pools of blood staining the cold stone floor. I stepped over the stand of an overturned brazier; I gazed at a tapestry that one of the girls must have pulled off the wall in a frantic effort to find escape from Salmelu and his murderous priests. But in this room of death, stark and narrow, there was nowhere to hide.

'The squire was right,' Master Juwain said, kneeling over one of the girls. With great weariness, he shook his head. 'There's nothing to be done here, Val.'

Maram walked over to me and laid his hand upon my shoulder. 'Let's leave these poor lambs to be buried, my friend.'

'Wait,' I told him, shaking my head. It seemed that I could still hear one of the girls screaming in agony – or rather, crying out for help.

I turned toward the room's only window, along the north wall. It was small and square, and open to the night wind blowing down from the mountains. I hurried over to it. Outside, the great, dark shape of Telshar stood outlined against the black and starry sky. I grasped the window's sill, and stuck my head out into the cool air to look out over it. Along the north side, the keep was built flush with the castle's great walls; it was a straight drop down more than a hundred feet to the rocks forming the steep slope upon which the castle was built. No one, I thought, could survive a fall from such a height. And no one, not even a young girl frantic to escape from a priest's evil knife, could climb so far down the castle's smooth granite walls.

'Here, Val,' Maram said to me as he joined me by the window. 'Such a sight would make any man sick.'

He placed his hand on my shoulder again. When he saw that I was in no danger of losing my dinner, he said, 'Let's get away from here.'

'Wait!' I said again. 'Give me a moment.'

The smell of pine trees and fear stirred something inside me. A soft voice, urgent yet sweet, seemed to be calling me as if from the stars. I pushed my head outside the window again, and twisted about to gaze up through the darkness. And there, some twenty feet higher up toward the tooth-like battlements, a small shape seemed fastened to the wall.

'A torch!' I cried out. 'Someone bring me a torch!'

One of the guards went out into the hallway and returned a few moments later bearing a torch in his hand. He gave this oily, flaring length of wood to me, and I thrust it out the window as I again craned my neck about to gaze up the castle's wall. And now I could see, faintly, what my heart had known to be true: by some miracle, a young girl had managed to climb out the window and claw her way up the windswept wall.

'What is it, Val?' Maram said to me. 'What do you see?'

The girl, perhaps nine years old, stood with her bare, bloody feet wedged into a narrow joint between the wall's white stones. Her hands had found a vertical crack and were jammed inside it. It seemed unbelievable that she had remained stuck to the wall thus for more than an hour. She was trembling, from cold and exhaustion, and was near the end of her strength. She looked straight down at me, the black curls of her hair falling about her frightened face. Through the dark, her eyes found mine and called to me with the last desperate fire of hope. Her certainty that I would not leave her to die here touched me deep inside and brought the burn of tears to my eyes. The wild beating of her heart was a sharp pain that stabbed into my own.

'The priests are gone!' I called up to her. 'Can you climb down?'

She shook her head slowly as if fearful that a more strenuous motion would loosen her precarious hold upon the wall. I felt the cold, rough knurls of the cracked granite through her sweating hands; I felt the slight muscles along her forearms bunching and burning and growing weaker with each of her quick, painful breaths. I knew that she could not climb back down toward the window, not even an inch.

'Let *me* see!' Maram called to me. He pulled me back into the room and tore the torch from my hand. And then it was his turn to look outside. I heard him mutter, 'Ah, poor little lamb – too bad, too bad.'

He pushed back from the window, careful not to let the wind blow the torch's flames into his face. He turned to look at me as he shook his head. 'Ah, Val, what can we do?'

Master Juwain and the two guards had now joined us by the window. I looked at them, and at Maram, and said, 'We have to bring her down.'

'Ah, Val – but how?'

One of the guards suggested sending for a rope and lowering it to the girl from the battlements high above.

'No, there is no time,' I said. 'We'll have to climb up to her.'

'*Climb* this wall?' Maram said. '*Who* will climb it?'

In answer, I unbuckled my sword and pressed it into his hand. It was first time since it had been given to me that I allowed it out of my reach.

'Are you mad?' Maram said to me. 'Let us at least search for a rope first before you –'

'No, there is no *time*!' I said again. I knew that the girl outside who had looked straight into my soul would soon lose her hold. 'Help me, Maram.'

I reached to pull at the rings of steel encasing me, but the sudden and silent plaint that sounded inside me told me that I didn't even have time to remove my armor. I moved over to the window again and gripped the cold sill.

'But, Val!' Maram protested, 'she's a *slave*. And you are . . . who you are.'

But who was I, really? While the guard held the torch for me, I again stuck my head out the window to descry my route up to the girl. She gazed down at me. And her dark, wild eyes showed me that I was a man who couldn't let a young girl simply fall to her death.

With everyone's help, I backed up and out the window, gripping the edge of the casement above it as I pushed my feet against the sill. The darkness of night fell upon me; the cold wind rattled my hair against the wall's ancient stone. Through empty space I stared down at the rocks far below. My belly tightened, and for a moment it seemed I might lose my dinner after all. How could I climb this naked wall? How could any man? Once each spring, I knew, my father walked around the entire castle inspecting it for any crack or exposed joint in its stones. Such flaws in the masonry were always mended, making it impossible for an enemy to scale the walls. But here, a hundred feet up, it seemed that no such repairs had been made for a hundred years. Who could have thought to prevent a simple slave girl, in blinding fear, from climbing out a window upon cold, cracked stone?

I drew in a quick breath and turned my gaze upward. The guard held the torch out the window, and its fluttering yellow light revealed a crack above my head. I reached up and thrust my fingers into it. I found another crack with my left hand. And then, as I fit the toe of my boot into a narrow joint in the stone to the right of the window, I slowly pulled myself up. Two feet I gained this way, and then a couple more as I pulled and pushed against other cracks and other joints.

It was desperate hard work in the dead of the night, and a single slip would kill me. My hands were slick with sweat; the rough granite soon abraded the flesh from my knuckles and left them bloody. I suddenly remembered the story of how Telemesh had fought his way up the face of Skartaru, the black mountain, to rescue an ancient warrior bound there. Lines of verse came unbidden into my mind:

> Through rain and hail he climbed the wall
> Still wet with bile, blood and gall . . .

I fought my way up another foot and then another. The torch's light soon weakened so that I could barely make out the features of the stonework above me. I nearly slipped, and tore my fingernails to the quick on a little lip of granite. The immense black weight of the sky seemed to lie upon my shoulders and push me back toward the earth

> Where dread and dark devour light,
> He climbed alone into the night.

But I was not alone. As if in answer to my silent supplication, Flick joined me there beneath the stars. His whirling, fiery form showed a crack about three feet above me that I would have missed. And the girl kept looking at me with wild hope. She called no encouragement, with her lips. But her eyes, clear and deep, kept calling me and urging me upward. They reminded me that I had a greater strength than I ever knew. This connection of sight and soul was like an invisible rope tied between us and joining our fates together as one.

At last I drew up by her side. My fingers clawed a little crack; the tips of my boots had bare purchase on a broken joint of stone. The trembling of my body was almost as great as the girl's. I felt her heart beating wildly a couple of feet from mine. The wind carried her scent of fear and freshly-soaped hair over my face. Through the dark I looked at her and said, 'Grab onto me!'

She shook her head. I knew that she didn't have the strength to let go her hold without falling.

'Wait a moment!' I said.

85

I looked about and espied a wider and deeper crack a little above me. I jammed my whole hand into it. Its sharp knurls bruised my bones. When I was sure of my hold, I reached out with my other hand to wrap it around the girl's narrow waist. Then, in one carefully co-ordinated motion, I helped her up and onto my back, even as she threw her arms around my neck and locked her bare legs around my waist. In this way, carrying her piggyback like the little sister I had never had, I began climbing back toward the window.

'Val!' Maram called up to me as he stuck his head out the window and held the torch high. 'Careful now! Only a little farther and I'll have you!'

It was much harder climbing downward. I had trouble seeing where to put my feet and finding holds for my hands. Although the girl was as slight as a swan, her weight, added to that of my armor, was a crushing force that burned my tormented muscles and pulled me ever down toward the hard and waiting earth. Twice, I nearly slipped. If not for Flick's guiding light, I would never have found holds in time to keep us from plunging to our deaths.

'Val! Val!'

And yet there was something about the girl that was not a grief but a grace. Her breath, quick and sweet, was like a whisper of warm wind in my ear. In it was all the hope and immense goodness of life. It poured out of her depths like a fountain of fire that connected both of us to the luminous exhalations of the stars. In the face of such a strong and beautiful will to live, how could I ever lose my own strength and let us fall? And so there, beneath the black vault of the heavens, for many moments that seemed to have no end, we hung suspended in space like two tiny particles of light.

As promised, when we reached the window Maram grabbed onto us, and he and the others helped us back into the room. The girl stood facing me as we regarded each other in triumph. Then she cast a long look at her murdered friends in the corner of the room. She burst into tears, and buried her face against my chest. I wrapped one arm around her back as I covered her eyes with my other hand, and I began weeping, too.

Master Juwain touched my shoulder and said, 'Val, this is no place to linger.'

I nodded my head. I was now trembling as badly as the girl. I looked down at her and asked, 'What is your name?'

But she didn't answer me. She just stood there looking at me with her sad, beautiful eyes.

One of the guards came up to me as I was buckling on my sword.

He said, 'It seems that the Red Priests' servants were all mute, Lord Valashu.'

'No doubt so that they couldn't tell of their masters' filthy crimes,' Maram added.

I bit my lip, then asked the girl, 'Was it Salmelu – Igasho – who did all this?'

The sudden dread that seized her heart told me that it was.

'Do you know if Salmelu kept company with a ghul? Might he have secreted such a man in the castle to steal the Lightstone?'

But in answer, she only shrugged her shoulders.

'Come, Val,' Master Juwain said to me again.

I started moving the girl toward the door, but then stopped suddenly. I said to her, 'Your name is Estrella, isn't it?'

She smiled brightly at me, and nodded her head.

'I must ask you something.' I bent over and whispered in her ear, 'Do you know who the Maitreya is? Is it I?'

It seemed a senseless thing to ask a nine-year-old slave girl who could not even speak. And she looked at me with her dark, almond eyes as if my words indeed made no sense.

Master Juwain cast me a sharp look as if to ask me why I still doubted what was almost certainly proven. And I said to him, 'I must know, sir.'

'Very well, but do you have to know it right *now*?'

The sight of the murdered girls was like a poisoned knife cutting open my belly. Around my neck I felt an invisible noose, fashioned by Morjin, inexorably tightening. My whole being burned with the desire to have answered a single question.

'There's so little time,' I said to him. 'Will you come with me, now, sir, to see what wisdom your gelstei might hold?'

Master Juwain nodded his assent, and so I went out into the hall. The guards remained behind to wait for those who would prepare the dead girls for burial. I did not know what to do with Estrella. When I mentioned giving her over to the care of a nurse, she threw her arms around my waist and would not let go until I promised not to leave her.

'All right then,' I said to her. 'If you're to show me the Maitreya, perhaps you can show me other things as well.'

And so I took her hand in mine, and led her and my friends back down to the great hall to stand before the Lightstone.

6

When we reached this room of feasts and councils, more people were gathered there. The sleeping Guardians had been moved off the dais and laid beneath it on the cold stone floor. Baltasar had deployed forty of the new Guardians to posts near the steps at either end of the dais. The remaining Guardians stood watch on the dais as usual, fifteen of them to either side of the Lightstone. Their hands gripped their swords, and they showed no sign of wanting to fall asleep.

My mother, hastily dressed in a simple tunic and shawl, stood over the sleeping Guardians talking with my father. Lord Tanu prowled about with his hand on his sword and looked very crabby from the loss of sleep. It seemed that the night's events had roused the entire castle.

I presented Estrella and gave a quick account of how she had escaped from Salmelu and his priests. My mother began weeping, whether from relief that I was still alive or from her sorrow for Estrella it was hard to tell. She came over to us and smiled at Estrella. She gently laid her hand on her shoulder.

But Lord Raasharu was not so kind. He came over to us and looked at Estrella, saying, 'Could this be the ghul, then?'

His question outraged me. I held out my hand to warn him back as I said, 'She's just a girl!'

'Forgive me, Lord Valashu, but might not the Lord of Lies make use of one so young even more easily?'

'No!' I said. And then, 'Yes, perhaps he could – but not this *one*, Lord Raasharu. She's no more a ghul than you are.'

The fire in my eyes just then must have convinced him of what my heart knew to be true. He bowed and took a step back, even as the awe with which he had earlier regarded me returned to his face. He seemed ashamed to have doubted me. 'Forgive me, Lord Valashu, but it was my duty as your father's seneschal to ask.'

'It's all right, Lord Raasharu,' I said, clapping him on his arm. 'This has been a long night, and we're all very tired.'

But this, it seemed, was not good enough for Lord Tanu. He marched straight up to us as his suspicious old eyes fixed on Estrella. 'If she's not a ghul, then perhaps she's a spy that Salmelu left behind. She came out of Argattha! How do we know that her true loyalties won't always lie with the Kallimun priests and the Red Dragon?'

My mother slipped her shawl around Estrella's bare shoulders. Then she gathered her closer, and stood holding her protectively. 'If this girl is a spy, then fair is foul and I'm as blind as a bat.'

Lord Tanu opened his mouth as if to gainsay her, but my father suddenly stepped forward and called out, 'Enough! The Red Dragon has set traps for us tonight, but it's not to be believed that this girl is one of them. Now, haven't we other concerns?'

We did have. For it seemed that there was still a ghul hiding somewhere in the castle. The thirty Guardians continued their unnatural sleep. And I still struggled to solve the great mystery of my life.

While the search continued, my father sent one of his fastest riders to the Brotherhood's sanctuary to retrieve a book about the lesser gelstei that Master Juwain requested. Master Juwain believed the sleeping men sprawled below the dais would awaken naturally in good time. But if they did not, he wanted to search in his book for mention of some tonic or tea that would rouse them.

'There must be some specific that will counteract the effects of the sleep stone,' he said. 'Just as there must be some specific *sequence* of thoughts that will open *this*.'

So saying, he drew out the opalescent little thought stone that he had brought from Nar. In the presence of the Lightstone, its colors seemed to swirl more vividly.

'Try, sir,' I said, urging him toward the dais.

He yawned and said, 'I'm afraid I would have a fresher mind if we waited until tomorrow.'

'Tonight *is* nearly tomorrow,' I told him. 'Haven't we waited long enough?'

Master Juwain's eyes flared with a new light. He loved nothing in life so much as delving into the mysteries of the mind.

And so we both went up upon the dais. The Guardians there made room for us. Master Juwain stepped straight up to the Lightstone, holding the little gelstei in the open bowl of his hands. I stood by his side as he closed his eyes. He fell so still that it seemed he was sleeping, too.

And so I waited to see if Master Juwain might discover some proof of my fate. What a great mystery the gelstei were! The secret of their making had been almost completely lost. But why, since there were still many ancient books describing how naked matter – the base elements of the earth – might be transmuted into these glorious crystals?

I remembered Master Juwain once explaining the answer to this puzzle: 'Because the gelstei are *living* crystals, and the knowledge that goes into their forging is individual and spiritual and alive.'

They could not, he had told me, be forged as if by recipe. And they could not be used that way, either.

And as it was with the lesser gelstei, so it was even more with the greater gelstei: the silustria of my sword, the healing varistei, the blazing firestones. And most of all, the Lightstone itself. It was said that the golden cup gleaming on its stand three feet away from me had been forged by the Galadin around a distant star many ages ago – but no one really knew. Certainly no one on Ea, for twice ten thousand years, had succeeded in creating another like it, for almost everything about the gold gelstei remained a mystery. All through the Age of Law, the Brotherhoods had tried to unlock its secrets, with only partial success. As Master Juwain had said to me, it was one thing to hold the Lightstone in one's hands, but quite another to wield it.

It was near the first hour of the new day – Moonday, I thought – when Master Juwain finally opened his eyes. He sighed as he squeezed the little gelstei in his hand. 'I'm afraid I've failed, Val. The conundrum remains: this crystal *might* contain knowledge about the Lightstone. But it seems we still need the Lightstone to open it.'

I gazed at the golden cup that we had fought through hell to bring to this place. It quickened the powers of each of our gelstei – and so quickened our individual gifts that enabled us to use them.

Master Juwain went on, 'I've tried all the formulae and incantations, in ancient Ardik, in Lorranda and Uskul, even the Songlines, but nothing has availed.'

My father's words rang in my head: that we *must* believe, for believing in a thing, we make it be. Then an old verse flashed in my mind:

> *The deeper dance of head and heart,*
> *The angels' grace, mysterious art,*
> *To weave light's thread so lucidly:*
> *True mind's resplendent tapestry.*
>
> *The sacred fire of heart and head*
> *Where sense and thought are sweetly wed,*
> *Through ancient alchemy is wrought*
> *A higher sense, a deeper thought.*

After I had recited these lines, Master Juwain looked at me and asked, 'Where did you learn that?'

'From a book in your library, years ago,' I said. 'Perhaps you might find these thoughts that are deeper than words, since as you say, none of your words has availed.'

'But, Val, thoughts *are* words. Language *is*.' He held up his little crystal. 'And *this* is called a thought stone – not a heart stone.'

I gazed off at our family's table, where my mother sat with Estrella tending her bruised and bloodied feet. Something about this mute girl, so wild and free, called forth the grace of an animal. An animal, I was sure, had thoughts and mind, ordered not with words, but with the deeper logic of life. Estrella, not being able to talk to others, had somehow learned to communicate a blazing intelligence as if unfolding a fireflower from out of the depths of her being. The smile on her face as my mother finished her work and kissed her spoke more clearly and purely than words ever could.

'But, sir,' I said to Master Juwain, 'doesn't thought arise from the deeper intelligence of the heart? Doesn't mind merely translate this intelligence into words, and then manipulate it and permute it?'

Master Juwain remained silent as he looked at me.

'And didn't you once teach me,' I went on, 'that the head and heart are two horses that draw the same chariot? And that the ancients made no such war between mind and body as do we?'

Master Juwain sighed as he nodded his head. 'Yes, yes, I know very well what you say is true. But, you see, sometimes I don't *know* . . . what I know.'

I pointed at the pocket of his robes and said, 'The varistei is a healing stone, yes? What if it could heal this rent in the soul? Why don't you try using it on yourself?'

He looked appalled as if what I had suggested to him was more painful than taking a knife to his own chest to perform a surgery. But he slowly nodded his head as he removed the emerald crystal from his pocket. He stood holding it in his hand in front of him.

The deeper dance of head and heart . . .

The healing stones, the green gelstei were called. And yet their powers ran much deeper than merely mending flesh together. Used in harmony with the natural forces of the earth, the varistei could awaken and strengthen the very fires of life itself.

The sacred fire of heart and head
Where sense and thought are sweetly wed . . .

Again, Master Juwain closed his eyes. I felt my heart beating in a quick but steady rhythm with his. The sounds of the room – jangling steel and creaking chairs and low voices – faded into a distant hum. I seemed to wait forever, all the while expecting Master Juwain to look at me and tell me that he had failed yet again. And then suddenly, the varistei came alive with a deep viridian light. The hall fell eerily silent as this lovely radiance enveloped Master Juwain's hand, his arm and then his entire body; it seemed to course *through* his body and illumine it as from within. I gasped, then, to see his heart pulsing inside his chest like a great, living jewel. It sent shoots of emerald light through his arms and his legs, and up in a great shimmering fountain through his head.

When at last he opened his eyes, I had never seen these twin gray orbs so luminous and clear. He smiled as he tucked his varistei back into his pocket. Then he looked upon the Lightstone. The golden cup overflowed with a clear light, which he seemed to drink in through his eyes. He stood thusly for a long time. At last he turned his attention to the thought stone that he still held in his other hand. He stood gazing at it, nearly lost in rapture, even as the first rays of the morning sun fell upon the great hall's windows and carried colors of crimson, gold and blue into the silent room.

'I see, I see,' he whispered to himself.

Now some of the sleeping Guardians began stirring and opening their eyes, bewildered. My father led Asaru and my brothers up upon the dais. Lansar Raasharu and Lord Tanu followed, and my mother, her arm covering Estrella's shoulders, slowly climbed the steps to hear what Master Juwain might say.

'You were right, Val,' he said, holding up the thought stone for all to see. 'Words were not the key to open this, though its contents were recorded *in* words. In High East Ardik, no less, which, then as now, was a language that only the Brotherhoods used.'

A fleeting look of triumph swept over Master Juwain's face as he continued,

'And *I* was also right. There *is* knowledge of the Lightstone in this gelstei. And knowledge of the Maitreya, too.'

'Go on,' I said as my eyes burned into his.

'I'm afraid it won't be as much as you hoped for.'

'Go on,' I said again.

Master Juwain sighed as he held his hand out toward the Lightstone. 'It seems that the Cup of Heaven may be used by anyone, each according to his virtue and understanding. But if a man is flawed in any way, the light leaks out from his deeds like water from a cracked cup.'

'Are you saying, then, that a man needs to be perfect in order to use the Lightstone?'

'No – only to use it perfectly.'

'And the Maitreya?'

'The words concerning *him*, at least, are clear enough,' Master Juwain said. 'The Lightstone is meant for the Maitreya.'

'But *how* is he to use it?'

'Only he will ever know.'

I turned toward the Lightstone, now pouring out a golden radiance as if it had caught the rays of the morning sun and was giving them back a thousandfold. Around the dais the last of the stricken Guardians were waking.

'But *who* is the Maitreya, then?' I asked Master Juwain. 'What does your stone say about that?'

'Very little, I'm afraid.' Master Juwain sighed again as he looked at me with all the kindness that he could find. 'This is the relevant passage, listen: "Just as the Lightstone is the source of the radiance that holds all things together, so the Maitreya is the light that draws all peoples and all kingdoms together toward a single source and fate."'

I looked at Master Juwain and said, 'Is there no more?'

'I'm certain that there is more recorded in the other thought stones in Nar.'

I drew Alkaladur and held it before the Lightstone. The Sword of Truth, it was called, the Sword of Fate. Its silver gelstei, gleaming as bright as a mirror, gave me to see a frightful thing: that I stood at the center of the whirlwind of forces that drew all the people of Ea toward a singular fate.

Lansar Raasharu suddenly cried out, 'Claim the Lightstone, Lord Valashu!'

'Claim it, Val!' Baltasar, his faithful son, repeated.

I looked around at my father and my mother, at my brothers and friends and all these people who were so close to my heart. Only hours before, Kasandra had warned of a ghul who would undo my dreams. I was sure that none of those present could be this evil being. And yet, in the deepest sense, I could be sure only of myself. Shouldn't I then claim the Lightstone, here and now, if for no other reason than to keep it safe within my grasp and guarded by my sword?

'Claim it, Val!' my fierce brother, Mandru, said to me.

The golden cup gleamed before me. If I were a false Maitreya and yet claimed it for my own, I would crack apart like a cup of clay and bring great evil to the world. But if I were the true Maitreya and failed to claim it, another would – and then the evil that he wrought with the gold gelstei would be just as great.

'Come, Val,' my brother Jonathay laughed out. His face, both playful

93

and calm, was lit up with his faith in me. 'If you're not the Lord of Light, then who is?'

At last I turned toward Estrella. She stood in the shelter of my mother's bosom silently sipping from the cup of warm milk and nutmeg that my mother had given her. Kasandra had said that this girl would show me the Maitreya. Without words to mar the way she saw the world and interpreted it to others, her whole being was a beautiful mirror like the silustria of my sword. This, I thought, was her gift. She smiled at me with her innocent and beautiful face, and in the quick, clear brightness there, it seemed that she was showing me myself just as I was.

Then I remembered the words of Morjin's letter: *You cannot be this Maitreya, either.* But Morjin was the Lord of Lies. I suddenly knew that he truly *did* fear that I was the Maitreya. And so, it seemed, I *must* truly be.

'All right,' I finally said, holding up my sword. I smiled at my good friends, at Sunjay Naviru, and at Skyshan of Ki and at others. 'All right. In eleven days, the tournament in Nar will begin. All the kings of the Valari or their seneschals will be there. Let this be the test of things, then: if I can persuade them to journey to Tria, there to meet in conclave with the kings of the Free Kingdoms and make alliance against Morjin, I will claim the Lightstone.'

At this news, Baltasar and Sunjay – Jonathay, too, and others – let loose a cheer. Asaru smiled at me and told me that he was glad that I would be accompanying Yarashan and him to Nar. But Lord Tanu remained skeptical. He pulled at his sour face and asked, 'And just how will you accomplish this miracle?'

'With all the force of my heart, sir.' I went on to explain that I would compete at sword and at bow, and at all the tournament's other competitions. 'If I do well enough, or am even declared champion, then the kings will have to listen to me.'

'If you're declared champion,' Asaru said with a smile, 'you'll have to defeat *me* first, little brother.'

'And *me*,' Yarashan put in as pride stiffened his handsome face.

I smiled at both of them as I bowed my head. Then I turned to Master Juwain. 'The tournament's champion, whoever he is, may ask of King Waray a boon. If fortune should favor me, I would ask that the Brotherhood school might be reopened.'

Master Juwain squeezed the thought stone in his hand. He was nearly as eager as I to enter the Brotherhood school and discover what knowledge its companion stones might hold.

'Very well,' Lord Tanu said to me. 'You young knights always want to go to tournaments. But is it fitting that the Knight of the Swan and the Guardian of the Lightstone himself should abandon his charge to go off seeking glory?'

'No, it is not,' I said to him. I held my hand out toward the Lightstone. 'And that is why we will have to take it with us.'

As I now explained to Lord Tanu, no less my father and Lansar Raasharu and everyone else, there were good reasons for risking the Lightstone by taking it on the road. First, I had vowed that all the Valari kingdoms would share in its radiance. Second, if King Waray should grant me or another Meshian knight the boon of entering the Brotherhood's school, the Lightstone would be needed to open any thought stones. Third, although there was obvious danger in taking the Lightstone out of the Elahad castle, there was perhaps an equal danger in keeping it here, as the night's events had proved. And fourth, if it should be proven that I was the Maitreya, the Lightstone must be close at hand for me to claim.

When I had completed my argument, everyone remained silent and looked at my father to see what he might say. He gazed at me for many moments before he finally spoke: 'It is hard to imagine losing this great light that has come into our castle so soon after gaining it.'

'We have each of us given our word, sir. Shouldn't we honor this?'

'Are you asking my permission to remove from my hall the greatest treasure in the world? And to take from my kingdom a hundred of its finest knights?'

He nodded at Baltasar as his radiant eyes looked past the Lightstone at the Guardians who stood around it. And then he turned back toward me.

'Yes, your permission, sir,' I said to him.

'Is that truly mine to give?'

'Should not a king command his own son?'

'His *son*, yes,' he said as he regarded me strangely. He bowed his head to me, slightly, then continued, 'A king is charged with the safe-guarding of his kingdom and ordering its affairs – and so commanding those who follow him. But he has a greater charge as well, and that is to the kingdom of the earth and all of life. This realm, however, he does not rule. If he should lose his son to this higher realm, how then should he presume to command him?'

A sharp pain filled my throat as I looked at my father. The great passages of life were always sad. I could find no words to say to him.

'Very well, then, Valashu,' he finally forced out. 'Take the Lightstone with you to Nar, if you must. But be careful, my son.'

He leaned forward to embrace me and then kissed my forehead.

95

'Will you come, too, sir?' I asked him.

He glanced at the Lightstone and shook his head. 'No, that's impossible, now. The Red Dragon has spoken of marching armies into Mesh. There's much to be done if these armies are to be kept away.'

I bowed to him deeply and then met his bright gaze.

'And now,' my father said to everyone, 'it is more than late. Let us retire to our rooms or take breakfast, as we will. Later there will be much to do.'

And with that, he put his arm around my mother to escort her and Estrella from the hall. Everyone else except the Guardians who would stand near the Lightstone through the morning prepared to leave as well. I remained for a few moments staring at this sacred cup that had caused so many to sully themselves and make murder. Then I went off to take a few hours of rest.

7

That afternoon the bodies of the scryers and the slave girls were laid to earth on a grassy knoll on the slopes of Telshar above the castle. There I buried as well the box that Salmelu had given me. I stood with my family and friends beneath a cloudy sky and listened to my father vow vengeance toward the one who had so defiled his kingdom. Never again, I thought, would he extend hospitality toward the emissaries of Morjin.

Late the next day, a messenger brought word of the Red Priests. It seemed that they had managed to keep ahead of the knights that my father had sent in pursuit of them; they had ridden straight across Mesh and into Waas before the kel keep that guarded the frontier could be alerted. Thus they made their escape. For the Waashians would allow no knight of Mesh into their realm, nor even suffer them to tell of Salmelu's infamy. This was according to King Sandarkan's command. Only a few years before, at the Battle of Red Mountain, we of the Swan and Stars had badly defeated the Waashians, and King Sandarkan still held great bitterness toward Mesh.

Neither did the search of the castle uncover the ghul. But then, that is a ghul's nature, to remain hidden inside another's mind or dwell deep within the flesh of a faithful nurse or a groom or even a friend. Now that it had come time to prepare for the Nar tournament, I was relieved to be putting behind me the castle's many residents and the many more town-dwellers who journeyed back and forth from Silvassu every day. It gave me some small comfort that I could choose my companions from those I was certain could not be a ghul. Baltasar and the hundred Guardians I trusted with my life – and more importantly, with the Lightstone. Lansar Raasharu, of course, was beyond reproach, as were my brothers, Asaru and Yarashan. Master Juwain would be riding at my side, as he had on the great Quest. And it turned out that Maram would be coming with us, too.

'Well, Val,' he said to me after a long day of laying in supplies and attending to the many details of organizing an expedition, 'you didn't really think I'd let you go off alone on another adventure, did you?'

'You're the most faithful of friends,' I said, clasping his hand. 'But your decision wouldn't have anything to do with another wedding postponement, would it?'

He smiled at me knowingly and said, 'Well, perhaps just a little. Let's just say that a journey to Nar will give me a little more time to make sure that Behira is truly the one meant for me.'

'But what did she say when you told her you were going away?'

'Ah, well, she wept, of course, too bad. But I believe that I was able to make her understand that duty called me to your side in your time of need. I promised her that if I were to win any of the competitions, I would bring back the gold medal and give it to her.'

I nearly coughed in astonishment. 'Are you really thinking of entering the tournament?'

'I? I? Go galloping about trying to cross lances with Valari knights? Do you think I'm mad? The point is, Behira *believes* I will be competing. This will soothe her. If I'm kept busy, you see, I'll have less time for dalliances. But when we actually reach Nar, I can always, ah, be incapacitated with a bad back or the flux, do you understand?'

I *did* understand, and I promised Maram that I would keep secret this little dishonesty. He seemed very happy with his plan, and gave thanks that fate always seemed to rescue him from Lord Harsha's wrath just when things looked darkest for him. But this one time, fate betrayed him. At the evening feast, when it came time for the rounds of toasting, Lord Harsha stood upon his game, old leg and called out, 'Tomorrow Lord Valashu and Mesh's finest knights will leave for the tournament in Nar. My daughter has just told me that Sar Maram Marshayk will be joining them and competing as an honorary Valari knight! We should all honor his courage! Let us all drink his *health*!'

Maram, sitting at Lord Harsha's table beneath Lord Harsha's upraised goblet, cast me a quick, sharp look from across the room as if to ask me if I had divulged his plan after all. I shook my head at him. And he shook his head at me in silent resignation and drank his beer even as two hundred lords and knights cheered him and wished him well.

Lord Harsha had yet another surprise for him. He was not an especially clever or imaginative man – except perhaps when it came to protecting his daughter. So it vexed Maram greatly when Lord Harsha clapped him on the back and announced, 'As many of you know, Sar Maram is to be my son-in-law. Since it is distressful for my daughter and me to see him ride off at this time, we've decided to journey to the tournament as well. We'll see to it that no harm befalls this brave knight!'

At this, Maram choked on his beer. His fat face reddened as he groaned and looked across the room at me for help. But it was all I could do to keep from laughing at this much-deserved plight that he had brought upon himself.

And so it seemed that all preparations for the expedition to Nar and our roster were complete. Yet one more addition remained to be made. Later that night, I met with my father and my family in his rooms. Estrella, whom my mother had practically adopted, took warm milk while the rest of us had brandy. When I told her that I would not be returning to Mesh for perhaps several months, she threw her arms around my legs and would not let go. She wept and seemed disconsolate, even when my mother promised to teach her the art of weaving and my grandmother sang her a comforting song. I knew then that I must take her with me, for our fates were somehow joined together. If I left her here in Mesh, I was afraid that the beautiful thing that had come alive inside her upon our meeting would wither and die.

'She's like a sister to me,' I said as I laid my hand upon her dark, curly hair. Her little triangle of a face, all quicksilver and wild, brightened to see me smiling down at her.

'Yes,' my father said, looking at us, 'but would you take your sister, and one so young, upon a dangerous journey?'

'She will have a hundred Valari knights to protect her,' I said. I placed my hand on the hilt of my sword. 'And myself.'

'Even so, she would be safer here.'

'Would she truly? With a ghul still on the loose? How do we know that this man wouldn't seek to complete Salmelu's evil work?'

My father thought about this as he studied Estrella's lively face. Then he said, 'But, Valashu, it's a hundred and fifty miles to Nar. And four times that distance to Tria.'

'Estrella,' I said, 'has come out of Argattha, and that is the greatest distance of all, for the road from hell is endless.'

I went on to tell of my sense that Estrella still carried much of this hell inside her, in her nightmares of memory, if not in her soul.

'You cannot know what an abomination Morjin has worked upon that place,' I said, to my father and to my family. 'Morjin has made children . . . to do unspeakable things. I would make for *this* child, at least, happier memories.'

My father's eyes grew deep as oceans. It sometimes seemed that he had the power to look straight through me. 'You wish to heal her of her affliction, don't you?'

'Yes,' I said, touching Estrella's long, delicate neck. 'There's nothing wrong with her that she shouldn't speak. Nothing wrong that Morjin hasn't somehow *made* wrong. If I am the one . . . whom many think I am, then with the aid of the Lightstone, it may be that I can give her back her voice – and perhaps much else as well.'

My father nodded his head at this, then said, 'And if you could work this miracle, then your healing of her would be that which showed you the Maitreya – is that right?'

'Yes,' I admitted. 'But even if she doesn't show me what it seems she must, she might show me another. Whoever the Lord of Light truly is, he must be found for the sake of all Ea.'

'For the sake of Ea and not your own?'

'One can only hope so, sir.'

In the end, it was decided that such a journey, on good horses over good roads, under the escort of a hundred knights, should not prove too arduous for this tough and resourceful girl. She wanted to come with me so badly that she locked the tips of her long, tapering fingers through the rings of my mail. If fate was moving us along the same road together, who was I to go against it?

One last matter regarding our expedition still had to be decided. By law, no knight or warrior of Mesh was allowed to leave the Nine Kingdoms wearing the marvelous diamond battle armor of the Valari – except on expeditions of war. This was meant to protect a lone knight against brigands who might murder him in order to divest him of the glittering treasure that encased him. So it was that I had journeyed across Ea and back wearing only my steel mail. But not all knights could afford two suits of armor; at least half of the Guardians were not so fortunate. Therefore, they must leave Mesh either unarmored or raimented in diamonds.

'It won't do to leave my knights unprotected,' my father said to me. 'The Red Dragon has spoken of sending armies against Mesh and has brought murder into my house. Very well, then – let it be as if you are riding to war.'

Early the next morning, on the 9th of Soal, all who would journey to Nar assembled in the castle's north ward. It was a day of drizzle and low, gray clouds that smothered the sky and promised only more rain. This stole some of the sheen from the knights' usually-resplendent diamond armor. At least, I thought as we all formed up, diamonds do not rust. I ran my finger across the misted, white stones affixed to the hardened leather along my arm. Diamond being lighter than steel, it was joy to move about unburdened, with nearly as much freedom as had a man wearing only woolens or a leather doublet.

I sat astride my great, black warhorse, Altaru, and I urged him past some squawking chickens toward the front of the formation. There, Asaru and Yarashan gathered, too. They wore, as did I, great helms with curving steel face plates and silver wings sweeping up from the sides. Black surcoats showing the silver swan and the seven stars of the Elahads draped cleanly over their shoulders and chests. Their triangular shields were embossed with the same emblem. These bore as well, near the point, marks of cadence that distinguished my brothers and me from each other. Asaru had chosen a small, gold bear while Yarashan displayed a white rose. My mark was that of a lightning bolt. It was burned into the black steel of my shield as it was into the flesh of my forehead.

Lord Harsha and Behira, with Maram, Master Juwain and Lansar Raasharu, took their places immediately behind us. Lord Harsha's emblem was a gold lion rampant on a field of bright blue. It covered nearly all his shield, except that the bordure around its rim showed a repeating motif of silver swans and stars against a narrow black field, for he had sworn allegiance to my father and must bear sign of it. So it was with Lord Raasharu, his family's emblem of a blue rose against a gold field being surrounded by the same bordure, and with all the other knights lining up behind him.

Baltasar, who would be that day's bearer of the Lightstone, had the position of honor at the center of the middle column of Guardians. Our small baggage train trailed this main body of our expedition, followed by strings of our snorting remounts and a rear-guard of twenty knights commanded by Sunjay Naviru. Estrella, I discovered, could not ride and had been brought to Mesh with her sister slaves locked inside a cart. And so the prospect of sitting all day by herself in one of the wagons distressed her. I decided that she should begin our journey riding with me. My mother escorted her through the courtyard, treading carefully through the squishing mud right up to the front of our assemblage. She helped her up onto Altaru's back, and the small girl seemed happy to sit in front of me dangling her feet over Altaru's sides.

'Neither of you will be comfortable this way for long,' my mother said to me as she stood there in the courtyard's churned-up mud. 'Please mind that she doesn't grow too tired or sore.'

I promised that I would take as good care of Estrella as she would herself.

'Goodbye, Valashu,' she said as she bent forward to kiss my knee. 'Whether you return as a Maitreya or just a man, make sure you *do* return.'

In the north ward that morning, lined up along the walls from the Aramesh Tower to the Telemesh Gate, blacksmiths and carpenters mingled with great lords such as Lord Tanu, and midwives waited in the rain with princes and even kings. Almost all the castle had turned out to see us off. At the front of this throng stood my father and grandmother, with my brothers Karshur, Mandru and Ravar. When it came time for us to ride forth, they braved the mud and joined my mother in making their goodbyes. Karshur made me promise to return with the gold plaque in swordsmanship. Mandru, adding a twist to my mother's theme, advised me to return with the gold gelstei – or not at all. This was meant to be a joke, of course, but there was a painful truth in his otherwise tender parting with me.

On this journey, my father had no gifts to give me other than the reassurance of his smile and the fire of his eyes. He spoke the same farewell as he had a year before. This time, in the light of what I sought, his words had an even deeper poignancy: 'Always remember who you are, Valashu. May you always walk in the light of the One.'

I nudged Altaru forward, and my powerful horse whinnied with excitement, glad to set out into the world again. And so I led the rest of my company through the castle's gate. A thousand iron-shod hooves struck wet paving stones, sending spray and a great noise into the air. The road wound down from the castle through an apple grove and turned into the North Road that led all the way toward Ishka and beyond.

It was not a pleasant day for travel. And yet the land through which we passed was still lovely. The fields around Silvassu showed the emerald sheen of new shoots of barley and rye; the wildflowers along the road were alive with bees and butterflies undaunted by the soft rain. To the left of us, the peaks of the mountains – Vayu, Arakel and Telshar – vanished into folds of silver mist. Soon we entered the forest filling the Valley of the Swans. With the oaks and elms in full leaf and the songbirds chirping gaily, it seemed churlish to chafe at a little moisture working its way into our garments or to long for the sun to burn its way through the clouds.

We rode all day at an easy pace so as not to tire the horses. That night we camped in the hilly country toward the northern end of the valley. On some nearly level pasturage well-watered by a swift stream, we laid out our rows of tents. Upon considering the warcraft I had learned from my mysterious friend, Kane, and from my father, I

102

insisted that our little camp be fortified by a moat and a stockade. This rudimentary fence was little more than some sharpened stakes pounded into the moist earth and logs and brush piled up to form a breastwork. Nevertheless, with Guardians stationed every twenty paces, we would be well protected against any thieves or murderers who might try to steal upon us in the middle of the night.

My tent, a large pavilion of black and silver silk in which the Lightstone would reside each night, covered a patch of moist grass in the middle of the camp. It was large enough to accommodate numerous people, and Estrella gave signs of wanting to lay out her sleeping furs inside and share it with me. But that would have been unseemly. For however much I thought of her as my sister, she remained a young girl of no true relation. And so I arranged a compromise: Lord Harsha and Behira would have the tent next to mine, and Estrella would sleep with them. We would take our meals, with Master Juwain and Maram, around a common campfire. If Estrella should cry out in the darkness, in her soundless way, her plaint might awaken me so that I could go to her and lead her out of the land of nightmare.

Our dinner that first night on the road to Nar was plentiful and good: beef and barley soup mopped up with a black rye bread thick with butter; roasted lamb and mushrooms; asparagus shoots picked from the shoulders along the road; apple pie that my mother had packed with a block of aged, yellow cheese. All this provender gave us good cheer against the fine, misting rain. The beer and brandy poured into our cups helped raise our spirits, too. I sipped this fine liquor by our fire, with Master Juwain and Maram on my right, while Estrella, Behira and Lord Harsha sat in a half-circle to my left. My two brothers, at the fire nearest us, held a little war council as they discussed their strategies for excelling at the tournament. Between the rows of tents around us, Baltasar, Sunjay Naviru, Sivar of Godhra, and all the other Guardians except the sentries, gathered around fires of their own.

For a couple of hours, I talked with Lord Harsha and Maram about the tournament and other worldly affairs. And all this time, I couldn't help stealing quick glances at Estrella. She seemed to pay no attention to these matters of great moment which so concerned me and my friends; perhaps she didn't understand our talk of statecraft or just didn't care. During dinner, she ate with abandon as if she had been starved and couldn't get enough of food, and of life itself. Later she played with a little doll sewn out of some bright bits of cloth. Behira, that truly kind young woman whom Maram so foolishly declined to marry, had given it to her as a present. It seemed the only possession

103

that Estrella had ever been allowed to keep as her own. It drew all of her attention. For this, too, was her gift, the way that a picked flower or a brightly colored bird and all the things of life absorbed her utterly. I watched as her dark, almond eyes seemed to melt into the doll's silken substance. I wondered at her origins. With her light brown skin and finely-boned face, she might have been Hesperuk, Galdan or Sung – or some marrying of all three. She was less pretty than beautiful. Her body was as slender as a willow; her slightly crooked nose suggested that someone had once broken it. What a mystery she was! What a mystery all human beings were! Argattha, I knew, had broken men as strong as bulls and yet here this little sprig of humanity sat in a soft spring mist happily playing with her doll as if none of the world's horrors could touch her.

After Lord Harsha and Behira had taken her off to bed, I remarked this inextinguishable quality of hers.

'Her soul . . . is so free,' I marveled. 'After a life in bondage, she's still so wild at heart. Like a sparrowhawk – like the wind.'

'People survive slavery in different ways,' Master Juwain said to me. 'I think that she retreats inside herself.'

'No, it is more than that,' I said. I told him, and Maram, that Estrella seemed able to look into a thing and perceive some part of its fiery essence as her own, and so to take refuge there. 'She *sees* things, sir. And what she sees, she reflects in her eyes, in her soul.'

'You're quite taken with her, aren't you?'

'She has a gift,' I said. 'Whether it's to show me the Maitreya or simply show the sun on a sunless day, who could know?'

'Yes, a gift,' Master Juwain agreed as he scratched his bald head. Soft lights began dancing in his eyes as if I had just given him a key piece to a puzzle. 'There *is* something about her. Consider how she found her way up the castle's wall in pitch blackness.'

I thought about this as I gazed through the fire's flames at the blue and yellow tent into which Estrella had retired for the night. I said, 'Perhaps she felt for the cracks in the stone.'

'Yes, but felt with her hands or with a different sense? Perhaps she has the second sight.'

'Like a scryer?'

'No, not exactly. A scryer's gift is to perceive things hidden in time.'

'Some scryers,' I said, thinking of Atara, 'can also see things hidden in space.'

'Yes, and there clairvoyance is wed with prophecy. But I'm thinking that perhaps Estrella is gifted otherwise.'

He went on to tell of a talent so rare that it had only an ancient name little used any more: that of a *seard*. A seard, he said, had a knack for finding lost things – by becoming, in spirit, that very thing.

I gazed at the sparks in the flames before me. They reminded me of Flick's fiery form whirling about nearby. I said, 'A curious thing happened this morning, sir: When I was packing my chess set, I discovered that one of the white knights was missing. I couldn't imagine how I'd lost it. But Estrella found it for me in Yarashan's room. It seems that he had borrowed it without telling me to replace a missing piece in *his* set. But how did Estrella even know to look there?'

Maram took a sip of brandy and said, 'Curious, indeed, my friend. But it's even more curious to think of a seard *becoming* a piece of carved ivory – or anything else. If she's to find the Maitreya for us, is she to *become* him as well, then?'

'Only in spirit, as I've said,' Master Juwain told Maram. He eyed Maram's glass of vanishing brandy as if to admonish him that such strong drink could cloud both memory and the wits. 'I would think that a seard might find the Maitreya through a transparency of the soul that nobody else would possess. By *seeing* him in a way that nobody else could.'

'Ah, you're speculating, sir,' Maram said, needling him.

'That I am. But how else is one to make sense of Kasandra's prophecy?'

I poked the fire with a charred stick, and this sent up even more sparks. I said, 'The true miracle is that Argattha didn't crush this gift from her. And that Morjin – or his priests – didn't discover it and use her as a sort of living lodestone to point the way to the Maitreya.'

'As you would use her?' Maram said, now needling me.

'It is different,' I told him. 'As different slavery and freedom. If Estrella follows me, this is *her* will and not mine.'

'One can only hope so,' Maram said to me.

Master Juwain pulled at his lumpy chin and said, 'I'm afraid it isn't always so easy to distinguish slavery from freedom. Or to tell a slave from one who is free.'

'How so, sir?' I asked.

'Consider Estrella, then,' Master Juwain said. 'She is starved her whole life of the one thing that a young girl most needs. And then you save her from death, but even more, you give her the sweetest thing in life. You, who loves so freely and fiercely, as your mother has said. You never count the cost, do you, Val, when you give your heart to a friend?'

'Are you saying that what is between Estrella and me, this thing that is so pure and good, this *love*, enslaves her?'

'No, love can never enslave – it is just the opposite. But our *need* for love, burning us up like a fever, *that* can enslave. For that which we most desire pulls at us and captures us, like moths around a flame.'

'But Estrella doesn't seem . . . captured.'

'No, I admit that she does not. She has great strength. She still retains her freedom, as she did in Argattha.'

'What do you mean?' Maram asked. 'The filthy priests captured her and forced her to their will.'

'Yes, they captured her *body* which is the least part of ourselves that we might lose,' Master Juwain said. 'Far worse it is to let another master your mind. And it is truly damning to give up your soul.'

He went on to say that slaves were the least useful of Morjin's servants, for a slave must constantly be controlled by whips and chains and the threat of being put to death. And that was because a slave's mind, while compromised by fear, often retained enough free will to plot revolt and the murder of his master, and to dream always of freedom.

'And that is why,' Master Juwain said, 'that the Lord of Lies would rather make men into true *believers* of his lies, for then, having surrendered their minds, they will do his bidding without question. Such men we do not call slaves, but they are less free than a mine-thrall.'

'Some of Morjin's men would march off a cliff for him,' Maram said. 'Remember the Blues at Khaisham? They're the perfect soldiers.'

'No, not so perfect as you might think,' Master Juwain said. 'For what a man believes, he might come *not* to believe. Men often change their allegiances to ideals like snakes shedding one skin and growing another.'

'Morjin,' I said, with a sudden certainty, 'would fear this.'

Master Juwain slowly nodded his head. 'Which is why he seeks to steal men's souls above all else. As the mind embraces the body, so the soul enfolds the mind. Control a man's soul, and you are the master of all that he feels, thinks and does.'

'It seems as if you're speaking of a ghul,' I said.

'I'm speaking of the path toward losing one's freedom,' Master Juwain said. 'This is not a simple thing. No one is completely free, just as no one is completely a slave.'

'But what *about* a ghul, then?'

'A ghul, Val, is only an extreme case of what we've been discussing. He is that certain kind of slave that not only surrenders his soul to one such as Morjin, but then becomes possessed by him body, mind and soul.'

I thought about this as I listened to the crickets chirping in the pasture beyond our rows of tents. Near the fire, Flick's luminous substance streaked up toward the sky like a fountain of little silver lights. He seemed to point the way toward a break in the clouds, where a single star shone out of the night's blackness.

I looked over at Master Juwain. 'Sir, you said that no one is ever truly free. But what about the Star People? What about the angels?'

Master Juwain considered this a moment, then said, 'Just as there is a path toward slavery, there is one toward freedom. A man begins this path by learning the Law of the One and strengthening his soul. If he is wise, if he is pure of heart, he will go on to walk other worlds as one of the Star People. And the Star People, the most virtuous, gain freedom from aging and so become Elijin. And the Elijin advance as Galadin, who are free from death. The Ieldra, it is said, being of light, are free even from the burden of bearing bodies. And the One – ageless, changeless, indestructible and infinitely creative in bringing forth new forms – is pure freedom itself.'

'Then Morjin,' I said, 'as one of the Elijin, should be more free than you or I.'

'He *should* be,' Master Juwain said. 'But an angel can lose his soul as surely as a man. And when he does, having a greater soul to lose, his fall is more terrible.'

He went on to speak of the fall of Morjin's master, Angra Mainyu, the greatest of the Galadin. Very little of this tragic tale was recorded in the *Saganom Elu*. But Master Juwain, in an old book discovered in the Library at Khaisham, had come across some passages concerning Angra Mainyu's seduction into evil and the cataclysm that had followed. Long, long before the ages of Ea when men had first come to earth, Angra Mainyu had been chief of the Galadin on their home of Agathad in the numinous and eternal light of Ninsun. But he had coveted the Lightstone for his own, and so his gaze had turned toward the world of Mylene, where the Lightstone was kept. After journeying there, through deceit, treachery and the fire of great red gelstei that had nearly destroyed Mylene, he had slain the Lightstone's guardian and had stolen the Cup of Heaven. He persuaded a great host of angels to his purpose, for there are always those who will challenge the will of the One. Among the Galadin who followed him were Yama, Gashur, Lokir, Kadaklan, Yurlunggur and Zun. And among the Elijin: Zarin, Ashalin, Shaitin, Nayin, Warkin and Duryin. They called themselves the Daevas, and they fled to the world of Damoom.

Then befell a great and terrible war, the War of the Stone, that was fought on thousands of worlds across the universe and lasted tens of thousands of years. Ashtoreth and Valoreth had led those angels still faithful to the Law of the One against Angra Mainyu. Master Juwain could tell us very little of this war. But it seemed that somehow Ashtoreth and the faithful Amshahs had finally prevailed. The Lightstone had been regained, and Angra Mainyu and his dark angels had been bound on Damoom.

'And there, on this darkest of the Dark Worlds, Angra Mainyu still dwells to this day,' Master Juwain said. He looked up at the clouds that hid the night's stars. 'And now he is master only of his own doom.'

I wasn't so sure of this. One of the reasons that Morjin wished to regain the Lightstone was to use it to free Angra Mainyu from his prison.

'In a way,' Master Juwain went on, 'we may think of Angra Mainyu and Morjin as ghuls themselves.'

'Morjin, a *ghul*?' Maram said.

'Certainly. For it is part of the Law of the One that you cannot harm another without harming yourself. All the evil that the Red Dragon has done has possessed him with evil. And so now his own evil purpose enslaves him.'

I couldn't help thinking of Kane, he of the black eyes like burning coals and a soul as deep and troubled as time itself. Kane, who was once Kalkin, one of the immortal Elijin sent to Ea with Morjin and other angels who had been killed long ago. Kane, I knew, had slain thousands, and he burned with a terrible purpose that consumed him with hate. And yet he still held within his savage heart a bright and beautiful thing that was hate's very opposite. By what grace, I wondered, did he retain his essential humanity and the freedom of his soul?

I spoke of this to Master Juwain and Maram, and then I said, 'It's hard to understand why one man falls and another does not.'

'Surely there always remains for each of us a choice.'

'Yes – but why does one man choose evil and another good?'

'That, in the end, will always remain a mystery. But the path toward bondage and evil is well known.'

He went on to say that just as Morjin had enslaved others through greed, lust, envy and wrath, these evils had captured him as well.

'Fear and hate are even worse,' he said. 'Hate is like a tunnel of fire. It burns away all the beauty of creation. It concentrates and attaches the will to one thing, and one thing only: the object that is to be destroyed. Is there any slavery more abject than this?'

'Kane,' I said, staring at the fire, 'hates so utterly.'

'Yes, and if he does not let go of it, one day it will destroy him – utterly.'

In the fire's hot orange flames, I saw Atara's beautiful eyes all torn and bloody – and burning, burning, burning. To Master Juwain, I said, 'It is not so easy . . . to let go.'

'Do you see? Do you see? But we *must* turn away from these dark things if we are ever to be free.'

'Is that possible?' I wondered aloud. 'To be truly free?'

'It *must* be possible,' Master Juwain said. 'But if the One is the essence of freedom, then it follows that only a man completely open to the will of the One could be completely free.'

'Ah, the will of the One, indeed!' Maram put in after taking a pull at his brandy. 'That still sounds like slavery to me.'

While Flick spun by the fire and the Guardians stood watch over us, I pondered this deep and paradoxical mystery. How, I asked myself, could any man know and work the will of the One?

'Is *this* what a Maitreya is, then?' I asked.

'I wish I could tell you,' Master Juwain said.

I wished that Estrella were awake and sitting by the fire with me so that I might see the answers that I sought somehow reflected in her eyes.

'Was there nothing about this,' I asked Master Juwain, 'in your gelstei?'

Master Juwain brought out the thought stone and held it up to the fire. 'There was only a hint that the Maitreya has some vital part to play in man's journey toward the One.'

I wished that Kane hadn't gone off on some secret mission to uncover the plans of the Red Dragon. If he were sitting here now, I thought, he might simply tell me what the Maitreya was meant for. And more, being of the Elijin and having lived long enough to know other Maitreyas in other ages, he might tell me if I could be this Shining One.

After that we went off to our beds. I slept fitfully, being disturbed by dreams of Kane stalking the Red Priests in darkness and killing them with his quick and savage knife. I was very glad when the new day dawned all clear and bright. The meadowlarks singing in the hills around us cheered me; the silvery spheres of dew on the grass caught the sky's blueness and the rays of the golden sun.

We traveled all that day up the North Road through the steadily rising hills. Toward noon it grew quite warm, but the sun did not heat up our armor as much as it would mail, for steel drinks in heat and light, while diamond scatters it in a resplendent fire of many colors. It was a glorious sight to see the hundred Guardians of the Lightstone formed up into three columns and riding forth all with the same bright purpose. The miles vanished beneath the clopping of the horses' hooves. In the late afternoon, we entered the thicker forest that covers the mountains to the north. We passed through the pretty town of Ki, and made camp outside it near a stand of oaks.

On our next day's journey, the road rose steeply toward the pass between Ishka and Mesh. The horses drawing the wagons had hard work to keep driving themselves against the ancient paving stones; the horses that bore us snorted and sweated, and were grateful when we stopped to give them rest and exchange them for our remounts. Finally we came to that great cut of rock called the Telemesh Gate. One of my ancestors, using a great firestone, had melted it out of the granite in the saddle between Mount Raaskel and Mount Korukel. On my last journey into Ishka, Maram, Master Juwain and I had been attacked here. Out the dark mouth of the Gate, a great, white bear had charged down upon us and had nearly torn us to pieces. It remained still unclear as to whether this bear was an animal ghul made by Morjin to murder us. Altaru, remembering his battle with the bear, let loose a tremendous whinny as we drew nearer the Gate. I had to pat his sweating black neck and reassure him that any bear mad enough to charge our company would be impaled on the Guardians' long lances.

I was less sure of what we would find on the *other* side of the Gate, for King Hadaru's knights had lances of their own, and many more than did we. And so I commanded my men to keep tight their columns, and keep even tighter their lips, and I led them straight into the den of an even greater bear.

8

nd so we crossed into Ishka. We wound our way down from the
pass through fir forests smelling of flowers and fresh spring sap.
A few miles farther, on a hill beside the road, we came upon the
great fortress that guarded this approach into Ishka. Lord Shadru was
its commander. When his lookouts in their towers espied our company
advancing into his king's realm, he alerted his trumpeters to sound
the alarm and rode out to meet us in force.

This proved to be two hundred Ishkan knights, part of the garrison
stationed at this important fortress. Lord Shadru, a stout old man
whose face had once been burnt with red-hot sand in the siege of a
castle in Anjo, led his knights straight up to us. He called his men to
halt, even as I did mine. Then he raised his hand in salute, even as I
did mine.

'Lord Valashu!' he called to me. His words came out stiffly, as his
lips were thick with scar. 'It is good to see you again, though I must
ask why you have entered our land uninvited and without permission?'

His hand swept out toward the knights behind me. From the grim
look on Lord Shadru's seamed and pitted face, one might have thought
that I led an invasion force into Ishka.

'These are the Guardians of the Lightstone,' I told him. 'And we wish
nothing more than to cross Ishka in peace.'

Lord Shadru's eyes widened as if he didn't believe me. He called
out gruffly, 'You speak of peace, and yet you ride forth in battle armor!
You speak of the Lightstone, and yet Lord Issur has told me that it is
your father's intention to keep it in Silvassu for as long as it pleases
him. Where is this Cup of Heaven, then, that you claim to guard?'

I motioned for Baltasar to join us, and my fiery young friend rode
up from between the columns of knights behind me. I asked him to
show Lord Shadru the Lightstone. When he brought forth the golden

111

cup and held it high for all to see, Lord Shadru's eyes widened even more.

'Well, well, it seems I was too hasty in my judgments, Lord Valashu.' I motioned for Baltasar to place the Lightstone in Lord Shadru's hands, and this he did. For a moment, it seemed that Lord Shadru was holding the sun itself. 'Well, well, *well*, King Hadaru will be very pleased, indeed.'

I told Lord Shadru that we were on our way to the great tournament, and hoped to see King Hadaru there.

'I've had word that the king will lead a company of knights to Nar, so you certainly *will* see him there,' Lord Shadru said as he handed the Lightstone back to Baltasar. 'But first, you will see him in Loviisa.'

'Then he hasn't set out yet?'

'No, I had word that he would leave in a few more days.'

I exchanged quick looks with Baltasar, and then nodded at Asaru who came up beside him. We had been hoping to ride straight to Nar, but now it seemed that there was no graceful way to avoid a meeting with King Hadaru.

Lord Shadru confirmed this when he said, 'Very well, you will require an escort to the King's palace.'

He motioned at the knight beside him, a long, lean man with six battle ribbons tied to his long, gray hair. He presented him as Lord Jehu and said, 'He will ride with you to Loviisa.'

Lord Shadru gave the command of the Ishkan knights over to Lord Jehu. He wished us a pleasant journey. And then he looked at Baltasar and said, 'May I see the Lightstone one last time?'

Again Baltasar drew out the Cup of Heaven, and Lord Shadru sighed out, 'Remarkable, remarkable – who would have thought I would live to see such a thing?'

We said farewell to Lord Shadru and watched him ride back up to the huge stack of stones that was the Ishkan's fortress. Then Lord Jehu formed up his knights: a hundred ahead of us as in a vanguard and a hundred following behind. In this way, like a small army, we continued down the road through the most rugged part of the mountains. We of Mesh did not mingle with the Ishkans, for we had fought too many wars with them to make friends so easily. But neither did we quarrel with them. When we made camp that night in a fallow field that a generous farmer lent us, only a little brook separated our rows of tents from those of the Ishkans. There was to be no going back and forth over this little water. But the songs we sang around our campfires were the same that the Ishkans sang around theirs; as the night deepened, we made a single music that winged its way up toward the stars.

We set out very early the next morning with the intention of reaching Loviisa by dusk. After some hours of working our way down through a series of gradually descending mountains and foothills, we broke out into the broad valley of the Tushur River. Here the forests and farms spread out in a patchwork of different shades of green for as far as the eye could see. The Tushur itself was a hazy blue band in the distance. Loviisa had been built around the point where the North Road bridged the river. We spent the rest of the day riding toward it at an easy pace. The gently rolling country was kind to our mounts and to the horses drawing the wagons; the hours melted away into the abundant sunshine of a long and warm afternoon. We stopped only twice, to water the horses. At our second break, I watched Estrella picking wildflowers in a field buzzing with bees, and Lord Jehu, standing with his horse on the road above, watched us both.

It was just past dusk when we crested a palisade on the south side of the river and rode up to King Hadaru's palace. The fountains and gardens fronting it seemed to invite us closer. In all the Morning Mountains, there was nothing like King Hadaru's Wooden Palace. Its pagodas were exquisitely carved and arrayed on many levels, to delight the eye with its perfect proportions as much as to provide protection from wind and rain and the assault of enemy men.

Lord Jehu insisted that the hundred Guardians were far too many armed knights to be allowed into the palace. I insisted that if the Lightstone was to be brought before King Hadaru, the Guardians must accompany that which they guarded at all times, for this they had sworn upon their lives. King Hadaru broke this deadlock by sending a herald to invite all of us into his throne room. The King of Ishka, it seemed, would not deign to show fear of a hundred Meshian knights.

And so, leaving our horses and baggage train to the care of the Ishkans, I led my brothers and the Guardians into the palace. The main hall was a splendid affair of great cherrywood and ebony columns carved like the pieces of my chess set. Its panels of shatterwood were as black and beautiful as jade. All this darkness contrasted with the room's floor, an almost unbroken expanse of white oak waxed and polished to a high gloss. The massive throne, at the center of the hall, had also been carved out of this wood which was as common as it was strong. King Hadaru sat upon it waiting for us to take our places before him. He seemed to disdain surrounding himself with a private guard. Instead, some of the greatest lords of Ishka stood by the sides of his throne.

I nodded my head toward Prince Issur and Lord Nadhru, a dark and difficult man who had once threatened to bind me with ropes and drag me out of Ishka. Lord Mestivan attended King Hadaru as well, and next to him stood Lord Solhtar who pulled at his thick black beard as he eyed us with a fierce pride of protectiveness of his king and his land. Devora, the King's sister, was not in attendance this evening, but his beautiful young wife, Irisha, stood near the very foot of the throne. Her hair was raven-black like Behira's and her skin was as fair as hers, too. But she had a fineness of face and form that the plump Behira lacked. Maram stared at her with a barely-concealed lust heating up his red face. And Behira, holding tightly onto Lord Harsha's arm, stared at Maram.

'Welcome to my house,' King Hadaru said as his black eyes caught Maram up in their cold light. He was a big, burly man – bigger even than Maram – and his large head and face reminded one of a bear. Many battle ribbons were tied to his thick, white hair. 'Prince Maram Marshayk, Lord Valashu, Lord Asaru, Lord Raasharu, and everyone – welcome all.'

I stood directly in front of the throne with my arm covering Estrella. Asaru, Yarashan and Lansar Raasharu took their places to my left with Maram, Master Juwain, Lord Harsha and Behira on my right. Baltasar and the Guardians were arrayed behind us. I made the presentations while King Hadaru nodded his head and smiled cordially. He regarded us as might a bear eyeing a herd of deer who had presented themselves as a meal.

Then he raised his hand, and Lord Jehu and his two hundred knights marched into the room and stationed themselves between the Guardians and the main doors. At the same time, the hall's side doors opened to let in another hundred knights. They crossed the room at speed to take their places near the throne. If King Hadaru didn't usually keep a private guard, he certainly had one now.

'Val!' Maram whispered to me as he nudged my side, 'we've walked into a trap!'

To my left, Asaru's hand came to rest on the hilt of his sword, and so it was with my brothers. I didn't turn to see if the Guardians behind me were also prepared to fight for their charge, any more than I would doubt the rising of the sun. King Hadaru gripped the hilt of his own sword, the famed kalama with which he had once beheaded Mukaval the Red of the Adirii tribe. And then he smiled his cold smile and demanded that I deliver into his outstretched hand the golden cup called the Lightstone.

As calmly as I could, I asked Sivar of Godhra to step forward. He was a diligent man who held his rather short body rigidly erect at all times. His face, steely and serious, was now lit up with pride because it was his turn to bear the Lightstone. He brought it forth and gave it to King Hadaru, even as I asked him. Then he stepped back and waited to see what King Hadaru would say – and what he would do.

'Very good, very good,' King Hadaru murmured. His fingers closed around the golden cup as his eyes drank in its light. He fairly trembled with lust, envy and greed at last fulfilled. 'Very good, indeed.'

'We *have* walked into a trap,' I whispered back at Maram. 'Let us hope that King Hadaru cannot escape it.'

King Hadaru, who missed little of what occurred in his palace, or in his realm, shot me a swift, hard look. His thin lips broke into another smile. 'Valashu Elahad, you must be honored for keeping your promise, after all.'

'My father said that the Lightstone would be brought into Ishka.'

'Yes,' King Hadaru said, nodding at Prince Issur, 'we had word of this. But no one thought it would be so soon.'

'Soon means soon,' I said, echoing my father's words.

'I confess you've caught us unawares. We've no stand on which to set the Lightstone, as your father keeps in his hall.'

Now my hand, which had never left the hilt of my sword, gripped its black jade and the seven set diamonds tightly. It had come time to dash King Hadaru's hopes, and I did not know what he would do.

'That's just as well,' I said, 'for no stand will be needed.'

The frostiness of King Hadaru's stare nearly froze my heart. 'What do you mean, Lord Valashu?'

'The Lightstone,' I told him, 'is on its way to Nar, even as are we.'

I turned to nod at the Guardians behind me, and I saw that Lord Jehu and his two hundred knights lined up behind *them* were ready to draw their swords at their king's command.

'What?' King Hadaru snarled out. 'What treachery is this?'

'No treachery at all, King Hadaru, but only need.' I explained that the events in my father's hall had impelled the decision to take the Lightstone on the road. 'As Prince Issur has reminded my father, the Lightstone is to be shared among all the Valari.'

'Yes, but first it was to be shared among the Ishkans!' King Hadaru thundered. 'This was the promise made on the field of the Raaswash!'

'And it *was* shared there,' I said, 'on the day that my companions and I returned from Argattha. Every warrior and knight in your army held it in his hands.'

To the side of the throne, Prince Issur's plain face lit up with wonder as if he well-remembered the feel of the Lightstone's gold gelstei. So it was with Lord Nadhru and Lord Solhtar and the many other Ishkans in King Hadaru's hall.

115

'And still it is being shared,' I continued. I pointed at the golden bowl that King Hadaru now gripped in both hands. 'Its light now graces your hall.'

'For a night? For two? You promised that the Lightstone was to reside in Loviisa as it did in Silvassu.'

'No, that promise was never made.'

'It was made in spirit.'

'No, not even in spirit, King Hadaru. If you search your heart, you will know this is true.'

King Hadaru glared at me with his cold, dark eyes. I knew him to be an honest man, with others if not himself.

'Am I to be made to accept then,' he said to me, 'that you intend to take the Lightstone from my hall tomorrow? You promise me a birthday cake and leave me with only crumbs. I had hoped, I had hoped . . .'

It was the great sorrow of his life, I thought, that so many of his hopes and dreams had turned to despair.

'The Lightstone,' I reminded him, 'was made to be possessed by no man.'

'No, possessed by none,' he muttered. His eyes stabbed into me like cold swords. 'But claimed by one.'

'No one has claimed the Lightstone yet.'

'No, not *yet*,' he said as he gripped the cup even more tightly.

'I'm only the Lightstone's Guardian,' I said. 'And as its Guardian, I'm charged with deciding –'

'Who decides matters in this hall?' King Hadaru broke in. 'Who is king in my kingdom? Who must protect all its treasures?'

'The Lightstone belongs to no kingdom on earth. Its first Guardian brought it from the stars only to –'

'The Elahad,' he interrupted me again, 'was the ancestor of the Ishkans, too. But even *he* did not claim to be the Maitreya.'

The bitterness in King Hadaru's voice was a poison in my veins. He stared at me with a strange mixture of loathing and longing. All kings wish for their sons great virtues and great deeds that prove them worthy of inheriting their realms. But on the Raaswash and six nights ago in my father's hall, I had proved his firstborn, Salmelu, to be nothing more than a murderer and a traitor. And more, it had been I who had brought the Lightstone out of Argattha and not Salmelu or Prince Issur. And so I brought great shame to King Hadaru and all his line; my very existence and presence in his hall was an insult that tore his heart with an anguish almost too great for him to bear.

'Do you remember standing in that ring?' King Hadaru asked me.

116

He pointed past my shoulder at the floor, where a great circle of red rosewood had been set into the white oak. The Guardians formed their lines behind it. I remembered too well standing in this ring of honor where the Ishkans fought their duels. There Salmelu's sword had pierced my side; there I had wounded him nearly to the death.

'You spared the life of him whose name we no longer speak in this house,' King Hadaru said to me. 'You should have slain him. Is this the compassion of a Maitreya?'

I stood with my hand on my sword as I remembered the faces of the dead scryers and the slave girls; I found myself wishing that I *had* slain Salmelu.

'Of course, it's also said,' King Hadaru continued, 'that the Maitreya will be a great warlord. Have you ever led men into battle, Lord Valashu?'

I looked at the rigid faces of Lord Issur and Lord Nadhru and those of the hundred Ishkans positioned near the throne. Behind me, lined up by the main doors, stood Lord Jelu and his knights, and their hearts beat with bloodlust and wrath. The Guardians I had led into Ishka trembled to test their swords against these men and take back the Lightstone from King Hadaru's clutching hand. It was possible, I knew, that a battle would break out in this room in another moment. King Hadaru desired this. Some shame burns so deeply that it seems only blood can wash it clean.

'It's my hope,' I said to him, 'that we will fight no more battles.'

He laughed his brittle, humorless laugh and said, 'You would end war, so I've been told.'

'Yes – we Valari were meant to be warriors of the spirit only.'

'Is that so? Then whom are we to war against? And how are we to war against them?'

With the valarda, I thought. *With all the force of our souls.*

'An alliance,' I said to him, 'must be made to oppose the Red Dragon. This is why we're journeying to the tournament.'

I felt the coldness of King Hadaru's eyes touching mine. And he must have felt a little of the fire of the dream that blazed inside me. 'An alliance?' he asked. 'Waashians stand with Taroners? Ishkans stand with warriors of Mesh?'

'Even as we stand together in this room, King Hadaru. Even as we stood at the Sarburn three thousand years ago.'

King Hadaru gazed at the little bowl. A soft radiance flowed out of it and spilled over him in a golden sheen. There was a burning in his eyes, and in my own. It came to me then that shame was only a bitter reminder of our instinct to be restored to our inborn nobility. King

Hadaru, I knew, might long for death in battle and the slaying of all his foes. But there was something he desired even more.

'Help me,' I said to him. 'Help me make this alliance.'

'Help *you*? How?'

'Journey with us to Nar. If the Valari see the Ishkans and Meshians riding together, they'll believe any miracle is possible.'

'If *I* saw that myself, I would believe in miracles, too,' King Hadaru said. He paused to look down into the soft, golden curves of the Lightstone. 'You speak of riding together, of sharing this cup. But those who guard it are all of Mesh. Are we of Ishka to follow in your train like dogs hoping for leavings from your plates?'

I exchanged glances with several of the knights framing King Hadaru's throne. Then I said to him, 'All right, then. Choose ten of your finest men, and they will take oaths as Guardians, too.'

These words had scarcely left my lips when a great sigh of surprise blew through the room. Some of the knights about me grumbled their disapproval of my suggestion, but many more seemed pleased.

'Ten knights?' King Hadaru said. 'Why not a hundred? Do think that Ishka is so poor in spirit that we cannot spare so many?'

'No one will ever say that of Ishka, King Hadaru. But it is my intention to journey from Nar into Tria. A hundred knights will be quite enough to alarm the Alonians, as they alarmed Lord Shadru. Two hundred Valari *will* begin to look like an invasion.'

King Hadaru thought about this as he studied the cup in his hand. Then he said, 'Yes, perhaps you're right. Fifty knights would be better.'

'That is still too many,' I said. 'Warders must be found for each of them so that Morjin's illusions won't touch them. And I must be sure of every Guardian.'

'Are you saying that you'll doubt the knights I choose?'

'No, King Hadaru. But the Guardians' first loyalty must be to the Lightstone, and to me. I must know the men I lead.'

'How long, then, would it take you to become acquainted with thirty of my knights?'

'Twice as long,' I said, 'as it would half that number.'

'Fifteen knights,' he muttered, shaking his head. 'Of course, all this is only speculation. Who could think that even fifteen Ishkan knights could ride with Meshians all the way to Tria?'

'Is it easier,' I asked him, 'to imagine twenty knights making this journey?'

'Perhaps. Surely you can understand that my knights would long for the company of their countrymen.'

'Then why don't you choose these knights now, since they stand with their companions?'

'Why *don't* I? Why, I don't because it hasn't been decided yet that the Ishkans will join the Guardians as you propose.'

He gazed at the Lightstone for what seemed an hour. Then he announced, 'It's said that *the* Gelstei is able to find all other gelstei and have power over them. It's also said to give immortality.'

He held out his old, scarred hand and studied it for a long few moments. And then again his fingers closed around the golden cup as if he were loathe to let it go. I, of all men, knew how he felt. To surrender the Lightstone to another was like giving up one's heart.

My eyes found his then, and he snapped out, 'What are you looking at? Don't look at me that way!'

All Valari, I remembered, aspired to polish their souls until they shone with the fire of flawless diamonds.

'Maybe you *are* the Maitreya,' King Hadaru said to me. He stared at the Lightstone for a moment before looking back at me. 'Maybe you aren't. But your hope of making an alliance is a good one. I have come to see that Morjin must be opposed, after all. He is like a spider who weaves his webs in dark places to ensnare the innocent.'

He leaned forward from his massive wooden throne as if to stand and give the Lightstone to Prince Issur. Then he seemed to think better of this impulse. He settled back into his seat as he pointed at Estrella. 'Others have suffered worse insults at the hands of the Red Dragon than have I. This girl, perhaps, who has lost her power of speech. And yet I have lost a son to him; it is like losing one's life. The one whose name I will no longer speak was not always a creature of Morjin's. He was hot-headed, yes, and proud – well, we all knew how proud he could be. But he was not born evil. Morjin made him so. Morjin is a stealer of souls, and I will do all that is in my power to make him pay for his crimes.'

So saying, King Hadaru finally rose from his throne. He stepped over to a tall, young knight with a noble face, whose long nose was like a pillar holding up his finely-boned brow. He extended the Lightstone to him and said, 'Sar Jarlath, will you guard this with your life? Will you swear to slay all enemies who would steal this cup from its rightful master?'

Asaru turned to look at me just then, and so did Maram and Lord Raasharu. Their faces seethed with anger and pride. As Guardian of the Lightstone, it was upon me to ask of Sar Jarlath the very questions that King Hadaru was now putting to him. But I did not gainsay him. I stood in silence watching the little miracle that unfolded before me.

And so King Hadaru continued, 'Will you agree to ride forth under Lord Valashu's command, and yet never forget that you are a knight of Ishka and carry with you the honor of your king and countrymen?'

Sar Jarlath gave his assent, and we watched with gladness as King Hadaru pressed the Lightstone into his hands. So it went with other knights, King Hadaru walking about the room and choosing out the finest of the men who followed him. Now, it seemed, they would follow me. When all twenty had been selected, they joined the hundred Guardians near the ring of honor. Then Sivar of Godhra gave over the charge of the Lightstone to Sar Jarlath, who would be its next bearer on the road to Nar and Tria.

After that, King Hadaru called for a feast. We all ate much meat and drank much beer. King Hadaru regaled us with accounts of valor of the twenty new Guardians whom he had chosen. Years seemed to fall away from his worn, old face. It was the first time I had seen him happy. I gave thanks yet again that it had been my fate to find the Lightstone. For a great king had touched the golden cup, and it had touched him.

When it came time for bed, Asaru took me aside and said to me, 'You gambled greatly in bringing the Lightstone here, little brother.'

'Yes – but all the other gambles seemed worse.'

'But how did you know that King Hadaru wouldn't try to take it?'

'I *didn't*. But one either believes in men or not.' I smiled to reassure Asaru and continued, 'King Hadaru is presumptuous, arrogant and vain. But he has the soul of a Valari.'

That night I took my rest in a richly furnished room reserved for princes and kings. I slept well, knowing that the new Guardians who stood watch outside my door would lay down their lives to protect me and the Lightstone.

9

In the morning, everyone assembled in the lane in front of the palace. King Hadaru, wearing a red tunic emblazoned with the great white bear of the Aradars, sat astride a big gelding. His standard-bearer held aloft a fluttering banner with the same charge. Prince Issur and Lord Nadhru rode next to the king. Fifty knights, King Hadaru's private guard, took their places behind them, followed by a considerable baggage train. Asaru and Yarashan chafed at having to trail after this company, but protocol demanded that we yield precedence to a king in his own realm. And so the Guardians and I lined up much as before, only now there were twenty more of us. I went among these Ishkan knights learning their names and those of their fathers. In appearance, they were little different than the knights of Mesh. They wore diamond battle armor glittering in the morning light. Their surcoats and shields, bordered with white bears, showed their various charges. I noted the black lion against the white field of Sar Kimball and the gold sunburst of Sar Ianashu, a slender and hirsute young man, who was Lord Solhtar's second son. As marks of cadence, to each of their charges, had been added a small golden cup. I considered letting the new Guardians ride together as a single squadron within our company. But they must become used to us, and we to them, and the sooner the better. And so I positioned Sunjay Naviru next to a Sar Avram and Sivar of Godhra next to Sar Jarlath, and so on. It would be many long miles, I thought, before these proud knights accepted each other in companionship, much less love. In truth, we would be lucky if we didn't tear into each other with mistrustful eyes and words – or even our swords.

The first hour of our journey took us down through the houses and shops of Loviisa, the largest of Ishka's cities, though still quite small. The cool air smelled of baking bread and coal smoke from the many smithies. The armorers here made good steel – though not quite so fine, I thought, as did my countrymen in Godhra. Our route led through winding streets back to the North Road, which gave onto a stout bridge spanning the raging Tushur river. Just beyond this dangerous water, in a square lined with several inns, we came to the intersection of the King's Road. This was a well-paved band of stone wide enough for six horses to ride down it side by side. It curved east through Ishka into Taron, all the way to Nar. King Hadaru led his knights onto it. And we who guarded the Lightstone followed them.

We had a fine day for travel, with many drifting white clouds to steal some of the heat from the bright spring sun. It was noisier than I would have liked, however, as the hooves of so many horses sounded a continual percussion of iron against stone, and the wagons' iron-shod wheels ground particles of grit into dust. It pleased me to hear the knights in my company keeping up a low hum of conversation or even singing one of the battle songs that all the Valari know. In truth, there were moments when both Meshians and Ishkans became too intoxicated with the passion of these old verses, and then their voices seemed to vie with each other in loudness and stridency rather than harmonizing. There were moments, too, when I thought I caught a rumble of discord or a brief flurry of heated words from the knights behind me. But that was the worst of things, and I gave thanks for that. The hours and miles passed uneventfully as we all kept the peace.

But later that afternoon, a quarrel broke out and threatened to turn into a brawl. We had stopped to water the horses at one of the little rivers that flowed down from the low range of mountains to the north of Loviisa. As I watched Altaru drinking his fill of the icy water, a shout rang out behind me; I turned to see Skyshan push the heel of his hand against Sar Ianashu's chest and nearly knock him off his feet. Then Sar Ianashu reached for his sword even as Tavar Amadan grabbed his arm to restrain him and Sar Jarlath knocked his shoulder into Tavar.

'Hold!' I cried out. I saw, all in an instant, that the Ishkans of King Hadaru's guard on the road ahead of us were all gripping the hilts of their swords. And so were Baltasar, Sunjay Naviru and other knights of Mesh. 'Hold, now, before it's too late!'

I ran down the road and threw my body between Sar Ianashu and Skyshan. I pulled them apart and shouted, 'Are you Valari knights? Are you Guardians of the Lightstone?'

My fury, if not my words, cut into them like a sword and seemed to empty them of breath. Tempers cooled, then. I stood listening to these men's explanations. It turned out that their quarrel was ancient. The ancestors of both of them had lived along the Diamond River, on opposite sides. Once a time – 939 years ago to be precise – one of

Skyshan's great-grandsires had fought a duel with one of Sar Ianashu's over a woman who had both Meshian and Ishkan blood. Both men had been killed. The resulting feud had lasted a hundred years, until the Diamond shifted its course, and Sar Ianashu's ancestors had been forced to move to another site higher in the Shoshan range of mountains. For reasons that I was not able to determine, both Sar Ianashu and Skyshan had decided to renew this feud after all these many centuries.

'But this cannot be,' I said to them. 'Your grievances are ancient. The very mountains have changed their faces in this time, but you have not. How are we to ride together this way? Is there an Ishkan knight who can't tell of sorrows more recent at the Meshians' hands or a man of Mesh who hasn't suffered the loss of kinsmen in one of our wars? My own grandfather was killed along that very same river scarcely ten years ago, and so were many others.'

Sar Ianashu, a violent man whose cheek muscles were popping beneath his taut ivory skin, finally opened his mouth as if to gainsay me. But then he thought better of such rashness and bit his lip. I was now his lord. He had made vows and would not break them. He bowed his head in shame, and so did Skyshan.

By this time, King Hadaru had walked down the road to see what trouble had befallen us. He watched in silence, both jealous that I should so address one of his knights and glad to see that I had calmed this little dispute even as he might have done. Then he returned to his place at the head of our columns. When it came time to get back on our horses, Asaru walked up to me and said, 'This cannot go on. Ishkans and Meshians, together – this is impossible.'

And I said to him, 'No, it will be all right.'

'But, Val, how can you be sure?'

'Because,' I said, 'either one believes in men or one does not.'

Despite my brave words, I kept a wary watch upon my men as we resumed our journey. But Sar Ianashu's and Skyshan's outburst seemed to let the bad blood between them rather than inflaming it. That night, we had a happy camp within sight of the mighty Culhadosh river. I gave the Lightstone into Sar Ianashu's keeping; Sar Ianashu surprised everyone by lending Skyshan his sharpening stone, which was a very fine one made of pressed diamond dust. After that they clasped hands and pledged their companionship. They both knew that, although I had made no threats, any more fighting would result in their expulsion from the Guardians. What would it avail for them to satisfy some point of honor a thousand years old if they must suffer such shame?

While our dinner of fresh lamb was sizzling over our cooking fires,

I gave Estrella what was to become the first of a series of riding lessons. She hated sitting all day by herself in a creaking wagon. With a few motions of her hands and her eager eyes, she indicated that she wished to ride next to me. And so I chose out a gentle mare from our string of remounts and sat Estrella upon her. With her skinny legs gripping the mare's brown sides, she seemed almost too small to ride a full-sized horse. And she could not speak to this fine animal as others might, with soft words and comforting tones that found resonance in the mare's easy nickers. Estrella, however, spoke to her in other ways. Her graceful hands caressed the mare's mane and communicated her faith that the mare would not hurt her. It seemed to me, watching how Estrella's quick, dark eyes met the dark eye of the mare's great turned head, that she immediately loved this beast and that the mare knew this with an animal's instinct. As I led both horse and girl about the fields along the river, I thought that it wouldn't be long before Estrella could ride with the knights and others of our company.

After dinner, I discovered that King Hadaru was a fine storyteller. He invited Asaru and me, and several others, over to his campfire to share some very good and very rare Galdan brandy. He recounted the deeds of the Ishkans' ancestors at the Battle of Rainbow Pass in the year 37 of the Age of Swords, which marked the first time that the Valari had defeated an invading Sarni army and had fought with a people other than themselves. Then, to the nightly ritual of warriors running their sharpening stones along their swords, he recited some ancient verses that were close to every Valari's heart:

A sword becomes a warrior's soul,
Its shining steel through pains made keen,
His strength and valor keep it whole,
His faith and honor keep it clean.

A warrior's soul becomes his sword:
It cuts through darkness, pain and fright;
Its diamond-brilliance points him toward
The brilliant, pure and single light.

When he finished, he raised his glass to me and told me, 'Some day, I would know more about this sword it's said you carry inside *you*, Valashu Elahad.'

Early the next morning we crossed the Culhadosh River, greatest of the waters that drain the Morning Mountains. And so we passed into Taron, the most populous of the Nine Kingdoms. It was a fair country with many farms spread along the Culhadosh. Out of this rich black soil, the Taroners grew barley and oats, wheat and rye – and not a few warriors and knights who had pledged their swords to King Waray in Nar. We met a small squadron of these who were on their way to the tournament. Their shields showed blue boars and black ravens and other devices unfamiliar to me. If the Taroners were chagrined to see such a large body of outland knights riding free through their land, they gave no sign of it. But their leader, a Lord Eladaru, remarked the strangeness of Ishkans accompanying Meshians, saying, 'If this is truly the end of the age, as has been prophesied, then this must be the first of its miracles.'

After King Hadaru proudly called up Sar Marjay, one of his nephews, to bring forth the Lightstone, Lord Eladaru blinked his eyes and said, 'It seems I misspoke. Meshians surrendering the guardianship of the Lightstone to an Ishkan – surely *this* must be the greatest of miracles. The next thing you know, maybe King Kurshan really will find a way to sail the stars.'

Lord Eladaru bid us a safe journey, then gathered up his men and rode on ahead of us. I watched them disappear along the road that wound up and around the low, green hills to the east.

We, with our heavy baggage train, followed them more slowly. We passed through fields of sunflowers and apple orchards, and then some miles of rolling pasturage given over to the grazing of goats and sheep. Toward the end of our first day in Taron, the finely paved road turned into a track of packed dirt. As there had been no rain for the past few days, the hot sun had dried out its surface. The horses' hooves, no less the wheels of the wagons, pulverized the dirt and sent up thick clouds of dust. Trailing behind King Hadaru and his Ishkan knights became a torment of stinging eyes and grit coating our lips and teeth. We had to cover our faces with our scarves so as not to choke. Maram complained about riding behind King Hadaru. As he wiped at his beard and blinked his powdered eyes, he said, 'Now that we're in Taron, the Ishkans should trail us. Let them eat *our* dust.'

On our second day in Taron, Maram had good cause to wish for the previous day's dust: toward noon, some thick, dark clouds came out of the west and let loose a downpour lasting for hours. The rain turned the road into a bog of sticky mud and potholes like little brown ponds. Twice, one of the wagons got stuck in this mire. Our pace slowed as the horses slogged along; I listened to the squish and suck of their hooves against the mud as I blinked my eyes against the slanting rain. The gray sky seemed too low, too heavy. The air was too moist and nearly smothered me. I felt something cold, wet and dark sniffing at my insides like the snout of some fell beast. I felt a pulling there, in my belly, as if sharp teeth were tearing into me while long claws hooked into my back. This odious sensation seemed to emanate from somewhere behind me; it reminded me of the time that the dreadful Grays had pursued Maram, Master Juwain, Atara and me through the wilds of Alonia. Only now, on this muddy road in the open country, whatever was pursuing me seemed to have no hate for me, but only a fierce will to rend and destroy.

We made camp that night in well-drained meadow above the road. After Estrella's riding lesson, I held council in my tent with Maram and Master Juwain – and with my brothers, too. I told them of my misgivings. And Maram immediately sighed out, 'Oh, no, not the Stonefaces! I'd rather face Morjin himself again than them. If it *is* them, too bad for us.'

'It will be all right,' I said to him. I remembered too well the unclean sense of how the Grays wanted to suck out my soul and torment me. 'This didn't *feel* like them.'

'Well, what did it feel like?'

'Like someone behind me wanted to murder me.'

Yarashan, who had little liking for the new Guardians, didn't hesitate to say, 'One of the Ishkans, then?'

'It can't be,' I said. 'Whoever is pursuing me, in his wish to slay . . . there is so much *power*.'

Yarashan shook his handsome head skeptically. This strange gift I had of sensing others' emotions disturbed him, the more so because he seemed to lack it. 'It *could* be one of the Ishkans, Val. King Hadaru chose them himself, didn't he? What if he's set one of them to murder you?'

He went on to say that King Hadaru could not want me to be the Maitreya. Even though King Hadaru had spoken nobly about uniting the Valari, very likely he himself wished to be the one to lead an alliance against Morjin. If I were killed, then King Hadaru might contrive a way to use the new Guardians to give him control of the Lightstone.

'You've a keen mind for plots and strategies,' I said to Yarashan. My brother beamed as if he had just beaten me in another game of chess and was proud to explicate my mistakes. 'What you say makes good sense – except for one thing.'

'And what is that?'

'King Hadaru is no murderer who would set an assassin upon me.'

'Can you be sure of that?'

'As sure as I am of Ianashu and the new Guardians. As sure as I am of Skyshan and Sunjay and the Guardians that I chose myself.'

Yarashan looked at Asaru as if in frustration of my naivete. And Asaru said, 'There is another possibility. The ghul may have followed us from Mesh.'

I shuddered at this suggestion as I looked out the flap of my tent at the darkening hills around us. If a ghul was hiding in the pastures or woods nearby, I could not sense him.

'We should post extra guards tonight,' Asaru continued. 'And we should post guards around *your* tent, Val. Men we can trust beyond doubt in case one of the Ishkans *is* an assassin.'

Each night, since we had set out on the road, it had become our custom that the Lightstone return to my hand and be kept in my tent at the center of our camp.

'No, there will be no guards around my tent,' I told Asaru. 'What would we tell them? That we mistrust the Ishkans, who are now their companions? And what would the Ishkans think of their calling as Guardians when they discovered that we of Mesh sought to guard ourselves against *them*?'

Master Juwain, who had been silent until now, sighed as he rubbed the back of his head. 'Very well, then, since the rain has stopped, I'll sit outside my tent as if taking a bit of fresh air. If anyone approaches *your* tent, Val, I'll find a way to detain him and give the alarm.'

'Ah, do you intend to sit up all night?' Maram asked him.

'Are you volunteering to relieve me and take a shift?'

Maram, who had been proposing no such thing, or so I thought, looked back and forth between Master Juwain and my brothers. Their unyielding black eyes fixed upon him as if to ask whether he was truly a Valari knight in spirit, as the two diamonds of his ring proclaimed him to be.

'I suppose it wouldn't hurt me to lose a little sleep tonight,' Maram finally said. He clapped me on my shoulder with his huge hand. 'I wouldn't sleep very well in any case knowing that a ghul was stalking my best friend.'

It was arranged then that Maram would take the second of the night's shifts. Asaru and Yarashan, whose tent was pitched next to mine, would keep watch during the last hours of the night.

And so everyone except Master Juwain retired to his bed. I spread out my sleeping furs inside my large pavilion; next to me I laid my chess board and the wooden box containing thirty-two ivory and ebony pieces. And on top of it I set the Lightstone. I lay back to look up at the stars through the open flap in the roof of my tent. I felt outside among the many Guardians for the cold knives of a desire to murder me; I felt nothing. I was certain that I would be unable to sleep. It pained me to think of Master Juwain sitting up for hours outside his tent while I tossed about here futilely trying for a bit of rest. Then I remembered a meditation that he had once taught me in the heart of the Vardaloon, when clouds of mosquitoes had whined in my ear for endless dark hours. I closed my eyes to practice it. My mind cleared as time began to dissolve. The little noises of the camp and the chirping of the crickets in the fields outside faded away; inside me there was a spreading calm and a desire to lose myself in the timeless realm of the One.

I was more tired than I knew; I must have dozed off quickly and slept for hours. I was not quite aware of what awakened me. Perhaps it was the swirl of little lights as Flick spun furiously about in the dark spaces above me. For a moment I lay suspended in that netherworld of unknowing, not quite able grasp onto the sights, sounds and smells of the earth, or even the sense of my own existence. And then conscious-ness came flooding into me like the crush of an icy river. I gasped for breath, and a surge of fear caused my heart to begin beating wildly. I opened my eyes to see the cloaked figure of one of the Guardians moving toward me. He held a mace in his upraised hand. Seeing that I suddenly saw him, he leaped forward in one furious motion and whipped the mace straight down toward my head.

My whole body convulsed with a terrible urge to escape this sudden death. I jerked my head away from the descending mace even as I rolled to my side and grabbed the Lightstone. I was not quite quick enough; the iron mace grazed the side of my head and stunned me. The knight above me raised back the mace again as he fell upon me; by some miracle I grabbed his arm so that he could not brain me. With his other hand, he grabbed at my hand that held the Lightstone. Thus locked together, he bore his weight down upon me, raging at me like a lion, twisting and pulling and trying to push his mace into my teeth even as he drove his knee at my belly. I smelled the sweat-stained leather of his battle armor and the essence of lilacs steaming off the white scarf tied around his neck. As we rolled about in this death struggle, he kept trying to bring his mace to bear. The insane power of his body and being shocked me. It could only be another moment before he fought free of my weakening grip and split my head open. I finally cried out with all the force of my lungs: 'No!'

From far away, it seemed, I heard the sound of swords being drawn from their sheaths. And then someone called out: 'It came from the pavilion! It must be Lord Valashu!'

The knight above me at last succeeded in pushing the mace into my throat. I slid my hand down toward the mace's wooden shaft and latched onto it. But I couldn't quite rip it from his grasp, and he pressed the mace downward with a sickening force. I choked and gasped for breath, even as the knight tried to rip the Lightstone from my hand. But I gripped onto the little cup with the last of my strength.

'Lord Valashu, we're coming!'

Suddenly, this murderous knight let go both my hand and the mace. He sprang up and lunged for the opening of the tent. Through the red haze of my stunned senses, as I struggled to breathe, I saw him open his mouth and call out: 'He's getting away!'

Then he rushed from my tent even as Sunjay Naviru and two other Guardians rushed in. They came right up to the side of my sleeping furs. While one of the Guardians held up an oil lamp, Sunjay began checking me for wounds. I struggled to sit up; I struggled to speak, but for a moment I could not. I pointed toward the tent's opening. Sunjay laid his hand on my chest and said, 'It's all right, Val. You'll be all right – whoever did this to you won't get away.'

Sunjay, I suddenly realized, believed that the knight who had tried to murder me was in hot pursuit of a would-be assassin. The two other Guardians in my tent, and the many others in the camp, must have believed this, too, for I heard a dozen voices pick up the cry: 'He's getting away!'

I shook my bleeding head back and forth as hard as I dared. I finally found my voice and croaked out, '*He* tried to murder me!'

'Who did, Val?'

'The one . . . who was here.' I realized with a start that I recognized the man who had left me holding his mace – and the Lightstone. 'The one you let get away: it was Sivar of Godhra.'

Sunjay burned with anger and shame to learn that he had been fooled by such a ruse. I burned with disbelief that one of my own, the faithful Sivar, could have betrayed me and then had the cleverness to fool Sunjay in order to make his escape.

I shook off the pain in my pounding head. I sat up and pulled on my diamond-studded boots. And then I ran from my tent, out into the camp which had come alive with men holding torches and shouting while others were ripping open their tent flaps to see if we had been attacked in the middle of the night. To the east, from the nearby encampment of King Hadaru and the Ishkans, came the flash of torches being lit and the cries of knights fearing a plot against their king.

'Search the camp!' I called out as I drew my sword. 'Find Sivar!'

It didn't take long for the Guardians to fulfill this command, for the camp was small and there was no place to hide except inside the tents or underneath them. A quick search turned up only one surprising thing: that Maram seemed to have fallen asleep outside his tent. Not even the clamor of a hundred and twenty knights hurrying about sufficed to awaken him.

And then one of the sentries to the north remembered seeing Sivar near the stockade just after all the shouting had begun. An examination of this wooden fence revealed some displaced branches where someone must have climbed over it. The sentry, Omaru Tarshan, was aghast that he had failed in his duty. But I eased his shame, pointing out that the stockade and the sentries had been meant to keep enemies from infiltrating the camp and not murderous Guardians from escaping.

Then King Hadaru and his knights arrived to reinforce us. King Hadaru made his way into our camp and called out to me, 'What has happened?'

'One of my knights fell mad,' I said. 'He tried to steal the Lightstone.'

After that, I ordered a search of the surrounding pasturage. Men holding bright torches spread out in a widening circle across the still-dark grass. A short while later, from a copse of mulberry to the north, one of the Guardians cried out that he had found Sivar. I led a charge toward these trees with twenty of the Guardians and King Hadaru close behind me. I followed the torchlight of the first Guardian into the copse. And there, fallen on his back next to one of the trees, I saw Sivar. He clutched a bloody dagger and stared at nothing because his throat had been cut from ear to ear. It seemed that he had died by his own hand.

'Here, now – what's this?' King Hadaru cried out as he came up to me. 'Look, then, a *Meshian* has turned traitor!'

'No,' I said, 'he was no traitor – not exactly.'

Asaru and Yarashan, with Lansar Raasharu, Baltasar and Sunjay joined me beneath the mulberry trees, with their darkly fluttering and coarsely-toothed leaves. Then Master Juwain came panting up to us followed by Lord Harsha, who limped along as quickly as he could. When his single eye looked past the light of the torches to take in Sivar's fallen form, he called out, 'This is terrible! My grand-nephew, whom I recommended as Guardian myself – how can this be?'

'Because he was a ghul,' I said. My heart ached with a sharp pain because there could no longer be any doubt of this. 'It must have been Sivar who used the sleep stone on the Guardians at the castle. He must have waited for this night, for a second chance to steal the Lightstone.'

I brought forth the golden cup to show everyone that it remained safe. But neither it nor anything, it seemed to me, would ever be safe again.

Lansar Raasharu's noble face was now a mask of anger. He pointed down at Sivar and said, 'But if this man was a creature of Morjin's, why did he kill himself?'

'To keep from being captured and questioned,' I said. 'In any case, once I had recognized him, he was useless to Morjin.'

'Yes, but why kill himself *here*? Could not the accursed Crucifier simply have commanded him to cut his own throat in your tent?'

We all looked at each other then. It seemed that the hand of Morjin lay heavy about us even from a thousand miles away, pressing down like a mailed fist upon this little stand of trees and reaching out to rip open the fabric of our tents in the encampments below us.

It was Master Juwain who had an answer for Lord Raasharu. He nodded his bald head toward him and said, 'Sometimes a ghul retains enough of his soul to hate his master, even to break free, for a few moments. It may have been so with Sivar. Until the Red Dragon found him hiding here in these trees.'

I held up my hand as if to ward off Morjin's evil eye. With Sivar dead, I knew that Morjin had no way to perceive this place or anywhere else nearby. But in that dark moment, with the blood filling the dark opening in Sivar's throat, it seemed that Morjin could look into any part of the world that he willed.

'A ghul,' Master Juwain said, his voice heavy with sadness. He turned to examine the gash that Sivar's mace had torn along the side of my head. 'It's a miracle he didn't kill you, Val.'

'He . . . was so powerful,' I said.

I didn't add that Sivar, moving to Morjin's will, had been possessed by all of his sorcerous strength.

'Here, Val,' Master Juwain said to me. 'Let me look at your eyes.'

As one of the Guardians held up a torch, a bright lancet of light stabbed straight through my eyes into my head. The kirax with which Morjin had once poisoned me seemed to flare up in my blood as if Morjin himself had breathed his fiery breath into me. It was like acid eating into every nerve in my body, making this pain a hundred times worse.

'Damn him!' Lansar called out as if my hatred of Morjin had become his own. 'Damn Morjin for doing this!'

After Master Juwain had finished testing me for concussion, Lansar Raasharu looked at me in thankfulness that I would be all right. I wondered if he might have possessed some small part of my gift. His devotion to me was like a shield held up to protect me, leaving himself uncovered, and I loved him for that.

'And damn Sivar for betraying us!' he added.

131

I looked down at Sivar's body and said, 'No, let's not damn him, for he has damned himself. It might be so with any man.'

'With any man who is weak, perhaps. With any man who is faithless and turns away from the Law of the One.'

I said nothing as I looked down into Sivar's dead eyes. Even great angels such as Angra Mainyu, I thought, had turned away from the One.

'What shall we do now, Lord Valashu?' Lansar asked me.

'Let's bury him,' I said. 'Before Sivar was a ghul, he was Sar Sivar, whom many of us loved.'

After that, one of Sivar's friends wrapped his body in his cloak, and six of the Guardians bore him back to camp to prepare for burial. King Hadaru and his knights went back to the Ishkan encampment, there to take a little rest in what remained of the night. I retired into my tent. Master Juwain met me there with some hot tea to soothe my savaged throat. Then he went to work stitching up the gash along the side of my head while I spoke with Asaru and Yarashan about the night's calamity. After a little while, Maram poked his head inside and joined us, too. Yarashan tore into him for falling asleep on his watch and nearly getting me killed. But Maram had kept many long watches through many long nights on our quest across Ea; I knew that he hadn't simply allowed himself to nod off. Maram confirmed this, filling in another piece of the puzzle of how Morjin had nearly worked my doom.

'I didn't *fall* asleep,' he huffed at Yarashan. 'Near the end of my watch, Sivar approached me with a cup of brandy. He said that he couldn't sleep, either, with all the excitement of the tournament beginning the day after tomorrow. He asked if he could join me in a little nightcap before sleeping. And why not, I thought, since I had only a few minutes left before I was to wake up Lord Asaru? Sivar was really a kind man, everyone said that about him, and I was grateful for this little kindness. But the brandy must have been poisoned with a sleeping potion. I remember talking with him about the lance-throwing competition . . . and then there was nothing.'

His suspicions were proved when he retrieved his cup for Master Juwain's examination. Master Juwain took one sniff of the still-moist brandy residue and pronounced, 'Nightstalk. The Kallimun use such potions. Probably Salmelu or one of the Red Priests supplied Sivar with it – along with the sleep stone that dropped the Guardians in King Shamesh's hall.'

For a while Master Juwain, with Maram and Asaru, speculated as to how Morjin had made a ghul of Sivar. Did Morjin have spies in Mesh who had somehow marked out Sivar as weak in the will? Had Sivar delved into the dark mysteries of the mind only to find the Red Dragon waiting for him in the deepest and most desolate of caverns? Nobody knew. After a while, Yarashan gave up trying to fathom the unfathomable and said to me, 'At least the ghul has been exposed and killed – we can be thankful for that.'

But Maram, who understood me better than almost anyone, looked at me and said, 'Ah, Val, the prophecy, too bad.'

'The prophecy? Which prophecy?' Yarashan asked. Although he was an intelligent man, he was not a particularly sensitive one. 'The scryer said that a ghul would undo Val's dreams. Well, she was wrong. Val fought him off, like a true Elahad, and so the ghul was made to undo himself.'

'No, Yarashan,' I said. The night's events had nearly ripped out my insides. 'I . . . was so certain of Sivar. Of all the Guardians. Their hearts, their beings: so bright. *This* was the dream. But how can I be certain of anything ever again?'

How could I, I wondered, ever claim the mantle of the Maitreya if I couldn't be certain even of myself?

Yarashan, of course, had no answers for me. And neither did Maram or Asaru, or even Master Juwain. We stayed up talking for the rest of the night. At last, with the sun rising like a ball of fire over the green hills to the east, it came time to break camp. A burial remained to be made. Tournament competitions must be faced, and if possible, won. And above all, Morjin, the Crucifier, the Lord of Lies, must be opposed at all moments with all the force and purity of our hearts – or else we might end up as had Sivar of Godhra, a man without a soul who was doomed to wander lost among the stars until the end of time.

10

Nar was the largest city in the Nine Kingdoms; it spread out across the rolling, green country to the west and north of the Iron Hills, where its founders had delved for ore and built forges to make steel. To this day, plumes of smoke rise over the shops of the Smithy District along the hills; there could be found the Street of Shields and the famous Street of Swords that was the ancient heart of Nar. We made our way east toward this oldest part of the city, for the King's Road took us straight toward a juncture there with two other highways: the Adra Straight, which led north out of the city across Taron's tree-covered plains, and the great Nar Road running from Tria all the way into Delu and bisecting Nar from the northwest to the southeast. It was said that once a wall had surrounded the city, but we saw no sign of it. The Narangians boasted that their swords were their walls. No enemy had beleaguered Nar since Athar had conquered much of Taron in the ninth century of the Age of Swords.

Word that the Lightstone was being brought into the city must have preceded us, for the people of Nar lined the road from the very outskirts to the west and on into the Valari District, where many knights and lords had fine stone houses. That morning, I had given the Lightstone to Tavar Amadan; as we rode along, he held high the shining cup for all to see. Great lords such as Siravay Jurshan stood in front of the shops with carpenters and bakers and other tradesmen, all of whom wore on their fingers the diamond rings of knights or simple warriors. And all of them – and many women and children, too – cheered as we passed by. And that was a rare and beautiful thing in this kingdom, for the thousands of Taroners to shower their accolades upon an armed company of Ishkans and Meshians riding into their midst.

After a while, we passed the old Tournament Grounds, which long ago had been abandoned and given over as a greenway. The road took us between the Knight's District to the north and the King's Palace, all the way to the great square in the heart of Nar. There, beneath the steep hills on which perched an ancient castle, the white Tower of the Sun rose up toward the sky. Although it was not nearly so great as the towers in Tria or Delarid – or even in Khevaju, Nazca, Ar and other cities of other lands – people came from across the Nine Kingdoms to view this shining wonder, for the Valari have never been great builders and nothing like it could be seen in all the Morning Mountains. There, too, at the edge of the square, we came to the intersection of the Nar Road and the Adra Straight, a finely made road that led past the smithies close to the hills along a district full of fine eateries and inns. Smells of roasting chicken and hot bread mingled with coal smoke and steaming dung which the many horses clopping down this thoroughfare left behind them. The Narangians crowding the street on either side seemed not to notice or mind this effluvia that tainted their air, as in any large city. They loosed their cheers upon us from mouths wide open at the marvel of the Lightstone. But the Ishkans riding ahead of us and many of Mesh pulled their scarves up over their noses, thus did they try to protect themselves from the dust of old, dried dung that the horses' hooves pounded into powder and kicked up into choking brown clouds.

At last we came to the Tournament Grounds, laid out between the Adra Strait and the Nar Road along a great greenway at the northern outskirts of the city. The site where the competitions were held every three years was itself large enough to contain almost a whole city. A paved road ran down its center for almost two miles from east to west. It gave access to the Chess and Sword Pavilions, and then to the acres of fields where knights rode at each other with flashing maces and long lances. At the far end of the Grounds, along the Nar Road, could be found the areas given over to lance throwing and archery. Smaller roads, of dirt, connected the various encampments set up around the competition spaces, along the Grounds' northern and southern edges. Witnesses from Taron and all across the Nine Kingdoms had taken up residence there with the knights and warriors who would display their feats of arms for all to acclaim.

First and largest of these encampments, on the southern edge, was that of the Taroners. Many of these had been unable or unwilling to find lodgings in Nar's crowded inns; therefore they had set up their tents or laid out their sleeping furs in neat rows near the brightly-colored pavilions of Taron's greatest knights and lords. King Waray himself occupied the greatest of these pavilions, a magnificent dome of red and white silk flapping in the morning breeze. By tradition, whenever a tournament was being held, he left his palace to dwell among the pilgrims who honored his city. He was said to be a great mediator of disputes who loved clasping hands and learning the names of knights from each kingdom. Many called him a peacemaker. But my father, who had journeyed here for more than one tournament, called him a cunning and difficult man who liked to play others as a knight does chess pieces, in order to achieve the kind of sly and blood-less victories that strengthened his kingdom without ever quite threat-ening real war.

The Meshian encampment, for thousands of years, had been laid out on the Grounds' northern edge between the encampments of the Lagashuns and the Ishkans. Many of my countrymen had arrived before us. We Guardians, strengthened by the twenty Ishkan knights, set up our pavilions near those of Sar Sulaijay and Lord Junaru and others who would be competing here on the morrow. To the blue and white of Lord Junaru's pavilion was added the black and silver of mine, and the reds, golds and other colors of my Ishkan knights, and if any of Mesh objected to this unprecedented mingling, no one voiced his concern. Neither did it alarm anyone when we surrounded our company with a moat and stockade. Word of Sivar's treachery spread quickly, and all Meshians, whether Guardians or not, seemed ready to fight for the Lightstone if any enemy should attack us. Of course, all along the Tournament Grounds flew the sacred white banners of truce. Anyone who broke this ancient covenant would be punished by dishonor and death. But here, on these much-trampled fields where the Valari had contended with each other for thousands of years, it was not impossible to imagine some lone knight or his kindred falling mad and fighting a real battle and spilling red blood to gain the greatest prize in all the world.

I spent most of the day settling into our camp and preparing for the next day's lance-throwing competition. With our bright pavilions arrayed only a hundred yards from the greenway along the Grounds' northern edge, we had relief in at least one direction from the bustle of the tournament. Tall oak trees rose up like a wall before us; birds piped out their songs, and the perfume of flowers wafted over us on a gentle wind. But in other directions there were other sights, smells and sounds. Between the encampments, food-sellers had set up stalls next to those of brewmasters, cloth merchants, astrologers, armorers and many others. Nearby, jugglers cast brightly-painted balls into the air while wandering minstrels made music around their campfires. It was good to hear their singing and the voices of the Valari that joined them; it was good, too, to smell the loaves of hot bread that the bakers took out of their ovens and the sizzling sweetmeats that old women prepared on their little charcoal grills. Down the road running along the encampments of the Lagashuns, Meshians, Ishkans and Kaashans paraded a continual stream of knights displaying their colors and their horsemanship. Many pilgrims passed by us, too. From their inquisitive glances, it seemed that they hoped for a glimpse of the Lightstone – or of me. While riding through Nar's streets and across the Tournament grounds, more than one person had looked at me as if to wonder if I might truly be the Maitreya. I tried to ignore these throngs who lingered in front of our camp. The urgent beating of their hearts was almost a greater sound than the pounding of hundreds of horses' hooves and the booming of the great war drums that reminded every knight that the tournament, above all else, was meant to demonstrate the Valari's readiness for battle.

Around midafternoon, a visitor called on me, and him I could not ignore. For it was King Danashu of Anjo, who strode into our encampment accompanied by only two knights. King Danashu was a large man with great shoulders and long arms swollen with muscle. In his youth, no knight had been able to cast his lance farther than he. His finely made face, too, was swollen – but from the effects of strong drink and participating too exuberantly at too many feasts. His blue tunic, emblazoned with a gold dragon, barely concealed a large belly that bulged out beneath his massive chest. Of all the kings of the Valari, he was said to be the strongest, in his body. But as ruler of his realm, he had less power than some of his dukes and barons who had torn his once-proud kingdom apart.

I invited him into my tent, where we sat and took tea with my brothers. King Danashu paid his compliments to our father and discussed the art of lance throwing with Yarashan. He spoke of the clear, blue skies above us and the fine weather he hoped would grace the tournament. And then he turned toward the point of his visit.

'It's said that you rode into Taron with King Hadaru.' King Danashu looked from Asaru to Yarashan, and then at me. 'Meshians and Ishkans together – this is not news that we of Anjo can be expected to celebrate.'

Asaru studied King Danashu for weakness, as my father had taught us, and I did, too. And finally, I said, 'It's time that all Valari rode together so that the Red Dragon doesn't fall against us one by one. If Mesh can make peace with Ishka, then so it can be with any of the Nine Kingdoms. And that is something that *all* Valari can celebrate.'

'Perhaps,' King Danashu said. 'And yet, I haven't heard King Hadaru speak of peace.'

I opened my mouth to proclaim that King Hadaru possessed little-recognized virtues, but just then Asaru cast me a quick, stern look. Although it was my prerogative to order all matters pertaining to the Guardians and the Lightstone, it was his, as our father's eldest son, to speak for Mesh.

'King Hadaru may not desire peace with Anjo,' Asaru said. 'But he desires war with Mesh even less.'

At this, King Danashu slowly nodded his head and wheezed out, 'Then this matter of your brother recovering the Lightstone has not changed your father's pledge?'

'A pledge is a pledge,' Asaru told him coldly. 'If Ishka invades Anjo, Mesh will march against Ishka.'

'But what if King Hadaru continues suborning my barons and dukes? He's nearly won Duke Barwan's allegiance and made Adarland part of Ishka. Forcing the duke to give up his young daughter to marry an old king – *that* was an ignoble deed.'

Asaru and I traded knowing looks. For King Danashu to speak of Anjo's nobles as 'his' was something like a hound claiming dominion over wolves. Duke Rezu of Rajak and Duke Gorador ruled their tiny realms without thought of King Danashu, while farther east, Baron Yushur had made war against Count Artanu of Onkar in an attempt to add to his possession and strengthen it in case King Hadaru conquered Adar outright and moved against Anjo's other baronies and duchies.

'My father,' Asaru told King Danashu, 'has no say over whom King Hadaru may marry. Nor over the affairs of your realm.'

This was Asaru's way of chiding King Danashu. But there was no scorn in his voice and little pride – only a heartfelt desire that King Danashu should somehow reunite his broken kingdom and rule it as more than a king in name only.

'No, no one has say over Anjo,' King Danashu said, 'except Anjo's king. We've had our time of troubles, but this must soon end.'

'We've heard that there were plots against you.'

'Against a king, there are always plots. But the assassins were caught and killed. The barons who set them upon me will be punished, I can promise you that.'

'Very well,' Asaru said.

'Anjo will be strong again,' King Danashu boasted. 'As it was in the old days.'

'We all pray that this will be so.'

'Yes, with the aid of friends such as Mesh, we'll be strong,' he muttered. Something in the way he said the word 'friend,' with both resentment and hope, caused me to sit up straighter on my tent's rug and pay closer attention. 'And then all will be repaid.'

138

'We of Mesh desire no repayment of any debts you may think you owe us,' Asaru told him. 'Only, as you say, your friendship.'

'But what if the Red Dragon were to attack Mesh?'

I felt Asaru's pulse quicken along with my own. Although King Danashu couldn't have known of the threats that Morjin had made in his letter, he must have feared such an obvious move and the repercussions it would have on Anjo.

'The Red Dragon *won't* move against Mesh,' I reassured him. 'Soon there will be a conclave in Tria. And we'll make an alliance against him.'

'You speak with such certainty,' King Danashu said as he looked at me. 'Do you really believe you can unite the sovereigns of the Free Kingdoms to your purpose?'

'We *must* unite,' I told him.

'Yes, well, the *Maitreya* would say such a thing. And perhaps the Maitreya, if the Maitreya is more than just a myth, could accomplish this miracle. But what would an alliance against Morjin be worth without the swords of the Valari kings?'

'Very little,' I admitted. 'Which is why our kings or their emissaries must journey to Tria.'

'Impossible, impossible. I'm afraid that not even the Maitreya could accomplish *that*. Why, I was speaking just this morning about this impossibility with King Waray.'

Something about the way he said King Waray's name made me look at King Danashu more closely. He was breathing quickly, which caused his big belly to rise and fall beneath his blue tunic. I could almost feel the beads of sweat running down his side there, too.

'Does King Waray, then,' I asked, 'share your discouragement?'

'*All* the Valari kings do, Lord Valashu. None of us wants to answer King Kiritan's summons to Tria.'

'Pride,' I said. 'The pride of kings.'

King Danashu pulled back his massive shoulders as he sat up straight. He regarded me with a flaring anger as he said, 'Don't think to judge a king until you've sat upon his throne. When I was your age, I, too, thought being a king, a Valari king, would be a simple matter of following simple principles. Always to be honest, to honor the Law of the One, to wield a sword like an angel and die in battle – to be *willing* to die for kinsmen and kingdom, this seems such a simple thing. But life is not so simple, is it? There are always complications and difficulties, so many, impossible to see. There are always those who would undo a king and destroy his honor, and so a king must stand strong at all times. You may call this pride, if you will. But do not blame the

Valari kings if they do not wish to abandon their realms to pursue impossible dreams in Tria.'

I sat looking at King Danashu for a few moments and then called for Sar Shuradan to enter my tent. At my command, this grizzled knight drew forth the Lightstone and placed it in King Danashu's hands.

'A year ago,' I said, 'King Kiritan called a quest to recover this cup. And the Valari kings, even yourself, refused to send their sons and knights to Tria. They said that finding it would be impossible.'

King Danashu's once-fine featuresface took up the light of the golden cup so that the beauty of his youth stood out from his tired face. His dark eyes flared with its radiance as he stared at the Lightstone. 'What you say is true, Lord Valashu. But there were so many uncertainties, it seemed foolish to waste men on such a quest.'

I smiled at him and said, 'Truly, many thought me a fool for setting out toward Tria. But what is considered foolish before an event occurs is often deemed otherwise afterwards. And so with the reverse. What will Ea think of the Valari if we allow Morjin to triumph, all because common wisdom deems an alliance against him to be impossible?'

'Some would say,' King Danashu told me, 'that Morjin could never triumph so long as *we* possess the Lightstone.'

King Danashu eyes were now blazing with a golden fire. And I said, 'It is one thing to gain such a prize, but another to keep it. Morjin has already set a ghul to try to steal the Lightstone, and nearly succeeded.'

'But he *must* not succeed, not a second time.'

'Will you help us, then?'

'What is it you would ask of me, Lord Valashu?'

'Only that you speak in favor of journeying to Tria.'

King Danashu stared at the cup in his hands and sighed out, 'That is indeed a great deal to ask. Do you wish that I should do this for Mesh or for you, Lord Valashu?'

'Do it for *yourself*,' I said. 'If Mesh should have to stand alone against Morjin, who will stand with Anjo against Ishka?'

King Danashu's heart surged with a wild hope, and I wondered at its source. He said, 'But if I speak in favor of the conclave, who will listen?'

'You're the king of Anjo,' I said. 'Everyone will listen.'

He nodded his head as if suddenly deciding something. 'Very well, then. I shall begin with King Waray. He, at least, is a reasonable man.'

'Thank you,' I told him. I watched as he turned the Lightstone around and around in his hands. 'It's a beautiful thing, isn't it? Will you help us guard it?'

'Help you? How?'

'As King Hadaru did. Twenty Ishkan knights are now Guardians of the Lightstone.'

'Twenty knights,' he muttered, shaking his head. 'I'm sorry to say that right now I have very few knights to spare.'

'How few, then? Fifteen? Ten?'

'No, five knights only could I lend you for this task.'

'Very well, then, five knights it will have to be. Choose your finest, King Danashu.'

'I shall choose them from among those who win honors at this tournament.'

We clasped hands then to seal this troth, and King Danashu reluctantly gave the Lightstone back to Sar Shuradan. He stood up and prepared to leave my tent. And then he said to me, 'It will be good to take meat with the sons of Shavashar Elahad at the feast tonight. But King Waray would speak with *you*, Lord Valashu, in private before the feast. He has asked me to convey his invitation.'

After bowing to me and my brothers, he collected his two knights posted outside my tent and left our encampment. I noticed him making his way toward some nearby jewelry stalls, perhaps to inspect their wares.

'He calls himself a king,' Yarashan spat out as he watched him stride forth. 'But it seems he's only a king's messenger.'

'No, Yarashan,' I said, 'he *is* a king, and could rule as one if only he turned his attentions toward winning his dukes and barons instead of other kings.'

Asaru said, 'It's clear enough, isn't it, that he's looking for meals at King Waray's table?'

'Yes, that seems certain,' I said, thinking of the surges of emotion pouring out of King Danashu whenever King Waray's name was mentioned. 'But does he seek a secret alliance with Taron? And does Taron seek alliance Anjo? For King Waray, that would be a dangerous game.'

'It would,' Yarashan agreed. He stood beneath the apex of my tent near Asaru and me, and looked back and forth between us. 'If King Hadaru gained word of this alliance before it was concluded, he might be tempted to march against Taron to preempt it.'

'But why,' Asaru asked, 'would King Waray take such a risk?'

I placed my hand on the hilt of my sword, and the hazy pattern forming up before my inner eye suddenly became vivid and clear. I said, 'King Waray has never liked giving battle, and the Ishkans have the largest army in the Nine Kingdoms. He's always counted on us to keep the Ishkans in check. But if Morjin should move against Mesh,

141

Ishka would be free to turn north against either Anjo or Taron – or both. And so King Waray might see making an alliance with Anjo as the *lesser* risk.'

'An alliance between Anjo and Taron?' Yarashan snapped. 'Does a lamb make alliances with a lion? Doesn't King Danashu realize that Taron would eat up Anjo in pieces?'

'His position, no matter which way he turns, is weak,' I said. 'Which is why his greatest hope is for an alliance of *all* the Valari.'

'But he believes this to be impossible!' Yarashan said. 'As it likely is. You heard what he said, Val.'

'Yes, but he also promised to speak in favor of the Trian conclave. And he has pledged five knights to become Guardians.'

'Do you think he'll honor his word?'

'Yes,' I said. 'He is an honorable man, despite his weakness.'

'Five knights,' Yarashan said. 'How is that you invite the Anjoris into our company while you seemed reluctant to accept the Ishkans?'

I said nothing for a moment as I looked at Yarashan's haughty face. And then Asaru answered for me, saying, 'Our little brother only *seemed* reluctant, isn't that right, Val?'

'Yes, that is true,' I said. 'It was likely that King Hadaru would insist on making Ishkan knights Guardians. The pride of kings, yes? And if all the Valari kings do likewise, they'll see that an alliance is not only possible but inevitable.'

Yarashan nodded his head as he smiled at me. 'You're more cunning than I ever would have thought. But what of King Waray, then? Our father has always said that he's more difficult than even King Hadaru. You certainly won't persuade him as easily as you did King Danashu.'

'We'll find out about King Waray soon enough,' I said. 'Now why don't we get ready for this feast that he's prepared for us?'

I turned to see to a bath and to fresh garments, and I considered what I would say to the man who styled himself as the greatest of the Valari kings.

11

An hour later I rode out alone to answer King Waray's invitation. Many knights, on their way to visit friends or kindred in other encampments, passed by in continual streams of snorting horses and brilliant surcoats flapping in the wind. A dirt road connected the Meshian pavilions with the Tournament Grounds' main road. At the intersection, where teams of workmen made busy preparing the Sword and Chess Pavilions for the coming competitions, I turned east and let Altaru gallop full out for a few hundred yards to give him a little exercise. Soon we came to the Taroners' encampment. I counted hundreds of pavilions sprung up from the soft green grass like so many brightly colored mushrooms. In a little field between them, many rows of tables were being set with plates and goblets for the evening's feast. Grooms working the firepits there roasted whole lambs on black, greasy spits while others nearby hurried to and fro bearing casks of brandy or baskets of bread. King Waray's pavilion, overlooking all this activity, was like a small palace constructed of red and white silk. After tethering Altaru outside it, I made my way toward its open door. I gave my name to one of the guards posted there, and he vanished inside the pavilion to announce me. A few moments later, a tall, dignified man came out to greet me. His long red tunic was emblazoned with the white winged horse of the House of Waray.

'Lord Valashu Elahad!' King Waray said to me. He clasped hands with me as if we were old friends. 'Welcome to Nar!'

With his aquiline nose and black, luminous eyes, he appeared the epitome of a Valari King. His high forehead seemed to radiate a shining intelligence. But as he thanked me for honoring his summons and began speaking of the friendship of our two kingdoms, the words that poured from his thin lips seemed sometimes to squeak like mice and at other moments to roar like mountain lions. His was a curious voice: pinched and nasal, gravelly and sweet – all at once. It might, I thought,

143

as easily disarm and charm a friend as it could flay an enemy. It was clear from the first that King Waray intended to charm me. He hailed me as the Lord of the Lightstone. He praised the beauty of my horse and my skill at mastering such a magnificent and ferocious beast. And then he laid his arm about my shoulders and gently urged me to walk with him through the Taron encampment.

'Yes, a fine horse, indeed,' he said as he watched Altaru's neck arch downward to graze on the rich spring grass. 'One of the Anjori wild Blacks, isn't he? We've all heard the story of how you risked your life, when you were still a boy, to break him.'

'Altaru,' I said to him, 'was never broken. He allows me to ride him, but no other.'

'Of course – well, it was still a great feat. Just as it seems more recently you've tamed the mighty Ishkan bear.'

'King Hadaru,' I said, fighting back a smile, 'might think otherwise.'

'Of course he would. But he has chosen Ishkan knights to join your Guardians, hasn't he? And he has ridden with an *Elahad* all the way from Ishka into Taron.'

'Truly, he has,' I said, watching as King Waray's bright eyes watched me. 'For at least a hundred miles, Ishka has made alliance with Mesh.'

King Waray smiled at me. 'King Hadaru and I spoke together earlier today. He has assured me that he favors an alliance of *all* the Valari, even as you propose.'

As we paused in front of his huge pavilion, I had to fight to keep the fire of hope from flaring too brightly on my face. I asked him, 'Do *you* favor such an alliance, King Waray?'

'Of course I do – how else are we to oppose Morjin?'

'My apologies, but King Danashu has given me to understand that you consider such an alliance an impossibility.'

'King Danashu sees impossibilities everywhere,' he said. 'Perhaps he heard me speak of the great difficulties in forging such an alliance and misconstrued this to mean I thought it would be impossible.'

'Then you *do* think it's possible?'

'My father, a very wise man, once asked me this: How is it possible that the impossible is not only *possible* but inevitable?'

My heart sounded in my chest like a thunderbolt. I said, 'That is my feeling, exactly. The Valari *must* unite. Any difficulties must give way like darkness before the light of the stars.'

'Beautifully said, Lord Valashu. And I have invited you here so that we might speak of these difficulties. Why don't we begin with King Hadaru, who is a very difficult man?'

'But you say that he has spoken in favor of the alliance.'

'Indeed, he has. But there was everything about his manner, the very tone of his words, that suggested *he* hopes to lead this alliance himself.'

King Waray, as we began walking between the Taroners' pavilions, slid this innuendo into me as smoothly as might an assassin a knife. He was a shrewd man and subtle. He had a cool, polished facade like the marble of his great Sun Tower, and his casual knowledgeability and seeming goodwill concealed a monumental arrogance and desire to control others. I knew that he wasn't telling me the whole truth, about King Hadaru or anything else. And yet I also knew that his sense of honor would not permit him to lie outright. He was, rather, like a knight facing formal combat or playing a game with strict rules of his own making. I recalled then that, in his time, for many tournaments, he had remained undefeated at chess.

'King Hadaru,' I told him, 'has always seen himself as the strongest of the Valari kings. And he doubts that I could be the Maitreya.'

'Many doubt this, Lord Valashu,' he said. And then he slid another knife into me and twisted it. 'I think you even doubt this yourself.'

I remained quiet for a moment as I stopped to look at him. And then I said, 'And you, King Waray? Are you one of the doubters, too?'

'Well, what does it really *mean* to be a Maitreya?' he asked me, giving voice to the question I most wanted answered. 'I can tell you that if any Valari deserves to be Maitreya, then surely it is you.'

'Thank you,' I said. 'One of my reasons for journeying here was to cast more light on this matter.'

'Of course – you hope to unite our people. If you accomplish this, you will prove yourself to be the Maitreya.'

I bowed my head to him and said, 'You are very perceptive, King Waray. But it's also my hope to search inside the Brotherhood school. There might be knowledge there that could settle this question.'

'The school has been closed,' he told me. 'Your Master Juwain has seen to that.'

'We were hoping you might be persuaded to reopen it.'

'Perhaps some day I might be.'

The light of the late sun glinted off the helm of a passing knight, and I suddenly realized something: *He does not want me to be the Maitreya. He does not want any Valari to be this Shining One.*

'What would it take, then, to persuade you, King Waray?'

'That is still to be determined. You see, the Brotherhood has gathered much knowledge that is difficult to interpret or is actually misleading. And this is a time where we Valari must not be misled.'

'Truly, we mustn't. And that is why the Maitreya must be found.'

'Of course, he must be found, if that is possible,' he said. 'But what if it should happen that Valashu Elahad is not the Maitreya? What if none of the Valari is? Even so, the Valari must find a way to unite.'

King Waray's black eyes were bright with dreams, and I suddenly realized something else: *He truly desires a Valari alliance – but with himself as its leader.*

'The way to unite is simple,' I said to him. 'Each king has only to pledge his support to every other, should Morjin threaten to march against any of our kingdoms. And then to meet in conclave in Tria.'

'Of course, it is simple to say this, but much more difficult to accomplish. King Mohan, for one, cares little for Morjin's threats.'

'That is because he knows little of Morjin.'

'He knows enough to determine that Morjin has problems of his own. Since you made off with the Lightstone, it's said that some of the Dragon Kings have plotted against Morjin and have tried to assassinate him.'

'And how has this news come to you?'

'A king always has his sources,' he said mysteriously. 'I've always striven for peace, always tried to understand the true concerns of those around me. To achieve this, one must know a great many things.'

'Does King Mohan favor a Valari alliance?'

'That is difficult to say. He certainly favors anything that would promote Athar's gaining glory, particularly if that occurred to the detriment of Lagash and King Kurshan.'

'The old dispute,' I said, shaking my head.

Long ago, in the Age of Swords, King Saruth the Great, whom King Mohan claimed as a distant ancestor, had made a bid for empire and had conquered parts of Taron and Lagash – and even Delu. The old tales told that King Saruth had captured and murdered King Thanasu of Lagash, and had forcibly taken his daughter as his wife to strengthen his line. The Lagashuns had never forgiven the Atharians for this ignominy. More recently, thirty years ago in one of the endless wars between these ancient enemies, both sides claimed the other had broken the rules of formal battle: Lagash accused Athar of commencing the fight before giving Lagash a chance to negotiate, while Athar held Lagash guilty of slaying captives out of hand.

'Of course, I've tried to reason with both King Mohan and King Kurshan,' King Waray said. 'King Kurshan speaks of sailing to the stars even as he builds a great fleet of ships. Who could blame King Mohan for fearing that King Kurshan will use this fleet to strengthen Lagash against Athar? Well, King Mohan is hot-headed and has an evil temper, and so I suppose we can *all* blame him for that. And so I've tried to find words to cool his heart. I count it as one of my greatest victories that during my reign, war between Athar and Lagash has thrice been averted.'

As I listened to King Waray's sweetly deceptive voice, I had a strange sense that his words had actually inflamed King Mohan's fear of King Kurshan – and perhaps King Kurshan's dread of King Mohan. I sensed that King Waray liked to fan the flames of such fires and then intervene with his talk of peace to put them out. In this way did he disarm the kings around him even as he gained their gratitude. In this way did he gain prestige and power.

We began walking again down the rows of the Taron tents. Knights dressed in fine tunics for the coming feast passed by us on their way to visit with friends or perhaps take in a game of dice before sitting down to table. Out of respect, they gave us wide berth – all the while straining their ears toward us and stealing glances at me as if hoping for a glimpse of the Lightstone.

And then King Waray lowered his voice as he said to me, 'It may indeed be difficult to win King Mohan to the idea of alliance, for he has grievances against many kingdoms, and Mesh not the least. However, King Talanu is a different question. As always, he will favor anything that Mesh does.'

King Talanu Solaru of Kaash, my grandfather, had been unable to journey to the tournament because of his failing health. But he had sent his son, Lord Viromar, in his place. Although my uncle's friendship was much more with my father than with me, he could certainly be counted on to speak for a Valari alliance, for Kaash and Mesh themselves were ancient allies and supported each other in almost all matters.

'Of course,' King Waray continued, 'King Talanu's unconditional advocacy of this alliance is itself a strike against it.'

'Because of Waas?'

'Exactly. Anything the Kaashans support, King Sandarkan will oppose on first impulse. The Waashians remain too bitter.'

For three hundred years, the Waashians had made war against Kaash in an attempt to recover a large chunk of territory lost in one of their formal battles. But the Kaashans' ferocity and their long swords – with the aid of Mesh – had defeated the numerically superior Waashians again and again.

'Bitter they might be,' I said. 'But they will never regain the Arjan Land through war.'

A little light flared in King Waray's eyes just then, but he kept his cool demeanor. His voice rolled up from his throat through his mouth and long nose: 'There speaks Meshian pride. Is it any wonder that King Sandarkan would speak against this alliance?'

I found that my hand had fallen upon the hilt of my sword. Too many of my friends, I remembered, had died beneath the Waashians' spears only a few years before. Even so, I commanded my fingers to relax. The war with Waas, I reminded myself, had been won. And if an alliance was to be achieved, Mesh and Waas must never make war again.

'King Sandarkan,' I said, 'would then speak against the very thing that preserves his kingdom.'

'Preserves it against Morjin, do you mean?'

'No, against the Valari. My father showed great restraint in not adding Waashian territory to his realm. But the other kings surrounding Waas would not be so kind. King Mohan looks always to the south, doesn't he? Even King Hadaru might be tempted to break truce with Waas if he saw the eagles gathering to rend her apart. Even yourself, King Waray.'

He shrugged his shoulders at this and told me, 'I've said many times that Taron seeks to gain no new territories. I've assured King Sandarkan of this. I believe I have his trust, and I also believe that I can persuade him of the necessity of an alliance.'

At what price, I wondered? Would he promise King Sandarkan the return of the Arjan Land in exchange for his support?

'If you could soften King Sandarkan's heart, that would be a great thing,' I told him.

'Of course – I would like to help you in any way I can.'

I realized then another thing about King Waray: that if he failed to gain the leadership of the alliance because I proved myself as the Maitreya, he would try to control me by making himself indispensable.

'King Sandarkan,' he said, 'journeys to Nar often. In time, I'm sure he'll see the sense of things.'

'We have little time, King Waray. The tournament begins tomorrow and lasts only a week.'

'Well, we mustn't rush things – this isn't quite the moment for the alliance you seek.'

'But the conclave will begin in Tria and the end of Marud! The Valari kings must be there.'

'Lord Valashu,' he said, catching me up in the command of his dark eyes, 'it is one thing for the Valari to come together in alliance with each other. But it is quite another to make alliance with outland kingdoms. That, I'm afraid, is impossible. And more, it is not even desirable.'

Inside my mind, the bright tower to the stars that I had been building suddenly cracked and threatened to crumble. I clamped my jaws shut to keep myself from crying out in anger at him.

'There *must* be an alliance,' I said to him. 'Of the Valari, first, and then of all the Free Kingdoms.'

Now it was his turn for anger. I felt it burning up through his heart even though he kept his face as cool as ice. 'Of course, the Maitreya would say that. Or, rather, the one who *believes* himself to be the Maitreya.'

'Others believe that, too.'

'Perhaps, but fewer than you might hope.'

'It is my hope,' I said, 'at least to gain the confidence of the Valari so that they might see what needs to be done.'

King Waray paused to look beyond the Taron encampment at the fields of the Tournament Grounds. Then his sharp eyes pierced me like arrows. 'You no doubt hope to excel in the competitions. But I must tell you what many are saying: that if you are to prove yourself as the Maitreya you will have to become champion.'

'Do *you* say this, King Waray?'

'I only repeat the common sentiment.'

'Well, someone must be champion,' I said.

'Three previous champions will be competing tomorrow. Do you really think you can defeat them?'

'Surely that is in the hands of the One.'

'Some would say that your fate lies in your *own* hands, Valashu Elahad.' He cast a quick, scornful look downward as my fingers gripped the hilt of my sword. 'You competed at the last tournament, and as I remember, your handiwork, while honorable, was not outstanding.'

'Much can change in three years.'

He laughed at me then as if enjoying a great joke. 'Many of my knights have made pilgrimage to Silvassu to view the Lightstone. They have watched you practicing at arms, and a few of them have even crossed lances with you. I'm told that there is no hope of your gaining more than a third at the long lance, and none at all of your pointing at lance throwing or the mace.'

'There is wrestling,' I said.

'At which you might possibly win fourth place.'

'There is archery.'

'A fifth, if you are lucky.'

'There is chess, too.'

He laughed again, harder this time, because he of all men knew that my mastery of this game was not of the highest.

'There is the sword,' I said, squeezing Alkaladur's hilt.

Now King Waray's laughter funneled from his nose like the blare of a trumpet. And he called out: 'The sword! Ha, ha, ha! Defeat Lord Dashavay? Impossible!'

For the past three tournaments, Lord Dashavay of Waas had won the sword competition by utterly destroying the defenses of his opponents. No one had ever come close to defeating him. Many acclaimed him the finest swordsman in a thousand years.

King Waray laughed for a few moments more, and then cast at me a criticism that would shame any Valari warrior: 'My knights have told me that no one has even *seen* you practicing at sword since you returned from your adventure.'

I said nothing as I stared down at Alkaladur's hilt, with its carved swans and diamond pommel stone.

'Clearly, then, you must have no hope of prevailing at the sword,' he told me. 'So clearly you cannot be champion.'

It was the rule of the Tournament that a knight must win at least one first place to be awarded the champion's medallion.

'We always say that a sword is a warrior's soul,' I told him. 'Do not be too quick to damn mine to defeat.'

'I hear it's a great sword you've gained,' he said to me. 'May I see it?'

I drew Alkaladur and the king's doubtful eyes squinted against the glare of its bright gelstei. 'Beautiful. But do not think that it will help you vanquish Lord Dashavay,' he said coolly.

No, perhaps it wouldn't, I thought as my sword showered its radiance upon me. Perhaps Lord Dashavay would win the sword competition as he had before, and be declared the Tournament Champion, as he had before. Or perhaps that honor would fall upon Lord Marjay or Sar Shivamar or another. Perhaps it was not my fate, after all, to be champion or even the Maitreya. Did that truly matter? Perhaps King Hadaru would overcome the hurts and suspicions of his many enemies and find a way to lead the Valari alliance; perhaps King Waray would do this himself. Why should it matter *who* led the alliance so long as all free peoples stood together against Morjin?

Because one, and one only, can unite the Valari. A voice whispered this inside me, begging me to listen. And then the sun above me seemed to empty itself in a stroke of lightning that ran down my sword and burned straight into my soul. And in the flash of this bright star's fire I saw my fate, even as the voice called to me again, now so loud that I could not ignore it: *Because you, and you only, are this one.*

'No,' I gasped out as I struggled to keep from falling down to the soft green grass below my feet, 'this sword will not help me vanquish

150

Lord Dashavay. But it *will* help me vanquish Morjin. And that is why I must speak, as soon as possible, with the Valari kings.'

I pointed my sword past the Taroners' tents toward the field where a hundred tables had been set for the evening's feast. At the largest and centermost table, decorated with vases of white starflowers, I would soon sit with King Hadaru and King Mohan – and with King Waray himself.

And now this proud and angry king shook his head back and forth, and he snapped at me, 'Speak at your own risk then, and of all that you desire.'

After that he left me standing alone by the tent of one of his lords, and he retired into his much larger pavilion to prepare himself to receive guests. I wandered about the Taron encampment, greeting various strange squires and knights. Several asked me to show them the Lightstone; I told them that they would have to wait for the feast to behold it, when the Guardians would arrive to join me. After a while, I made my way toward the many stalls in the area adjoining the Tournament Grounds' main road. I watched a fire-eater sucking in flames and an acrobat walking along a tightrope stretched between two poles; I gave a few coins to a minstrel who played for me on his mandolet a few sad songs. A haruspex beckoned me closer, and a Tarot master offered to tell my fortune. But I did not want to believe that a few colorfully painted cards chosen at random could hold the key to my future.

At last, from all across the Tournament Grounds and the inns of Nar, King Waray's guests began arriving. Knights from Athar, masters of the Brotherhood, lords and ladies from the rich country beyond the Iron Hills – they all urged their mounts down the various roads and poured into the Taron encampment. At its border, where many posts had been pounded into the ground so that the horses could be tethered, I met Master Juwain and Maram, who rode with Lord Raasharu, Lord Harsha, Behira and Estrella. There, too, I greeted the Guardians and took charge of the Lightstone. My brothers joined me there as well; with them was my uncle, Lord Viromar, who had brought with him a contingent of twenty of Kaash's finest knights. Two of these – Sar Yarwan and Sar Laisu – had fought by my side in Tria against assassins, and they had also made their own quest for the Lightstone. Lord Viromar, whose emblem was a white snow tiger upon a blue field, was a dark, impassive man of few words. But he was a great warrior renowned for his presence of mind in battle, no less his love of justice, and my father always said that he would make a fine king.

In a stream of brightly colored cloth and glittering diamond armor, we all made our way toward the Field of Feasts, where we joined King Waray's others guests. It seemed that King Waray had invited everyone in the city to dine with him, for rows of tables were laden with endless of platters of food. Lord Harsha, Behira and Estrella took their places with Maram and Master Juwain not far from the head table, while the Guardians were seated closer still. Properly, only kings or their heirs to the throne should sit with King Waray. But since I was Guardian of the Lightstone, King Waray had invited me to join Asaru at his table. In an act of kindness that surprised me, he included Yarashan in this honor so that he wouldn't feel slighted. We pulled out three chairs together, and bowed our heads as my uncle, with King Hadaru, King Danashu and the other kings, seated themselves around King Waray.

The feast began, and it was much like many others that I had attended. Much food was eaten; casks of brandy and beer were emptied as their contents found their way past the lips of King Waray's guests, and none more so than Maram. He made a fine toast to King Waray's hospitality. Others stood and made toasts, too: to all the knights who would be competing on the morrow; to their success in arms; to the tournament's past champions. Here King Waray, sitting at the center of our table, paused to cast me a cold look. It grew even colder as one of the Kaashan knights raised his goblet and praised me for leading the quest to find the Lightstone. He called for a minstrel to come forth and tell this tale. When many of the other knights present added their voices to this demand, King Waray was forced to summon his own minstrel, a man named Galajay, who sang out words that King Waray could not want to hear.

At last it came time for me to bring forth the Lightstone and show it to all assembled on that broad field. This I did. I held the golden cup high so that it caught the light of the torches and the night's first stars. Then I gave it to my uncle, who held it a moment before setting it into the hands of King Danashu. And then he passed this shining wonder down the line of the other Valari kings.

Baltasar, my hot-blooded and faithful friend, of his own impetuousness, suddenly stood and called out toward me, 'Lord of Light! Maitreya! Lord of the Lightstone!'

Others, at the Meshian tables, picked up the cry. Almost immediately Sar Laisu and half a dozen Kaashans added their voices to this acclaim, and soon many knights at the tables of the Ishkans, Lagashuns, Anjoris, Taroners, Atharians and even the Waashians joined in:

'Maitreya! Maitreya! Maitreya!'

So loud did this chant become that I was finally forced to stand

and hold up my hand for silence. As the hundreds of voices died down, I called out, '*That* is still not proven!'

Sar Tadru of Athar, who had also stood with me in Tria to make vows, now called back, 'What would it take then to establish this proof?'

'That, too, is still not determined,' I told him. 'But it would make a mockery of the One's design if the Maitreya were to come forth only to see the Lightstone regained by Morjin. And this Morjin will certainly attempt if the Valari don't stand together against him.'

I looked down at the kings at my table. It had come King Sandarkan's turn to hold the Lightstone. He was a tall, thin man with a predatory look about his lean face. His body seemed all angles and long limbs, and he reminded me of nothing so much as a huge preying mantis. And now he gripped the Lightstone in his hands as if he never wanted to let it go.

'If the Valari are to stand together,' his thin voice croaked out, 'let us first put our own house in order. And how are we to do that when certain Valari enter the rooms of others to take priceless objects that are not theirs?'

Here he turned slightly to glare at the impassive Lord Viromar, and I couldn't help remembering what King Waray had said about Kaash's conquest of the Arjan Land. I noticed King Hadaru eyeing King Danashu as a hungry bear might a wriggling salmon, while King Kurshan and King Waray sat side by side separated by a wall of mistrust. The Valari kings, I thought, shared this table like a single family. And like a family they seethed with resentments, jealousies and old wounds.

'King Sandarkan!' I called out. 'You fret over lost objects when our house itself is on fire and threatened with destruction. Will you help put out this fire before you lose *everything*?'

'You ask a great deal of Waas.'

'No more than of any Valari kingdom,' I said. 'You've spoken of rooms within our small house. But the Valari were sent to Ea to build mansions and whole cities glorious beyond anything we can even dream.'

'Myths,' he said, shaking his head.

'If the Valari unite,' I said to him, 'the time of wars between us would come to an end. All would be restored to Waas, and much more. The whole world would lie before us, waiting for us to create an indestructible kingdom beneath the stars.'

'Miracles,' his voice croaked out. Again, he shook his head, but his eyes were bright. 'Are such miracles truly possible?'

I looked at the golden cup that he held in his long, lean hands. It came to me then that while families were sometimes riven by malice, an opposite and deeper force ran within them like a river of light.

'Maitreya!' a young knight of Waas suddenly called out. 'Maitreya!'

It seemed to me that the time had come to bring about one of the miracles King Sandarkan had spoken of. But then the man sitting next to him, King Mohan of Athar, impatient as always, suddenly turned in his chair and snatched the Lightstone from his hands with all the speed of a snapping turtle. He held up this prize to regard it with his small, hard eyes. He himself was small, for a Valari, and hard in his body and spirit from the fierce disciplines he forced upon himself. His face was rather ugly, despite his fine features, because of his seething irritability, arrogance and love of strife.

'Lord Valashu,' he said to me, 'you have regained the Lightstone for all the Valari, and for this you have earned our thanks. And now you try to gain a Valari alliance. But who is to lead it? *You?*'

I counted the beats of my heart as I listened to some knights at one of the Anjori tables begin chanting again: 'Maitreya! Maitreya! Maitreya!'

King Mohan didn't wait for me to answer; he cast me an angry, smoldering look and fired out another question: 'Do you ask us to approve your leadership, here, now?'

'No,' I said, 'at this time, it will be enough if the Valari kings agree to the alliance, itself. And agree to journey to Tria. There it will be decided if I am the Maitreya.'

'No,' he shot back at me, 'that must be decided here, on the Tournament Grounds, with lance and sword. If you are truly the Maitreya, you must prove it. And how else but by becoming champion?'

I saw that King Waray was regarding King Mohan as if very pleased with the words he had just spoken.

Now Maram, both very drunk and very incensed, rose out of his chair and pointed his finger at King Mohan as he said, 'The proof you desire lies in your hands. Who but the greatest of champions could have fought through half of Morjin's army to bring the Lightstone to you?'

'Yes,' King Mohan sneered out, 'we've all heard of this great deed, sung by minstrels. But who has seen it? An old Master Healer and a fat prince of Delu?'

Delu and Athar were ancient enemies, and Maram's face flushed red with rage. I was afraid he might even draw his sword and fall upon King Mohan. But he restrained himself. He drew in a deep breath and said, 'A prince of Delu I was born, but I am now also a Valari knight.'

Here he held up his silver ring, with its two bright diamonds, for all to see.

'A Valari knight,' King Mohan said, 'needs more than a ring to make him so. Prove *yourself* in the competitions, and we might believe you had the skill at arms to judge Lord Valashu's deeds and to report them truly.'

Maram opened his mouth as if to shout down King Mohan, but I caught his eye and shook my head slightly. If he pressed King Mohan, this rapacious king would only turn upon him like a cornered wolverine and defend his position all the more fiercely. And so, with a loud grumble, Maram assured King Mohan that he would prove his worth as both a Delian prince *and* a Valari knight. And then he took his seat.

I nodded at King Danashu and at King Kurshan. I said to them, and to all the kings at our table, 'King Mohan appears to speak for all of you. But I would ask you each, as kings of your own realms, to speak for yourself.'

I believed that if four or five of the Valari kings pledged to meet in Tria, King Waray, as a great conciliator, would suddenly find himself in favor of this journey as well. And then King Mohan would be forced to follow his lead – or to stand alone.

'Lord Viromar,' I said to my uncle, 'will you go to Tria?'

And this taciturn prince of Kaash replied with a single word: 'Yes.'

'King Kurshan, will you make the journey as well?'

King Kurshan looked up at the dark sky. It seemed that he was trying to decide the very fate of the world. And then he smiled, and his scarred visage lit up as if with dreams of sailing from Tria itself straight up to the stars. He said, 'If the other kings agree to this, so does Lagash.'

'King Danashu,' I said, turning to Anjo's nominal sovereign, 'will you meet in conclave with the outland kings?'

King Danashu pulled at his heavy chin as beads of sweat formed up on his brow. He had promised me that he would speak in favor of meeting in Tria, but now he seemed unable to meet me eye to eye.

'It must be said,' he finally forced out, 'that we Valari should make an alliance. Of course we should. And we Valari kings should meet with the other kings in Tria. We *should* do this, unless other matters prevail upon us here. King Sandarkan is right that we should first put our own house in order. Let us do this. Let us *then* journey to Tria, or to another meeting place, perhaps even in Nar – perhaps next year.'

As he fell silent, I saw King Waray regarding him triumphantly.

A sudden heaviness weighed at my belly as if I had swallowed a ball of lead. And I asked King Sandarkan, 'Will you meet in conclave?'

King Sandarkan glanced at King Danashu and then at King Waray.

He was like a great bird of prey alert for any shift in the direction of the wind.

'No, I will not journey to Tria, not now,' he said. 'The idea of an alliance is a good one, but it's time is not yet.'

Now it seemed that a whole ocean of molten lead burned inside me as I turned to King Hadaru and asked him the same question.

'The Valari must make alliance against Morjin,' he said to me and to all those present. 'But who is to lead this alliance? Valashu Elahad? I, for one, do not doubt his deeds. They are truly great. And it may be that he is this great Shining One whom many hope him to be. But at the Battle of Red Mountain, it's known that he hesitated in engaging his enemy who stood before him. Even as, in my own palace, in a duel, he refused to slay the one whose name I will not speak. Let us not forget that he has led four men and two women only into Argattha. If he would lead the whole of the Valari against Morjin, let him first overcome these hesitations; let him prove himself in battle as a warlord. Or, failing that, let him prove himself as this tournament's champion. And then we may speak of journeying to Tria.'

He, at least, the great Ishkan Bear, did not hesitate to stare straight at me. In his grim, old eyes was a promise that he would do what I had asked of him only if I did what he had asked of me.

'King Waray,' I said, finally turning to the gloating host of this feast, 'will you meet with the sovereigns of the Free Kingdoms?'

King Waray's polite face hid the most savage of smiles as he told me, 'Perhaps, Lord Valashu. But let it be as King Hadaru has said.'

Now only King Mohan remained to query. This I did. And he told me, 'Win the championship, and we will see about the conclave.'

As it had now grown late and the lance-throwing competition began early the next day, many of those present began saying their good-nights and returning to their respective encampments. More than a few knights walked up to my table to wish me well. Their words of encouragement were sincere, and yet they were proud men who would yield before me only if I truly outfought them.

At last, King Kurshan returned the Lightstone to me. I stared at this simple cup that held the light of the bright stars above. I remembered too well how I had fought and killed many men to gain it for the Valari. And soon, at dawn, I would have fight many Valari, if not quite kill them, so that the cup might be preserved for my quarrelsome people and an alliance be forged. It seemed yet another strange turning of my fate.

12

The next morning, to the sound of trumpets blaring in the cool morning air, I rode forth with Maram and the others of our encampment in our columns of whinnying horses and watchful Guardians, and we made our way toward the Tournament Grounds' main road. There our company had to pause while long lines of Lagashuns and Taroners passed before us. King Kurshan, resplendent in his diamond armor and blue surcoat showing a great Tree of Life, led his men past the Sword Pavilion and then on to the fields reserved for the long lance. King Waray and the more numerous Taroners followed them in a brilliant stream of flapping banners and knights displaying their emblems: gold bears and white wolves, crossed swords and sunbursts and roses, and many others. We of Mesh – and my Ishkan knights – joined this great procession. We paraded west more than a mile to the area given over to lance throwing. There we joined the companies of Waashians, Atharians, Anjoris, Ishkans and Kaashans who also converged there. An open pavilion, covered with a great red cloth, held the stands where the Valari kings and other luminaries would sit and bear witness to their knights' feats of arms. Other stands, lower and uncovered, adjoined the pavilion on either side, and these were already full of the many townspeople of Nar who had arrived before dawn. They had come in such numbers that most had to take seats on the grass beside the stands or keep to their feet in hope of being able to see what occurred before them.

On fields of grass still sparkling with dew, many targets had been set up in a long line running north and south. The targets were nothing more than open circlets of wood attached to poles planted in the ground. And the lance-throwing competition was a very simple, if very difficult, one: knights would spur their horses and gallop toward the targets, loosing lances at set intervals in hopes of seeing their pass through their circlet, eight inches in diameter. A long blue line, parallel to the line of targets, had been painted across the grass at a distance of ten yards. Any knight failing to loose his lance before reaching this line, or failing to transfix his target, would be eliminated. Those who succeeded would advance to the next round and would ride toward the next line, the yellow one, at a distance of twenty yards. And so with the orange line ten yards farther out and the white one beyond it. Any knights who remained in competion after riding at the red line at fifty yards would then ride at each other.

'And *that*,' Maram said to me as we made our way toward the staging area with Asaru and Yarashan, 'is the very part of this competition that makes no sense.'

'How so?' I asked him. I reached down to pat Altaru's neck, and my great black warhorse whinnied with excitement.

'Think of it, my friend. A knight such as you, or I, against all the odds, succeeds in a practically impossible feat. And his reward is having to face another knight throwing a lance at *him*.'

'But the lances are blunted,' I pointed out.

'They're not blunt enough. They can still crush a windpipe or an eye. It's happened before.'

'You worry too much.'

'And you worry too little. I'll never understand you Valari!'

I noticed him gripping his lance with his sweaty hand; the two diamonds of his ring sparkled in the early light. I said, 'Perhaps you *should* understand us then, since, as you have said, you are now one of us.'

I clapped him on the shoulder and then rode over to Sunjay and Baltasar. They were two of only twenty Guardians who would be competing in the tournament; the rest of our companions would carry out their duty while they watched from beside the stands. With Asaru and Yarashan and the forty other knights of Mesh who had journeyed here before us, the number of my countrymen casting their lances that day would be sixty-two – sixty-three if Maram were counted as riding for Mesh.

The other Valari kingdoms fielded similar numbers of knights. We assembled in the staging area, Meshians with Meshians, Taroners with Taroners, and so on. But when it came time to line up for our ride toward the targets a hundred yards away, we took our places according to the drawing of lots and not by our respective kingdoms. Once, long ago, the tournament had been a proving ground where each Valari kingdom tried to gain pre-eminence. But for many centuries, the competitions had been dedicated only to the proving of an individual's prowess: that a knight might gain glory and thereby demonstrate the magnificence of the One's most glorious creation.

While the judges took their places near the targets across the field from us, the first wave of knights was called to line up. This they did, to the cheers of the thousands of people in the stands behind us. Each knight turned his mount toward his distant target; as it happened, Maram and Yarashan, with Skyshan of Ki, were three of these. And then the heralds gave the signal for them to charge. And fifty knights, in their polished armor and surcoats bearing their bright emblems, urged their mounts across the field. They quickly gained speed as one whole line of knights; it marked a man for shame if he sought advantage in a slower charge and lagged behind the others. Across that broad field they thundered, past the long red line at fifty yards, and soon crossing the white line at forty yards, and then the orange and yellow lines. The boldest of the knights – and Yarashan was one of these – reached the blue line first and cast their lances first. But moments later the other knights caught up and cast their lances as well. The judges held up flags to proclaim the knights' success or failure. A white flag signified that a lance had sailed smoothly through its wooden circlet; a black flag denoted a miss. And red was the flag of disqualification, indicating that hit or miss, a knight had loosed his lance *after* crossing the blue line. It seemed a great, good omen for the success of the tournament that in this first wave of knights, only white flags were raised to herald their prowess.

'Well, that wasn't so bad,' Maram said to me, as he and the other knights of the first wave rejoined us in the staging area. Both he and his horse were covered in sweat. 'There's no danger at these distances at least – unless you fall off your horse and break your neck.'

I was called up in the fourth of the ten waves to ride toward the blue line. At the heralds' signal, Altaru leapt forward as if he understood deep in his bones the task that must be accomplished. Knights on their mounts to either side of us galloped toward the targets, too. Wind whipped into my face and fought its way between my helmet and sweat-soaked hair. I felt Altaru's huge hooves beat into the ground and churn it up in clumps. His great body was heavy with muscles that bunched and exploded with a tremendous power. For a few glorious moments, my horse and I moved together across the field as if we were a single beast encased in a shining black hide and diamond armor, fused together in our purpose and in our love. Hundreds of pairs of eyes transfixed us like lances, for Altaru would not suffer any other knight or rider to outpace him, and he insisted on taking the lead in the charge. And so we were the first of this wave to reach the blue line. Seconds before Altaru crossed it, I set my boots in my stirrups and loosed my lance; the thrust of Altaru's hindquarters and the perfect coordination of his body with mine helped me. I had never been particularly good at this act. But I watched with a wild joy as my lance sailed cleanly through its wooden circlet.

Nearly all the knights of this wave were successful as well. But young Sar Eshur of Waas, who had never been tested in a real battle, waited a moment too long to cast his lance and was disqualified. So it went with a few other knights in the succeeding waves. By the time all five hundred and thirty-three of us had charged the blue line, thirteen knights had been eliminated by such fouls while another nine missed their targets altogether.

The next rounds, marked by their respective lines at ever greater distances, took an increasingly greater toll. More knights were eliminated at twenty yards and many more in their ride toward the orange line at thirty yards. At forty yards, I missed my target while Maram fouled. He complained that the trampling of so many horses preceding him had nearly obliterated the white line so that he couldn't see it. It saddened me that I had come so close to riding toward the last line, the red one, and thereby gaining a chance to point at this competition. Maram professed to share my disappointment, but I sensed that he was really quite pleased with himself for lasting longer than most of the other competitors – and avoiding the dreaded riding of knight against knight.

We met in the staging area with the other Meshians to watch this climax of the day's feats. Only four knights faced the red line successfully, and these were Asaru, Yarashan, Lord Karathar of Lagash and Lord Dashavay. I watched this last famous knight ride slowly among the other Waashians in their part of the staging area. He seemed a perfectly proportioned man and more handsome in face than even Yarashan. Although he couldn't have been more than forty years in age, his hair showed streaks of white along with the battle ribbons tied there. His emblem was white lion on a green field; around his neck he wore the gold medallion of championship that he had won at the last tournament.

At last the heralds blew their trumpets, and Lord Dashavay rode out into the field to face Asaru. They charged each other, loosing their blunted lances at each other as they pleased. Lord Dashavay managed to catch Asaru's lance on his triangular shield; with perfect timing, he waited until Asaru was unbalanced from his cast, and then aimed *his* lance so that it sailed straight and caught Asaru's shoulder with a loud clack of wood against diamond. The judges awarded the victory to Lord Dashavay. Asaru congratulated him, and rode back to join us.

'Lord Dashavay is a great knight,' Asaru said as he pulled off his helmet and wiped his sweating brow. 'Three years ago I rode against him as well, and his skill at the lance has only grown.'

By the time that Yarashan and Lord Karathar rode out to face each other, the sun was low in the western sky. Lord Karathar quickly vanquished Yarashan as everyone expected, and then Yarashan lost again to Asaru in the fight for third place. In the culminating battle, Lord Karathar and Lord Dashavay charged each other three times before Lord Karathar succeeded in casting his lance straight against Lord Dashavay's chest. It missed his throat by an inch, and Maram looked at me in silent reproof even as the many people in the stands cheered Lord Karathar and hailed him yet again as the victor of the first competition.

'Five times he has won the lance throwing,' Yarashan complained. 'He'll have to die in battle or of old age if anyone else is ever to prevail.'

While the judges awarded points – ten for first place, five for second, and three, two and one for third, fourth and fifth – all the knights who had competed that day made a procession and rode past the pavilion where King Waray and the other kings were seated. He bowed his head to honor us. Then he called forward Lord Karathar, Lord Dashavay, Asaru, Yarashan, and Sar Tarval of Athar, who had won fifth place. He presented each of them with finely made lances bearing gold plaques that told of their feats. I pressed Altaru through the mass of men and mounts in front of the pavilion so that I could congratulate my brothers. As I clasped hands with them and tested the balance of their new weapons, I noticed King Waray looking at me as if to ask when it would come my turn to be honored.

'Ah, that was a day,' Maram said to me as we rode back to our encampment near the woods. 'I'm ready for a long glass of beer.'

'You did well,' I said to him.

'I *did*, didn't I? So did you. But not quite well enough to satisfy King Athar. Or King Waray. Did you see the way they looked at us?'

'Tomorrow is wrestling. We'll do better.'

'*You'll* do better, my friend. I'm afraid I've never wanted to practice much at that particular art.'

'That's because you've been too busy wrestling with Dasha Ambar and the other ladies.'

As our horses walked along the Tournament Grounds' main road, Maram eyed a beautiful silk-seller hawking her wares in a stall and then a haruspex at another who smiled and beckoned him closer. He turned to glance at Behira riding with Lord Harsha behind us; he sighed and said to me, 'And *that* is a better exercise of my talents.'

'You could excel at wrestling, if only you'd apply yourself. It's said that practice makes perfect.'

'No, no, my friend, practice makes only broken bones. When I was a boy, I smashed my knuckles wrestling my eldest brother. And, by bad chance, my cousin dislocated my jaw and nearly gouged out my eye. And the truth is, I'd rather look down and find a woman in my arms than some strange, sweating man.'

I smiled because I shared this particular sentiment. The next day we gathered with all the other knights and witnesses in the great Sword Pavilion, which also housed the wrestling competition. There Maram and I, with the knights of Mesh, faced those of Taron, Ishka and the other kingdoms; we also faced each other. It was a long day of grappling with opponents: locking arms and trying for choke holds and throws, as well as strikes with knuckle, elbow and knee at the body's various vulnerable points. By the noon meal break, many knights had been eliminated from this savage competition and too many suffered from various injuries: jammed fingers and crushed noses; boxed ears and popping joints and concussions.

My brothers and I sought sustenance to endure the coming rounds, and so we walked into the area to the north of the Sword Pavilion, where a small city of stalls and kiosks was laid out along narrow lanes. As I was eating cherries with Asaru and Yarashan at one of the fruit sellers' stalls, Lord Harsha and Master Juwain hurried through the crowds straight toward us. Lord Harsha, his hand on the hilt of his sword, limped up to me and asked, 'Have you seen Sar Maram?'

I looked past a hatter's stall at a line of vendors preparing roasted pheasants, mutton joints and other sizzling viands. I said, 'He told me that he was off to look for a slice of cherry pie.'

'That's not all he's looking for, it seems,' Lord Harsha said. He went on to explain that Behira had caught him exchanging whispers with a beautiful woman from Lagash, and she feared that he had made an assignation. 'My daughter is very worried – and so am I.'

Yarashan, eating a cherry almost daintily as if he didn't want its juices to stain his fine face, let loose a little laugh. 'You'd do better to worry that Maram doesn't find his pie. How that man can eat! He's likely to stuff himself so full that he won't be able to compete this afternoon.'

'If he doesn't present himself soon,' Asaru said, looking up at the sun, 'he'll miss the next round and be disqualified.'

My brother held a plum to his puffy, split lip as if its coolness might soothe it. I rubbed my sore elbow, which had been pulled straight and nearly bent back the wrong way. Master Juwain looked at us with all the compassion he could summon, for he had spent all morning tending such injuries – and much worse. And then he said, 'Disqualification might be exactly what Maram seeks.'

'That would be a pity,' Yarashan said. 'Who would ever have thought that he would do so well? Vanquishing five fine knights, and him taking hardly a scratch.'

In fact, one of Maram's opponents that day had managed to jam a fingernail into Maram's eye, leaving him with a rather serious scratch that Master Juwain had been able to treat only with difficulty.

'Let's look for him then,' I said. 'He can't have gone very far.'

'Unless he's gone back to the Lagashuns' encampment with that woman,' Lord Harsha said. 'But why don't we hope for the best and at least try the pie-sellers first?'

Without waiting for agreement, he clamped his hand around his sword again and pushed off into the crowds. I positioned myself close to him, while Asaru, Yarashan and Master Juwain hurried after us. As quickly as we could, we searched around the stalls of every pie seller, baker and pastry cook in that area of the Tournament Grounds; knowing Maram as we did, we also searched amongst the beer sellers, vintners and brandy kiosks – to no avail. And then the first warning trumpet sounded from the Sword Pavilion behind us.

'Surely he'll hear that and make his way back to the competition,' Asaru said.

'If Sar Maram is doing what it seems he might be doing,' Lord Harsha said, 'he'll be hearing other trumpets – calling him to his doom.'

So saying, his eyes narrowed, and he drew forth his sword a few inches so that its steel caught the light of the sun.

Finally, following an intuition that flashed through my mind, I led the way toward the edge of the kiosks in that area. And there, at one of the dice stalls, we found Maram standing before a table and casting a pair of cubical, carved bones. A pile of coins was heaped up on the table before him. Many people stood watching him – and his pile of coins – as if they hoped his luck would hold and would magically be bestowed upon them.

A sigh of relief broke from Lord Harsha's tight, old lips as he beheld this sight. But Asaru was less forgiving. He stormed up to Maram and said, 'Didn't you hear the trumpet?'

'Ah, what trumpet?' Maram asked, shaking the yellow dice in his huge hand.

'It's nearly time for the next match. You don't want to be late.'

'*Don't* I?' Maram said as he glanced at his pile of coins.

'No, you don't,' Asaru said, reaching out to close his hand around Maram's. 'What's wrong with you? Playing dice at a time like this? You're a Valari knight, and you shouldn't stoop to such vice.'

'Well, it's said that every man needs one vice.'

'Yes, but you drink and make a glutton of yourself. You womanize.' Here Asaru cast a quick look at Lord Harsha whose hand remained clamped around the hilt of his sword. 'And now it seems you gamble as well.'

'Ah, I'm still deciding which vice will be mine.'

I couldn't help smiling at Maram's incorrigibleness, and neither could Yarashan. Even Asaru seemed amused by this comment – but he kept his face stern even so. And he told Maram, 'You should concentrate on your virtues instead of your vices. You might point at wrestling, you know.'

Maram looked at his pile of coins and then at the other dice-throwers around the table. He rubbed his red eye and said, 'I prefer to gamble gold pieces rather than body parts, which are more precious to me.'

Just then the second warning trumpet sounded as if from far away.

'Are you ready to withdraw from the tournament then?' Asaru asked.

'What if I am?' Maram said, staring at him. 'I've been injured, haven't I?'

Yarashan scoffed at this, saying, 'If you call a scratch an injury.'

The sudden fire in Asaru's eyes warned Yarashan into silence. And Asaru said to Maram, 'Don't you want to give the lie to King Mohan's insinuation that you are unqualified to judge Val's feats of arms? Don't you want to help Val?'

'Help him be acclaimed the Maitreya?'

'Yes, if that is what it takes – to help all of Ea.'

Asaru stood staring at Maram, and so bright did his eyes become that Maram was finally forced to look away from him. He gripped the dice in his fist and muttered, 'Ah, well, let's go and wrestle, then.'

Angrily, he cast the dice one last time across the table. The six-sided bones tumbled about and then came to a stop. One of the other dice-throwers examined their carved faces and shook his head in defeat as he called out, 'Double dragons! This knight has too much luck!'

After the table's owner took his share of Maram's winnings, Maram scooped up his coins and dropped them into a leather purse. He gave a few of them to some tatterdemalions standing nearby, and then began walking back toward the Sword Pavilion even as the last warning trumpet blared.

That afternoon, it seemed that Maram was touched by the angel of fortune herself. Four sturdy knights he faced on the wrestling mats, and he sent each of them tumbling down or managed to demonstrate a kill with some vicious strike or choke hold. Thus did he vanquish even Asaru. As Lord Harsha sat in the stands with Estrella and Behira, they watched these moves with great concern – and even greater surprise. From my place at the edge of the wrestling ring, I overheard Lord Harsha say to his daughter, 'How is this possible? It would take more than luck alone for Maram to defeat Lord Asaru.'

In the final round, however, Maram lost to Sar Rajiru of Kaash. At the ceremony afterward, they stood before King Waray to be honored – along with Yarashan, Asaru and me, for we had won third, fourth and fifth places. It was a great day for the knights of Mesh, and even King Mohan offered his grudging appreciation as he glared at us and shook his head in wonder.

Before dinner that night, Maram, Asaru, Yarashan and I bathed our battered bodies in one the wooden tubs set up at the edge of our encampment. As Maram laved handfuls of steaming hot water over his mountainous frame, Asaru seemed to look beneath his layers of fat, and he said, 'You've grown stronger since you set out on your quest.'

'Fighting dragons,' Maram said, 'will make a man so.'

'So it seems. But that doesn't explain your skill on the mats. Strength alone never prevailed at wrestling.'

'No,' Yarashan added as he poked his finger into Maram's big, hairy belly, 'it seems our guest from Delu must have been practicing.'

'Maram,' I said, 'has given me to understand that he doesn't practice wrestling.'

As we all looked at Maram, his face flushed bright red, whether from shame or the heat of the bath, it was hard to tell. 'Ah, Val, I said only that I didn't *like* to practice wrestling. When I was a boy, my father made me drill at hand to hand because he was always afraid that an assassin would jump out from behind a curtain and stick a knife into me.'

Despite the water's permeating heat, I shuddered as I thought of how close Sivar of Godhra had come to murdering me. To Maram I said, 'You learned well.'

'Well enough, I suppose. At my father's court, no one could beat me.' Maram held up his knight's ring and shook the water from its two diamonds. 'Then, too, ever since your father gave this to me, I've engaged Sar Garash to renew my skills.'

So, I thought, the mystery of Maram's second in wrestling was finally

165

explained. Old Sar Garash, years ago, had won firsts in this savage art many times before retiring from the competitions to teach young knights such as Asaru, Yarashan and myself.

'You've been practicing in secret then?' Asaru asked him. 'But why?'

'Because of Valari pride, that's why,' Maram told him. 'Think of it: if it became known that I was any good at wrestling, every knight in Silvassu would have wanted to challenge me to a match.'

I smiled as I said to him, 'You'd rather your other talents become known so that women challenge you to other more pleasurable matches.'

'Just so, my friend. Just so.'

'Lecher,' I said to him.

Maram laughed as he splashed a handful of water at me and said, 'At least I practice my talents. At least I keep *my* sword sharp, if you know what I mean.'

This sentiment seemed to touch upon Asaru's righteousness and familial pride. He turned to look at me through the bath's steam and said, 'You should practice with *your* sword, Val.'

'Perhaps,' I said to him. 'But the woman I love dwells far away, and will not marry me in any case.'

Asaru frowned at this; with too-great a seriousness, he said, 'I'm not speaking of *that* sword, as you know well enough.'

I looked over the edge of the tub, where Alkaladur in its lacquered sheath rested against the tub's cedar staves, ready to be drawn at an instant's warning. Every morning and every night, in the privacy of my room, I drew it forth to practice the forms that I had been taught as a boy – and to renew the lessons that the incomparable Kane had drilled into my bones. But since the quest, I hadn't crossed swords with another, in combat or in practice.

'In the end,' Asaru said to me, 'the tournament will likely come down to the sword competition. But how can you hope to win it, Val? Have you given up, then, as King Waray has said?'

'No, not yet – our father taught us never to give up, didn't he?' I lathed some hot water over my aching elbow and added, 'besides, it's premature to speak of swords when we all have to survive tomorrow's mace-work.'

At the mention of this brutal competition, Maram groaned and looked down into the water's steamy surface as if hoping to catch sight of his reflection. And then, to himself as much as me, he muttered, 'Ah, my friend, perhaps you should have left me alone with my dice after all. I confess I've always loathed the mace ever since the day that assassin nearly brained me. Survive, indeed.'

The next morning, on the wide fields also given over to the long lance, Maram did quite well for three rounds of the mace competition. But I did not. In the very first round, riding against Arthan of Lagash, fortune betrayed me. Or rather, my gift did. Arthan was scarcely twenty years old, untested in battle and of no renown. In fact, he was a simple warrior who had yet to win the two diamonds of a full knight. But he was a fury with the mace. As the Valari kings and five thousand witnesses watched from the stands fifty yards away, he charged across the green grass straight toward me wielding his mace with a mighty and tireless arm. His horse nearly collided with mine. Five times, as we wheeled about, as our horses panted and tore up the turf with their great, driving hooves, he swung this cruel, clublike weapon at me. And five times I either evaded the heavy iron head or deflected it with my shield even as I aimed blows at him. Although some said that mace-work was much like fighting with a sword, I had always found the mace to be a cumbersome and ill-balanced weapon, impossible to wield with finesse and difficult to check. The truth is, I loathed the mace and had no feeling for it. Arthan sensed this about me. Thus he urged his horse in too close to Altaru to press his advantage. This was a mistake. Altaru, who loved the snorting violence of battle, would suffer no other horse or rider to hurt me if he could help it. And so my fierce stallion whinnied in wrath as he drove his shoulder against Arthan's exposed leg, nearly breaking it. Arthan cried out from the sudden pain, and so did I, for it had been too many months since I had wounded another in battle and I was unprepared for the sudden agony that poured through me. Arthan recovered more quickly than I did. As I was gasping for breath, he feinted toward my side, and then with great power, changed the arc of his blow. The mace's head stopped in the air only inches from my temple. I should have given thanks that Arthan had enough restraint to check the mace before knocking my brains out. But with this difficult maneuver, he had demonstrated a kill and had knocked me out of the competition.

His victory cast doubt upon my will to do battle. For King Waray and King Mohan, and many others watching in the stands, saw my moment of debility as hesitation. As I rode back toward the competition's staging area, King Mohan shook his head at me and spoke words to King Waray that I was sure I did not want to hear.

It gained me no favor that Arthan, despite his injured leg, to the astonishment of all, went on to win the competition. He was the youngest man in two hundred years to do so. To honor his feat, King Kurshan bestowed upon him his double-diamond ring and knighted him right there on that field before the cheering multitude.

Of the knights of Mesh, Yarashan was the only one to win points that day, taking second place. This put his tally for the tournament at ten points, even with Lord Karathar, Sar Rajiru and Arthan (now Sar Arthan), all of whom had won firsts. Some there were who said that the tournament's scoring system was unfair, that a knight such as Yarashan who had pointed at three successive competitions should have more honor than single winners. But that was not the way of things in the Nine Kingdoms. When it came to battle, victory was honored above all else save honor itself, and such pre-eminence was accorded the greater proportion of points.

That day saw the first deaths of the tournament. Sar Ishadur's horse, in his wild charge against Lord Marsun of Ishka, stumbled in the churned-up earth and threw his rider headfirst into the ground, which broke his neck. Not even Master Juwain, with his healing crystal, was able keep him alive. And later that afternoon, a very tired Sar Sharald of Anjo failed to check a savage blow aimed at Athar's famous Lord Noladan. The mace sank deep beneath Lord Noladan's forehead with a sickening crunch and a great gout of blood, killing him almost immediately. For his failure to exercise restraint, Sar Sharald was disqualified and banished from the tournament. His shame was great, but all the knights witnessing this horror, including myself, knew that such misfortune might some day fall upon them.

Pilgrims and other wayfarers in the Morning Mountains were often shocked by the violence of the Valari and our triennial tournaments. But in centuries past it had been far worse. In the Age of Law, when the men of other lands had beat their swords into spades to build the great Towers of the Sun and had bowed to the will of the Council of Twenty Kings, the Valari had mistrusted this peace. And so we had kept our swords – and kept them sharp. Although war among the Valari, for a while, died as it did in Alonia and Galda, its spirit did not. Kingdom vied with kingdom in elaborate war-games in which entire armies would take the field to maneuver against each other and strive for victory. Sharshan these games were called – but the Valari had prosecuted them with a deadly seriousness. Warriors, like living chess pieces, moved and fought each other across designated battlegrounds according to precise rules. Unlike chess pieces, however, a wild sword or a chance spearthrust might lay them low or kill them outright. Many were the wounds and deaths at Sharshan.

Over time, as darkness fell upon Ea and the Age of the Dragon began, Sharshan had developed in two directions. The Valari took to meeting in Nar to display their prowess at arms, in mêlées in which companies of warriors and knights from each kingdom fought each other. When

168

these brutal affairs still killed too many, they were finally disbanded, to be replaced by competitions between individual knights. The Valari, when disputes between kingdoms grew too acrimonious, also took to meeting on real battlefields, in Ishka, Anjo, Taron or Athar, to fight real battles. At first, for a few centuries, many of the rules of Sharshan carried over to ameliorate the worst consequences of war. But gradually these rules became fewer and simpler. Now, in our formal battles, the Valari agreed only on a very few things: that the battle would commence at a set time and place; that opposing kings would give each other a chance to negotiate; that prisoners would not be harmed and would be released after the defeated king surrendered; that the battle would not overflow into other parts of the kingdom and so become a real war in which lands might be plundered, women ravished or men murdered or enslaved. It was my fear that even these rules would one day break down as war's essential savagery took hold of men's hearts and burned away all restraint – and then burned the beautiful lands of the Morning Mountains from Mesh to the Alonian Sea.

Everyone at the tournament, I thought, from King Waray down to the lowliest groundsman or groom, was glad when the day of the mace ended. The next two days were given over to the chess competition. This was meant to be a time of rest before archery the following day and then the very strenuous long lance and sword competitions. And rest it was, for our bodies. But the intricate play of ivory and ebony pieces across sixty-four black-and-white squares sorely vexed the mind. I won five of my games and fought two others to a draw. Yarashan lost only a single game, to Lord Manamar, who took first place. After Yarashan had received his gift for taking second – a silver knight as long as a man's open hand – he pulled me aside by the rows of chess tables to speak with me. He held up his prize, and with uncharacteristic graciousness, he told me, 'This should have been yours, you know. Or even Lord Manamar's gold knight.'

'Perhaps it should have been,' I said. 'But prizes aren't given for ninety-ninth place.'

'You played brilliantly,' he said. 'As you always do, for twenty or thirty moves, you played like an angel. But then, as you almost always do, you made a weak move or blundered outright. Why, Val, why?'

Why, indeed? I shook my head because I had no answer to his question.

But Yarashan did. With a surprising gentleness, he laid his hand on my shoulder and smiled at me. 'Might it have something to do with this gift of yours? You're so used to closing yourself off from others to protect yourself that you fail to perceive their plans to defeat you.

169

And so in trying to checkmate them so single-mindedly, you overlook obvious threats to your own king.'

I looked at my handsome brother in wonder. For a man I had always considered to be vain and rather shallow, this was a penetrating insight.

'And as it is with chess,' he added, 'so it is with life. It's our weaknesses that defeat us, not our brilliance that saves us. Take care, Little Brother – take care.'

As he walked off, holding high his prize so that the day's witnesses might applaud him, I thought deeply upon what he had said to me. I vowed to examine myself for weaknesses and flaws, as I might my armor before a battle. I sensed that some day, and soon, the fate of many beside myself would depend on my ability to avoid blunders and the traps of my greatest enemy.

13

With Yarashan's second at chess, he now had fifteen points, which made him the tournament's leader. According to the rules, however, he was unlikely to become champion since he must win one of the next three competitions outright, and this even Yarashan admitted he could not do.

At archery the next day he failed to point. But Asaru won a fourth while I barely edged out Sar Avram of Ishka for fifth. And Maram surprised everyone, again, by winning third place. When we met in my tent afterward for a glass of brandy, he explained his feat thus: 'I truly *haven't* been practicing with the bow. At least not very much. But Atara is the finest bowman – ah, bow-*woman* – in Ea. Watching her fire her arrows with such skill, I think, must have got into my blood.'

'Well, you've now pointed in two competitions,' Asaru told him. 'That should satisfy even King Mohan.'

Of the five hundred Valari knights competing at the tournament, few would point at all, and fewer still point twice.

'Eight points I've won,' Maram said, holding up the bronze arrow that King Waray had given him. 'That's more than you, Val.'

Indeed, it was five more than my paltry three points – more even than Asaru's six. But we all knew that Asaru was likely to win a first at the long lance, and so add ten more points to his tally. And sixteen points was often enough for a knight to be declared the tournament's champion.

The next day dawned dark and cloudy with a moisture in the air that augured rain. But for all the long hours of the morning, the sky seemed to hold back its threat and tormented us knights with that cloying stillness that precedes a storm. Sweating in our stifling armor, we couched our long lances beneath our arms and charged at each other across grounds that had already been trampled in the mace competition. Asaru, again and again, outmaneuvered his opponents

171

and touched the blunted point of his lance against the bodies of all who faced him. And so did I, for Asaru had taught me all his skill with this difficult weapon; for much of my youth we had ridden at each other on the practice fields, brother against brother. Lord Bahram of Waas likewise prevailed, as did Athar's Sar Tarval. By late afternoon, with lightning strikes rending the dark sky over the distant Iron Hills, the four of us had advanced to the long lance's penultimate round.

Sar Tarval, however, who had added thirds in the mace and chess to his fifth at lance throwing, had taken a nasty wound to the neck in one of the preceding rounds. One of the Atharian healers had extracted the splinters of a broken lance from the muscle there and had bandaged his neck as best he could. He called for Sar Tarval to withdraw from the tournament. But Sar Tarval was a brave man and the nephew of King Mohan; he wouldn't so easily abandon the opportunity to ride against me and ruin my chances. And so, with difficulty, he climbed on top of his warhorse to seek victory and the favor of his bloodthirsty king.

We waited with each other in the staging area while Asaru rode out to face Lord Bahram of Waas. Their battle was long and brutal, for they were both knights of great prowess. Ten times they charged each other, trying to touch their lances against belly or chest. Finally, in the eleventh charge, Asaru's lance found its way past Lord Bahram's shield and took him square over the heart. This was a clear kill. I watched in horror, however, when the button came loose from Lord Bahram's lance, even as Asaru's shield deflected it upward. The exposed steel point found a seam in the diamonds of Asaru's armor and drove straight through into his shoulder. Asaru cried out from the pain of it, and so did I. The blow nearly knocked him from his saddle. But he recovered enough to sit up straight like the victor he was and to guide his horse back to the staging area. Lord Bahram shook the blood off the tip of his lance; he shook his head in anger, because there was only shame and defeat in wounding an opponent in a part of the body that was not meant to be a target.

Asaru managed to ride back to the staging area, straight up to me. I looked at the blood staining his black and silver surcoat, and I asked, 'Is it bad?'

And Asaru, who knew me well, shook his head. 'Not bad enough to keep *you* from defeating Sar Tarval. Keep your mind on his lance, Val.'

And with that, he smiled at me and waved off the grooms who would have borne him away on a litter, and he insisted on riding by himself to the white pavilion set up near the edge of the field as a house of healing.

Then the heralds signaled Sar Tarval and me to take the field. We rode out fifty yards, and then charged each other. Our horses thundered across the torn turf and there was the noise of lance beating against shield. Again we charged, and yet again; we wheeled about and closed, maneuvering to strike our lances at our opponent's body. After a few moments of some violent thrusting and the buttons of our lances slamming into our steel shields, we broke apart and rode off a hundred paces for another charge. But Sar Tarval suddenly slumped in his saddle as he clapped his hand to his neck. The bandage there was soaked through with blood. The judges, seeing this, called for a halt to our combat. They rode out into the field to examine Sar Tarval. It was determined that his wound needed to be re-dressed. And so the competition was suspended until this could be done.

I followed the grooms who carried Sar Tarval across the Tournament Grounds' main road to the house of healing. And Maram and Yarashan, and others, followed me. There, beneath the pavilion's flapping white silk, in a large space that stank of boiling herbs and blood, the grooms set Sar Tarval on a cot next to Asaru. Master Juwain had removed my brother's armor and was already working on his pierced shoulder. Another healer, from Nar, began cutting away Sar Tarval's red bandage. Thirty-six knights lay on other cots, and one of these was Baltasar, who had a badly cut hand. A worried Lansar Raasharu stood over him. I greeted both of them. And then I turned to touch eyes with my brother.

'The wound *is* bad, isn't it?' I said to him. Master Juwain's body blocked my view of Asaru's shoulder, and I was glad for that.

Asaru ignored my question and asked me, 'Did you prevail?'

'No, not yet. As soon as Sar Tarval is ready, we'll cross lances again.'

But this, it seemed, was not to be. Just then the low buzz of voices around the cots died to a silence as King Mohan entered the pavilion. He strode quickly forward with powerful steps as if his tight, small body could barely contain the fires that burned inside him. His hard face seemed softened by his concern for Sar Tarval. He moved right up to the edge of his cot, and he gave no care that his fine tunic – gold and emblazoned with a blue horse – might be stained with Sar Tarval's blood.

After speaking with the healer who attended him and looking at his neck, King Mohan smiled down at his nephew and said, 'I must ask you to withdraw from the tournament.'

Sar Tarval's dark eyes flashed toward me before turning back to his king. He said, 'I would rather die, sir.'

'I understand – but I would rather you didn't. Your life is dear to me.'

173

Sar Tarval nodded his head, and winced from the sudden pain. 'Yes, you saved it at the Silver River. At great risk to your own.'

At the mention of this fierce battle with Kaash, King Mohan's eyes flared brightly. And then he asked Sar Tarval again, 'Will you withdraw?'

Again Sar Tarval looked at me for a long few moments. And he sighed out, 'If that is your will, sir.'

Maram, standing by my side, clapped his hand against my shoulder and smiled at me. With Sar Tarval's withdrawal, I was assured of at least a second at the long lance, and five precious points.

King Mohan now turned to stare at me. His face was full of simple emotions: anger; disappointment; pride; jealousy; love. I said to him, 'I don't understand, sir. I thought you wanted me to lose.'

'What I *want*,' he told me, 'is of no importance.'

I shook my head at this because these were not words that I expected this willful man ever to speak.

'A king,' he said to me by way of explanation, 'has desires, as does every man. He acts to bring them to fruition, and this is right and good. But he can never be sure his acts will lead to the desired result; he can only be sure of the acts, themselves. Therefore each act must be good and true, as and of itself. It is upon me to guard the lives of my knights as I would *my* own life. Or failing that, not to risk them carelessly. A king who doesn't live for the good of his men and his kingdom is no true king.'

This was a noble thing for him to say. I bowed my head and told him, simply, 'Thank you.'

But this only angered King Mohan. He stared up at me as he gritted his teeth. Then he said, 'You owe me no thanks. I have done what I must, and now so must you. If you are to be the Maitreya, you'll win the tournament no matter what anyone does to help or hinder you.'

With that, he turned back to Sar Tarval and clasped his hand. Then he walked up and down the pavilion, greeting other Atharian knights and listening to the stories of how they had come by their wounds. They all looked at King Mohan with utter devotion, as did Sar Tarval. I overheard King Mohan promising a great feast in their honor when they returned to Athar. And then he said his goodbyes and walked out of the tent.

Master Juwain, who had finished bandaging Asaru's shoulder, said to my brother, 'You should withdraw, too.'

Maram seized upon this as a beggar might a gold coin. He added, 'Yes, if you withdraw, Val will win the long lance by default. The ten additional points will give him thirteen. Then he'll need only a second at the sword to win the tournament.'

Yarashan, standing next to Maram, slowly nodded his head. Lord Dashavay had won a fourth at chess, which gave him seven points altogether. Ten more from a win at the sword would put him at seventeen, one behind me if I should do as Maram had said.

'But what if Val fails to take second in the sword?' Yarashan asked. 'Then both he *and* Asaru would fail to gain the championship.'

Master Juwain waved his hand at these speculations as he might shoo away a cloud of biting flies. 'King Mohan spoke truly. An action is either right or wrong. And it is right that Asaru should withdraw, as did Sar Tarval.'

Asaru had so far endured in silence others' opinions as to what he should or should not do. And now he said, 'What is right for Sar Tarval isn't necessarily so for me. My wound poses no danger to my life.'

'Does it not?' Master Juwain said. 'What if, in riding against Val, you reopen it? What if you bleed to death before I can help you again? Or what if you grow faint and break your neck falling off your horse?'

Now it was Asaru's turn to wave off Master Juwain's speculations.

'All right,' Master Juwain said with a sigh. 'But I'm afraid I must tell you that Lord Bahram's lance tore a nerve. I was able to begin healing it, but it needs time to regenerate fully. If you ride now, you risk the use of your arm, Asaru.'

Asaru winced as he exerted all his will to raise up his arm and test it by flexing muscles and fingers. Seeing this, Yarashan began cursing Lord Bahram. Lord Bahram, he said, had hated Asaru ever since the Battle of Red Mountain when Yarashan had put his lance through Lord Bahram's son. Yarashan as much as accused Lord Bahram of loosening the button on his lance and wounding Asaru deliberately. But Asaru would hear no such slander against a Valari lord, not even his enemy. He returned to the matter at hand, saying, 'Some risks must be taken for the sake of honor.'

'But there is no dishonor,' Master Juwain told him, 'in a wounded knight remaining in his bed.'

'In this instance, there is grave dishonor. If I withdraw, many will say that I did so only to help Val win the long lance.'

'Ah, who cares what anyone says?' Maram asked him.

At this, Yarashan shook his head in disgust as if Maram might point at a hundred competitions and still not understand what it meant to be a Valari warrior.

Asaru and I met each other's eyes. I deeply cared what others would say, and so did Yarashan – as would Baltasar and the other Guardians of the Lightstone. Our father would care, and our grandfather, if he were still alive, and all our family and friends who remained in Mesh.

175

'And it is more than that,' Asaru said as he looked at me. In his steady gaze there was something that recalled our climbing mountains together beneath blue sky and sun, something so bright and beautiful that I could hardly bear to behold it. 'If you were you to win the long lance this way, Val, and so the whole tournament, you would always doubt when others called you "Lord of Light".'

'Yes,' I said to him as we clasped hands together, 'that is true.'

'And *that*,' Asaru said, 'is why I cannot remain here. Now help me up, and let's finish out the day before it rains.'

By the time we took the field again in front of King Waray's pavilion, big drops of rain were already splatting down upon our helms and horses. My brother and I charged each other across broken, blood-stained grass. Our lances, with a tong of wood against steel, glanced off each other's shields. Asaru held his with his left hand, and the force of my blow shivered up his arm into his bad shoulder, causing him to bite back the shock of pain which stabbed through him. I winced, as well. I considered lowering my shield on the next charge so that Asaru might win this overlong competition and return to his bed. But the flash of anger in his eyes as we faced each other again told me that he knew what I was thinking. It told me, too, that if I lost to him intentionally or fought half an inch beneath my best, I would make a mockery of his valor in riding against me.

And so I charged him with all the fierceness and speed that I could summon from my horse. It would be better, I thought, to finish this as quickly as possible. Asaru clearly thought this, too, for I sensed him straining every muscle and nerve in his battered body to shift his lance at the last moment and score a kill against me. But he had taught me too well; I deflected his lance with my own even as I tried to touch its tip against his chest. He slipped sideways in his saddle then, and my lance touched only air. He smiled to have evaded me this way as the joy of battle, for a moment, washed away its agony.

Six more times we made passes at each other. Thunder boomed closer now as rain began falling in silver, slanting sheets. After our eighth pass, made slower by the slick and sodden turf, Asaru quickly reined his horse around and closed with me. There followed a minute of furious, thrusting lancework as our horses screamed and struggled for purchase in the sucking mud, and lightning flashed above us. Finally, in a brilliant stroke, Asaru parried my lance with his and thrust forward quickly. His lance tip scraped across the edge of my shield and slammed into my chest. One of the judges riding nearby then held up his lance, signaling Asaru's victory.

It was Asaru's greatest feat so far that he kept to his saddle as he rode up to King Waray to receive his prize. But there, in front of the stands, as Yarashan and I came up to him, he fell down into my arms, and we helped the grooms lay him on a litter. They bore him to the healing pavilion where Master Juwain went to work on him again. Master Juwain was already exhausted from many days of such exertions. The fire he summoned from his emerald varistei was scant. But it was enough for him to hope that Asaru might yet heal fully, if he were well-tended and fever did not take hold of him. Toward this end, I arranged for Asaru to be brought back to my tent. I laid him on my bed. I spent the night with him there, and Estrella and Behira helped me bathe him and feed him sustaining broths. By the time morning brightened my pavilion's windows, he was able to sit up and exchange a few words with me.

'You fought well,' he said to me. His breath came out almost as weak as a whisper, for he had lost much blood.

'You fought *too* well,' I said to him. 'You look as pale as a ghost.'

'And you look tired. You should have gotten some sleep.'

I yawned as I stretched my bruised body. How could I have slept when, for hours, I had been afraid that my brother *would* become a ghost?

'Today is the day,' he said as he looked at the light streaming in the window. He watched me fasten my armor and then buckle on my sword. 'Now you'll *have* to win, won't you? Walk with the One, Val, and watch Lord Dashavay's sword.'

He smiled at me as he clasped my hand weakly. And then I walked out into cool morning air to face Lord Dashavay and others.

In the Sword Pavilion that day, the mats had been pulled up from the fencing rings to reveal nine circles of polished oak. Facing them were the center stands where King Waray and King Mohan sat between King Sandarkan and King Kurshan. Lord Viromar was present, too, and my uncle took his place next to King Danashu, who kept his wary eyes on King Hadaru as if expecting a knife in the belly for his plotting against Ishka. But King Hadaru, like the many lords, ladies and knights in the rest of the stands around the pavilion, looked straight ahead toward the three rows of fencing rings where the four hundred and forty knights remaining in the tournament would face each other with our bright kalamas.

By good chance I drew a bye in the first round, and so I had a few moments of rest to watch Lord Dashavay at work, along with other great swordsmen such as Lord Marjay and Sar Shivamar. But by bad chance I drew Lord Dashavay as my opponent in the second round. Maram, sitting with Yarashan and me on one of the many waiting benches between the stands and the fencing rings, grumbled loudly, 'Do you suppose King Waray arranged this to knock you out early so that you don't even point?'

'No,' I told him as I looked up at the stands where King Waray sat glaring at me. 'Surely it was just the luck of the lots.'

Usually, in these first rounds of the competition, matches were fought in all nine rings at once, for there were many knights to be eliminated. But because King Waray and many others wished to witness my match with Lord Dashavay undistracted, the heralds called forth only Lord Dashavay and me. We took our places in the center ring. Lord Dashavay wore his green surcoat with its white lion over his gleaming armor; he was helmless, as was I. We both found places for our bare feet on the shining white wood. He drew his sword and faced me with an almost palpable confidence. He studied me with great intensity. His first match with Sar Araj had lasted exactly nine seconds, long enough for him to beat aside Sar Araj's sword and stop the arc of his own three inches from Sar Araj's head.

I should have studied my famous opponent, too; I should have looked for weakness on his striking face or in his preternaturally calm black eyes. Instead, I stared at the bloodstains that reddened the wood of our circle. I listened to the thunder of my racing heart as I waited for the judge to approach and give the signal for us to begin.

From the bench where Lord Issur sat with Lord Mestivan and the other Ishkans, I heard Lord Nadhru call out to me, 'Now we'll see if it was luck that you defeated Lord Salmelu in that shameful duel!'

I drew Alkaladur then, and many men and women in the pavilion gasped at its brightness. Flick appeared to turn a spiral around my sword's silver length before winking back into nothingness. A flicker of doubt broke the coolness of Lord Dashavay's demeanor.

And then the judge, Old Lord Jonasar of Taron, cried out: 'Begin!'

Lord Dashavay sprang at me without the slightest hesitation. I met his sword in a clash of steel against my sword's silver gelstei. We leapt back from each other, circled and closed again. Our swords whipped out, once, twice, thrice. The clanging of the blades was deafening; the burn of bright steel past my eyes nearly blinded me and struck fear into my heart. It was not fear for myself, or for losing this match; it was a gut-twisting dread that I might wound or kill Lord Dashavay. I knew that I could. For Kane, the bright angel of death who was my friend, had taught me too well. All the enemies that I had fought with this sword on the road to Argattha and within its dark hell of cold rock and bitter hatred had taught me, too. Something dark now dwelled within my sword as if it had drunk in these many deaths and demanded

178

more. Or rather, something incredibly bright blazed down its shimmering length into my hands and heart, and called me to prevail at all costs even if others must be utterly destroyed. And this, I knew, was why these many months I had practiced alone with this terrible and beautiful sword.

Lord Dashavay, with perfect timing and sense of distance, aimed another blow at me, and another, and then a whole series of cuts, feints and thrusts. I parried them all. The faster he moved, the more quickly I whipped Alkaladur about to knock his blade aside. As I began to perceive the pattern of his attack, my silver sword wove an impenetrable pattern about me, like a fence of light. Frustration furrowed Lord Dashavay's sweating brow. He gasped from the pain of his burning muscles as his heart pushed hot blood through his veins and he swung his sword at me, again and again. Now his sureness was broken by dismay, and dismay began to give way to a fear that ate into his spine. I took a step toward him and then another. I turned my blade, right and then left, parrying and using the momentum of his sword striking mine to whip my sword around in an arc back toward him. I felt no tiredness, only an inexhaustible strength that my sword drew down from the sun and poured into my arms. Yarashan had warned me to beware of my weaknesses. But here, in this circle of honor, with this bright sword ringing against Lord Dashavay's well-tested blade, I knew that I would make no mistakes.

I struck with great speed at his head, and he took a step backward. Again I attacked him, and again. Alkaladur flared and flashed like a cloud of light, like entire whirling constellations of stars. The Sword of Light, men called it. And now Lord Dashavay's fear deepened to awe as I showed him something beautiful about this terrible art of ours that he had never hoped to see. The light of my sword pursued him and chased him about the circle; he couldn't escape it any more than he could strokes of lightning. And neither of us could escape our fate. I pressed him ever backwards, pounding at him relentlessly. My heart pounded out bright bursts of joy, for suddenly my fear left me, and I knew that I had the power to score against him rather than to slay. And so, as his sword swept by me for the hundredth time, I thrust forward with a savagery that tore away my breath. And I stopped the point of my blade an inch from his heart.

'Hold!' Lord Jonasar cried out. 'Match to Lord Valashu Elahad!'

I stood there gasping for air as the cries of hundreds of Valari in the stands came roaring into my ears.

'Lord of Light!' I heard someone call out. 'Maitreya!'

Lord Dashavay looked down at my bright blade that had stopped

him cold. His astonishment burned away in the flame of sudden understanding. He gasped out, 'Brilliant, Lord Valashu! I never knew. Perhaps
some day we can make another match.'

He bowed his head to me then, and I bowed to him. Then we walked
out of the circle to rejoin our friends where they sat with the other
knights of our respective kingdoms.

'Champion! Champion! Champion!'

Maram rose from our bench, threw his arms around me and
pounded me on the back. Baltasar, taking care of his wounded hand,
joined him in congratulating me, as did Sunjay Naviru and Yarashan.

Of course, their celebration was premature, for I had won only my
first match of the morning. There followed a long day of other matches
and other rounds, with Lord Marjay, Sar Siraju of Lagash and others.
I vanquished them all even more quickly than I had Lord Dashavay.
Between my matches I watched other knights fence. It was a good day
of excellent swordsmanship and only one death. Late in the afternoon,
I drew my sword for the last time in that tournament and sheathed it
scarcely half a minute later, after I had swept away Sar Shivamar's
fevered defenses – and nearly his head. The judges awarded me my
ten points, and King Waray was forced to drape around my neck the
gold medal of the tournament's champion.

'Lord of Light! Lord of Light! Lord of Light!'

At the edge of the stands, I stood before King Waray as the many
people in the pavilion rose to their feet and cheered me. Lord Viromar,
with the Valari kings, bowed their heads to me. And then King Mohan,
as blunt and honest as he was contentious, said to me, 'Sar Maram
was right about you. That was the finest swordwork I've ever seen. No
knight has ever deserved the championship more.'

'Thank you, King Mohan,' I said. 'Do I then deserve to ask if you
will make the journey to the conclave in Tria?'

'You do.'

'Will you?'

His black eyes seemed bright with the light of my sword, and something else. He said, 'Yes, I will.'

I turned to King Kurshan, and I asked him the same question, as I
did Lord Viromar; they both gave their assent. After I had queried King
Danashu likewise, he hesitated a moment as he looked to King Waray
for sign of what he should say. And then he seemed to find the best
of his own will inside himself, and he said, 'Perhaps this *is* the time
to meet in Tria. I won't be the only Valari king to stay behind.'

I bowed my head to him and then looked at the gaunt, disbelieving
King Sandarkan. We locked eyes together for a moment before he

looked away. And he said, 'Perhaps we *could* put our house together, at least for as long as it takes to ride to Tria and then home again.'

'King Hadaru,' I said, turning toward the old Ishkan bear. 'Do you agree?'

King Hadaru fastened his hard eyes upon me as he pulled at the battle ribbons in his white hair. 'I *do* agree, at least to journey to Tria. You've earned your chance to speak there in favor of an alliance.'

Now only King Waray remained uncommitted to the conclave of all of Ea's Free Kingdoms. I stood beneath the stands as the gold medallion that he had bestowed upon me pulled at my neck. And I asked him, 'King Waray, will you journey to Tria?'

And without hesitation, this suave, cunning king smiled at me as if I were a son who had honored him, and he said, 'Of course I will. Together we'll make a procession into Tria that hasn't been seen for three thousand years.'

And with that, the thousands of people in the pavilion let loose a great cheer. Baltasar and the other Guardians stood together in the stands, and they cried out, 'Maitreya! Claim the Lightstone!'

They made a procession of their own, nearly a hundred and twenty of them, down into the pavilion's floor. Then Sharash of Pushku, whose turn it was to keep the Lightstone that day, approached me, holding high the golden cup.

'Lord of Light!' he cried out to me. 'Claim the Lightstone!'

A hundred voices from the stands called out as well, 'Claim it! Claim the Cup of Heaven!'

I stood there for a long time looking at this golden cup that showered its light upon the many men and women there. I waited for the pavilion to grow quiet. I looked up at Estrella, who sat with Lord Harsha. She seemed bright and happy as she smiled at me and waited to see what I would do.

At last, I motioned for Sharash to lower the Lightstone. And then I called out as loudly as I could, 'After the conclave is successfully concluded and an alliance is made, then – and only then – I will claim the Lightstone.'

Out of the silence that fell across the stands, King Waray said to me, 'Is there nothing you would ask for yourself, as is a champion's right?'

His broad smile hid the churning inside him, and I knew it cost him a great deal to ask me this. And I smiled at Master Juwain before turning back to King Waray and saying, 'I would ask only that the Brotherhood's school be reopened and that Master Juwain be allowed to complete his research there.'

'Of course,' King Waray said, as his hands clenched into fists. 'It will be my pleasure to grant you this. Now why don't we all retire to our tents to prepare for the feast tonight?'

As he made his way from the stands and out of the pavilion, many people followed him. Many more, however, came down to congratulate me. To Yarashan and Baltasar, to Lord Raasharu, Skyshan and Sunjay Naviru, I showed my champion's medallion. It was a great moment, made poignant only by Asaru's absence. But Maram's hand thumping on my back and the deep quiet of Estrella's dark eyes gave me to hope that I would fulfill all my dreams, and soon.

14

I spent most of the next day in my tent with Asaru, tending his wound and recounting the events of the tournament, especially the sword competition which he had not been able to watch. With Master Juwain filling his torn body with the green gelstei's magic light, he seemed to gain strength every hour. By the time the following morning dawned clear and bright, Master Juwain felt confident of my brother's recovery.

'I've done all I can for Asaru,' he said to me as he took me outside. 'Now he'll have to heal of his own light – and by the One's grace.'

'Thank you,' I said to him as I looked off at the rising sun.

'And now we should go up to the school. With King Waray's prohibition, it might take many days to search through the thought stones.'

King Waray, even as I had feared, had forbidden Master Juwain to remove any artifact from the Brotherhood's sanctuary.

'We don't have *many* days,' I said to him. 'We should leave for Tria as soon as we can.'

With time pressing at us, Master Juwain and five others of his Brotherhood organized a little expedition to reopen their school in the hills above Nar. The Guardians and I joined them, for it seemed certain that the Lightstone would be needed to open any gelstei Master Juwain might find. To our numbers was added a company of Taron knights under the command of a Lord Evar. They would escort us to the school and make certain that King Waray's wishes were obeyed.

And so later that day we left Yarashan, Lord Harsha, Behira and Estrella behind with Asaru, and we rode out from the Tournament Grounds. With the fifty Taroners in the lead, we made our way through the smoky Smithy District up into the green hills overlooking the city. The Brotherhood school – a collection of old stone buildings spread out across the top of one of these broad hills – rose up before us as if the very bones of the earth had been exposed by wind and weather and the relentless wear of time. I liked the feeling of this ancient site. As with other Brotherhood schools, there was a quiet magnificence here and a harmony with heaven and earth that suggested an eternal quest for mysteries. The library formed the center part of the Brother's sanctuary. It was fronted by perfectly proportioned columns beyond which loomed its great wooden doors. Lord Evar, a tall man almost as gaunt and grim as King Sandarkan, drew forth a great iron key and made a show of formally unlocking these ancient doors.

While the five other masters went off to attend to various duties and the Guardians stood watch before the doors, Master Juwain showed Maram and me into the library. It was nothing so grand as the immense Library of Khaisham and collection of books that had perished in flames. But with its many aisles and shelves of musty, leather-bound volumes and manuscripts resting in the quiet beneath its great dome, I guessed that it held more books than all of Silvassu. Along its curved walls were many cabinets containing relics that the Brothers had rescued over the ages. Master Juwain, with a key that a Master Tavian had given him, approached one of these cabinets and unlocked one of its long, flat drawers. He slid it out halfway to reveal many opalescent stones which rested in pockets scooped into the wood. In front of each pocket was inscribed a number. Each stone ran with shifting colors that ranged from ruby to bright violet; each of them seemed nearly identical to the stone that Master Juwain had opened in my father's castle and which he now drew forth.

'Do you see?' he told Maram and me as he turned the stone between his fingers. 'It's as I said: there were too many to remove to Mesh.'

I looked deeper into the drawer and saw that there were ten rows of ten stones – or should have been, for near the back of the drawer, one stone was missing from the ninth row.

'But how did you choose *this* stone?' Maram asked him.

'By chance,' Master Juwain said. He tapped his finger against the three drawers below the opened one. 'These, too, contain gelstei believed to hold knowledge of the Lightstone. I had to pick one of them and test it.'

'Four hundred stones,' I said, shaking my head.

'Three hundred and fifty-three, to be precise,' Master Juwain told me. 'The fourth drawer is only half full.'

'Even so, to open and read all of them would be like reading as many books, wouldn't it?'

'Yes, but it may be that the knowledge in the stones is indexed and cross-referenced, as in the books of the better libraries. If so, then I might be able to follow a stream of knowledge to the one we seek.'

'*Any* knowledge about the Lightstone, you should seek,' I said to him. 'About the Maitreya. Now, if you will, please begin.'

As in the great hall of my father's castle, Master Juwain used his varistei to prepare his head and heart for the task before him. Then I brought forth the Lightstone. Master Juwain set his thought stone back into its place in the drawer and removed another one. His gnarled fingers squeezed it tightly as he held it before the Lightstone. This time, he had much less trouble opening it. The Lightstone flared with a sudden radiance as the thought stone's colors seemed to catch fire. I saw these colors swirling in bright patterns in the black circles at the centers of Master Juwain's eyes. So intently did he stare at this little gelstei that it seemed he might never move again.

'I see, I see,' he whispered. And then, after some moments, while my heart beat quickly, he said, 'Brother Maram, please give me number nineteen.'

Without turning his head, he handed Maram the little stone, which Maram set back in its place before retrieving the one that Master Juwain had requested. He pressed it into Master Juwain's hand. And for what seemed a long time, Master Juwain stared at this thought stone, too.

'Number eighty-two!' Master Juwain finally called out. 'Third drawer!'

And so it went for the rest of the day and far into the night, Master Juwain calling for specific thought stones and Maram delivering them faithfully – even as I stood in front of Master Juwain holding up the brilliant Lightstone.

At last, Maram patted his rumbling belly and suggested that we should take our evening meal. Master Juwain then broke off his researches. He looked across the large, circular room at the blazing candles that he had only grudgingly permitted Maram to light. And then he told us, 'The thought stones *were* indexed, perhaps thousands of years ago. But the system has been lost – until today.'

He began to explicate this system but I held up my hand to stop him. 'Excuse me, sir, but we've little time. What did you discover?'

'Much less than we'd hoped, I'm afraid,' he said. 'That is, the thought stones *do* contain a great deal of knowledge. But most of this is recorded in the *Saganom Elu.*'

'Is there nothing new, then? Nothing that might be able to help us?'

'Only bits and pieces,' he said. 'Only hints.'

'Tell me, then.'

'Well, there is *this*,' he said. 'There are passages indicating that the Maitreya is one who must make a great sacrifice.'

'Of his life?' I asked.

Master Juwain's news did not accord with the *Saganom Elu's Book of Remembrance*, where it was written that: 'The Maitreya will gain the greatest prize; he will reach out and take the whole world in his hands.'

Master Juwain shook his head and told me, 'No, I had no sense that the Maitreya must *die* for others, not exactly. Only that he must forsake some great thing.'

'Is it love, then? Marriage?'

'No, I don't think so. It has something to do, rather, with the Lightstone.'

I squeezed the golden cup that I still held in my hand. 'But the Lightstone was *meant* for the Maitreya. How, then, should he give it up?'

'I'm not sure he must. I'm not sure he can.'

'What do you mean?'

'Do you remember the passage from the *Beginnings*?: "The Lightstone is the perfect jewel within the lotus found inside the human heart."'

'A beautiful metaphor,' I said.

'Beautiful, yes – and perhaps something more.' Master Juwain gazed above us at the dome's clear windows that let in the light of the stars. 'You see, there are the infinities.'

'Sir?'

He looked back at me and showed me the thought stone. He said, 'This little gelstei is a finite thing, as is the knowledge it contains – as are all *things*. The One, of course, is infinite. But the Lightstone, somehow, is both.'

Now all of us, even Maram, stared at the golden contours of the Lightstone as if seeing it for the first time.

'And as with the Lightstone,' Master Juwain continued, 'so with the Maitreya. We know that he is the one who has a perfect resonance with it. There is a sense that in order for this to be so, he must sacrifice his finiteness – his very humanity.'

I gripped the Lightstone so tightly that it hurt my fingers. I shook my head because I did not know what Master Juwain's words could mean. I said, 'If only there was more.'

'I'm afraid that's all I gleaned from this first pass. But if I'd had more time . . .'

His voice died off into the library's half-light.

'Yes?' I said to him.

'Well, you see,' he said, 'there *was* one stream of recordings, more like a rill, actually, that I might have followed. A hint of a hint about some great store of knowledge concerning the Lightstone.'

I looked out the window at the great constellations wheeling slowly about the heavens. I said to him, 'We have all of tonight – and tomorrow, too, if need be. If you are willing, sir.'

The gleam in Master Juwain's luminous eyes told me that he was more than willing. When Maram groaned that we could not possibly go on without sustenance, I sent him to retrieve a loaf of barley bread and some goat's cheese from the stores that the Guardians had shared out for their dinner. And then, after we had eaten, Maram returned to retrieving thought stones for Master Juwain as our old friend set to work.

Thus we passed the rest of the night. As Master Juwain gained proficiency at opening and reading the stones, this strange business went more quickly. At times he called out the numbers of new stones so suddenly that Maram was hard put to replace the old one before drawing forth the new. He puffed and sweated as drawers slid open and slammed shut and the marble-like thought stones rattled in their wooden pockets. Finally, near dawn, Master Juwain gave back to Maram the last of a long sequence of stones. He looked at us and smiled. Although his eyes were red with weariness, he was almost hopping with excitement.

'I believe,' he told us, 'that there is a gelstei containing the true knowledge of the Lightstone. A gelstei unlike any other. It's called an akashic crystal.'

'That name is unfamiliar to me,' I said.

'Akashic is a word meaning "great memories". It seems that the knowledge contained in this crystal, compared to an ordinary thought stone, is as an ocean to a pond.'

I considered this as I gazed at the little stone that Maram had yet to put away.

'It may be,' Master Juwain continued, 'that the akashic crystal holds the wisdom of the Elder Ages.'

The ancient stones of which the library was made suddenly seemed small and cold. The Brotherhood school, built in the Age of the Mother, was many thousands of years old – almost as old as any building on Ea. And yet it was said that even this great span of time was really very little. As a year is to an age, so is an entire age of Ea to one of the Elder Ages, before Elahad and the Star People bore the Lightstone to earth.

'But how could it?' I asked. 'The knowledge that Elahad and his kindred brought with them perished with them. This is known. This you taught me, even when I was a boy.'

Master Juwain sighed and said, 'It would seem that some of what is known is known wrongly.'

'Then how do you know,' I asked, pointing at Maram's thought stone 'that the knowledge contained in *this* gelstei, and the others, is true?'

'I don't,' Master Juwain said. 'It must be tested, as all knowledge and supposition must be. But it *has* been tested, many times, by the ancients who placed it there. And I have tested it against all that I know and have experienced, and through reason. There is a certain flavor to that which is fact and another to wild fancies.'

I bowed my head to him that this was so. I told him, 'If you believe it's true, that's good enough for me.'

'I *believe* that the wisdom of the Elder Ages was preserved. Somehow. And that, once a time, this akashic crystal did exist. The question is, does it still? And where might it be found?'

'Not in Khaisham, I hope,' Maram put in. 'When I think of all the books that burned there, the people, too . . . and the gelstei, so many, too many, too bad.'

For a moment, Maram lost himself in memories of that horrible night in which Count Ulanu the Cruel had ordered the destruction of one of Ea's greatest wonders. But Master Juwain, I saw, was looking toward the future instead of the past. His eyes were bright with dreams.

'It would seem,' I said to him, 'that you believe the akashic crystal *does* still exist. And that you know where it might be found.'

We smiled at each other then, and he said, 'Well, Val, I admit that here knowledge must yield to supposition. But late in the Age of Law, a Master Savon recorded that the akashic crystal was hidden away to keep it safe. There are verses that tell of this. Do you remember the famous one about Ea's vilds?'

I remembered very well the Lokilani's magic wood which Master Juwain called a vild and the verse that described it:

> There is a place 'tween earth and time,
> In some forgotten misty clime
> Of woods and brooks and vernal glades,
> Whose healing magic never fades.
>
> An island in the greenest sea,
> Abode of deeper greenery
> Where giant trees and emeralds grow,
> Where leaves and grass and flowers glow.
>
> And there no bitter bloom of spite
> To blight the forest's living light,
> No sword, no spear, no axe, no knife
> To tear the sweetest sprigs of life.

The deeper life for which we yearn,
Immortal flame that doesn't burn,
The sacred sparks, ablaze, unseen –
The children of the Galadin.

Beneath the trees they gloze and gleam,
And whirl and play and dance and dream
Of wider woods beyond the sea
Where they shall dwell eternally.

As I recited this well-known work, the words seemed to hang in the library's still air like dreams. Flick flamed brightly and whirled about to the verses' music. When I had finished, Master Juwain smiled at me and said, 'Very good. And very true, as we have seen. But someone – I couldn't determine who – rewrote these lines to tell of *another* Vild where the crystal must have been hidden. Listen:

There is a place 'tween earth and time,
In some secluded misty clime
Of woods and brooks and vernal glades,
Whose healing magic never fades.

An island in a grass-girt sea,
Unseen its lasting greenery
Where giant trees and emeralds grow,
Where leaves and grass and flowers glow.

And there the memory crystal dwells
Sustained by forest sentinels
Of fiery form and splendid mien:
The children of the Galadin.

And they forever long to wake,
To praise, exalt and music make,
Breathe life through sacred memories,
Recall the ancient harmonies.

Beneath the trees they rise and ring,
And whirl and play and soar and sing
Of wider woods beyond the sea
Where they shall dwell eternally.

'Do you see?' Master Juwain said. 'If Kane told true, we know that there are at least five Vilds somewhere on Ea.'

'Kane told true,' I said with sudden assurance.

'And if these *verses* tell true, there must be a lake somewhere in the middle of one of Ea's grasslands, and an island in the middle of it.'

'Why a lake?' Maram asked. 'The Vild we discovered in Alonia was in the middle of the forest, and yet the verses described it as "An island in the greenest sea".'

'Because the *new* verses,' Master Juwain said, 'tell of a *grass-girt* sea. That can only be a lake.'

'Metaphors,' Maram grumbled as he yawned. 'Poetic fancies.'

'No, I think not,' Master Juwain said. 'There is a certain precision here. The maker of the verse might have written of a *grassy* sea, mightn't he? Why grass-*girt*, then?'

'Ah, who could ever know?'

Master Juwain smiled at Maram's crabbiness, then said, 'I once read of an invisible island in the middle of a lake. Until tonight, I thought *that* story was a fancy.'

Something sounded deep within me and I looked at Master Juwain through the candles' flickering light. 'And where was this lake, then?'

'At the edge of the Wendrush. Where the grasslands come up against the curve of the Morning Mountains, above the Snake River.'

I nodded my head, for I had once seen this lake on a map. 'That's Kurmak country – perhaps Atara has finished her business in Tria and has returned there.'

I gazed out the windows at the stars in the sky to the west. It seemed that, just then, these bright bits of light could be no brighter than my eyes.

'Val!' Maram half-shouted. 'I hope you're not thinking what I *think* you're thinking!'

'I must know,' I said to him.

'But Val, why do we need to go looking for this Vild and some old crystal? Almost everyone already *believes* you to be the Maitreya. And when we reach Tria, I'm sure you'll prove this to everyone's satisfaction.'

'I must know, Maram,' I said again. 'Before we reach Tria, I must truly know.'

I drew my sword then and held it straight out toward the west. Once this bright blade of silustria had pointed me toward the Lightstone; now it pointed me toward my fate.

'This lake,' I said, 'lies along the way to Tria.'

'A way without roads,' Maram grumbled. 'A way through the Kurmak's lands and then through unknown parts of Alonia.'

'The Kurmak will give us safe passage,' I said with sudden certainty. 'Sajagax will. He is Atara's grandfather, and he'll have to offer her friends hospitality.'

For a while, as dawn's red glow brightened the windows, we stood among the books and little gelstei telling tales of Sajagax, the Kurmak's famous chieftain. We debated whether to seek the akashic crystal in his lands. Master Juwain seemed willing to risk his life – if not the Lightstone itself – in discovering what knowledge the crystal might contain. I held that we would face risks along whatever road we took, and of what use would the Lightstone ever be if we never learned its secrets?

And so in the end even Maram agreed to this new quest. Master Juwain locked the drawers containing the thought stones and returned the keys to Master Tavian. Then we rejoined the Guardians where they waited in the cool air in front of the Library's doors. It fell upon me to tell them what we had decided. Only a few of them seemed dismayed at the prospect of venturing into the Wendrush. But Baltasar – and many others – counted it as a reasonably safe journey. They reaffirmed their allegiance to me as Knight of the Swan. In the end, as Baltasar said, it was upon me to decide whither the Lightstone should go.

We rode back down to the Tournament Grounds in the quiet of a lovely morning. Dew sparkled from the blades of grass by the road, and bright birds chirped all along the way. It was good to see our familiar pavilions flapping in the breeze. The news that the Guardians would be riding through the Wendrush spread quickly through our encampment – and then through the whole of the Tournament Grounds. Lord Lansar Raasharu approached me to request that he accompany us on our way toward Tria, and I could not refuse him. Estrella, at first, clung to my waist, and then followed me about like a lost puppy for the rest of the day. Finally Lord Harsha took me aside and said to me, 'She refuses to return home with our other country-men. The girl is half-mad, it seems, and is determined to remain with you.'

'Yes, it's impossible to dissuade her,' I said. 'And perhaps there's no need. She can ride well enough now to keep up with us.'

'You shouldn't be taking her on what might be a dangerous journey, Lord Valashu. But since you're determined, yourself, it should be said that a young girl should not go forth alone in the company of a hundred and twenty men.'

'What do you propose, sir?'

'That she rides with Behira and me, and sleeps in our tent as she did along the way to Nar.'

191

'Very well, then,' I said. 'But would you take *your* daughter into dangerous lands?'

Lord Harsha sighed and rubbed his crippled leg. His single eye fastened on me like a grappling iron, and he said, 'It would seem that Behira is determined, too. We're a determined people, aren't we? The Wendrush *might* prove dangerous. But Tria certainly will, for Sar Maram, who seems determined to drink or dally his way to his doom. And that is why we, who still love him, must go with him to protect him.'

'Oh, it's a matter of *love*, is it?'

'Indeed it is. My love for my daughter and my hope for her happiness, in whatever strange soil it might take root.'

'My friend will no doubt be pleased with your devotion.'

'Well, Sar Maram has proved himself a great knight, hasn't he? Then, too, it's said that no one should die before he's seen Tria.'

In the end, I agreed to take Lord Harsha with me. I would be glad for the fellowship of this crusty old warrior, not to mention his sword. Then, too, as he had said, it would be good for Estrella to keep company with Behira, who was almost like a mother to her.

Late that afternoon, our numbers increased by five more. True to his word, King Danashu chose his finest knights to take vows as Guardians. One of these – Sar Hannu of Daksh – had won a fourth in the long lance and had done quite well in archery and the sword. The other Valari kings, seeing this, insisted that their knights should join us, too. I could not refuse them. And so by the time evening settled over Nar, our encampment swelled with these new knights: ten Lagashuns and ten from Waas, and fifteen Atharians. My uncle, Lord Viromar, found twelve Kaashans eager to ride with us, and one of these was Sar Laisu who had made his own quest to find the Lightstone. So far, this put 171 Guardians under my command. Although I felt sure of every one of them, I remembered too well that I had possessed similar confidence in Sivar of Godhra. I remembered, too, that it had been Lord Harsha who had originally proposed Sivar for the Guardians. He still suffered from the shame of this misjudgment. Therefore, to redeem him in the eyes of his friends, and in his own, I asked his help in approving these new knights. This he gave. After some hours of grilling them and looking at them closely with his blazing eye, he found all of them worthy. And so he found himself worthy to give service to his king's son, and we were both glad for that.

The last king to ride into our encampment with a contingent of knights was King Waray. He held his sharp nose high as he presented Sar Varald, Sar Ishadar, Lord Noldru the Bold and seventeen others.

Although he didn't say it, I knew that he wished to choose at least as many Taroners as there were Ishkans for the Guardians. I was glad for these new men, and told King Waray this. But, as I had with King Hadaru, I admitted that it would not do to take more than these 191 Guardians into the Wendrush and then into Alonia.

'Sajagax will have to welcome Master Juwain, Maram and me,' I said to him. 'It's to be hoped that he'll also welcome knights who ride with me – but certainly there is a number beyond which even he will grow wary.'

'Your concern for the concerns of our enemies is touching,' King Waray said.

'Sajagax is no enemy of the Valari.'

'Is he not? He has fought two battles with the Ishkans and has thrice tried to invade Anjo.'

'Yes, but there has been peace between them these last ten years.'

'Even so, he would not welcome King Hadaru or King Danashu on his lands. And likely not King Sandarkan, King Mohan or myself. Neither King Kurshan. And so we all must take the Nar road to Tria.'

'It's likely to be the safer road.'

'It is. And that is the point. We believe that the Lightstone should take the safest route.'

'The Lightstone,' I said, 'will be safe enough with the Guardians. You have my promise that we'll bring it into Tria.'

'By yourselves. As you'll bring *yourself*, Lord Valashu. But you should know that some of the other kings believe your place is with us.'

'Does King Mohan say this, then? King Hadaru?'

'Well, no, not yet. They're inclined to ride with their own retinues, by themselves, to Tria. But if the Maitreya – the man who would be proclaimed as such – if *he* were to take the Nar road, then all of us might be persuaded to ride with him.'

It was a grand thing that King Waray proposed: the kings of the Valari riding together into Tria, their helms and armor shining brightly, their emblems bold beneath the sun – and with me and the Lightstone in the lead. For a moment, I was tempted to abandon my quest to recover the akashic crystal. But then I shook my head and said to King Waray, 'You know why I must journey into the Wendrush.'

'Yes, I *do* know why,' he said. 'And you must be honored for this. Just as you must be honored for another thing.'

Beneath the noise of our encampment, King Waray's shining eyes grew quiet with a sad sincerity. For a moment, I trusted him. I saw that he was truly a man of aspirations who had never been able to live up to his ideals.

'Lord Valashu,' he told me, 'it's said that you have the power to make others feel what is in your heart.'

'Sometimes, that is true.'

'Then you must also have the power *not* to persuade others this way. You must know how I, of all men, appreciate your restraint in this with me.'

I *did* know this, and I bowed my head to him. I said, 'You speak of honor, King Waray. But how can one honor anyone while doing violence to his soul?'

'How indeed, my young friend? Perhaps you *should* ride with us to Tria. But since you can't, perhaps *I* can keep the spirit of your dreams alive among the other kings.'

'Thank you,' I said, bowing my head again. 'You honor me.'

'Excellent,' he said. 'Now I must excuse myself and wish you well on your journey. Until we meet in Tria.'

And with that, he clasped my hand in his and rode off into the night.

The following morning, the Guardians assembled along the road outside our encampment. With hundreds of horses pawing the earth and men laughing in the early light, I arranged for the new knights to ride among the old, as I had with the Ishkans. I left Baltasar to see that this was accomplished. And then I went inside Asaru's pavilion, where my brother had been moved, to say goodbye to him. For in a few moments I would be traveling north and east, while he must recuperate here before returning to Mesh.

'*This* farewell,' he said, 'pains me almost more than when you set out to find the Lightstone. And it truly pains me more than my shoulder.'

He winced as he sat up in his bed and looked at me. Yarashan, who had hardly moved from his side for most of two days, handed him a cup of steaming tea, and said, 'All right, then, we'll remain here until Asaru is well enough to ride. Another week, and we can –'

'Two weeks would be better,' I broke in. 'As Master Juwain has prescribed.'

'All right, *two* weeks, then,' Yarashan muttered. 'Long enough that we'll miss the conclave, even if we start out after you.'

Asaru smiled at him and said, 'We'll have to hope our little brother can conclude this affair without us.'

His eyes were like two stars as he looked at me. He seemed to sense that my becoming champion had changed something in me. He grasped my hand and pulled me closer to him so that he could embrace me.

'Farewell, Valashu,' he said to me. 'Return home soon.'

After I had embraced Yarashan as well, I went outside and climbed on my horse. And so I led the Guardians out of Nar along the King's Road as we had come. As in our entrance into the city, many people lined the way to cheer us along. And to cheer me. Cries of 'Champion!' 'Lord of Light!' rang out into the air and almost drowned out the thunderous clopping of the horses' hooves. The gold medallion that King Waray had given me pulled heavily at my neck even as the Lightstone (now borne by Sar Hannu) impelled me down the road toward the west, where I might finally learn its secrets.

It was good to go forth with friends and companions into the fresh summer breeze blowing across the land; soon we reached the rippling wheatfields outside the city. I remained alert for sign of discord among the Guardians, for now it wasn't just Meshians and Ishkans riding together, but Anjoris, Kaashans, Atharians, Taroners, Waashians and Lagashuns. Now there were many more possibilities for knight falling out against knight and renewing old hatreds. But *these* knights, it seemed, during the week of the tournament, had grown tired of fighting – at least of fighting each other. In their easy laughter and recounting of feats, I sensed a camaraderie growing as it often did with men who suffered dangers together. Then, too, they were men of honor who strove to honor their vows and their charge to guard the Lightstone. They could not do this as quarrelsome individuals loyal to their kings, but only as Valari knights who rode with me. My gaining of the championship, I knew, had been vital in gaining the devotion of these proud men. For no Valari warrior likes to be led by one of unproven prowess, and in my victory they saw the possibility of their own achievements and the realization of their deepest dreams.

That day I rode at the head of our three long columns, and Estrella rode beside me. She had a calm and gentle touch with her little gelding; I had never seen anyone learn a horse's ways so quickly. Riding in the open air seemed to please her immensely, as did the wind and sun and smell of the summer flowers in the rolling fields about us. Her slender body was stronger than it looked. She had good stamina for continuing on mile after mile and taking only a few breaks, to water and feed the horses and to feed ourselves. Thirty miles we covered on that first day of our journey out from Nar and as many the next. The unaccustomed abrasion of sitting in a saddle all day must have pained her, but she made no complaint – neither with her ever-silent lips nor with her dark, expressive eyes. Often she would brush aside the soft curls from her face and look at me happily. She seemed always to want to be near me, to serve me, to remind me of the best parts of myself. It made her happy to make *me* happy, and I loved her for that.

And yet, beneath her radiant smiles and quicksilver expressions of delight, something dark and heavy seemed to pull at her heart like a great weight. I felt this most keenly on the evening of our third day of travel, when we reached Loviisa. We made camp by a stream in the hills overlooking the city; above us on the nearby hill loomed the old Aradar castle, abandoned when King Hadaru had built his wooden palace. As the sun set in the west beyond it, this huge pile of stone changed colors, from bone white to an almost glowing and blood-filled red. Estrella sat with me and my friends around our campfire, and she flitted about refilling my bowl with some succulent lamb stew and pouring water into my cup. And in the middle of tendering these little devotions, something about the castle caught her eye. She froze like a fawn caught in a snow tiger's icy stare. As she stared at the castle's keep, at its flaming western wall, fear rushed through her little chest like poison, and her bright and dreamy face fell ashen with nightmare. She began shivering violently. Was she recalling the murder of her sister servants in my father's castle and her helplessness at being trapped outside on its pitch-black wall? Or was she reliving some hideous torment visited upon her in Argattha? She couldn't tell me. All I could do was to cover her with my cloak and hold her next to me until this evil spell had passed. But the immense sorrow that welled up out of her was too much for me to bear. It was like listening to the cries of a million children who had lost their mothers. I found myself suddenly bowing down my head and weeping into Estrella's thick hair even as she broke open and wept as well.

Later, after Behira had taken her off to bed, I walked alone up toward the castle. I stood beneath its towering battlements and looked up at the stars. Why, I wondered, were there so many black spaces between these brilliant islands of light? Why must darkness descend every night upon the world, and inevitably, upon men's souls? Was there no help for suffering, then? Men called me the Maitreya, but the cold wind falling down from the sky made me shiver and doubt this, for I couldn't even ease the anguish of a single little girl. As the wolves howled in the hills around me, I wanted to throw back my head and howl, too: at the lights in the heavens, at the pain of the world, at the fire that ignited inside me and made me burn for deeper life.

The next day was one of bright sun and skies as clear and blue as sapphire. Our way for the next forty or fifty miles, until we reached the mountains, was through a rolling and gradually rising country of rich farms and even richer pastures where countless sheep covered the green hillsides like blankets of white wool. No good roads led this way, only dirt tracks winding around wheatfields and occasionally cutting straight through acres of rye or barley. The Guardians, however, had no trouble negotiating such terrain. Upon abandoning our baggage train in Loviisa, we moved even more quickly and easily, though along somewhat less straight a path. In many places, our three columns had to be consolidated to two or even to one: a single long line of Valari knights strung out like glittering diamonds on a necklace. Late that morning, Maram suggested that we ride together behind the rear of the columns so that we might have a space to talk.

'You take too much to heart,' he said to me.

'No, in truth, too little.'

'You can't help what you can't help, Val.'

'But it *must* be helped,' I said. 'Everything must be.'

'But the world is the way it is. The way the One made it to be.'

I thought about this as I tried not to choke on the dust that the hundreds of horses ahead of us kicked up into the air. I thought of the letter Salmelu had delivered to me, and I said, 'Sometimes it seems that Morjin was right, after all.'

Maram always seemed to know what I was thinking. He asked, 'Do you mean, that we should hate the One? Do you . . . *hate*, then?'

'Sometimes, I almost do,' I said. 'When I remember Khaisham, when I think of Atara. And now, when Estrella can't even tell me what she suffers.'

'Morjin wrote that such suffering ultimately leads to our salvation – as I remember, through torturing innocents and rising above them.'

'Yes, and there he errs. In this lies much of his evil. But he is surely right that we were meant to rise, to be as angels. The world is the way the One made it to be, you say. And so are we. Surely the One made us to *make* a better world.'

'Well, ending war is one thing. But you can't end suffering itself.'

'Perhaps not. But what is the *meaning* of the Maitreya, then? What would the meaning of my life be if I didn't at least try?'

For much of the morning, as we rode through the pretty country of Ishka, we discussed the prophecies about the Maitreya recorded in the *Saganom Elu* and Master Juwain's hope of discovering much more in the akashic crystal. By noon we had put ten miles behind us, and by the end of the day, another ten. When we made camp in a fallow field that evening, our talk finally turned to more immediate things: to the fine weather we were enjoying; to the high spirits of the knights of eight kingdoms riding as brothers; to the lofty, white peaks of the Morning Mountains rising up before us to the west. As always, Maram feared encountering bears in these wooded heights. His fear increased mile after mile the following day and did not abate, not even when we began digging the fortifications for our nightly camp in the forest below Ishka's largest lake. For he remembered that just to the north of this lake lay the Black Bog.

'There are worse things than bears there,' he said. 'Dark creatures and dragons, I think.'

'But we encountered none on our passage of it.'

'Did we not? What was that ugly thing that flew across the sky?'

The Black Bog, it was said, was a portal to the Dark Worlds. On our nightmare journey through it, we had walked on one or more of these worlds before miraculously finding our way back home. It worried Maram that if we could wander out of the bog onto the familiar soil of Ea, so could other things from other places.

'What of the Grays?' he said to me. 'And what if there are worse things than those Soul-Suckers? What of the Dark One himself?'

To the sound of the Guardians digging a moat in the black earth around our encampment, I thought of Angra Mainyu, once the greatest of the Galadin – and now, if Master Juwain was right, the greatest of ghuls who would bring evil to all worlds. What shape had this once-bright being taken on? Was he still fair of form and wondrous in aspect? Or had the vile work of ages twisted him like a blackened worm so that he was hideous to behold?

'Angra Mainyu,' I reassured Maram, 'is bound on Damoom.'

'So Kane says – but what if he's wrong? And what if Morjin finds a way to free him?'

'He won't,' I said, 'as long as we guard the Lightstone. Now, why don't we finish making camp and raise a glass of beer – and forget all this talk of dark creatures and such?'

That night Maram raised more than one glass of thick, dark Ishkan beer. But he did not quite forget his dread of things that might come for him out of the night. And neither did I. Although the Black Bog lay a good twenty-five miles to the north of us, a hint of its terrors wafted across the lake in the faint fetor of rotting vegetation and mires that could suck a man down into the earth. It seemed to cling to our garments and to work its way inside us, even as we broke camp early the next morning and began climbing into the clearer and sweeter air of the mountains. A sense of overwhelming wrongness pervaded me. I felt something pursuing me, not necessarily from behind us or from any direction in space, but rather in time, from the past – or perhaps the future. It had the feel of Morjin. But in it also was Angra Mainyu's hatred of life, and all life's cruelty to life; it reeked of blood and screams and the sickness of the soul in surrendering to its worst nightmares. Didn't all evil, like decaying flesh, have the same foul odor? Didn't suffering, too? It came to me then that the terrible pain Estrella carried inside her might not have its source in Argattha after all. For if all things took their being from the One – fallen angels and swords no less flowers and trees and bright, singing birds – then might not the blame for Estrella's suffering be laid at the workings and will of this terrible One?

For the next two days, this realization oppressed me. I did not speak of it to Maram or Master Juwain, for they had trials of their own. Our passage through the mountains was difficult. The roads over these great peaks of the Shoshan range were slanted and bad. Fierce summer rains found us working our way up or down steep tracks of stone and dirt, which turned to streams of slippery mud beneath our horses' driving hooves. On one of the numerous switchbacks snaking up the sides of the slopes, Sar Jarlath's horse lost its footing and fell against some rocks near a spruce tree, breaking its leg with a sharp crack and ripping open its belly. Sar Jarlath plunged into these rocks as well; miraculously, he suffered only a broken arm. It was not a bad break, and Master Juwain mended it quickly. But the horse had to be put to death. This mercy killing saddened all of us, for he was a great-spirited warhorse that Sar Jarlath had ridden to an honorable seventh place in the long lance competition.

On the last day in the mountains, we passed by the Ishkan fortress of Karkallu and came down into the narrow valley of the Snake River. Beneath gray, heavy skies, we followed its bends and rapids toward the west. It was drier in this broken land, and the silver maples and oaks around us soon gave way to cottonwoods and hawthorn that grew along the watercourses of the Wendrush. We had our first view of the great grasslands late in the afternoon on the fifth of Marud. I led our company up a rocky hill at the mouth of the valley, and there before us for many miles lay a sea of green. Far out to the curving horizon – west, north and south – these dark plains lit up with flashes of lightning from the even darker clouds pressing down upon them. Their oppressive flatness was broken only by a few hummocks and the blue-gray track of the Snake River winding its way toward the much greater Poru a hundred miles farther on. To the south of the Snake, the Adirii tribe of the Sarni held sway; they were allied with the Kurmak, whose lands stretched out north of the river and west of the mountains. Into this open country of antelope, sagosk and lions, I sent three knights: Sar Avram, Lord Noldru the Bold and Baltasar. They were to seek out the headmen of the Kurmak's clans, and if possible, Sajagax himself. For I did not want to lead a force of nearly two hundred knights into unknown country without the permission of those who possessed it.

We made camp on a little triangle of land at the confluence of the Snake and a mountain stream that flowed into it. We fortified it heavily. It would be a bad place to be caught in the event of a thunderstorm and a flood. But there, at the gateway to the Wendrush, I feared raging Sarni warriors on horses more than I did raging waters.

And so we waited there for four days, resting, repairing ripped tents and other gear, polishing our armor and sharpening our swords. I took to spending part of each morning with Estrella. She gave signs that she wanted me to teach her to play my flute, and this I did. She learned its ways even more quickly than had riding her horse. In her long, tapering fingers, this slip of wood came alive with bright, happy sounds. She seemed to speak with music, with her beautiful hands, with the expressions of her lively face. And most of all, as her notes trilled sweetly to harmonize with the piping of the birds and the rushing of the river, the flames of her being seemed to pour forth like liquid fire from her lovely eyes, and that was the most marvelous music of all.

And yet there were moments, as at the monstrous Aradar castle, when her songs swelled with an unutterable sadness. It seemed that some black and bottomless chasm opened inside her and cut her off from that which she most desired. Then her music became a plaint and a plea that hurt me to hear and filled my heart with an unbearable pain. Listening to her play this way one morning, I knew that I must find a way to help her. I had no power to straighten crooked limbs or mend torn flesh, as Joakim the blacksmith's son, was said to do; this I had proved in my failure to cure a cripple I had encountered along the road to Nar and again with Asaru at the tournament. But might I, somehow, be able to heal a broken soul? Baltasar would say I could; so would his father, Lansar Raasharu, and many others. The words of Kasandra's prophecy sounded inside me like trumpets then. It came to me that Estrella *would* show me the Maitreya: but only in the act of my easing her long, deep and terrible suffering.

On the last morning of our sojourn, I found a spot on some rocks by the stream to sit with her. The air was sweet with spray and the song of two bluebirds warbling at each other: *cheer cheer-lee churr*. Estrella brought forth my flute, and I brought forth the Lightstone. All along the way from Mesh she had shown little interest in the golden cup. But now she held out her hand for me to give it to her. This I did. If I expected it to flare brightly and bathe her in its magical light, I was disappointed. The cup remained quiescent and

200

shone no more brightly than did ordinary gold. She sat for a long while gazing at it with her deep, wild eyes. Then she smiled and dipped the cup into the stream. She held it to her lips, drinking down the clear water in three quick swallows. It seemed that she was only thirsty.

'The Lightstone holds more than water,' I said to her as I took back the cup. 'Here, let me show you.'

As she breathed lightly on the end of my flute, her bright eyes were like mirrors showing *me* the deepest parts of myself. And calling me to bring forth the music inside me. She sat watching me and waiting as she played my flute and looked into my eyes. She looked at the Lightstone, too. The sun's rays streamed down from the sky and filled it with a golden radiance. I felt some part of this heavenly fire pass through my hands into me. It warmed my blood with an unbearably sweet pressure that broke open my heart. Everything that was there came pouring out of me and into her. Her face lit up like the sun itself then. She put aside my flute and laughed in her sweet, silent way until her eyes glistened with tears. She stared at the Lightstone, now shining with a numinous intensity. Its brilliance dazzled her; she sat frozen by the stream, her eyes wide open to the clear, blue sky and the shimmering cottonwood trees. I had a strange sense that she was seeing not just their billowing canopies but millions of separate silver-green leaves. It was as if she was aware of the One pouring out its light through all things. And shining with its greatest splendor in her. For a moment, it seemed, she was swept away by both these outer and inner luminosities, and there was no difference. She seemed to remain in this river of light forever. At last, her eyes blazed into mine as she returned to the world. The smile on her face made my heart sing. I sensed that, at least for a time, the ground of her being had knitted itself together and she was made whole again.

Something changed in me, too. Some of the terrible doubt that had oppressed me for many miles suddenly left me, like a wound lanced and emptied of poison. Estrella and I returned to our encampment to take our midday meal, and it seemed I stood straighter and walked with a lighter step. Sunjay Naviru, Lord Raasharu and others looked at me strangely, as if I had donned a magical garment woven of light.

And then later that afternoon, my happiness swelled like the sea, for out of the steppe to the west, three riders crested a knoll and galloped toward us. I recognized the blue rose of Baltasar's emblem and those of Sar Avram and Lord Noldru. They brought straight to me two pieces of great, good news: the lake told of in Master Juwain's verses had been located near the Snake River only thirty miles to the west. And Trahadak the Elder of the Zakut clan had invited us, in the name of Sajagax, to cross his lands freely on our way to seek out Sajagax and Alonia.

15

At dawn the next morning I led the Guardians out onto the Wendrush. The plains to the west blazed red with the fire of the rising sun, while the cool turf over which we rode remained steeped in the mountains' shadow. But soon the sun rose higher, and we broke free from the zone of darkness into the sun's strong, streaming rays. The air clicked with the sound of grasshoppers and buzzed with bees. Long grasses swished beneath us, scraping our horses' flanks and across our diamond-sheathed legs. We followed the general course of the winding river toward the lake that Baltasar had told of. If he was right about its location, we should reach it near the end of a long day's ride. And if he was right about Trahadak the Elder's assurance of safe passage, we should encounter no Sarni warriors that day.

'The Zakut encampment lies forty miles to the north of the lake,' he had told me during our council the night before. 'Along the river, at this time of year, the Zakut – all the Kurmak – do not pitch their tents.'

'And why is that?' Maram had asked him.

'Because it seems the river is given to flooding.'

'*Flooding*, you say? Ah, well, water is only water. But can this Trahadak be trusted?'

'The Sarni are savages, it's true,' Baltasar had admitted. 'But we've given them a gift of gold, and they have always been known to honor their word.'

It vexed me more than a little that I had to rely on Trahadak's word in crossing this unknown country. And so I sent outriders ahead us and behind to scout for bands of warriors that Trahadak might not know of. I did not really fear attack from any small numbers; it seemed that the only force capable of threatening us was that led by Trahadak himself. Even so, I did not want to be unprepared.

All that morning, however, we saw no beings that went on two legs, except ourselves and some flocks of ostrakats who waved their long necks at us and hissed fiercely to warn us away. The Sarni, of course, even though they are human beings like any others, do not go forth on two legs, for they are masters of the horse and worship this noble animal as others do the sun and sky. A Sarni warrior, it is said, measures his wealth by four things: the gold beaten into the ornaments that encircle his limbs; the shaggy sagosk that he herds; the women he has taken as wives; and the number and quality of horses that he rides. A man, it is also said, might have to wait many years to marry; he might be stripped of gold and lose all of his sagosk in raids. But a man must possess at least one horse, or he is not counted a man.

As we rode along in our three columns, we kept the curves of the river to our left, sometimes at a distance of a mile, sometimes only a hundred yards away, for we wanted to follow as straight a course as possible. Around noon, though, we had to circle to the north to avoid a herd of wild sagosk grazing along the river. But in so doing, we managed to flush a pride of lions that stalked the sagosk and preyed upon their stragglers and young. Seven great, yellow-eyed beasts burst from the grass in a shock of bunching muscles and unleashed power. The huge cats frightened our horses, who screamed and reared up, kicking out their legs and bucking Sar Viku and four other knights from their backs. The lions, perhaps frightened by the glister of our diamond armor and nearly two hundred long lances pointed at them, ran off into the grass. It was a wonder, I thought, that Sar Viku and the others took only bruises from their violent falls.

Toward the end of the day, with the sun bloodying the clouds on the western horizon, we crested a hummock and finally sighted the lake about five miles ahead of us in a depression in the earth many miles wide. The Snake River flowed into it. Somewhere to the west of this hazy blue body of water, it must also flow out. I wanted to ride closer to get a better look at this mysterious lake; I had considered making camp on its shores that night. But it had grown too late. It would be better, I thought, to dig our moat and build our stockade from the fallen wood down by the river to the left of us. There, with the river bending sharply south through the grassy steppe before bending back north and west, we would be protected by water on three sides.

And so we rode down into this sheltered pocket of land and set to work. Guardians sheathed their lances and drew forth spades from the packhorses to dig in the tough, sun-seared turf. I posted Sar Kimball and three other Guardians as sentries on a rise a few hundred yards farther out on the steppe, away from the river. It was one of these, Sar

Varald, who broke the peace of that quiet place. The sudden blare of his trumpet seemed to shatter the very air. I looked to the north to see these four Guardians galloping toward us.

'Mount!' I cried out. I ran over to where Altaru was tethered to some branches that we had intended to fashion into a fence. All around me, between tents lying limp on the ground, in the chaos of our camp, Guardians were running for their horses, too. 'Mount and form up!'

As Sar Varald and the others came pounding up to us, I commanded the Guardians to array themselves in three lines facing north toward the rise overlooking the river. Twenty of these, by arrangement, remained unhorsed. They were our best archers, and I posted them, ten to either side of us, on our flanks. While the rest of us sat upon our snorting horses with our lances pointing north, the archers strung their great longbows and began building a fence of arrows in front of them by sticking many long, feathered shafts point-down into the ground.

'Treachery!' Sar Kimball cried out as he and the other sentries reined up his huge sorrel at the front of our lines. There, at our center, with the late sun making brilliant the diamond armor of two hundred Valari knights, I waited with Maram and Lansar Raasharu to my right, while Baltasar and Sunjay Naviru sat on top of their mounts to my left. 'Treachery, Lord Valashu! The Sarni are upon us!'

'How many?' I asked him. I gazed at the grassy rise a few hundred yards away, waiting.

'Two hundred,' he said. 'Perhaps more – it was hard to tell.'

I turned to look past the two lines of knights backing us up. There, behind our center, Lord Harsha sat on his horse, and Behira and Estrella sat on theirs. Skyshan of Ki, who bore the Lightstone, was with them, along with Sar Adamar, Sar Jarlath and Sar Hannu of Anjo. If the worst befell, these knights would die to a man protecting Skyshan, even as we protected them. And Lord Harsha would certainly fight to the death in defense of his daughter and Estrella.

'Two hundred,' Lord Raasharu repeated in his calm, clear voice. No man in our lines had more experience of battle than he. 'Even odds.'

He said this, I thought, to inspirit us. For the odds were not equal. I remembered what my father had taught me as a boy: that while we Valari were nearly always invincible on the ground of the Morning Mountains, here, on the endless grasslands of the Wendrush, against the Sarni, our heavily armored knights were at a great disadvantage.

'There they are!' Maram suddenly cried out as he pointed ahead of us.

Along the line of the rise, some two hundred and twenty men on horses suddenly appeared against the cloud-dappled sky. They wore conical helmets polished brightly and black leather breast-pieces, hardened and studded with steel. Gorgets of gold gleamed around their necks, and many of these barbaric warriors sported golden circlets on their bare arms. Their faces were painted blue. Long, drooping, yellow moustaches spilled down beneath their chins. Each of them held in his hand a double-curved bow made of sinew, wood and horn. These powerful bows – and the arrows they fired – could work quick slaughter of their enemies from distances that matched the range of our longbows. If not for a miracle, I thought, they might slaughter *us*: we Valari, who were the most ancient and hated of their enemies.

'Baltasar!' I cried out as I stared at these wild men. 'Which one is Trahadak – can you point him out?'

I vowed to myself that if the Sarni charged us, the treacherous Trahadak the Elder should be the first to die.

Baltasar held his hand to the ridge of his helmet as he scanned the warriors before us. He shook his head, saying, 'The distance is too great.'

'Damn them!' Maram said. I saw that he had taken out his firestone. The cracked crystal remained useless in his hand. 'Damn this gelstei! If this were made whole again, I'd give them a little fire for turning against us. Do you think they've come for more gold?'

I couldn't say. It seemed certain that they couldn't have come for the gold of the Lightstone, for Baltasar had kept it and our mission a secret. But surely the Sarni wanted something of us, if only our horses, our arms and perhaps our lives.

'Do you think they want to parlay?' Maram asked. 'Surely they'd want to parlay before giving battle. Wouldn't they?'

I scanned the rise ahead of us. I saw no white flag raised, only standards embroidered with various animals that might be emblems of various clans. To the west, the clouds along the horizon broke apart, and the sun's rays streamed low and glinted from the Sarni's two hundred and twenty helmets. I did not know what they were waiting for.

'Perhaps they're only the vanguard,' Maram said. 'Perhaps more of them are coming. Should we retreat?'

We could not retreat. With the cold, rushing river to our back and to either side of us, we had no escape in those directions. Escape, in any case, out on the steppe, was impossible. The lithe and swift Sarni ponies could overtake our heavy warhorses even as the Sarni warriors, at full gallop, fired arrows at us and picked us off one by one.

'If only we'd had time to finish making camp,' Maram muttered.

'Then we'd be safe enough, wouldn't we? Ah, well, if they wait much longer, it will fall dark, and perhaps we can raise up a stockade against their arrows.'

But this hope, too, was futile. Surely our enemy, if they were indeed our enemy, would not allow us simply to go about our business of fortifying our camp. And even if they did, what would *we* do then? Cower behind our flimsy breastworks while the Sarni besieged us and waited for our food to run out? It seemed that I had led my men into a trap, though I couldn't see how I could have done otherwise; for us Valari, the entire steppe of the Wendrush was one enormous trap, from the Morning Mountains to the white peaks of the Nagarshath four hundred miles away. At no time in my life, except in Argattha, had I felt so helpless.

'What should we do, Val?' Maram asked me.

Two hundred silent knights along the lines to my right and left looked my way, and their black, blazing eyes seemed to ask me the same question. They were the finest of Valari warriors, and yet they were still men whose insides churned with dread as if they had swallowed whole bellyfuls of writhing worms.

There is always a way, I told myself, remembering how we had fought our way out of Argattha. *Always a way toward victory.*

I nudged Altaru out a few paces before turning right to ride down our line and then back to the left. I spoke no brave words to my men. But I looked at each of them eye to eye. I opened my heart to them. And so I passed to them the flaming torch that blazed inside me. An understanding passed back and forth between us, growing brighter and brighter, driving away fear and doubt.

'Champion!' they seemed to shout at me. 'Champion! Champion!'

A radiance lit up the center of my being with all brilliance and sound of a thunderbolt.

'Lord of Light! Lord of Light! Lord of Light!'

And then, as I remembered my purpose and who I really was, another thought came over me: *And there must be a way to end war.*

I returned to my place at the center of our line. To Maram, I said, 'What we will do is to fight like angels, if fight we must. But first we will seek peace.'

I called for a white flag of truce then. Sar Artanu brought the banner forward, and I took it from his hand.

'No, Val!' Baltasar called out as I made ready to ride forward. 'You forget yourself – your place is here, in command. Let me go instead.'

I considered giving the banner to him. But just then, from the rise before us, a harsh tattoo blared out from one of the Sarni's battle horns. The entire host of blue-faced warriors let loose a long and terrible battle cry. And then perhaps a hundred of them spurred their horses forward and charged down upon us.

'Oh, Lord!' Maram called out to me. 'It seems we'll have to fight, after all.'

In my haste to draw my sword, I dropped the white flag to the ground beneath us. Alkaladur's blade flared bright silver in the setting sun's light. I dreaded the thought of reddening it in the bodies of these screaming savages. My stomach tightened into a hard knot of pain; although it was not a warm day, sweat slicked my body beneath my diamond armor. My sword arm burned with a sick heat even as the shake and shudder of Altaru's trembling body beneath me filled mine with a rage to ride down our enemies and trample them into the grass.

Our archers began loosing their arrows before the Sarni did, for their longbows, cut of mountain yew, slightly outranged the Sarni's bows. The whine of feathered shafts split the air like huge insects flying furiously to drink blood. Three of the arrows found targets, but their companions all had bows of their own, and they were more than a hundred to our twenty archers. As they thundered closer, they began firing off arrows of their own. Hundreds of them hissed forth in a hazy cloud. The Sarni were the finest archers on earth. Even the difficulty of aiming at distant targets from on top of bounding ponies, it seemed, would not keep them very long from decimating us.

As I struggled to slow the wild beating of my heart, a great many arrows struck straight into us. Only our armor saved us. Arrow points broke against the rows of diamonds encasing our chests and limbs or glanced off altogether. The clacking of steel against these sparkling crystals was horrible to hear. And even more horrible to bear. An arrow bounced off my shoulder, bruising it. Another slammed into my belly, and nearly knocked the wind from me. A third pinged against my helmet. It was like being caught in the open in a hailstorm of death.

'Oh, Lord!' Maram called out next to me. 'Oh, Lord, oh, Lord!'

The Sarni drew closer, and I held my shield over my face. Five arrows struck against it; four of them pierced the silver swan and stars etched into its black steel and stuck there, rendering it useless. I cast it down on top of the white flag beneath me. Then Lansar Raasharu nudged his horse over to me and extended me *his* shield. 'Damn them! They've singled you out, Lord Valashu. Please take this and keep your face covered!'

'No, this is too much,' I said to him. 'You'll have nothing to cover yourself.'

208

'They're not concentrating on me. Now, please, take it and remember to angle it so that the arrows glance off.'

I nodded my head as more arrows whined past me. I strapped on his shield and said, 'Thank you.'

Down the line from me, Aivar of Taron cried out as an arrow pierced his eye. Other arrows found chinks in the diamond armor of other knights, killing or wounding them. An arrow tore into the flank of Sar Eladaru's horse, which screamed out its agony. In despair, one of the younger knights, Sar Shivalad cried out, 'Why don't they just kill *all* our horses and be done with us?'

But the Sarni do not kill horses; they would rather kill their mothers or wives. Any warrior who knowingly took aim at a horse in battle would be seized by his fellow warriors and staked out on the grass for the lions to eat. Even so, in any battle, even the finest of Sarni archers sometimes missed their marks.

'This is too much!' Maram muttered against the whine and clacking of the arrows and the Sarni warriors' terrible screams. 'What should we do, Val?'

'Wait,' I told him.

'But it's hopeless! If they don't kill us all on this charge, they will the next – or the one after that.'

'No!' I told him, remembering what Kane had said to me in Argattha. 'There might yet be a chance!'

With every yard that the hundred Sarni gained toward us, their arrows found their targets with ever greater accuracy and frequency. Three of my knights cried out as they fell from their horses, and then four more. I sensed that this emboldened the Sarni, even as our archers struck down three of them. Closer and closer they galloped, yelling at us and firing arrows with an almost drunken frenzy.

'Too close,' I whispered to myself as I peered over the rim of the shield that Lord Raasharu had given me. I studied the grassy undulations of the rapidly shrinking ground between our lines and the rampaging Sarni. And then I called out, 'First line! Lances ready! Charge!'

Not a single knight in the first line of the Guardians hesitated in spurring his horse forward. In truth, after the horrible helplessness of enduring the arrow storm, my knights exploded into action with a violent joy. Horses whinnied out their fury as my sixty knights drove them to a full gallop. The Sarni, it seemed, had been expecting just such a maneuver. For their tactics in battle were almost as old as the steppe itself: torment or tantalize the enemy into breaking ranks and charging – and then quickly retreat in order that they and their brethren might shoot their arrows from a safe distance. But the commander of *these* Sarni, I thought, had miscalculated the distances here. Either that, or he had no experience in battle against Valari knights.

Seeing us now thundering down upon them with our steel-pointed lances, the Sarni reined in their horses and wheeled about with amazing skill. Like a flock of birds suddenly changing direction, they began racing back toward their companions still waiting on the rise toward the north. They knew, even as I did, that their smaller ponies could always outdistance our heavy warhorses. That is, they could could either gain upon us or escape us over *long* distances.

Altaru, my fierce, black stallion, like the other horses along our charging line, was a sprinter. His great muscles gathered and exploded to the rhythm and beat of his driving legs. He snorted and sweated as we fairly flew through the air with my sixty companions a scant few yards behind us. Wind whipped into my face. I felt the fear of the Sarni warriors ahead of us, and smelled the blood of their wounded. We had the advantage of momentum and rushing upon them at a full gallop even as they were still building speed from their abrupt halt. We gained on them quickly. Many of them turned in their saddles to fire off quick shots at us; one of these sizzling arrows crashed into my hip with a sharp, piercing pain that enraged me. It enraged Altaru, too. He bore down upon the Sarni like a black fury ready to smash our enemy into the bloody grass with his great, pounding hooves.

BA-ROO! BA-ROO! BA-ROO!

One of the Sarni's warhorns blared out three times, and again, they halted and wheeled about. They had no intention of letting us ride them down and putting our lances through their backs.

'Death to the Valari!' their leader cried out. He was a large man with long blond hair flowing out beneath his shining helm and blue diamonds painted on his cheeks and forehead. 'Death to the Elahad!'

The Sarni faced us at close range over the trampled grass. Some shot arrows straight at us, and they killed three more knights. Many, though, had run out of arrows. These drew their curving sabers and clutched their little leather shields. Then, to their leader's command, they screamed as they spurred their horses toward us.

'Death to the Valari! Kill them all!'

They were a hundred to our sixty – now fifty-seven – but we were Valari knights, and so now the odds favored us. All along our charging line, one by one, my knights came up against the Sarni warriors. A dozen lances tore through leather armor and through the bodies of our enemies. Blood and froth sprayed the air as the screams of the dying shook the earth. A Sarni warrior shot an arrow straight into the mouth of Sar Jonawan; three others fired arrows at me that broke upon my armor. Two more warriors – one a huge man whose blue paint couldn't hide the scars on his face – charged at me screaming out their battle-cry. The scarred man reached me a moment before the other, and him I cleaved through the neck, splitting the gold gorget there and sweeping off his head in a single stroke. And on the backstroke, I turned in my saddle and lunged out toward the other side of me in a furious thrust that split open his friend's chest and pushed Alkaladur's point clean through his back. As I wrenched free my sword, it was as if my own heart had been wrenched from me. I screamed in agony. My enemies, in their last pulse of malice, seemed to grab my ribs from the inside and pull me down with them into death. Only Alkaladur saved me. My shining sword connected me to the sky and drew upon the deep currents of the earth. It drove back the icy nothingness, for a time, and filled me with new life.

'Sar Jarlath!' someone cried out.

I turned to see this large knight beset by four Sarni warriors. I whirled Altaru about and charged into them. I struck out to the right and left trying to protect him. My sword split open leather and skin and sent founts of blood spraying into the air. When the four warriors lay dead in the grass, Sar Jarlath raised his red-tipped lance toward me in gratitude for saving his life.

'Lord Valashu – behind you!'

In the melee of our two forces crashing together, a Sarni warrior on a dappled mare tried to sneak up behind me. Lansar Raasharu raced forward and intercepted him with a savage lance-thrust that tore through the man's eye. Other warriors screamed and descended upon us. Lord Raasharu, now shieldless, stabbed out with his lance again and again, even as I cut and lunged with my sword. A rage to kill leapt along my blood like fire. I felt it touch Lord Raasharu – or perhaps it was his own fury that burned into me. So it went all about us, my Guardians thrusting with their lances or whipping free their long kalamas in a rare rage to protect me and destroy our ancient enemy.

Soon many of the Sarni lay hacked and pierced on the grass. Our horses trampled their bodies; to the sound of steel clanging against steel was added the sickening crunch of iron-shod hooves breaking skin and bones. Those Sarni warriors not immediately engaged began racing back toward the position that the main body of their company still held on the rise. And then, one by one, any of these blue-faced savages who could broke off their engagements and joined the retreat. And we, of the long swords and the Morning Mountains, slaughtered the rest.

'Val, are you all right?' Maram gasped out as he rode up to me. His sword was red, and his face was white as he gazed at the carnage all about us. 'Oh, Lord, what a day! These Sarni have courage – but no care for their brothers.'

He pointed toward the hundred and twenty Sarni warriors watching from the rise, and he shook his head as if he couldn't understand why Trahadak the Elder, whoever he was, didn't order his men forward to aid their brethren. But if Trahadak had commanded such an advance of his reserve, so would I have done – as I still could.

I turned back toward the two lines of Guardians still waiting behind us across the sun-streaked steppe. I cupped my hand around my mouth and shouted, 'Archers mount! First line, to us, and charge! Second line follow at half speed!'

I nodded at Maram and at Lord Raasharu. To Baltasar and Sunjay Raviru and all the other knights who gathered about me in the middle of that bloody field, I called out, 'Let's break them!'

Again, I urged Altaru to a gallop, and fifty of my finest knights charged with me toward the rise. The remnants of the Sarni that we had butchered reached their line in a confusion of shouting men and bounding horses. As we surged up the slope, arrows rained against us and off of us; a few found their marks and killed my men. And all at once, the Sarni broke. The entire company turned their horses to the north and galloped off as quickly as they could.

'After them!' Baltasar shouted from my side as we pounded up the rise then reached its crest. His face was red from the heat of battle and bloodlust. 'Let's kill them all!'

'No, hold!' I shouted at him. I reined Altaru to a halt, and called to all my other knights as they crested the hill as well. 'Hold here and reform our lines!'

Our rearguard, with Sar Adamar, Sar Jarlath, Sar Hannu and Skyshan of Ki, finally arrived and joined the rest of us. Lord Harsha and Master Juwain were with them. My heart surged with relief as I met eyes with Estrella; she remained unharmed, as did Behira. The Sarni do not slay women or girls any more than they do horses. As before, we arrayed ourselves along the top of the rise in three lines facing north across the steppe. Our enemy had now halted about four hundred yards away. Their steel helms glistened in the last light of the day as they regrouped themselves and faced us.

'Look!' Maram called out as he waved his sword at them. 'Why don't they just go away? Don't they know when they're beaten?'

We had lost sixteen Guardians killed and almost as many wounded; some forty of the Sarni lay dead or dying on the grass behind us. And yet, our enemy was certainly not beaten. They still had a good one hundred and eighty effective warriors, as did we. They still had their bows and arrows and their swifter ponies, and all the advantage of fighting in the open. I watched as they brought up their packhorses bearing sheaves of fresh arrows.

'They *are* beaten, aren't they?' Maram said. 'If they attack us again, we'll ride them down again, cut them to pieces. Won't we?'

I hated to utter any words that might dispirit my men, but the truth had to be told. And so I said to Maram, 'No, they won't come so close again. If we charge, they'll hold back and cut *us* down with arrows.'

'So many dead, too many – too bad,' Maram said as he glanced behind us. His blustery optimism suddenly drained from him like blood into the ground. 'What have we gained, then?'

'Time,' I told him. I looked along the rise where my Guardians made ready for another round of battle. I looked out into the sweeps and undulations of the Wendrush where our enemy gathered. 'And now we hold the high ground.'

'Time to do what?' Maram muttered. 'Wait here on this rise and behold our doom?'

I leaned over in my saddle and grasped his arm. 'Do not speak so. Do you remember Argattha?'

'Ah, how could I forget?'

'There's always a way,' I told him. 'Always a chance.'

Just then the wind rose and seemed to carry on its currents a soul-shivering sound, like the cry of a hawk. My sword's silvery gelstei, now shaken clean of blood, caught the day's last light and cast it into my eyes. I turned away from its dazzle, turned to look out at the Sarni in the depression below us, and then beyond. Something moved just beyond the dark green curves of the next rise. The Sarni, from their vantage, could not see it. I barely could. I waited as it drew closer.

'Val, what are you looking at?' Maram said to me. He held his hand to the edge of his helmet along his forehead. Then he cried out, 'Oh, no! *More* Sarni! They've brought up reinforcements! This is the end!'

As my heart beat with an unbearable pain to the deeper rhythms of the earth, I made out a body of warriors on horses moving quickly toward us. I counted nearly a hundred conical helms; I caught glints of yellow hair against steel and black leather armor.

Now Baltasar and Lord Raasharu, Sunjay and Sar Kimball and all the other Guardians cast their gazes beyond the enemy at this new band of Sarni bearing down upon us. My knights made no complaint or utterance as had Maram. But their black, silent eyes filled with the darkness of death.

213

'What should we do, Val?' Maram said to me.

Baltasar looked at me as if to ask the same question. Sunjay looked at me, too, as did Sar Kimball and Sar Jarlath and all the rest of the Guardians. Lord Raasharu's noble face fell ugly with wrath and a spreading hopelessness.

I shielded my eyes to gaze at this new company of Sarni. In the glare of the setting sun, their chief's horse seemed almost red with fire. There was a white gleam about the chief's face. Alkaladur gleamed brightly then, filling my eyes with its silver lightning, and my heart seemed to swell like the sun.

'We'll charge,' I said to Maram, and to the others. 'Lances ready!'

Maram, who thought he understood, spoke now with the resolve of a true Valari: 'Yes, better to die swinging our swords against this new enemy than stand here and be shot down one by one.'

I smiled at him and said, 'Take courage, Sar Maram. You're not going to die. These new Sarni are our friends.'

And with that I turned to issue my orders: 'First two lines, charge with me! Third line to follow in reserve! Hammer and anvil!'

I struck my sword's diamond pommel against my fist and nodded at Lord Noldru the Bold and Sar Shuradan, who were in command of the second and third lines. Then I pushed Altaru to a gallop. Our entire company, in three long lines, flew down the slope through the long grass. Hooves beat the ground like a thousand mallets striking drums. Our enemy watched us approach and began shooting arrows at us. One of these shafts lodged in Sar Avram's arm, but no one was killed. When we drew too close, Trahadak the Elder or some other chieftain gave the order for the Sarni's retreat. As I had said, they wouldn't engage us at close quarters again. And so they pointed their horses toward the rise behind them and raced away. They must have smiled to think that they were luring us to our doom out on the endless spaces of the steppe.

A few moments later, however, the new company of Sarni burst over the top of the rise shooting arrows into the faces of our enemy. They had the advantage of surprise, and many of their whining arrows found their marks. Our enemy's chieftain, a large man whose face was painted entirely blue, looked upon these new Sarni and their chief, and he cried out, 'Imakla, imakla!'

Seeing that his men were about to be caught between two forces, he veered sharply to the right, shouting at his men to follow him and to escape the hammer of my knights bearing down upon them. He and perhaps half his men managed to gallop off before I and my first line of knights closed with his brethren, driving them against the sabers

214

and arrows of the new Sarni. What followed then, as steel cut at flesh and my knights cast their throwing lances into the bodies of our enemy, was a quick and terrible slaughter. Three of my men were killed with arrows. But all of our enemy who remained there on the field that day fought savagely and died. Their brethren left them to the fury of our long swords. And they disappeared into the darkening swells of earth to the west.

'Thus to the treacherous!' Baltasar cried out. He pointed his bloody kalama at the bodies of our fallen enemy. He was weeping because his friend, Sar Viku, lay among them. 'Let us follow and kill all the rest!'

But Baltasar's hot blood, as usual, clouded the reason of his brain. Our horses were nearly spent, as were we, and we could not have overtaken our enemies in any case. At least, it seemed, they were finally defeated.

Lord Raasharu rode up to me and raised his sword in salute. He called out, 'Lord Valashu Elahad! Lord of Battles! Lord of Light!'

His son, Baltasar, picked up this cry, and so did Sar Jarlath and Sar Kimball and the other Ishkans. Then Sar Hannu of Anjo urged his horse closer and added his deep voice to the chant, as did Sar Varald, Lord Noldru the Bold and the Taroners. And then all at once, the Kaashans, Waashians, Atharians and Lagashuns joined in, and all the Guardians shouted as one: 'Lord of Battles! Lord of Light!'

And then old Sar Shuradan called out, 'Victory is ours! Valari forever! Valari! Valari!'

We all knew that the Valari hadn't fought together since the Tarshid an entire age before, and that battle had ended in terrible defeat.

'Valari! Valari! Valari!'

In truth, however, the victory was *not* ours – not ours alone. Across the field where the bodies of our enemy lay broken and bleeding on the grass, the new company of Sarni had halted facing us. Some wiped their bloody sabers; others gripped curved bows no different than the ones our enemy had turned on us. Their silence was deep and unnerving. But what shocked my men more than anything – Sar Jarlath and Sar Ianashu, Baltasar and Tavar Amadan and all the rest – was that the faces of our saviors were smooth and unpainted and bore the softer, unmistakable lines of women.

'What's this – women dressed as warriors?' Sar Jarlath cried out. Then he gazed upon their efficient and violent work, and shook his head. 'No, woman *warriors*, truly. But who has ever heard of such a thing?'

As it happened, Lord Raasharu and Sar Shuradan had, and so had some of the other knights. Maram and Master Juwain knew of these terrible woman, as did I. They were of the Manslayer Society: Sarni women who lived apart from the rest of their tribe and trained at war as did men. They were fierce in battle, and they took vows to kill a hundred enemy men before marrying.

'Oh, Lord!' Maram said as his gaze fell upon these Manslayers' chief.

I, too, had eyes only for this woman. She sat tall and regal upon a great roan mare. A lionskin cloak draped from her shoulders. Her accouterments were those of the men that we had fought, and her hair was gold like the hoops encircling her bare upper arms. The golden torque protecting her neck was inlaid with the bluest of lapis. Her eyes would have picked up this bright color if it hadn't been falling dark – and if she hadn't been violently blinded. A white cloth was bound across her face just beneath her forehead. It was the glint of this cloth from across the steppe that had stirred my memory and ignited the fire of my heart. For this blind warrior, who had somehow found me in the middle of the Wendrush and saved my life, was Atara Ars Narmada, the woman I loved more than I did life itself.

16

I wanted to race over to her, to clasp hands with her and embrace her; I wanted to kiss her full lips and the cloth covering the hollows where her eyes used to be. I did not. I was the commander of nearly two hundred knights exhausted from battle. And she, it seemed, was the chief of her sister warriors. They were Sarni, and we were Valari, and although we had fought the same enemy that day, there was yet no love between us. All gathered there beneath the darkening clouds stared at Atara and me as they waited to see what we would do.

'Atara!' I called out to her. 'Atara Ars Narmada!'

She shook her head slightly and called back to me: 'Here, I'm just "Atara the Blind", Lord Valashu – *Lord* of Light.'

She smiled at me as she always had when playing with words or having fun. But beneath her welcome was a formality that I was unused to and a hint of coldness that immediately chilled my heart.

'How did you find us here?' I asked her. 'Why were we attacked?'

'Good questions, Lord Valashu. But why don't we answer them later? There's much to be done if you don't want to leave your fallen for the wolves.'

With night coming on, the rich greens of the steppe and the sky's patches of blue bled away into a solid gray that spread across the heavens and covered the earth like a shroud. Soon it would be too dark to see our companions where they lay in the long grass. We must find them and bury them before the wolves and other scavengers swarmed around them. And, it seemed, we must also bury the bodies of our enemy.

'We must have slain a hundred of them,' Lord Harsha said, 'so it will be hard work. But the dead are dead, Sarni or no, and they must be buried.'

'No, they must *not* be buried,' Atara called out to him. She nudged her mare, whose name was Fire, closer to us. It unnerved Lord Harsha,

I sensed, to see the blind Atara unerringly guide her horse around the bodies of the slain Sarni. 'At least, they must not be buried as *you* Valari bury men. Here we have different ways.'

The Sarni, in fact, do not dig graves in the very tough turf of the steppe. Instead, they divest their dead of all weapons, ornaments and clothing, and lay them on the grass with their eyes open to the sky and their arms opened outward as an offering to any beast who would take them. Naked a man came into the world, and naked he must go out of it.

'Barbaric,' Lord Harsha said to Atara when he discovered this. 'It's wrong to let your companions be devoured by wolves.'

'Is it better,' Atara asked him, 'to let them be devoured by the worms?'

Lord Harsha, who was unused to being faced down by women, particularly not one so young as Atara, allowed his hand instinctively to rest on the hilt of his sword. And almost instantly, the bows of ninety of Atara's sister Manslayers were raised and their arrows pointed at him.

'Come,' I said, riding over to Lord Harsha. I rested my hand on his arm and watched as he relaxed his fingers. 'We've enough burying to do already, however we're to do it. Let the Valari bury the Valari, and the Sarni attend the Sarni.'

We worked far into the night. While Atara and her Manslayers rode about the steppe looking for the enemy we had killed and six of their own, we of the Morning Mountains located our companions and bore them across our horses back toward the river. There, in hard soil bound with many roots, we began digging graves: twenty-one altogether, for two more knights had died from their wounds. We drew the arrows from the bodies of our companions. We bathed them and anointed them in oil. After placing their hands around their swords, we wrapped them in their cloaks and laid them in the ground. Then we gathered and gave voice to songs of mourning, to exalt and remember and sing their souls up toward the stars.

And all this we had to accomplish in the deepness of night, with wood fires blazing so that we could see, with Guardians posted in case our enemy should return. The Manslayers made camp fifty yards from ours. Our own camp that night we had to lay out without the traditional moat and stockade. With the sky clearing toward midnight, we erected only one tent: the pavilion where Master Juwain went to work on the wounded. He drew many arrows, and filled many holes in flesh, with his healing powders and the light of his green gelstei. It was a miracle that no more of my men died. But in addition to the twenty-one Guardians who would remain here forever by the river's bend, at least four more would keep them company until they were well enough to ride again.

When it finally came time for sleeping, it seemed that many of us needed company and talk even more. I sat with Atara and a middling-old woman named Karimah by a fire stoked with logs of deadwood. Lord Raasharu and Baltasar joined us there, with Sunjay Naviru, Lord Harsha and Maram. Lord Harsha held an old bottle of brandy, which he poured into cups and gave out to us. Baltasar watched with amazement as Atara reached her hand straight out and grasped her cup with all the precision of a diamond cutter. But his wonder at this feat quickly gave way to anger, for he was was still wroth over the death of Sar Viku, who had been as a brother to him.

'After we've visited this lake of yours, Val,' he said to me, 'we should lay waste Trahadak's encampment and slay those who escaped us today.'

Atara laughed at this in a voice that was clear and clean and sweet. She said to Baltasar, 'If you rode into Trahadak's encampment with lances and drawn swords instead of gold, it would be *you* who was slain. Trahadak is Kurmak, and Zakut at that.'

'Whatever he is, he's a treacherous dog.'

Atara smiled at this and told him, 'You should be careful how you speak of men on the Wendrush. We of the Manslayers might speak of a man this way, of course, but you should not. And you should know that we eat dogs here. And if Trahadak heard of your slur, he'd roast and eat *you.*'

Baltasar paled at this, for every child in the Morning Mountains is told stories of the Sarni's cruelties. Then he stroked the hilt of his sword and said, 'He would first be greeted by steel, as he was today.'

'Indeed? Tell me, Sar Baltasar, at the Zakut's encampment you paid tribute to Trahadak yourself, didn't you?'

Now Baltasar's hand tightened around his kalama's grip as he huffed out, 'We Valari pay tribute to no one. The gold was a gift, to honor Trahadak for his hospitality.'

'Very well, a gift then,' Atara said, smiling. 'But you sat as close to Trahadak as you and I sit now, did you not?'

Baltasar, who sipped from a cup of brandy with only his father and Maram between me and Atara, nodded his head.

'Very well,' Atara continued, 'then you know Trahadak's face as well as my own. Tell me, brave knight, did you see him on the field today?'

'Of course. That is, it *must* have been he who led that cowardly retreat. The truth is, it's hard to tell. All you Sarni look alike.'

This caused Karimah to burst into laughter. She scooted even closer to Atara and pressed the side of her face against Atara's cheek. Then she laughed out, 'Oh, yes, and we of the Manslayers, who are all *sisters*, especially look alike. I'm sure you can't tell Atara from me.'

We all had a good laugh at this. Where Karimah's long hair was bleached almost white from many years of sun, Atara's hair shone like living gold. Karimah's face was plump and pretty, except for the round scars on either side where an arrow must once have driven straight through her cheeks; Atara's face was square and smooth and beautiful. In her arms and body, Karimah was almost stout enough to have been *Maram's* sister. But Atara was long and lithe, clean-limbed and a wonder to look upon, even with the white cloth breaking the perfection of her countenance.

Baltasar, seeing these two women together, flushed with heat as if he had sat too close to the fire. He said, 'What I meant was, with your faces painted blue, who could tell one Sarni from another?'

'*We* certainly can,' Atara said to Baltasar. 'And that is why I must tell you that it was not Trahadak or any Zakut that we fought today. Nor any clan of the Kurmak, who always keep their word. No, the men we killed were Adirii.'

While I traded knowing glances with Lord Raasharu and Baltasar's face flushed an even angrier red, Atara went on to tell us that a band of warriors of the Adirii's Akhand clan had crossed the Snake River and invaded the Kurmak's country to hunt us.

'But how did they know to find us here?' I asked. 'And the Adirii, for them to ride through Kurmak country, risking war and slaughter, they must have been desperate.'

Desperate for gold, I suddenly thought. *Desperate to steal the gold gelstei.*

In her eerie way, Atara turned her head toward me as if she could see me and look into my heart. 'All the Sarni on the Wendrush know to find you here, or soon will. The Red Dragon has many spies, and word of your route toward Tria has preceded you and spreads like a wildfire.'

'But this is terrible news!' Maram cried out. He took a long drink of his brandy, and then another.

'No, Maram, perhaps not so terrible as you fear,' Atara reassured him. 'The Red Dragon, it's true, has promised a great weight of gold to anyone who will deliver the Lightstone to him. The Akhand clan must have learned of this and fallen mad with greed. For them to have crossed the Snake, they broke the truce between our tribes and the will of the Adirii's chieftain, Xadharax, who loathes Morjin nearly as much as do we Kurmak.'

Now it was Baltasar's turn to drink deeply of his brandy. To Atara, he said, 'My apologies, my lady – it was wrong of me to have impugned Trahadak, who treated me well.'

'He treated you more than well. When he learned that your company would be making its way toward the lake, he sent messengers to alert our Society where we were encamped scarcely half a day's ride away.'

'But if Trahadak knew the Adirii were after us, why didn't he send his own warriors to intercept them?'

Atara held a cup of brandy in her hand, but she did not drink of it. She said, 'Because Trahadak *didn't* know. Indeed, when Sajagax learns of what happened here today, he will be hard put to keep Trahadak from leading all the Zakut across the Snake against those greedy Akhand.'

'But why then,' Baltasar persisted, 'did Trahadak alert *you*?'

Atara smiled at him. 'Because he knew Valashu Elahad and I were companions on the great Quest.'

'Very well, my lady, but why did *you* ride here with so many of your sisters? How did you know to find us here?'

It was the same question that I had first asked her. While a sliver of moon spilled a little light down upon us and the wolves out on the steppe howled out their long, soulful hungers, I looked at Atara to see what she would say. And so did everyone else.

In answer to Baltasar's question, Atara brought forth a clear crystal as round as a child's ball. The white gelstei caught the fire's flames and sparks in little flickers of orange and red. Inside its polished curves, for the briefest flash of a moment, I thought I glimpsed an entire world burning up in bright flames.

'You're a scryer,' Baltasar said. He nodded his head as if a great mystery had been made clear to him. 'We've all heard that one of Val's companions was a scryer. But *who* has ever heard of a scryer without eyes who yet can see?'

Atara's entire being seemed to chill as if she had drunk deeply from an icy stream. She said, '*Can* I see? Sometimes it seems I almost can. And sometimes . . .'

Her voice died off into the night. The brandy I sipped burned my throat down into my chest; it reminded me that while Atara could often 'see' the forms and features of the earth down to the thinnest blade of grass a hundred yards behind her, at other times she was truly blind – as blind as if the hand of fate had cast her into a black cave.

'Scryers, it's said,' Baltasar went on, 'can see things distant in time. But whoever knew they can see things near in space?'

'Few scryers can,' Atara told him.

'Is that why the chief of the Akhand called you *imakla*? What does that mean?'

It meant, as I remembered, that Atara was not entirely of this world, that she rode with the immortal warriors of ages past and could not be touched by the hand or arrows of man.

'Please,' Atara said as she put down her brandy and squeezed her crystal sphere, 'let's speak of other things.'

Atara's cup was still full, while Karimah's was as dry as bone. Seeing this, Lord Harsha stood up and limped over to her. From his bottle, he poured forth a few ounces of brandy into her cup. Then he stoppered the bottle with a cork, and laid his hand on Karimah's bare arm, saying, 'Perhaps then we should speak of the beauty of the Sarni women. Perhaps we should make a toast to this and –'

Almost quicker than belief, Karimah drew forth a dagger and held its razor edge to Lord Harsha's wrist. With a smile on her jolly face, she said to him, 'Take your hand from me, Lord Knight, or you shall lose it as you have your eye.'

Lord Harsha's single eye blinked with astonishment. With surprising speed of his own, he jerked back his hand as if from a heated iron. Then he coughed out, 'Forgive me – I forgot myself. It seems that my son-in-law's flirtatious ways have corrupted me.'

Here he nodded at Maram, who mumbled, 'Son-in-law, is it? I thought I was still a free man, at least until next spring, when it might be a good time for a wedding. And as for my ways, I make poems, too, but I'm never accused of corrupting anyone when he is moved to recite verse.'

Karimah smiled at this and turned back to Lord Harsha, and said, 'You are certainly forgiven, then.'

But this wasn't quite good enough for Lord Harsha, who went on to explain, 'You see, it was only my intention to honor your beauty. So fair you are! In the Morning Mountains, we have no women like you.'

Karimah's smile grew broader and bolder. 'Well, you certainly may honor my *beauty* – from a distance. Indeed, I'd be honored if you did.'

'Then are you *imakla*, too?'

'*I*? No, Lord Knight, but I *am* a warrior of the Manslayers.'

'Then are men forbidden to touch you?'

'Forbidden? Do you mean by law? No – there is no law. There is only this.' Here Karimah held up her dagger, and her smile showed her strong, white teeth. 'It is *we* who forbid men this. Or not, as we please.'

Maram, who was now a little drunk, couldn't help making a little joke. 'And I must tell you, my, ah . . . *father-in-law*, that what pleases them usually is *not*. They may not marry or bear children.'

'Not until we've slain a hundred of our enemies,' Karimah said.

'And how many have *you* slain, then?' Lord Harsha asked her.

222

'In my life? After today, eighteen.'

'It is more than most Valari knights ever account for.'

'Perhaps – I wouldn't know,' Karimah said. 'But it is fifty-three fewer than Atara the Blind has sent to the wolves.'

Karimah brushed back the hair from Atara's face as if to array her in splendor so that we all might honor her for this rare and terrible feat. But after Argattha, Atara no longer took pride in slaying men. She sat pressing the white gelstei against her forehead, and she sighed out, 'Please, may we speak of other things?'

'Let's speak of sleep, then,' Lord Harsha said. 'It's been a day of battle, and who knows what tomorrow will bring? Maram, are you coming to bed?'

'Soon,' Maram said, yawning. 'As soon as I've finished my brandy. And perhaps had a little more.'

'You've had enough already,' Lord Harsha said to him as he tucked the brandy bottle inside his cloak. After nodding at Karimah, he looked back at Maram and said, 'But at least this is one night we won't have to worry about you wandering into the women's quarters.'

So saying, Lord Harsha limped off toward a nearby fire where Behira and Estrella lay sleeping. Shortly thereafter, Lord Raasharu and Baltasar said goodnight as well, and so did Sunjay Naviru. As promised, Maram drank down the last dram of brandy before belching and ambling off to bed. Karimah, however, seemed reluctant to leave Atara alone with me. She stroked Atara's hand and said, 'My dear one, the wolves will be out tonight, the lions, too. If the darkness falls about you, how will you find your way back to us?'

'If I fall blind, truly blind,' Atara said, 'I'm sure that Lord Valashu will accompany me.'

Karimah looked at me long and deeply as she might search the Wendrush's dark grasses for lions. Then she kissed Atara's hand and said, 'Very well, then. We'll be waiting for you.'

And with that, she stood up and walked off toward the Manslayers' campfires glowing against the shadowed steppe away from the river.

'Your Lord Harsha,' Atara said to me, 'should be careful of Karimah.'

'Do you mean, careful of his hands or careful of her knife?'

'I mean, careful of her heart. As long as we make our camp close to yours, there will be a danger for both our people.'

'But surely your sisters must often encounter men.'

'Yes, of course – but not men such as you Valari.'

'Are we so different from your Sarni warriors, then?'

'Yes, you *are* different. You have no care for counting your cattle or your gold, or boasting of the women you possess.'

223

'We do not think of ourselves as *possessing* our women. Is a woman a thing to be owned?'

'Do you see?' Atara said as she faced me. 'Do you see?'

I remained silent for a moment as I gazed at her golden skin and her long, golden hair. Then I said, 'We're warriors, Atara. We slay men, too.'

'Yes, you slay your enemies with such terrible, terrible fierceness, but not because you love killing – only to protect those you love.'

'Sometimes, that is true,' I said. 'But sometimes we're savages.'

'You *are* savages of the sword,' she said to me, 'truly, truly. And yet at other times so gentle. So quiet, inside. You sing songs to the stars! And I think the stars, sometimes, sing back to you. In light, in fire. And this fire! It burns so brightly in you. So hot, so clean, so sweet.'

At that moment I was almost glad that she could not let her eyes find mine, for I did not know if I could bear what I would see there.

'And *that*,' she said, breathing deeply, 'is why it is good that we don't make our camp with yours or take our meals together. In any case, what would *your* women say if Lord Harsha or the others had their way?'

'Lord Harsha,' I told her, 'is many years a widower. And the Guardians have no women.'

'So much the worse,' she said. 'But do you mean, no wives or no one to whom they have pledged their troths?'

'No wives. We have pledges, of course. We have our hopes.'

Here I reached out and clasped her hand in mine. This beautiful hand – long and delicate and yet strong from years of working her bow – seemed stiff and cold as if the fire's warmth had touched only her skin but had failed to penetrate deeper inside. Gently, but with unrelenting force, she pulled her hand away from mine.

'No, no, you shouldn't touch me,' she told me.

'Why – because you're a Manslayer who puts knives to men? Or because you're *imakla*?'

'Because I cannot bear to be touched this way. And neither can you.'

'Has nothing changed, then?'

'Should it have?'

'Yes,' I said, 'truly it *should* have.'

I thought of Master Juwain's hurrying to my father's castle to show me his star charts and of what had later occurred between Baltasar and me in the great hall. I thought of Estrella sitting by a little mountain stream and sipping water in all her innocence from a small golden cup.

'I still have my vow,' Atara reminded me.

'You've slain seventy-one men,' I said, 'yet you've only loathing to slay another.'

'And yet I must if war comes, as it seems it must.'

'But war must *not* come,' I told her. 'We must not let it. And as for your vow, you made it to the Manslayer Society, didn't you?'

'Yes – and to myself.'

'But there are always higher vows, aren't there? Merely in being born, you made a vow to life and to the One, who gave you life.'

She finally picked up her cup of brandy and took a long sip. She said, 'Do we honor life then by breaking our vows?'

'The old age and the old ways are nearly finished, Atara. This is a time of *new* life – and so for making new vows.'

'To you, then?'

'Yes, to me – to us and all the world. To the new life we'll bring forth.'

'But I'm still blind,' she said. 'Nothing will ever change that.'

I gazed off at the sky, at the constellations spread out across the heavens like a shimmering tapestry of diamonds and black silk. Solaru, Aras and Varshara, the brightest of the stars, poured down their clear, lovely light.

'If this is truly a new age,' I told her, 'then it is truly a time for new hopes.'

She pulled at the cloth binding her face and said, 'Morjin took my hope when he took my eyes.'

'Yet you have your sight – greater than it was before.'

'It is not the same,' she said. 'When *you* see, as I once did, the sun touches a thing: a stone, a flower, a child. The whole world . . . gives back the light into our eyes, touching us, in glory. Everything is so bright, so warm, so sweet. But now, what you call this sight of mine – it is so cold. It is like trying to touch the world through the iciest of waters.'

'You have your hands,' I told her. 'You have your heart – a heart of fire. No woman could love a child as you could.'

'A child, Val?'

'Our sons. Our daughters.'

'No,' she said, shaking her head. 'That can't be, don't you see?'

'But why?'

'Because it's all buried beneath this shroud,' she said, touching the white cloth. 'Because . . . in the light of a mother's eyes, a newborn learns to be human.'

I said nothing as I turned to stare into the fire. Flames still worked at a good-sized log, blackening it, and the coals beneath seemed hellishly hot, covered with ash and glowing a deep red. I remembered the coals of another fire in Argattha that had burned Atara's eyes to char; my hands could almost feel the hard edges of the box that Salmelu had delivered to me out of that forsaken place. If we learned to be human from our mothers, who was it that later taught us to be beasts?

'There's always a way,' I murmured. 'There's got to be a way.'

'Your way of hopes and miracles?'

'Miracles, yes, if you call them that.'

'What *should* I call this wild hope of yours then? What should I call *you*? Lord Valashu? Lord of Light?'

I nodded toward her scryer's crystal, but she seemed not to perceive this slight motion. I asked her, 'What have seen in your kristei, Atara?'

'Too much,' she said.

'Have you seen the Maitreya, then?'

'I've seen many people . . . who must have held the Lightstone. Who *will* hold it, almost certainly, and always *are*. But there will come a moment. Then there will be one who will make the cup shine as no one else can. Him I cannot see. No scryer can. In the same way it's impossible to see the Lightstone, we're blind to him in this moment, for their fates are as one.'

'Have you seen who the Maitreya is *not*, then? Is it possible that I could be he?'

'Do you wish to be?' she asked. She sat very still, and her voice was full of longing and mystery.

'It's said that if the Maitreya fails to come forth, then a Bringer of Darkness will claim the Lightstone instead. And yet this might not be the worst of such a failure.'

'What could be worse than this?'

'That the Maitreya would then also fail to bring forth miracles.'

Atara took another sip of brandy, and I felt the fiery liquid clutch and burn inside her chest. She took a deep breath and held it for a moment. The long, deep pain she held inside herself made me want to weep.

'You must know that these miracles you desire,' she said to me, 'I also desire. Desperately, desperately. But I mustn't, don't you see? And you mustn't either.'

'But shouldn't I desire what should be?'

'Do you *know* what should be, then?' The cold anger in her voice cut me like a knife.

'My grandfather,' I said to her, 'believed that a man can make his own fate.'

She smiled sadly at this and said, 'You have dreams. Miracles – you would work this beautiful thing you hold inside on moments yet to be. And on yourself. But, Val, you should know that the future has as many plans for us as we do for it.'

'Tell me of these plans, then.'

'Tell yourself. Listen to your heart.'

'But what of *your* heart?' I said. 'Do you remember the passage from the *Healings*? "*If we bring forth what is inside ourselves, what we bring forth will save us. If we do not bring forth what is inside ourselves, what we do not bring forth will destroy us.*"'

As Atara sat breathing softly and the fire crackled and moaned, I brought forth the Lightstone which I had earlier taken from Skyshan. Atara must have sensed if not seen it. She shook her head even as a ripple of dread tore through her. She murmured, 'No, Val, not this, please!'

'There's always a way,' I said to her. 'There must be a way.'

'No – not *this* way.'

A child, I thought, is born perfectly formed out of her mother as her mother is from the earth. And the earth, and all the earths and all the stars, take their being from the One, as all things do. And the One's essence, this divine will to create, was just love. In the One's fiery heart was the secret of creation itself. And didn't all human beings hold some of this bright flame inside? In the *Healings* it was also written that the Lightstone is 'the perfect jewel inside the lotus found inside the human heart'. Might not this jewel, I wondered, be used to quicken this flame until it blazed like a star? And might not Atara once again bring forth the perfectly formed being that she held inside herself?

'Atara,' I whispered. I cupped my hands beneath the Lightstone and held it between us. I felt its radiance penetrate my diamond armor and fill up my chest like the sun; I felt her heart beating in perfect rhythm with my own. For a moment, we were like two stars giving out light to each other in brilliant, golden pulses. 'Atara, Atara.'

And then she shook her head as something seized her with a terrible will. It seized me and seemed yank me away from her; it ripped my heart from my chest. And then there was only darkness. Inside me there was a hole, black and bottomless as empty space. The cold was so bitter and deep that I wanted to cry out in anguish.

'No, no,' Atara said, 'this mustn't be!'

As the Lightstone fell quiescent once more, I squeezed it between my hands until my fingers hurt. I said, 'Why, Atara, why?'

In the fire's red light, her face filled with both resolve and a silent anguish of her own. And she asked me, 'What if you fail in this miracle?'

'What if the sun should fail to rise on the morrow?'

'So sure you are of yourself! But if you fail, this sureness will turn to despair.'

'I won't let it.'

'Can you help it? Could you help the despair that would then finish *me*? You, with your *valarda* and the way you've always looked at me?'

Could I help it, I wondered? Could I bear to live if the brightest star in all the heavens suddenly died and shone no more?

'It would kill your dream,' she said to me softly. 'And so it would kill you, the finest part. How could I let that be?'

My eyes filled with a moist, stinging pain too great to hold in. And I gasped out, 'How you love me!'

'More than you could ever believe. Almost as much as you love me.'

'And that is why,' I said, 'I would take the chance.'

'Yes, you would risk it, for yourself. And so might I for myself. But we do not live for ourselves, alone.'

I stared at the white cloth covering her face. I wanted almost more than life to rip it from her and see revealed the two brilliant blue eyes that had once shone there.

'The Maitreya, men call you,' she said to me. 'But if you fail to work this miracle, what will you call yourself?'

'Would that matter, then?'

'More than you could ever believe.'

'If I fail, I fail. It must be put to the test. I must know.'

'Yes, indeed you must,' she said. 'But not by such proofs. Do you need it proven to yourself that you are alive? That deep inside, you are beautiful and sweet and good?'

'But *how* will I know, then, who I truly am?'

'As with anyone, that is for you – and you alone – to discover.'

I gazed through the fire's wavering flames at the many Guardians laid out on their sleeping furs in silent rows. Beyond them others stood watch against the line of trees down by the river. I listened to this dark, rushing water and to the crickets chirping in the grass; I listened to the wolves howling far out on the steppe and to the faint, far-off whisperings of the stars.

'This I know,' I said to her. 'Nothing about the future matters to me unless you are there to look at me as you once did.'

'Please, don't say such things. What of your friends and family? What of your people? The whole world?'

'The world can take care of itself,' I said. 'It always has.'

At this, she shook her head almost violently, then held her hand out toward the north, and then east and west. She turned for a moment as she beckoned south, toward the river. Her hand swept upward as

228

if reaching out to the stars, and she faced me once again. 'The Golden Band grows ever brighter. Sometimes I can *see* it. It's not really golden, of course. It has no color, but if it did, I would describe it as glorre: it's all softness and shimmer and carries inside it an infinity of hues. Infinity, itself. It . . . has touched me. You were right that my sight grows greater. And that is why I must tell you what I must tell you. Fate lies balanced on a sword's edge infinitely sharper than that of the knife Karimah put to Lord Harsha. *Your* fate, and that of the world. If you turn from it, all will fall into darkness.'

With a deep sigh, she set down her kristei and held out her hand to me. 'Please, may I have the Lightstone?'

I extended the golden cup straight toward her. For a moment, she fumbled about, trying to find it in the cool air of the night. Then I leaned closer and pressed it into her hand.

'Thank you,' she said. 'Now you take this.'

She gave me her crystal, and I held it in my hands not knowing what she wished of me.

'Look into it!' she told me.

'But this is a scryer's sphere. Am I a scryer, then?'

'Look into it!' she said again.

With the fire giving out just enough light with which to see, I looked into the kristei. It was of white gelstei and as clear as my sword's diamond pommel. There was nothing inside it.

Atara drew in a deep breath even as the Lightstone came alive in her hands. A clear, deep radiance spilled from the cup and spread outward to envelop me. It illumed the crystal sphere. Suddenly, with a gasp, I saw myself inside staring back at myself. I shuddered and blinked my eyes, for the eyes I saw boring into me were so black and bright with dreams that I couldn't help pitying their owner. I tried to put down the sphere then, but I could not because I found myself holding my sword instead. I tried to look away from the sphere, but I could not; through its clear surface I beheld myself holding the sphere as I sat with my back to a crackling woodfire, with the warriors of our encampment lying still behind me. I cried out in fear. No one heard me. The sphere's glittering surface suddenly hardened, and the world of my birth disappeared. All around me and above was a cold, curving brilliance like that of a mirror. With a shock, I realized that somehow the sphere had seized me and held me captive inside it. Everything fell cold then, like an icy blue inside blue, like a sky behind the sky. I felt myself falling, down and down into a shimmering neverness. Its depths were infinite. It opened outward and upward, and inward, forever.

For an endless moment I hung suspended in space like a feather buoyed upon the wind. I could see outward in any direction to the end of the world. There was an immense clarity. I looked down a million miles as from the height of a star. Below me blazed a city by the sea. I beheld the great, white Tower of the Sun and the Tower of the Moon; the palace of the Narmada kings sat on top of a hill overlooking a great river. The city, I knew, was Tria, and it was all on fire: the palaces and houses and gardens spread across its seven hills. Men and women, burning like human torches, ran screaming through its streets. I screamed out that this must not be, but still no one heard me. I reached out toward this City of Light, and found that I still held my sword. Blood flowed down its silvery length and drenched my hand. I tried to rub it away with my other hand, but it would not come off. It was, I knew, the blood of an innocent: perhaps a child who had got in the way of my killing wrath. For my fury to destroy the evil one who had set fire to the city filled me with a terrible burning of my own. My bright sword suddenly leapt with a terrible flame that ignited the fields and the forests around Tria. Faster than I could believe, it spread outward to the grasses of the Wendrush and the Morning Mountains and the sands of the Red Desert until all of Ea was on fire. There was no help for it; it burned with a fury that consumed even naked rock, down to the very bones of the earth itself. The world blazed and blazed in the vastness of space until only a small charred sphere remained and the fire burned itself out. And then the light died, too, and a darkness fell across the heavens like an impenetrable black smoke and smothered the radiance of the stars.

Darkness smothered me and stole the light from my eyes. For what seemed a million years, I was blind. And then I felt myself once again holding in my hand a small crystal sphere. A glimmer of its white gelstei broke through the blackness enveloping me. And then there were stars once more: the bright lights of the Swan and the Seven Sisters and all the other constellations filled the sky above the steppe. The leaves of the cottonwoods along the river fluttered in their radiance. Atara's white cloth reflected the dancing red flames of the fire. She still sat holding the Lightstone in her cupped hands. Her face was white and grave.

'Do you see?' she said to me softly. 'Do you see?'

I coughed at the dryness in my throat as I shivered. I gripped the kristei in my hand and stared into its clear depths.

'*Did* I see?' I asked her. 'Did I see the same vision you saw?'

'One of them – there are millions of others. Millions of millions.'

'But how is that possible?'

'It seems that the white gelstei not only quickens a scryer's visions but records them.'

'I didn't know it had that power.'

'Few do, even scryers. I didn't *know* myself until tonight. Until I quickened it with the Lightstone.'

I gazed at the golden cup gathering in the lights of the heavens. Who knew what other wonders this little vessel might work? Who knew *how* it could be made to work them?

'This future you showed me,' I said to her. 'Is this what I am supposed to fear if I fail to heal you?'

'Oh, no,' she said. 'It is what will befall if you *succeed* – and are then led to believe you are the Maitreya when you are not.'

I looked down into the crystal again, and I gasped to see Atara looking back at me. Her lovely face filled the whole of the sphere's luminous interior. Her blindfold was gone. In its place were two eyes as clear and sparkling as blue diamonds. And then my exaltation blazed out from deep inside me. It fell upon her like a dragon's red *relb* and burst into flame. The screaming of her eyes was worse than any sound I had ever heard. It took only a moment for the fire to burn her flesh down to the bone so all that remained was skull encased in char.

'Enough!' I cried out as I thrust the sphere away from me. One of the Guardians posted by the river looked my way, but I held up my hand to signal that everything was all right – even if it really wasn't. 'Take back your crystal, Atara. I would see no more.'

I gave the kristei back into her hand, and she returned the Lightstone to me. For a while we sat facing each other, saying nothing.

'You were right about one thing,' I finally said. 'These visions of yours, this way of seeing – it's too clear, too cold.'

Something of this terrible cold, I knew, would remain with me. It bit into my bones and recalled the ice mountains of the Nagarshath.

'You *do* see,' she said to me. 'This is the world where I live now.'

'But, Atara, there's another world.'

'*Your* world,' she said bitterly. 'And whether you're the Maitreya or not, you must do what you can save it.'

All the coldness inside her seemed to come pouring out, all at once. She *made* herself cold, toward me. And then she was no longer a woman of golden skin and warm breath and dreams; she was a scryer encased in the eternal freeze of glacier ice.

'Atara, Atara,' I said to her.

'No, Val – we will not speak of this again!'

I bowed my head to her, and then tucked the Lightstone back inside my armor. Perhaps she was right, after all. For we both knew that if

231

either of us weakened, I might risk all the fires of the heavens and hell to make her whole again.

'It's growing late,' she said to me.

The frigid tone of her voice was almost more than I could bear; it was more than she could bear, for I felt in her an intense desire to fall weeping against me – if only she'd still had tears with which to weep. I wept then to see this noble being hold herself so straight and still. Her restraint made me love her all the more. I longed for a sword to swing and crack open the icy tomb of this sacrifice that had stolen her away from me.

'Tomorrow we'll have to rest here,' I said. 'But the next day, we'll journey on to the lake.'

'To find this akashic crystal of yours?'

'Yes.'

If not a sword, I thought, then perhaps this great thought stone that might hold the key toward apprehending my fate.

'It's growing late,' she said again. 'We should go to bed.'

She stood up abruptly and started off in the direction of the Manslayers' camp. But she tripped over a fresh log, and it was all I could do to rise up and catch her, to keep her from falling face-first into the fire. I took her cold hand in mine, and she said to me, 'It seems that I might need help after all.'

And so we walked away from the fire around the rows of the sleeping Guardians, out into the steppe. We passed the dark, mounded graves of other Guardians who had fallen in battle only hours before. Their sleep was much deeper, and they would not arise to greet the new day. We had not been able to inscribe stones and set them into the places on earth where they lay. And so I silently whispered their names: Karashan and Aivar, Jushur and Jonawan, and those of their eighteen companions. I promised them that their sacrifice in risking the wilds of the Wendrush should not be in vain. I promised myself, and Atara, that I would find the akashic crystal and make it yield its secrets. I knew no other way. For as she had told me, it was upon me, and me alone, to pierce through to the heart of the mystery of my life.

17

I had hoped that all the wounded would be able to ride when we set out two days later. But despite Master Juwain's best efforts, the four Guardians who bore the worst wounds would have to remain here at least a few days while they recuperated. I saw to it that they were well-provisioned, and I appointed four others to nurse them and guard them against wolves and lions – or the return of vengeful Adirii. They were to follow us to the lake, if they could. But if we failed to rendezvous there, they were to return to their respective kingdoms in the Morning Mountains. It would not do for wounded knights to go trotting off after us across the endless miles of the Wendrush.

Thus our company was reduced to 165 Guardians. With the sun caught like a knot of fire in a notch in the mountains behind us, we formed up as we had before. I rode at the head of our center column, with Maram and Lord Raasharu to either side, and Estrella right behind me. It pained me that she had to endure the dangers of our journey. But during the battle, she had evidenced no sign of terror or panic. I attributed this to an inner strength that I was only beginning to understand. To see her sitting on her horse so peacefully in the morning's quiet, with the long grass swaying in the breeze and sparkling with dew, one might have thought that she was hardened to suffering and death. I knew she wasn't. As we passed the graves of the fallen Guardians, a dew of tears filled her eyes, and she wept in silence.

The ninety Manslayers, on their rugged steppe ponies, rode a hundred yards ahead of us as a vanguard. That morning, Atara did not lead them. Indeed, it was Karimah who led her, for Atara's blindness did not evaporate with the rising of the sun. Karimah held a string tied to Fire's bridle, and this fine mare seemed to understand that she must trail after Karimah and bear Atara patiently. Atara, I sensed, had little patience with the darkness embracing her. I dreaded that the Adirii might return and catch her in such a helpless state. But neither

Atara nor the other Manslayers seemed to fear this. As Atara had told me the day before, 'The Adirii took a great enough risk in hunting you. But to seek battle against Valari *and* Sarni – well, that would be madness.'

In truth, although the battle had cost us dearly, I had learned in my bones a great and agonizing lesson: that the only way the Valari could defeat the Sarni on the steppe was with the help of other Sarni.

Later that morning, when we took a break by the river to water the horses, I rode up to Atara and spoke of this. We found a place of privacy beneath a gnarly old cottonwood, and I remarked the wonder of our two peoples riding as one. I asked her if it was possible that her grandfather, Sajagax, might be persuaded to attend the conclave in Tria. For if Morjin could behold the greatest Sarni chieftain sitting peacefully at table with the sovereigns of the Free Kingdoms, then he might truly fear an alliance.

'Sajagax detests cities,' she said to me, 'but it *is* possible.'

'Is it likely?' I asked her. 'Have you *seen* this, then?'

'I mustn't speak to you any more about what I have or haven't seen.'

'But there's so much that I *must* know,' I said to her. 'This prophecy of Kasandra's. What did she mean that a man with no face would show me my own? And that Estrella would show me the Maitreya?'

Atara fell silent as she leaned back against the deep creases of silver bark. Then she said, 'A scryer shouldn't speak of another scryer's visions.'

'Please, Atara. For Estrella's sake, if not mine. It torments me to have to take her into danger.'

'It can't be helped,' she told me. 'What will be will be. The girl will be with you to the end.'

'To the end of *what*?' My life? Until I claimed the Lightstone or reached the darkest of places, wherever and whatever that was?

But Atara would say no more; indeed she had told me too much already. For a few minutes, as our hundreds of horses up and down the stony banks of the river lowered their heads and drank up bellyfuls of sweet, clear water, we spoke of other things. She gave me news of our companions on the Quest. Liljana continued to reside in Tria and plot the downfall of Morjin. As head of the Maitriche Telu, she was gathering Sisters from all across Ea to their secret sanctuary there. And against thousands of years of tradition, she had begun to instruct Daj in their witches' ways. The little boy that we had rescued out of Argattha had flourished under Liljana's care. His starved body had filled out from the nourishing foods that Liljana cooked him; and his starved mind had filled up with knowledge that the Maitriche Telu had preserved and kept secret ever since the Age of the Mother.

'And what of Kane?' I asked.

'Kane left Tria in great urgency five months ago.'

'Business with this Black Brotherhood of his?'

'I don't know – he wouldn't say.'

'Did he say when he might return?'

'I don't know that either. I hope in time for the conclave.'

I hoped this, too. There were many questions I wished to ask this strange, immortal man. He might have answers for me that not even the akashic crystal could tell me. It was with the thought of this fantastical gelstei, and him, that I ended our little sojourn by the river and climbed onto my horse. We still had many miles to go.

We reached the lake early that afternoon, cresting a rise to behold an expanse of glittering blue beneath a perfectly clear and deep blue sky. The lake seemed to be many miles wide, but we could not see very far out into it, for a wall of mist rose up from its surface in a thick swathe of gray.

'The Lake of Mists,' Baltasar called out from behind me. 'Surely this must be it.'

Surely it was. At least, that is what the men and women who lived near the lake called it. They were short and thick set with curly black hair and skins nearly as dark as burnt grass. They made their village of little huts hewn of cottonwood; they used the lake's water to irrigate fields won in bitter battle with their hoes against the steppe. It seemed that they grew only one crop: a yellow grain called rushk. Atara called them the Dirt Scrapers; she said that they had come up from the south, perhaps from Uskudar, two thousand years before at the time of the Great Death. The Kurmak allowed them to live here in exchange for a tribute paid in sacks of rushk, which was said to be nearly as sustaining as meat. The Kurmak also protected them from the Adirii and other enemies.

'Ah, they don't seem very grateful of their protectors,' Maram said to me as we rode across the narrow band of their fields. Several of the lake men, stripped to the waist and sweating in the sun, paused in their labor to watch the Manslayers ride past them. They glared at these warrior women with their dark eyes and gripped their hoes as if wishing they might put their blades into the Manslayers instead of hacking at weeds in their fields.

Some of these people, to our good fortune, did not scrape dirt at all, but were fishermen. Following the Manslayers, we rode straight down to lake's shore where an old man bent over caulking his beached boat. The joints of his hands were swollen with a lifetime of grinding work, and were much-scarred – probably from the many fishhooks

235

that had caught in them. Karimah, quirt in hand, demanded his name, and he said that he was called Tembom.

'Well, Tembom,' she told him, 'we have need to borrow your boat for the day, and perhaps more.'

Tembom straightened up his creaky body and stared at me – and the men that I led – as if he had never seen Valari knights before, which he undoubtedly hadn't.

'But why would you need my boat, Mistress?' he asked her.

'Why would you ask me *why*?' Karimah said, snapping the quirt against her hand.

While the Manslayers edged the shore and sat haughtily on their horses and my knights waited behind me to see what would transpire, Tembom looked out at the lake's quiet blue waters and the mist that rose up from it perhaps a mile away. He said, 'If it's fish you want, we have a good catch of carp, Mistress.'

Karimah's blue eyes flashed at him and she snapped, 'My lady and her friends are going fishing after more than carp. Now we'll need your boat.'

I, of course, had told Karimah nothing of my purpose in seeking a boat, and neither had Atara. But Karimah must have guessed much, for her eyes were like glittering gelstei as she stared out into the lake.

Maram liked boats even less than I did, and he dismounted to come up close and take a better look at this one. 'Well, she seems sturdy enough to hold up even if we're lost in that mist for a few hours.'

Tembom's old eyes widened with alarm. 'But, my lord, we never sail out that far. The mist is cursed.'

'How so?'

'It's said that any who sail into it do not return.'

'Cursed, you say? But when was the last time anyone fished there?'

'I don't know. Not in my lifetime or that of my father.'

Tembom stared out toward the center of the lake and shuddered. 'When I was a boy, my uncle, Jarom, said that he didn't care about curses. On a day as peaceful as this, he rowed into the mist – and it ate him alive, along with his boat.'

He rested his hand on the boat's rails as he might the head of a child. I fished a few gold coins from my purse and handed them to him, saying, 'If we don't return, use these to buy another boat.'

Karimah edged her horse right up to the boat, and whipped her leather quirt against it with a quick crack. She said to me, 'This man should not receive *gold* for rendering a rightful service.'

'He owes *me* no service,' I said to her. 'In any case, he must be indemnified against the chance that his boat will be lost.'

'But what of the chances we Kurmak take in protecting him? Hai – pay your gold coins to *us*, I say.'

But I had already given gold to Trahadak the Elder for safe passage across the Kurmak's country, and I wasn't ready to surrender up any more. Then Atara took Karimah aside to confer with her for a few moments. And Karimah said to me, 'Very well, then, we'll wait here with your Valari until you return. But please see that you *do* return. Atara is more precious to me than any gold.'

And with that she smiled as she stroked Atara's long hair. It seemed that she could tender little kindnesses to those she loved as happily as she could put her knife or her arrows into her enemies.

I lost no time in seeing to it that the boat was emptied of its nets, gaffs and other fishing gear. We stowed beneath its weathered seats enough supplies for several days. Then I took the Lightstone from Sar Ianashu and stood on the sandy beach with Lord Raasharu, Baltasar, Lord Harsha and others who were close to my heart.

'You will be in command,' I said to Baltasar. 'Take care that none of the Guardians speaks with Karimah's women.'

'*Guardians*,' Baltasar huffed out. 'What are we to guard then, if you take the Lightstone out into that accursed mist?'

'Guard the shore against our return,' I said, clapping him on his shoulder. I glanced at the Manslayers sitting on their ponies, at their golden hair and long, tanned arms bound in shining gold. I smiled as I added, 'And guard yourselves against *yourselves*.'

I was loathe to leave Altaru behind, for I well-remembered how this noble animal had led us to the first Vild through the trackless tangle of Alonian forest. But there was no way my great stallion could stand inside a little fishing boat. As it was, there was barely room for Master Juwain, Maram, Atara and me – and for Estrella, too, for at the last moment, as I stood in the shallows pushing the boat out into the lake, she broke away from Behira and splashed through the water up to my side.

'All right, all right,' I laughed out as Estrella jumped into my arms. I remembered for the thousandth time Kasandra's prophecy – and now Atara's. 'We won't leave you here.'

I lifted her into the boat, and then climbed in myself. I sat with her near the stern. Maram, to my surprise, volunteered to pull the oars, and he settled into the deep seat in the middle of the boat. Atara and Master Juwain, up near the bow, faced outward toward the center of the lake and the omnipresent gray mist that covered it.

To the sound of little waves lapping against the boat's sideboards and the long, wooden oars dipping into water with steady rhythm, Maram rowed us out into the lake. It was a calm day, and a clear one;

except for our uncertainty as to what we would find in this lake, it seemed that we had little to fear except the radiance of the sun, which in the middle of Marud was hot, constant and fierce.

My diamond armor threw back much of its light in a splendid display, and I could be thankful that I was wearing it instead of my much hotter steel mail. But I was quite hot enough. I sweated in saltwater streams that stung my neck and trickled down my back and sides. The sun burned my face. It seemed to suck the moisture straight out of my boots and leggings, which had soaked through when I had pushed off the boat. The still air was like a blast from an oven searing my eyes.

And then Maram rowed us straight into the wall of mist, and it immediately fell cold. It was like being wrapped in a blanket soaked with ice water. I began shivering, and so did Estrella. I covered her with my wool cloak, but it didn't seem to help very much. The mist dewed our hair and clung to our garments in a slick of moisture. It filled our nostrils and mouths with every breath we drew. There was no escaping it. I turned my head right and left, but this cold, gray cloud seemed equally dense in all directions. It lay so thickly about the lake that I could barely see Atara and Master Juwain near the prow as they drew on their cloaks and shivered, too.

'I can't see a damn thing!' Maram complained as he paused and pulled up the oars. 'I can't see where to row!'

'You can see *me*,' I said to him from only a few feet away. Even so close, there was a moist, smothering grayness between us that seemed to steal the clarity and substance from Maram's considerable form. 'Keep rowing, straight ahead, and we'll be all right.'

'But what is straight, then?'

In answer, I placed my fingertips together like the roof of a chalet and pushed my arms out straight toward the prow of the boat.

'Are you sure, Val? Do you remember how your sense of direction failed you in the Black Bog?'

'This isn't the Black Bog,' I said. 'We set out from the north side of the lake. If Master Juwain's verse tells true, the island must be at the lake's center, toward the south.'

Maram turned to look behind him into the swirling mist, and he said, 'And you're sure that way is south?'

'As sure as a swan flying toward Mesh at the fall of winter.'

'Well, you've always had this uncanny sense. Of course, it did fail *again* when we approached the first Vild, didn't it?'

'Just row, my friend,' I said to him, 'and we'll be all right.'

With a grunt of doubt, Maram went back to working his oars. The sleek wooden blades dipped into the water again and again. Other than this soft sound, it was almost deathly quiet. The whoosh of Maram's breath bubbling out into the air seemed almost as loud as a storm wind.

'It's colder here,' he said suddenly. 'Do you feel it, Val?'

Out of nowhere, the mist grew suddenly thicker, as if it were a wall of cold water pushing against us. It chilled my bones. Something in the air and in the gray lake beneath us – some strange, unsettling and powerful thing – seemed to warn us away in a shiver of dread that tore through the deepest parts of our bodies.

'Accursed mist!' Maram muttered. 'This can't be natural.'

'You know it's not,' Master Juwain said to him from the front of the boat. His voice sounded thin and distant. 'We know the Lokilani protect their Vilds with barriers beyond mists or walls of trees.'

'Invisible barriers,' Maram muttered. 'But felt keenly enough by the heart and soul. Atara! Can you *see* anything?'

'Less than you,' she said pulling at the blindfold across her face.

Estrella, sitting next to me on the moist wood of our seat, pushed herself against the hardness of my armor as I pulled my cloak more tightly about us. I brought forth the Lightstone in the hope that its radiance might show our way through the ever-thickening mist. In my cold hands, the little cup poured forth a glossy, golden light. But the tiny particles of mist threw it back into my face and scattered it so that the air surrounding the boat scintillated and dazzled the eye, making it even harder to see.

'Put it away!' Maram cried out, letting go his oar to cover his face. 'It's no help here!'

I did as he asked, and sat in the darkening grayness as the swells of water beneath us moved the boat gently up and down. The reek of rotten old fish emanated from the boat's creaking boards; the mist seemed to grab this stench, smothering us with it and nauseating us.

'Row, then,' I said to Maram. 'What else is there to do?'

For a while, Maram rowed with as much effort and as steadily as he dared. His fat cheeks puffed out with every stroke, and his beard beaded up with moisture, whether from sweat or the mist, it was hard to tell. After a while, he stopped and asked me, 'How long do you think I've been rowing?'

Water lapped against the boat's sideboards, and I said, 'Not long enough.'

'At *least* an hour, I should say. If I've pulled true, why haven't we reached this damn island yet?'

'We will, soon. Just keep rowing.'

With a soft curse, Maram began working the oars again. And each time he heaved his massive body backward in completion of a stroke, he muttered something under his breath.

Time passed. In this neverland of icy mist that devoured the sun, it was hard for me to tell exactly how much time. It might have be minutes; it might have been days. And then I listened more closely to the words Maram forced out with his heavy breath, and I heard him say, 'Five hundred eighty-one, five hundred eighty-two . . .'

'What are you doing?' I asked him.

He shook his head against the brown curls plastered to his face and told me, 'Counting strokes. If each stroke requires three seconds, then after twelve hundred strokes, well, that's an hour.'

'Yes, very good,' Master Juwain called out from behind him. 'But supposing each stroke requires *two* seconds or four. Then –'

'It doesn't matter,' Maram said. 'I'm just trying to get an idea of how long I've been at this. There's something strange about time here. Can you feel it? It seems like I've been rowing for five days.'

He went back to work with the oars and back to his count. After an even longer time – he didn't say what number he had reached – he shipped oars and slumped forward, resting his head on his hand.

'I'm tired,' he said. 'I'm cold. Val, how about a bit of brandy?'

I brought out a bottle of brandy and poured some into a cup. I handed it to him; he drank it in three quick swallows, then returned the cup to me for another round.

'There's something very wrong here,' he announced. 'I'm sure we're caught in a current. Doesn't anyone feel the boat moving?'

We all kept a silence as we felt for motion of wood over water. It seemed to me that we *were* moving, backward toward the north.

'Yes, yes, a current, of course,' Master Juwain said. 'In the Vilds, the telluric currents are very strong.'

I tried to imagine these invisible, firelike flows that knotted and gathered in certain places in the earth. Like the wheels of light that concentrated at certain points along the body's spine, Master Juwain called them chakras. The great earth chakras, as he now explained to us, could not only open doors to other worlds but work wonders on the forms and substance of this one.

'How else are mountains raised up?' he asked us. 'Why does the ground shake and split apart in some places on earth but not others? And so with the currents of the sea – or even a lake.'

'Very well,' Maram said to him, 'but I had never heard that anyone could wield these earth currents to move wind and water.'

'Neither have I,' Master Juwain said. 'I should very much like to meet these Lokilani and learn their arts.'

240

'We'll meet them soon enough,' I said. 'If there's a current here, we can row out of it.'

So thick was the mist blinding us that we could not test the water's movement by casting slivers of wood out into the lake. There was a slight wind, but this shifted about strangely, and it was difficult to tell if the current caused it by pushing us through the air. It was enough, I hoped, to sense the current's flow: away from the island and toward the north. All we had to do was to row hard against it.

This we now did. I gave Maram a rest and exchanged places with him. I began working the oars as quickly as I could, lifting them out of the water and dipping down as I pushed forward, only to lower them into the lake a moment later and pull backward against its dark, dense grayness with all the power in my legs, arms and back. Again and again, I heaved against the current; I gasped in cold, wet air through my mouth and gave it back in hot bursts of breath. The boat seemed to sail through the water. And yet it seemed that we moved nowhere.

After a long time, I gave up. I shipped oars and rested my arms on my legs as I fought to breathe against the mist that was choking me.

'It's not so easy, is it?' Maram grumbled at me. 'Row out of the current, you say. Row out of this damned mist, *I* say. Let's return to shore while we still can.'

I sat up straight and looked off into the mist past the boat's stern, in the direction from which we had come if we had rowed straight. That way must be north, I told myself. Therefore the boat's prow should still be pointed south.

'For pity's sake, take us out of this!' Maram said to me. 'Turn the boat around, Val.'

As my heart thumped inside my chest and pushed pulsing currents of blood up into my throbbing head, it seemed that water beneath us was slowly turning the boat around – and around and around. Or perhaps it was the turning of the world itself that I felt or some fiery current swirling deep inside it. Whatever it was, some strange and irresistible force seemed to take hold of me deep inside, spinning me about and obliterating my sense of direction.

'We're lost, aren't we?' Maram said.

I looked past his great shoulders at the wall of gray behind him. I looked to the right and left, and the grayness swirled no less densely in those directions. Which way was south? There was mist in my mind, and I could not see it.

'Take heart, my friend,' I said to Maram. 'At least this isn't as bad as the Black bog.'

'Take heart, you say,' Maram sputtered. 'Every time we get in a fix,

241

you remind me that it's not as bad as that filthy, evil place, as if that's supposed to encourage me. Well, so what if this *isn't* as bad? What's bad enough for you? We could still starve here, couldn't we? We could sink in a storm. And if there are currents protecting the island, then why couldn't there be whirlpools, too? To be sucked down into this damn cold water . . . no, no, that's not *quite* as bad as wandering around that stinking Bog until we rotted, but it's bad enough for me.'

I had nothing to say against this rant. For a while, we all fell quiet. Then Master Juwain said, 'The current might not flow back toward the shore. It seems to me that the Lokilani could better protect their island by a current that flowed *around* it, like a ring.'

'Oh, *that* certainly encourages me,' Maram said. 'To think we're caught in some whirl of water that turns around and around their island forever.'

'Take heart,' Master Juwain said to Maram. 'If only we could determine the direction of this flow, we could row crosswise, and so escape it – to go back to shore or continue on to the island, however things fell out.'

But here, caught in this cloud of gray that smothered our senses, moving in our wooden tub as the water moved, there was no way we could think of to feel out the currents of this lake. Can one feel the turning of the earth beneath one's feet?

We were all hungry, and so we paused to eat a meal of cheese and bread. The mist dampened the little yellow loaves that Tembom's wife had given us and caused them to taste like old fish. Not even the brandy that I poured into our cups sufficed to take this rancid taste away.

After that, for many hours, Maram, Master Juwain and I took turns in rowing crosswise against the current – or rather, against the direction we supposed the current to flow. We got nowhere. The mist seemed to grow only darker and thicker about us. I blinked my eyes against its blurring moisture as I tried to make out Atara sitting straight and quiet at the front of the boat. Was her world, when it fell dark, one of perpetual mist? How did she bear it?

'Ah, maybe we shouldn't have cast out those hooks and nets,' Maram said to me. He took a moment to rest from his labor at the oars. 'We could survive a long time here on the fish we could catch.'

'You'll like the Lokilani's food better, when we reach the island,' I told him.

'Yes, if there *is* an island somewhere in the middle of this damn fog. But I'm beginning to think it was all a myth.'

I felt his fear gnawing at his insides like a rat. Master Juwain, sitting again at the front of the boat, fought his growing doubt by keeping his mind whirling like a wheel. Even Atara was perturbed by the uncertainty of our situation. Her being felt steeped in a cold foreboding that made me shiver. Of all of us, only Estrella betrayed no apprehension. Every time I looked at her, she smiled at me in utter confidence that I would lead us aright. Her deep, trusting eyes seemed to show me a bright flame inside myself that not even the mist's smothering dampness could put out.

'The island can't be a myth,' I said to Maram. 'And there must be way to find it.'

Master Juwain, to occupy himself, began reciting the verses that had led us here:

> There is a place tween earth and time,
> In some secluded misty clime
> Of woods and brooks and vernal glades,
> Whose healing magic never fades.
>
> An island in a grass-girt sea,
> Unseen its lasting greenery
> Where giant trees and emeralds grow,
> Where leaves and grass and flowers glow

For no good reason, I drew my sword and pointed it toward the boat's bow and stern, and then port and starboard. Once, its gleaming silver blade had pointed the way toward the Lightstone. But now that I kept the golden cup so close, Alkaladur shone brightly at all times, no matter in which direction I swept it.

> And there the memory crystal dwells
> Sustained by forest sentinels
> Of fiery form and splendid mien:
> The children of the Galadin.

My sword's bright blade now showed only mist: millions of silvery droplets spinning through space like a spray of stars. The swirling pattern recalled a fiery form that was dear to me. I gripped my sword as I interrupted Master Juwain, calling out: 'Has anyone seen Flick?'

'Not for the last hour,' Maram said. 'Or maybe it's been a day.'

As always, Flick flamed into being or unbeing according to no rule or logic that any of us had ever been able to determine. Whether whimsy or will moved his swirls of little lights, perhaps not even the angels knew.

243

'Flick!' I suddenly called out. 'Do you know the way to the island? Can you take us there?'

It was a wild hope, but I wondered if Flick might be able to sense his brethren Timpum on the island that must lie somewhere beyond this mist.

'He can't hear you,' Maram said to me. 'And he certainly can't answer you, any more than Estrella can.'

'Flick!' I called out again. 'Flick! Flick!'

Maram, gripping the oars in his big fists, looked at me as if I had fallen mad.

'Don't you remember Alphanderry's little farce on the way to the Tur-Solonu?' I said to Maram. 'Flick seemed to understand much of what Alphanderry said.'

'Ah, he *seemed* to.'

'And many times since, he's had an uncanny knack of appearing just when we need him the most.'

'Well, we certainly need him now – where is he?'

'Flick!' I said again. 'Flick!'

'He's never come just because anyone called his name, Val.'

As Maram said this, my sword flared brighter. A memory flashed in my mind. At the pass of Kul Moroth, as Alphanderry had sung back an entire army with a voice of unearthly beauty, he had finally beheld Flick's sparkling lights. And just before Alphanderry had died, he had recreated the language of the Star People and had sung out Flick's true name.

> And they forever long to wake,
> To praise, exalt and music make,
> Breathe life through sacred memories,
> Recall the ancient harmonies.
>
> Beneath the trees they rise and ring,
> And whirl and play and soar and sing
> Of wider woods beyond the sea
> Where they shall dwell eternally.

'Ahura!' I suddenly sang out. 'Ahura Alarama!'

Out of the heart of the mist above the boat, a shimmer of lights burst into brilliance. Flickers of scarlet and silver swirled about like a top turning through space.

'Ahura Alarama!' I said again as I looked at Flick. 'Can you show us the way to the island, where the children of the Galadin sing?'

Flick hung suspended in the air only two feet from my face; at the center of his being sparkled a lovely blueness that reminded me of an eye. I looked into it, and it seemed to look into me. And then, without warning, Flick shot off into the mist, toward starboard, like a flock of tiny, twinkling birds suddenly taking flight.

'Turn the boat!' I cried out to Maram. 'Turn the boat and row!'

Maram needed no encouragement from me to begin pulling the oars. Within seconds, he was huffing and sweating and straining with every fiber of his huge body to keep up with Flick. Never had I seen him work so hard, not even in pursuit of wine or women.

'A little more to starboard!' I called out to him as I pointed my sword past his shoulder. 'That's good – now row!'

And row he did. He pulled at the oars with such speed and ferocity that I feared they would break. I feared that *he* might break. But he set his jaw and furrowed his forehead as he called upon reserves inside himself that seemed as vast as the sea. It always astounded me how he could transform himself from a wastrel into an angel of purpose at need. And now the need for furious and directed motion was very great, or so he must have deemed. I could feel his urgency not to lose Flick in the wet grayness, as well as his will to pull free from the onstreaming current. And so he heaved backward against the unseen waters of the lake, again and again, many times as I called for him to turn the boat, right or left, according to the direction of the little light that burned through the mist like the brightest of stars.

Somehow Flick seemed to know not to venture too far beyond us. He remained always a few feet beyond the prow of the boat, whirling in a silver ring of radiance. How long we followed him thusly I couldn't say. Maram couldn't count his strokes, and I was afraid to – afraid that his heart might burst or that he would fall to a stroke of sudden death. And then, with a mighty pull and a grunt from Maram as loud as a bear's, we broke free from the mist into the light of the setting sun. And in its blindingly brilliant rays, straight ahead of us, we sighted land. It was an island covered with giant trees that reached their shimmering green canopies two hundred feet upward toward the clear blue sky.

18

The Lokilani were waiting for us on the beach. There must have been a thousand of them: men, women and children packed four or five deep and lining the sands just beneath the wall of huge oak trees towering above. Like the Lokilani we had met in the first Vild, they were slight of stature, wearing mosslike skirts of some silvery substance over their lithe bodies. They had the same large, leaf-green eyes. But many of them showed hair almost as black and curly as Estrella's, and they were darker of skin than their cousins: their naked arms and legs were smooth and satiny brown like chestnuts. Much to Maram's relief – and my own – none of them bore bows and arrows or any other weapons they might turn against us.

They watched us beach our boat and climb out of it. And then one of them, a little man wearing a necklace of rubies, pointed at Flick, and his large eyes grew even larger with astonishment as he cried out, 'The Big People bring one of Timpirum! So bright! So bright! How is this possible?'

The moment that we set foot on the island, Flick's fiery form grew even more brilliant. His shades of crimson blazed like the rubies around the little man's neck; the blues near his center shone like sapphires, while his whirling bits of silver shimmered diamond-bright.

'The Big People *see* the Timpirum,' the man said, looking at me. 'How is *that* possible?'

And then there occurred what must have been to him the greatest of impossibilities, for many of the Lokilani children, who are not permitted to look upon the Timpum, began jumping up and down and crying out as one: 'I see the Timpirum, too! I see him, I see him!'

'You bring miracles here,' the man said to me. He spoke with a strange lilt that was alike and yet different from that of the Lokilani we had met the year before. Then he walked straight across the beach toward us as if it never occurred to him to fear our swords. He had a

246

bold, inquisitive face. He presented himself as Aunai, and asked our names. These we told him. And then, as if a signal had been given, the entire tribe of the Lokilani ran across the narrow beach and swarmed about us.

'Behold this one's hair!' a little woman cried out as she caught her hands in Atara's flowing mane. 'It's all gold, like an astor leaf!'

'And this one *has* no hair!' another woman said as she reached up to pat Master Juwain's shiny pate.

'And behold the hairface!' a young man said, upon daring to touch Maram's thick brown beard. 'He looks like bear!'

'He's as fat as bear,' one of his friends said, poking him in the belly.

Estrella, small and dark as she was seemed less strange to them, but the little men and women looked up at me in wonder. Many of them pressed close to me, and they ran their little fingers across the diamonds of my armor, the four diamonds set into my silver ring, and the great diamond pommel of my sword. Aunai eyed the scar cut into my forehead. Everything about us seemed a marvel to them.

And we marveled to have discovered another of Ea's vilds. The sun streaking down from the blue sky seemed stronger and brighter here, and yet strangely less harsh, with no burn to its brilliant golden rays. The soft wind carried sweet scents that refreshed our tired bodies and breathed a spirit of joy and celebration into us. Everything around us seemed clearer, deeper, lovelier. The very earth upon which we stood fairly trembled with ancient secrets and a primeval power.

'Beautiful, beautiful,' Atara said as she bent to pick up a little diamond that sparkled in the sands of the beach. 'I had forgotten how beautiful.'

Behind us, out over the lake's turbid waters, the mist waited like a dark ring of doom; but ahead, the Vild's great trees seemed to call us into their abiding greenery, where we might find rest and rejoicing and the fulfillment of our deepest dreams.

One of the Lokilani women, older and taller than most of the others, pressed through the throng and stepped up to us. She wore emerald earrings and a diadem woven with tiny emeralds around her silver-streaked hair. Her face was rather striking, with fine features and an expression that conveyed great sensitivity and kindness. Through her eyes poured a radiance like the sun's light through elm leaves. Aunai presented her as Ninana. I immediately took her to be the Lokilani's queen, but I was wrong.

'We do not have this word "queen",' Ninana said to me after I had tried to explain the ways of the world to her. 'It is a strange idea to

247

us, that one of us should tell others what to do, or should have a greater say than others in what occurs in the Forest.'

Here she turned to look at the great and silent trees rising up along the rim of the beach.

'Sometimes it seems strange to me, too,' I said to her. 'But so it is everywhere – even in your people's other Vild.'

I told her of our journey through Alonia and our sojourn in the Vild that had remained hidden in the deep woods there for many ages; I told her how Maram, Master Juwain, Atara and I had eaten the sacred timana fruit and had been gifted with sight of Flick and all the other Timpum that dwelled there.

'And that is even stranger,' Ninana said. 'To think that you Big People have found your way into the Forest where our cousins live – and now you have found your way here.'

The hundreds of Lokilani standing around us nodded their heads and murmured their amazement at our feat. And I said, 'Has it been long since anyone has come here, then?'

'No one ever comes here.' Ninana stared out into the lake and added, 'No Big People, that is. We allow the birds to come, and the butter-flies – and a few other things.'

'*Who* allows this, then? If you have no queen, is there another with whom we should speak? A man or woman of power? A sorceress?'

I tried to explain my mystification at the barriers that had nearly kept us from the island, and to determine who had summoned them. Ninana listened to me patiently as she gazed up at me. Then she touched the fabric of her skirt and told me, 'It takes only two hands to weave the angel moss into our garments. But it takes many hands – many, many – to weave the mist around the Forest.'

'Very well,' I said, smiling at the Lokilani encircling us. 'But we have so many questions, and we can't speak with all of you.'

'You *must* speak with all of us. And we must speak with you. We have many questions to ask you, too.'

Ninana watched as one of the Lokilani children, a little boy, danced around Flick's silvery swirl, all the while clapping hands and singing and piping out sounds of delight.

'Come, now, come,' Ninana said to us. 'We've agreed that you shall sit with us in the Forest and take refreshment with us, if you are willing.'

Like a flock of birds suddenly changing direction, the Lokilani all turned away from the lake and began walking toward the woods. We followed them. When we reached the line of the trees, the air suddenly fell cooler and quieter, almost alive in itself like the great green sentinels all around us. Giant oaks and elms predominated here, but there were

248

silver maples, too, and many groves of fruit trees laden with apples, pears, cherries and long blue fruits, bright as lapis pendants, which I had never seen. There were more flowers than I had remembered from the first Vild: goldthread, queen's lace, periwinkles, and tiny white starflowers that grew in bright sprays across the forest floor. There, too, out of the earth, grew amethysts and rubies, sapphires and perfect diamonds as big as a man's fist. We had to watch where we stepped for fear of trampling these pretty jewels with our boots. The Lokilani, however, seemed to follow invisible lines through and around the trees. With precision, and yet with naturalness and grace, their leathery feet found their way across the carpet of gold leaves laid out before us. Many of these had been shed by the splendid astor trees, whose fluttering leaves seemed to have soaked in the essence of the sun so that their canopies shone like clouds of gold, even at night. The astors' fruit, the sacred timanas, were golden, too: all round and brilliant like clusters of little suns.

But the loveliest of lights to grace the Forest were those of the Timpum. There were thousands of these twinkling beings, millions. They came in as many kinds as the squirrels, deer, bluebirds and other animals of hoof and wing that dwelled here. No flower unfolded its bright petals without one or more Timpum hovering over it like an even brighter butterfly woven of pure glister and radiance. No tree there was, however great, that did not emanate an aura in glowing curtains of green and gold, violet and silver and blue. As we walked deeper into the woods, Flick made acquaintance with his brethren beings, and he whirled with them in an ecstatic dance of white and scarlet sparks, and some part of his brilliance seemed to pass into them, and theirs into him. The Vild quickened him and made new his splendor with a living presence that was a marvel to behold.

About two miles from the beach, we came to a place were hundreds of mats woven from long shiny leaves had been laid out in a grove of astor trees. On each mat were set bowls of food: fruits, greens, nuts and other nourishment provided by the Forest. Maram eyed the pitchers of berry wines, which he had learned to like better than beer or brandy. He also drank in the beauty of the young Lokilani women as they took their places around the various mats with the men and children. I felt his belly rumbling in anticipation of the feast, even as his blood burned for more fleshy pleasures.

'Ah, Val,' he murmured to me. We sat down with our friends across from Ninana and two other Lokilani women whose breasts were, as he put it, as ripe and perfect as pears. 'I think I've finally come home.'

'Careful, my friend,' I said to him, 'and remember why we're here.'

'Can not a man as large as I contain multiple purposes?'

I smiled at him and said, 'Is that why you agreed to this little quest with so little complaint?'

'Indeed it is. Since I've risked death venturing here, shouldn't I, ah, now enjoy the sweetest fruits of life?'

He smiled at the pretty woman across from him, whose name proved to be Kielii. Then he added, 'I'd like to see Lord Harsha interrupt *this* feast.'

Just then Aunai joined us with a muscular young man he presented as Taije, who turned out to be Kielii's husband. When Maram learned this, he seemed crestfallen. But only for a moment. Upon looking about the woods at all the women kneeling around their mats, he said, 'Ah, well, a bee doesn't forego flowers just because all the nectar has been gathered from the first one he sees.'

I looked about us, too, trying to descry any sign of the Lokilani's village. Through the spreading astors and out between the great columnar trunks of the oaks beyond, I saw nothing that looked like a human habitation. When I asked Ninana where her people's houses were, she looked at me in puzzlement.

'And what is *house*?' she asked me.

I tried to explain the kinds of structures in which all people everywhere lived at least part of their lives. 'Even your cousins in Alonia make houses,' I said.

'Is that true?' Ninana said. 'It has been long – long past long – since any of us has journeyed there.'

'But where do you take shelter when winter comes?'

'Here there is no winter.'

'But what about when it rains and falls cold?'

'Here it rains only when we wish it to rain – and then we bathe or wait beneath the tallest trees to keep dry.'

'But where do you sleep, then?'

Ninana waved her hand toward the mosses blanketing the ground. 'We sleep wherever we fall tired.'

Maram, growing irritable at the sight of all the delicacies spread out before him that he hadn't yet been able to sample, growled out, 'But what of the bears, then? Don't you wish for a good fire at night and a stout wall to keep them away?'

But his words only mystified Ninana and the others. This necessitated another long round of explanations that delayed our meal even further. I tried to tell Ninana how other peoples made fire, which she had seen kindled only by lightning. And Maram tried to describe the eating habits of his huge, hairy friends.

'The bears here,' Ninana said at last, 'eat as we do. Do *your* bears really kill animals to eat them?'

'Sometimes,' Maram said.

'Do they eat people?'

'Not if we can help it,' he said with a nervous smile.

Ninana bent over to confer with Kielii; their soft, lilting words flowed back and forth between them like the music of a brook. And then Ninana asked us, 'Do your *people* eat people?'

'No!' Maram and I said upon the same breath. But then, upon recalling the horrors of Argattha, I added, 'Only in the house of the Red Dragon. Your cousins call him the Earthkiller.'

Ninana's face fell grave as she said, 'The Mora'ajin – yes, we know this one. He lives inside a mountain like a worm. He would eat up the very earth, itself, if he could.'

As Atara's hands clutched at the leaves beneath us, I traded quick looks with Master Juwain. It was astonishing that the Lokilani could know so little and so much.

'But come!' Ninana said, gazing at Atara. 'Our talk has turned sad, too sad, and now it is time to eat and be happy. Later we will speak of these dark things, if we must.'

All around the grove, the hundreds of Lokilani at their little leaf tables had already begun their meal. So then did we. We feasted on foods so sweet and full of life it was as if an elixir filled our bellies and hot spring sap coursed through our veins. Maram drank many bowls of elderberry wine but strangely seemed to fall only a little drunk. We talked of many things: of the ways of their cousins' Vild and the towers of Tria and the dolphins that swam in the sea and sang songs to those who would listen. At last it came time to pass around a bowl laden with ripe timanas. Estrella was not of age to partake in this part of the feast, but the rest of us were ready to eat this sacred, if dangerous, fruit. Once, its sweet, numinous taste had nearly killed Atara. But now that she and all of us had survived this initiatory vision, we had nothing to fear.

And so we feasted on the flesh of the angels, as the Lokilani called the golden fruit. And our vision was renewed. The Timpum appeared to us with even greater brightness and presence than before. Atara was the first to notice a new thing about Flick. To his usual swirls of silver, scarlet and blue had been added a brilliant tinge that we had first beheld deep within the crystal faces of Alumit, the Mountain of the Morning Star. We called this color glorre. It was as distinct from all other colors as blue was from red. It was as if the resplendent steps of the rainbow led to this numinous hue, a secret color that contained

251

the essence of all others and was somehow both their source and culmination. Most men and women could not see it. Certainly none of the Lokilani ever had.

'Look!' Aunai cried out jumping to his feet. 'Look at the Timpirum that the Big People brought!'

Bright bursts of glorre now rippled through Flick's being like waves of water catching the light of the sun. He whirled about beneath the astors as if drawing their unearthly beauty into him.

'The colors!' Aunai cried out. 'The colors!'

All at once, the Lokilani at the other tables rose to their feet to catch sight of the wonder that Aunai pointed out to them. Flick now hovered ten feet above my head, and so the hundreds of men and women in the grove were able to look in amazement upon his vivid swirls of glorre.

'A new color!' Aunai cried out. 'How is this possible?'

I, myself, wondered this, too. Had our eating of the timana made clear to us what had so far remained invisible? Or had the Vild so strengthened the flames of Flick's being that he was now able to bring forth this brightest and loveliest of colors?

Even as I sat motionless gazing at Flick, many of the Lokilani came over to our table to get a better look at him. In the light of their wondering eyes, the bits of glorre sparkling within him blazed ever more brilliantly.

'You bring miracles here,' Aunai said again. He turned to look at Ninana. 'As you said it would be.'

Ninana used a leaf to wipe a bit of timana juice from her lips. Then she looked me and explained, 'Some of us knew of one of these miracles. It was why we allowed you to come here.'

'Knew *how*?' I asked her. 'Are you scryers, then?'

'And what are scryers?'

I stole a quick glance at Atara, then turned back to Ninana. 'Can you see the future?'

'No, no – we see only what *is*. The Timpirum, sometimes, if we look very, very hard, show us what we need to see.'

'Show you . . . *how*?'

'Even as your Timpirum has shown us all the color you call glorre.' Ninana paused to moisten her lips with a sip of elderberry wine. Then she said to me, 'Won't you show us this *other* miracle you keep hidden, Vala'ashu Elahad? The jewel that gives the golden light?'

I looked into Ninana's wise old eyes, amazed yet again by what she knew. Then, with hundreds of the Lokilani crowding about our table, I reached inside my armor where I had tucked the small cup that I had brought out of Argattha. I stood up and held the Lightstone high for all to see. It flared in my hand. At first its radiance was golden, even as Ninana had said, but soon the light grew more intense, deepening to a brilliant white.

'Too bright! Too bright!' Aunai said, shielding his eyes with his hands. 'The jewel is too bright!'

As night had fallen several hours before, the world about us should have been dark. But the Timpum lit up the woods like countless candles, and the astors' canopies were like great, glowing domes above us. And in my hand I held a blazing star. At first its light dazzled almost everyone. But soon its brilliance deepened even more so that it fell perfectly clear – as clear as the air on a crisp winter day. One by one, the Lokilani were able to look upon the Lightstone without taking hurt through their eyes. But their hearts ached with the sweet strife of wonder, as did Estrella's, Atara's and mine. For just then Flick soared into this clear light, and the flames of his entire being blazed deep with a singular color, and that was glorre. Other Timpum, drawn to him like bright-hued moths, danced about with him in the vast silence that fell over the woods. Some of Flick's fire passed into them. Sprays of glorre brightened their forms, too. And then these Timpum spun off to rejoin their brethren deeper in the woods, passing on the flame from one to another like a fire spreading outward through dry grass. It took only moments, it seemed, for all the millions of Timpum in the Forest to come alive with this lovely angel fire.

After a while the Lightstone quiesced, and the Lokilani could see that it was just a plain golden bowl, and not a jewel as Ninana had said. Flick quiesced as well. He returned to a bright whirling of silver and scarlet sparks. But within his little form remained many brilliant bands of glorre. So it was with the other Timpum illumining the silent woods.

'A very great miracle,' Ninana said, gazing at the Lightstone as I sat down again. 'May I hold this jewel, Vala'ashu?'

I gave the Lightstone into her little hands, and she squeezed it a moment before passing it to Aunai. I told her something of the tale of how we had fought our way into Argattha to wrest the Lightstone from Morjin's throne room.

'You've given much, so very, very much, to find this Jewel of Light,' she said to me. She studied Atara's blindfold for a moment before turning her gaze on me as if looking deep into my heart. 'But why, why?'

I tried to tell her of the Star People's purpose in sending the Lightstone to earth. I told her of the battles that had been fought over

253

the ages to claim it. I said that the golden cup held inside it the fate of Ea and all her peoples, even the Lokilani.

'Tonight,' I said, 'we've all beheld what you call a miracle. The Lightstone works many such. But there is one miracle, the only true one, for which it was meant.'

Ninana waited for me to continue and then said, 'Please, tell us.'

I traded glances with Master Juwain and said, 'That we have not been able to discover. It remains one of the Lightstone's secrets. But we do know that there is one, and one only, who was meant to work this miracle.'

'And who is that?'

'We call him the Maitreya.'

At the mention of this name, Ninana drew in a deep breath, and Aunai nodded at Taije. Then a murmur of recognition rippled outward through the men and women gathered around us.

'We know this one, too,' Ninana said to me. 'We call him the Matri'aya, the Lightning. He is the one who opens the sky. The way to the worlds where the Forest covers all the earth. But we have never known that the Matri'aya would use a Jewel of Light to make this opening.'

Although I tried to keep my face calm, her words disturbed me deeply. I said nothing of how Morjin would use the Lightstone to open ways of his own: to the Dark Worlds and wastelands where the trees had been cut long ago and now not even a bird remained to sing a bright song.

'I think you have come to the Forest to look for the Matri'aya,' Ninana said to me suddenly. 'But the Matri'aya is not *of* the Forest, as are the nightingales and the fritillaries and the deer – and the Lokilani. This we know. The Matri'aya is the one who will come to the Forest from another place and take its most precious seed back to this place so that the trees will grow again in all lands.'

I looked off at Flick, who was now hovering beneath an astor tree. Weren't the Timpum, I wondered, in some sense the vital seeds from which the Forest's great trees germinated and took their deeper life? And wasn't Flick, this bright being of flame and glorre, the most precious of all these seeds?

'We *have* come here to seek the Maitreya,' I admitted. 'Though as you have said, we did not think to find him among the Lokilani.'

At this Master Juwain nodded his head and added, 'You see, we hope to recover the knowledge of *who* the Maitreya is and how he might be recognized.'

Ninana's eyes lingered on the lightning bolt scar cut into my forehead. Then she asked me, 'Are *you* the Matri'aya?'

My breath caught in my throat, and I took a quick drink of the Lokilani's cool, sweet wine. And I said, 'That must be tested. That must be known.'

'Then did you come here hoping that the Timpirum would make this known to you?'

'Not exactly,' I told her. 'But it's said that they guard a crystal that might tell us the secrets of the Lightstone – and the Maitreya.'

'In the Forest, as you have seen,' Ninana said, touching her emerald earrings, 'there are many crystals.'

'This one is called an akashic crystal.'

'I don't know that name.'

'It is a kind of thought stone. It holds memories of the Elder Ages.'

Ninana looked knowingly at Aunai just then, and my heart began beating faster. She nodded her head and said to me, 'The Jewel of Memory. Yes, we know this crystal. It was brought here long ago.'

Now Master Juwain rubbed his hands together and leaned forward toward Ninana. 'But how long ago, then? Three hundred years? Three thousand?'

The lines of Ninana's face drew up into a puzzled frown. 'And what is *year*?'

I smiled at Master Juwain's consternation. What, indeed, was a year to a people who had no winter, but only eternal spring?

'A year is twelve months,' he said to her. 'When the moon waxes full twelve times, that is a year.'

Now he smiled, too, very pleased to have found so easy a measure to match the time of the outside world with that of the Vild. But his satisfaction melted away a moment later as Ninana said, 'The moons come and go like the fruit on the trees, and who counts them? And why, why?'

'*Why*, do you ask? Why, to gauge time, my lady. To keep track of history and when events occurred.'

Ninana's face tightened as if she had chewed a bitter fruit. She said, 'You bring miracles into the Forest, but many distasteful words, too. The history that you have spoken of is nothing more than war and evil happenings. But here, there is only eating and singing, making babies and dying. Nothing ever *happens* that you would call an event.'

Master Juwain seemed inclined to want to argue with her. I could almost hear him lecturing her on the need to know the past so that its evils weren't visited upon the future. I reached over and squeezed his gnarly hand to silence him. And to Ninana I said, 'You've told us that the akashic crystal was brought here long ago, is that right?'

'Yes, before any of our grandmothers' great-grandmothers were born.'

255

'But you've also told us that none except the animals come from the outside. But it can't have been a bird or a butterfly who bore the akashic crystal to these woods.'

'No, indeed, it cannot,' Ninana said. 'I'm sorry that I didn't speak more clearly. I should have said that no *man* ever comes here.'

Maram patted his bulging belly as he stared across the table at a small, elegant woman standing in close with the other Lokilani. He said, 'You mean it was a *woman* you allowed past your damn mists?'

'No, indeed not,' Ninana said. 'No woman ever comes here, either.'

Maram held up his hands in helplessness as he looked at me. Then Atara, who had said very little during the feast, showed a bright smile. She had almost as good a head for puzzles as Master Juwain, and she could often see more.

'The Timpum are called the children of the Galadin,' she said to Ninana. 'Your cousins believe that the Galadin walked their woods long before long ago, and left the Timpum to light the trees.'

'Yes, the Galad a'Din *did* walk the world when it was all the Forest,' Ninana said. 'But the one who brought the Jewel of Memory was not of them. Like, but not so bright. And he could die, even as we die and all things do except the Bright Ones.'

'One of the Elijin,' Atara said softly.

I thought of Kane, who was once called Kalkin and might some day be again. In Argattha, he had told me about a band of immortal brothers who had come to Ea with him from the stars. Their names had been written in my memory with fire and blood: Sarojin, Averin, Manjin, Balakin and Durrikin. And Iojin, Mayin, Baladin, Nurijin and Garain. In the savagery of the Age of Swords, all had been killed – all except Kane and Morjin.

'What was this Elijin's name?' I asked Ninana.

'That is not remembered.'

'But you have preserved the story of his coming and the crystal that he brought. And you say that he could die – how do you know that?'

'Because he died *here*, in the Forest. We have set the Jewel of Memory above his grave.'

This news pleased Master Juwain even more than the sight of so many lovely Lokilani women enchanted Maram. Atara sat silent and still as if trying to behold this akashic crystal that we had come so many miles to find. Estrella nibbled on a pear, and gazed up at the astor's glowing leaves as if our stories and quests were not her concern. But Ninana's words cut me to my heart. That one of the great Elijin should have died here did not seem possible.

'Where is this grave, then?' I asked Ninana. 'May we see it?'

'Of course you may. But not tonight. Now it's time for singing and dancing, and sleeping. Tomorrow will come soon enough, soon, soon.'

The ways of Ninana and her people were really not so different from the Lokilani we had known before. A hundred of them, or more, made circles inside circles and danced about to songs that might have been as old as the Forest itself. With their bright green eyes and their spinning and whirling, they reminded me of the Timpum who spun with them. We all joined them and danced, too, even Estrella who could not add her voice to ours. But I gave her my flute, and with this little piece of wood she made a sweet music, to the Lokilani's delight. She danced about with a little boy who might have been her brother, all the while piping out perfect melodies. I had never seen her so happy, and this gladdened my heart.

At last, with the hundreds of Lokilani finding places to rest in the woods about us, we laid out our cloaks and made our beds on soft mosses. Atara cradled Estrella in her arms, and they soon fell asleep. And so did Master Juwain, for all the rowing earlier that day had exhausted him. As it had Maram and me. But I lay awake gazing at the new color that brightened Flick's form. It made me wonder what marvels might light up the akashic crystal that we would try to open on the morrow.

19

In the morning, after a light breakfast of fruit and nuts, we gathered
in the grove. Ninana and Aunai were to lead us to the Elijin's grave
and the great crystal planted there. Fifty of the Lokilani decided to
join us on this early stroll through the woods. Aunai led forth, with
Ninana walking behind him with the grace of a doe. Atara and Estrella,
holding hands, followed closely, with Maram, Master Juwain and me
only a few feet behind them. The fifty Lokilani fanned out behind us,
taking no care to walk in line or any kind of order. They chatted gaily
and piped out friendly words to each other like the birds in the trees
singing their songs. They had no fear that anyone should hear them;
they had no mind for marching or hurrying against time. To my frustration, they stopped frequently, as Ninana and Aunai did, to drink from
a clear brook or to pluck a pear to eat or to exclaim over the beauty of
a flower. As we passed deeper into the woods, many were their cries of
delight, for it seemed that the Timpum here all retained the bright new
color that Flick had bestowed upon them. A few Lokilani paused to
dance with these glorious beings, and a few more lost interest in our
mission and dropped out altogether – perhaps to dance with each other
in some secluded glade. What would it be like, I wondered, to live with
no thought for the future, as if each day were complete in itself and
might go on forever? To know nothing of hatred, killing or war?

About two hours into our journey, Atara stopped suddenly and
turned as if to look off through the trees. I looked too, and so did
many others. And there, only twenty-five yards away, a strange animal
stood munching the browse from a bush. It was about the size of a
deer and had much of that animal's grace, and yet it had something
of the goat and the lamb about it, too. It looked, however, more like
a small horse. Its fur was all white, and a single horn, straight and
showing spiral swirls like a seashell, grew out of its head. It seemed
utterly unconcerned that we should stand so close watching it.

'It's beautiful – what is it?' Maram said. 'In all the world, I've never seen anything like it.'

'In all the world you won't,' Ninana said to him. 'The *asherah* is of the worlds where the Bright Ones dwell.'

'Then how did it come to be here?'

Ninana waved her hand at the great trees growing all around us. She said, 'This is all that remains of the Forest that once was. You have called our home an island. But on all worlds everywhere, there is *one* Forest. Sometimes here, in certain places, when the stars are bright and the earth sings songs from deep inside, the trees remember this. Then our Forest and *the* Forest are truly one. And then the asherahs sometimes wander into our woods.'

'Is that *all* that wanders in?' Maram asked. He scanned the woods as if looking for dragons or other fell beasts.

'Yes,' Ninana said with a smile. 'The Galad a'Din allow only the asherahs to come here. They are blessed, blessed. They remind us of the deeper Forest where the Lokilani will walk some day when the stars call us home.'

I gazed at the asherah, standing in all its perfect whiteness, and the innocence of its bright, black eyes stunned me into silence. But Maram persisted in his inquisition: 'But why don't your people just follow the asherahs *back* to the Galadin's worlds?'

'Because once they come, they do not leave.'

And so it was with all the peoples of Ea, I thought. Our ancestors had come to earth thousands of years before, and here we remained on our much greater island as exiles on a war-cursed world.

'Ah, too bad,' Maram said, studying the strange beast standing before us.

'No, it is not so,' Ninana said to him. 'The asherahs give us great hope. For some day, they *will* leave – some day, some day. Their horns have great magic. It's said that they point the way back to the stars.'

Upon hearing this, Estrella's eyes lit up with wonder. And then suddenly, before I could stop her, she broke away from Atara and dashed off through the trees, straight toward the asherah. The animal should have been startled into a burst of furious motion, either fleeing from Estrella's wild charge or lowering its head to bring its wicked horn to bear in its defense. But it just stood there, regarding Estrella with its bright eyes. And then, as Estrella came closer and drew up in front of the asherah, it *did* lower its head. And Estrella reached out her slender hand and touched the asherah's horn. Estrella's whole being danced with delight. Her joy seemed to pass into the asherah, for it nuzzled Estrella's face and licked her ear. And all the while,

Estrella kept her hand wrapped around the asherah's great, shining horn.

I sensed within the asherah a great power; I knew that it could fiercely battle, with hoof and horn, lions or bears or any who attacked it. I sensed, too, that Estrella was in no danger. And yet, despite myself, I moved to protect her. I took only a single step forward. But it was enough for the asherah to regard me warily with its deep, knowing eye, and then to shake off Estrella's hand and bound off into the woods.

Estrella ran back to me and looked at me as if to ask why I had driven away this magic animal. What could I tell her? I hardly knew myself.

After that we resumed our journey, and all of us watched the woods hoping for the asherah to return. We walked beneath the great oaks and maples, where many birds called to each other from their branches. After a while, we paused to drink from a cool stream. And Maram said to me, 'There's something strange here, Val. Stranger even than that one-horned horse. We've been walking for at least three hours with the sun behind us. And so we should have covered a good ten miles. I didn't think this whole island could be half that wide.'

Neither did I. And neither did Master Juwain, who wiped his wet hands against the back of his bald head as he sighed out, 'Perhaps the old maps were wrong.'

'Is our sense of the lake's size wrong?' Maram asked. 'Is our sense of this island? It seems that it must go on for another fifty miles. Strange, strange.'

The Lokilani's Vild, I thought, was full of marvels and mysteries. We walked through the sweet-smelling woods for another two hours after that. And then we came to a place where an astor grove was spread out over a few small hills. And there lay buried the greatest mystery of all.

Aunai led us along winding ways beneath the beautiful trees, with their silver bark and their lovely leaves a yellow-gold brilliance against the blue sky. Many of them were in flower: bright bursts of white petals enveloped their boughs like clouds of light. Ninana told us that each tree had been planted from a seedling over the grave of one of their ancestors.

'The astors,' she said softly, 'are our fathers and mothers. Do you see, do you see? The Lokilani can never *really* die.'

Suddenly, as with the asherah, Estrella broke away from us and ran on ahead of Aunai. At first, I thought that she must have sighted another of these strange animals. I hurried after her, as did Maram and Master

Juwain, Aunai and Ninana and many others. But as we rounded the base of a hill, I could see no large animals of any kind through the open trees. And then I realized that it was not one of the asherahs that had drawn Estrella onward. For she stopped abruptly before a long mound, covered with grass. Aunai's exclamation of astonishment told me that she had led us unerringly to the Elijin's grave.

'But how did the girl know?' he asked me.

'She has a gift,' I told him. As we drew up next to Estrella and gathered around the grave, I explained that Estrella was a seard who could sense within herself the essence of the crystal that we sought.

This Jewel of Memory, as the Lokilani called it, was set upon a cairn of stones above the grave. I stopped breathing for a moment because I had never seen anything quite like it. It was round and flat, like a discus; its center was as clear as Atara's white gelstei and encircled by bands of translucent violet, blue and the other colors of the spectrum. Many Timpum, like hummingbirds, hovered above it. It was the first time I had seen these bright beings drawn to something that was not alive.

'Look!' Aunai said. 'Your Timpirum has come, too.'

Flick, I saw, appeared among the other Timpum and flitted about with them. Their colors caught up the hues of the akashic crystal. And this great thought stone reflected theirs, for its clear center suddenly shone with the singular brilliance of glorre.

'The verse did tell true,' Master Juwain said, staring at it. 'For here, surely, the memory crystal dwells.'

'And here the one who brought it to this island also dwells,' Maram said, shuddering as he pointed at the grave. 'But why isn't an astor planted here? Surely the Elijin deserve to be honored as do the Lokilani.'

'Surely they do,' Aunai admitted. 'But many times, it's said, so very many times we have tried to plant the sacred seeds here. But they would not grow. And so we planted grass instead.'

Maram nudged the mound with the toe of his boot and said, 'There's good dirt here like any other. I don't understand why grass should grow from it but not these pretty trees.'

'Why, why?' Aunai said to him. 'We have asked ourselves why for many, many of what you call years, but we do not understand.'

I drew my sword then, and stared at its mirror-like silustria. The Lokilani, too, stared at this new wonder that shone in their woods. And then, as I touched my finger to Alkaladur's edge, Ninana cried out in dismay to see blood welling up from the slight wound it made.

'What have you done?' she said to me. 'And why, Vala'ashu?'

In answer, I walked over thirty paces to the nearest astor tree. Ninana

261

and Aunai and a dozen other Lokilani followed me. So did my friends. I came up to the tree's lowest bough, which was laden with many clusters of white flowers. I held out my finger and let a single drop of blood fall upon one of these. The little red ball rolled along one of its white petals before gathering into a tiny pool at the flower's center. I waited while my heart beat three times. And then, to my horror, I watched as the flower's petals blackened as if from flame and curled inward into a dark, withered knot.

'What have you done?' Ninana cried out again. 'Why, why?'

I sheathed my sword and sucked on my finger for a moment before pointing back toward the grass-covered grave. 'The Elijin did not just die here; he *came* here to die.'

Master Juwain's gray eyes lit up like the sea under a bright sun as he said, 'Do you think it is Balakin that lies here, then?'

'It must be he,' I said. I turned to Ninana and tried to explain. 'The Beast we call Morjin led a quest to recover the Lightstone, long, long ago. And he killed others of his kind whom he feared might find the Lightstone. It's said that one of these, Balakin, he poisoned with kirax.'

'But what is *kirax*?'

'It's made from the kirque plant,' I told her. I tried to describe this blue weed that grew in more mountainous climes. 'It's the deadliest of poisons.'

She looked at me in utter mystification. 'But what is *poison*?'

I drew in a deep breath to cool the burning inside me. I tried to explain this, too, saying, 'It's all life's bitterness and hatred of other life distilled into an evil essence. The kirax consumes life like a fire does leaves.'

'Oh, that is bad, very bad,' Ninana said. She reached up and plucked the dead flower from among the many others still living along the silver bough. 'The astor is the most blessed of trees, but it will grow only in blessed soil.'

She led the way back to Balakin's grave, if indeed it was he who had been buried here. She held out her hand above this green mound and said, 'Then the kirax has . . . *poisoned* the earth here. So that is why only grass will grow.'

'Yes,' I said, 'so it must be.'

'But you say this Balakin and his kind were immortal?'

'Immortal, yes – but they could still be killed. Even though it would take much kirax to kill one of the Elijin.'

'And this kirax,' she said, holding out the dead flower, 'did the Mora'ajin poison you, too?'

'Yes,' I told her. 'One of his men did.'

'But you still live. You're as beautiful as a flower but you must be as tough as grass.'

I noticed Atara smiling at this, and I smiled sadly, too. And then I said, 'No, that is not it. The amount of poison in me is minute. And yet, one day it will kill me, too.'

One day, I knew, I would strike my sword into an enemy trying slay me or someone I loved. The kirax, which tormented every nerve in my body like tendrils of fire, also ignited my gift of *valarda* and left me even more open to others' agonies, especially those I inflicted upon living flesh. And so one day I would kill, and the terrible pain of it would carry me down into death.

No, I told myself, *that must not be.*

'Is there no cure for it?' Ninana asked me. She laid her cool hand on the scar cut into my forehead. 'No rain to put out the fire?'

I brought forth the Lightstone and held the little cup over Balakin's grave. 'It was my hope to find a cure in this.'

'And have you?'

'Almost,' I said. 'Almost, I have.'

'I don't understand.'

I gazed at the little cup, all golden against the golden canopies of the astors spread out around me. I said, 'You speak of rain to quench this anguish that burns all beings, and yet there are lakes inside me, truly, entire oceans. Inside all people, if only we could find them. Once, when I held the Lightstone, I did. And many times since . . . almost.'

Ninana nodded her head and looked at me sadly but hopefully. 'Then is the Matri'aya also the one who would show the way to these oceans?'

'We believe so. He must have the power to use the Lightstone this way. We believe that the akashic crystal will tell of this.'

I handed the Lightstone to Master Juwain. And he stepped closer to the head of the grave, where the akashic crystal showed its bands of brilliant colors.

'Might I try to open this crystal, my lady?' he asked Ninana.

'Open . . . how?'

Ninana looked at him doubtfully as if suspecting he might use the Lightstone to hammer at the crystal like a boy cracking open a nut.

'There are resonances between the Lightstone and the crystal,' he tried to explain. 'As with people. We speak words to each other, and this opens each other's minds.'

Ninana thought about this as she studied the Lightstone. Then she looked at Aunai and asked, 'Do you think this is all right?'

Aunai nodded his head and told her, 'I can't see the harm of it.'

Then he turned to a man named Ekewai and asked the same question of him, and so it went, men and women conferring with each other until all the Lokilani present consented to Master Juwain's proposal.

And so Master Juwain held the Lightstone before the great crystal. I expected him to have at least as much difficulty unlocking its secrets as he'd had with the thought stone in my father's hall and those in the Brotherhood's sanctuary in Nar. So it surprised me to see him give a gasp, even his eyes deepened like the sea and Lightstone poured forth a radiance full of glorre. It touched the crystal's center and rippled outward, changing its bright bands one by one until the crystal's entire surface shone with this new color. I felt my heart beating hard inside my chest, and it seemed that the akashic crystal pulsed with a deep and secret light. Master Juwain, it seemed, was drinking it in through his eyes and every particle of his being.

I feared that he might stand there all day in rapture. And so it surprised me once more when, a few moments later, the Lightstone's splendor faded along with that of the akashic crystal, and Master Juwain's eyes grew focused and hard.

'What time is it?' he called out, looking up at the sun pouring down through the trees.

'Scarcely past noon,' I said to him. 'Why do you ask?'

His ugly, old face radiated excitement. 'Noon, yes, of course – but what *day* is it?'

Maram stepped up to him and touched his shoulder. 'Ah, it's still *today*, sir. The thirteenth of Marud, I think.'

'Impossible,' he said, giving the Lightstone back to me. He stared at the akashic crystal sitting on top of its pile of stones. 'Days have passed, it seems, weeks.'

Atara smiled at him and said, 'So it is sometimes when a scryer looks into her crystal.'

'Yes, it must be,' Master Juwain said.

To the gasps of the Lokilani, Maram reached out to touch the akashic crystal's colored bands. 'Then I gather you opened this?'

'Opened it? Indeed, I suppose you could say I did. But does one open the sea when cast into its cold waters?'

I smiled to see waves of happiness spreading across his face, transforming him from something squashlike into the loveliest of human beings. 'Then there is much knowledge in the crystal, as we hoped?'

'Knowledge, Val? You can't even begin to imagine.' Master Juwain was almost hopping about as if he'd drunk ten cups of coffee. 'A

264

common thought stone holds great knowledge, but compared to this, it's like a drop. *I* can't imagine it myself. If all the words in all the books in the Library at Khaisham were written here, there would still be room for a million more such libraries.'

'Tell me of these words, then,' I said.

Now Master Juwain's face fell sad and sick as if he had discovered a store of grain that had gone moldy. 'I cannot, I'm sorry. You see, all the knowledge bound in this crystal, all the words – it was all recorded in the language of the angels.'

For a thousand miles across the forests, mountains and deserts of Ea, Alphanderry had tried to recreate this strange and beautiful language of the Elijin and Galadin that no man understood. And at the pass of the Kul Moroth, for one brilliant moment, in an outpouring of perfect song that shook the very heavens, he had succeeded. But it seemed that the secrets of this language had died with him.

'Ah, too bad,' Maram said. 'Then there's no hope of ever understanding it.'

'No, there must be hope,' I said. 'There must be a way.'

Master Juwain brightened a bit and said, 'Alphanderry sang out the words of this language. If only we could remember them and learn their meaning, we might be able to use them to decipher it.'

I drew my sword again and held it pointing toward the sky. Its silvery surface reflected the golden astor trees and the immense blue dome above the world. Flickers of the Timpum's colors danced along the blade. The Sword of Truth, men called Alkaladur, the Sword of Memory.

'Alphanderry,' I said suddenly, 'sang *these* words before Morjin's men slaughtered him: "*La valaha eshama halla, lais arda alhalla.*"'

'Are you sure, Val?' Master Juwain asked me.

'Yes, to the word – I am sure.'

'But we don't know what this means.'

I gazed long and deeply at my sword, and I said, 'Almost, I do, sir. There's something about this language. In hearing it, it's like *knowing* that I know the lines to a song from childhood that I had thought forgotten. It's as if the song is right *there*, just beneath my deepest memories, but I can't quite bring it to mind.'

'I wonder if it must have been that way for Alphanderry, too,' Master Juwain said. 'Can you remember more of what he sang out?'

'Almost, I can.'

'Well, you may, in time.' He rubbed his hand across the akashic crystal with the reverence he might have reserved for a book. 'We need more time. Time to gain more words, and time to learn their meaning.'

'How much time, sir?'

'I don't know. Many days, I should think. Maybe months.'

I sheathed my sword, and I, too, touched the opalescent crystal. It was cool like any other stone. So, I thought, it had come to this, as I had feared it might. I looked at Ninana and said, 'We would like to borrow this, if we may.'

She looked at me as if I had suggested borrowing one of the Lokilani's children. 'Do you mean, to take the Jewel of Memory from the Forest?'

'Yes,' I said to her. 'We can't remain here, and neither can this crystal if we are to learn from it what we must.'

'I understand,' Ninana said, moving closer to the head of the grave. 'But the jewel is dear to us, very dear.'

Aunai stepped forward and touched her shoulder. 'There was a time when the jewel did not dwell here, and a time when it will not again.'

Ekewai, a slight, comely man who seemed as gentle as a sheep, pointed at the crystal and said, 'The Ela'ajin brought this here for a purpose. To keep it safe, yes?'

'To keep it safe,' Aunai said, glancing at me, 'or to keep it for the Matri'aya?'

Ninana held out her wrinkled hands toward the Timpum sparking and shimmering above the akashic crystal. They seemed to gather up its colored lights as bees might a flower's nectar.

'It would be a great loss to us,' Ninana said sadly.

'It is a great decision to have to make,' I told her. 'Perhaps you could call together your elders and hold council.'

'No, that is your way,' she said. 'Our way is this: since the loss would be all the Lokilani's, all the Lokilani must decide.'

And with that, she turned to Ekewai and a young woman named Noehela and others, and she asked them if they would call their people from across the island to gather here. They agreed to this, hurrying off through the trees in different directions – or rather, walking a little more quickly than was usual for them and with new purpose.

And so we waited there in the astor grove all the rest of the day for the great council to commence. As dusk fell and the woods deepened with whatever darkness ever touched this enchanted island, the Lokilani began arriving in twos and tens. Delectable foods were brought forth, and we sat among the mosses and flowers feasting far into the night. We listened to the katydids calling in the trees; we watched the Timpum brighten the grove even as the stars lit up the sky. And still the Lokilani had not gathered in all their numbers, and so we laid out our cloaks and slept. Early the next morning, a few hundred more of the little people came singing and dancing into the grove as if to a birthday celebration. By noon, I counted some twelve hundred men, women and children crowding the ground about Balakin's grave.

Ninana finally came up to me and stood with me above the akashic crystal. The emeralds in her black and silver hair sparkled with a green fire as she said, 'We are ready.'

'Very well,' I said, looking at Maram and Master Juwain. Atara sat nearby working a comb through Estrella's curly black hair. 'Do you need us to withdraw while you make your vote?'

'Vote?' she said.

I explained to her how certain of the free peoples chose their kings or made their laws.

'Oh, no,' she said, 'that is not our way, either. We must speak with each other and reach an understanding. We must be of one mind.'

'But a thousand people can't be of one mind!' Maram said. 'And they certainly can't all speak with each other. It would take a year!'

But it seemed that the Lokilani could – and that it might take nearly as long as Maram feared. Ninana gathered in all the goodness of her voice, which was pleasant but not strong; she spoke to all assembled, giving as clear and truthful account of our quest as anyone could. When she had finished, she asked me if I or any of my friends had anything to add. We didn't. And so the Lokilani began the long work of deciding what should be done.

They broke into perhaps two hundred groups, and sat in little circles, spread out across the hills of the astor grove. For an hour or more, they did nothing but talk. The sound of their small voices was like the buzzing of the bees that flew from flower to flower spreading pollen. From time to time, one or more of them would break away from their group and walk over to join another, adding other voices to what was one continuing conversation. This mixing and mingling occupied another few hours, by which time many of the Lokilani had grown hungry, as had we. And so they sat in their circles, and they ate their berries and bearseed bread and drank their, cool, sweet wine. And all the while they talked and laughed and sang their sweet songs, and it was hard to believe that they were engaged in an argument of great moment.

Toward the end of the day, while we waited near the akashic crystal, the Lokilani merged into larger groups of twenty or thirty. And still they gave voice to their thoughts, many of which seemed opposed to giving up their great jewel. That the Lokilani children felt free to speak as equals with their mothers and fathers surprised me. More than once, like kittens dancing around a butterfly for the first time, two or three of them would come over to get a better look at me and my friends;

267

some of them even dared to ask me questions or tried to prompt me into laughter or song. Their parents came, too, and these looked harder at me, at the scar marking my forehead, and their questions were harder and more pointed. At dusk it came time for yet another meal as the men and women of the woods reassembled into yet larger groups. Finally, late that evening, with the Timpum lighting up the flowers and grasses like fireflies, the Lokilani sat all together as one, a little army of little people ready to protect that which was dearest to them, as any people would.

As emissaries, Ninana and Aunai, with Taije and Kielii, came over to us. The look on Ninana's face was both hopeful and grave. My friends and I all stood as she addressed us: 'We have spoken together all day, and still there could be more talking, much more – but we know that you desire to return to your own lands.'

'Have you reached a decision?' I asked her.

'We have, Vala'ashu.'

My chest swelled like a bellows as I waited for her to say more.

'We have decided that we cannot decide, I'm sorry. We are still of many minds, many, many.'

I felt the air explode from my lips as if someone had punched me in my belly. I said, 'Then no decision is a decision.'

'If you could stay here longer, perhaps a moonful of days, or two, then we could discuss this further, yes?'

I thought of the great conclave in Tria that would begin in only two more weeks, and I said, 'We cannot remain here. But even if we could, what would change your people's minds?'

'Many look for the wisdom to make this decision in the lights of the Timpum. Many of us look for a sign.'

I, too, looked for a sign of what to do. My friends could not help me. Master Juwain brought out his journal and stood writing down the few words of the angels' language as if he might never hear spoken any others. Atara rolled her scryer's sphere between her hands, but her face remained as blank as the white cloth that covered her eyes. Maram stared greedily at the akashic crystal as a pirate might regard treasure. I was afraid that he might counsel me to seize the crystal and fight our way off the island. And Estrella simply smiled at me as if to ask why I concerned myself with glittering gelstei when all I needed to know dwelled like a bright light within my heart.

At last I brought out the Lightstone and held it toward the akashic crystal. In its presence, the colors of the translucent disc began swirling and flaring with greater radiance.

'A sign,' I whispered. 'A sign.'

A vivid light flashed in my mind then, and to Master Juwain, I cried out, '*Lais* – the Galadin's word for sign is *lais!*'

Even as my voice died off into the sounds of the wind and the distant song of a nightingale, Flick blazed into being and whirled above the akashic crystal. The lights of his fiery form rippled in a pattern that seemed at once familiar and utterly strange. I could almost read these colors of crimson, silver and glorre as I might letters on a page of a book. Two spots of a deep brown, like eyes, formed up out of this swirl and seemed to gaze at me. And then, to my astonishment – and that of Master Juwain, Ninana, Aunai and all those gathered around us – from Flick's luminous center, a beautiful music poured forth. It rose and swelled in perfect syncopation with the pulses of radiance he gave to the night. In its lovely harmonies was the sweetness and clarity of water running over smooth rocks and all the brilliance of a star. It sounded almost like the song of the angels, in which music and words were as one.

'A sign,' Ninana murmured. 'A sign.'

'The Timpirum sings!' Aunai cried out. 'I hear him! I hear him!'

We all did, and that was very strange, for no one in the Lokilani's wood had ever heard any of the Timpum utter the slightest sound.

'A sign,' Ninana said again, this time more loudly. 'This is surely a sign that this Timpirum belongs with the Jewel of Memory.'

'And that the jewel belongs with the Timpirum,' Aunai added. 'As the Timpirum belongs with Vala'ashu.'

'A sign, a sign!' Taije and Kielii cried out with one voice. Now the entire tribe of Lokilani rose to their feet and rushed over to us, shouting, 'It is a sign! The Timpirum sings – listen, listen!'

For a while, we all did listen to this marvelous music that hung in the air like the sky's constellations. And then Master Juwain recited part of the verse that had led us here:

> *And they forever long to wake,*
> *To praise, exalt and music make,*
> *Breathe life through sacred memories,*
> *Recall the ancient harmonies.*
>
> *Beneath the trees they rise and ring,*
> *And whirl and play and soar and sing*
> *Of wider woods beyond the sea*
> *Where they shall dwell eternally.*

I finally put away the Lightstone, and Flick fell silent as a deep peace spread outward through the grove. Then Ninana stepped forward. She

269

lifted up the akashic crystal from its cairn and set it into my hands. It was lighter than I had thought it would be.

'But not all of your people have spoken,' I said to her.

Ninana looked out into the circles of Lokilani gathered around us. Their eyes were nearly as bright as the lights of the Timpum.

'No, we *have* spoken,' she said to me, 'with our hearts. Can you not hear what we say?'

Twelve hundred hearts beat as mine did, and those of my friends, joyfully and with great hope. And with great trust that I would use this precious jewel wisely.

'The Lokilani,' Ninana said to me, 'do not protect the Forest only for the Lokilani. A day will come – soon, soon – when the Matri'aya will light the way back to *the* Forest. It will grow again even in the deserts. The trees, Vala'ashu! Our children, who take their life from flower and leaf, and give it back in joy and song. This is more precious to us than any jewel.'

So saying, she drew forth a small bag woven of silklike fibers. She pressed it into my hand. Inside it were many tiny black seeds: the timana's seeds, from which would grow great astor trees.

After that there was much singing and dancing. Maram whirled about with a pretty young woman as hundreds watched. Estrella played with the Lokilani children; her delight was sweeter to me than any of the Forest's fruits. Even Atara, for a few hours, emerged from her palace of ice. Ninana, and four other Lokilani women, brought out green gelstei crystals like unto Master Juwain's and tried to heal her blindness. They failed. It seemed that no new life would ever grow in the sacred soil of her face which Morjin had blackened. It didn't matter. For as Atara told me, 'I've seen you gain what you hoped to find – *and* the children of the Galadin. What could make me happier than that?'

She smiled at me and squeezed my hand; the warmth of her fingers remained with me far into the night, when it came time to try to sleep. But I could not sleep. After Maram stole off into the woods, I lay on my cloak gazing at the akashic crystal which I had set down into the moss beside me. I gazed at the still forms of Atara, Estrella and Master Juwain, and all the Lokilani spread out nearby beneath the golden gloze of the astor trees. Most of all, I gazed at the Timpum. And listened. For the woods around me seemed to fill with a ringing like bells as the Timpum came alive in their blazing millions and sang songs of glory as old as the stars.

20

We spent most of the next day walking through the great woods back to our boat. On the beach, with the lake's waters lapping gently against coarse sands, we said goodbye to Ninana and Aunai and the several dozen Lokilani who had accompanied us. We launched our boat and rowed straight out toward the mist with a fair wind at our backs. When we reached this wall of cold, gray cloud, a swift current caught us up and bore us away from the island. Our strenuous work at the oars further speeded us along, for we did not wish to spend any great time beneath this wet blanket that blinded us. After what seemed less than a mile, we broke free from the mist, out into the sunshine of a hot summer day. It did not take us very long to make our way back to the lake's northern shore and find the little village of the Dirt Scrapers.

Tembom was very glad to see us, for he had given up his boat – and us – as lost. Baltasar and the Guardians met us by the shore, as did Karimah and the Manslayers. It was very good to see my men formed up on their great warhorses; the diamonds of their armor sparkled brightly in the sun, almost as brightly as the Timpum of the mist-shrouded island across the lake.

'Baltasar!' I called out as I greeted my friend. 'Sunjay! Lord Harsha! Lord Raasharu!'

Skyshan of Ki held the reins to my horse, and I greeted Altaru with as much gladness. I climbed onto his back and said to Baltasar, 'You seem ready for a journey.'

'That we are,' he said. 'As soon as your boat was sighted, we broke camp. It was thought that with such a long delay, you would want to ride as soon as possible.'

The tightness of his voice told me that he had worried we would never return; the faces of my Guardians told me the same thing. Valari

271

restraint kept them from voicing their concern. But the ways of the Sarni warriors were very different.

'Atara!' a strong voice cried out. The moment that Atara set foot to land, Karimah jumped off her horse with several other Manslayers. Karimah rushed forward to kiss Atara, and she began weeping and talking, all at the same time, wailing out, 'Four days you were gone! I thought you were dead – we all did. What kept you, my dear?'

Atara said nothing of the Lokilani and very little of the wonders of their woods. It wouldn't do to tempt the Sarni to their doom seeking treasure on the island, nor Tembom and the Dirt Scrapers, who stood about watching us, too. But Atara did admit that our quest had been successful.

'A great thought stone was hidden on the island long ago,' she said. 'With the aid of the Lightstone, we found it.'

At this, I brought out the akashic crystal for all to see. Flick spun above this little discus, and all gasped as glorre passed from his form into the gelstei and back again.

'What is this!' Baltasar said as he marveled at this new color. 'You have stories to tell, Lord Valashu.'

'We do,' I said to him. I looked from him and my other knights across a little dirt lane to where the Manslayers gathered on their horses watching us. Their naked arms showed bands of bright gold, and their sun-burned faces showed desire – whether for my men or something else, it was hard to say. 'And it's to be hoped that you *don't* have stories to tell.'

Something stirred inside Baltasar as he glanced at a handsome woman named Chinira. She stared back at him, boldly, and he said, 'We kept the peace, as you commanded. But it's well that you returned when you did.'

We were not the only ones to have rejoined our companions, for only the day before, Sar Sharath and Sar Manasu had arrived with the other knights whom we had left behind after the battle. The four wounded ones had recovered well enough to ride, and that was good, as many miles still lay between this misty lake and Tria.

Although it was growing late, we set out that very afternoon. Karimah and the Manslayers pointed their horses toward the west, and rode away from the Dirt Scrapers' village without a glance backward. I paused only long enough to thank Tembom for the use of his boat and his people for the loaves of rushk bread that they gave us freely.

It was a hot day for travel. The sultry air almost immediately caused Maram to slump in his saddle and nod off. I rode up next to him and nudged him awake with an elbow in the ribs. And I said to him, 'You should have gotten more sleep last night.'

'Ah, I should have gotten *any* sleep last night. But Akia wouldn't let me.'

'And who is Akia?'

'Who is *Akia*?' he said. 'Did you not see me dancing with her? She of the honey lips and breasts that turn up toward the stars? Ah, well, I promised her that we would meet and dance all night *beneath* the stars, if you know what I mean.'

'Too well,' I said, turning to look at Lord Harsha and Behira where they rode with the wounded knights near the end of our columns. Then I said to Maram, 'Are you all right? You've never begrudged losing sleep to do your midnight duets before.'

'No, I haven't, have I? But it seems Akia took me at my word; all she wanted to do was to *dance*, if you know what I mean – too bad.'

I told him to close his eyes and meditate, since the day would be long and he had lost his chance for deeper rest.

'Meditate? On what? On my dwindling powers? I'm losing my charms, I know I am.'

I looked out at the grasslands to the west, and I said, 'Take heart. A lion chases five antelopes and counts himself lucky if he catches one.'

'Yes, and the old lions lose their teeth and starve. I'm getting old, my friend. I can feel it in my bones.'

'But you're only twenty-five.'

'I'll be twenty-six next month. No, no, it's time I engaged a new life. I've decided that I *shall* marry Behira. I'll make the announcement in Tria, after *you* claim the Lightstone and announce yourself.'

'That,' I said, 'may depend on what Master Juwain finds inside the memory crystal.'

'Even if you find air inside it, you'll be forced to make a decision, and soon,' he told me. 'You can't play coy with your fate, any more than I can keep putting off mine.'

I thought about this as we made our way around the shore of the lake and then followed the river that flowed out of it. We kept well to the north of its windings, which snaked across the sun-seared steppe like a blue ribbon edged with green. The leaves of the cottonwood trees, with their silver shimmer that I had always thought so glorious, seemed dull against my memory of the great oaks and astors of the Lokilani's island. And the yellow grasses of the Wendrush seemed almost dead. I thought of the even harsher terrain of Yarkona and the great desert said to lie to the south of it. Would the Red Dragon, I wondered, bring the fire of war out of the west so that all of Ea became a blackened wasteland? Or would peace prevail and the earth be made green again? As I scanned the dun-hued distances about us, I squeezed the bag of seeds that Ninana had given me and dreamed of a new world.

And yet *this* world, I thought, still had its own beauty. And the plains of the Wendrush still teemed with life. The Manslayers, who rode on ahead of us; seemed to appreciate this in a way that we of the Morning Mountains could not. I tried to apprehend this stark land through their eyes and feel the wind through their senses. And when I did, its dried-up grasses seemed less a desolation than a great, golden shield stretching out in all directions to meet the blue sky. Chirping crickets and countless insects made their homes here while the prairie dogs built their mounded villages and kept vigil outside their holes for hawks and wolves and other predators. We passed great herds of antelope and sagosk who ate the grass with as much pleasure as men at a feast. The long, swaying strands also concealed prides of lions, with their tawny coats and their watchful yellow-green eyes. It seemed a million of them could have lain in wait about us. Maram feared these great beasts, as did some of my men, even those knights who bore the lion on their shields as their charge. But Atara and the Manslayers gave them less thought than the biting flies who took pieces out of flesh and drew blood from the horses. Instead they turned their wariness toward searching the rolling country for any sign of their enemies.

These, in this part of the Wendrush, were mainly the Janjii, who sometimes raided east of the great Poru River and even a few rogue bands of Kurmak who would not follow Sajagax and had no love of the woman warriors of the Manslayer Society. All the rest of the day, however, we encountered none of these, nor indeed any other human beings. We made camp that night near the river, and the Manslayers watched with amusement as we fortified our rows of tents with a moat and a stockade built of cottonwood logs. Their strategy, if attacked in the middle of the night, was different than ours: they would simply mount their horses at a moment's notice and flee into the dark steppe. Either that, or else they would maneuver across the grasses, fighting their arrow duels if moon and stars gave enough light, or closing and slashing with their sabers if all else failed.

We traveled early the next day. We kept a good pace toward the west, but not so fast that the riding would further weaken my wounded warriors. I gave the Lightstone to Sar Marjay to bear and the akashic crystal to Master Juwain. He spent hours delving into its incomprehensible contents, and many more with pen and paper trying to comprehend them. Over a midday meal of the nut-sweet rushk bread and roasted antelope, I heard him repeating otherworldly words and muttering, half to me, half to himself, 'Let's see, we have *valaha* and the root there must be *val*, which could be star as with Ardik or indeed our own language. And then there is *arda*. Fire, perhaps, or heart or soul. Or maybe all three. And with *halla* and *alhalla* we have a pairing that . . .' And so it went, Master Juwain puzzling out meanings and scribbling down possibilities in his journal. I tried to remember more of Alphanderry's death song, and Master Juwain seized upon each word that I brought forth as if it were a precious jewel.

Late that afternoon we came to the confluence of the Snake and the Poru. This mighty river my companions and I had swum the year before – but in Valte and farther to the south where it was not as wide. Here, with the summer-swollen waters of the Diamond and the Snake added to it, the Poru was a great band of brown flowing swiftly across the steppe. We decided to make camp at the very point where the blue Snake flowed into it. It would be our last night of drawing and drinking clear water. The Sarni, it is said, like the taste of the Poru and draw strength from this Mother of Rivers. But to me and my men, the prospect of dipping our pots and cups into its turbid flow was as appealing as drinking mud.

For the next three days we followed the Poru's course westward and turning gradually toward the north. Except for afternoon thunderstorms when the sky opened up with lightning and rain fell upon us in sheets, we had good weather for riding. And the Wendrush, however much a Valari knight might feel ill at ease here, was a good place to ride. The turf was easy on the horses' hooves, with few stones and fewer hills to climb. And it was easy for the horses to keep up their strength, with all the fodder they needed growing out of the black soil beneath them. The grass, rich and heavy with seed, sustained them and relieved us of the burden of having to carry oats or other grain. It was one of the reasons why a Sarni army could cover great distances quickly, for they could ride to war without a baggage train weighing them down.

During this part of our journey, the Manslayers kept to themselves and Atara kept mostly to her sister warriors. Occasionally, however, she would ride with us, visiting with Maram or Master Juwain, making Behira's acquaintance and chatting happily with Estrella. At these times, she seemed warm and content with life, and she took joy in the singing of the meadowlarks and the sweet burn of the sun upon her face. But when she spoke with me, the frigidity returned to stiffen her being. She kept these interchanges brief and to the business at hand. So it was that as we drew nearer to the Sajagax's summer encampment, she explained why her grandfather had chosen this place on the Poru at the northeast corner of the Kurmak's lands: 'There's good water for the horses and herds here, of course, even if you Valari are too pure to want to drink it. Then, too, the Janjii are most numerous just to the other side of the river, and beyond their lands, only fifty miles, are the Marituk. Sajagax likes to keep his enemies close.'

'Does that include Alonia?' I asked her.

Atara smiled sadly, for her very life was the result Sajagax cementing an alliance with Alonia in her mother's marriage to King Kiritan. 'Let's just say that while Sajagax no longer regards my father as his enemy, the same is not true of all his dukes.'

'But what of the Adirii, then? We are far here from their lands.'

'Yes, but we have been at peace these many years. If any more truce-breakers, like the ones that nearly annihilated you, crossed the Snake in force, Sajagax would move south to annihilate *them*.'

I was eager to meet this great warrior renowned across Ea for his deeds in battle. We came upon his encampment late on the fourth day of our journey from the Lokilani's lake. In truth, the vast assemblage of men, animals and dwellings spread out along the Poru's eastern banks was much more like a movable city. Acres of animal pens – holding horses, sheep, goats and lowing sagosk – formed a barrier around its northern, eastern and southern sides. Even from a mile away I could smell these thousands of animals and the dung they dropped onto the ground. I smelled, too, the slaughter yards nearby where the Sarni women worked, hanging fly-covered joints on spits and smoking strips of meat over fragrant fires. Farther in toward the river were the many open-air shops where the Sarni tanned leather, crafted bows and beat red-hot steel into arrow points, sabers and studs for their armor. The core of the city was reserved for habitation. There, hundreds of rows of tents, with dirt streets running through them, were laid out as neatly as in any Valari encampment. But the tents were much larger, being circular and fitted over wooden frames. The Sarni made their coverings from a thick felt, either of sheep's wool or the long, soft hairs of the sagosk. A few of the tents, though, were larger still and woven of finer materials. These belonged to Sajagax's captains. The largest tent of all, at the city's center, was that of Sajagax himself: a huge dome of quilted silk rose up almost like a palace.

No guards impeded our entrance to the city. The Sarni are the freest of the Free Peoples, or so they like to claim, and therefore they do not deign to keep any warrior from riding among them. Even the sight of a hundred and seventy-three Valari knights arrayed for war did not unnerve them, as unprecedented as our arrival must have been. At a moment's notice, Sajagax could summon five thousand warriors to his standard. Then, too, word of our crossing of the Kurmak's lands had gone ahead. Indeed, Sajagax's outriders had tracked us across the entire course of our journey from the lake. And so the Sarni had been made ready to receive their most ancient of enemies, not with bows and arrows but rather with wine and beer and roasted meats for a great feast.

As we rode down dusty streets lined with men, woman and children eager to look upon us, Atara dropped back to accompany me. With her lion-skin cloak and white blindfold, she made a striking figure: the great *imakla* woman warrior who had been blinded yet somehow could see. She greeted the Kurmak warriors whom she had known for years, calling out their names with her clear voice: 'Tiagax, Orox, Turkalak!' And the women, too, 'Ghita, Tyraya, Sarakah!' As anyone would have to admit, they were a handsome people: tall, clean-limbed and strong, with long blond hair and eyes that gleamed like gemstones of blue or green. Nearly all of them claimed descent from Sarnjin Marshan, son of Bohimir the Great, the Aryan warlord who had sailed out of Thalu at the end of the Age of the Mother to conquer most of Ea. They were a proud people, as honest and open as they were brutal. Their word for stranger was *kradak*, which meant simply 'enemy'. Their eyes fell upon us like hundreds of steel-tipped arrows. It seemed that they might be happier roasting *us* over their fires instead of haunches of sagosk or lamb.

We drew nearer to the center of this barbaric city, and Atara pointed out the tents containing the treasury and armory, and those of Sajagax's concubines and main wives. And then we came to the tent of Sajagax. Its outside was hung with lion skins, while inside, as I would soon discover, it was decorated with sable and ermine and sheets of beaten gold. The Kurmak's great chieftain was waiting for us outside its open doors. To either side of him stood his greatest captains: Urtukar, Mansak, Jaalii, Yaggod, Braggod and his son, Tringax. All were big men, like unto form and appearance with Sajagax.

But in Sajagax himself, I thought, there concentrated the essence of a Sarni warrior. He wore a doublet of antelope skin embroidered with gold and lapis beads. He was an inch taller than I and massive in his gold-girded arms and across his chest. The weight of gold chains hanging from his bull's neck would have bowed down a lesser man. In his thick hand he bore like a staff of kingship his great bow: a double-curved welding of wood, sinew and horn so heavy and thick it was said that none but Sajagax could draw it. His face was heavy, too, and cut in harsh planes like the sun-seared steppe. His gray mustaches drooped down beneath his stoney chin; his long hair was golden-gray, braided and bound with golden wire. He had the same brilliant blue eyes that had once sparkled from Atara's countenance. He did not stand on pomp or ceremony, for he gazed upon his grand-daughter with an outpouring of adoration for all to see. No one, however, would mistake him for a good-natured man. He radiated ferocity and willfulness as the Marud sun does heat. As Atara had told me, he could be cruel. Once, when a merchant named Aolun Wohrhan had betrayed him in a business dealing, Sajagax had allowed that Aolun should have all the gold for which he had lied and cheated. And so he had commanded that the greedy Aolun be staked out on the ground and molten gold poured into his eyes, ears and mouth.

'Atara!' he called out as we all dismounted. His voice was gravelly and bigger even than Maram's, like a battle horn blowing, and blunt as a war hammer. 'My beautiful granddaughter!'

She rushed up to embrace him, and he kissed her lips, and tears welled up in his eyes. His captains looked on disapprovingly, not at his display of emotion but because the Sarni are seldom kind to women.

Atara presented me and many of my companions. Then Sajagax called out, 'Valashu Elahad, Lord Guardian of the Lightstone, you and your warriors are welcome in my house! Never have I had the privi-lege of entertaining Valari warriors before, except with arrow and sword. But tonight, at least, let there be peace between our peoples. Come! Rest! Eat! Sit with me and let us talk of your journey.'

Urtukar, a fierce old man with a saber scar cutting his face from ear to chin, objected to allowing such a large company of armed Valari knights into Sajagax's tent. But Sajagax gainsayed him. He waved off his concern as he might shoo away a biting fly, bellowing out, 'Do you think I fear these knights? Let them bring their swords to the feast, their lances, too, if they wish. I care not. They are the Guardians of the Lightstone. How are they to guard it if they are stripped of their weapons?'

He was less generous, however, in inviting Behira and Estrella to take meat with him, for Sarni warriors will sit at feast with warriors only. And so Sajagax's eldest wife, Freyara, was summoned to take them to a more private feast with the women in her own tent.

Sajagax led the way into *his* great tent. So huge was this billowing silk structure that it would have required a frame the size of my father's hall to hold it up. Instead, great wooden poles, nearly as long as the masts of a ship, were planted in the ground as the main supports. The guy ropes, I saw, were braided silk. The entire floor was lined with rich and intricate carpets, mostly of blue and gold, for Sajagax was fond of these colors. I looked for a chair or any furniture that might be construed as a throne. But Sajagax required nothing of the sort; indeed he had as much disdain for chairs and other decadances as did my father. With a painful stiffness due to many old wounds, he sat down against a mound of cushions near the tent's center. His captains sat in a half-circle to his right, while Maram, Lord Harsha, Lord Raasharu, Baltasar, Sunjay, Atara and I took our places to his left. Other prominent Kurmak warriors sat in similar circles throughout the tent, as did the rest of the Guardians. The question arose of what to do with Master Juwain, for he bore no weapon and was therefore counted no warrior. Tringax, a young man with bellicose blue eyes, suggested that Master Juwain should dine with the women and children. But I stared at him coldly, and informed him that Master Juwain had stood by my side the length and breadth of Ea and had fought his way into Argattha, a place that even the boldest of the Kurmak warriors might not dare to go. In the end, Tringax relented, and Sajagax invited Master Juwain to sit with us.

The feast began abruptly, with no speeches of welcome or fanfare. The Sarni, given to the extravagant in their possessions, were simple in their taking of food and drink. They cared little for delicacies and not at all for the fine art of cooking. What mattered to them, it seemed, was the abundance of meat. And of bread and beer and bowls of mare's milk, for this is most of what the Sarni consumed. Beautiful young women wearing long silk robes served us legs of lamb, roasted sagosk livers and other steaming victuals on great golden platters. Many of them bore bruises on their faces and on their naked arms, and they were subservient in their manner. Baltasar mistook them for slaves. He was astonished, as I was, when Sajagax told us that they were his newer wives. Sajagax only laughed at our outraged Valari sensibilities. He slapped one of these wives on her rear as he bellowed out, 'What need have we of slaves when we have women?'

Atara, I saw, sat quietly sipping from a goblet of wine as Baltasar and others looked at her. I said to Sajagax, 'But women are the mothers of your children! The mothers of you and all your warriors!'

Sajagax laughed again as he tore off a huge chunk from a lamb's leg with his strong white teeth. 'Yes, and that is what woman are good for.'

'We Valari,' Lord Raasharu said sternly, 'believe that women are meant for much more.'

'Yes, they are good at cooking and gathering sagosk dung, and some of them can even sing.'

Now Baltasar, picking up on his father's reproach, said to Sajagax,

'If a man spoke thusly in the Morning Mountains, he would have to sleep with his sword instead of his wife.'

'Do you fear your women, then?' Sajagax asked. 'You, who are always so fearless in battle?'

'We don't fear them,' Baltasar said. 'But we don't command them, either. Does one command the sun to shine?'

'No, but a *man* was made to master his women. And women were made to be mastered.'

Sajagax looked down at his great hand, thick with callus and scars along his knuckles. It was then that we learned that a Sarni warrior who refused to beat his wife was called a man without a manhood.

I looked at Atara again and said, 'Some women, it seems, are not so easy to master.'

'Indeed, they are not,' Sajagax said, smiling at his granddaughter. 'That's the beauty of the world, isn't it? Most women are sheep but a few are born to be lionesses.'

'From all you've said, it seems surprising that the lions would let them be.'

'*Let* them?' Sajagax called out. 'Does one *let* the sun shine? No one lets a women become a warrior.'

I bowed my head toward Atara, and then glanced at Karimah and three others of their Society who sat with the warriors in another circle. I said, 'The Manslayers are few; your warriors are many. Surely you could keep these women picking up dung, if you chose to.'

'*Could* we? At what price? Have *you* ever tried to make a Manslayer pick up dung, Lord Valashu?'

I admitted that I had not. And then Sajagax continued, 'If we tried to do this, then *we* would have to sleep with our swords at the ready – and our bows and arrows, too.'

I smiled at him and said, 'Do you fear your women, then?'

Sajagax laughed heartily and clapped me on my shoulder to acknowledge that I had scored a point in this verbal jousting that the Sarni relished. And he said to me, 'The Manslayers are *warriors*. They claim for themselves, out of strength, the right to kill. Thus they make others fear them. *They* fear death not. Thus they are twice feared. They escape from having to pick up dung by their willingness to die and to deal death. And in this, as with all warriors, they claim their freedom.'

In his rough, old voice I heard echoes of the words that Morjin had written to me. I said to him, 'Then is it only the strong who can be free?'

He took a long drink of wine from his goblet as he nodded his head. 'That, too, is the beauty of the world, its terrible beauty. The strong do as they will; the weak do as they must.'

For a few moments I thought about this as he waited to see what I would say. Finally I spoke, and the answer I gave him was what I might have told Morjin himself if he were sitting with us:

'It is the will of those who are truly strong,' I said, 'to protect the weak. They fear neither death nor other men. Only being unkind.'

But kindness among the Sarni, as I saw, was regarded less a virtue than a boon of the victor toward the vanquished. Their warriors were even more brutal with each other than with their women. Their continual verbal sparring often turned violent; twice during the feast, two of Sajagax's men came to blows, standing and smashing at each other's faces with their fists. Such unseemly displays would never occur in Valari society without swords being drawn in a duel to the death. I watched in amazement as these yellow-haired barbarians quickly spent their fury and then returned to their places, eyeing each other malevolently. They bore each other deep grudges in this testing of their manhood. They, and all who witnessed their combat, would remember who had bested whom. And so it went all their lives. The strongest of them became captains over warriors and chieftains over clan or tribe. In their bluffing and bullying of each other, I better understood a Sarni saying that Atara had told me earlier:

'Every tribe against every tribe; every clan against the tribe; every family against the clan; every man against his family. And all the tribes against the *kradak*.'

The Sarni's enmity for me and my men boiled barely beneath the surface like a geyser that might erupt at any moment. Sajagax's warriors stared at the glittering armor of my knights as if counting the diamonds there and mentally adding these white gems to their treasure chests. So it had gone for ages. How many times had the Sarni invaded the Morning Mountains hoping to seize our vital mineral wealth? No other people had made war against the Valari so often or with such savagery. And now, here in Sajagax's tent, the Kurmak fired different kinds of arrows at us. Fell words flew from the lips of these wild warriors and stung my men like so many barbs. I overheard one warrior at a nearby circle taunting Sar Hannu of Anjo: 'You look familiar. Weren't you one of the knights who fled from my company at the Battle of the Crooked Field?' This, I told myself, was only more testing; in anticipation of this, I had issued strict orders that my men should not trade insult for insult, nor under any circumstances draw their swords. Lord Raasharu and my other counselors feared that Sajagax might use such an incident to provoke a battle – and then after I and all the Guardians lay slaughtered on Sajagax's blood-drenched carpets, Sajagax would claim the Lightstone for himself.

When at last the time for singing and serious drinking was at hand, Sajagax called to see the Lightstone. Sar Elkald of Taron stood and came over to hand the golden cup to me. And then I gave it to Sajagax to hold.

'Beautiful,' Sajagax said as his eyes lit up. The cup seemed lost in his huge hand. 'But so small.'

His hot breath steamed out into the even hotter air of his tent. I could see his image, all fierce with longing, reflected from the numerous golden sheets hung from the tent's walls. Threads of gold showed in the tapestries also displayed there, and the tent's great poles likewise were sheathed with this most precious of metals. So rich were these furnishings, it made one wonder what was left to lock away in Sajagax's treasury.

'So this is the *true* gold,' he said to me as he gazed at the cup. 'Let us hear the story of how you gained it.'

Maram, his face flushed with wine, was only too happy to stand and give an account of the great Quest. He told Sajagax and the Kurmak warriors of all our battles, paying particular attention to his heroics at Khaisham and the arrow wounds he had received there. Our hosts struck their bows against their goblets in acknowledgment of these feats. They were less inclined to believe Maram's description of the invisible bridges that spanned the gorges of the Nagarshath and the great Ymanir who had built them, for it displeased them to imagine a people larger and stronger than themselves. And they would have dismissed the story of Flick altogether if this strange being hadn't suddenly appeared to amaze them with a brilliant display of lights. But they listened in wonder as Maram explained how he had used a firestone to burn an opening into Argattha and then later to wound the great dragon named Angraboda. And when Maram reached the climax of his tale, when the blinded Atara had stood upon Morjin's throne firing arrows into our enemies and felling them by the dozen, many of these grim-faced warriors burst into tears of pride and called out, 'Atara Manslayer! Atara for the Kurmak!'

'Great deeds!' Sajagax exclaimed as Maram sat back down. His hand still gripped the Lightstone, and a golden sheen fell upon his face. He turned to Atara and said, 'You are a glory to our people. The Kurmak have always fought Morjin. And we always will.'

Sajagax now stood to sing out the tale of how the Kurmak and other tribes of the Sarni had ridden to war against Morjin at the Sarburn two whole ages before. His voice blared out like a battle horn, and he needed no minstrel to recall the verses that extolled the deeds of great warriors six thousand years dead. According to his version of this story, it was only through the heroics of his Kurmak ancestors that the Lightstone was wrested from Morjin's hand. That many of the Sarni tribes had fought on Morjin's side he neglected to tell.

After he had sat back down, I said to him, 'We of the Morning Mountains still sing of the wonder of the Sarni riding with the Valari to battle. But it should be remembered that it was Aramesh who wounded Morjin and took the Lightstone from him.'

'True, Aramesh claimed the Lightstone according to the ancient right of guardianship.' Sajagax stared at the golden cup in his hand with all the passion he might have reserved for a new bride. 'The right *you* Valari have always claimed for yourselves. But are not *all* those willing to shed blood in the Lightstone's defense its rightful guardians?'

Everyone, I thought, knew the story of how the Valari tribe long ago had been riven when Aryu had slain his brother and had stolen the Lightstone. But I doubted if Sajagax and the Sarni also knew that Aryu's descendants had used a varistei to alter their forms and so become the Aryans. a strong and rugged people whose blue eyes and fair skin were better suited to Thalu's cold mists. And with the exile of Sarngin Marshan, the Aryans had become the Sarni, and how should these fierce warriors want to believe that they were therefore descended from a murderer and the greatest thief in all history save Morjin himself?

'It was Elahad who brought the Lightstone to earth,' I told Sajagax. 'And it is *his* descendants who must bear the burden of guarding it.'

'So you say,' he muttered as he gazed at the little curve of gold that he gripped so tightly. 'So you Valari have always claimed.'

Lansar Raasharu fingered the hilt of his sword as he huffed out, 'We claim this: that the Lightstone was meant for the hand of the Maitreya and no other.'

'So you say,' Sajagax muttered again as he looked at me. '*I* say it was meant to be used to defeat the Red Dragon.'

I tried to smile at this quarrelsome old chieftain but I could not. I said to him, 'Truly, it was. But defeat how? With the blood of yet more battles? Or defeat in light?'

Sajagax looked at me strangely. 'I've also heard it said that Valashu Elahad claims to be this Maitreya.'

'No, not yet,' I told him. 'We're hoping that the crystal we recovered from the Lake of Mists might tell if a claim should be made.'

'What is there to tell, then? The Maitreya would be the greatest of warriors, the boldest and the strongest.'

His blue eyes bored into me, and his fierce gaze burned with blood-lust, pride and challenge.

The Sarni, it is said, covet gold as a drunkard does spirits, but they revere three things: the horse, the sky, and their given word. Sajagax had promised us safe passage through the Kurkmak's lands. This could not include despoiling us of our possessions. Atara had also once told me that her grandfather, though sometimes cruel, was always true. I had gambled everything upon this. Either one believes in men or not.

'My father,' I said to him, 'taught me that the greatest strength of all lies in following the will of the One.'

I looked at the Lightstone and held my hand out toward him.

Sajagax's hardened fingers only gripped it more tightly. His eyes narrowed with a terrible concentration; his jaws ground together as if trying to snap a bone. He seemed to fight a ferocious battle within himself. And then, with a sudden laughter that rumbled up from deep in his chest, he found his *own* immense will and slapped the little cup into my hand.

'Here, take it!' he roared out. 'Guard it with your life, if that's what you want! It matters not to me.'

I held the Lightstone for a moment before setting it down on the cushion in front of me. I said, 'It matters to *me* that you would help us in our purpose. It matters to all Ea.'

'Help you *how*? By having my men enlist as Guardians under your command? No Sarni warrior would have the stomach for that.'

'No,' I told him, 'we've Guardians enough already. But why don't you ride with us to Tria? As it was in the ancient days?'

He chewed at his mustache a few moments before saying, 'Kiritan has called a council of the kings of all the Free Lands. *Kings*, Valashu Elahad. Why would a Sarni chieftain wish to sit with such as these?'

A stew of emotions bubbled inside him, and I misinterpreted his sensibilities. I said to him, 'But surely King Kiritan has invited you to the conclave as well. Surely he would welcome you, even if you don't call yourself a king.'

'No, that I don't. That I never will,' he called out. 'Kings compel the service of their subjects as if they were women, and what satisfaction is there in that? *I* am a free man, and a leader of free men who follow me or not as they please. What business have I among *kings*?'

'The business of defeating Morjin,' I told him.

'Morjin,' he spat out as he might a piece of moldy bread. 'We Kurmak will fight him no matter what your kings decide.'

I looked around the circle at his captains. Yaggod and Braggod were like great, tawny lions trembling to rend and slay, and Tringax and the scarred Urtukar seemed no less eager for war. All the Kurmak warriors in Sajagax's tent, I thought, would gather to his standard and would die sooner than admit to a fear of the Red Dragon's armies.

'Yes, you will fight, and you are to be honored for that,' I said to Sajagax. 'But wouldn't the chance for victory be greater with others by your side?'

'*What* others, then? King Hanniban of Eanna? King Marshayk of Delu? They are weak.'

At the mention of his father's name, Maram bristled but said nothing. He took another sip of wine and glared at Sajagax.

'The Valari kings will fight,' I said to Sajagax. 'In the end, if it comes to war, they will have to fight.'

'*Kings*,' Sajagax spat out again. 'Valari.'

'Yes, Valari,' I said. 'You've fought us many times, but you've never understood us. None of our kings rules except through the will of warriors as valiant and free as your own.'

Sajagax looked at the circles of grave-faced Guardians who sat watchfully throughout his tent. Then he traded looks with Jaalii and Mansak. He said to me, 'And you've never understood *my* people, either.'

Maram saw his chance for vengeance over Sajagax's slight, and he said, 'We understand that Morjin is buying the service of other Sarni tribes with gold.'

'Gold,' Sajagax said sadly as he gazed at the Lightstone. 'We love it too much. Ever has it been our downfall. Even now the Zayak demand a tribute of Morjin and believe that they have thus gained dominion over him. But in the end, as in ancient days, it is he who will make slaves of them.'

'The Zayak we fought on our way home from Argattha,' I said. 'And now it seems that the Adirii have gone over to Morjin, too.'

'No,' Sajagax said. 'Only one of their clans. And they shall be punished.'

'And what of the Marituk, then? They are your enemies. Have they thus become Morjin's friends?'

Sajagax turned toward the west as if he could gaze through the silken walls of his tent and far out across the Poru river into the Marituk's lands. 'We've had word that Morjin has sent many treasure chests to the Marituk. Will they make alliance with him? That is hard to say. They hate the Beast – but perhaps less than they do Alonia and the Kurmak.'

He went on to say that, as always, the Janjii would follow the Marituk, for they were under their fist.

'And what of the other tribes?' I asked him.

'In the south, the Siofok and Danyak stand ready to ride with Morjin. And the Usark and Tukulak are inclined to join them.'

'That is bad,' I said. 'And what of the Mansurii?'

'They hate Morjin – almost as much as they love his gold.'

I looked off at the gold-shod pillars holding up the tent, but I said nothing.

'The southern tribes are weak,' Sajagax said. 'But most of the central tribes remain strong enough to oppose him.'

'The Niuriu? Their chieftain gave us shelter on our journey.'

'Yes, Vishakan is a good man and will never yield to Morjin. And neither will Artukan and the Danladi.'

'But what of the Urtuk?' I said, naming the Sarni's most numerous tribe and Mesh's ancient enemy.

'The western Urtuk remain undecided,' Sajagax said. 'And the main clans would carve the livers from any emissaries Morjin sends and despoil them of their gold. The eastern Urtuk hate the Valari enough that they might join Morjin just for the pleasure of carving out *your* livers – and your hearts, as well.'

'Then the Sarni tribes each go their own way, as always.'

'Not *always*, Valashu Elahad. Even in Mesh, they must sing of Tulumar the Great.'

Truly, we *did* sing of this bloodthirsty warlord, but none of our songs were happy ones. In the year 2073 of the Age of Swords, Tulumar Elek, having united all the Sarni and gone on to conquer more civilized lands, took the title of Emperor of the Wendrush, Delu and Alonia. It was said, if not sung, that Morjin had aided Tulumar in his bid for world dominion and then betrayed him to his death with poison.

'As it was in the ancient days, so it is now,' Sajagax told us. 'Morjin cannot win without the Sarni. And if my people ride with him, he cannot lose.'

'Then that is all the more reason that *you* must ride with us to Tria. If an alliance is made against Morjin, if you and the Kurmak take part in this and the other tribes behold this miracle – then might not the Sarni be persuaded to ride *against* Morjin?'

'That is possible,' he said. 'But if the alliance fails, it will go badly. Few of the tribes will want to fight on the losing side.'

'The alliance won't fail,' I said.

'How can it not? What could bring the Valari together with Valari – and with Alonians and Delians? The Maitreya?'

'Yes, he.'

Sajagax pulled at the golden wire binding his braided hair as he looked at me. 'You ask a great deal. For me to ride to Tria at this time, with the Marituk raiding in the north and the Red Dragon to be watched – and all on the hope that some untested youth might be the Shining Warrior out of legends none know to be true. No, no, this is too much.'

Baltasar started to reply to this, but Maram laid his hand on his knee and spoke instead: 'Lord Valashu is not untested. Haven't you listened to what I've said? In Argattha, he slew as many as did Atara. And under his leadership, we vanquished the Adirii as well. And only last month, he defeated all at the great tournament and became its champion.'

Sajagax nodded his head as he continued to regard me. And Braggod, a red-faced man with the longest and most impressive of mustaches, spoke for his chieftain: 'Sajagax has led us to victory in thirty-three battles. And as for your tournament, you didn't invite *Sarni* warriors, so what honor is there in claiming its championship?'

'Valari *knights*,' Maram said, glancing at the two diamonds of his ring, 'are matchless at arms.'

'With the sword, perhaps,' Braggod allowed. He lifted up his bow and shook it at Maram. 'But not with a truly noble weapon.'

'Our archers hit their targets, too,' Maram said.

'You say "our" as if you are truly a Valari. But no matter the diamonds you wear, you'll remain a fat prince of Delu.'

Maram's face flushed as red as Braggod's. He said to him, 'This *Delian* won a second in wrestling. And a third in archery.'

'In what *you* call archery. Shooting at targets that don't shoot back can hardly be counted as sport.'

'And what do you call sport, then?'

'Why, shooting at each other from horseback, fat man.'

Now Sajagax and everyone in our circle looked at Maram, who seemed ready to choke on his bile and throttle the rude Braggod. I was afraid that despite himself, Maram was about to blunder his way into a duel. And so I gripped Maram's arm to steady him; to Braggod and the others, I said, 'Our Valari longbows weren't made for such work. And while in your lands, my knights may not engage in any sport that might draw Kurmak blood.'

If I had hoped to cool Maram's and Braggod's rising tempers, I hoped in vain. Braggod suddenly stood up, and the muscles along his ruddy neck and arms stood out like snakes swollen with blood. He shook his fist at Maram and said, 'We've other sports then, fat man. Why don't we see if you're as good at holding the horn as in blowing your own fat horn?'

'What do you mean?' Maram asked, now as puzzled as the rest of us.

'It's a test,' Braggod said. 'Each of us is given a horn of beer. We drink. The horns are refilled, once, twice – as many times as it takes. The one who holds his beer and remains standing is the better man.'

Maram's eyes gleamed. Braggod might as well have suggesting a test to see who could deflower the most virgins.

'Bring on your horns!' Maram called out with a smile. He fairly jumped to his feet. 'It's time we tested your Kurmak beer!'

Sajagax's warriors in their circles cried out: 'The *kradak* will drink against Braggod! Give him room to fall!' They stood and gathered around us, and so did many of my knights.

The Sarni cut their long, curved drinking horns from the heads of the greatest sagosk bulls. Such horns, it is said, are the measure of a man. Some are shorter, some longer, their lengths varying according to the amount of beer a warrior can consume. But the horns used in such contests as this were always of the longest: a tall man's arm scarcely sufficed to reach from the horn's mouth to its tip.

Sajagax's wives brought forth two horns, equal in length, brimming with frothy beer. Braggod took one and Maram the other. They stood eyeing each other. Braggod was slightly taller than Maram and seemed stronger, with long, lean muscles that showed beneath his sun-burned skin. He was thick through the body and hips, with massive legs from a lifetime of squeezing the ribs of horses. At a signal from Sajagax, they both lifted up their horns and threw back their heads as they drank deeply.

'Ah, not bad,' Maram said as he smacked his lips and then belched. 'In fact, it's really quite good. You brew your beer from that yellow rushk grain, don't you?'

Braggod belched, too, and licked the foam from his drooping mustache. His large blue eyes seemed as watery as a lake.

'Well,' Maram continued, 'it's more potent than Meshian beer, I'll give you that. Why don't we refill our horns?'

Braggod consented to this, and Sajagax's wives poured the yellow-brown beer into their horns. They raised them and began again.

'Come, Braggod!' Yaggod called out, 'drink it down!'

'Drink *him* down!' a nearby warrior called back.

'No one has ever outdrunk Braggod before.'

'And no one ever will.'

'Especially not some fat *kradak*. Look at that belly!'

It took Braggod and Maram slightly longer this time to drain their horns. When they had finished, Maram stood staring at Braggod, whose eyes were glazing and losing their focus. The big warrior seemed a little unsteady on his feet.

Again their horns were refilled, and again they were emptied.

'Do you see?' Maram said, patting the ball of fat pushing out above his belt. 'A belly is a great, good thing. In form, like unto a globe, like . . . ah, the world itself. And so it is a reservoir of great strength. It centers a man. And more to the point of this fine sport of yours, it gives a man a greater capacity to enjoy your fine beer.'

He began reciting verses that extolled the beauty of the belly. I could not tell if he was composing these in the moment. I appreciated his strategy: rather than immediately calling for another horn, he seemed happy to let the beer bubble in Braggod's belly and do its work.

'Bring on another horn!' Tringax finally said. 'No one has ever finished a fourth horn.'

Now both Maram and Braggod were weaving and shifting about, trying to find their balance. Freshly filled horns were pressed into their hands. Again, they began to drink.

'Down, down, drink it down!' the Sarni warriors called out. And my Valari knights standing with them picked up the chant: 'Down, down, drink or drown!'

Maram and Braggod stood with their horns thrust out toward each other as they eyed each other and drank. Somehow, to the amazement of Yaggod and Urtukar and others who were expert at these contests, they both managed to drink their beer to the last drop. When they lowered their horns, both of them seemed sick, as if they stood above a precipice on slippery rocks.

'Ah, that was very good,' Maram said with a belch. 'A very, *very* brew. Ah, I mean, a very *fine* brew. Very fine, indeed.'

He began rambling on about his liking of the Kurmak's beer, all the while watching Braggod. This great captain now began staggering, lurching forward and checking himself, desperately trying to pull himself erect before staggering again.

'Ah, had enough, have you, Braggod, my drinking man?' Maram took a step closer to him. He looked around at the warriors watching him. 'I do believe he's about to fall. May I help him?'

'You may not lay your hands upon him,' Sajagax told him. 'That would be wrestling.'

Maram belched again and muttered, 'May not lay my hands upon him, so you say. Well, I won't then. But he must go down.'

Maram stepped even closer to Braggod, whose eyes were almost rolling back into his head. Suddenly, Maram let loose a tremendous belch. The blast of his breath seemed further to stagger Braggod. 'Down,

down, like a drunken clown!' Maram called out. Then he pushed out his belly against Braggod, nudging him slightly. It was just enough to make Braggod teeter and lose his balance altogether. With his arms flailing, he finally collapsed, falling down into his pile of cushions. All present laughed wildly and cheered to see such sport.

'Down, down to carpet-covered ground!' Maram rambled on. He stood weaving above Braggod and smiling at him. 'Well, my good man, I think you *have* had enough to drink, too bad. But Maram Marshayk has not. Bring on your best beer! Fill my horn! Fill your eyes and watch how a Valari knight and a *prince* of Delu drinks. Behold!'

Once again, one of Sajagax's young wives poured a stream of dark beer into Maram's horn. This time, it took Maram much longer to drink it, but drink it he did. Proud Sarni warriors stood dumbfounded at this feat; they knocked their bows together with a fearsome clacking. Never in living memory had any of them heard of a man finishing five horns of beer. And so Tringax called out: 'A five-horned man! Maram of the five horns!'

'Five horns?' Maram said. 'Why not make it six? Yes, I like the sound of that better: "Six-Horned Maram"!'

So saying, he held out his horn yet again. But when Sajagax's wife came forward to refill it, Maram's face fell sick and he shook his head as he thought better of his impulse. 'Ah, enough, enough – I think I've had very enough.' And to the cheers of hundreds of warriors, both black-haired and blond, he fell backwards down to his cushions, too.

Braggod lay close-eyed and moaning as if felled by an axe, but Maram still had his wits – and his pride. As everyone looked on, he smiled at Sajagax and said, 'Do you see? Do you see, great chieftain? And you thought we Delians *weak*!'

No one could challenge Sajagax thusly and expect such a man to keep his silence. Sajagax nodded at Maram and said, 'You're not weak in the belly, I'll give you that. Nor in the mouth. If you weren't so drunk, we'd put the strength of your arms to the test as well.'

'My arms are as strong as those of any Sarni.'

'You think so, fat man?'

'As strong as yours, old man.'

Sajagax's eyes flared with anger. He said, 'Prove it, then.'

'Gladly. How?'

In answer, Sajagax stood up and leaned his body into his bow as he bent it and strung it. He handed it to Maram and sat back down. 'Let's see if you can draw this, then.'

Although Maram was unused to working a bow from a sitting posi-tion, he held the great bow out before him with his stiffened arm. He

290

grunted and groaned and exerted all the power of his arms and back to pull the bow's string to his ear. Then a moment later, he relaxed the string and called out, 'There!'

Yaggod and Urtukar nodded their heads at this feat, Tringax, too. And Sajagax said to Maram, 'You're stronger than anyone would think, I'll give you that. That was more than most of my warriors can manage. But that is not what we mean by drawing a bow.'

'What is, then?'

Sajagax handed him an arrow fletched with raven feathers, one of the heavy ones used for piercing armor. He said to Maram, 'You must hold this at full draw for a count of at least five.'

'Only five? Can Five-Horned Maram do any less?'

And with that, he knocked the arrow and again drew the string back to the side of his head. Sajagax tried not to blink as Maram pointed it past his head toward the roof of the tent.

'One!' Sajagax cried out.

Maram grunted and seemed to swallow back a belch. He gripped the arrow between his sweating fingers with a fierce concentration.

'Two!' A hundred voices cried this out together.

Beads of sweat rolled down Maram's face as he gasped for breath. Both his arms began trembling with the strain of pulling the great bow.

'Three!'

'Look at him!' a warrior called out. 'Five-Horned Maram is going to hold the count!'

'Four!'

But even as everyone in the tent, myself included, shouted out this number, Maram's arm buckled and he lost his grip on the bowstring. With a loud crack, it sent the arrow whining through the air. A dozen warriors ducked low their heads. And three hundred more looked up to witness the neat hole that the arrow had punched through the silk of Sajagax's tent.

Seeing this ruin, three of Sajagax's wives looked at Sajagax and cringed. Everyone else looked at him, too. The great chieftain's face grew as red as the Marud sun. His eyes fixed on the hole like arrows of his own. Even Yaggod and Tringax dared not speak.

At last, like the sky breaking open during a storm, Sajagax let loose a tremendous laugh. He threw back his head and pounded Maram's shoulder, all the while pealing out a huge, happy thunder. We all laughed with him. And then Sajagax dried his eyes and took back his bow.

'Well, Sar Maram,' he said, 'that was better than anyone would have expected. None of the Kurmak will ever question your strength again.'

Maram squinted as he looked up at the stars showing through the hole he had made. He belched and said, 'I'm sorry about your tent, Sajagax.'

'That's all right – it was growing stuffy in here, and we needed a little ventilation.'

I took a sip of wine, glad that I had this spirit of the grape to drink instead of beer.

'Here, Lord Valashu!' Sajagax said, smiling at me as he held out his bow. 'Let's see if you can draw it.'

I smiled back at him and said, 'No one has ever called *me* an archer.'

'But you placed fifth in archery at this tournament of yours, didn't you? You won the gold medallion of championship, didn't you?'

I admitted that I had as I looked at Sajagax's huge, knotted bow.

'Take it, Lord Valashu,' he said to me. The smile suddenly fell from his face. His eyes grew hard as diamonds and seemed to press into me. 'Take it. Surely the one that Five-Horned Maram follows must be the strongest of men.'

Yaggod and Tringax and all the Kurmak captains in our circle except the senseless Braggod turned to look at me. Master Juwain and Maram, Lord Harsha, Lord Raasharu and Baltasar – all my friends' eyes fell upon me with an uncomfortable light. Even Atara seemed to be waiting to see what I would do.

'Surely the one that Sajagax rides with, *if* he rides,' Sajagax went on, 'must be strong enough of heart at least to *try* to draw this bow.'

I knew that I was not as strong as Maram. I looked at the thick, curved bow that Sajagax gripped in his huge fist. If I refused to take it, I would bring shame upon myself. But if tried to draw it and failed, I might bring worse than shame.

'Come, my friend,' Maram said to me. 'If I can draw it, you can.'

'Show him what a Valari warrior is made of!' Baltasar added.

And then for the first time during the feast, Atara spoke, and her voice was as clear as a bell: 'Take the bow, Val.'

I took the bow. It was even heavier than I had thought it would be. Sajagax gave me an arrow, and I knocked it to the bow's string. I raised up the bow and tried to pull back the arrow as far as it would go.

'Valashu Elahad!' Sar Avram called out. 'Lord Valashu for the Valari!'

A terrible weakness burned through the muscles of my arms and back as I struggled to draw the great bow. I gasped at the pain of it. I knew with a sick and sudden certainty that I didn't have the strength for this feat, any more than I could lift a rock the size of Sajagax. Inch by inch I pulled back the arrow; when the bowstring was about three inches from my ear, my arm seemed blocked by a wall of stone, and I could draw the bow no further.

'That's about as good as *I* can do,' Tringax admitted as I trembled and strained and finally relaxed the bow. 'No one except Sajagax will ever draw this.'

'The Elahad *will* draw it!' Sunjay Naviru said. 'He's only taking a moment to get a better grip.'

I could grip the bowstring with the claws of a dragon, I thought, and still not be able to draw this massive bow. Just as I was about to give up hope and betray my weakness yet again, Flick began spinning above the Lightstone. All the Timpum possessed qualities such as brightness, calmness or curiosity that made one think of people's faces. I had always seen Flick as a sort of mischievous but well-meaning child. But now I saw something strange in the array of lights before me. Flick's usual colors began giving way to a swirl of topaz, incarnadine and soft browns. Glorre contained the essence of all colors, and out of this brilliant hue, for one lightning-quick moment, a distinct face flashed into form. it was that of Alphanderry. A sharp pain stabbed through my heart. Why, I wondered, did this beautiful man have to die? So that I might go on to find the Lightstone?

As Flick faded back into nothingness, my memory of Alphanderry and his impossible feat at the Kul Moroth burned inside me. I could almost hear him telling me, in the language of the Galadin, that nothing was impossible. I gazed down at the Lightstone, which seemed to fill with a marvelous liquid the color of glorre. I drank it in through my eyes. And the more that I drank, the more that the golden cup poured forth this luminous substance. I knew that the little Lightstone could hold much more than ten thousand drinking horns – and I could hold much more than I ever dared dream.

'Come, Val,' Maram said to me.

A tingling warmth flowed down my spine, into my arms and hands and every part of me. It touched fire to my blood and filled me with a great strength.

'Come, Val,' Atara said to me. 'Draw the bow.'

I lifted up this massive working of wood and horn; it now seemed as light as my flute. With one swift motion, to the gasps of Tringax and Urtukar and others looking on, I drew the nocked arrow straight back to my ear. Atara and Maram called out, 'One!' with a single breath. Hundreds of other warriors did, as well. The next numbers came in succession to the slow and even beating of my heart. When the count reached ten, I eased the tension on the bow, and gave both it and the arrow to Sajagax.

'One hole is enough,' I said to him as I looked up at tear in the tent's roof that Maram had made.

'Lord of Battles!' Baltasar called out. 'Lord of Light!'

Sajagax breathed heavily as he looked at me. He pulled on his bow as if testing it to see if someone had somehow slipped a lighter one into his hand. And then, quickly and surely, he nocked the arrow and turned as he drew it back as far it would go. He sighted on the hole in the roof. He held the bow at full draw for what must have been a count of twenty. Then he let fly the arrow. It burned through the air invisibly and vanished through the star-sparkled hole.

'One hole *is* enough,' he agreed, smiling at me.

Hundreds of knights and warriors gasped to see such marksmanship. I blinked my eyes, not quite daring to believe what I had witnessed. Not even Atara or Sar Hannu or any other archer I ever heard of could have made such a shot.

'If I ride with you to Tria,' Sajagax said to me, 'if an alliance is made and you are proclaimed the Maitreya, what then, Lord Guardian?'

'Then Morjin will not be able to move against the Free Peoples.'

Sajagax's eyes blazed with a blue fire. 'No – but *we* will be able to move against him.'

'Perhaps, but we must not.'

'*Why* not?'

'Because we can defeat him without making war.'

'Defeat the Red Dragon without *war*, you say?'

His eyes burned into mine. Sitting at the center of his great tent, with hundreds of his warriors gathered around him and thousands more at his call, he looked deep inside me for any sign of weakness or fear. At last, I touched his bow and then laid my hand on the hilt of my sword. I said, 'We were meant for much more than this.'

'What, then?'

'To make a new world.'

Now I stared at him as the anguish of all those I had slain and seen slain came pouring into me. My eyes burned, and burned into *him*. Why, I wondered, had so many suffered so much for me to have recovered the Lightstone? I felt the fire of this golden cup blazing inside me, brighter and brighter. I could not hold it. I stared at Sajagax without blinking in a test of will that seemed to last an hour. Finally, he looked away from me and sat rubbing his eyes as if they were tired and gave him pain.

'You Valari,' he said to me, 'are strange.'

I held out my hand to him and said, 'Will you ride with me to Tria?'

'All right, Valashu,' he told me, 'on the morrow, the Valari and Kurmak will ride toward this new world of yours.'

He smiled as he took my hand. His grip was strong enough to crush bones, and it took all my strength to hold the clasp without crying out.

After that, there was more drinking and singing, far into the night. Sajagax offered one of his daughters in marriage to Maram; Maram, under Lord Harsha's scathing eye, told Sajagax that he was already betrothed and that as a Valari warrior he might take only one wife. When it came time for sleeping, Sajagax noticed that Atara's blindfold was soiled with dust and splashed beer. He called for a fresh, white cloth to bind her eye hollows. With his own hands he tendered this service. After he had finished, he sat combing back her golden hair with his calloused fingers. Tringax and Yaggod and others, displeased at his kindness, glared at him in reproach. And Sajagax glared right back and called out, 'If the chieftain of the Sarni's greatest tribe can't do as he pleases in his own tent, what's the point of being chieftain?'

He picked up his bow then, and stared down his captains one by one. Although they might have dreamed deep in their hearts of a new world in which no man would ever yield to another, no one was willing to challenge the great and fearsome Sajagax.

21

In the morning, with the smells of freshly baked bread and roasting meats hanging heavy in the air, we gathered in the great open area outside of Sajagax's tent. My Guardians formed up in their three columns; Sajagax had summoned his own private guard: fifty Kurmak warriors, all of the Tharkat clan. All wore conical steel helmets over their long, blonde braids; their armor was of black leather studded with shiny bits of steel. This covered only their upper bodies, and left their arms bare and free for drawing their powerful bows. It was much lighter than the suits of diamonds that encased a Valari knight from neck to ankle. Being unused to battle at close quarters, the Sarni carried no shields, nor throwing lances, nor long lances either. Thus the load that their horses had to bear was lighter than that of our stout warhorses. Being unused to roads as well, they did not bother to draw up these lithe animals into anything resembling columns. The only order I could detect in the horde of snorting horses and fierce men that gathered to Sajagax was that Sajagax would ride foremost among them.

Just before we set out, however, he nudged his horse, a young piebald stallion, over to where I sat at the head of my knights. He looked long and deeply at Altaru and said, 'It's a great horse you ride, Valashu Elahad. He has beauty and grace. A little too thick for speed over distances, but I would guess he's a terror in a short charge.'

Sajagax and his guard led the way out of his city of tents, and this took some time. When we reached the open steppe, his warriors fanned out to either side of him in a formation that reminded me of a flock of geese. We followed them at a distance of a hundred yards. They did not really need to lead the way toward Tria, for the during the rest of our journey, we would parallel the Poru as it wound its way through grassland and forest to the Northern Ocean.

Atara and Karimah, who had said farewell to the Manslayers so that they could attend the great conclave, rode with me and my Guardians. Despite what Sajagax had said about the Sarni warriors respecting the Manslayers, the Manslayers did not really trust their own men and preferred to keep a distance from them. Of course, they did not trust *my* men either. But as Karimah had with Lord Harsha, she kept her knife ready (and her sword and bow), and so my knights were careful how they looked at this jolly but violent woman. And as for Atara, everyone knew that she and I had been comrades-in-arms and perhaps something more.

In truth, I welcomed the chance to be near her even though she seldom consented to speak with me. Her coldness along the sere miles of the endless steppe was a winter that I longed to melt away as with the waxing of the hot spring sun. I knew well enough the source of her silence toward me. And so I understood why she pulled her red mare next to Karimah, Behira or even Estrella, to speak with these females in a way that she no longer could with me – or perhaps any man. They comforted her in a way that I could not. It made me want to reach Tria all the sooner, to unlock the Lightstone's secrets and claim it as my own – and then to begin the great work of healing that I thought I must be born for.

Toward this end, I spent as much time as I could with Master Juwain trying to recreate the language of the Galadin. With every mile of grass that our horses trampled beneath their hooves, it seemed that I remembered more words of Alphanderry's last song. Master Juwain, in an elegant and precise script, dutifully wrote each of them down in his journal. When I confessed that I had seen Alphanderry's face take shape out of Flick's shimmering form, Master Juwain grew very excited. He brought forth the akashic stone, and he said, 'Ever since we drew near the Lokilani's island, there's been something strange about Flick. And then in the astor grove, the music, his song, so like Alphanderry's – strange, strange.'

On our first night out from the Kurmak's city, we made camp below some rocky bluffs overlooking the Poru. Master Juwain and I sat with Maram, Lord Raasharu, Atara and Estrella discussing the difficulties of unlocking the akashic crystal. Master Juwain held the rainbow disc in front of a crackling woodfire and watched its play of colored lights. Just then Sajagax, with two burly warriors named Thadrak and Orox, rode into our encampment. Sajagax had with him a bottle of Sungurun brandy that he wished to share. He took his place by the fire, sitting between Atara and me. He gazed at the akashic crystal with little curiosity, as if it were a mere jewel to be appraised and claimed as treasure. But when Flick appeared to whirl above it, his blue eyes lit up with wonder and dread.

297

'The imp returns,' he said. He made a sign of a circle above his fore-head and held out is hand as if to ward off evil.

'Flick is no imp,' Maram said. 'More like a spirit of the little people's wood.'

'No, *more* than a spirit, I should say,' Master Juwain told us. 'Perhaps much more.'

Sajagax hastened to fill our mugs with his fiery brandy, which was even better than our own good brandy that we had brought with us from the Morning Mountains. He gripped the bottle's long neck with great force: I sensed, to keep his hand from trembling. 'If not a spirit, what then?'

'The Lokilani,' Master Juwain said, 'believe the Timpum to be some part of the Galadin.'

'But what are the Galadin if not the greatest of spirits?'

'The Galadin,' Master Juwain said as he took out his worn copy of the *Saganom Elu*, 'are men – and something much more. Would you like to read the passages that tell of them?'

'I cannot read,' Sajagax said, making another circle with his finger and staring at the book suspiciously. 'I care not to learn that art.'

'Not read! But why?'

Sajagax tapped his finger against his head and said, 'To depend on words written on paper – this weakens the memory. And so the mind.'

'But there are so many books!' Master Juwain said. 'So much know-ledge! Far too much for anyone to remember!'

'Books! Knowledge!' Sajagax spat out. 'What does a man really need to know? To shoot an arrow straight; to live like a lion; to die bravely. What good are books for this?'

'But there is so much more! Why, the ways of the stars and the secret of making the gelstei, and –'

'A *man*,' Sajagax said, holding up his great bow, 'teaches his son how to make his weapons and the ways of the wolves and other men. Your books might speculate as to where the sun goes at night and why winter comes. But it is better to know where the sagosk go *when* winter comes.'

'But all of history!' Master Juwain said. 'The Chronicles! The Songs! The Prophecies! To understand why we are here and where we were meant to –'

'We are *here*,' Sajagax broke in again, 'that we might know joy. And as for the past, it is like the future: dwelling in these little tents, we lose the pleasure of life in the here and now, beneath the open sky. It is enough to know the deeds of the *imakil* and one's ancestors. These are told of in the sagas, and passed down from father to son. *These* words are written in the blood and heard in the heart, and so they never lie.'

The implication that the writings in his book might not all be entirely accurate disturbed Master Juwain and angered him. But he took a deep breath to calm himself. He pointed at Flick and said, 'This Timpum has somehow learned to sing. If we could hear *his* songs in our hearts, we might understand the Galadin's language. And so we might better understand the Law of the One.'

'What is there to understand?' Sajagax, disdaining our clay mugs, brought forth a golden goblet and filled it with brandy. He drank half of it in a single gulp. 'The Law of the One is simple: "Be strong. Do what you will. Keep your word. Seek glory. Bear no shame. Honor –"'

'You speak of honor?' Master Juwain called out, now interrupting him. 'You, who honors not the wisdom of many great men who have given their lives to gain it?'

Sajagax's eyes narrowed as he studied Master Juwain. He seemed puzzled that an old man who bore no weapons should yet bear the courage to dispute with him. 'I *do* speak of honor,' he continued. 'As it is spoken of in the Law of the One: "Honor your father. Honor your horse. Honor the wind, the sun and the sky. Honor your honor above all."'

He paused to drink the rest of his brandy. And Master Juwain asked him, 'And is that all you know of the Law, then?'

Sajagax peered at the scarred opening of Master Juwain's ear, which Morjin's priest had enlarged with a red-hot iron. And Sajagax said to him, 'No, I know this last thing, that my father taught me: "Live free or die."'

Master Juwain sighed as he rubbed the back of his bald head. He said to Sajagax, 'And I know what the masters of my Order taught me.'

He squeezed his leather-bound book and thumbed through its pages.

'If that is different than what I have said,' Sajagax growled out, 'then it is a lie, and I wish to hear it not.'

'Is that why your people have always turned away the Brothers we sent to instruct them? Either that, or burnt them?'

'Yes,' Sajagax said. 'We do not abide liars.'

'The truth is only ever the truth,' Master Juwain said. 'And the Law is the Law. But men, according to their knowledge, according to their powers, understand it differently.'

'Words, and more words,' Sajagax muttered.

Master Juwain looked at the blazing logs before us. 'A man teaches his young son not to play with fire, does he not?'

'Of course – what's your point, wizard?'

'And when his son is older,' Master Juwain continued patiently, 'the same father teaches him to *make* fire.'

Sajagax, like a lion sensing a trap, now only stared at Master Juwain. 'A father,' Master Juwain said, 'makes rules for his children, but requires different things from an infant, a boy, or a youth.'

Sajagax now gripped his bow with such force that had it been a man's skull, he would surely have crushed it. 'Are you saying that we Sarni are children who cannot understand this Law of yours?'

'It is not my Law, but *our* Law – the Law of the One. And all who dwell on earth are as children in their understanding of it.'

He went on to say that the Star People knew more of the Law, while to the immortal Elijin, much more was revealed. 'And the Galadin,' he told us, 'are given the sight and senses to apprehend the Law perfectly.'

Maram, listening to his old master with great care, asked him, 'And what of the Ieldra?'

'The Ieldra *are* the Law, the perfect working of the One's will upon the world and all the stars.'

At these words, I couldn't help gazing up at the brilliant constellations illumining the sky. Somewhere, in this whirling array of lights, the Golden Band poured forth all the Ieldra's beauty, goodness and truth. But most men were too blind to see it.

'If we could understand the Law of the One as the angels do,' Master Juwain said to Sajagax, 'then we would understand how the Lightstone might be used. And who might use it.'

At this, I brought out the gold gelstei and sat turning it beneath the stars. Sajagax asked to hold it. I set it into his massive hands. The moment that the little cup touched his skin, his eyes brightened with a new light. He shook his head in wonder. I felt something change inside him then. The core of his being seemed like an iron heating for a long time in a fire and suddenly turning colors from black to red-hot.

He gave the Lightstone back to me. Then he pointed at Flick and said, 'And you truly believe this imp might help in this understanding?'

'We truly do,' I told him.

Sajagax again made the sign of the circle with his finger. Then he gathered in all his courage and waved his hand at Flick as he might try to ward off a cloud of flies. We all watched as his hand swept through Flick's sparkling lights without disturbing them in any way.

'All right,' he said. 'Speak, imp. Tell me of the Law of the One.'

At that moment, Flick's radiance coalesced into the shape of Alphanderry's face. I gasped to see Alphanderry's curly black hair, large brown eyes and fine features now woven of light instead of flesh. It was as if our old friend stared luminously out of the dark air before us.

Sajagax jerked back his hand as if from a flame. And his eyes opened wide with astonishment as words poured forth from Flick's glowing mouth: 'Speak, imp. Tell me of the Law of the One.'

Sajagax tried to making his warding sign yet again, but he couldn't seem to make his arm move. He stared at Flick, dumbfounded, as we all were. For the voice that had boomed out into the night was *not* that of our dead minstrel but the gravelly blare of Sajagax himself.

'Alphanderry was a great mimic,' Maram reminded me. 'Do you remember how he made fun of King Kiritan?'

I nodded my head because I remembered very well. And Sajagax shook his fist at Flick and said, 'Well, he better not make fun of me.'

And Flick stared right back at him and said, 'He better not make fun of me.'

Sajagax forced a smile and tried to put on a bold face. He muttered, 'Never ask an imp to tell you the Law of the One.'

And then a moment later, still speaking in Sajagax's voice, Flick amazed us yet further, saying, 'To tell you the Law of the One: "Be strong and protect the weak. Work your will in accordance with the higher will. Keep your word as you would the truth. Seek the glory of the One."'

And so it went, Flick adding to or altering slightly the words that Sajagax himself had already spoken. I heard him command the great Kurmak chieftain to honor both his father *and* his mother. And he finished by saying, '"Live free and die gladly into the light of the One."'

For a while no one spoke as we stared at Flick's numinous new face. The sounds of the world suddenly seemed too loud: the popping and hissing of the wood in the fire; the crickets' chirping; the wolves far out on the steppe howling at the moon. Many of my men, sitting around fires in front of their tents, sensed that something extraordinary was occurring between me and my friends. They looked our way. But it seemed that Flick was not visible to them from such distances.

Then Master Juwain turned to me and said, 'I think that Flick might be able to do more than simply mimic our words, Val.'

'Val,' Flick said, now in Master Juwain's voice, and he looked up at the stars.

'*Val*!' Master Juwain cried out. 'Do you see? Look where he's looking! *Val* – this *is* the Galadin's word for star!'

Master Juwain set down his copy of the *Saganom Elu* and brought out his journal. He opened it to the first page and said, '*Arda!*'

And Flick replied, '*Arda*,' as he looked through the fire's wavering flames straight at Lord Raasharu's chest.

'All right, then,' Master Juwain said, smiling happily, '*arda* is "fire" or "heart", as I thought. Now then, we have *halla*, which could be harmony or beauty or –'

'*Halla*,' Flick repeated, and he looked at Atara sitting straight and still next to me, as cold and beautiful as chiseled marble. Then Flick's soft brown eyes fell upon Estrella, and his face lit up with a beauty of his own as he repeated one more time: '*Halla*.'

This testing of words continued for some time. Sajagax poured more brandy into our mugs, and we sat sipping this sweet, old liquor as we listened to Flick speak. After a while, Flick seemed to grow tired of this labor. He closed his mouth and stared at Master Juwain. A twinkle of lights danced in his eyes. His face came alive with all of Alphanderry's old playfulness. And then, in Alphanderry's own voice, he sang out with heartpiercing beauty whole shimmering streams of song. When he had finished, even Sajagax had tears in his eyes. Then Flick smiled at him and laughed softly, and he winked once again into neverness. But his lovely voice lingered: it seemed to hang in the air like the after-tones of silver bells.

Master Juwain, who had been scribbling furiously in his journal, put down his quill and said to me, 'Too much, too quickly – do you remember anything of what he said?'

'Yes,' I told him. When I closed my eyes, I could hear Alphanderry's song inside my heart. 'I remember.'

'Good. Well, we still have some hours before dawn.' Master Juwain again picked up his quill. 'Let's get to work, shall we?'

I yawned and looked up at the Swan constellation shining above the horizon. 'Whatever Flick really is, sir, *I'm* still a man and have to sleep.'

'We all do,' Sajagax agreed as he looked at me strangely. 'Summer nights are short, and at dawn we'll ride hard for Alonia. And you Valari will be hard put to keep up with us. We don't want you falling off your horses.'

He grabbed his brandy bottle and leaned over to kiss Atara good-night. Then he stood up and muttered, 'Horses! What was it that imp said to me? "Honor your horse – and all the creatures of the earth"' But how can anyone honor the worms and blowflies alongside the horse?'

And with that, he stood up and summoned Thadrak and Orox, and they walked back to the Kurmak's encampment.

All the next day, during our hot, long ride by the river, Flick did not return to enchant or mystify us. But I called up his words for Master Juwain to record in his journal. It amazed me that he managed to write with such a neat hand sitting on top of his swaying horse. His need to learn the Galadin's language, I thought, was nearly as great as my own.

We covered a good distance that morning, for the Sarni always rode swiftly, and we who guarded the Lightstone desired to reach Tria as soon as we could. Some of my knights complained of the monotony of our journey; the world was flat here, nothing more than endless miles of yellow and green grassland beneath a sheeny blue sky. There was little to engage the eye. Bees buzzed among the wildflowers, and we caught sight of some lions fighting over an antelope they had killed. I worried that my men, irritated by the heat and bloodflies that bit their faces, might themselves take to fighting: Meshians against Ishkans, Waashians against Taroners, Atharians against Lagashuns. But the truce that we had forged during our journey from King Hadaru's hall and tempered since the tournament held true. It touched my heart to see Kaashans and Anjoris treating each other with goodwill, as if they were brothers. It helped, I knew, that we Valari were all strangers in a strange land here, where the wind blew wild and fierce across the sere emptiness of the Wendrush. If it came to battle, we must fight as one – or die as knights of separate kingdoms. That there was something more in their giving up old grievances, Lord Raasharu reminded me during a brief rest along the bank of the Poru.

'You are the Lord of Light,' he said to me as his long face brightened with reverence.

I shook my head as I told him, 'That is still not proven.'

'The more you doubt yourself, Lord Valashu, the less others do.'

I looked off at Sar Avram and Shivathar and my other knights up and down the river watering their horses in the Poru's turbid flow. Sar Jarlath, who had come so close to death in the battle with the Adirii, smiled at me and waved his hand in salute. To Lord Raasharu, I said, 'They might do well to doubt. Much depends on the truth or falseness of that which they call me.'

'The men love you,' he said to me simply. 'They do not doubt this, any more than they doubt that you love them.'

His words pierced my heart like so many swords. My father had once said that leading men as a band of brothers was the greatest of joys – and that leading them to their deaths in battle was the greatest anguish.

303

'They would follow you, you know,' he said to me, 'even if you weren't the Maitreya.'

I carried this thought with me as we resumed our journey. Most of the time I rode at the head of our columns, exchanging words with Master Juwain. I kept watching Sajagax and his warriors, who rode easily and skillfully ahead of us. The Kurmak, at least, had no love of me or my knights. Perhaps, in their fierce way, they loved or honored Sajagax, for they were all of Tharkat clan, as was he. Certainly they feared him. He had demanded of each of them that they give their word not to fight with my men. It was to this, more than anything, that I attributed the uneasy peace between our two companies.

But the Kurmak continued to fight or contend among themselves. From time to time, a pair of them would shout at each other or break from their ragged formation to gallop across the grass in a race. They shot their arrows at lions and sometimes charged singly toward a pride of them, vying with each other to see who could come the closest before these great beasts either charged *them* or fled. They whistled and cursed and laughed at each other's jokes. A few of Sajagax's most willful warriors guzzled beer, even during the day, and their loud, brash songs of challenge to the sky frightened the birds away.

Once, as I rode next to Atara, I asked her why she had left Alonia to live with her grandfather among these rude, wild people. And Atara told me, 'We Sarni *are* violent, it is true. But so it is almost everywhere. On the Wendrush, at least, if a warrior wishes to kill you, he will do so openly and honestly. We do not plot and scheme or poison each other, either in body or mind. We keep our word and our laws, as cruel as you might think they are. We like singing and dancing. And we love life, Val. Despite what my grandfather said about the flies and worms, if he were forced to spend much time in a castle or some grand house of marble, he would go mad, as would any of my people.'

Later that day, we came to the place where the Poru was joined by the Astu. This great river, fed by the Blood, the Jade and other waters that streamed down from the White Mountains, added to the Poru's flow and swelled it so that the distance from its east bank to the west was nearly a mile. Sajagax and the Kurmak now took to scanning this mighty brown river, and both its wooded banks, for directly across it was the land of the Marituk. Only the bravest and most determined of warriors, I thought, would dare swim their horses and themselves through treacherous currents that had drowned more than one raiding party. The Marituk were such warriors. And so were the Kurmak. When we camped that evening and treated Sajagax to some of the succulent antelope that one of my knights had killed, I overheard Orox begging

Sajagax to add a little fun to our journey and strike out toward the west in order steal women, horses and gold.

But Sajagax had not won thirty-three battles and great wealth by being so easily diverted from his purpose. He had given me his word that he would ride with me to Tria, and so ride we did, as straight and quickly as an arrow flies, or so the Sarni like to say. By noon the next day, with the sun like a hot orange fire turning the world into a furnace, we neared the northern bounds of the Kurmak's country. We had to turn a few miles toward the east, for here the Poru overflowed its banks, making a mire of the steppe's long grasses and soil. The cause of this, I soon learned, was not any natural configuration or depression of the earth. The hand of man alone had wrought a structure – the greatest on earth – that blocked the river like a dam. And this massive work of granite and mortar was called the Long Wall.

From miles away, we saw it cutting across the steppe like an upraised scar of stone. Towers, every fifty yards, surmounted its endless line of battlements, biting at the sky like teeth to the east and west for as far as the eye could see. Alonian soldiers stood garrison duty in the towers, though few were stationed here, for Alonia and the Sarni were not presently at war. But the Alonians dreaded the Sarni, as they always had. Late in the Age of the Mother, King Yarin Marshan the Great had drawn a line from the southern end of the Blue Mountains six hundred miles east to the Gap in the Morning Mountains. All the lands to the north, he had claimed for Alonia. But the kings who had succeeded him had not been able to hold back the tide of the Sarni's swelling numbers. After nearly a thousand years of war and rapine, King Shurkar Eriades had gained enough power to begin building the Wall along the Line of Yarin. Two hundred years it took for the Alonians to complete it. By 1124 in the Age of Swords, the Alonians thought themselves well-protected against the yellow-haired hordes of the south.

But the Wall had a weakness, and that was the Poru river. Indeed, the original Wall had a break in it a mile wide, for its makers had built it only to the points, east and west, where the Poru overflowed its banks during the spring floods. But the Sarni found that they could mount autumn and winter attacks along the corridors to either side of the Poru when the river went down. A few of these, despite the heroics of the Alonian soldiers defending the corridors, were successful. And so the Alonians labored another fifty years to extend the Wall to the Poru's east and west banks, driving pylons deep into the muddy earth to support its great weight of stone. And still the Sarni had continued their aggressions, building boats and rafts and simply floating their armies down the river into Alonia. And so finally the

Alonians had spent another hundred years – and thousands of lives – planting their pylons into the bedrock beneath the river itself. They then built the Wall out over the river like a massive bridge. Three feet only, during the Poru's lowest flow, separated the base of the Wall from the waters of the river. And when it was in flood or running high, during the spring and the summer raiding season, the base of the Wall was submerged, impeding the river's flow so that spilled over its banks and created a mire three miles wide.

As we drew closer to the Wall, Sajagax halted his horse on a low rise and sat staring at it. A short while later, with my Guardians behind me, I drew up to him, and he said, 'There it is, Lord Valashu. A dunghill made of stone.'

He swept his hand even with the Wall and continued, 'Do you see how it cuts the earth? Like a belt too tight cutting a man in two. The sagosk cannot cross it; neither the hares nor the antelope nor even the lions. The wild horses can no longer run free! Here, where we Sarni are constrained to live, the steppe is open and the grass grows as long as it pleases. And on the other side . . . well, you will see.'

Maram, Baltasar, Lord Raasharu and others of our company, gathered around to marvel at this great stone wall. Orox, sitting on his horse near Sajagax, pointed out a place on the wall a quarter mile to the east of us where its gray-green granite had been replaced by a stone pinker in color. He said, 'There is where Tulumar broke the Wall.'

In the year 2057 of the Age of Swords, Tulumar the Great of the Urtuk tribe, with the aid of Morjin, had spread a red substance called *relb* over the wall and melted its stones to lava. With the Breaking of the Long Wall, as this event was called, Tulumar had led his armies through the huge, smoking hole and had gone on to conquer Alonia and much of Ea.

'I'd break it myself and grind the stones to dust, if I could,' Sajagax said. 'If I had a firestone, I'd burn the whole wall back into the earth.'

Maram, who possessed what might have been Ea's last remaining firestone, shoved his hand down into the inner pocket of his surcoat as he stared at the Wall in silence.

'This is one day,' I said to Sajagax, 'that the Sarni will need neither relb nor firestones to pass through the Wall. Shall we make our way to the gate?'

A few hundred yards ahead of us, across the windswept grasses, a massive iron gate was set into the Wall. Two great, round towers stood to either side of it. The soldiers posted on top of these had seen us approaching before we had seen them. They had hoisted red pennants

306

challenging us to announce ourselves or face a storm of arrows fired by the Wall's archers.

And so, leaving our two companies of warriors waiting behind us, Sajagax and I rode side by side down to the Wall. The sally port set into the gate creaked open, and a mail-clad knight bearing a white lion against his green surcoat rode out a few paces to greet us.

'I'm Sajagax, chieftain of the Kurmak,' Sajagax called out to him.

'Lord Valashu Elahad of Mesh,' I said, presenting myself. I looked back at my knights and added, 'And of the Valari.'

Upon this word, the thick-set knight stared at me in amazement. The sun reflected off the diamonds of my armor seemed to dazzle his eyes. 'Yes, Valari indeed – you must be,' he said. 'But what are Valari knights doing riding across the Wendrush in the company of the Kurmak?'

I did not wish to tell him of my reason for seeking the Lokilani's island, nor that my knights and I bore the Lightstone.

'We are journeying to the conclave that King Kiritan has called,' I said. 'Surely you must have been told to open your gates to any who have been summoned to Tria.'

Lord Halmar, for that proved to be the knight's name, scratched his bearded jaw and said, 'That I was, Lord Valashu. But it was thought that only Sarni would pass this way, if indeed any chose to attend the conclave. What is your business with the Kurmak?'

'Only peace,' I told him, looking at Sajagax. 'We are emissaries of peace.'

Lord Halmar studied my knights spread out on the rise behind us. 'Emissaries bearing lances and swords. And nearly two hundred of you, if my count is right. That is a great many to guard the chief emissary, even if he is a lord of Mesh.'

'These are dangerous times,' I said to him.

'And miraculous times, as well. I've heard that one of the Valari has regained the Lightstone.'

His sharp blue eyes fixed on me like grappling hooks, and would not let go. I held his gaze and said to him, 'We have heard that as well.'

After a few moments, Lord Halmar looked away from me and muttered, 'Very well, then, I will send heralds to Duke Malatam, and he will decide whether or not you may pass.'

On the other side of the Wall, as Atara had told me, lay the demesne of Tarlan, whose lord was Duke Malatam.

'And how far from here is his castle?'

'Two days' ride.'

'Then it will be four days before your heralds return. The delay might well cause us to miss the conclave.'

'I'm sorry, Lord Valashu, but that can't be helped.'

Sajagax finally lost patience and shook his fist at the wall as he thundered, 'It must be helped! I have been summoned to the conclave, and Lord Valashu rides with me. And so does Atara Manslayer, also known as Atara Ars Narmada. If you delay us, Lord Halmar, *you* will have to explain to King Kiritan why you kept his granddaughter and the father of his queen from joining him to decide great matters. Now open your cursed gate!'

At this, Lord Halmar paled. I sensed that he was caught in the unenviable position of having to face King Kiritan's wrath or that of his lord duke. 'All right,' he told us, 'you may pass. Call your companies forward and wait here.'

Without another word, he turned his horse and rode back through the sally port, which slammed shut with a loud ringing.

I said to Sajagax, 'It seems he has guessed the nature of the little trinket that we bring to Tria.'

'Indeed. You're not very good at lying.'

'I never denied that we bear the Lightstone.'

'No, but you didn't affirm it either. The truth evaded is a lie.'

So it was. So my father might have told had he been here sitting on his horse in Sajagax's place. I looked at Sajagax and bowed my head to him. I said, 'I don't think you're very good at lying, either.'

'No, I'm not. But then I haven't had much practice.'

Sajagax and I returned to our companies, and we led our men down to the very foot of the gate. There, with the Long Wall towering above us and blocking the sight of half the sky, we waited for the gate to open.

With much shrieking of rusted iron, rattling chains and men shouting, its two doors swung slowly inward. Sajagax led his warriors through the Wall, and I followed him with the Guardians of the Lightstone riding in their columns behind me. Lord Halmar had assembled the entire garrison here, lining up a hundred knights and some four hundred men-at-arms on either side of the road leading north into Tarlan. Only the knights, I saw, were permitted to display their own charges on their shields and surcoats, for that was the way of things in Alonia. The common soldiers, standing stiffly with their long, rectangular shields before them, each wore two badges, one on either arm. The right badge bore the arms of King Kiritan: the gold caduceus on a blue field. And the left badge showed the black saltire and red roses of Duke Malatam. It seemed that Lord Halmar had called up his men to honor us. But as Lansar Raasharu told Lord Harsha in a low voice, it was more likely that they stood ready to do battle with us: 'How can this Lord Halmar be sure that Sajagax hasn't hidden the whole Kurmak horde on the steppe behind us? And that we and his warriors won't fight to keep the gate open?'

Indeed, more than once over the ages, the Sarni had won their way into Alonia through assaults on the Long Wall's gates. Where siege engines or heroic storming of the walls had failed, often bribery of the gates' guards with gold had won the day. But on *this* day, at least, Lord Halmar and his garrison had little to fear, for Alonia and the Kurmak had been at peace for more than twenty years, ever since they had sealed an alliance through the marriage of King Kiritan and Sajagax's favorite daughter, Daryana. Even so, after the last of my knights had passed through the gates, Lord Halmar's men hastened to shut them once again.

The road before us led through a patchwork of canals and irrigated farmland bordering the river. Two men on horses, I saw, were galloping northward along it. I guessed that Lord Halmar must have sent them to alert Duke Malatam that we would be passing through his lands.

Lord Halmar invited us to take refreshment with him in one of the guardhouses built into the base of this side of the wall. But as Sajagax put it, not caring who heard him, 'I've little liking to set foot inside one of these stone coffins. In any case, we must be on our way.'

And so we thanked Lord Halmar for his hospitality and set out down the road after the heralds. A hundred and fifty miles of good roads and peaceful country lay between us and Tria, and I hoped to make this journey in only four or five more days.

22

For fifteen more miles that afternoon, we rode north along the eastern side of the Poru. Farms to the right and left of the road had been hacked out of the once-open steppe. Instead of grass, the Alonians grew wheat and other grains. An intricate system of canals carried water from the river and watered these fields, which were broken up into green rectangles and squares. Every half mile or so, we crossed a little bridge spanning one of the larger canals. Sajagax and his warriors hated being forced onto the road in order to make these crossings – and more importantly, to keep from trampling the fields. And they had nothing but contempt for the men and women who worked stripped to the waist and bent over under the hot sun hoeing and weeding and scattering buckets of manure to fertilize their crops. As Sajagax said to me during a break to water our horses from one of the canals, 'Look at these dirt-scrapers and dung-carriers! They're practically slaves of whatever lord owns this land. They'd be better off if we ended their miserable lives by using them for target practice.'

Here he lifted up his bow and winked at me. Horrified, I placed my hand on his arm and said to him, 'Be strong and protect the weak.'

For a moment, I felt a flame of compassion ignite inside Sajagax. And then he shook his head even as he shook his bow at the tamed countryside around us. 'They're *kradaks* like everyone else here, and they've no right to live on the Wendrush like real men. We should level all of Alonia and convert it to pasturage for our horses.'

I looked at him to see if he was serious. He was. No wonder, I thought, that we Valari had fought these savage Sarni for three long ages.

And then, just as I had given up all hope for this barbarian with his braided gray hair and fierce mustaches, he surprised me. As we were passing through a village whose name I never learned, he stopped to give a gold coin to a blind woman begging alms. When I bowed my head to acknowledge his kindness, he said to me, '"Be strong and protect the weak." It's a hard law you've laid upon me, Valashu Elahad. There are too many of the weak. But that woman could have been my own granddaughter.'

The Alonians, sad to say, did not return Sajagax's largesse. We made camp that night on a fallow field of a wealthy landowner. This was a soft and haughty young knight, who it seemed had never been to war. Although he did not charge us for pitching our tents on top of his weedy field, he demanded gold for the bread and beef that he wished to sell us – at extortionate prices. After Sajagax had heard him out, he nearly put an arrow through his eye. The knight retreated behind the walls of his estate. And Sajagax bent down to plough his rough, old hand into the black soil beneath his boots. He held it out before me and said, 'I'd rather eat dirt than pay for that weakling's food. On the Wendrush, we either kill strangers passing through or give them so much meat and drink that they can't move.'

Our dinner that night was more of the tough, dried sagosk that we had gnawed on our journey and the inevitable biscuits that Valari called battle bread and the Sarni knew as rushk cakes. Our breakfast the following morning wasn't much more appetizing. But it was enough to sustain us on a long day's ride through the sun that baked us and a few hours of rain that drenched us and slicked the paving stones beneath our horses' clopping hooves. Late in the afternoon, we came to a place where the road turned west and crossed the Poru along a great stone bridge. On the other side was the town of Tiamar, a square assemblage of sparkling stone buildings from which Duke Malatam ruled the lands of Tarlan. The Duke, however, was not in residence in his palace above the river. With other nobles, he had fled the summer heat of these sweltering lowlands for his family's old castle in the hills twenty miles to the north.

'It's just as well,' Sajagax said to me when a passing tinker gave us this news. 'If this duke tried to charge us for his hospitality, too, I *would* put an arrow through him. And then King Kiritan would have to decide if he wished to make war with his own father-in-law.'

None of us wanted to delay our journey by seeking out this great duke in his castle so that we might pay our respects to him. But it was he who sought us out instead. We stopped that night outside the city on a short-grassed commons used for grazing sheep. In the morning, with the sun a glowing red disc above the eastern horizon, we were preparing to break camp when a thunder of hooves sounded on the road to the northwest. I came out of my tent to see a company of thirty knights bearing down upon us. A black cross divided their leader's white shield into quarters, and each of these quadrants showed a repeating motif of red roses: the arms of Duke Malatam.

The Duke and his knights drew up their lathered horses on the commons between the Kurmak's camp and that of my men. I walked out twenty yards to greet him, followed by Lansar Raasharu, Lord Harsha, Maram, Atara and others. But Sajagax insisted on mounting his horse and riding the short distance from where his warriors sat around little fires eating their rations of dried sagosk. No Sarni chieftain, I thought, would bear being unhorsed and looking up to face an Alonian.

'Well, then, I see that the Sarni and the Valari *do* ride together, after all,' Duke Malatam said. He was a smallish man of middle years. He had a thin face like a ferret, and he sported a sleek brown beard. 'Though you do not camp together, I see. Old enmities are hard to put aside, aren't they? You've done well to come this far in peace, and I must tell you that my domain is a peaceful one where mayhem is not tolerated. But *emissaries of peace* are of course welcome.'

To Sajagax's consternation, he dismounted and walked over to clasp my hand warmly. This obligated Sajagax to dismount as well. He climbed down from his horse slowly, and I could feel the aches and pains of old wounds in various parts of his body, which was stiff and cold in the morning air. But Sajagax neither grunted nor winced to give sign of any of these torments. He walked up to us and grasped the Duke's elegant hand. 'We accept your welcome,' he said.

Duke Malatam stood gazing up at Sajagax as he thoughtlessly wiped his moist hand on his white surcoat, which draped over a fine suit of mail. I wondered why, if Tarlan was so peaceful, he was wearing armor on such a calm, bright morning.

'We've ridden all night to reach you before you continue north,' he said to us. 'I have business in Tiamar. I'd like to invite you to join me at my estate and enjoy my hospitality. The Kurmak's greatest chieftain should feast on the finest foods before taking to the road. And so should a prince of Mesh.'

So, I thought, this little duke had recognized my name where Lord Halmar had not. His soft, little eyes danced over mine as if trying to win my confidence with his obvious good will. But his charm felt hollow to me, like an egg sucked dry of its contents. And Sajagax, though flattered, was suspicious of him as well.

'We must ride, and ride quickly,' Sajagax said, 'or we might miss the conclave.'

'But surely a few more hours spent strengthening yourselves for your journey won't matter. I can offer you bread, summer lamb and the finest beef in all of Alonia.'

At the mention of this meat, taken from an animal that the Sarni regarded with disdain, Sajagax pulled out a strip of leathery sagosk and said, 'We have good food of our own – would you care to join *us* for breakfast?'

Duke Malatam's nose wrinkled in disgust as he eyed this piece of dried flesh. It was said that the Sarni softened such rations by stuffing them down beneath the saddles of their warm, sweating horses. I knew this to be true.

'I wouldn't want to consume supplies that you'll need on your journey,' the Duke said. 'I think we would all be happier taking breakfast at my palace.'

'My apologies,' I said to him, 'but we haven't the time.'

'But we've much to discuss, Lord Valashu.'

The Duke nodded his head at a portly, fair-haired knight, whom I took to be the captain of his men. This knight dismounted, as did the thirty others of Duke Malatam's guard. They each bore various charges on their fine, fresh surcoats: a golden eagle; white roses; a black boar. Their mail was brightly polished, and I could detect in these shining, interlocked rings no mark of a sword blow or dent of a battle-axe. Their faces, too, seemed unmarked by the horror of war. How should they, in a realm that for many years had known mostly peace?

'I would speak with you about the conclave,' Duke Malatam said to me. 'And about the great Quest.'

He fingered the large medallion that hung from a chain around his neck. It showed at its center a little cup with seven rays streaming out of it – as did my own medallion that I wore over my armor. I looked at the medallions of Atara, Maram and Master Juwain shining in the morning sun.

'I had heard,' Duke Malatam continued, 'that an Elahad of Mesh had found the Lightstone. But one hears so many things these days. It's hard to know what to believe or not, isn't it?'

At this, Atara stepped forward and answered for me, 'It *is* hard to know. Lord Valashu stood with me and my friends in front of my father's throne to make vows to seek the Lightstone. But I don't recall seeing you there to receive your medallion.'

Her words seemed to tie the Duke's insides into knots. His fair skin flushed as he asked her, '*Could* you recall seeing me, Princess, since your sight has been taken from you and you can no longer see anything at all?'

'Her second sight hasn't been taken,' I said.

Duke Malatam stared at the cloth bound around her head. He coughed into his hand and told us, 'Well, in fact, there was an illness in my family, and I came late to Tria – too late to take vows with you and the others. But not too late to receive my medallion. King Kiritan gave it to me with his own hand.'

'And in what land,' Maram asked, looking at Duke Malatam's medallion, 'did you make your quest?'

The Duke's face burned an even brighter shade of red as he coughed out, 'In my own lands. Of course, I *would* have gone to the end of the earth for even a glimpse of the Lightstone. I *wanted* to go with you to Argattha. Of course, I didn't know that you and your companions would dare what must be the greatest deed of this or any other age. But I guessed that the Lightstone never left Argattha. I like to think that this guess – I should say that it was really more of a deduction based on the old legends – somehow lent spirit to the heroes who *did* find the Lightstone. It's said, isn't it, that all true hearts beat as one? Even across hundreds of miles or the whole of the earth? I believe that your great valor touched fire to the hearts of all who truly sought the Lightstone. Certainly it touched mine. If only I could, I would have stolen past Argattha's gates myself.'

Master Juwain turned his good ear toward him, and then pulled at it as if it wasn't quite good enough to make sense of the Duke's wild claims. He asked him, 'And why didn't you, then?'

'Well, King Kiritan asked me to remain in Tarlan. When one's king makes such a request, even the greatest of nobles must grant it, even though his heart yearns for greater adventures.'

'King Kiritan,' I said to him, 'used the Quest as a reason to send Alonia's other nobles *away* from their domains. Why not likewise send you?'

Duke Malatam bowed his head toward Atara. 'The Princess will have told you much about Alonia. But it's hard for one from a faraway kingdom to understand the affairs of another realm. It's hard for the Princess herself, having lived among her grandfather's people for so long, to understand. Yes, King Kiritan asked Duke Ashvar and Baron Maruth to make their quests in distant lands. One could almost say that he even shamed them into this. But this is a peaceful way, isn't it, to limit the mischief of nobles whose loyalty is in doubt? Raanan has been the most rebellious of domains ever since King Sakandar tried to reunite Alonia two generations ago. And the Aquantir has ever been a hotbed of plots and schemes against the royal house. Our neighbor to the west fancies itself the greatest of Alonia's domains, and its lords have never knelt easily to any king in Tria. Is it any wonder, then, that King Kiritan should ask a loyal duke to keep watch on the Aquantir? And so, yes, although I should have died from my desire to storm Argattha with you, it was perhaps my greater destiny to remain here and help keep Alonia strong. The day is coming, even as you know, Lord Valashu, when Alonia must lead an alliance against Morjin and . . .'

He continued chattering on in a like vein as the sun rose higher and warmed the grassy commons. It seemed that he was trying to eat up time as the day does the sky.

'A loyal lord,' I said to him, breaking in, 'would be a strength to any king. This is a time when all free kings and lords must stand together.'

Duke Malatam fairly beamed at what he took as a compliment. He said to me, to his knights and to all gathered about us: 'Everyone knows I have always stood by my king. When I first came into my possession fifteen years ago, there was rebellion in the Aquantir. I'm proud to say that I led my knights to aid King Kiritan in putting it down. We defeated Old Baron Maruth at the Battle of Angels' Crossing. I had the honor of leading the charge against the Baron's right flank, which collapsed in the face of the valor of my knights.'

Here he paused to smile at his portly captain, whose emblem was a black boar on a red field.

'A great battle, was it?' I asked him.

'A great victory. We outnumbered the Aquantirings two to one. When we outflanked them and began hacking down their infantry from the rear, they laid down their arms and surrendered. We lost only twenty eight knights killed and fifteen wounded.'

I bowed my head to him and said, 'And has the new Baron Maruth never sought revenge?'

'He wouldn't dare to lead an army into Tarlan. We are too strong. Even brigands that bedevil other domains fear to ply their trade here.'

'Very good,' I said, 'then our journey will be a peaceful one. And now we must excuse ourselves and be on our way.'

The Duke placed his hand on my arm as if to keep me there. 'I really must insist that you join me for breakfast at my palace.'

I looked at his small, pale hand pressing down upon my diamond armor. Baltasar looked at this hand, too, as if he were trembling to whip free his sword and slice it off.

'Are you commanding us to join you?'

'Command you?' His hand suddenly slipped off me, and he dried it again on his surcoat. 'No, no – of course not. Alonia is a free kingdom, and Tarlan is the freest of her domains. You may go where you will. It's a rare, good fortune that a Valari prince and his knights should pass through, and so I felt I should insist on offering my hospitality. But since you are in a hurry and have already offered yours so gracefully, perhaps it would be better if we took a bit of breakfast with you. We're all very hungry.'

He smiled at me warmly; if he were a dog, I thought, he would have wagged his tail and licked my hand. And yet there was something greedy and rapacious in him, like a weasel driven to try to steal chickens when a farmer is sleeping. The last thing that I desired was to take breakfast with this vain and manipulative man. But Sajagax *had* offered him hospitality, and so there was nothing to do but sit with him and eat a quick meal.

And so sit we did, by a campfire where Master Juwain fried up a few eggs that we had bought in Tiamar. While Sunjay and other Guardians took care of Duke Malatam's knights, the Duke invited his captain, Lord Chagnan, to eat with him, as I did Maram, Atara, Karimah, Lord Raasharu and Sajagax. The eggs were devoured in only a few minutes, but that was the only part of the meal that was quick. When Sajagax then brought forth much dried sagosk, Duke Malatam insisted on partaking of this leathery, horse-scented treat. He took a very long time chewing it, as if his teeth were weak. I watched the sun slowly rising in the east.

'Yes, your deed in gaining the Lightstone will be sung for ages,' he said to me as he continued chatting between bites of meat. His little jaws worked much more quickly at speech than in getting on with the business of breakfast. 'I must tell you how I've dreamed of the Cup of Heaven. It's as if the angels themselves have put visions in my mind. And now it seems the angels have sent *you*, Valashu Elahad, so that I might have a vision of a more immediate nature.'

I traded quick glances with Maram and Master Juwain, and I said, 'What makes you think we have brought the Lightstone with us?'

'Come, come, Lord Valashu! Would the one who claimed the Cup of Heaven leave it with another? Why else would you ride with so many armed knights into my domain?'

I looked about us where the Guardians were finishing breakfast or busy folding up their tents. Sunjay Naviru and Skyshan of Ki – and others – kept a close watch on Duke Malatam's knights as they, too, worked at their tough, dried meat.

'Please, young lord,' Duke Malatam said. 'Won't you allow an old and faithful quester of the Lightstone a glimpse of it once before he dies?'

He sat all hopeful and still as his medallion reflected the sun's bright rays into my eyes. How could I refuse such a heartfelt plea? He might be both conceited and avid for glory, but hadn't the Lightstone been made precisely to cure men of such ills?

'Sar Ianashu!' I called out. This tough young knight came hurrying over to us. I asked him to bring forth the Lightstone, and this he did.

'Splendid!' Duke Malatam cried out as Sar Ianashu held up the golden cup. It seemed almost as bright as the sun. 'May I hold it?'

I hesitated a long moment as I looked upon Sar Ianashu's noble face. If I could allow a knight of Ishka to hold the Lightstone, why not a great duke of Alonia who had once vowed to seek it unless illness, wounds or death struck him down first – and above all, to seek it for all of Ea and not himself?

I nodded at Sar Ianashu, and he placed the Lightstone into the Duke's moist, little hands. He sat staring at it as if peering through a portal to a finer and more beautiful world. 'Splendid, splendid – I've never seen anything so splendid. I *would* have died if only I could have gained this to bring others light. And I'd die right now, a thousand times, if only I could see this used to undo the Dragon's darkness. Isn't this what the Cup of Heaven is *for*? It's for the Shining One, who would give his life that others might have greater life. This is written in the *Saganom Elu* – I'm an educated man, and I know. And I know that he *will* come forth. He will be the bravest of men, the best of men. A Lord of Battles, perhaps. A master of war who will make war against the Great Darkness itself.'

He chattered on and on like the meadowlarks in the pasture singing their morning songs. But the morning was quickly passing, and soon the little yellow-breasted birds would fall silent. And soon we must take to the road again if we were to bring the Lightstone into Tria before it was too late.

And so I gently pried the cup from Duke Malatam's sweating hands. I gave it back to Sar Ianashu. The Duke had the dazed look of one who has been struck on the helmet by a mace. I said to him, 'Thank you for the pleasure of your company, but now we really must be on our way.'

Duke Malatam slowly came to his senses. He then offered to supply us with fresh meat, flour and other provisions. I was tempted to top off our saddlebags with this food. But as we would have to return to Tiamar and spend half the day going about the butchers and millers to do this, I politely declined.

'Very well, then, Lord Valashu,' Duke Malatam said to me. After we had finished the last work of breaking camp, we all stood by our horses. The Duke clasped my hand in his and told me, 'May you go with the One.'

I wished him well, too, and mounted Altaru. Estrella, Maram, Atara and my other friends, with the Guardians, formed up behind me.

Ahead, Sajagax and his blond warriors were already waiting on the road. The Kurmak nudged their horses to a quick walk, and so did we. Duke Malatam led his thirty knights in the opposite direction, back toward Tiamar.

We rode in silence for most of two miles as the air began heating up and our horses' hooves rattled the worn paving stones of the road. I looked past the green, checkerboard country behind us, and the Duke and his knights were nowhere to be seen. Ahead of us, the road seemed to curve north and west through a steaming land of canals and farms.

Sajagax confirmed this a few minutes later when he rode back to have a word with me. He pulled at the gold wire twining his mustache and said, 'I remember this from my last journey through this country, more than twenty years ago now. The *kradaks* built their cursed road as close to the river as they could. But it bends back to the west ahead of us, to avoid the hills to the north. If we rode straight toward the northwest, we could cut across this bend – and cut a few miles from our journey.'

He left it unsaid that we could also leave the cultivated strip along the river for the more open land of the Wendrush.

Lord Harsha's single eye surveyed the rolling country to the left of us, and he said, 'Duke Malatam seemed too keen to delay us. It won't hurt for us to take a path that he might not anticipate.'

'All right,' I said, agreeing to this proposal. 'Let us then keep a watch behind us as well as ahead.'

And so we left the road. Sajagax, almost gleefully, led the way through a cabbage field, and he didn't care if his warriors' horses kicked to pieces what the Sarni considered to be a stinking vegetable. After a few miles of trampling black dirt and splashing through shallow canals, the farms gave out, and we came to the open steppe. Even I breathed a sigh of happiness at the sight of the sea of grass opening before us.

But we had not ventured very far out upon it when a familiar feeling began eating at my spine. A sharp sensation like pinpricks horripilated the flesh at the back of my neck. I knew, with a sudden dread, that someone was following me.

Sajagax seemed to know this, too. Perhaps he possessed something of my gift of *valarda*. Perhaps the cries of the hawks above us alerted him to approaching dangers or the wind carried faint scents to his nostrils, for more than once he paused and sniffed the air behind him as might an old lion. His clear blue eyes fixed on me as I too often turned in my saddle to look across the undulating acres of grass behind us. He sent scouts to ride back along the line of our route. And then, once again, he urged his horse back to me and my columns of Valari

318

knights. He suggested that we ride off a dozen yards so that we might confer together.

'You're as nervous as an antelope,' he said to me as we walked our horses parallel to the columns of Guardians. 'I haven't seen you like this.'

'We're being followed,' I said to him. 'By whom remains uncertain.'

Sajagax nodded his head and glanced behind us. 'I think it is Duke Malatam. To behold the Lightstone is to love it like life itself, but he loved it *more* than anyone should, if you know what I mean.'

I stopped for a moment and tried to feel through Altaru's sturdy legs for any shaking of the earth; I looked behind us for any sign of a dust plume rising into the clear blue sky. To Sajagax, I said, 'Do you ever grow tired of battle?'

Sajagax seemed to swell like a bellows ready to deliver a blast of air into a furnace. 'Ask me if I grow tired of living. Should I want to give up that which stirs the greatest life within me? I love battle as all men should: as the sun loves the world, as a man does a woman.'

At this, I looked off at Atara riding next to Karimah as the columns of my knights passed by us. The beating of my heart was a deep pain inside me. Sajagax followed the line of my eyes, and he breathed out a heavy sigh.

'Sometimes I *do* grow tired,' he admitted. For a moment, he sat slumped on his horse, deflated and spent like an old man. 'There's been so much slaughter. Eleven of my sons. Seventeen grandsons. My first wife.'

'Isn't Freyara your first wife?'

'No, when I was a young man like you, I took a bride from the Haukut clan. Her name was Aliaqa.'

Sajagax wiped the sweat stinging his eyes, and a great sadness came over him.

'Was she killed in battle, then?'

'No, a Marituk warrior stole her from my tent.' He sighed again and then forced himself to sit up straight as a red rage began building inside him. 'Torok was his name. I swam the Poru and then followed his track a hundred miles to where his family had their camp. Four days I spent waiting for my moment. And then I took my Aliaqa back.'

'And Torok, his family – they didn't follow you?'

'No, I had driven off their horses. But when Torok saw me riding off with Aliaqa, he fired an arrow into her back. To spite me. To take from me my greatest treasure. He could have fired his arrow at me.'

I reached out and clasped his hard hand in mine. Tears filled his eyes. He squeezed back with such a fierce grip that I feared my hand might break.

'After I gave Aliaqa back to the world,' he continued, 'I waited four more days. I returned to their camp. When everyone was sleeping, I cut through their tent, which belonged to Torok's brother. His name I never learned, but I put my sword through him first. I woke up Torok so that he knew who it was that killed him. The noise woke everyone else up, too. The brother's wife was like a she-wolf: she could have been a Manslayer. She came at me with a knife, and I had to cut her down, too.'

Now the old rage that had tormented him for so long turned inward and began eating at his insides like a ravening lion. I sensed that he wanted to tell me more, so I said, 'And then?'

'And then I killed the brother's children, too. The oldest boy couldn't have been more than five; the youngest was a baby, a girl with milk on her mouth. I told myself that it was a mercy, that they couldn't have survived the jackals and wolves with their elders dead, thirty miles from any other Marituk encampment. But I know not, Valashu, I know not.'

Sajagax bowed his head as he stared at the grass. It was a terrible thing that he had told me. He sat beneath the hot sun sweating and blinking his eyes. Then he looked at me. In a deep, angry voice, he forced out, 'I didn't make the world! Battles all true men must fight. We try to work our will on the world, but it may be that the world works its will on us. Who can see the end of it all?'

Again, I looked off toward Atara, who now rode a couple of hundred yards ahead of us. Seeing this, Sajagax's fierce, old face suddenly softened. 'If battle should find us here, I want you to stay by my granddaughter's side. She's a warrior, the greatest of the Manslayers, but she is still the woman you love, and you must protect her.'

He clasped hands with me yet again as if to seal an agreement. Then he dug his heels into his horse and galloped back to where his warriors made their way across the steppe. I rejoined my company, riding side by side with Atara. Thus we proceeded for perhaps an hour before one of Sajagax's scouts came pounding over a rise behind us. He galloped straight past our columns and cried out, 'The Alonians! They have betrayed us!'

At this news, Sajagax turned his warriors and waited for us to catch up to him. Then he rode forward, with Thadrak and Orox. I joined them there, on a grass-covered knoll, accompanied by Atara, Lord Raasharu, Lord Harsha, Baltasar, Maram and Master Juwain. Then the scout, nearly breathless from his dash across the steppe, gasped out:

320

'Duke Malatam leads a great many knights – I saw his standard with the rose flowers!'

'How far behind us?' Sajagax asked.

'Five miles.'

'How many knights?'

'Nearly five hundred. And thrice as many remounts.'

At these numbers, Maram's face paled as if a demon had drained him of blood. And Lord Raasharu said, 'Duke Malatam could not have assembled such a force this quickly, not since breakfast.'

'No,' I agreed. 'The call must have gone out when he first had word that we had passed through the Long Wall.'

'Then he *did* try to delay us outside of Tiamar,' Baltasar said. My hot-blooded friend's face filled with all the color that Maram's lacked. 'He would have waylaid us there – like a filthy brigand!'

'He'll waylay us here if we don't ride!' Maram called out.

Atara, who had remained silent, faced back toward the line of our march, to the southeast. We all faced that way, too. The sun was bright above the wavering, golden grasses, and hurt all our eyes. We had to squint to make out the plume of dust rising from the earth into the sky.

'Let's ride,' I said. 'We have a good lead. Perhaps we can outdistance them.'

I turned my black warhorse toward the cloudless sky in the north-west. I looked at Atara sitting so peacefully on hers. Despite my hopeful words, I feared that battle *would* find us here, and that soon I would have to slay many man to protect her, as she would me.

23

Sajagax and I led our warriors in a race across this vast, open country. The Sarni set a pace that would soon exhaust our horses, and our remounts, too, which pounded and panted behind us.

After while, as the sun rose higher and poured down its orange fire upon us, we saw that no matter how fast we rode, Duke Malatam's knights drew closer and the dust plume behind us grew larger above the horizon. We stopped by a small stream for a little water. As quickly as we could, we unbuckled our saddles from our sweating horses and slapped them onto the backs of our remounts. Altaru hated me riding another horse, but seemed to sense that he had to preserve his strength for greater exertions still to come. The Kurmak warriors who joined us by the stream likewise exchanged horses. Sajagax chose a gray stallion and rode up to me as I mounted my new horse.

'You Valari ride well,' he said to me, 'but you ride slowly.'

'Yes,' I told him as I sweated inside my casing of diamond armor. It seemed as hot and heavy as molten lead. 'Slower, at least, than your Kurmak warriors. Why don't you escape, while you still can?'

'You mean, forsake you?'

'This is not your affair,' I said to him. 'You haven't taken vows to protect the Lightstone.'

'No, we haven't,' he said to me. Then his heavy face split wide with a grin as he looked at Baltasar, Sar Jarlath and others of my knights. 'But you have told me that we *should* protect the weak.'

I smiled back at him, and clapped him on his bare shoulder. Then we resumed our flight across the wide, rolling plains of Tarlan. It grew even hotter. Our horses snorted and panted and coughed. They beat their hooves into the sun-baked turf and sent up dust devils of their own. The dry air sucked the moisture from our sweating bodies, parching us and cracking our lips and tongues. I worried that my knights who had been wounded in the battle with the Adirii would not be able to keep up this killing pace – much less Estrella and Behira. But Behira, schooled by her father, rode determinedly and well. And Estrella surrendered to the torment of this long chase. Her slight body seemed to merge with her charging horse; as we sped along mile after mile, she rode near me, and her dark, wild eyes showed distress but no complaint.

And still the small army pursuing us gained on us, by inches, it seemed. I turned in my saddle many times to look behind us; I scanned the endless grasslands ahead of us, trying to calculate distances and time. Maram, panting almost as loudly as his horse as he rode beside me, suggested that we might last out all the day and flee into the cover of darkness. But unless some clouds came up, it seemed that the rising moon would give Duke Malatam enough light to keep after us – especially once he and his men gained a clear line of sight as to our long lances and sparkling armor. And I did not want to be caught in the open at night.

'Atara!' I called out as she sat beside me urging on her horse. The pounding of hundreds of hooves was nearly deafening. 'Do you know what lies ahead of us?'

She shook her head back and forth. The cloth wrapped around it was powdered brown with dust. She said, 'I've never been this way before.'

'Of course – but what can you *see*?'

She fell silent for a couple of hundred yards as we continued our jarring journey across the steppe. And then she said, 'What would you want me to see?'

'Is there any broken country about?'

'Yes,' she gasped out, coughing against the dust.

'Can you describe it?'

'Yes. Seven miles ahead of us – or eight – there is a line of hummocks, exposed rock and . . .'

Her voice died into the hot wind whipping at our faces.

'That might be perfect,' I told her. 'Tell me more of what you see.'

She patted the neck of her lunging horse and shook her head. 'It would be better if you saw for yourself.'

With all the skill of the Sarni warrior that she was, she gripped her bow in one hand while unbuckling her saddlebag with the other. She brought out her scryer's sphere and held it sparkling in the sun.

I called for a halt then. As Atara gave the kristei to me, the Guardians sat on their horses behind me, fighting to breathe against the cloud of dust enveloping us. Sajagax and his Kurmak warriors halted, too. He led them back to us as I peered into the clear crystal.

323

'What witchery is this?' he shouted out to me.

But this was no time for explaining the mysteries of the white gelstei. I stared into its shimmering substance. And there, preserved within like an ant inside amber, was a perfect image of the kind of topography that I had been seeking.

'We'll fight!' I called out. 'On the ground ahead of us, we'll stand and fight – if that's what Duke Malatam truly wants.'

'We'll fight with you!' Sajagax said, nodding at Orox and his other warriors. 'But tell me what you're thinking?'

'We'll set a trap within a trap,' I told him. 'Lead your warriors back the way we came. Ride past Duke Malatam's knights, keeping a good distance from them. Let the Duke believe that we have quarreled.'

'And what if he tries to stop and question us? What story would you have us tell him?'

'He won't try to stop you. So you won't have to lie to him. We'll take some blood, wrap a few of your men in bandages. The Duke will *want* to believe that the Sarni and the Valari can never ride together.'

'I see,' Sajagax said, nodding his head. 'Then the blood and bandages will lie for us.'

I said nothing to this remark as Sajagax barked out orders. The Sarni, when they are hungry and rations are scarce, sometimes open their horses' neck veins and drink their blood. Orox and Thadrak now came forward with knives and cut at the necks of two of the Kurmak's remounts. They caught the blood in their mouths, and then spat it onto some fresh bandages. These red-soaked cloths they wrapped around the heads and bare arms of three warriors, named Uldrak, Tringall, and Ragnax. Sar Kandjun, a fearless and clever knight from Pushku, then suggested a way to elaborate our ruse. I reluctantly agreed. And so he borrowed a few arrows from Orox. He forced the point of one of these down between his armor and his neck, leaving the feathered shaft sticking out. He called for more blood, which Orox smeared over him. Sar Jaldru and Sar Marjay volunteered to plant arrows about their bodies as well. Then they all lay down in the grass in awkward positions, playing dead.

'Do not,' I said to Sajagax, 'attack the Alonians unless they attack us first. We might yet be able to avoid a battle.'

Quickly, for Duke Malatam's men were drawing nearer, I led my knights forward across the steppe. And Sajagax and his warriors galloped off in the opposite direction.

After about a mile, we veered toward the west. The cloud of dust behind us grew larger as our pursuers gained on us. Now we could make out Duke Malatam's standard flapping at the front of the cloud:

the red roses against the white field, like the blood against the bandages that bound three of my men. I no longer feared that the Duke's army would overtake us, but I did dread that they might trample Sar Kandjun and the other knights in their haste to waylay us.

Soon the terrain that I had seen in Atara's crystal came into sight. Along the horizon, limned against the blue sky, a long sweep of bare rock topped with grass rose up before us. The rock looked like granite, for it showed streaks of pink and little silver flickers of various minerals. It was sheer, as if cut by the hand of man. In one place a huge notch, half a mile wide, was formed by the granite walls to either side of it. It seemed that it might once have been a quarry from which the ancient Alonians had cut the stones for the Long Wall. It seemed, as well, that it might be a break in the escarpment before us. I knew that it was not. I led my columns of knights straight toward it.

And still Duke Malatam and his men gained on us. When I turned to look at them, I saw the Duke like a little bit of cloth and shining steel on top of a charging white horse, leading a mass of armored knights our way. We drew closer to the escarpment. Its curving heights would have prevented any easy retreat to our right or left. And so we continued on, riding into the mouth of the notch. Once, its ground must have been all bare rock, but now acres of sere grass grew over it. It was shaped like the wedge of a pie, its point pushing into the granite walls to either side of us. Now we could clearly see where it dead-ended only a few hundred yards farther on.

'Halt!' I cried out. I whirled my horse about and cupped my hands over my mouth. 'Change out horses, and lances ready!'

With Duke Malatam's force bearing down upon us, we again changed horses. I worked quickly to resaddle Altaru and mount him, as did my men with their best battle horses. Then I deployed a hundred and twenty of the Guardians in a single line two hundred yards long across the notch, anchoring our flanks by the sheer walls to either side of us.

We all faced outward, toward the east where the Duke's retainers were thundering closer. Behira and Estrella, with Master Juwain, waited on their horses behind us, as did Baltasar and fifty other knights in reserve. One of them, Sar Juralad of Kaash, bore the Lightstone. I took my place at the center of our line. To my right, Maram sat on his horse gulping for air and muttering at the cruelty of life; to *his* right were Lord Raasharu, Lord Harsha, Skyshan of Ki and others. To the left of me, Atara calmly stroked her mare, Fire, whose mane fell about her long, lithe neck like a mass of flames. In Atara's sun-burned hand was clasped her deadly, double-curved bow. Karimah, likewise accoutered, sat close by her side, followed by Sunjay Naviru, Sar Kimball, Lord

Noldru and nearly sixty others down the line: the finest knights in all the world. Their lances were all couched beneath their arms; the points formed a line of their own, drawn in triangular lengths of sharp, shining steel. Between their horses was a good spacing, not so much that Duke Malatam's men could easily force their way through, but enough for them to maneuver and swing their maces and long swords when the time came.

There was nothing to do now but wait, and wait we did. The blazing sun above us moved scarcely a hair's-breadth as the Duke's little army poured into the mouth of the notch and then ground to a halt before us. The Duke rode about on a brown gelding calling out commands in his high, nervous voice; in short order, he formed up his five hundred men in lines facing us. Then one of his heralds hoisted the white flag of parlay. The Duke, with the herald and his stout captain, Lord Chagnan, rode forward to offer us terms of surrender.

I did not go forth to greet him. This was an insult, implying as it did that I did not trust him to honor the peace of the parlay. I did not. But more importantly, I wished for all my knights and his to know that I did not consider him to be an honorable man.

'Lord Valashu!' he called out to me. He halted his horse twenty yards from our lines. His dusty, feral face turned toward Atara and Karimah as he eyed their bows and quivers of arrows slung on their backs. 'Let us talk as one lord to another, as men who could be friends!'

I waved my lance at the lines of Alonian knights facing us. On their hundreds of surcoats and shields were emblazoned their various charges: boars and bears, lions and dragons and crossed swords. I called out to the Duke, 'Is *this* the hospitality of a friend? Treachery, it is!'

Duke Malatam's face reddened, as if I had slapped it. And he shouted back to me, 'You speak of treachery, you who have claimed the Lightstone for himself?'

'Nothing has yet been claimed,' I told him. 'We only guard it.'

'So you say. But for *whom* do you guard it? You took a vow, in King Kiritan's hall, to seek the Lightstone for all of Ea. And it is to King Kiritan that you must surrender it.'

'How do you know that isn't much of our purpose for journeying to Tria?'

'Is it really? I must tell you that it is *my* purpose to see that the Lightstone is placed in King Kiritan's hands. I have searched my heart, and I know that my king would ask this of me.'

'You lie,' I said to him. 'It's written on your face.'

Duke Malatam unwittingly rubbed his hand across his bearded

cheek as if trying to scrub away the stain of shame that burned there. And then he shouted at me, 'You're the liar, Valashu Elahad! Surrender the Lightstone to *me*, now, or there will be battle between us!'

'Let there be battle, then!' I shouted, feeling my blood surging hot and wild inside me. Then I took three deep breaths and held the last one for a count of seven seconds as Master Juwain had taught me. In a softer voice I said, 'Or remember what is right and true, and let us pass in peace.'

'You shall not pass,' he said to me, 'so long as you keep the Lightstone. Surrender it, and you may keep your lives.'

'Surrender yourselves! Lay down your lances and swords – and *your* lives will be spared!'

Duke Malatam looked at me as if I had fallen mad. Then he shouted: 'You Valari! Your day has passed! You fight with everyone, even your Sarni scouts, who have abandoned you! Look at your knights, Lord Valashu! Look how you have betrayed them! You have ridden blindly into my domain, knowing nothing of it. And so you stupidly led your men into a trap.'

He paused to suck in a fresh breath of air, and he shook his fist at the walls of rock rising up behind us. 'You're caught between an anvil and a hammer. Look at *my* knights! We outnumber you three to one. We'll fall against you with a great weight of steel, and crush you like worms. No quarter will we give, no quarter! We'll slaughter all of you! We'll strip your bodies of your diamonds and sell them in Tria. And you. *You*, Lord Valashu. I'll cut off your ears and gut you! And feed your entrails to the wolves!'

Again he fought for breath as his small eyes fell upon Atara and then moved on to stare at Behira and Estrella behind us. He shouted, 'And I'll give your women to my men, the girl too, and they will . . .'

His voice died into the echoes of the rock walls about us as Lord Chagnan looked at him in horror. Duke Malatam seemed suddenly to remember that he was a lord of one of Alonia's greatest domains and not some ravishing brigand. He seemed to realize, too, that he had gone too far. And so he had. At his reference to Estrella, Atara whipped out an arrow and nocked it to her bowstring. Although she did not aim it at Duke Malatam, his face blanched with fear. He cringed and held up his hand as if to ward off a blow. He cursed and shouted out to me, 'All that comes is upon you!' Then he jerked his horse about and dug his spurs into its bloody sides. With Lord Chagnan and his herald, he galloped back to his lines.

'Well, that's one way to end a parlay,' Maram said to Atara. 'Would you really have shot him?'

327

In answer, she pulled back the arrow, sighting on the Duke where he sat between Lord Chagnan and another knight. Her face was fell and cold as she suddenly loosed it. It burned through the air and crossed the two hundred yards separating our forces in the blink of an eye. But Lord Chagnan had covered his Duke with his shield, and the arrow glanced off it with a clack of steel against steel.

'Oh, Lord!' Maram cried out. 'Oh, Lord! Now there will surely be a battle!'

'There was no help for it,' Atara said.

'But what about your grandfather and his warriors?' Maram asked. 'Weren't they supposed to fall upon Duke Malatam's rear by now? And *discourage* him from giving battle? Wasn't that the whole point of our strategy?'

I looked off at the rolling, open steppe beyond the mouth of the notch behind the lines of Duke Malatam's men; so did Maram and a hundred and seventy of my knights. There was nothing to be seen there except miles of grass.

Where is Sajagax? I wondered. To Maram, I said, 'Not quite the whole point. If fight we must, we hold a strong position here.'

'*Strong*, you say? We're trapped, my friend, even as that filthy-mouthed duke has said! Truly we are. And three of them to every one of us, and . . . '

He suddenly fell silent as he noticed Lord Harsha, Lord Raasharu, Skyshan of Ki and Sar Kimball – and many others along our line – staring at him. He gulped and looked at me as he seemed to remember something. Then his deep voice boomed out: '. . . and we're Valari knights, all of us! One Valari is a match for any three of them! Of course we are! Why did I forget this? Why must I mouth such faithless words when faith blazes so brightly inside me? Truly it does. So what if I'm afraid? Who isn't? But I grow tired of it. As you must grow tired of me. I'm tired of myself. Ah, Maram, my friend, you don't have to be *that* afraid. "Act as if you have courage, and courage you shall have" – so it says in the Book of Battles. All right, I will! I survived Khaisham and Argattha, and fought the Dragon himself. I've slain better men than these. And I fight with the best men of all! Valari! My friends, my brothers!'

Maram hadn't really meant to make a battle speech, but all at once Lord Harsha and Sar Kimball and all the other knights up and down the line and behind us let loose a great cheer as if they were of one mind and one heart: 'Valari! Valari!' Maram looked astonished, at them, but at himself most of all. He sat up straighter on his horse. He gripped his lance with a steady hand and pointed it at Duke Malatam's men.

'It works!' he said, leaning closer to me. His brown eyes were full of fire. 'I'm not afraid any more!'

I smiled because I was no longer afraid for him.

And then one of Duke Malatam's heralds blew a trumpet, and the five hundred knights facing us spurred their horses forward. They quickly built up speed to a full gallop. The Duke had massed his knights in two lines along his center and three deep on either wing. I knew that he planned to crash into our flanks and break them. The Duke himself rode in the second line, leading from the rear, as they say. It seemed a cowardly thing. But he needed the knights in the line ahead of him to act as a shield against Atara's and Karimah's arrows, for these two warrior women fired shaft after shaft, as quickly as they could, at the target formed by the black cross over Duke Malatam's chest. It was a target, however, that they could scarcely sight on let alone hit. One of Atara's arrows pierced the gorget of the knight ahead of the Duke, and he fell off his horse even as another knight closed in to take his place. A moment later, Karimah's arrow struck the new knight's shoulder, but glanced off his mail. So it went as Duke Malatam's army thundered closer.

Where, I wondered, looking at the plains beyond them, *is Sajagax*?

It does not take a galloping horse very long to cover two hundred yards. And so Duke Malatam had little time to perceive the folly of his deployment and correct it. As his knights pushed down through the notch, its angled, rocky walls acted as a funnel driving both rider and horse closer together, packing them into an ungainly mass of snorting beasts and men furiously trying to maintain control of them. The five hundred knights drew nearer to us, and many of their horses collided with each other, in several places stumbling and breaking legs with sickening snaps as their riders flew into the ground and were trampled by the horses behind them. I gritted my teeth against the hideousness of jangling steel, crunching flesh and screams. Another of the Duke's miscalculations worsened this disaster. He had counted on the force of his greater numbers to break our line. But the weight of massed and heavy horse is mostly in the mind. Charging knights *can* break a wall of infantry – but only if the warriors with their shields and spears panic and flee. For horses are not stupid, and they will not willingly throw themselves onto spears or drive their bodies into anything that appears to them as solid. And so they are likewise loathe to crash straight into other horses.

And so as my knights steadied their mounts and pointed their lances at the men bearing down upon us, the horses all along Duke Malatam's first line began whinnying wildly and digging their hooves into the ground in a frantic effort to come to a halt. The knights behind them, with Duke Malatam himself, were bunched too close to avoid colliding with them and pushing them toward us. More horses screamed, and men, too, as my knights' lances tore through arms, chests, bellies and faces. A few of the boldest of the Duke's men managed to strike their lances into my knights' shields, which knocked Sar Shagarth and Sar Galajay from their horses. A few more drove their horses through our line in brave attempt to create openings. But they were quickly met by the lances of Sar Varald and Sar Shuradar and other knights from our reserve that Baltasar sent forward to close with them. A great noise of clashing steel, ringing shields and men crying out challenges and shrieking pitifully rived the air.

With great effort, I closed myself to all this fear, agony and death. And then the tide of battle swept me under. A knight bearing a red ram's-head on his black shield tried to spear Atara, who was firing arrow after arrow point-blank through the mail of the knights massed in front of us. I urged Altaru forward to cover her, as Sajagax had commanded me. The point of my lance took the knight through the mail rings covering his chest, killing him instantly – and nearly killing me. Before I could rip my lance free, another knight's horse crashed into his, knocking both horse and knight to the ground. The force of the fall snapped my lance, which I cast down as useless. And yet another knight of Tarlan used that moment to lift high his mace and close with me. Atara shot an arrow straight through his face. And then I drew Alkaladur. Its gelstei flared like a silver flame. Many of Duke Malatam's men cried out in dismay to see this shining sword; they covered their eyes at its brightness and tried to back their mounts away from me. But two knights, braver than the rest, pressed forward to hack at me with *their* swords. The first of these, Atara killed with an arrow through the throat. The second, I beheaded. It sickened me to behold how easily my sword cut through the mail protecting his neck even as it sent a shock of fear through the Duke's knights.

A few more of them them came at me and Atara, and my sword sheared their armor as if it were quilted cotton. The air became a red haze of spraying blood, cleaved bodies and screams all about me. Up and down the line, a hundred individual battles were being fought. My knights' long kalamas, though not quite the equal of my blade, sliced through shields and rings of steel. And Duke Malatam's knights worked their weapons against us. As the great mass of men and horses behind the front line pushed them onto our lances and swords, the Tarlaners began fighting with the fury of desperation. A mace crashed into Sar Kimball, who cried out in anguish. Steel broke against glittering diamonds. I gasped to see a lance drive into Lord Noldru's chest. His blood spread like a flower of death across his surcoat, and was as red as that of our enemy.

Where is Sajagax? I wondered. *Where is Sajagax?*

On my right, knights beset Maram from either side. He snorted and bellowed like a bull, crying out: 'Come! Come! Do you think I'm afraid of you?' He panted and puffed as he lunged with his sword, then straightened, parried and lunged again. Then he swung his kalama in a quick and furious stroke that cleaved the helm of the closer knight. The other knight died as one of Karimah's arrows pierced his eye.

More arrows suddenly whined through the air. Armor-piercing shafts drove through rings of mail. Ten of Duke Malatam's men cried out almost as one, and then ten more as arrows shattered their spines or transfixed their backs. I looked beyond the snarl of men and horses pressing at me. Fifty yards beyond the killing zone, Sajagax and his warriors sat on their steppe ponies in a line gleefully firing round after round of arrows into Duke Malatam's men from the rear. A panic seized the hearts of these beleaguered knights and spread through them like a shaking illness, for they knew with a sick and sudden certainty that it was *they* who were caught between a hammer and an anvil.

'Come!' Maram shouted as swung his sword. 'Come one, come all, and test your courage against Maram Marshayk of the Five Horns!'

I cut down the last of the knights blocking my way toward Duke Malatam. Altaru seemed to sense my wrath to slay this little man who had brought so much death to this field this day. My raging black stallion charged down upon him. The Duke's white surcoat was stained with sweat, but the only red upon it was that of embroidered roses. He cringed in his saddle, gripping a bloodless sword in his trembling hand. As I steeled myself to slay him and raised back my sword, he suddenly cast down his and cried out, 'Quarter! I beg quarter of you! Mercy, please!'

Hearing this, all through the mob of men and horses that his neat lines of knights had become, the Tarlaners began dropping their weapons and pleading with us: 'Quarter! Mercy! We surrender!'

'Hold!' I called out. I commanded my arm to freeze with my bright sword pointing straight up toward the sun. I looked at my knights to the right and left and called out again, 'Hold, now! Quarter has been asked, and quarter will be given!'

Nearby, Lord Raasharu held his kalama at the ready as the Duke's knights across from him threw down their swords, and thus waited Sunjay Naviru, Skyshan of Ki, Lord Harsha, Sar Shivathar and more than a hundred others. But still the arrow storm raged from the Kurmak warriors' bows, striking down the Duke's men by the dozen.

I sheathed my sword and cupped my hands around my mouth. As loud as I could, I shouted, 'Hold, Sajagax! Tell your men to hold!'

Sajagax, caught up in a killing fury, fired a last arrow through the mouth of one of the Tarlaners, who had turned his horse in an attempt to flee. Then he shook his head like a boy who has been told to cease playing a game. He lowered his great bow and shouted to his warriors: 'Hold! Hold now, but let none of the *kradak* escape!'

Upon these words, the last of the Duke's men surrendered. I commanded them to dismount their horses. This they did. To Sar Adamar, I appointed the task of organizing a detail to cast the Tarlaners' weapons and shields into a great heap. I sent Sunjay Naviru and twenty other knights to drive their mounts into a herd toward the south side of the notch. At the other side, my knights herded our defeated enemy beneath the points of lances held at ready. The Duke's men stood in their torn and bloody surcoats, with their heads bowed and their eyes cast upon the ground. All across the notch's reddened grass lay the wounded and the dead. A few men still screamed at the agony of chopped bellies and severed limbs. Many more were whimpering and moaning, but most of them would never again utter any complaint.

One of Sajagax's warriors, a thick-armed giant named Trallfax, was going about slashing his saber through the throats of the wounded Tarlaners. I urged Altaru toward him as I cried out, 'Hold your sword! There's been enough killing today!'

Trallfax shot me a savage look and then nearly chopped off a wounded knight's head. He moved quickly over to another knight, who was writhing on the grass. Seeing this, Sajagax whipped his horse forward toward Trallfax. The great Sarni chieftain leapt off his horse and grabbed Trallfax by the arm.

'Hold, nephew!' Sajagax said to him.

'But uncle,' Trallfax shouted, pointing at the Tarlaners strewn about the ground, 'these *kradak* are all wounded, and it is the law.'

'There is a new law!' Sajagax thundered. His voice fell off the rock walls around us like a bolt from the heavens. 'An old, old law that will seem as new: "Be strong and protect the weak."'

The fire in Sajagax's eyes seemed to chasten Trallfax. He bowed his head to his uncle and chieftain, and Sajagax let him go so that he could sheathe his sword.

'You came late,' I said to Sajagax as I looked at the carnage all about us.

'Better late than not at all,' he told me. 'After we had put some miles between us, Thadrak said that we would be ill-fated to make battle on the side of the Valari, and Baldarax called for an omen. So we had to sacrifice a mare, that her entrails might be read.'

I stared at Sajagax, not quite knowing what to make of him. Who could trust these savage and superstitious Sarni?

Soon after that, Lord Raasharu came up to me with a count of those who had fallen that day. It seemed that in the span of only a few minutes, with the Kurmak's help, we had killed more than hundred and sixty of Duke Malatam's knights and wounded half as many.

'And what of the Valari?' I said to Lord Raasharu. 'How many of my men were killed?'

'None, Lord Valashu. And only twelve wounded, none to the death.'

None killed! I thought. It seemed a miracle. *None killed!*

Lord Noldru, whom I had given up as dead, walked slowly up to me. Master Juwain had removed his armor and bandaged his chest. It turned out that the lance that had pierced it had driven through armor, skin and muscle but had gone no deeper.

'Eight score of the enemy killed and none of us!' he called out to me. 'A great, great victory, Lord Valashu! Who has ever heard of such a thing?'

And then Baltasar rode his horse forward and cried out, 'Lord of Battles! Lord of Light!'

As one, all of my knights upon that killing field drew their swords and held them toward me as they shouted: 'Maitreya! Maitreya! Maitreya!'

It came time to deal with Duke Malatam. I rode over to where he stood huddled with his knights. I dismounted and stepped up to him. I looked around at the bodies of his wasted knights, and I had to command my fist, covered with its diamond-studded gauntlet, not to strike his face.

I said to him, 'You may keep all the provisions that you brought with you; we will give you extra bandages, for it seems that you have not brought enough. Two of your horses you will be allowed to keep so that you might send heralds back to Tiamar for help with your wounded. The others we shall drive off, that you cannot follow us where we must go. Your lances and swords –'

'Please, Lord Valashu,' Duke Malatam broke in, 'allow us to keep our swords! On our honor, we will –'

'You have no honor,' I told him. 'To attack wayfarers to whom you have offered your hospitality is an ignoble thing. Your armor you may keep, your shields, as well. And your lives. But your swords shall be broken.'

333

At this, the Duke bowed his head, and so did the knights gathered around him. Across the field could be heard the terrible sound of snapping steel as my men carried out my command.

'Your armor you may keep,' I told the Duke. 'Your shields, as well. And your lives.'

Duke Malatam looked at me, and his eyes filled with tears. 'You are merciful, Lord Valashu. I see now what I should have seen before. Forgive me, but the sight of the Lightstone – the very thought of it – drove me mad. But you have taught me compassion. They call you the Maitreya. I believe this, now, with all my heart. If you'll let me, I would take up a new sword and ride with you to Tria, as part of your guard.'

He looked at me with all the devotion of dog. I wanted to accept his homage; I wanted to forgive him and take him into my confidence. But that much vanity and trust I did not have.

'No,' I told him, 'you shall go back to Tiamar and await your king's command. We shall go to Tria to hold conclave with him.'

I turned my back on him to walk across the field and visit with my wounded knights. A mace had broken Sar Kimball's arm, and a lance taken out the eye of Sar Gorvan. Others had other wounds. But by the One's grace, all of them would live.

None killed! I thought, giving thanks to the wind. *None killed*!

But as I stepped around the bodies of the fallen Tarlaners, I knew in my heart that *too* many had been killed. Five-Horned Maram, my fat friend, had himself slain five of the enemy that day, more than had any of my knights. But the dead no longer looked like enemies to me: they were only dead. They were all men who should have lived to take wives and sire children and fight the true enemy, called the Red Dragon. They were all *men*, luminous beings beneath their coverings of flesh, created in the likeness of angels. And now, like all the other countless souls who had once stridden the earth in all their pride, they walked among the stars.

24

The next morning, we rode away from that blood-drenched place. The Tarlaners were too ashamed to put a name to the terrible defeat that had befallen them, but it would ever after be known among the Valari and the Kurmak as the Battle of Shurkar's Notch. King Shurkar Eriades, I thought, would have been appalled that the stone taken from the quarry there had failed to protect his realm from this small force of Sarni who rode with us. I, too, was appalled by the slaughter that we had wrought together. It occurred to me that with these splendid warriors on our side, working with the Valari as a man's thumb might coordinate with his fingers, I might at last reunite the two estranged kindreds of the tribe of Elahad and forge a weapon of terrible power, efficiency and deadliness.

Our pace away from the escarpment was slow, for we were all tired, and I did not want to press my wounded knights. One of these was Sar Kandjun. It seemed that a Tarlan knight, while Sar Kandjun had been playing dead, had used him for target practice, sticking his lance into Sar Kandjan's thigh. Sar Marjay and Sar Jaldru had testified that Sar Kandjun had borne this insult without uttering a sound. But after the Duke's host had passed, Sar Kandjun had arisen from the grass, bound his leg with some cloth torn from his surcoat and had whistled for his horse. Then he led the others toward the notch. These three brave knights thus came late to the battle, but with Sajagax's warriors, they had fallen upon the Tarlaners' rear with a vengeance that brought honor to their names.

Our flight across the Duke's lands had taken us too far west, almost all the way to the Aquantir. And so, to cut the road leading to Tria, we had to journey north and slightly east, toward the hills that glowed a golden-orange beneath the sun. I did not think that Duke Malatam was mad enough to try to gather his scattered horses and mount a pursuit. And I doubted if his beaten men would follow him if he did.

Even so, we kept a watch behind us. Sajagax sent outriders to patrol in that direction as well as ahead.

The steppe stretched before us, a sea of long swishing grasses that seemed as endless as the sky. But according to Atara, who had been this way before, we were approaching its northern bounds. After about eight miles of easy travel, we saw single trees pushing up out of the turf like lonely sentinels. A few miles further on they were joined by a sprinkling of their cousins. And then suddenly, after we had crested a rise, we came upon a line of trees stretching from east to west for as far as the eye could see. Alonia's Great Northern Forest stood before us like a wall of green. Sajagax and his warriors seemed even more loathe to enter it than they had been to cross the Long Wall.

'Trees,' Sajagax said to me as we sat side by side in front of our companies surveying the country ahead of us. 'So many trees.'

I pointed at a band of stone about a quarter mile ahead of us and to our right. I said, 'Look, there's the road. From here, if Atara is right, it's scarcely more than a hundred miles to Tria.'

'About such things, Atara is always right,' he said. 'Though I passed this way once, before she was born, and it seemed like much more than a hundred miles.'

We made our way onto the road, with Sajagax riding foremost and his guard strung out behind him. I led my knights in three columns following them. After the soft ground of the Wendrush, the road's paving stones seemed too hard and the sound of our horses iron-shod hooves against it too loud. And then we passed into the archway of trees before us, and their fluttering green canopies suddenly blocked out the sun. It grew cooler, and the air thickened with the moist breath of the forest. Several of the Sarni warriors ahead of us made signs as if to ward off evil.

We ambled up the road for several more miles. This closed country of wooden pillars and shrubby ramparts seemed to chasten our yellow-haired allies. Many of Sajagax's men, I thought, had never seen more than a scattering of trees in all their lives. Although Thadrak and a few others had ridden on raids into Anjo, that broken kingdom's patchwork of woods was nothing like this expanse of vegetation that went on a hundred miles to the north and more than twice that to the east and west. The forest's gloom fell over them like a dark, green blanket and smothered their easy laughter, which I had come to relish as I did the wind and sun. Even I, who had grown to manhood among the great oaks and elms of the Morning Mountains, found myself wishing to come upon an open field or a crag that might give a good view of the sky. But the only high ground nearby was the hill land along the Poru to the east of us, and these old, rounded mounds of earth were covered in trees as thick and tall as those towering above us.

Late that afternoon, however, we came upon a great clearing to the side of the road. It seemed large enough to encamp an army. Indeed, although we were still in Tarlan, King Kiritan had ordered it cut out of the forest in order to accommodate *his* armies, should he have need to march this way. It was one of many such sites along the roads leading through Alonia. We decided to spend the night there. When we were finished laying out our firepits and pitching our tents, acres of sweet green grass surrounded us, and this made Sajagax's warriors happy and all our horses even happier.

During the night, a thick shroud of clouds came up to cover the stars. It began raining hard before dawn and continued all the next day. Big drops of water and occasional bursts of hail pelted us in millions of silver, streaking missiles. My wounded knights felt this assault most grievously, although they did not complain of it. I gave my cloak to Sar Kandjun to keep out this wet, driving cold. It helped him, a little, I thought. I wished I had two hundred cloaks, for all of us who had fought the Tarlaners suffered from aching limbs and a stiffness that penetrated to the bone.

Atara, wrapped in her lion skin, kept warmer than most – at least in her body. Her soul, however, remained as cold as the little bits of hail that fell down from the dark clouds above us and broke against the diamonds of my armor. It was like a wall of ice between us. I wanted to melt it and heal her of her deepest anguish as badly as I wanted the sun to return. I knew that she pushed me away only to drive me into myself, to learn the truth of who I really was. It cost her a great deal to maintain her aloofness. In her heart was a deep hurt that choked her and would not go away. I wanted to weep at this strange and terrible compassion of hers, as cold and hard as the crystal of her gelstei.

As we trod down the road and our horses kicked up a muddy spray, I brooded over what she had told me about the world's fate hanging balanced upon the edge of a sword. I felt my own fate, pulling me on toward Tria. I felt, too, something dark and too-familiar pursuing me from behind. Then the road led us past the last of the hills to the east, and a sense of dread and doom fastened its claws into the bones of my back and would not let go. That night, lying on ground so sodden that my sleeping furs soaked-through, I dreamed that I was trying to ride away from my own shadow. But the faster I rode, the stronger and more defined it grew. When I told Master Juwain of this the next morning, he interpreted it to mean that I was afraid of my fate of being the Maitreya.

'All men,' he said to me as he pressed a cup of hot tea into my hand, 'fear the great, shining thing inside themselves and try to flee from it. How much worse this must be for the Lord of Light.'

I gulped the tea and scalded my throat. I said, 'But this is no shining thing. It is dark. It is cold, like death.'

'As I've said many times,' he told me, 'there is an identity of opposites. The light that is too bright burns and blinds. And is it not written that the silver swan is born anew from the ashes of its own funeral pyre?'

'"To live, I die,"' I said, quoting from the *Valkariad*. '"Out of the deepest darkness, the brightest light."'

'Do you see, Val? Do you see?'

'Perhaps,' I said to him. 'You know a great deal about dreams. But whatever it is that's after me *feels* as real as this rain that won't stop.'

After that we broke camp and set out into the wet morning. We crossed into Old Alonia, and the rain seemed to grow only stronger as did my sense of something following me. At last, I felt obliged to take Sajagax into my confidence. I told him of my fears. He looked at me strangely and said, 'Sometimes, Valashu, I think that you are like the *imakil* who ride in another world. They have senses that we of this world lack. You say that something hunts us. *I* sense this not – and I have the eyes of an eagle, the nose of a wolf, the ears of a horse. But this is not my country; these cursed trees devour the wind and sky. Very well then, I will send out riders again to look for signs.'

I sent out riders, too: Sar Avram and Sar Elkad, Sunjay Naviru and Skyshan of Ki. They galloped back down the road and beat through the forest to either side of it searching for anything that went on two legs or rode on top of anything with four. With Sajagax's scouts, they returned to report that they had seen nothing more suspicious than five deer, a black bear with her cubs, a woodcutter and a merchant making his way up the road toward Adavam with a cart full of silks to sell.

It occurred to me that Estrella, as a seard, might be able to find whatever my men could not. She rode beside me, now covered in Atara's lion skin, which Atara had draped over her shivering body to protect her from the rain. When I tried to describe my sense of being steeped in shadow, she just looked at me as she always did and smiled mysteriously.

As we made our way north, the road bent back toward the Poru and took us through a rich farmland mostly cleared of trees. The huts of peasants stood out against misty, emerald fields. The rain eased and then softened into a drizzle that sifted down from the gray sky. Some time after noon, we came to Adavam, second largest of Alonia's cities. It had been built on marshy ground where the Istas river flows in from the west and meets the Poru in a great joining of waters. We spent a few hours riding along its crowded streets, buying meat and bread for my hungry men and oats for the horses. We might have found accommodations for the night with one of the nobles who had estates outside the city – or with a Lord Palandan, who dwelled in the great, ancient castle rising up at the city's center. But after our encounter with Duke Malatam, we'd had enough of Alonia's nobility for the time being. And so we pressed our tired mounts onward, and we crossed the great Delikan Bridge that spanned the Istas. We made camp that night five miles to the north, in the fields of a peasant who owned his own lands. Although he was too poor to feed us, he surprised everyone by producing a cask of beer, which he and his eldest son helped us drain to the last drop.

We awoke the following morning to skies as blue as a robin's egg. The sun came out to dry the sodden lands through which we rode, and a rainbow arched across the horizon. Its vivid colors seemed to drive back the chill of dread clinging to me. We passed along a stretch of road where the farmland gave out into forest again. I smiled to see the millions of leaves above us letting through a lovely, green light. Estrella, riding to my left, smiled her bright smile as if to show me this radiance inside myself. Master Juwain, on my right, sat on top of his horse holding the akashic crystal in his gnarly hands. He softly sang out words in the angels' language that he called Galadik. He had come to understand at least a part of this musical tongue, and he worked very hard to unlock the knowledge stored in his glowing disc.

Late in the afternoon, just as we crossed a stream flowing down to the Poru, Master Juwain's crystal began shimmering more brightly than any rainbow. Hues of scarlet, viridian and sapphire blue spun about its center and seemed to whirl right off the disc and fill the air with a brilliant sheen.

'Hold!' I called out, raising up my hand. I reined-in Altaru, while behind me, Maram, Karimah and Atara brought their mounts to a halt as well – along with the tens of Guardians behind them. 'What is this?'

'I don't know,' Master Juwain said as he gazed at the crystal. 'Look how it flares!'

Even as he spoke, the entire crystal filled with glorre, as it had in the Lokilani's wood in the presence of the Lightstone. But the Cup of

Heaven now resided with Sar Hannu, who sat on his horse in the middle of our columns nearly a fifty yards behind us.

'Look, Val, look!'

Now the glorre spilled out and enveloped us in a shimmering cloud. Seeing this, Sajagax galloped back down the road straight toward us. He called out, 'What magic do you summon now, wizard?'

'I don't know,' Master Juwain said again. 'But this gelstei – it's as if it's seeking something. It *wants* something of me.'

'How can that be?' I asked him.

'I wish I knew.'

Maram came forward to get a better look at the crystal. 'But how do you *know* it wants something of you?'

'I wish I knew that, too.'

Just then Flick appeared like a comet falling out of the sky. In a swirl of sparkling lights, he turned circles around the crystal in Master Juwain's hand. Then he shot off into the woods. His luminous form paused between two maple trees as if he waited for us to follow him.

'Flick wants something of us too,' I said. 'Perhaps the same thing.'

'What?' Maram said. 'To go wandering about these wild woods?'

I looked off through the trees. Then I turned to Atara. 'Is there anything unusual nearby?'

But Atara only shook her head. Even when she could 'see,' she could not do so perfectly.

'Let's go with Flick,' I suggested. I smiled at Maram. 'These woods are a tangle, but nothing so bad as the Vardaloon.'

I nodded at Sajagax and Lord Raasharu, and they seemed almost as eager as I was to solve this new mystery. And so I led off into the trees, toward Flick. My knights trailed after me at a walk, followed by Sajagax and his warriors. Our hundreds of horses let loose snorts of unease as their hooves cracked the deadwood littering the forest floor. The undergrowth was mostly bracken and maidenhair, which Altaru pushed past or trampled down. But patches of it were cinnamon fern and royal lady growing four feet high, and this I chopped through with my sword. Flick seemed to have no sense that such vegetation might impede us. He streaked around stem, leaf and tree trunk with the ease of sparkling water and all the impatience of a child.

Thus we continued for perhaps an hour. Flick led us on a course that seemed as straight as the flight of a blazing arrow. And all the while, with every furlong deeper into the woods that we rode, Master Juwain's crystal flared brighter and brighter.

Without warning I came to a break in the trees through which I could see a wall of sandstone before us. Altaru pushed through the last of the bracken, and we came out onto a wide strip of shingled ground that fronted an unusual rock formation. It rose up perhaps three hundred feet and curved around toward the right and left. The mound seemed circular in shape; I guessed it might be a quarter of a mile in diameter. Baltasar and rest of my knights joined me there between the mound and the trees. So did Sajagax and his warriors. We watched with amusement – and amazement – as Flick rose straight up the rockface like a flaming bird that could simply soar over the barrier in front of us.

'There must be something at the top,' Maram said, looking up at the smooth rock above us. 'If I had wings, I'd follow him.'

'If you had wings, they'd break,' Sajagax said as he nudged his horse closer to Maram and poked his finger into his big belly. Then he looked at me and asked, 'How are we to follow this imp of yours?'

Long cracks ran vertically in many places through the mound's sandstone, and sprays of ivy covered much of it, but it was otherwise as smooth as a girl's cheeks. I looked at this rock doubtfully, and I said, 'It might be scaled.'

Sajagax examined the wall with even more doubt written across his florid face. 'You Valari may be men of the mountains, but even a goat would have a hard time of such a climb. There must be another way.'

Master Juwain held the akashic crystal toward the mound, and the gelstei blazed like a little sun in his hands.

'Let's ride around this,' I said, pointing at the wall. 'Let's see what we can see.'

Carefully, for the ground was broken with many splinters of sandstone, I led forth in a slow walk around this great bubble of rock. Everyone followed me. So did Flick. Although his form remained free of anything resembling a face, he seemed somehow frustrated with me and the limitations of my all-too-human body.

Suddenly, before we had rounded less than half the mound's circumference, I came up a much larger crack splitting the rock from ground to summit. The sandstone to either side of it, draped in more ivy, was carved into great, pillar-like figures that might have been Elijin or Galadin. Wind and water and the slow work of time had worn smooth the details of their faces. The opening beckoned like an entrance to a great building. I watched with smile as Flick shot through it and disappeared from sight.

'Let's follow him,' I said to Maram. I peered inside the crack, which was wide enough for two horses to navigate side by side. I looked at Master Juwain, who sat on his horse clutching the akashic crystal. 'Will you come, too, sir?'

'If a dragon guarded this gate,' he said, pointing at the crack, 'it couldn't stop me.'

Atara said that she wanted to accompany us, and so then did Karimah and Sajagax. Estrella gave signs that she would not be separated from me. Her bright eyes reminded me that she might help us find inside whatever it was that excited both the akashic crystal and Flick.

Then Lansar Raasharu nudged his horse forward and said, 'Let me come with you, Lord Valashu. We don't know what lies within, and you might need my sword.'

Baltasar likewise shared his father's concern and volunteered to ride before me as a single knight acting as my vanguard. I smiled at him and said, 'Thank you, my friend, but you would best serve me if you would remain here in command of the Guardians.'

'Very well,' Baltasar said, peering through the dark crack, 'but at least send five knights into this, that they might report back to you that the way is safe.'

This seemed prudent, and so I chose out Sar Shevan, Sar Varald, Sar Ishadar, Juradan the Younger and Sar Hannu to make this little mission. Sar Hannu gave the Lightstone into my keeping, and then led the others into the crack. I listened as the sound of their horses' hooves clacking against rock died into echoes.

And so we waited there between this great, mysterious mound and the darkening forest. We did not wait very long. Soon Sar Hannu returned by himself and told me, 'The way *is* safe, Lord Valashu. And it leads to a great open area that you must see! Come, come!'

His enthusiasm communicated to Maram, Master Juwain and Lansar Raasharu, no less than Sajagax, Atara, Karimah and Estrella, whom I now led into the crack. Its walls, I saw, were smooth as glass, as if a red gelstei had melted this corridor through the sandstone. The day's fading sunlight filtered down to illuminate the many fallen rocks, which our horses had to step over with care lest they turn a leg. The corridor was not straight, but bent first right and then left, like the length of a snake. Sar Hannu and I rode side by side, followed by the others. The sound of his breath steaming out into this dim, closed space added to the creaking of diamond armor and iron-shod hooves striking stone like the hammers of miners delving for hidden ores.

And then the corridor straightened and gave out into the open area that Sar Hannu had told of. We rode out toward the four other knights who waited near its center, looking about themselves with awe coloring their faces. For the mound, as we all could see, was hollow. Its insides seemed to have been scooped out of the rock – or melted – in the shape of a perfect cylinder. Above us, above the mound's curving sandstone rim three hundred feet high, the twilight sky was a circle of dark blue showing the night's first stars. Our horses stood within a lower circle, the eastern half of which was given over to rounded, rising rows of stone benches like those of the great amphitheater at Nar. In its western half, which seemed like a staging space, a few elms grew out of cracks in the ground. This might once have been solid rock, but now was covered by layers of old leaves, mosses and dirt that must have blown in over the years. But the circle that caught my gaze and held it was formed by the cylinder's walls. At first, in the deepening gloom, I had thought that they were of fused glass, like the walls of the corridor leading into this strange place. Now, however, as Master Juwain dismounted and brought forth his akashic crystal, these hollowed sweeps of rock began to scintillate and glow.

'Look, Val, look!' he called out.

I dismounted, then, and so did everyone else. I stood gazing at the rock, which now swirled with colors like those of the akashic crystal before it had fallen full of glorre.

'What *is* this place?' Maram said.

Sajagax and Karimah both made warding signs, even as Atara stood quietly holding Estrella's hand. Lansar Raasharu, with Sar Hannu and the other knights, waited nearby gripping the hilts of their swords.

'In all the books I've ever read,' Master Juwain murmured, 'I've never come across mention of anything like this.'

Atara smiled coldly and said, 'Some scryers can look backward into time as well as ahead. Although I've never had this gift, my sense of things here is that no scryer who ever lived could look far enough back to see its making.'

'It feels *old*,' Maram agreed. 'If Ymiru told us right, Argattha is at least six thousand years old, but this feels older still – much older.'

I drew my sword, and its long length of silver gelstei reflected a bit of the heavens' light into my eyes. Without quite knowing how, I suddenly knew that Maram was right. I said, 'Surely, then, this must be some wonder from the Elder Ages.'

But this did not ease Maram's anxiety. He looked at me and said, 'Something from *before* the Star People came to earth? Who, then, built it? Who, then, sat on those seats?'

He pointed at the eastern half of the amphitheater, with its many benches carved out of stone.

'Others must have visited Ea before Elahad,' Master Juwain said. 'Perhaps the Elijin. Perhaps, as the little people thought, the Galadin themselves.'

At his mention of these great, inextinguishable beings, Estrella clapped her hands together and smiled as if she had found a fireflower in some lightless wood. But Maram's disquiet only deepened. He looked about the amphitheater and muttered, 'Angels, you say, and we can only hope you are right. But what if other things came here? Dark things out of the Dark Worlds? Or worse, ghosts? I must confess, this place feels haunted to me. Can't anyone else *feel* this? There's a *presence* here.'

He waved his hand in front of his face as if to feel for hidden entities. Although it was a summer evening and not at all cold, he shuddered and drew his cloak about himself.

'I'm less concerned with ghosts,' Master Juwain said, pointing ahead of him, 'than with the miracle of those walls. They seem to be of the same substance as this gelstei.'

He rapped his knuckle against the akashic crystal. It was now sending out pulses of glorre as with ripples of water from a stone tossed into a quiet pool.

'I need to get a better look,' he said.

He strode off to examine the jackets of opalescent crystal now pulsing with soft lights all around the amphitheater. Maram accompanied him. Estrella started to dance off by herself toward the benches, but Atara did not approve of her being alone anywhere in this mysterious place at the fall of night, and so she went with her. I swept Alkaladur up toward the stars as if my shining sword might slice open the very heavens to reveal their secrets. Sajagax and Karimah made more warding signs, while Lansar Raasharu and the five Guardians stood ready to draw their kalamas. The night grew darker.

And then, near the benches, out of the wavering air, a figure of a man appeared. His whole being glowed with a soft light. I could not see his face, but he was tall, with long, black hair draping down upon a blue tunic embroidered with silver and gold. Estrella, upon perceiving this man, clapped her hands so loudly that the sudden *crack* drew Maram's attention. He turned away from the crystal of the wall, and shouted, 'Oh, my Lord! If *that* isn't a ghost, then I never hope to see one!'

This 'ghost,' or whatever he was, took a step toward Estrella and Atara, who were sitting on the first and lowest of the benches. Seeing this, almost quicker than thought, Sajagax whipped an arrow from his quiver and fitted it to the string of his great bow. Before I could cry out for him to stop, he drew back the arrow and fired it at the man. The arrow shrieked forth and seemed to streak right through his ethereal body in a shimmer of little lights. It slammed into one of the higher benches, and its steel point broke against the stone and sent up a spray of chips.

344

'Hold, Sajagax!' I called out as he drew another arrow.

'A ghost!' Maram shouted again from across the amphitheater. 'Surely he must be a ghost!'

The ghost now turned to look at Maram, and then at Sajagax and me. His face was of noble mien, with a long nose like an exquisitely sculpted pillar and a broad forehead. His eyes, black and bright as the sky above us, were like the eyes of my father and grandfather and many other Valari. He smiled at us and beckoned with his long, strong-looking hand toward the benches as if inviting us to sit down.

'Come!' I called out. 'Let's sit then. What else is there to do?'

At that moment, Flick fell out of the air and turned flaming spirals around the ghost. This being's otherworldly face glowed with a smile as if he were greeting an old friend.

'Come, Sajagax, put down your bow! Come, Maram, Master Juwain, and everyone, and let us sit!'

I led the way toward the sandstone benches where Atara and Estrella sat watching the ghost. Everyone converged there and joined them on the first bench – except for Lansar Raasharu, who insisted on standing behind me to guard my back.

Then the ghost faced us and astonished us by singing out in a deep, lovely voice: 'Aulara, Auliama.'

The words echoed from the amphitheater's walls, now sparkling even more strongly with bright colors.

'It sounds like the language of the angels,' Maram said.

'Perhaps he is an angel,' Sajagax said, aiming his sharp eyes at the being before us. 'Pray that he is not a demon or other evil spirit, as I feared.'

'Aulara, Auliama,' the ghost said again.

'But what does that mean?' Maram asked. He turned to Master Juwain. 'Sir, do you know?'

'Yes,' Master Juwain said with a happy smile. 'It is an invitation: "Ask, and be answered."'

'Ask what?' Sar Hannu said, pulling at his heavy chin. 'Is this some sort of ancient oracle, then?'

'If it is,' Sar Varald said, 'then we should beware. This ghost could twist words and our understanding of them as might a scryer.'

At his careless words, Atara shot him a frosty look and said, 'You know little of scryers, it seems, and even less of what we've found here.'

Sar Varald, who did not want to dispute with the woman I loved, bowed his head and stared down at the old leaves upon which the ghost stood.

'It seems to *me*,' Maram said, 'that none of us understands anything about this place.'

Master Juwain sat gazing at the discus-like crystal in his hands. Then he rubbed his head as if it ached and looked at me. 'The voices inside this – they sing to the walls here. And the walls sing, too. Can't anyone hear them?'

I stared at the curved, colored expanse of gelstei glimmering beyond the ghost. I shook my head. Master Juwain might have learned to read the akashic crystal and perhaps its much greater cousin spread across the walls surrounding us, but I lacked the art.

'Whom do the walls sing *to*?' Maram asked Master Juwain.

At this question, the ghost smiled as if he could understand Maram. He lifted back his head and looked up at the stars.

Atara said to Maram, 'If this *is* an oracle, you should be careful of what you ask. We might have only three questions – or one.'

As she said this, the ghost looked straight at her and repeated again, '*Aulara, Auliama.*'

Master Juwain nodded at me and said, 'Ask him your question, Val.'

'All right,' I said as the ghost now looked at me. I drew in a quick breath and asked, 'Who *is* the Maitreya?'

My heart drummed hard inside my chest as the ghost stood there staring at me. His eyes, made of light or some shimmering substance, looked right through me. And then he spoke what seemed a single word: '*Laravari.*'

'But what does that mean?' Maram asked.

'I think it means: "wait",' Master Juwain said.

'Wait for what? It's already past dinner time.'

Again the ghost looked skyward, and then he let loose a torrent of music as he sang out, '*Lanila eli la Ieldara lumiara ar Ininasuni . . .*'

Thus he continued for quite a while before finally falling silent. And Maram asked Master Juwain, 'Do you understand what he said, sir?'

'Some of it, I think. I believe he is waiting for a certain star, or stars, to rise. Our name for this would be Ninsun.'

I looked up at the black circle of sky, studded with many stars as bright as the diamonds of my armor. Various constellations edged the sandstone rim high above us. I made out the splendid Firwe and Salwe, the Eyes of the Tiger, and other points of light. I watched and waited as the world slowly turned its dark face to the heavens.

'Ninsun,' I whispered. I knew this name out of legend only, as the dwelling place of the Ieldra.

And then, just as the first of the stars forming the necklace of the

Mother appeared, my heart seemed to stop and I could not breathe. For this brilliant star poured its light straight down into the amphitheater like a stream of glorre. The numinous color touched the walls, which blazed with a sudden surge of radiance, giving back the light a thousandfold. Master Juwain's crystal flared brightly, too. The air filled with a strange song, and then ten thousand songs as voices both beautiful and terrible made a music that I could hardly bear. I wanted to stop my ears with my fingers and cover my eyes. But the music, bright as dreams of angels, compelled me to listen and look.

'*Aulara, Auliama,*' the ghost said yet again.

What happened then was hard to understand. My consciousness seemed to divide in two like a silk cloth torn by the wind. All the while, I remained aware of the amphitheater and all it contained: the rustling leaves of the elms, the ghost talking to me, the hard stone bench beneath the even harder stones that encased my legs. And yet I found myself in other places, too: soaring through the sky like an eagle above primeval forests, standing on a burning plain, floating in the dark sea of space that envelops other worlds. All that I experienced occurred within time, like grains of sand falling through an hourglass one by one, but time itself seemed to open into a bright infinity that contained all things. I smelled flowers whose scents were utterly strange to me. I felt the earth of distant worlds through the paws of animals for which I had no name.

I listened to the moans of women giving birth and the clash of steel against steel and the rapture of a silver swan singing its death song. I heard a great deal and saw much more.

And this is what I saw: by the shore of a blue ocean on some watery world, a great host of men and women gathered. There must have been a million of them. They were raimented in garments finer than silk, and fillets of silver encrusted with emeralds and diamonds shimmered against their dark hair. The music that poured from their lips gave me to know that they were of the Galadin. Their eyes and hands, shining from within, told me this, too.

They interlocked hands as they danced in ever-widening circles around a golden cup that floated in the air. And as they danced, they sang and the cup gleamed and grew ever brighter. Time passed, perhaps a day, perhaps a thousand years, and then their voices joined into one and filled the world with a single, heartpiercing chord. The flames of their beings suddenly brightened beyond belief and passed around their circles from man to woman as quick as breath – and passed into the shimmering cup, back and forth, from them to it and it to them. The little cup flared so brightly that it outshone the sun. Then a ball of fire exploded outward from its center into space and consumed the Galadin and their world. The light of the great event filled all the universe.

And out of this pure and infinite light, the first gelstei crystallized like the colors of the rainbow falling out of the sky. They were seven in kind, and they sparkled more splendidly than rubies, sapphires and diamonds. And as they poured out great pulses of violet or red, yellow or blue, they vibrated like a mandolet's strings in seven fundamental notes. This music of creation, almost too bright and too beautiful, fell upon the expanding sphere of fire and interfused every part of it. And so the Galadin, who had now become much more, sang the new universe into being.

And out of this angel fire, stars were born. There were millions of millions of them. And from the substance of these luminous orbs, countless worlds formed in this lovely new universe that as yet had no name. And still the Ieldra sang, and from the world's blue oceans and rich, fecund earth arose the fishes and flowers, the whales and butterflies and trees, and all the other forms of life. And finally, men and women, who possessed minds to wonder at the mystery of themselves and to find their purpose in the great play of creation.

And so they planted seeds in the ground and harvested and made flour into bread, as men do; they dug up iron from the same ground and forged it into hoes and ploughshares. They quarreled over who owned this ground, and then made swords instead, and they slew each other in great numbers until their various earths ran red with rivers of blood.

But they were strong, these first men and the women they took as wives. The great song of life fired their beings; the music of memory carried them forward into the brilliant future. Out of the red, roaring oceans inside them came children and their children's children, in numbers too great for swords to cut down. They built cities in which to live and walls around their palaces and great, soaring towers.

And then to the greatest of these worlds, Erathe, the Ieldra sent the Lightstone. It found its way into the hands of a man with fire in his eyes and a great, blazing heart. People called him Maitreya, the Lord of Light.

He journeyed from city to city and land to land, bringing light wherever he went. And men put down their gleaming swords and polished their souls instead. And glorious cities greater even than Tria filled all the lands until all of the world shined with the splendor of a great civilization and peace at last reigned on Erathe.

Then men, tall men with bright, black eyes, looked toward the stars. The boldest of them walked from world to world bearing the Lightstone and giving it into the hands of other great-hearted beings who arose from their various earths. These, too, filled with cities as true civilization spread across the heavens.

At last, after many millions of years, the Lightstone returned to Erathe. There, one of the Shining Ones claimed it and brought it before the throne of a great king, a Starwalker who had journeyed to the center of the universe where the great geistei were kept and had gained great powers of the body, mind and soul. And this mighty warrior came down from his golden throne and knelt before this one. The radiance that poured from the Cup of Heaven washed away the last of the king's ephemerality and quickened the flames of his being so that his lifefire could never die of its own. And when he straightened yet again, the stars themselves crowned him in light, and there stood the first of the universe's immortals.

The king then gave up his throne to visit other worlds and help others prepare to make the same journey as had he. And the Lightstone followed him, always borne by the sons and grandsons of the tall, bright-eyed men. And the Cup of Heaven was given to other Shining Ones, who raised up other kings and queens to the order of the Elijin. And the greatest of these – Ashtoreth, Valoreth, Arwe, Urwe, Artu, Mainyu, Arkoth, Varkoth and Ahura – came to preserve the Lightstone's radiance inside themselves so that they shone and no particle of their beings could be harmed in any way.

And so the great Galadin went forth and summoned others of their kind to the world of Agathad, also known as Skol. And there they waited to fulfill their destiny. At the end of the ages, they would gather by the shores of a silver lake, and sing, and set free the bright infinity within themselves in an explosion into light. They would become beings of pure light: the Ieldra of the new universe to which they would give birth. And life would continue on its journey toward the One: ageless, indestructible, indwelling deep inside the depths of all things.

And all this, as the stars poured down their radiance into the amphitheater and I sat frozen to the bench beneath me, I saw and sensed and tried to understand.

The Maitreyas truly are Bringers of Light, I thought. *And they are the Makers of Angels*.

And then, like two pieces of silk knitted into a whole cloth again, my consciousness was made one, and I returned to staring out at the amphitheater's layers of leaves and glittering walls – and at the ghost

349

who stared right back at me.

'Ah, *that* was like a drunkard's dreams,' Maram said as he rubbed his eyes. Where before he had shivered, now beads of sweat formed up on his fat forehead. 'Did everyone else see what I did?'

For a while, as the constellations turned slowly above us, we sat there exchanging accounts of what we had seen. They were much the same. Our understanding of them, however, was not.

'The men who guarded the Lightstone,' Sajagax said to me, 'seemed much like you Valari. But why? Who chose *them* for this glory?'

Maram nodded at me and said, 'And what of the king, then? Certainly *he* must have been Valari. He looked like you, my friend.'

The king still stood out in my mind's eye, at once as strange as the distant world of Erathe and utterly familiar: he might have been my brother, my father, myself.

'It was the first Shining One who bore Valashu's aspect,' Lord Raasharu said. 'For surely it is not the cast of a man's face or the color of his eyes that contains his essence, but his heart and soul.'

This provoked yet more comment, from Sar Hannu and Sar Varald and the other knights, who were inclined to believe that the ghost's sole purpose in giving us these visions was to show me my destiny as the Maitreya.

'There is much that we still don't comprehend,' Master Juwain said. 'The movement of man is always toward the One, even as we of the Brotherhoods have always taught. But it seems that this rise can be hindered, or even forestalled altogether. From other sources, we know of Angra Mainyu's fall and the War of the Stone. But we were told nothing of this tonight. How is the Lightstone to be used and why did the ancient Maitreyas fail with the Dark One?'

No sooner had this question left his lips than the ghost stepped forward and said, '*Aulara, Auliama.*' Then he began singing out a song that filled all the amphitheater and shook the very stone surrounding us.

'No, wait!' Master Juwain called out, glancing up at the sky. 'That may not be the question that would be best to ask. It is growing late, and there are other things of vital importance that must be . . .'

His voice died before the vastly greater voice of the ghost as it became clear that this mysterious being intended to answer Master Juwain's question whether he liked it or not. I listened to the ghost, enraptured, even though I could understand little of what he was saying. For a single word repeated again and again, and that was *Alkaladur*.

Again I drew my sword and held it pointed toward the stars. Its silustria rang out like a bell and seemed to sing in harmony with the ghost's music.

'What is he saying?' Maram called out in a voice nearly as big as the ghost's. 'I don't understand any of it.'

Master Juwain, gazing at the ghost, said to him, 'There's too much, too fast, for *me* to understand either. But I believe that he is telling the story of Angra Mainyu's fall and the attempt of the Galadin and Elijin to heal him of his madness.'

'Then why doesn't he tell it in words that make sense?' Maram bellowed out.

At this, the ghost suddenly ceased singing and stared at Maram. Then he smiled and began reciting:

> When first the Dragon ruled the land,
> The ancient warrior came to Skol.
> He sought for healing with his hand,
> And healing fire burned his soul.
>
> The sacred spark of hope he held,
> It glowed like leaves an emerald green;
> In heart and hand it brightly dwelled:
> The fire of the Galadin.
>
> He brought this flame into a world
> Where flowers blazed like stellulars,
> Where secret colors flowed and swirled
> And angels walked beneath the stars.
>
> To Star-Home thus the warrior came,
> Beside the ancient silver lake,
> By hope of heart, by fire and flame,
> A sacred sword he vowed to make.
>
> Alkaladur! Alkaladur!
> The Sword of Love, the Sword of Light,
> Which men have named Awakener
> From darkest dreams and fear-filled night.
>
> No noble metal, gem or stone –
> Its blade of finer substance wrought,
> Of essence pure as love alone,
> As strong as hope, as quick as thought.

Valarda, like molten steel,
Like tears, like waves of singing light,
Which angel fire has set its seal
And breath of angels polished bright.

Ten thousand years it took to make
Beneath their planet's shining sun;
Ten thousand angels by the lake:
Their souls poured forth their fire as one.

In strength surpassing adamant,
Its perfect beauty diamond-bright,
No gelstei shone more radiant:
The sacred sword was purest light . . .

As the ghost continued reciting verses that reminded me of others that Alphanderry had once spoken to me, I gazed at my shining sword. The one who forged it, I thought, had named it after another sword, made many ages ago not of silustria but *valarda* – a sword of the soul. *The true Alkaladur.* A hundred questions sprang into my mind. Why couldn't one of the Maitreyas heal Angra Mainyu? And was the ancient warrior of whom the ghost spoke the same as the warrior mentioned in Alphanderry's epic: Kalkin, the immortal Elijin who had somehow become Kane, my companion and friend? And if so, why had Kalkin taken the lead in this quest over the much greater Galadin such as Ashtoreth and Valoreth?

I listened as the ghost told of the great war between the Amshahs, who sought to preserve the Law of the One, and the Daevas who followed Angra Mainyu:

In ruth the warrior went to war,
A host of angels in his train:
Ten thousand Amshahs, all who swore
To heal the Dark One's bitter pain.

With Kalkin, splendid Solajin
And Varkoth, Set and Ashtoreth –
The greatest of the Galadin
Went forth to vanquish fear of death.

And Urukin and Baradin,
In all their pity, pomp and pride:

352

The brightest of the Elijin
In many thousands fought and died.

Their gift, valarda, opened them:
Into their hearts a fell hate poured;
This turned the warrior's stratagem
For none could wield the sacred sword.

Alkaladur! Alkaladur!
The Brightest Blade, the Sword that Shone,
Which men have named the Opener,
Was meant for one and one alone.

   As the night deepened and the wind fell down from the stars, the
ghost went on singing for a long time, for his tale was a long one. He
told of how Marsul had called a great crusade to wrest the Lightstone
from Angra Mainyu by force of arms. Half of the Amshahs had joined
Ashtoreth and Valoreth in seeking Angra Mainyu's defeat through
finding a way to wield the Sword of Light; but half of them betrayed
the One's injunction that the Elijin and Galadin may not take life, and
they had gathered to Marsul's standard. And not just angels, it seemed,
but the Star People who were my ancestors:

And by their side Valari knights
Like stars a hundred thousand strong,
Their diamond armor gleamed like lights;
Their shields were hard, their swords were long.

What followed then, as the ghost finished his account of the War of
the Stone, saddened me for he told of my friend's wrath and near-fall
into evil:

At last the faithful Kalkin broke:
With sword in hand, with bitter breath,
Upon his soul an oath he spoke:
He vowed to bring the Dragon's death.

Then Mainyu fled across the stars
With Yama, Kadaklan and Zun.
The Daevas with their soul-dark scars –
They hid beneath a silver moon.

On Erathe, oldest world of Man,
The Amshahs found their ancient foe.
With Marsul, Kalkin, in the van,
Their helms on high, their swords aglow.

The armies met in summer's heat
Upon Tharharra's sun-seared plain;
No pity, quarter or retreat
No breath of wind nor drop of rain.

Alkaladur! Alkaladur!
The Sword of Love, the Sword of Life,
Which men have named the Quickener
Of dreams of death, of peace and strife.

All day the angels' armies clashed
Across the blazing, grassy sea,
Where steel and gelstei cruelly flashed
In deeds of dreadful savagery.

The sky burned black, the sea ran red –
At last the warrior seized his foe
Who stood as dead among the dead
By might of empathy laid low.
For Kalkin, with black stone in hand,
Now touched upon the depthless dark;
He brought him to that lightless land
And dimmed the Dragon's sacred spark.

And Marsul seized the golden bowl
While Manwe worked the Dragon's doom:
With aid of angels sent from Skol
He bound the Dragon on Damoom.

Alkaladur! Alkaladur!
Triumphant Sword, the Righteous Blade,
Which men have named the Vanquisher
Of woe and evil men have made.

Then Marsul, mad with long-held lust,
Beheld the golden bowl that shone.
He broke the Amshahs' sacred trust,
And claimed the Lightstone for his own.

354

But Kalkin fought him sword to sword
Across Tharharra's blood-soaked field,
Contending for the ancient hoard,
He forced his furied friend to yield.

Bereft of that which maddened him,
Brave Marsul's ageless eyes grew clear;
He found that place of grace and glim,
And faced his fate without a fear.

And now this Galadin so bright,
Atoning for his killing pride,
Vanished in a cloud of light –
Thus Marsul, mighty Marsul, died.

Alkaladur! Alkaladur!
The Blade of Grace, Mysterious Sword,
Which men have named the Deepener –
To ruthless ruth will be restored.

The Amshahs then grew cold with dread
At setting of the bloody sun;
On ground where so much life was shed
They saw an even Darker One.

But he who'd touched the Sword of Light
Perceived the Lightsword had touched him.
While angels watched, his heart blazed bright,
His eyes, his hands and every limb.

The warrior gave to Valakand
To guard the ancient golden bowl;
He set the vessel in his hand,
Thus cooled the fire of his soul.

And though the dark was not undone,
A light within the darkness hides;
While Star-Home turns around its sun
The Sword of Light, and Love, abides.

Alkaladur! Alkaladur!
The Sword of Fate, the Sword of Sight,

Which men have named Deliverer,
Awaits the promised Lord of Light.

As the ghost finished chanting, other beings appeared in the staging area. All were men, or something more, and all wore armor of various kinds: plate or steel mail or rings of silvery silustria – and not a few, diamond armor like my own. Many gripped swords or maces dripping with blood. They gathered among the bodies of the dead, who lay fallen all across the amphitheater's ground. One man, whose bright eyes shone like the diamonds he wore, stood tall and straight as another placed the Lightstone in his hand. This other man smiled a savage smile at me. I gasped to see Kane, or some apparition of him, gazing out at us through the darkness of the ages: He had the same cropped white hair, bold face and blazing, black eyes that I knew so well.

And then, as quickly as these new ghosts had come into the amphitheater, they were gone.

'Ah, that was *worse* than any dream,' Maram said. 'I hope never to see another battlefield, even one from the Elder Ages. If that is indeed what we saw.'

He looked at me to make sense of the ghost's verses and the haunting tableaux that had appeared before us. But where before I'd had a hundred questions about the past and future, now a thousand tormented me.

Master Juwain, sitting beside me, rubbed the back of his smooth head as he looked up at the sky. There were clouds in the east, and the stars of the Mother were falling toward the amphitheater's western rim. 'It's growing late, Val,' he told me. 'We've learned much, but I'm afraid you still don't know what you must, do you?'

'No, not yet,' I told him. I turned to look at Sajagax and Lansar Raasharu, who were watching me.

'If our need to journey on wasn't so great,' Master Juwain said, 'we could return here tomorrow night, and for the next year of nights, until we had our answers.'

Hearing this, the ghost again said, '*Aulara, Auliama.*'

I gazed at his wavering form, and I murmured, 'It *is* late. The others will be worrying about us.'

I turned to Sar Varald and said to him, 'Will you go back out and inform Sar Baltasar of what we've found here? And that we will be delayed yet a short while longer?'

Sar Varald bowed his head to me. Then he stood and began walking toward the crack in wall by which we had entered the amphitheater.

356

'*Aulara, Auliama*,' the ghost said to me.

And then, because I could bear it no longer, I stood and asked the question that I, like all men, most wanted answered: 'Who am I?'

I did not know what to expect. Perhaps, I thought, the ghost would begin reciting more verses or tell me that such a mystery was impossible ever to apprehend. So it surprised me when he beckoned for me to come forward and stand within the staging area. He likewise beckoned Maram, Master Juwain, Atara and Estrella. There was nothing to do but walk out and position ourselves in front of the benches as he indicated.

'*Agalastii!*' the ghost said, pointing at my chest, where I had tucked the Lightstone down beneath my armor. I sheathed my sword and drew forth the golden Cup of Heaven. '*Agalastii!*'

And then, as quick as a breath, the amphitheater again filled with luminous figures. Many of them, it seemed, were kings: I recognized King Waray's fine, dignified face and the much-scarred King Kurshan, who bore the white Tree of Life on his blue surcoat. Other Valari lords stood nearby, next to a man who could only be King Hanniban Dujar of Eanna, for his shield showed blue lions rampant on each of its gold quadrants. King Aryaman looked at me with eyes as blue as Sajagax's, while King Tal of Nedu watched me, too. And so did the kings of the lands ruled by Morjin or who had made alliance with him: a lithe man wearing the bronze, fish-scaled armor of the Hesperuks regarded me with awe, as did another with soft, almond eyes, whom I knew as King Angand of Sunguru from his unique emblem of a white heart with wings. Many chieftains of the Sarni gathered there, too. And then, one by one, as the Lightstone flared brighter in my hand, they bowed their heads to me and knelt down, touching their knees to the crunching leaves upon the ground.

And then I looked behind me toward Estrella, who was looking back at me, and through me, as if she had at last found what she had been seeking all her life. And the sun rose over the world. The sun was *inside* me, shining with a light that I knew could never die. I knew, too, that I could bring it forth and share it with others.

'*Auliama!*' the ghost chanted.

'Lord of Light!' the kings called out as one. And then, from farther away, another voice: 'Lord Valashu!'

It seemed that I had my answer. Surely I would never be more certain of my fate than I was at that moment. And yet. And yet. I stood there watching the bright star of the necklace of the Mother set, and I longed to ask still one more question.

'Lord Valashu!' Sar Varald called out again. I turned to see this thick-thewed knight enter the amphitheater and run toward me. 'They are all gone!'

357

'What?' I felt stunned as if by the blow of a mace. 'What is it, Sar Varald?'

He came panting up to me with his sword drawn, and said yet again, 'They are all gone!'

At that moment, the star fell behind the amphitheater's dark rock, and all the kings kneeling before me returned whence they had come.

'*Who* is gone?' I said to Sar Varald.

'Baltasar! Sunjay Naviru! All the Guardians – the Sarni, as well!'

Hearing this, Sajagax leaped up from his bench and charged toward us gripping his great bow in his hand. Lansar Raasharu and the other knights followed closely behind him. So did Karimah. And I said to the sweating Sar Varald, 'Are you sure they're gone?'

'Yes, Lord Valashu. I searched the woods outside the amphitheater, calling out their names. And no one answered back.'

'That's impossible!' Sajagax said. His heavy face furrowed with anger.

'Perhaps they grew tired of waiting and decided to make camp *deeper* in the woods,' Maram said. 'Or perhaps something scared them off.'

'That's impossible,' Sajagax said again.

'Yes, truly it is,' I said, agreeing with him. 'The Guardians were posted by the entrance pillars. They would have died to a man before yielding to anyone or being driven off.'

'And so with my warriors,' Sajagax said.

'But what if it were *ghosts* they faced?' Maram said. 'Or something worse?'

As everyone looked at him, I bent down and put my finger to the moss beneath me. It was wet with fresh blood. I quickly straightened and stepped over to Sar Varald, who was trembling. I gripped his arm to steady him. 'You didn't see any signs of battle?'

'No, none.'

I rubbed the scar on my aching forehead, utterly bewildered by what he had reported.

'Come!' Sajagax said to me as he started for his horse, which he had tethered to one of the elms along with the other horses.

I turned toward the ghost, who cast me one last, deep, piercing look as he said, '*Aulara, Aulara, Aulara.*' Then he, too, winked into unbeing and vanished into the neverness of the night.

'All right,' I said to Sajagax. I began running toward Altaru, who pawed the ground in his eagerness to leave this haunted place. 'Let's find out if men can disappear from the earth as easily as ghosts.'

For the moment, at least, this was the greatest mystery of my life.

25

When we came out through the crack leading from the amphitheater, we found the shingled ground surrounding the rock formation deserted, as Sar Varald had said. The starlight falling down from above like luminous rain showed nothing except chips of sandstone strewn about. I asked Atara if she could perceive anyone in the woods around us or beyond, but she couldn't. I cupped my hand over my mouth and called out as loud as I could, 'Baltasar! Sunjay! Guardians of the Lightstone!' No one answered back, neither from the right or left, or from straight ahead, where the dark woods were quiet except for the clicking of the katydids. I bade Maram and Sajagax, with their battle-horn voices, to call out as well, to no good end.

'We should be quiet now,' Atara said to me as she stood holding the reins of her horse. 'Why announce ourselves to whatever drove them off?'

'But what *could* have driven them off?' Maram said. 'Nothing that I'd like to imagine.'

'*Nothing* could have driven them off,' I said with certainty.

'Not even the Grays?'

At the mention of these dreadful men who had once nearly devoured our souls, both Atara and Master Juwain shuddered while Sajagax and Karimah made signs to ward off evil. And I said, 'The Grays might have frozen them with fear, though from what Kane told us, probably not so many. They could not have compelled them to abandon us.'

'Then what did?' Maram asked.

'That we must discover,' I said. 'But whyever Baltasar led the Guardians away from here, he must have had a good reason.'

My faith in him was unshakable. And after what I had experienced in the amphitheater, so was my faith in my fate.

'Let's look for sign of them,' I said.

Of all of us, Sajagax had the greatest craft at hunting and tracking, and the sharpest eyes. And so he took the lead in retracing our steps around the rock formation. We walked our horses slowly across the treacherous, rattling shingle, all the while searching the wall of trees that rose up before us. Soon we came to the place where the trampled ferns and broken deadwood showed where we had come through the forest, from the southeast. Sajagax dropped to his hands and knees, peering through the near-blackness as he traced his fingers around the divots the horses' hooves had left in the earth. Then he straightened and said, 'I don't think they passed back this way. Let's go on.'

We continued our journey around the great bubble of rock, which loomed in the starlight like the bald head of a giant. After about a hundred yards, Sajagax stopped suddenly. I stared so hard through the darkness that my eyes burned, and I could just make out the broken vegetation between the trees. Then Sajagax again entered the woods and dropped to the ground. A few moments later, he came back to me and said, 'They *did* pass this way. The track seems straight and leads northeast.'

'Back to the road,' I said. 'But by a different direction.'

'So it would seem.'

'Then it would seem *we* have a choice. We might return to the amphitheater for the night. Or go on.'

There were good reasons, I said, for spending the night in the amphitheater: its entrance was narrow and easy to defend, and we were all too tired to go bushwhacking through the dark forest. But the prospect of returning to that place of ghosts disquieted Sajagax and Karimah – and Maram most of all.

'I'm hungry and thirsty, and we have little food or water,' he said as he patted his horse's saddlebags. 'And more to the point, I don't *like* that place. What if there are secret entrances to it that we can't guard? There's *some* secret about it that we haven't learned. And *that* might have something to do with why the Guardians abandoned us.'

Sar Hannu looked toward the rock formation, and I felt a shuddering beneath his armor. Then he said to me, 'We would be immobilized inside there. In any case, the Lightstone should not be separated from its Guardians.'

'Nor the chieftain of the Kurmak,' Sajagax said, 'from his warriors.'

'All right then, let's follow them,' I said. 'Perhaps we'll come across them farther up the road.'

It was too dark to ride through the trackless woods, and so Sajagax strode forth at a slow walk, leading his horse through the bracken. I followed him, pulling gently on Altaru's reins; Estrella, Atara, Karimah,

360

Maram and Master Juwain came next, and then Sar Hannu and the other knights, while Lansar Raasharu brought up the rear. It was hard work, pushing through the ferns and trying not to trip over the old, downed trees and rotting splinters of wood almost impossible to see. We made too much noise, gasping as we stubbed our feet against half-buried rocks or snapped dry branches. Maram worried that bears might be hiding behind the shadowed oaks; certainly, he said, there would be snakes slithering across the dark mosses and poison ivy leaving its flesh-eating oils all over our garments. But he reserved his greatest fear for things not of the earth: 'What if the amphitheater also contains malevolent spirits?' he whispered. 'And what if they can take form and follow us?'

I touched my finger to my tongue and tasted the iron tang of blood. Then I pressed my finger to my lips and whispered, 'Shhh! You'll frighten Estrella. You'll frighten yourself.'

'Ah, you're right, my friend – I don't *have* to be afraid, do I?' He fell silent for a moment as he puffed and pushed his way through the swishing ferns. And then I heard him muttering to himself, '"Act as if you have courage, and courage you shall have." Well, whoever wrote that never saw a ghost.'

We continued on thusly for more than an hour, making our way through the towering trees. It was well past midnight when they finally gave out onto the road. Sajagax led his horse onto this dark, smooth band, and so did I. The striking of Altaru's iron-shod hoof against the naked paving stones was like the sounding of a gong announcing us to anyone who might have been hiding in the woods to either side of the road.

'Ah, here we are at last,' Maram said, looking right and then left. 'The question is, which way did they go?'

'Surely toward Tria,' Master Juwain said, coming up behind him.

Sajagax walked his horse toward the north, sniffing at the air and staring down at the nearly black stones of the road. After about ten yards, he espied a pile of dung, most likely, as he said, left by one of the Guardians' or his Kurmak's horses.

'They went this way,' he announced. Then he motioned toward Karimah and pointed down as he told her, 'Test it, woman.'

Quick as the flash of a shooting star, Karimah drew her knife and hissed at him, 'Test it yourself, mighty chieftain.'

It was too dark to make out the features of Sajagax's face, but I sensed that he was smiling. I sensed as well his sudden affection for this handsome woman. The Sarni are a sudden people, and he said to her, 'If you weren't a Manslayer, I'd take you as a wife.'

'If I weren't a Manslayer,' she told him, 'I'd let you. But since I am, if ever I kill my hundred, I'll take *you* as a husband.'

By tradition, any Manslayer completing her vow was free to chose among the men of her tribe a mate, who was then assured of siring great warriors.

We all had a good laugh at her besting of Sajagax, Sajagax most of all. I liked it that he could laugh at himself. And I liked it even more that he wasn't too proud to stoop down and test the dung with his finger, even as he had suggested to Karimah.

'They passed this way two hours ago,' he said. 'Or perhaps three.'

'Then we will have to ride hard to overtake them,' I said.

Without another word, I mounted Altaru, and so did the others their horses. I urged Altaru to a canter. The rhythmic, three-beat tempo of his hooves against the road was like a stately dance that the other's horses joined in, too.

Soon, however, it became apparent that we could not keep up this gait. The clouds drifting in from the east thickened and smothered the faint flickers of the stars. It grew nearly pitch black. We slowed our horses to a jolting trot and then a fast walk. I could barely see the road in front of us. Maram kept yawning and complaining that he couldn't keep his eyes open *to* see the road. Master Juwain rode stiffly as if each one of his old bones and joints pained him. We were all exhausted, from the battle four days before and all our hard riding and everything that had happened since. Twice, Estrella fell asleep and nearly slid from her little horse. The third time this happened, Atara stopped me and said, 'We can't go on this way, Val. She's only a girl, and needs rest. We all do.'

Even Sajagax, who was used to spending whole days and nights in the saddle, agreed with this. He came up to me and said, 'We passed a clearing off the side of the road a few hundred yards back. Let us camp there for the night and continue on in the morning.'

Maram held out his hand in the dark air and said, 'I do believe I felt a raindrop – it would be madness to ride through such a night in the rain.'

At last, I bowed my head to the inevitable. 'All right, then, we'll stop for a few hours. But we must be on our way by dawn, if we can.'

By the time we found the small clearing that Sajagax had spoken of, more drops of rain were splatting down, pinging from our helms and soaking into our garments. It was too late and we were all too tired to gather wood or dig trenches to fortify our encampment. It was all we could do to set up our only two tents in the deepening rain. Each tent could sleep four comfortably and six at a squeeze. Sajagax

ordered Estrella, Atara and Karimah to take the first tent for themselves, and not even Karimah disputed this. He insisted on wrapping
himself in his cloak and lying down on the wet ground outside its
entrance flap. Maram needed no encouragement to spread out inside
the second tent, nor did Master Juwain. But Lansar Raasharu balked
when I suggested that he join them. And Sar Hannu – with Sar Varald
and Juradan the Younger – rebelled altogether against my command
that they should rest.

'It is you, Lord Valashu, who must take some sleep,' Sar Hannu said.
'Who knows what tomorrow, or even the rest of this night, will bring?
The Lord Guardian of the Lightstone must be of a fresh mind to face
it.'

'The *Lord Guardian*,' I reminded him, 'must sometimes make sacri-
fices for the sake of that which he guards and the others who help
him guard it.'

'Truly spoken,' Sar Hannu said. 'Thus surely the Lord Guardian must
be willing to put aside his compassion for a few hours, if not his pride.'

In the end, I was forced to relent, as was Lord Raasharu. While Sar
Hannu, with Sar Varald, Sar Shevan, Sar Ishadar and Juradan the
Younger, posted themselves around our encampment, we went inside
the tent. I lay down next to Master Juwain, who had taken out his
akashic crystal and seemed to be meditating on it. It took only a few
minutes for Maram to fall asleep, and not much longer for Lansar
Raasharu. After a while, in a near-whisper, I told Master Juwain, 'You
should sleep yourself, sir.'

'In moment,' he murmured. The disc in his hands glowed with a
soft glorre that lit the tent faintly. 'This crystal seems to be alive now
in a way that it wasn't before we found the amphitheater. The voices
– so strong, so strong!'

'Is Kane's voice one of them?'

'I'm not sure,' he said. 'I'm not sure I've yet found the way to go
where I must inside this. There are whole worlds there – a universe
full of worlds.'

'If Kane were here,' I said, 'then surely he could show us the way to
them. If the ghost spoke truly, then Kane was involved with the War
of the Stone from the first.'

'Yes – and it's strange that he was the one to lead in the forging of
the first Alkaladur, this Sword of Light.'

'It would be good to know more about *that*,' I said. 'Why did it take
so long to forge it? And why did the Amshahs fail to heal Angra
Mainyu?'

Master Juwain sighed as he slid his knotted old hand across the smooth crystal. 'I think the answer to both those questions is clear enough. The Sword of Light was made of the collective compassion of ten thousand Elijin and Galadin. Surely it must have been difficult beyond our comprehension to achieve the attunement of so many. And as for their failure, the *valarda* is a double-edged sword, even as you've discovered. At the moment they struck out to touch Angra Mainyu with their love, when they were most open, he must have struck back in hate.'

'To kill this way with hate,' I murmured, 'could anything be more evil?'

At this, Master Juwain fell silent as he rolled over on his side and looked at me. I drew my sword from its sheath and watched as its silustria took on the tones of glorre. I said, 'Then Kane named this in mockery of the true Alkaladur.'

'Perhaps, Val, perhaps,' he said mysteriously. 'But there is much that we don't know about either sword.'

'And much that we still don't know about Kane.'

'True enough. It seems that he resisted breaking the Law of the One for the longest time. But finally he followed Marsul to war.'

'Our friend ever finds hate inside himself,' I said. 'But ever the opposite, too.'

'Yes – and it took great faith for him, at the last, to surrender the Lightstone to Valakand. Even as in Argattha, he gave it back to you.'

I sheathed my sword and brought out the Cup of Heaven instead. The small golden bowl was warm against my hand. 'The touch of this, it seems, drove Marsul mad – as it had Angra Mainyu. But why?'

'Because the Lightstone was made for the hand of the Maitreya, and no other,' he said. 'This much I *have* discovered. The Elijin, even the Galadin, are not permitted to use it.'

'But why?' I said again. 'What is the secret of this gelstei?'

'That I don't yet know, Val. But it's clear that during the Elijin Satra, all the angels who tried to use the Lightstone failed – and fell.'

The word 'satra,' I remembered, meant 'true age': the great and very long ages of the universe. As the rain pattered against the fabric of the tent above us and its interior filled with the sounds of Maram snoring and Lansar Raasharu's heavy breath, Master Juwain told me more about the history of these elder ages. The first of them, he said, in the immense span of time after the creation of our universe, Eluru, was called the Dark Satra. Over ten billion years, on countless worlds, life came forth and strove always towards the highest, at last attaining to Mind when the first human beings appeared. These men and women of the earth, the Ardun, gave their name to a new satra that saw all the worlds of

Eluru flower with people. The Ardun Satra progressed more quickly than the first, lasting only a tenth as long. But it was long enough to achieve a great civilization on Erathe. On that world, the first Maitreya used the Lightstone to raise up the Ardun to a new order: that of the Valari. This name had originally meant, simply, the 'Star People'; and now, during a glorious age called the Valari Satra, men and women of the stars learned to walk from world to world, bringing to the Ardun peoples the seeds of Civilization. And bringing the Lightstone as well. It became a sacred tradition that the best way to use this golden cup was to give it into the hands of a Maitreya who would then help quicken a world's peoples to a higher order. As there were very many worlds in the universe, however, the whole process progressed rather slowly over a hundred million years.

By the end of the age, when many had achieved World-Mind, it seemed that the design of the One – and the Ieldra – was unfolding much as it should. As time went on and knowledge of all manifestations of the One gradually accumulated, men and women began to gain great powers of body and mind. Finally, on Erathe, oldest of Civilization's worlds, a great king was raised up to the order of the Elijin. His first charge, according to the Law of the One, was to vow never to take human life. His second charge was to help others gain his high estate. And so he journeyed across Erathe and then out into the stars to carry out this noble mission. After thousands of years, as the Elijin Satra progressed, this first immortal was joined by many others. These angels, as they were called, acted as messengers of the Ieldra, visiting troubled worlds and helping them toward Civilization.

But not without a struggle. The Elijin, enjoined never to kill, had to work by the power of persuasion and teaching, as well as touching people's hearts with their great, golden auras. From time to time, one or more of the Elijin would break the Law of the One and fall into murder. Many, too, tried to use the Lightstone to gain still greater powers and become greater beings. But for some mysterious reason, all who tried failed and fell – even as Master Juwain had said. It was only after a great many years that the Elijin laid down a law that only the Guardians of the Lightstone and the various Maitreyas were allowed to touch it.

'If we could learn *why* the higher orders may not use the Lightstone,' Master Juwain said, pointing at the cup in my hands, 'we might understand *how* the Maitreya can.'

I squeezed the Lightstone's smooth, glowing gelstei, said to be the hardest and most impenetrable of substances. I whispered to Master

Juwain, 'I *must* know this, sir. Keep searching in your crystal, if you will.'

'I certainly will, Val. But I must tell you the search might last years.'

'Years,' I whispered. 'I'm no immortal, you know.'

Master Juwain looked at me strangely and said, 'Perhaps not.'

'And the world won't wait forever.'

'That it certainly will not,' he said. His face fell troubled and grave. 'The Cosmic Maitreya, the Great Shining One, must come forth and soon. The age is ending, Val. Not just the Age of the Dragon, here on Ea, but the Galadin Satra itself. There must be a progression, a great progression.'

'What do you mean, sir?'

He sighed and held his hands out from his chest. 'When a man, with the aid of the great gelstei that we call the seven openers, becomes an Elijin, that is a progression. And so with the passage of the Galadin, as when Marsul freed the light inside himself in transcending his human form. But once in every universe there comes a moment toward which all time and history has pointed. This is a Great Progression. The word for this has been carried down as the *Valkariad*.'

I thought about this name, which was one and the same as the epic preceding the penultimate book of the *Saganom Elu*. I said, 'I thought that meant "the passage of the stars".'

'That is one translation. A better one might be: "the creation of the stars". For at the moment of the *Valkariad*, all the Ardun of the universe are raised up to the Valari order, even as the Valari become Elijin and the Elijin advance as Galadin. And the Galadin, as we saw in the amphitheater, transcend themselves in creating a new universe.'

'We *did* see that,' I said. 'But how can that be possible? The Galadin are only finite beings, yes?'

'True, true. But just as all beings and all things arise from the infinite One, all things contain the seed of the Infinite inside themselves.'

I thought of the bag of timana seeds that Ninana had given me. Each one, if planted in the right soil, would magically burst forth into a great astor tree. But even these golden glories were as nothing against the splendor of the stars.

'The Valkariad is coming,' he said to me. 'Angra Mainyu and the War of the Stone have delayed this moment, but it *must* come, and soon.'

'And then?' I asked.

'And then,' he said simply, 'the Age of Light shall begin.'

I lay back against the earth, trying to ignore the discomfort of my armor's diamonds grinding into my back. The tent's air steamed with the smells of wet wool and Maram's beery breath, but I paid this no

366

mind. For inside myself, I felt quickening a bright, silver seed. There were stars there, a whole universe of stars. When I closed my eyes for a moment, I walked the heavens' incandescent heights.

And then, even as I looked out into the tent again, Flick appeared in a swirl of gold and glorre. I smiled at him and said, 'Well, little Flick, what do you think about this business of men becoming angels?'

I didn't really expect any kind of an answer. And so it surprised me, and Master Juwain, when a sweet voice like the piping of a bird issued from Flick's sparkling form, and he told me, 'Beware the Skakaman!'

I blinked my eyes in incomprehension, and then he was gone.

'"Beware the Skakaman,"' I whispered. I turned to Master Juwain. 'Do you know what that means?'

But he only shook his head as he patted his colored crystal. 'Perhaps I'll find that word in here.'

'Perhaps you will,' I said to him. 'But not now. We both must sleep, or else go out and stand watch in place of Sar Hannu and Sar Varald.'

Master Juwain put away his crystal then, and the tent fell dark as a cavern deep inside the earth. Sleep claimed him first while I listened to the rain breaking against the tent roof and the quieter beating of my heart. Then I passed into a lightless land that wasn't quite life and wasn't quite death. Nightmares tormented me. A black shape, as indistinct as a shadow, seemed to take hold of me and pull me down into a dreadful coldness. There was a gurgling, like rain running off the tent and being sucked down a hole. I couldn't breathe. I knew, somehow, that I lay sweating and writhing on the ground, unable to wake up.

And then, at last, I *did* come awake, to the sound of a long, deep scream. It took me a moment to realize that I had cried out in my sleep with a terrible pain that ripped open my throat.

'Val, what is it?' Maram said. He knelt next to me, shaking my shoulder. It seemed that my cry had awakened him – and everyone else.

'Valashu!' A voice like that of a sagosk bull bellowed from outside our tent. I tried to shake the sleep from my head as Sajagax called out yet again: 'Valashu! Atara! Everyone! Weapons ready! We are attacked!'

I whipped Alkaladur from its sheath and leaped up as I practically tore through the opening of the tent. Outside, the day's first light pushed through sodden grayness still smothering the world. Sajagax, I saw, was standing off in the trees, staring down at something as he gripped the hilt of his saber. I began running toward him. I was only dimly aware of Lansar Raasharu, Master Juwain and Maram bursting from our tent even as Atara, Karimah and Estrella hurried out of theirs.

I drew up beside Sajagax. Although it was hard to see through the twilight, I made out the form of Sar Shevan sprawled on the wet, rotting leaves. I knew without looking that he was dead. The gorget had been ripped away from his throat, which was slashed open. His eyes were as empty as balls of glass.

'Oh, my Lord!' Maram cried out as he joined us. 'Oh, my Lord!'

He gripped a drawn kalama, as did Lansar Raasharu, who stood beside him. Karimah came up clutching her bow while Atara had a saber, as did her grandfather. Master Juwain held nothing more deadly than a wet stick that wouldn't serve to drive off a dog. But it was he, with his clear, gray eyes, who espied Juradan the Younger lying dead in a pool of blood a dozen paces deeper into the woods. A quick search through the bracken nearby turned up the bodies of Sar Ishadar and Sar Varald, who had likewise been murdered.

And then Estrella came running up to me. She grabbed my arm and pulled at me, all the while pointing at the woods on the opposite side of the clearing. I turned, dreading what I would see. But there was nothing there, it seemed, except trees. And then Estrella broke away from me. Before I could catch her, she bound off like a young doe and sprinted across the clearing. I followed her as quickly as I could; so did everyone else. She led us straight to the last of my fallen Guardians. Sar Hannu lay in a clump of bloodstained lilies. But he was still alive, and his dark, haunted eyes found mine and would not let go.

'Sar Hannu!' I cried. I dropped to my knee, and lay my hand on him. His throat, too, had been cut, but along the windpipe and not across it. 'Who did this to you?'

With the last of his strength, his bloody hand locked onto mine. And he gasped out, 'You . . . did.'

And then he died. Not even Master Juwain's green gelstei or Estrella's frantic, pounding hands could bring him back to life.

'What did he mean?' Maram asked me as he stood over us. The falling rain beat against Sar Hannu's closed eyes and washed his blood into the earth. 'Does he blame you for leading him here, to his death?'

'Yes, that must be it,' I said. And I thought: *As he should.*

'But what killed him then? An assassin? No, no – how could any assassin lure five Valari knights into the woods and slit their throats?'

Sajagax and Karimah looked at each other as they made warding circles with their fingers. Nearby, Atara stood in the rainy dawn with her blindfolded face turned toward the woods as if looking for something that no one could see.

'*Something*,' Maram said, 'from the amphitheater must have taken form and followed us here. If you hadn't awakened when you did, surely it would have murdered you – and maybe all of us.'

Beware the Skakaman, Flick had said to me. I did not want to believe that any of the beings who had lit up the amphitheater could be evil. Nor did I want to believe that they could take form and go stalking about the earth, even as Maram had suggested.

'If it *was* a ghost that murdered them,' I said to Maram, 'it seems unlikely that it would have refrained from entering our tent to murder me just because I screamed.'

'Then what *did* murder them?' he asked.

But I had no answer for him; neither did Master Juwain or anyone else. We stood there in the pouring rain staring down at Sar Hannu's torn body in the cold, gray light of the dawn.

'We should ride now, as quickly as we can,' Sajagax said. 'Whatever did this might return.'

I pointed my sword toward the looming trees and said, 'I pray that he does.'

'Come, Valashu,' he said, taking my arm. 'Let's leave this cursed place.'

'No, we can't leave our friends unburied.'

'Let us then strip off their armor and bury them as we Sarni do.'

'No,' I said again. 'They are Valari knights and will be buried in their armor, with their swords over their hearts.'

It took us all morning to do as I had said, for we only had two shovels among us and I would not consent to making shallow graves that some scavenger might easily dig up. As it was, the task that I had appointed us would have been impossible if the ground of the clearing hadn't been free of tree roots and softened by the rain. I regretted only that we had no headstones to mark the places on earth where these five Guardians of the Lightstone would rest in eternity.

We broke camp with rain beating against our covered heads. We rode away from that place of slaughter as quickly as we could. The gurgling of water running down the road's gutters reminded me how terrible it was to have one's throat cut and die.

For most of four hours we kept up a quick pace. Baltasar and the Guardians, if they had fled for Tria, were likely halfway to the city by now and might be impossible to overtake. I didn't care. I wanted to charge up the road, sweeping from my path any impossibilities or obstacles. I couldn't help hoping that whatever murdered my knights would try to waylay us. For in the clear light of the day, I would draw Alkaladur and cleave him in two, whatever dread substance he was made of.

Late in the afternoon we came to a village straddling both sides of the road. There wasn't much of it: a blacksmith's forge, a carpenter's shop, and a mill above a swift-running stream – and perhaps thirty little stone houses. As we slowed to a walk, one of the villagers came out of her house with some cakes to sell. She called out to a man blowing glass over a glowing kiln inside: 'Look, Amman, more Valari – Sarni, too!'

I halted before her doorway, and the others drew up behind me. I called down a greeting to this little woman, whose fine wool tunic and silver bracelets suggested that she and her husband made a excellent living selling their goods to wayfarers. I asked her, 'Have you seen our friends? Did they pass this way?'

'Early this morning, my lord,' the woman said. 'But they've not yet left Silver Glade, which is what we call our village. They've set up in Harbannan's wheat field by the river.'

She pointed up the road where a little bridge spanned the silver water that she called a river. The mill stood to the right of the road on the water's far bank. If there was a wheat field to the left, the curve of the road and the houses obscured it.

I thanked the woman and gave her a coin for her cakes. Then I urged Altaru forward, and we cantered down the village's main street, followed by Sajagax and the others. A few moments later, we pounded across the bridge. There the road turned to the left, and the houses gave out onto an expanse of ripening wheat. And there, on a triangular field between the road and the river, my scores of Guardians were drawn up on their horses in a long line as if for battle. Across the road, in an apple orchard, Orox and Thadrak and all of Sajagax's warriors gathered beneath the trees with their bows strung and their sharp, blue eyes fixed on the road.

'Baltasar!' I called out as I crossed the field. I could easily make out the blue rose that stood out from the gold of his surcoat. He waited on top of his horse at the center of the line. Sunjay Naviru sat nearby, and so did Sar Kimball, Lord Noldru, Lord Harsha and many others whom I was glad to see. 'What are you doing here?'

I pulled up in front of my Valari knights, with Sajagax and Lansar Raasharu, who looked at Baltasar as if afraid his son had taken leave of his senses. Atara and Karimah joined us there, too, and a few moments later, Thadrak and Zekii galloped in from across the road and greeted Sajagax with puzzled looks.

'What are *we* doing here?' Baltasar said to me. 'What are *you* doing here, Lord Valashu?'

'What do mean?' I asked him. I didn't know whether to be dumbfounded or furious with the actions of my hot-headed friend. 'Why did you desert us?'

Now it was Baltasar's turn to regard me as if I had fallen mad. He blurted out, 'But you commanded me to!'

'What do you mean?' I said again.

'Outside the bald rock in the woods, you commanded me to lead the Guardians and the Kurmak here!'

'Never!' I told him. 'Why would I do such a thing.'

'Because, you said that you had discovered inside a great treachery.'

'What treachery, then?'

'That Duke Malatam had gathered a new army and was pursuing us again.' Baltasar looked back and forth between me and Sajagax, who was glaring at him. 'You commanded me to intercept the Duke's army here, in this village. You were to take the Lightstone into Tria by a different route. That's what you said.'

'*Someone* might have said that,' I told him. 'But it was not I.'

'But it *was* you!' Baltasar said. 'You came up to me outside the rock. I *saw* you. So did Sunjay, Skyshan, Adamar – everyone. You stood two feet from me, face to face!'

Along the line of my knights, Sunjay Naviru and Lord Noldru nodded their heads gravely in affirmation of what Baltasar had said. They all stared at me as if to assure themselves that I really was Valashu Elahad.

'But how *could* I have come up to you outside the amphitheater?' I asked Baltasar. 'Since the Guardians were posted across the entranceway?'

'Well, you said that you had found a secret entrance.'

At this, Maram shot me a swift, knowing look and muttered, 'Ah, what did I say? What did I say?'

'You told me,' Baltasar went on, 'that you had come out on the side of the rock opposite us. And then you circled the rock and approached us from the woods. And commanded us to ride toward Silver Glade immediately.'

'No, it was not I,' I said again. 'It was something else.'

I motioned for the Guardians to break their formation and gather around me. Then I told them everything that had happened inside the amphitheater and since then.

'But this is terrible!' Baltasar said to me. 'What if Sar Maram is right? What if some ghost from the amphitheater took on your form and commanded me to desert you? And then followed to slay you and steal the Lightstone?'

Beware the Skakaman! I thought. I was almost convinced that Maram's fear had somehow been made real.

'Perhaps,' Sunjay said, 'it was only an illusion sent by the Lord of Illusions himself.'

He touched the warder stone that hung from his neck, and so did many other knights around us. And Master Juwain said, 'I don't think these gelstei failed to protect you.'

'No,' I said agreeing with him. 'What happened to Sar Hannu and the others was no work of illusion. Someone struck cold steel into them.'

At the mention of the murdered Guardians, the men around me bowed down their heads. Lord Noldru, I saw, was weeping, for Sar Varald had been his friend.

'What are we to do, then?' Baltasar asked me.

Although the rain had stopped and the sky was clearing, soon it would be dark. I looked about the wheat field and the orchard across the road. I said, 'It's late, and so we shall camp here for the night – after we've paid Farmer Harbannan for trampling his wheat. Tomorrow, we'll ride into Tria.'

The camp we made then was the strongest of our entire journey. Deep moats we dug in poor Harbannan's field, and we gathered wood from a nearby stand of oaks to build up a stockade around our rows of tents. I issued a password, *Alumit*, that anyone approaching my pavilion must know. I gave orders that anyone resembling me should be examined to make sure he was wearing the gold medallion of the Quest and that of the Tournament Champion. Master Juwain and Maram volunteered to act as my safe-keepers, that everyone might see that I had not left their presence –and that they had not left mine.

I dined with them and Atara inside my pavilion that evening. I desired only the companionship of those who had borne the uncertainties of the Quest with me. And so I regarded it as the working of fate when I heard a faint clopping of hooves along the road and then two visitors announced themselves at the perimeter of our encampment. For they proved to be friends I loved as mother and brother: Liljana Ashvaran and a little boy named Daj, whom we had brought out of Argattha.

26

The Guardians posted behind the stockade would not let them pass. After being summoned, I hurried out of my pavilion and down the rows of tents to see two figures dressed in traveling cloaks and standing by their horses outside the stockade in the swishing wheat. Twilight was darkening the world, but I could still make out Liljana's pretty, round face and Dajarian's sharper features. The months since the Quest had wrought changes upon them. Liljana's once-plump form had thinned, and her cheeks seemed gaunt and hollowed. Daj, however, stood half a head taller and had filled out, probably from Liljana's sumptuous cooking. In his fine tunic, cleaned up as he was, he seemed almost a different boy. From beneath a mop of black hair, his almond eyes looked out at me and met mine with great gladness.

'Val!' he called to me. And then, impulsive as always, he blurted out, 'Your armor really *is* made of diamonds!'

Liljana nodded at him in a kindly way, then turned to me. 'Well – are you going to keep an old woman waiting all night in the dark?'

Liljana, I thought, was hardly old. Although her hair was gray as iron and her skin deeply creased, she was only of middling years and still robust. She possessed a strength of body and spirit that a much younger woman might have envied. Indeed, many did, for she was the Materix of that secret Sisterhood known as the Maitriche Telu.

'Sar Avram! Sar Tavar!' I called out to the sentries. 'These are my friends – let them through!'

Sar Tavar, a long-faced knight, stared past the thin logs of the stockade and shook his head doubtfully. 'What if the thing from the amphitheater has taken on this woman's form?'

Liljana's forehead creased with puzzlement. I felt her bristling with anger at being kept waiting for what must have seemed no good reason. But I sensed her resolve to control this impulse and sort things out in a calm, careful and even relentless way. The flames of her being blazed with a bright will toward goodness, truth and beauty, and if she were really a skulking murderer in disguise, then I might as well give up all hope, for the world had ended and the sun would not rise on the morrow.

'Let her pass,' I said to Sar Tavar again.

Sar Tavar and Sar Avram reluctantly pulled open the stockade's rudimentary gate, and Liljana and Daj stepped inside. Just then, Master Juwain, Maram and Atara came hurrying up behind us. Liljana greeted them warmly, then told me, 'I can see that my identity is questioned, though I really can't imagine why. You have stories to tell me, as I have you. Very well. But I'm the same Liljana who cooked your meals and darned your socks across the length of Ea. Of course I am.'

She bowed her head toward Atara, and then stared at me. 'Don't you remember what I said to you in the White Mountains about what a woman truly desires?'

'Do *you* remember?' I asked her.

'Of course I do.' She stepped closer to me, which caused Sar Tavar to grip the hilt of his sword. Then, as I leaned down, she cupped her hands over my ear and whispered, 'To be someone's beloved.'

If Atara had still possessed eyes, they would have filled with anguish just then. Somehow, she must have known what Liljana told me. She stood tall and still as one of the sculptures that the Frost Giants carve out of ice. I didn't want to look at her.

And then Liljana rushed forward and threw her arms around Atara. She kissed the cloth binding her face, and stroked her long hair. Tears streamed from her soft, large eyes as she said, 'It's good to see you again, my dear.'

I felt Atara weeping inside as she embraced Liljana and kissed her. And then, in a quavering voice, with only a little irony, Atara said, 'It's good to see *you*, too.'

Daj ran up to me, and I grabbed his sides and raised him up in the air. He laughed as he looked at me eye to eye. Once, his lively face had held the aspect of one much older than his nine or ten years. But under Liljana's care, much of the boy had returned to him. I set him down, and rumpled his hair. And he ran his finger over the diamonds encrusting my chest. He told me, 'Liljana taught me my letters. Ten times, maybe more, I've read the story of how Aramesh and the Valari defeated Lord Morjin at the Sarburn. I didn't know *anyone* had ever defeated him before . . . before you did in his hall. They call the Valari the "Diamond Warriors". But I never really believed your armor was made of *diamonds.*'

His words caused Sar Tavar and Sar Avram to beam with pride. Other

374

knights had broken away from their meals to get a look at these two companions from the great Quest. Baltasar and Lord Raasharu crowded in close next to Skyshan of Ki, Sar Kimball and Sunjay Naviru. And then Lord Harsha and Behira, with Estrella, made their way down the lane between the tents. When Daj met eyes with Estrella, a smile as bright as the sun broke upon his face. He pushed past the tall knights nearby and ran straight up to her. 'Estrella!' he cried out. 'Estrella! Estrella!'

He hugged her to him, and then stood back as they both fairly danced with delight. And Liljana called to him: 'You *know* this girl?'

'Yes, from the Dark City where she served one of the priests,' he said. 'She's my sister.'

We were all astonished to hear this, for during the many miles of our flight from Argattha, Daj had never spoken of any relation that he might have left behind. Upon questioning, however, Daj now admitted that Estrella was his sister in spirit only.

'Her mother was a slave, too,' Daj said. 'She belonged to a weaver on the fourth level. That's where Estrella was born.'

I stepped closer to these two mysterious children. I looked at Daj and asked, 'But how could you know that? Was there a time when Estrella could speak?'

'Of course there was,' he said. 'I mean, there is. She speaks to me now.'

I turned to Liljana, who held in her hand what seemed a little piece of driftglass cast into the shape of a whale. But I knew it to be of blue gelstei, the stones that quickened the powers of truthsaying and listening to the whisperings of the mind. I looked into her wise, old eyes, and asked, 'Have you . . . ?'

Have you taught him how to speak mind to mind?

Liljana had once promised me – and our other companions – that she would never look into another's mind without his leave. But she didn't need to exercise this power now to understand my unfinished question. She shook her head slightly as she said to me, 'No, I haven't.'

'Then what does Daj mean?' I asked.

I watched as he looked at Estrella, widening his eyes and pursing his lips. Estrella nodded as she gestured with her hand back toward the road. Then she slashed her finger across her throat. Her face darkened with a frown. I didn't need the gift of valarda to perceive the sadness that fell over her.

For a while, the two children stood there facing each other, flashing hands, smiles or knowing looks at each other. It seemed they were talking to each other in a secret language much deeper than words.

Then Daj broke off his silent communications. He looked at me and said simply, 'It's after you.'

'*What* is?' I said to him.

'The Skakaman,' he told me.

Baltasar, Skyshan and other knights moved in closer. Their eyes filled with dread as they regarded Daj warily. Dread seized my innards with cold claws, and I looked at Daj with amazement, for I had spoken this evil-sounding word to no one except Master Juwain.

'And what is *that*?' I asked Daj.

Daj held up his hands and shook his head. 'I don't really know. But I heard Lord Morjin speak of the Skakaman once. I think it's something he sends to hunt people down when they're asleep. It . . . steals their faces.'

Baltasar muttered something to Sunjay then, and Lansar Raasharu's hand tightened around the hilt of his sword. Other knights looked at each other as if seeking to confirm their worst fears. Seeing this, Master Juwain stepped over to me and said, 'Perhaps we should return to your pavilion. I'm sure our friends would welcome a little dinner.'

At the mention of food, Daj's eyes lit up. In Argattha, he had often had only rats to eat – that is, when he'd had anything at all.

And so I bade the Guardians to return to their meals or posts. I led Liljana and Daj back to my pavilion, where they joined Atara, Maram and Master Juwain inside. Since Daj and Estrella seemed inseparable, I invited the girl as well. In the soft light of the oil lamps that I meant to keep burning all night, we sat in a circle and shared our simple meal of roasted pork loin and some fresh bread and onions that we had bought in the village. The walls of my tent, lined with white silk, danced with shadows. Because they were so thin, we kept our voices low as we discussed all that had happened along the way from my father's castle toward Tria – and what had occurred in that great city over the last few days.

'A tinker traveling up the road,' Liljana said to me, 'passed your knights earlier today. When he reached Tria, he told of a company of Valari a few miles outside the walls. The word has spread quickly. Ever since King Waray and King Mohan arrived, everyone has been expecting you, myself most of all. I had to hurry to leave the city before they closed the gates for the night. And so here I am.'

'Why the urgency?' I asked her. 'Don't tell me that it's just because you're glad to see an old friend?'

'I *am* glad to see an old friend, my young friend,' she said, reaching out to squeeze my hand. 'But there are things I must tell you before you go into the conclave tomorrow.'

'Then has it already begun?' I asked.

'It has,' she said. 'King Kiritan wouldn't wait upon your arrival. Your Valari kings, of course, objected to that, since, as they said, it was your father who called for the conclave in the first place. But King Kiritan shouted them down. There has been much shouting in his hall. For two days, that's all these glorious kings have done, shout and argue with each other.'

Between bites of bread and pork, she told of some of these disputes. The sovereigns of the Free Kingdoms, it seemed, could not even agree upon the nature of what they were supposed to agree upon. Were they met to make an alliance against Morjin or only to discuss means to forestall his aggressions? Old King Hanniban of Eanna, for one, professed little fear of Morjin. He claimed that the southern kingdoms had fallen to Morjin's perfidies and plots because they were weak. But the Free Kingdoms, he said, were strong. He boasted that the combined navies of Eanna, Thalu and Nedu could easily blockade the Dragon Channel against Morjin's warships. And if Morjin's armies tried to attack Eanna by way of the much more arduous land route through Surrapam, then Eanna, with aid from Thalu alone, could easily beat back the invaders.

'King Hanniban,' I said, upon listening to this, 'is shortsighted. He thinks only of his own kingdom.'

'So it is with each king, I'm afraid,' Liljana said.

'And he underestimates his enemy,' I said. 'Morjin will soon fall against the Ymanir and destroy Elivagar. He'll reinforce Yarkona from Sakai, then order Count Ulanu to attack Eanna from its soft underbelly in the southeast, even as his Hesperuk armies move up through Surrapam. He'll crush Eanna between these two jaws. King Hanniban must be blind not to see this.'

As I said this, Atara's lips tightened. But she sat across from me in silence.

'Well,' Liljana said, 'other kings *do* favor an alliance.'

'Which kings?' Maram asked from beside her.

'Well, your father,' she said. 'I think he's very eager to make alliance with Alonia and the Nine Kingdoms. He fears that Delu will be attacked from Galda across the Terror Bay, as in ancient times.'

'Ah, well, he's a fearful man,' Maram said. 'But in this case with good reason.'

'Too true,' Liljana said. 'And if reason alone prevailed, Alonia would promise aid to Delu. But King Kiritan doesn't want to commit forces that might be needed in defense of his own kingdom – unless others first commit to him. They're selfish men, these kings.'

377

'Then all must commit as one,' Master Juwain said. 'There simply *must* be an alliance.'

'And that is precisely what King Theodor Jardan has said. Of course, being of the Elyssu, he's a reasonable man.'

'Of course,' Master Juwain said. He, who had been born on this island kingdom, smiled at Liljana. But she did not smile back.

'But I'm sorry to say,' she told him, 'that King Theodor favors an alliance only with Alonia and Delu – and possibly with the Nine Kingdoms. The western kingdoms he doesn't trust. It's been only twelve years since the Elyssu warred against Nedu.'

She watched as Master Juwain's ugly face fell into a frown. From the moment these two luminaries of their respective Brotherhood and Sisterhood had met, they had taken to sparring verbally with each other.

And then Maram put in, 'Is there anyone besides my father who favors an alliance of *all* the Free Kingdoms?'

'Well, there is Atara's father,' Liljana said, looking at Atara. 'King Kiritan has almost persuaded King Tal and King Aryaman of the need – King Theodor, too. If he succeeds, King Hanniban will likely go along with them. But it seems he won't succeed.'

'But why not?' Atara asked, breaking her silence.

'Because the kings dispute everything,' Liljana said. 'Are the Free Kingdoms merely to make a pact to come to each other's defense in case of invasion? Or are they to form an army and navy of their own, and themselves invade the lands held by the Red Dragon? And if so, how many battalions of foot is each kingdom to contribute? How many archers and knights? How many warships? What should be the Alliance's strategy?'

'Fourteen kings,' I said, 'will likely offer fourteen different strategies.'

'Of course they would,' Liljana said, brushing bread crumbs from her lap. 'Of course they have. And that is why everyone realizes, even if they won't admit it, that only one of them can lead the Alliance. King Kiritan is exercising all his power to ensure that *he* is that king.'

'That,' I told her, 'can never be. The Valari kings would never accept any but a Valari to command the Alliance.'

She nodded her head as she wiped her hands on a moistened cloth. 'King Hadaru has made this clear to everyone. King Waray, too. And King Mohan has said that the only one of Valari who could be Lord of the Alliance would be the Lord of Light himself.'

Liljana, having finished eating, turned to look at me with clear eyes that missed very little. I sensed her searching for something deep inside me. I could almost feel her congratulating herself that any noble qualities she found there were at least partly due to her cherishing my soul.

I wiped my hands, too, then broke out a bottle of brandy, which pleased Maram greatly. After filling all our cups, I turned to Liljana and said, 'Then have the Valari kings spoken much of the Maitreya?'

'*All* the kings have spoken of him,' she told me. 'And throughout the whole of the city, there is talk of little else. You can't know how much we Trians have awaited the fulfillment of the ancient prophecies.'

I noticed Atara holding her head utterly still. She seemed to be looking at something outside my tent, past the shadowed, silken walls of time. To Liljana, I said, 'Then is it possible they would entertain the thought of the Maitreya being of the Valari?'

'If that Valari lord was he who had brought the Lightstone out of Argattha,' she said, squeezing my hand again, 'they would welcome him with open hearts and trumpets blowing.'

'And you, Liljana?'

'Why, the questions you ask!' she said, squeezing my hand even more tightly. 'I'd be *overjoyed* for you to claim the Lightstone – if that is truly your fate.'

She paused to take a sip of brandy as she looked at first Atara and then Estrella. And then she said, 'Of course, I'd always hoped that the Maitreya promised to bring in the Age of Light would be a woman.'

We all smiled at this, except Liljana herself. She had never been one to take herself or her own words lightly. But more to the point, ever since she had looked into Morjin's mind in Argattha, she had lost her ability to smile, even as Atara had warned her.

Now it was my turn to squeeze her hand. I said to her, 'But what of the kings at the conclave, then?'

'Some are almost ready to *accept* Valashu Elahad as the Maitreya,' she told me. 'Most of your Valari kings, of course. King Marshayk. And, I think, King Theodor. Even King Aryaman.'

'Ah,' Maram said, staring at his cup, which he had already emptied, 'it is one thing to accept Val as the Maitreya but quite another to make the Maitreya the Lord of the Alliance.'

'True, true,' Liljana said. 'But better the Maitreya as Lord, many say, than King Kiritan himself. Few except Lord Kirriland and the nobles closest to King Kiritan want to see him as a King of Kings.'

'But would they want Val any more?' Maram asked.

'It is to Val's advantage,' Liljana said, 'that he is *not* a king, nor ever likely to be.'

Master Juwain sighed as he rubbed the back of his shiny head. 'From what I remember of Val's last meeting with King Kiritan, it seems unlikely that he will ever accept Val as the Maitreya, much less as Lord of the Alliance.'

'Not unless the other kings accept him first,' Liljana said. 'Then King Kiritan will be forced to bow to their will – either that or to stand alone.'

'My father,' Atara said suddenly, clenching her hands, 'will not suffer *anyone's* will, not even that of thirteen other kings.'

'But he can't want to oppose all the Free Kingdoms!' Maram said.

'No, of course he doesn't,' Liljana told us. 'Which is why he also won't suffer anyone calling Val the Maitreya. And *that* is why I've come here tonight – one of the reasons.'

She put down her cup and brought out her little whale figurine. For a few moments she stared at this bit of blue gelstei. Then she looked at me and said, 'King Kiritan means to challenge you, Val.'

I noticed that Maram and Master Juwain were also staring at me intently. To Liljana, I said, 'To challenge me . . . as man or Maitreya?'

'Perhaps both,' she told me. 'But he will certainly try to discredit your claim to the Lightstone.'

'But how?' I asked her. 'And how do you know?'

I glanced down at her figurine, and so then did Maram. He had always feared that she might peer into his mind as easily as she might open the pages of a book, regardless of all her promises.

'As for how I *know*,' she said to me, 'that is easy to tell. One of my cousins is one of King Kiritan's tasters. She's sniffed out his intentions, so to speak.'

'You mean, one of your sisters of the Maitriche Telu,' Maram said. 'And you mean, she's spied on him.'

Liljana reached out to tap Maram's empty cup as if blaming the brandy for loosening his tongue. 'You should be careful of what you say, young man, and where you say it.'

She looked at Estrella, who sat across from her limned against the tent's thin walls.

'The girl has all our trust,' Maram told her. 'Besides, she's unlettered, and she couldn't tell anyone of what she hears.'

This last, of course, had proved not to be true. All this time, Estrella had sat next to Daj, flashing bright smiles at him, speaking to him in their private way and seemingly ignoring the conversation of her elders.

'Estrella,' I told Liljana, 'is one of us now. Her fate is tied to my own.'

'Do *you* trust her?' Liljana asked me.

Estrella's dark, wild eyes found mine just then, and I said, 'With all my heart. With my life.'

No sooner had these words left my lips then Daj looked me and laughed out, 'Estrella trusts you, too, Val. She even trusts Liljana.'

He turned to smile at Liljana, but she just sat across from him regarding him sternly. And she muttered, 'Impertinent boy.'

Daj, in Argattha, had faced a fire-breathing dragon bravely, but he now fairly wilted beneath Liljana's disapproval. Seeing this, Liljana leaned over and touched his arm. Her voice softened as she said, 'These are matters of life and death, Daj. And not just *our* lives, either.'

Most other boys, and even men, would have looked away from Liljana's relentless gaze. But Daj met her eye to eye. His love for her, I thought, was as deep as his desire to please her. And she obviously loved him as a son. During their months together, it seemed that she had lavished her care and ideals upon him – and forged new chains even harder than the iron shackles that had once encircled his limbs.

After a few moments, Liljana turned toward Estrella and said, 'I'm delighted that you trust me, young lady. But would you trust me with all *your* heart? And with your life?'

Estrella cocked her head as if to ask, 'What do you mean?'

In answer, Liljana held up her blue gelstei and told her, 'I would speak to you with this, in the privacy of our minds, if you'll allow me.'

As we all waited to see how Estrella would respond, she looked deep into Liljana's eyes. She seemed utterly without fear of this powerful woman. Quick as a bird, she nodded her head and smiled at Liljana.

'Very well,' Liljana said, closing her eyes. 'Then listen, listen.'

As my heart beat slowly in my chest like a drum stroke measuring out time, Estrella closed her eyes, too. Liljana sat facing her in silence. She remained utterly still. Not even a jog of her head indicated that she might be hearing anything inside Estrella's mind. Estrella's breaths fell and rose, steady and deep, like my own.

And then, after what seemed an hour, Liljana opened her eyes and sighed. She looked at Master Juwain and then at me. 'It's no use. I can speak to her, but she cannot speak to me.'

'Then her muteness,' Master Juwain said, 'is of the mind as well as the mouth?'

'I think it is *only* of the mind,' Liljana said, gazing at Estrella. 'She has a beautiful mind: most of it is perfectly clear. Like a diamond. Thus she is able to understand others' words. But the part of it that *makes* words of her own and tells her tongue to speak them has been darkened. By Morjin – damn his soul to burn in dragon fire! I saw this in her memories! When she was very young, he used a green gelstei

381

to make her mute, as I presume he did the other slaves that he gave to his priests.'

Every abomination, I thought. *Every twisting of that which is beautiful and good.*

Master Juwain drew out his varistei and regarded it with his sad, gray eyes. How many times, I wondered, had he tried to heal Estrella of her wordless silence?

Liljana reached out to take Estrella's hand in her own. 'Poor girl!' she told her. 'You poor girl!'

Estrella pulled away from her and sat staring at her hand as if grateful that she still had the ability to move her long, expressive fingers as she willed. Her lovely smile told of her delight in her own being, just as it was. Having no pity for herself, she did not welcome Liljana's.

To turn Liljana's attention from her, I looked at her and asked, 'Liljana, you said that King Kiritan would challenge me – do you know how?'

'No, I'm sorry, I don't. I only have my suspicions.'

I took a sip of brandy, then nodded at her to say more. Liljana's suspicions were often more valuable than most people's certainties.

'The one who claims the Lightstone,' she said, 'must also be able to wield it, yes? But wield it *how*? This is the key to everything, I think.'

I brought out the Lightstone then and sat holding it in my hands. For a while, as the little noises of the camp outside my tent quieted and the night deepened, we talked of the ways that it might be used. Liljana hoped to find within its golden hollows the power to grow more gelstei, particularly the green and the blue. With other blue crystals similar to her own, she said, she might speak mind to mind with her sisters in other lands and so coordinate a secret alliance against Morjin. Then, after the great Red Dragon was finally overthrown, new green gelstei could be made to pour out their healing light and restore Ea to the glories of the Age of the Mother. Master Juwain reminded us that Ymiru and his people hoped to use the Lightstone to forge more gold gelstei. He pointed out, too, that the gold gelstei might open doors to other worlds: whether for ill, as in freeing Angra Mainyu from Damoom, or for the great good of inviting angels to walk once again on Ea.

'I don't believe,' Liljana said, 'that King Kiritan will challenge Val to summon Ashtoreth into his hall. Nor to stamp out new gelstei as his mint does coins. No, the power of the Maitreya that most people speak of is the power to heal.'

He will be a healer, I thought, recalling the words of 'The Trian Prophecies.' *From his eyes will pour a healing light.*

I looked at Liljana and said, 'To heal, yes – but heal *how*? To take away people's hatred? To end war?'

Master Juwain nodded toward me and said, 'In the amphitheater, the ghost spoke of healing Angra Mainyu of his fear of death. What great beings we all would be if this evil were lifted from our hearts!'

I felt my own heart beating hard and quick. And then Liljana told me, 'People are saying that the Maitreya will heal the crippled and the ill.'

I glanced at Atara, but if she was aware that I was looking at her, she gave no sign of if.

'King Kiritan,' Liljana said, 'has invited the blacksmith's son, Joakim, to stay at the palace. No one knows why.'

'We heard a story,' Maram said, 'that this Joakim had healed the blind.'

Now we all looked at Atara. She pulled at the cloth binding her face, but said nothing.

'*That* story,' Liljana said, 'has been embellished. In Joakim's village, they claim only that he healed an old man of an eye catarrh and straightened the legs of a girl with rickets. But this might be enough for King Kiritan to put him forth as the Maitreya.'

I squeezed the Cup of Heaven between my hands and watched its golden contours catch the lamp's flickering light. I asked, 'What sort of man is Joakim?'

'I should hardly call him a *man*,' Liljana said. 'He's still a beardless boy, really, and simple like his fellow villagers. Some say *simple-minded*.'

'Then he would not be one to be considered to lead the Alliance?'

'Hardly.'

Maram picked up the brandy bottle and refilled his cup. He said, 'How convenient for King Kiritan.'

Master Juwain nodded his head, then asked Liljana, 'Then is King Kiritan to use this story to discredit Val? His own emissary has witnessed Val's healing of Baltasar's *spirit*. Surely this miracle should weigh against any mere healing of the flesh.'

As he spoke, he turned his green gelstei between his rough, old fingers. I had seen him use this crystal to mend a fatal wound that an arrow had drilled into Atara's lung – all in a matter of moments. But how many times, I wondered, had he failed to heal her of her blindness?

'I don't know what the King intends,' Liljana said. 'But stories are only stories. King Kiritan – and all the kings – might want it proved to their eyes that Val is who he claims to be.'

'So far,' I said, gazing at the Lightstone, 'nothing is claimed.'

'So far,' she said wryly. Then she searched my face and asked, 'What is it *you* intend, Val?'

I took a deep breath and held it a moment before saying, 'The Lightstone holds the powers of all the other gelstei, yes? Thus it has the power to heal. I *know* that it does.'

'Go on,' Liljana said, fixing her large eyes upon me.

I looked at Estrella, who was smiling at Daj, and then at Atara sitting so still and grave as she waited for fate to unfold. I said, 'It's not a question of bending King Kiritan to my will, or to anyone's. He must be won. It must be proven to him that I am the Maitreya.'

'Go on,' Liljana said again.

'If I could make Estrella speak again or Atara to see, then –'

'No, Val!' Atara said suddenly, cutting me off. 'Not this way! Not in my father's hall!'

'I must know,' I said to her as gently as I could. I felt the Lightstone giving a soft, warm radiance into my hands. If I had touched a piece of coal just then, I thought, it would light up like the sun. 'Everyone must know. Surely the time has come.'

It nearly broke my heart to see Atara clenching her hands as she silently shook her head.

'It may be,' I said, 'that King Kiritan thinks to bring forth this black-smith's boy as a sort of champion to make his challenge. But what if it were *I* who first challenged him?'

'That's it, Val,' Maram said after gulping down some more brandy. 'Take the battle to the enemy!'

I did not like thinking of King Kiritan as the 'enemy.' But the principle that Maram espoused was sound enough. If I were the one to issue the challenge, then it would take much of wind out of King Kiritan's sails.

Master Juwain tapped his fingernail against his green crystal. He bowed his head toward Atara. 'What you propose is dangerous! To give eyes once more to Atara might be beyond the ability of even the Maitreya.'

'Perhaps,' I said. Then I turned toward Estrella. 'But Liljana has told that Morjin has darkened a part of this girl's mind. I *know* that the Lightstone can be used to brighten it again.'

Master Juwain rubbed his smooth head and frowned at me. 'Even if you're right, Val, even if you *are* the Maitreya, which I believe with all my heart, I'm afraid it will take time to learn to use the Lightstone once you've claimed it. There is still much we have to learn.'

So saying, he put away his varistei and took out the akashic crystal instead. Its swirls of gold and glorre, I knew, contained much wisdom. But surely the Lightstone held the very secrets of the universe.

'What if you fail?' he asked me. .

I looked into the gleaming surface of the Lightstone and saw a bright being of adamantine resolve looking back at me. 'I won't fail,' I said.

'But what if you do?'

'If I fail, I fail. Then the kings will have to choose another to lead the Alliance.'

Master Juwain gazed at me. Finally, he said, 'There are still some hours between now and tomorrow. Will you at least reconsider your plan?'

And Liljana added, 'Please do think about this carefully.'

Atara's cold, beautiful face, as I looked across our circle, reminded me that no one could see all the consequences of an act. Even Estrella seemed unsure whether she wished to be made whole again. Daj assured me that she desired with all her heart to be able to talk to birds and sing songs to the sunrise. But then he added that she could do that, in her own way, already. As I gazed at this luminous and happy child, playing with the curls of her dark hair, I wondered, who was I to think of taking her from her secret, silent garden into the wider world where people might twist her utterances to their own ends and ensnare her in webs of words and yet more words?

'I wish Kane were here,' I said, turning to Liljana. 'He, of all men, would know about the Maitreya. Have you *seen* him, then?'

'Not since Viradar, when he left Tria without warning me,' she told me. 'But that brings me to the second reason I've come here tonight. I have a letter for you.'

She reached into the pocket of her cloak and removed a square of ivory paper, sealed with a bubble of blood-red wax. She handed it to me and said, 'This arrived two weeks ago. The man who delivered it said that I was to give it to you before you entered the conclave. He said it was urgent that you read it as soon as possible.'

'This man,' I said, pressing my finger against the letter's hard seal, 'was he of the Black Brotherhood?'

'I believe so. But he wasn't any more eager to tell me about himself than I was to tell him about *myself*, if you know what I mean.'

She drummed her fingers against her palm, waiting for me to open it. I sensed that she was near the end of her patience. The letter was addressed to me in a bold, clear hand. I drew out my dagger and broke the seal. The letter was a single sheet of paper dated the 30th of Ashte, 2813 – barely a week before Salmelu and the Red Priests had defiled my father's hall and I had set out for the Tournament at Nar. The words set into the paper in black ink, on both sides, were also bold, but less clear, as if Kane had written them in great haste. This is what I read:

385

Valashu,

I am sending copies of this to Liljana in Tria and to your father's castle, for it is vital that you know why I have taken to the road again. I am not sure where this letter will find you, but find you it must. For you are in great danger. Morjin has recovered from the wound that you dealt him, as I said he would. He seeks his revenge. I have learned that he has summoned three assassins from the world of Khutar. You must know their nature, for they are not human – not just human. They are called the Skakamen. You may think of them as the Half-Elijin: they who have gained some of the virtues of greater beings but have been denied immortality due to a sickness of the soul. Even so, they possess great hardiness, strength, cunning and the ability to heal their flesh of almost any wound. So, they have the power to shape their own flesh as they will. Thus they can take on the shape of the victims that they hunt and slay – or any shape at all.

The first of these assassins, Elman, I have hunted, and I have sent him back to the stars. I have found the trail of the second assassin, Urman, and him I will pursue as well. The third assassin has eluded me. His name is Noman. Beware this Skakaman, for he will use all his wiles to murder you and steal the Lightstone. Trust no one! Watch your back! Look into the hearts of everyone, even those closest to you! If any bear you ill will, slay him out of hand before he slays you!

I will help you execute this Skakaman, too. I expect that you will make the journey to Tria, with all the others who would join against Morjin. Look for me there. Look to the Lightstone and guard it for the Maitreya. Morjin must not gain it back! That he has summoned three Skakamen from Khutar without its aid bodes ill. So, he must be close, very close, to being able to open a portal to Damoom and freeing Angra Mainyu as well.

Know that if he succeeds, it will be the end of everything. I may have led you to believe that with the Baaloch's defeat, the War of the Stone was concluded. It was not. The war goes on, and has been fought on other worlds all during the ages of Ea. I believe that it will be won – or lost – here on our world within the next few years. You cannot know the peril. You have been told of the Dark Worlds. But the Ieldra will never allow the whole of Eluru to darken. Just as the universe was created in the progression of Galadin into the Ieldra, the Ieldra will be forced to destroy their handiwork if the Galadin fail to lead a great progression into the Age of Light.

And so the Lightstone must be placed in the Maitreya's hands, and soon. And so we must bring Morjin down at any cost. **At any cost!**

Kane

386

'Well,' Maram said to me when I looked up from the sheet of paper that I was clenching, '*another* letter. Aren't you going to read it to us?'

I took a sip of brandy to moisten my throat. And then I did as Maram had requested. After I had finished, I sat gazing at the lamp's little light.

'Dark worlds, indeed!' he cried out. 'The end of all things! Too much! Too much!'

Again, he refilled his cup with brandy, and downed it in nearly a single gulp. He wiped the tears from his eyes and coughed out, 'A Skakaman, too! Well, now we know what killed our poor knights. A shape-shifter, as in the old tales! Ah, well, I suppose that's better than a ghost.'

Daj and Estrella sat holding hands as they stared at each other in dread of this new horror that had been unleashed upon their world. Atara stared off into a dark landscape of her own that I did not wish to behold. And Master Juwain tapped his finger against Kane's letter and said to me, 'I see, I see. It's all made clear now. All that has happened for ill since that night in your father's castle was wrought by this Noman.'

He went on to say that Noman must have entered Mesh disguised as one of Salmelu's emissaries. No doubt Salmelu murdered Kasandra and the scryers, in part to keep them from explaining their prophecy that a man with no face would show me my own, and so give Noman away. It was certainly Noman, he said, who used a sleep stone to incapacitate the Guardians; only my timely arrival kept him from stealing the Lightstone from my father's hall that very night. And it was Noman who had nearly assassinated me outside of Nar.

'The Skakaman,' Master Juwain said to me, 'must have followed us from Silvassu. And when we made camp, he must have followed Sivar of Godhra into the copse where he went to collect firewood. And there murdered him. And there mimed him, taking on his form. And then returned to camp to murder *you*.'

I looked at the Lightstone where I had set it down in front of me. I rubbed my head where Noman, disguised as Sivar, had nearly brained me with his mace. Then I looked up and said, 'Then I wasn't wrong about Sivar! He was no ghul!'

'No, he was not,' Master Juwain agreed. 'He was just another knight whose face Noman stole. As he stole *your* face, Val. He must have followed us to the amphitheater and tricked Baltasar and the Guardians away from their post. And then followed us. It wouldn't have been hard for him to lure Sar Varald and the others into the woods, to their doom, if they thought he was you.'

Maram poured some more brandy into my cup, then asked the question on all our minds: 'Do you think he's still miming you? And if he's not, who is he now?'

None of us wished to venture a guess. But Atara suddenly turned toward me and said, 'He'll murder and mime someone in my father's palace.'

'Have you *seen* this, Atara?' I asked.

'Only with the eye of reason,' she said with a grim smile. 'Morjin will want to keep you from claiming the Lightstone – at any cost. And so he'll want Noman to strike you down before you can unite the kings against him. Where better to murder you except in the palace, or in its grounds?'

Where, indeed, I wondered as I looked at the blindfold encircling her head? And then I asked her, 'But what does this Noman look like when he's *not* miming another?'

'I don't know,' she told me. 'I can *almost* see him. Almost.'

We all fell quiet for a few moments and sat sipping our brandy. And then Maram muttered, 'Ah, this is too much, too much.'

'Courage, my friend,' I said, clapping him on his shoulder. 'Three times Noman has failed to murder me and steal the Lightstone. I *know* that he will fail again.'

I smiled at him, and felt all my bright hope for the future passing into him and warming his insides with a fire more sustaining than that of the brandy.

'All right, all right,' he said, 'courage I shall have, or at least act as if I have. What else is there to do?'

He smiled back at me and clasped my hand with his fat, strong fingers.

'It's late,' Liljana announced, looking at us. 'We should all go to bed and get some rest for tomorrow.'

As it seemed there was nothing more to say, we took Liljana's words to heart and bade each other goodnight. Atara kissed Liljana, and went out to rejoin Karimah. An extra tent was found for Liljana and Daj, while Estrella went off to sleep next to Lord Harsha and Behira. Master Juwain and Maram spread out their sleeping furs inside my pavilion.

Despite the need, I slept poorly that night. I mourned Sar Hannu and Sar Varald, and the other fallen Guardians. I wondered whose face Noman would take on next? And most of all, I lay awake looking out at the stars and dreaming of the fulfillment of all my plans in Ea's most ancient city. Kings were waiting for me there. All of time and history, it seemed, was waiting for me to enter Tria and finally claim the Lightstone.

27

On a brilliantly clear morning, with the sun pouring down like liquid gold upon my columns of knights, we passed through Tria's Varkoth Gate. Its immense, iron doors, wrought with the likeness of the great Galadin for which it was named, were flung open, and once again we looked upon the City of Light. Ahead of us rose three of Tria's seven hills, covered with fine marble houses and gardens and palaces – and the Tower of the Sun and the Tower of the Moon. These great spires were cast of living stone, which shimmered in the early sunlight like the whitest and purest of pearls. Indeed, much of the city was raimented in this glorious substance. It seemed to breathe its radiance into the very air so that Tria's thousands of buildings sent streamers of light, like invocations, toward the heavens.

This ancient place, I thought, bespoke humanity's highest aspirations and hopes – as well as our failings. On top of Tria's greatest hill stood King Kiritan's enormous palace, with its nine golden domes gleaming above the emerald trees and lawns of the nearby Elu Gardens. But to reach this lofty abode, we first had to pass through a district of tenements and dark alleys whose rotting timbers suggested that nothing ever built on Ea could attain to the eternal. That was the way of things in Tria, splendor amid squalor, nobles living elbow to elbow with beggars, the perfume of flowering trees tainted with the reek of rubbish and ordure that people dumped into the gutters of the streets.

I, who had once beheld the rainbow hues of Alundil, the jeweled City of the Stars high in the White Mountains, knew that much more than this was possible. For I had seen the dwellings of the Star People, there and in my dreams. These, no less the Lightstone, I brought with me toward the conclave of the kings. My spirits soared like a flock of swans. Although the deaths of my five Guardians saddened me, I knew that they had died protecting the Lightstone, even as they had vowed. And now I must live to fulfill my fate.

From the moment that our columns of horses clopped up the street leading from the Varkoth Gate, Trians in their hundreds and thousands came out of their houses and lined the way. Rich and poor, dressed in silks or rags, they crowded in close to witness the astonishing sight of Sarni warriors and Valari knights in our diamond armor entering their city together. An old man shaking a tin cup cried out that the Maitreya had come among them again, as the ancient prophecies had foretold. Well-dressed women bearing baskets of flowers cast rose petals at me and onto the street ahead of me. They clamored for a glimpse of the Lightstone as they ran up to me and laid their hands on my legs or tugged at the fabric of my surcoat.

Liljana gave me to understand that King Kiritan had forbidden such displays. But many of our welcomers were of the houses of the Hastars, Eriades, Kirrilands and Marshans: four of the ancient Five Families who, for thousands of years, had contended with the Narmadas for the throne. And so they ignored the wishes of their king. They opened their hearts to me. And I, who had passed so hopefully through the walls of their city, finally threw open the gates in the walls surrounding my own heart. I drank in the cheering of the multitudes as a parched man might water. It seemed that I could not get enough of this wondrous sound. In the cries of those who swarmed around me was an ageless and beautiful yearning. I felt this great dream inside myself, ennobling me and washing clean all my fears. As the Trians' joy raised me up to the greatest heights, where I could almost lay my hand upon the sun, I felt myself immortal.

For most of an hour we climbed up Hastar Hill, with its fine palaces, and then made our way through Eluli Square and up the higher Narmada Hill overlooking the whole of the city. I gazed out upon miles of gleaming buildings offset by spaces of green. The great Star Bridge, also called the Golden Band, spanned the Poru, which divided the city into east and west. Far out in the glimmering blue bay into which the river emptied loomed the skull-shaped island of Damoom. For all the Age of Law, Morjin had been imprisoned there. I knew that soon he would be thrown down and brought there again – either that, or slain. From the thousands of people crowding the streets, I heard demands for deliverance from Morjin's evil that had lain so heavily upon the world for so long. And so I promised them, and myself, that I would never rest until the Red Dragon was utterly defeated.

At last we crested the hill and came to a gate set into the low wall surrounding the King's palace. A small army of guards dressed in the blue-and-gold livery of the House Narmada met us there, for word of our arrival had gone ahead. Although these grim-faced guards did not cast rose petals or give voice to cheers, their eyes seemed to sparkle and shower me with hope. But they were watchful and wary, too, at the sight of so many Valari knights and Sarni warriors making their way toward the great dwelling of their king.

Waiting with them was a herald named Jasson, who escorted us along the oak-lined road leading to the palace. This small, punctilious man informed us that we had missed most of the morning's proceedings. As we rode with him past lush lawns covered with chirping sparrows, he also warned us not to trample King Kiritan's precious grass; anyone caught hunting the King's deer in the woods of the nearby Narmada Green, he said, would be put to death. This injunction, with all the other rules and protocols that he laid upon us, provoked Sajagax's proud warriors. When we dismounted in front of the white colonnades of the palace, Baldarax and Thadrak stalked about the grass gripping their bows and threatening to shoot arrows into any of the grooms who came to take their horses. I felt their sharp, blue eyes, like daggers, chiseling off the gold veneer from the gleaming domes above us. If it hadn't been for Sajagax's fierce scowls, they might have blundered their way into a battle with the ranks of guards posted on the steps leading up to the palace.

Sajagax looked up at the magnificent dome of King Kiritan's Throne Room that soared above us. 'The Trians have always been great builders,' Sajagax said, 'but the curve of the open sky pleases me more.'

In truth, he hated almost everything about being locked up inside this city within a city. He was loathe to enter the palace and sit in chairs, as he put it, 'With a dungheap of stones piled up above my head.' I noticed his thick finger tracing out zagging signs in the air as if to strengthen any enchantment that kept the palace from collapsing into a pile of rubble.

Jasson informed us that Sajagax's guard and my knights would have to remain outside. He invited our men to encamp on one of the lawns behind the palace. Ten companions only, he said, we each might take with us into King Kiritan's hall. And so Sajagax chose out Baldarax, Zekii, Orox, Thadrak and six other warriors to act as his escort. I asked Lansar Raasharu, Baltasar and Sunjay Naviru to accompany me. And Skyshan of Ki, Sar Shivathar, Sar Jarlath and Lord Noldru the Bold – Sar Juralad and Sar Kimball as well. And, of course, Lord Harsha. Maram was accounted a prince of Delu, and therefore allowed into the conclave on his own right. And so with Liljana, as a scion of one of Tria's oldest families, and Daj as her servant. Master Juwain was honored as were all of his Brotherhood. The herald reluctantly permitted Behira and Estrella, who bore no weapons, to remain with us. And as for Atara, who bore both a saber *and* her great bow, who could think to deny entrance to King Kiritan's daughter and only legitimate child?

And so Jasson led us into the palace and through the southern doorway of King Kiritan's throne room. This immense circular space, with its great dome glowing with sunlight high above, teemed with people, living and dead. The mighty of ages past seemed to haunt the hall like ghosts. Here, in 2736 of the Age of Law, the aged King Eluli had stood before the Council of Twenty and proposed that Katura Ashlan of Delu succeed him and so become Ea's first High Queen. Two centuries later my ancestor, King Julamesh, had brought the Lightstone here from Mesh and had delivered it into Godavanni's hands – only to see Godavanni murdered by Morjin and the Lightstone stolen. I remembered very well standing here myself with three thousand others little more than a year ago and vowing to gain it back. I could almost hear the voices of the many Questers raised up in hope and echoing from the curved, white stones of the walls. I could almost hear, as well, the cheers of the thousands who had come here today to witness the forging of a great new alliance and fill their eyes with the golden radiance of the Lightstone.

Jasson's high, piercing voice rang out like the whine of a saw as he announced us to the throngs of Alonians, Delians, Thalunes and others who crowded the hall. We made our way down the aisle leading to the great, jewel-encrusted throne raised up at the hall's very center, and all eyes turned upon us. In the hall's northern quadrants were gathered brightly-dressed men and women of almost every station: artisans, lordless knights, lesser merchants and even peasants, all of whom stood packed together shoulder to shoulder craning their necks. A long line of guards held back this mob with their rectangular shields locked together.

The hall's southern quadrants were full of many long tables lined up on both sides of the aisle. The favored and the high sat at these in comfort to witness the great proceedings. To my right, at the table nearest the throne, I saw Breyonan Eriades, Ravik Kirriland, Davinan Hastar, Hanitan Marshan and other princes of the Five Families. The great lords of Alonia's domains crowded the table next to them like so many lions growling at each other over a kill: Baron Monteer of Iviendenhall, Baron Maruth of the Aquantir, Duke Ashvar, Count Muar and Old Duke Parran of Jerolin, whose cleft nose and harsh gray eyes reminded all that he was a fighting lord among lords used to battle and death. It shocked me to see Duke Malatam sitting next to him. Why had he come here, I wondered? This little man rubbed his thin face nervously and regarded me like a whipped dog begging me to forgive him for soiling a carpet.

On my left, also near the throne, was the table of the greatest of Tria's Five Families: the Narmadas. There sat a bull-necked lord named Belur Narmada and the King's cousin, Count Dario, whose cool blue eyes peered out at me from beneath his rings of flaming red hair. There, too, Queen Daryana should have joined him taking morning tea with King Kiritan's other kinsman. But I looked across the room to see this handsome woman sitting on the *other* side of the aisle, at the table behind that of the Five Families. As I soon learned, she had quarreled with King Kiritan. A queen, she had argued, when entertaining guests, should always sit at table with her king. But on this day, at least, King Kiritan had proclaimed that he would sit only with other kings or their heirs. And so he had commanded her to sit next to Count Dario. Because she would not be commanded, she had taken a chair with the dozen chamberlains, scribes, stewards, chancellors and others of King Kiritan's household. She gazed at Atara, and at me, as we made our way down the aisle toward the largest table in the hall.

This was a great wheel of white oak set just beneath King Kiritan's throne. King Kiritan had ordered it crafted and carved just for this occasion. Around it were placed massive chairs occupied by the sovereigns of Ea's Free Kingdoms. It was King Kiritan's conceit that at such a table, none could claim precedence by sitting at its head. But I noticed that King Kiritan's chair was positioned precisely in front of the throne. The sculptures of the sacred animals on the steps leading up to it, and the great golden throne itself, thus seemed to frame King Kiritan and to impart to him much of their magnificence. I noticed, too, that the kings he deemed most important were seated closest to him. On his right, next to an empty chair, were King Theodor of the Elyssu and Maram's father, King Santoval Marshayk. And on his left: King Hanniban, King Tal, and King Aryaman of Thalu, who was well-named, for in this yellow-haired giant of a man was said to live again the Aryan sea kings of old. The Valari kings, I saw, had been relegated to the table's southern half, farthest from King Kiritan. Next to King Aryaman sat King Waray. And next to *him*, around the wheel of the table, sat King Sandarkan, King Danashu and Prince Viromar, who had turned to bow his head to me as I walked nearer. The chair next to my cousin was conspicuously empty; next to it waited King Mohan, also turned toward me, and then King Kurshan and King Hadaru. This old bear of a man fixed his black eyes upon me as if to say, 'Well, Valashu Elahad, we Valari have gathered here, as you asked us. Now what will you *do?*'

At a word from King Kiritan, all the kings at the central table, and the men and women at the other tables, rose to their feet. King Kiritan invited Sajagax to sit next to him; he motioned for me to take the empty chair directly across the table from him. In his strong, rich voice, he called out to me: 'You come late to our conclave, Prince Valashu. But we should all be glad that you have indeed finally come. The world might not wait upon laggards, even one who calls himself the Lord Guardian of the Lightstone. We, however, have waited. With great patience. And so, please, sit and unburden yourself.'

As he stood staring at me with his piercing, blue eyes, someone from the mob behind him cried out, 'Maitreya! Lord of Light!'

Two of the guards immediately drove into the mob gripping their heavy spears and using their shields to shove people aside. They closed in on a large, shaggy peasant, whose gray wool tunic was eaten with holes. I could not hear what the guards said to him. But the man suddenly bowed his head as the guards pressed him from either side and escorted him down the line of guards and out of the hall.

King Kiritan did not deign to turn and witness this chastisement. His square, stern face was stamped with his will to order his realm and all that his prideful eyes looked upon. He stood stiffly and almost too straight; his large, well-made head seemed to push the nine points of his golden crown up toward the heavens as if in challenge. He was splendidly attired, in his white ermine mantle and his blue tunic embroidered with gold lions. In his golden hair was a little more silver than I remembered, and his red beard was shot full of gray; even so, he seemed somehow even more vital and powerful, as if the great events of the last year had ignited a fire in him and called him to greatness. I couldn't help staring at the circular scar on his cheek, where Queen Daryana had once bitten him in one of their disputes. She, at least, held no awe for Ea's foremost king.

Following his lead, we all sat at his round table, and the others in the hall took their places. Liljana and Daj walked over to a table in the third row to my right, behind a table of King Kiritan's retainers and in front of a dozen richly dressed merchants. Maram contented himself with joining Lansar Raasharu, Baltasar and the other Guardians at a table that had been set aside for them along the aisle back toward the hall's southern doors. They were in good company, though, for the knights in the retinues of the Valari kings shared the tables nearby. On the opposite side of the aisle, Master Juwain greeted others of his Brotherhood whom King Kiritan had summoned to the conclave. Atara might have shared a table with Orox and Sajagax's warriors or taken an empty seat next to Count Dario and the other

Narmadas; instead, she decided to sit with her mother. Many people watched with amazement as she strode straight down the lane between the tables. And then, suddenly, her second sight seemed to fail her, and she was reduced for the last few paces to feeling her way with her unstrung bow, tapping its horn-hard end against the floorstones and the edges of the tables.

King Kiritan glanced at his daughter without compassion, and then returned to staring straight at me. He called out, 'We have heard that you have brought the Lightstone here, as you vowed to do. Let us see it, then!'

The hall grew quiet. And so I stood and drew it forth. I held it high above my head.

'It *is* the Lightstone!' someone cried out. 'Truly it is!'

I saw that King Aryaman was staring at me as a wolf might his prey. King Hanniban, a thickset and ruthless man renowned for his cunning in having survived Kallimun plots for most of his seventy years, regarded me as he pulled at his snowy beard. It was said that he thought about death too much, and feared it mightily. It was said, too, that he drank mothers' milk at his meals in order to forestall the ravages of old age. His greed to lay his old hands upon the Lightstone sickened me. I could almost hear him calculating how to relieve me of my burden.

'We must congratulate you,' King Kiritan said to me, 'on stealing this from the Red Dragon's throne room. Now, deliver it to us, as you also vowed.'

I moved not an inch as I stared right back at him. And then I told him, 'I made no such vow. None of us did who entered Argattha or undertook the Quest.'

'You swore to seek the Lightstone for all of Ea and not yourself!'

'And here it is,' I said, 'brought through mountains, steppes and forests, guarded by great knights from brigands and treacheries, for Ea, and not for myself.'

'That is not what we have heard,' King Kiritan told me. 'Even now, here in this hallowed house of Ea's High Kings, the safest of all places, you grip the golden cup as if it were an heirloom of *your* house that you claim by right.'

I glanced at Baron Monteer and then Count Muar, a rapier-thin man whose deadly stare gave one the impression that he could strike as quickly as a snake. Absent from the table of these great lords was Baron Narcavage, who had been killed the year before on King Kiritan's own lawn in a plot to assassinate King Kiritan – and me. I looked farther out into the room, at the heavily armored guards lined up behind the throne and posted by the four doors. Any one of these, I thought, any one of the knights and nobles sitting at the tables or the tradesmen standing and staring at me might be the Skakaman, Noman, in disguise. How many hundreds of men and women, in their coverings of cloaks, bright tunics, armor and flesh were gathered in this great hall, the safest of all places?

'Nothing has yet been claimed,' I said once again, turning back to King Kiritan. 'And I *am* the Lord Guardian of the Lightstone, and so it is upon me to see that it is placed in the hands of the Maitreya.'

'Maitreya,' he snapped out. 'Lord Guardian. Who appointed you so? By what right? And from whom do you guard the Lightstone? King Marshayk? King Kaiman? Ourselves?'

Next to King Hadaru, King Kaiman nodded his red-haired head toward me. And next to *him*, King Santoval Marshayk, who looked much like an older and even fatter Maram, flashed a jolly smile at me, showing his brown, sugar-eaten teeth.

Without warning, from behind me, Baltasar suddenly leapt up from his table and pointed his finger at Duke Malatam. He cried out, 'We guard the Lightstone from your own back-stabbing lords, King Kiritan!'

Duke Malatam's face flushed bright red. Count Muar's hand fell upon the hilt of his sword. Lansar Raasharu, without rising, reached out to grasp his impetuous son's arm and pull him back to his seat. And King Kiritan barked out, 'Duke Malatam has journeyed here to make apologies for his misjudgment. He shall himself be judged at the appropriate time. In any case, we are not in Tarlan but in Tria.'

He continued staring at the Lightstone as he addressed me, 'If you truly guard this for all of Ea, Valashu Elahad, then allow all of Ea to behold it – and to hold it in our hands, even as you do.'

So saying, he nodded at Prince Viromar, sitting to my right, and at King Danashu next to him.

It seemed that I had no choice but to pass on the Lightstone, and so this I did. Prince Viromar took the cup from me and studied it for a few moments before giving it to King Danashu. The Valari kings were no strangers to its radiant warmth, and they did not linger over it. Quickly the cup made its way to King Sandarkan and King Waray, who hesitated only a moment before setting it into King Aryaman's hands. It seemed lost there. King Aryaman was bigger even than Sajagax, with a bushy red beard, yellow hair and eyes as blue and cold as ice. His arms were as thick as most men's thighs, the better to swing the axe that was buckled to his waist. An old wound to his lip made him seem that he was sneering at others, even when he was not. He was the strong king of an island people ravaged and weakened by centuries of

396

blood-feuds, and I could feel in him a raging desire to make Thalu great again.

'The Cup of Heaven!' he called out in a voice like rolling thunder. 'What a great weapon has been given us, if only we have the wit to use it.'

He gripped the little cup so hard that it seemed he might crumple it. But one might as well try to crush a diamond. With a heavy sigh, he passed the cup to King Tal, said to be a great scholar of the gelstei and perhaps the most intelligent of Ea's kings. He looked at it for a long while, turning it around and around in his long, lithe hands. Then he gave it to King Hanniban. This old man held it close to his mouth as if he could drink in its light with his bluish lips. It took all his will, it seemed, to turn it over to King Kiritan.

The moment that this aspiring King of Kings touched the Lightstone, I nearly whipped out my sword and lunged across the table at him. For I felt *his* will to claim the Lightstone for himself as surely as I did the wild beating of my heart against my ribs. All of his vainglory and lust for power – and his malice toward me – beat against me like a battering ram. It crushed the air from me, and for a moment I could not draw breath.

'Very good, Valashu Elahad,' he said to me. His blue eyes were now lit up like glowing sapphires. 'Very good.'

He glanced toward the hall's west door at a tall, scarred graybeard decked out in full armor and gripping the hilt of his sword. I took him to be the captain of the guard. The way that King Kiritan looked at him sent a thrill of fear shooting through me.

'Indeed,' he said, speaking to King Aryaman, and to everyone present, 'the Lightstone *has* been given us to be used for a great purpose – the greatest of purposes.'

His rough, strong hands folded around the golden cup as if making a prayer. It seemed that he was waiting for something.

My attention was drawn to a young man sitting at the Narmada table and I knew without being told that this must be Joakim, the blacksmith's son. He was about my age, and his hamlike hands were blackened from coal dust. He seemed uncomfortable in a new tunic stretched too tight across his massive chest and shoulders. His thick forehead, broad face and dull, brown eyes gave him something of the appearance of an ox. His easy smile was full of longing and wonder as he gazed at the Lightstone.

I sensed King Kiritan's awareness of him, and I expected that he might turn and address him. But he ignored him. Instead, he gripped the Lightstone even more tightly, and called out into the hall: 'Surely it is the will of the One that the Lightstone has returned to Tria, where it belongs. Its promise has drawn Ea's free kings here, to make alliance. What a great thing this is! When we called the Quest a year ago on our birthday, we knew that fate would deliver it into our hands. Many of you made vows to regain the Lightstone for all of Ea – but how is all of Ea to use this greatest of all the gelstei? Surely one, and only one, can wield it in Ea's name.'

'The Maitreya!' Baltasar suddenly cried out, again leaping up from his chair. Only Lansar Raasharu's steely grip on his arm kept him from drawing his sword. 'This we all know: the Lightstone is for the Maitreya!'

'Indeed, indeed,' King Kiritan said, 'but until he comes forth, others must use it as best they can.'

Now I pushed back my chair with a harsh, stuttering of wood against smooth stone, and I stood up, too. I called out to King Kiritan: 'No, others may *not* use the Lightstone as you say.'

'*You* say this, who has used it to draw your Valari kings here?'

'It is one thing,' I said, 'to call others to gather around a great light. It is another to wield this light oneself.'

The sound of another chair scraping over the floor broke out into the quiet of the hall. And Count Muar stood and called out, 'Prince Valashu confuses the issue! By what right do the Valari keep the Lightstone? By *force*, I say, they keep it – as I've said before. And by force alone they will be compelled to surrender it!'

His words caused all the Guardians to spring up and clasp the hilts of their swords. And Baltasar shouted at Count Muar, 'Are you calling for a battle? Then battle you shall have!'

King Kiritan turned his bright gaze from me to regard the fierce King Mohan and King Kurshan, and the other Valari kings, whose hands also gripped their swords. The knights in their retinues, sitting at their tables, looked toward them for sign that they should draw and set upon Count Muar and his men – or upon anyone who challenged a Valari's honor. On the lawn outside the palace, all my other Guardians stood ready to battle to the death, if only I could call to them. Even Sajagax and his warriors seemed unprepared to see King Kiritan appropriate the Lightstone.

'When the time comes, the Lightstone *will* be taken by force,' King Kiritan said, gripping the cup between his hands. 'But by the force of reason, fate, even love. Until then, it will be guarded as it has been. No one has suggested otherwise.'

And with that, he glared at me even as he passed the Cup of Heaven to Sajagax. He motioned for Count Muar to take his seat, and we all joined him in sitting back down in our chairs.

Sajagax traced his calloused finger around the contours of the golden cup as he regarded King Kiritan. Although King Kiritan had reserved the place of honor for him, I knew that Sajagax took little honor in sitting to King Kiritan's immediate right. 'Keep your friends close, and your enemies closer' – this was a cherished Sarni maxim, no less that of the more civilized Alonians. King Kiritan had wed Sajagax's daughter only to blunt the arrows of one of his deadliest enemies, and he had never ceased treating Daryana as something of a barbarian. Sajagax's love for Daryana, with her still-golden hair and bright, blue eyes full of adoration for her father, was like an arrow piercing my own heart. I wondered if King Kiritan suspected that Sajagax regarded Daryana as too good for him, and not the opposite.

'Reason,' Sajagax said to King Kiritan in his bull's horn of a voice, 'is a great, good thing. It was reason, was it not, that impelled us to ally our lands by marriage when a thousand years of bad blood would have it otherwise? And thus reason should prevail in leading others into alliance with us in order to bring this light that Valashu Elahad speaks of into *all* lands. And to bring the Law of the One. Why else has the Cup of Heaven come to us? I care not to hear more arguments as to claims and rights. Prince Valashu has spirited this gelstei out of Argattha and guarded it successfully so far. Let him continue to guard it until the Maitreya comes forth.'

So saying, he gave the Lightstone to King Theodor, who rather quickly passed it on to King Santoval Marshayk. This great whale of a man was the largest in the room – indeed, in almost any room. He was the only king besides Kiritan to wear a crown: a splendid working of gold set with large rubies on each of its points. His fingers were heavy with fat and jeweled rings, his jewel-embroidered silks glittered almost like Valari battle armor. Even as he examined the Lightstone, he nibbled on a honey cake, which he washed down with copious amounts of mulled wine. His face was as red as a beet. Jasson had told me that he had brought with him part of his harem, and had taken over several rooms of the palace. He was, I thought, what Maram might have become if not for the grace of the One.

'So *this* is the little trinket that Prince Maram Marshayk lifted from the Dark City,' he said. Because he was wroth with Maram for taking on the sword of a Valari knight, among other things, he would not look at him or refer to him as his son. But he didn't mind loudly speaking his name, the better to call more glory to the house of Marshayk. 'If the Lightstone remains here in Tria, then surely it will invite the Red Dragon's attack. I would like to say again that should his armies march, Delu stands ready to march to Alonia's aid.'

His blustering speech prompted cheers from his retainers at the Delian table, but from no one else. Everyone doubted his willingness to fight the Red Dragon – and his ability.

With a lingering look, he gave the cup to King Kaiman. At thirty years of age, he was a young king, and a bold one. He had curly red hair and restless blue eyes; he was himself restless, moving about in his chair like a flaming torch aggravated by a hot, southern wind. Some said that he was a king in name only, for with the fall of Surrapam, he had been forced into exile. About him was an air of desperation to return to his land and free his conquered people.

He stared into the Lightstone's mirror-like surface as he said to King Marshayk, 'Would you then pledge to march as far as Surrapam to fight the Dragon's armies there?'

'To march to the end of the world?' King Marshayk said. 'Of course! If we make alliance, of course I will.'

King Kaiman passed the cup to King Hadaru, and it quickly made its way around the table to King Kurshan, King Mohan, and then to me. I set the gleaming gelstei in the middle of the table for all to behold.

For the moment, at least, the business of the conclave seemed to have returned to more practical questions. And so King Kiritan fixed King Marshayk with his cold eyes and said, 'As for that, you haven't yet declared how many men you will pledge.'

King Kiritan, I thought, was quite eager to obtain this number. And King Marshayk, like a fish wriggling away from a spear poked at him, said, 'Surely more than five thousand.'

'Indeed, but how *many* more, then? Two thousand? Ten?'

'Perhaps. Perhaps even more. But a king never knows how many men will muster to his standard until he makes his call.'

King Marshayk, of course, did not wish to commit any great numbers of his army to defending Alonia – or any other realm. But he was even more loathe to understate Delu's strength, and so invite enemies (or friends) to perceive his kingdom as weak. It was a dilemma that all the kings at the table faced.

King Kiritan now looked over at me and said, 'And what of Mesh, Prince Valashu? If we *were* all to make alliance, how many knights and foot will King Shamesh pledge?'

I felt hundreds of people watching me and waiting for my answer. It was clever of King Kiritan, I thought, to have called for the conclave to be held in public. It was hard not to commit all of Mesh's forces with the eyes of so many upon me.

'When last Mesh and Ishka lined up for battle by the Raaswash,' I said, 'we fielded ten thousand knights and foot.'

'Ten thousand? We had thought that the Valari's proudest kingdom could do better than that.'

'If it came to war with the Red Dragon, perhaps we could.' I waited a moment, then cast King Kiritan's barb back at him. 'What of Alonia, then?'

'If it comes to war, Prince Valashu, a *hundred* thousand Alonians await our command.'

'That,' I said, 'is a large army. But probably too many to maneuver effectively.'

'Indeed, too many for an *inexperienced* commander,' he said, gazing at me, 'to lead into battle.'

Upon hearing this, King Hadaru pulled at the colored ribbons tied to his long, white hair. He held up his hand as if to call for silence, then he said, 'Once again we return to the question of who is to lead the Alliance, if there is really to be one. Commanding larger numbers is no measure of a warlord. Were it so, Duke Malatam would have defeated Lord Valashu's Guardians at the battle they fought only a week ago.'

As Duke Malatam, sitting at his table, bowed his head in shame, King Kiritan addressed King Hadaru. 'Are you saying that this young prince of Mesh is fit to lead *all* the armies of the Alliance?'

King Hadaru turned to fix me with his lustrous black eyes. I knew that this irascible king still bore me much ill will. So it surprised me when he said, 'Fit? Yes, it would seem so. And even more, fated.'

'But only two days ago,' King Kiritan said to him, 'you claimed precedence over all other kings, even ourself, as having fought the most battles!'

'Two days ago,' King Hadaru said, 'Duke Malatam hadn't arrived to tell of Lord Valashu's victory. And what a victory! A hundred and sixty of the Duke's knights killed against none of Lord Valashu's! As far was we Valari are concerned, that was to be the measure of things, that he prove himself as a warlord.'

'The measure of what, then?'

'The measure of him as the Maitreya.'

Many people in the mob behind King Kiritan began murmuring and vying with each other to get a better look at the great, round table. Two men, almost with one voice, cried out, 'Lord of Light!' And King Kiritan's guards quickly escorted them from the hall.

King Mohan waved his hand impatiently as the fine features of his face contracted with fierce concentration. 'As King Hadaru says, we keep circling back to the same question. Who else *except* the Maitreya could lead the Alliance?'

'Only the greatest of kings,' King Kiritan said.

'Yes, but which king is he?' King Mohan said, looking around the table. 'Which king will the other kings suffer to command them?'

A wicked gleam flared in King Kiritan's eyes as he said, 'Perhaps you, King Mohan.'

At this, King Sandarkan shook his head violently, and King Kurshan's scarred face fell into a scowl. 'Never!' he said. 'The breaker of the rules of *sharshan* to lead other kings in battles with no rules? Never!'

King Kurshan continued scowling at King Mohan, and for a moment I was afraid that these two enemies might renew their old dispute and draw on each other. It was beneath King Kiritan's dignity, I thought, to so provoke Valari kings into rancor toward each other, for this was too easy to do. But thus did he strive to control the conclave.

'It seems that the Valari,' King Waray said, playing the peacemaker, 'are of a single mind regarding the Alliance's leader: he must be the Maitreya.'

'*Must* he?' King Marshayk said from across the table. It seemed that he was mouthing words he imagined King Kiritan would wish him to speak. 'What if no Maitreya comes forth? Is there to be no Alliance then?'

And King Aryaman growled out, 'We don't even know what the Maitreya really *is*.'

He is the lightning in the darkest night, I thought. *He is the sun that lights up the day*.

'It is written,' King Mohan said, 'that the Maitreya will be the greatest warrior in the world. Who is that? The minstrels will sing ten thousand years of Lord Valashu's feat in fighting his way out of Argattha.'

King Aryaman, I noticed, fingered his axe as he glared at me in challenge. I knew that he would have liked to put my prowess to the test.

Here Master Juwain, sitting with other masters of the Brotherhood, rose to his feet and drew forth his battered copy of the *Saganom Elu*. He thumped his hand against the old leather and called out, 'Your Majesties, may I speak? It is indeed written as King Mohan says. But the Valari have always striven to be warriors of the *spirit*. Surely the Maitreya would conquer through the force of his soul and not his sword.'

He sat back down, and King Hanniban cleared his throat as if to warn everyone to silence. He said, 'Whether the Maitreya wields soul or sword begs the question. How will he conquer at all if there is no Alliance? I, for one, doubt that an alliance is possible, even led by the Shining One.'

'That is because,' King Theodor said, 'you refuse to risk even a single battalion in defense of any land other than your own.'

'Or any warship,' King Tal said.

'I'm still not convinced of the need,' King Hanniban said. 'But be assured that my shipwrights are building more even as we speak.'

King Aryaman's fingers tightened around the haft of his axe as he called out, 'Yes, warships that can sail toward Thalu as easily as Surrapam, should the Red Dragon's threat prove to have no teeth.'

'Be careful, King Aryaman, of what you say,' King Hanniban warned him. 'During my reign, Eanna has known only peace because peace we have sought. But, at need, that can change.'

'We of Thalu,' King Aryaman said to him, 'have warships of our own.'

'Which you have encouraged to fall on *my* merchants' caravels!' King Tal called out from next to him.

King Aryaman now turned his bellicose gaze on King Tal as he half-shouted, 'Be careful of what *you* say, King Tal! How many times must I affirm that the losses you bemoan were caused by a few rogue raiders?'

'Affirm it all you will, but in doing so, you only admit that you cannot rule your own kingdom.'

'I rule *this*!' King Aryaman said, drawing his axe and shaking it at King Tal. 'What do *you* rule?'

As King Tal stared coolly at the shiny steel of King Aryaman's axe, King Theodor called out from across the table, 'How is it that King Tal berates King Aryaman for loosing his sea-raiders when it was King Tal's own barons that forced Nedu's entire fleet to sail against the Elyssu?'

'What choice did I have?' King Tal called back to him. 'Since you insisted on letting Duke Brayan keep Ilian Island?'

'But Ilian Island is *ours*, and has been since the Channel War!'

For a while, the other kings at the table watched as the debate among King Tal, King Theodor, King Hanniban and King Aryaman grew ever more heated. Finally, when King Tal warned King Aryaman to keep his raiders away from the important fishing waters off the Northland Banks, King Aryaman lost his patience. He rose to his feet and lifted up his axe. Then he swung it down toward the center of the table. With a thunderous crash, its steel blade bit deep into the white oak as he shouted out, 'But no one can reason with these men! Any alliance of our realms is impossible!'

With King Kiritan glaring at him as he might an errant child, King Aryaman pulled free a purse of coins and tossed it jangling onto the floor. 'For your table, King Kiritan,' he said.

He stared at his axe planted only inches from the Lightstone; so did King Kiritan and King Hanniban, and all the other kings seething with their own resentments and doubts.

I gazed across the table at this huge, yellow-haired king steeped in the violence of his long and ancient line. And I said to him, and to everyone else in the hall, 'No, King Aryaman, you're wrong. An alliance is not only possible – it's inevitable.'

I stood up then, and the eyes of all gathered there turned my way. The sunlight streaming down through the dome fell upon the Lightstone and caused it to gleam like a golden jewel. It seemed to sear my lips like fire. The time had finally come, I thought, to tell everyone how the world might be.

28

And this is what I said to them: 'All men, even brothers, contend with other men, for that is the way of the world. Each protects his own interests and his own self, and that is right and good. It is thus with all people: each man, woman and child is an island, whole and complete – a glory to the earth. But all islands, beneath the sea, join with each other through the motherland and the very world that gave them birth. So with human beings. Islands we are, yet we are also part of something greater. What man wouldn't stand with his brothers, out of love, to protect their family against brigands who would burn their fields and steal their cattle? And what family wouldn't give its sons to die in battle protecting their kingdom against the armies of an invader? But what is greater than any kingdom? Surely the world we call Ea. If the Red Dragon's armies tear it apart, which of you kings will be left to pick up the pieces of your shattered realms? Which of you loves your people so little? Which of you loves *Ea* so little? Who will not look beneath the blood-red sea of ancient enmities to behold that which connects us, land to land, brother to brother, heart to heart?'

I paused in my speech to take a quick breath and look at the Lightstone. I drank in its splendor. And it touched into fire all that was within me: my dreams, my hopes, my soul. The longer that I gazed at the golden cup, the brighter and deeper this fire grew. King Aryaman must have sensed it raging through me, for his face had fallen fearful yet softer, almost childlike, as he looked at me strangely. King Hanniban and King Marshayk were looking at me, too. All the kings at the table, I thought, were waiting for me to pass on this beautiful flame. To work this miracle seemed the simplest thing in all the world. I need only open my heart to them.

'King Tal!' I called out. 'Would you not give up arguing over a few fish to see your sons and daughters stand strong and free?'

His cool gray eyes touched mine and warmed with a new light as he nodded his head.

'King Theodor!' I said. 'There are hundreds of islands off Nedu and the Elyssu. Why fight over one of them only to lose all of them?'

'Why indeed?' he said, gazing at me.

I walked around the kings in their chairs at the rim of the table until I came to King Aryaman. I leaned over and grasped the rough wood of his axe's haft. With a quick wrench, I freed it and handed it to him. 'There are greater adventures than raiding merchants' caravels. Did not Thalu's own King Koru-ki build a fleet of lightships to sail up to the stars?'

The wild gleam in King Aryaman's eyes told me that I had guessed right about him, that he shared King Kurshan's dream of setting forth to new worlds. He pushed his axe down into his thick black belt as he stared at me in amazement.

And so it went as I moved around the table, speaking in turn to each of the kings. The fire inside me grew brighter and brighter, like the heart of a star. I sensed that I could wield the Lightstone like some sort of cosmic hammer, to forge a finer sword than the length of silver gelstei I wore sheathed at my side. The Sword of Light, the Sword of Love. Which king, which man, could stand against it?

'King Hanniban!' I said, looking upon this sad, old man. It seemed that he could hardly breathe. 'Will you not pledge to join the Alliance?'

He blinked his red-rimmed eyes as if he could hardly bear to look at me; years seemed to fall away from him as he sat up straighter, made new by a finer elixir than mother's milk. To the gasps of many watching us, he called out, 'I pledge my whole army and all my warships!'

Now a dozen men and women in the mob pressing the guards cried out, 'Maitreya! Lord of Light!' The captain of the guards tried to identify them and cut them out, but even as he began issuing orders to his men, three score peasants and landless knights picked up the cry and shouted, 'Lord of Light! Lord of Light! Lord of Light!' They were too many to drive from the hall unless the guards were willing to spear their own people.

At last I came to King Kiritan. His cool blue eyes were now hot with anger as he glared at me. He seemed still to be waiting for something. And I said to him, 'We make alliance not just for the sake of Ea, but for *all* worlds. The Lightstone was sent here for a great purpose.'

But I could not move him. He pressed his thin lips tightly together for a moment before snapping out: 'To be placed in *your* hands?'

'Maitreya!' half a hundred men and women shouted. 'Maitreya!'

As I locked eyes with King Kiritan in a silent battle, Duke Malatam stood and begged permission to speak. King Kiritan broke off staring at me and said to him, 'Speak then, if that is what you wish.'

Duke Malatam smoothed his sleek brown beard with his little fingers, all the while turning his ferret's-face right and left toward the many kings and nobles watching him. And in a voice full of both bombast and pleading, he said, 'Many of you know that I have had great success in battle until I met Lord Valashu Elahad and his knights. My defeat has been told of – and Lord Valashu's victory. But the true nature of this victory has *not* been told. For in the end, it was my victory as well: a victory of the spirit. I confess that when I first laid eyes upon the Lightstone, the wanting of it drove me mad. Lord Valashu healed me of my madness, not with steel and death, but with mercy, compassion and new life, for myself and my knights whom he spared. I do not know *what* the Maitreya is; perhaps no one does. But I do know *who* he is.'

And with that, with a flourish of his hand, he bowed deeply to me, and then returned to his seat. And many people cried out, 'Maitreya! Healer! Lord of Light!'

But not everyone in the hall shared their enthusiasm. At the nearby table of the Five Families, a lean, wolfish man about King Kiritan's age fixed all his attention on me. Although he affected a casual interest in the shouts of the mob and never actually looked at me directly, I felt his resentment and malice toward me sliding between my ribs like a quick and vicious dagger. His name, I recalled, was Ravik Kirriland. He had unusually colored eyes that I hadn't remembered being quite so vital and dark, like violets.

King Kiritan, even more, could not bear the cries of the multitudes around us. He finally lost his patience as he stood and shouted out: 'Silence! Silence, or we will have the hall cleared!'

At once, the chanting ceased as impassioned words died on the lips of hundreds of men and women. The hall grew quiet. Even across the room, I could hear Maram and Master Juwain, and others, gathering in their breaths. And then King Kiritan snapped at me: 'They call you the Maitreya.'

'Yes,' I said, staring at him.

'All of us have dreams, Valashu Elahad, but *we* have tried to discourage false hopes until it is known whether you are truly this Shining One who has been prophesied.'

'It *is* known, as well as it will ever be!' Maram suddenly called out. He looked at me long and deep as if in warning.

'No, it is *not*,' King Kiritan told him.

407

'No, it is not,' I agreed, turning away from Maram. Although Atara had no eyes, I felt her staring at me from her table across the hall. 'It must be put to the test.'

A flicker of surprise flashed across King Kiritan's face. Then he said, 'Yes, we agree, it must be tested.'

King Hanniban and King Aryaman, as well King Hadaru and every other king at the great, round table, were watching me and waiting. And I called out, 'It is said that the Maitreya will be a healer.'

Now it was King Kiritan's turn to surprise me. With a quick glance toward Joakim sitting nervously at the Narmada table, he said, 'Healing is no measure of a Maitreya. Were it so, we would all bow down to simpletons. Or elevate the Brotherhood's Master Healers to the highest throne.'

Here he smiled thinly and looked right at Master Juwain. Master Juwain took this as a challenge: to himself, and even more, to me. He regarded me for a long few moments. An understanding passed between us. And then, with great dignity, he stood up and walked between the rows of tables toward the Guardians' table immediately across the aisle. He came up to Estrella, who sat between Lord Harsha and Behira. He placed his gnarled, gentle hand on top of her head and sighed out, 'Even I, with the aid of a green gelstei, have been unable to heal this girl.'

So saying, he opened his other hand, and many people gasped in wonder at the beauty of his emerald crystal that he showed them.

'What ails her?' Count Muar called out, turning toward me.

'She is mute,' I told him.

Count Muar scoffed at this as his face darkened with doubt. 'Do you propose to heal this girl, who is in your charge, of that which might require no healing at all?'

'What do you mean?' I asked him.

'Is it a miracle to summon forth words from one who perhaps willfully swallows her own words? What kind of test is that?'

'She cannot speak,' I said.

'Cannot or will not?'

'Do you challenge *my* word?' I said to him.

I commanded my hand move away from the hilt of my sword. And King Kiritan's eyes filled with a dark light as he looked from Count Muar to me.

'In the end, a knight's word is all he has,' he told me coldly. 'Therefore, it is upon us to ask you a simple question: Are you the Maitreya?'

My heart beat three times, like a hammer against hot steel, and I gasped out, 'But that is what must be tested!'

Although I knew he was trying to maneuver for advantage, I did not see the nature of the trap.

'Indeed,' he said, 'and surely *this* must be the test of things, the only test, that you give us your word, yea or nay.'

He stood up as tall and straight as the carved pillars set into the walls as he gazed across the table at me. And then he spoke words to an ancient verse that I knew too well:

> About the Maitreya
> One thing is known:
> That to himself
> He always is known
> When the moment comes
> To claim the Lightstone.

'Do you deny, Valashu Elahad,' he said to me, 'that you came to Tria to claim the great gelstei?'

I looked away from him toward the center of the table where the little cup I had sought for so long sat gleaming in the sunlight. And to King Kiritan, I said, 'No, I don't deny this.'

'Very well, then tell us, in truth, what you must know in your heart,' he said to me. 'If you are the Maitreya, then we shall pledge our entire army and all our warships to the Alliance, to be led by you. If you are the great Shining One told of in the prophecies, then we shall ourself place the Lightstone in your hands.'

The sudden shout of a thousand men, women and children shook the stones of the hall – and struck straight into my heart: 'Maitreya! Maitreya! Maitreya! Maitreya! . . .'

This is the moment, I thought. *This must be the moment.*

My eyes were pure fire as I gazed across the hall at the mob clapping their hands and beating their fists against the guards' long shields. The kings sitting in their chairs were all watching me. Nearby, where many nobles were rising up from their tables, Liljana, Master Juwain and Maram were all looking at me, too. Estrella flashed a bright smile at me, but she had already shown me all that she could. Atara still sat in silence with her beautiful face turned toward me. I felt time boiling away like drops of mist beneath a blazing sun. Inside me, the terrible, hot flame of kirax burned my blood. But it was nothing against my deep, consuming desire to know who I really was. It came to me then, like a lighting stroke, that if only we could ask the right and true questions, with all our hearts, we would be answered.

'Ashtoreth,' I whispered, 'blessed Mother, I must know: am I the one for whom the Lightstone was meant? Should I claim it?'

At this, King Mohan looked at King Kurshan and called out against the noise filling the room, 'Listen, the Elahad calls on the angels!'

'Ashtoreth,' I said again, a little louder, 'am I the Maitreya?'

Above the Lightstone, in the wavering air over the center of the table, brilliant colors burst into being. This must be Flick, I thought, yet never had I seen him shine so vividly. So bright was this radiance, it astonished me that no one seemed to perceive it except myself.

'*Ahura Alarama,*' I whispered, speaking Flick's true name.

As I held my breath, the colors brightened even further, and deepened to a splendid glorre. And out of this marvelous hue, Alphanderry's face and form took shape. My old friend, shimmering with a secret light, seemed to stand on air. He smiled at me, and in his lovely eyes was all of his old grace and joy in being human – and something more.

And then his lips parted, and I did not understand why no one else could hear the words that he spoke to me: **'The Lightstone was meant for the Maitreya, and you are not he. The Shining One is always of the Ardun, never the Valari. He is the one who forsakes the path of the angels to die from the world: willfully, joyfully, triumphantly.'**

I looked up into the light of Alphanderry's eyes, which were bright as stars. A terrible, wild fear ripped through me. And I whispered, 'What *is* the Maitreya then? Is he not the one who will vanquish death?'

'Listen,' someone called out as if from far away, 'the Elahad *talks* with the angels.'

And Alphanderry said to me, **'Angra Mainyu once held the same dream as do you. He, too, wanted to end death, suffering itself. He deceived himself, as have you, Valashu.'**

And someone else, from behind me, said, 'The Elahad talks to the air! Or talks to himself. Surely he is mad.'

I am not he; I am not he; I am not he . . .

I had a hundred more questions that I wished to ask Alphanderry. But then he smiled at me in silence one last time, and his eyes filled with sadness, compassion, warning and hope. And then he vanished into a swirl of sparks that soon burned themselves out, leaving behind only darkness.

'Lord Valashu,' King Kiritan called out to me in his sternest voice, 'Did you hear what we said?'

I could hardly hear King Kiritan even now, for Alphanderry's words shrieked like shattered steel in my mind. I knew that all he had told me was true. I denied it. The voice whispering inside me, forever it

410

seemed, told me much the same thing. I didn't listen. I didn't *want* to listen. How could I, with Atara still sitting broken in her chair and waiting to be made whole again, with Estrella and all the other children in the hall, and in the world, waiting to die beneath the spears and nails of the Red Dragon's armies – or simply to die upon the fiery cross of life: horribly, meaninglessly, agonizingly?

'Lord Valashu,' King Kiritan said to me, 'we must ask you to tell us what is in your heart.'

Blackness was in my heart, bitterness and blame. I looked around the table at Ea's kings who waited upon my answer. If I denied that I was the Maitreya, they would lose hope, and there would be no Alliance. King Kiritan might lead Delu and the Elyssu in a separate and smaller coalition of their realms, for a while, but in the end Morjin would defeat them, as he would the Valari kingdoms, one by one. He would free Angra Mainyu from the hell of Damoom, and unleash hell on earth – and everywhere – and that would be the end of all things. And as Kane had warned me, that must never be.

'Valashu Elahad,' King Kiritan said again, 'we must ask you formally, before all the sovereigns of Ea's Free Kingdoms, before the witnesses gathered here today, before the entire world: are you the Maitreya?'

I am he who must find him to place the Lightstone in his hands.

I looked straight at King Kiritan and opened my mouth to tell him this. But I spoke only the first three words, 'I am he –' For just then, a great tumult shook the hall as many people began crying out as one:

'Lord of Light! Lord of Light! Lord of Light! Lord of Light! . . .'

'I am he,' I whispered to myself. A thousand men and women had heard this as my affirmation. 'I am he.'

For a moment, I gazed at the Lightstone and felt within myself a great power still to realize all my dreams. I looked over at Atara whose lips were silently forming the words: 'No, no, no, no . . .' Yes, I thought, yes. I knew it was wrong for me to blind myself this way. I knew, too, that I could not escape the evil of it. Evil had seeped into the pores of my skin in the sickening stench of Argattha and into my blood in the kirax upon the arrow that Morjin's priest had fired into me. It had poisoned my mind in the black ink of the words of Morjin's letter. And most of all, it had stricken my soul with the screams of all the men that I had put to the sword. All that I could do now, I thought, was to choose a lesser evil over a greater. And so I, too, retreated into silence, letting stand my lie.

Then King Kiritan called out to me in a voice like thunder: 'No, you cannot be the Lord of Light!'

He motioned toward Atara's table, where a scribe picked up a huge,

411

old book and brought it to our table. King Kiritan took it from him, and thanked him. Then he opened it to a page that had been marked with a slip of red silk. Again he called for silence in his hall. As the mob grew quiet, King Kiritan read this to all assembled beneath his golden dome: *'They who are born of the earth, love the things of the earth; they of the stars look always back toward their home and love heaven's light above all other things. The Maitreya, loving life, loving others' lives as his own, is always earth-born. Never is he of the Valari. They might seek in the stars for the source of creation's splendor until the end of time, but the Lightstone is not for them.'*

King Kiritan slammed shut his book, and shouted at me, 'Not for them! Not for *you*, Valashu Elahad!'

I stood staring at him as he stared at me. I couldn't move; I could hardly breathe. It was as if he had driven a spear through my chest.

While many hundreds of people around me let loose murmurs of anger and looked at King Kiritan in astonishment, Master Juwain came forward and stood by my side. He said to King Kiritan, 'Lord King, what is that book that you have brought here?'

'It is a chronicle written by Balakin, who was one of the Elijin sent to Ea in the year 795 of the Age of Swords.'

This news prompted exclamations and curious looks from the nobles sitting nearby. Master Juwain pointed at the crumbling volume on the table in front of King Kiritan and said, 'Where did you find this?'

King Kiritan grew instantly wroth as he barked out, '*We* don't have to answer to *you*. However, since this is a matter of the utmost moment, we will tell you that we found it in the library of our ancestors only last night.'

'I'm afraid I know of no such book written by any of the Elijin.'

'Indeed? Then the erudition of the masters of the Brotherhood fails them.'

Now it was Master Juwain's turn to glower at King Kiritan. My small teacher and friend, standing in his plain woolens at the table of the kings, seemed to swell with anger and pride. And then he called out to Ea's greatest king: 'Our erudition is no small thing. It has led me to a lake on the Wendrush, where I recovered *this*.'

So saying, he drew forth his akashic crystal. The great lords and nobles of Tria, no strangers to the gelstei, leapt up from their tables to get a better look at the swirls of color spilling out of this unique gelstei over Master Juwain's hard little hands.

'In this stone,' Master Juwain said, 'is recorded Balakin's testament and annals of the Elder Ages – and much else. Nowhere have I found lines similar to those that you have read to us.'

'Indeed? Then perhaps you weren't seeking them diligently enough.'

'Not diligent enough!' Master Juwain cried out. 'I have spent nearly every waking hour between the Lake of Mists and Tria seeking in this crystal for knowledge of the Shining One and the Lightstone!'

'Seeking *how*, then?'

'As you would a single book in your library that you were able to locate . . . only last night.'

'Then that,' King Kiritan said, resting his hand on the book that his scribe had brought him, 'is your problem. Balakin tells in here of the stone you have found. It is a gelstei, and one from the stars – and therefore alive in the way of these crystals. Did you ever think simply to ask it for the knowledge you sought?'

'*Ask* . . . this crystal?' Master Juwain said, staring at the pulses of green and glorre lighting the air around him.

'Indeed, indeed. Why don't you ask it, here, and now?'

Master Juwain cupped both his hands around the rim of the crystal as he murmured, '*Aulara, Auliama.*'

At once, a great light blossomed out of the crystal. And there, beside Master Juwain, beside me, stood the ghost from the amphitheater. His noble face and bright eyes fell upon Master Juwain as he said, '*Aulara, Auliama.*'

'Sorcery!' Belur Narmada cried out as he jumped up from his table. 'This Master Healer summons ghosts!'

Throughout the hall, others picked up this cry: 'Sorcerer! Sorcerer!' Count Muar and Count Dario – and many of those around us – looked at Master Juwain with loathing and dread. I heard Maram murmur to himself, 'How did *he* get inside *that*?'

Master Juwain seemed as perplexed as he was. He seemed reluctant, as well, to ask the question that King Kiritan had suggested to him. And so King Kiritan asked it for him: 'Well, wraith, will you tell us about the Maitreya and the Valari?'

Without hesitation, the ghost began singing out in the angels' musical language that only Master Juwain could understand: '*Li Ardonaii irri jin lila . . .*'

This time he recited fewer words, more slowly, and Master Juwain was better able to understand them. By the time he had finished, Master Juwain's lumpy old face had fallen gray and grim. And King Kiritan called out: 'Well, you of the Brotherhood claim to understand all the ancient languages. Can you translate for us?'

Master Juwain slowly nodded his head. He looked at me and whispered, 'I'm sorry, Val.' And then he began reciting for all to hear:

413

The Ardun, born of earth, delight
In flowers, butterflies, bright
New snow beneath the bluest sky,
All things of earth that live and die.

Valari sail beyond the sky
Where heaven's splendors terrify;
In ancient longing to unite,
They seek a deeper, deathless light.

The angels, too, with searing sight
Behold the blazing, starry height;
Reborn from fire, in flame they fly
Like silver swans: to live, they die.

The Shining Ones who live and die
Between the whirling earth and sky
Make still the sun, all things ignite –
And earth and heaven reunite.

The Fearless Ones find day in night
And in themselves the deathless light,
In flower, bird and butterfly,
In love: thus dying, do not die.

They see all things with equal eye:
The stones and stars, the earth and sky,
The Galadin, blazing bright,
The Elijin, Valari knight.

They bring to them the deathless light,
Their fearlessness and sacred sight;
To slay the doubts that terrify:
Their gift to them to gladly die.

And so on wings the angels fly,
Valari sail beyond the sky,
But they are never Lords of Light,
And not for them the Stone of Light.

Not for them! I thought, looking at the Lightstone. Not for me.
Bitter acids burned inside my belly, and I was sick to my soul. From

414

across the room, Maram reached out with his eyes as if to steady me. His fat face was full of outrage, relief, pity and recognition.

King Kiritan pointed at Master Juwain and said, 'Out of the mouth of Lord Valashu's own teacher, the truth is made known!'

I looked over at Liljana, who was sitting next to Daj and weeping.

Now King Kiritan pointed his finger at me and cried out, 'You knew, all the time, you surely knew! Therefore, you, Valashu Elahad, are a liar!'

What he said was surely true, but it was too much for Baltasar to bear. He rose up from his seat and whipped out his sword, all in one blindingly quick motion. This time, Lansar Raasharu failed to restrain him. Indeed, my father's faithful seneschal drew his own sword and aimed it at King Kiritan as he shouted: 'Lord Valashu is not a liar! All we've heard are some words from old books and this ghost. They're nothing against the truth of what Lord Valashu has done and who he is. He *is* the Maitreya! We all know he is!'

At this, Sunjay Naviru and Lord Noldru and the Guardians at their table raised up their voices to acclaim me as the Lord of Light. So did many of the knights in the retainers of King Kurshan and Prince Viromar at their tables – and King Kurshan, King Mohan and Prince Viromar themselves

Then King Kiritan cast his cold eyes upon them, and upon the other Valari kings, one by one. And he called out, 'Valashu Elahad stands betrayed as the liar he is! To have pretended to be the Maitreya so that he could gain power for himself – what a foul crime this is! But he is not alone in this misdeed. The Valari kings and their knights have joined him in lying, hoping to see him proclaimed as Maitreya so that the Valari could rule the Alliance – and so rule the Free Kingdoms, and perhaps all of Ea! And rule *how*? With a despotism like unto that of the Red Dragon himself!'

A deathly silence descended upon the hall. For a moment, King Hadaru and King Waray and the other kings sat stunned and staring at King Kiritan in disbelief. Then many things happened at once. King Mohan rose up from his chair and drew his sword. So did King Sandarkan. The sound of other swords slipping from their sheaths rang out into air. King Kiritan called out to his guard captain, who hurried toward our table with a dozen of his men. From the hall's southern door came the sound of rattling mail, boots pounding against stone and shouting. Across the hall, the mob surged against the wall of shields, and in several places broke through. Around the tables lined up on both sides of the aisle, angry men and women began standing up and yelling at each other, some declaring that I must surely be the Maitreya, others crying out: 'Liar! Fool!' Next to Atara's table, two burly merchants had come to blows, and it seemed that the retinues of King Aryaman and King Tal might at any moment draw swords and fall against the nearby Valari knights – or against each other. Resentment and rage filled the air like black clouds just before a thunderstorm.

Then I saw Ravik Kirriland push aside King Kiritan's scribe and chamberlain as he made straight toward Atara's table. His lean face and dark violet eyes fixed on her. There was murder in his heart – I was sure of this. Hate knows hate as the blind know the dark. It came to me then that Ravik must be the Skakaman called Noman. Under the cover of the chaos sweeping the room, he would come up beside Atara and slip a dagger into her, quickly and savagely, without being noticed. Thus he would silence the one person who might warn me who Noman was. And then he would come to murder me as well and steal the Lightstone.

'Atara!' I called out. I whipped free my sword. I leaned across the table and swept up the Lightstone, clasping it against my chest. 'Atara!'

There was no time to say more, no time to shove through the crowds and fall upon Ravik, for he was quickly closing in upon her. I wanted to die myself then. My heart swelled inside me with an unbearable pain that nearly choked me and made me gasp for breath. This red-hot anguish of love gathered at my core like a knot of fire. And then the alchemy of evil transmuted love into hate. I hated Morjin for loosing this merciless creature upon Atara – and upon the world. I hated the One for making the world this way, with evil digging its filthy black claws into all things and dragging even the most beautiful of beings down into despair and death. Most of all, I hated myself. For I should be as clean as new snow and as flawless as a diamond; I should have roses and starlight and life without end. Instead I held within myself pure dragon fire, black as soot, for all the light had burned out of it. As the man everyone called Ravik Kirriland drew up to Atara, this terrible flame built hotter and hotter in my heart until it was like hellfire itself.

'Atara!'

In my left hand, the Lightstone blazed like the sun; with my right hand, I gripped my sword and pointed it at Ravik. It was as if I held a lightning bolt, so brightly did the silver silustria flare. Then, as a dazzling darkness filled my eyes and the world stood still, all my fury poured out of me. It flashed through the air and struck straight into Ravik. He cried out in agony, arching his back as he turned toward me and grasped at his chest. Even across the room, I could see the light

416

die in his eyes. Then he fell to the floor with a sickening slap of flesh against cold stone, never to rise again.

'Lord of Light!' someone called out. And then another voice, even louder, 'Lord of Death!'

Across the hall, all eyes not staring in horror at Ravik's body fell upon me. The shock of what had happened stunned nearly everyone into motionlessness. Many of the merchants and nobles at the tables near Atara's were coughing, clasping their chests, bending over and retching from the terrible killing force that had spilled into them. Many looked at me in awe, and in dread, for no one had known that I had the power to slay this way.

'There was death in his eyes!' one of King Kiritan's magistrates called out. 'We all saw it!'

In his eyes, I thought, recalling an old verse, *a healing light.*

'Murderer!' A thin, pretty woman about Ravik's age stood up from his table and hurried over to kneel above him. I took her to be Ravik's wife. She pointed her finger at me and said, 'Why did you murder him, who only ever spoke praises of you?'

I took a step toward the place where Ravik lay crumpled on the floor, and everyone standing in my way moved aside as from a rabid dog. To the woman, I said, 'That is not your husband. He is a Skakaman, an evil thing sent by Morjin to assassinate King Kiritan's own daughter – and myself.'

'It *is* my Lord Ravik!' the woman shouted, bursting into tears as she stroked his face. 'What's the matter with you? He's the King's own friend – Atara's, too!'

As I moved closer to them, one of King Kiritan's chamberlains, an elegantly dressed man with warm, honest eyes, attested that Ravik used to play chess and other games with Atara when she was a child. He looked up at me and said, 'Ravik loved Atara as if she were his own daughter. If he was rushing upon her, it was only to protect her from the violence you brought here this morning.'

I hesitated, looking down at Ravik's still form. In death, all his malice toward me had bled away.

Then Atara, still sitting in her chair above Ravik and his wife, turned her blindfolded face toward me. And she said to me, 'Oh, Val! What have you done? What have you done?'

Now I wanted to retch myself, but there was nothing inside my belly except bitterness and pain. I reached my sword out toward Ravik's body, and I said, 'He *is* the Skakaman. He must be.'

Just then the commotion outside the hall's southern door grew louder. A voice I knew as well as my own called out to the guards

417

there: 'Let me through, I say! Do you not see this medallion? So, I stood before the throne a year ago to make vows with everyone else, and I *will* stand here again. Let me through!'

I looked over then to see Kane brazen his way into the hall. My mysterious friend made his way straight down the aisle toward the round table where King Kiritan stood staring at him in alarm. His white hair, thick as a snow tiger's fur, was cropped close, as I remembered. Although he was as old as the stars, he moved like a young tiger stalking his prey. His large body rippled with a barely-contained fury; beneath his travel-stained cloak and steel mail, his muscles bunched and relaxed with an almost palpable power. His bold face turned right and left as his black, blazing eyes scanned the people standing about him. As he strode closer, he seemed more kingly than any of the kings standing about watching him.

He turned past a row of tables and came up to me. He looked down at Ravik and said, 'He is not the Skakaman.'

'Are you sure?' I said. 'How can you be sure?'

But Kane didn't answer me. He returned to drilling his hard, black eyes into the nearby knights and nobles, one by one.

'I thought he was a monster,' I explained to Duke Parran, who was standing nearby.

He, and many others, cast me evil looks as if it were *I* who was the monster. They made warding signs with their fingers; a few even spat at me. They regarded my sword – and even the Lightstone – with loathing and dismay. Their fear of me made me sick.

'Then he was innocent,' I whispered, sheathing my sword. Then, much louder, 'Innocent!'

'What man, born of the world,' Kane growled out, 'is truly innocent?'

Maram came up to me and laid his hand on my shoulder as he shook his head. Then he repeated the words of Kasandra's prophecy: 'The blood of the innocent will stain your hands.'

I put away the Lightstone then. I stood looking at the hand that had pointed my sword at Ravik. I couldn't bear the sight of it. I raised it to my mouth and bit my palm as hard as I could. My teeth ripped through my skin; I tasted blood. Then I pressed my hands against my face and stood there weeping.

'So,' Kane said, grasping my arm. 'So.'

When I finally drew my hands away and looked out through the veil of tears clouding my eyes, I saw Kane scrutinizing the kings at the round table, one by one. Finally his gaze fell upon King Kiritan. Something violent, like lightning, passed between them. And Kane shouted out to the hall: 'Ravik Kirriland was not the Skakaman! But *he* is!'

'You're mad!' King Kiritan shouted back at him as he motioned to his guards.

'Noman!' Kane called out to him. 'Did you think that you could hide behind that face you stole?'

King Kiritan – or Noman – turned to his guard captain and barked out: 'Seize those liars! Slay that madman and that murderer where they stand!'

But the guard captain and his men were reluctant to follow such a command. Seeing this, King Kiritan drew his sword and charged toward me. Twelve of his men, shamed at allowing him to expose himself, suddenly rushed forward, too. One of these cast his spear at me. With a clash of steel against diamond, its point struck me beneath my chest, nearly breaking against my glittering armor and knocking the breath from me. Master Juwain, to my right, held up the akashic crystal as he might a shield. One of King Kiritan's men drove his mailed fist into his arm, knocking the crystal from his hand. It struck the floor and shattered into pieces. The light died from each shard, one by one. Then Baltasar and my Guardians pushed through the throng to protect me – and the Lightstone. As two of King Kiritan's men closed in on Kane, to be met with the fury of his flashing sword, King Kiritan fell upon me with *his* sword. I could scarcely breathe, and so I was slow to draw my own. And in my moment of debility, he struck at me with a terrible savagery. Baltasar cried out, 'Val!' even as he jumped in front of me to intercept him. But he was off-balance, and King Kiritan's sword slid past his kalama. The force of the thrust split apart the diamonds encrusting Baltasar's armor as the sword drove deep into Baltasar's chest. So quick and shocking was this death-blow that Baltasar did not even scream. *I* screamed, however, in agony and hatred as I finally freed my sword. I rammed the silver blade past Baltasar's shoulder; it ripped through the golden lion of King Kiritan's tunic and struck straight through his heart. He died cursing me with his hateful eyes. He fell to the floor along with Baltasar, his sword still lodged in Baltasar's bleeding body.

'The King is dead!' someone called out. 'The Elahad has slain the King!'

'Murderer!' someone else called out. 'Slay the king-slayer and all his murdering kind!'

Kane had now succeeded in hacking apart the shields of his two adversaries; in a moment more, he would knock aside their spears and cut them down. My knights had fallen against King Kiritan's guards with a desperate wrath and a deafening clanging of steel against steel. Near the round table, the Valari kings and their retinues stood ready to bring battle into the hall – and war into Alonia. Just then the strong, steady voice of Count Dario called out to everyone: 'Hold! Put down your swords! The King is dead, and let there be no more killing here today!'

'The King is dead!' men and women from the mob shouted. And then a hundred more joined them in their mournful cry: 'The King is dead! The King is dead!'

Nearly everyone froze then as they eyed those around them with a terrible tension like that of a drawn bow. Count Dario, a brave man, stood up straight and made his way from the Narmada table past King Hadaru and King Kurshan. He turned his red-bearded face toward King Mohan as he laid his hand on the blade of King Mohan's sword. 'Peace,' he said to him. 'Let us not make war with each other.'

Seeing this, Belur Narmada shouted out: 'The King is dead! And so Count Dario must be King!'

'By what right!' Duke Parran shouted back. Baron Maruth and Duke Ashvar joined him in outrage, and Count Muar called out, 'Count Dario has no claim upon the throne!'

Count Dario nodded his head toward these great lords, and he said, 'It may be that my claim is not strong enough, but I shall be regent until a new king is crowned. Does anyone dispute me?'

Even as he said this, a new company of guards a hundred strong, led by a young Narmada lord, burst through the hall's great southern doors. They wore the blue and gold livery of the royal house and brandished heavy spears. They marched straight down the aisle toward Count Dario and stood by his sides. And then Count Muar and Baron Maruth reluctantly sheathed their swords.

Accompanied by a dozen of these men, Count Dario strode toward me. On the floor beneath me lay the corpse of the man that I had thought was King Kiritan. There, too, lay Baltasar's still-warm body. Lord Raasharu knelt beside him stroking his hair as he cried out, 'My son! My son! My beautiful son!'

Now Count Dario stared down at the man that I had slain, and his eyes widened in horror. So it was with Duke Parran and King Kiritan's scribes and chamberlains, and everyone else gathered close to us. And myself. For in death, Noman's face could not hold the shape of King Kiritan's countenance. I watched with dread as the skin and bones beneath seemed to ripple like bubbling tar and transform into a face that I hated more than any other. The lines of the jaw and cheekbones were fine, almost delicate, and would have made for a beautiful being

420

but for the sagging, grayish flesh mottled with broken blood vessels. The eyes, red as blood, were still open and stared up at the great nothingness. They were the eyes, I thought, of Morjin.

'*That*,' Kane said, pointing down at him, 'is how I was sure Ravik was not Noman. In death, a Skakaman's face returns to that of his master.'

'More sorcery!' Belur Narmada shouted, crowding in closer. He motioned toward Kane, Master Juwain and me. 'These men are all sorcerers!'

But his kinsman, Count Dario, was not so easily persuaded that we were workers of the black arts. He listened patiently as Kane explained about the Skakaman and his kind that Morjin had summoned to earth. He pressed his lips together in grim silence as Kane said, 'So, this Noman must have entered the palace yesterday and contrived a way to murder and mime King Kiritan. Likely your king's body will never be found.'

Hearing this, Atara, who was standing next to me, bowed down her head and began sobbing beneath her blindfold. And Queen Daryana came up to her daughter and held her against her bosom. She herself, however, shed no tears for her murdered husband and king.

'So,' Kane growled, kicking his boot into the cheek of the man who had killed King Kiritan, 'likely we'll never know the shape of this thing's true face, for the Skakaman is truly a man with no face.'

At this, Maram and Sunjay Naviru and Lord Harsha – and many others – looked at me. The dread in their eyes recalled the last part of Kasandra's prophecy: that a man with no face would show me my own.

Now King Waray, accompanied by King Hadaru and King Mohan and all the Valari kings, pushed past the men and women crowding around the tables and stepped up to me. His proud, eagle's nose pointed straight toward me as he regarded me with his flashing eyes. And he called out to me in his nasal voice, made firm with rectitude and resolve: 'It's clear that this thing called Noman tried to trap you. Therefore all his words and questions must be suspect. Even so, one question must be asked, and it is upon me to ask it: Are you the Maitreya?'

There was still hope in him, I saw to my amazement, wavering like a candle flame on a windy night. And in my uncle, Prince Viromar, and in many others, this mysterious will of life that things should move toward the good. Once more the hall fell quiet as everyone gazed at me. I could hear Atara and Lansar Raasharu weeping softly, and the blood rushing in my ears, but little else. King Theodor Jardan and King

Tal, with the huge King Aryaman and Sajagax, drew in close, along with King Hanniban, King Kaiman and King Marshayk. They joined the Valari kings, and a thousand others, in waiting for me to speak.

I looked down at my sword then. The blood from my bitten hand caked the black jade hilt and the diamonds set into it. But Noman's heart-blood would not cling to the bright blade. In its gleaming silustria I beheld my tormented face – and my fate. An alliance of Ea's Free Kingdoms, I saw, *still* might be forged. If I could not lead it in light, even love, then I could compel others to follow me through awe, fear and hate. I could throw down Morjin and make the world safe for a new and better age.

I am he, I thought. *I am he.*

'No!' I whispered to myself, loathing what I saw in my shining sword, 'no, no, no, no!'

I looked down at Ravik's dead body. Once, I remembered, Morjin had prophesied that I would use my sacred gift of valarda to slay in fury, and so I had. How easy it was, I thought, to turn away from all that was bright and beautiful and be cast alone into darkness.

'Valashu Elahad,' King Hadaru said to me, 'King Waray is right: the question must be asked, and the truth must be told. Are you the Maitreya?'

The truth must be told!

I slammed my sword back into its sheath. I licked my bloody lips; I gulped in a huge breath. And then I cried out, 'No, I am not the Maitreya! I am Morjin! I am Angra Mainyu!'

For a long few seconds, no one spoke. No one dared to look at me. I could feel everyone contemplating me in horror and mystification. Then Lansar Raasharu stood up before me. His cheeks were streaked with tears. He grasped my arm as he pointed down at Baltasar and cried out, 'My son did not die in vain! You *are* the Maitreya! You mustn't deny it!'

'No, Lansar,' I said gently, 'I am not.'

Lord Raasharu's dark eyes fell as black and bottomless as the deep hole of hatred that had opened inside him. He hated Morjin, I sensed, even more than I did for stealing his son away from life. For a moment, it seemed, he even hated me. Although he tried to hold his plain, noble face stern and still, as befit a Valari lord, he was mad with grief. And he said to me, 'Do you remember the third part of that witch's prophecy? That a ghul would undo all your dreams? I *won't* let the Dragon fulfill this!'

A shipwrecked man, drowning at sea, will try to grasp onto the slightest stick of wood. I wrapped my still-bleeding hand around his hand and told him, 'It's too late, sir. The prophecy has already been fulfilled. *I* am the ghul.'

I tried to explain that my very dream of vanquishing the Red Dragon and all his evil had made me a slave to him. For my terrible wrath had blinded me, and for one vital moment, had robbed me of my soul.

Now Duke Malatam came forward and said, 'If Lord Valashu is not the Maitreya, what is he, then?'

What, indeed? When the light goes out, what is left?

'He is a murderer,' Belur Narmada said, pointing down at the floor. 'He slew Lord Ravik and then King Kiritan.'

'By his own words, he stands condemned,' Duke Parran said to Count Dario. 'He should be put to death.'

Lansar Raasharu gripped the hilt of his sword as he glared at him; Maram, Sunjay Naviru and the other Guardians gathered in close to me, ready to swing their kalamas and begin battle anew.

'He cannot be put to death,' Count Dario said. 'No matter his crime, he is an emissary of King Shamesh.'

'He is a king-slayer!' Belur Narmada shouted.

'That may or may not be,' Count Dario said, looking down at Noman's corpse doubtfully.

'He certainly killed Lord Ravik!' Count Muar said. 'We all saw this!'

'Yes, he killed Lord Ravik,' Count Dario said, 'in the heat of passion, even as once he saved young Baltasar's life. Manslaughter this might be, but we shall not in turn slay him for this.'

'Then imprison him on Damoom, and seize the Lightstone as wergild for these deaths and the ruin that he has brought into this hall!'

At this, Lansar Raasharu and the Guardians unsheathed their swords, and so did I. Then Sajagax, his great bow in hand, fit an arrow to its bowstring and called out, 'I care not to hear more talk of imprisoning or slaying Valashu Elahad! Who speaks of this again shall himself be the first to die!'

King Kiritan's guards surged forward to disarm Sajagax, but then Count Dario held up his hand to stop them. 'Hold!' he commanded them. 'There shall be no more violence here today!'

'But what shall be done with Lord Valashu?' Belur Narmada asked.

'Let him go!' Sajagax bellowed out to Count Dario and all the nobles standing nearby. 'Unless you wish a war with all the Kurmak, let him go!'

I looked around at King Hanniban and King Aryaman, King Tal, King Theodor and King Marshayk, who had come so far to unite in a noble purpose. I hoped that they might speak for me, as Sajagax had.

They stared at me in a cold silence. So it was with even the Valari kings. King Hadaru and King Kurshan, King Waray and King Danashu and King Mohan – they all turned their dread and enmity on me, even as they turned their hearts away from me.

'Valashu Elahad,' Count Dario told me in a voice as heavy as lead, 'this conclave has come to an end, and you have no place in the company of kings. Leave Tria before the sun sets tonight. Leave Alonia as quickly as your horse will carry you. Do not return.'

He drew in a deep breath as he pointed at the pocket of my cloak into which I had placed the Lightstone. And then he added, 'Take that cursed thing from our land.'

After that, there was nothing to say and little to do. Kane, sword in hand, stood by my side flashing deadly looks at any and all who would dare challenge me. Master Juwain bent to scoop up the pieces of his shattered crystal, then pressed close to me, as did Maram. Liljana, with Daj and Estrella close behind, came over to me and met my eyes with a sweet, motherly look that told me she would always see good in me, even when I could not see it in myself. Atara finally broke away from Queen Daryana. She stepped up to me and gently touched my wounded palm. It made me weep to feel the warmth that had returned to her and passed into to me, hand to hand.

Then Lord Raasharu, Lord Harsha, Sar Shivathar, Skyshan of Ki, Sar Juralad and Sar Kimball raised up Baltasar's body to their shoulders. Sunjay Naviru, with Sar Jarlath and Lord Noldru, formed a vanguard ahead of them. At my command, they stepped forward with drawn swords, and my friends and I followed them bearing Baltasar's body down the long aisle and out of the hall.

29

O n the lawn outside the palace, we said goodbye to Sajagax and Queen Daryana. King Kiritan's death had at last freed her from her despised marriage vows, and she had decided to return with her father to her childhood home.

'There's no point in my trying to rule,' she explained, standing up straight and regal. 'The barons would never accept a Kurmak as their sovereign.'

As Sajagax's warriors brought up their horses and my knights gathered around us, Maram said to her, 'But what of Atara, then? She is King Kiritan's daughter as well as yours.'

Daryana looked at Atara, who was embracing Karimah in farewell, and she said, 'Yes, Atara is our *daughter*. The Alonians might once have bowed to a High Queen, but that was in another age.'

'Then who will rule Alonia?'

Daryana waved her hand in front of her as if warding away a hornet. 'Perhaps Count Dario. Perhaps Baron Maruth. I care not. Let the Five Families and the barons fight with Kiritan's bastards over the throne.'

Just then one of her servants came out of the palace bearing a gem-encrusted box. I presumed it contained Queen Daryana's jewelry: all that she would be taking with her from Alonia. She grasped the box and said to Atara, 'Besides, our people will need me now.'

Sajagax laid his muscular, sun-burned arm about her shoulders as he looked at Atara and said, 'As I warned Valashu, in the event of the conclave's failure, there will be trouble with the Marituk. Trouble all across the Wendrush. We'll ride south as quickly as we can. Won't you ride with us?'

'No,' Atara said, standing by my side and squeezing my hand. 'I'll ride with Val. My place is with him, now.'

Sajagax stepped forward to kiss Atara, and so did Daryana. They took their leave of each other in the brusque Kurmak way. Then Sajagax clasped my hand and said, 'You shouldn't blame yourself for what happened here. Fate is fate, is it not? But we're still free, and we still have our bows – and swords. Let us use them to fight Morjin and bring the Law of the One into all lands.'

He grinned at me, then mounted his horse and added, 'You'd better ride quickly, too, Valashu. No matter Count Dario's words, I trust these Alonians not at all. And your Valari kings hardly more. Maybe we'll meet again in better times. Until then, death to our enemies – and seek the glory of the One! Farewell, my Valari friend!'

And so we parted ways with the great Sajagax and his wild, yellow-haired warriors. They rode out of Tria as they had come. I gathered the Guardians to me and prepared to leave the city by a different route. And then Liljana surprised me, announcing that she and Daj would accompany me, too.

'I didn't fail you on the road to Argattha, did I?' she said to me. 'Did you think I'd desert you now just because the road ahead seems a dark one? No, no, of *course* I'm coming with you!'

We hastened to leave Tria then. With my columns of knights behind me, my friends and I made our way across the city down broad avenues lined with people who had turned out to witness my disgrace. No one cheered me. No one cast rose petals onto the streets. Our retreat took us down to the Poru and across the great Star Bridge, gleaming golden in the late sun. Near the ruins of the Old Sanctuary of the Maitriche Telu, we stopped at a large house for Liljana to retrieve a few cooking pots and other essentials she might need on our journey. And then we passed the city's walls through the Ashtoreth Gate, which slammed shut behind us as the Trians sealed in their city against the fall of night. The Nar Road lay before us, for hundreds of miles, through deep forests and across mountains. As Liljana had said, it seemed a dark way, its worn paving stones already fading to shades of gray and black as the day's light failed all around us.

I learned much later that with the deaths of Noman, Ravik Kirriland and Baltasar (and King Kiritan, whose body was never found), the great conclave did indeed come to an end, even as Count Dario had said. But for the next few days, most of the kings lingered on in Tria as King Waray tried to rally the Valari kings and persuade the others to sit once more in good faith at King Kiritan's round table. But then King Mohan quarreled with King Kurshan, and they nearly came to blows. King Kurshan rode off with his retinue, as did King Sandarkan, who had renewed the old dispute with Prince Viromar over the Arjan land. King Waray himself had to take the defensive when King Hadaru accused him of conspiring against him and Ishka. In the end, the old

426

Ishkan bear stormed out of the palace threatening war with Taron. Things went not much better with King Aryaman and King Tal, and the other kings. They left Tria in betrayal and anger, never to return. And as for Count Muar and Baron Maruth, *they* each vowed to return at the head of their domains' armies should Count Dario press his claim to Alonia's throne.

Late the next day, thirty miles from Tria outside the town of Sarabrunan, we buried Baltasar on a little knoll covered with oaks. He would rest in good company. For all about us, beneath the woods and grass, were buried the ten thousand Valari who had fallen at the Battle of the Sarburn two entire ages before. Beneath some moss, I found a white stone that had once marked the grave of one of these men. Time had nearly worn smooth the ancient headstone. I called for a hammer and used a sharp tent stake to renew the lettering cut into the hard granite: *Here lies a Valari warrior*. Sunjay Naviru declaimed that I should chisel Baltasar's name and feats into the stone, but Lansar Raasharu would not hear of this. He said that his son would have more honor lying in the ground as did the other heroes who had fought against Morjin and defeated him. And so I planted the stone above Baltasar's grave and said a prayer for his soul.

That night, we camped in a fallow field beneath the Hill of the Dead, as the knoll had once been called. We dug a deep moat around our rows of tents and made a palisade of sharpened stakes driven into the loamy earth. Sunjay Naviru posted one of the Guardians at every twenty paces to watch for Belur Narmada's knights – or anyone else who might have thought to pursue us. My men ate a cold, quick meal and hurried off to their beds. They bade me goodnight with deep looks of mourning. It was a quiet, cheerless camp, and I listened in vain for the singing of the Sarni warriors who had accompanied us along many miles of our journey toward Tria.

After we had eaten the last of our cheese, bread and dried sagosk, I sat for a long time with my friends around a fire outside my pavilion. I asked Lansar Raasharu to join us in council, but he said that we companions who had faced Morjin in Argattha should take our tea and brandy together. He told me that *he* would face Morjin alone on the Hill of the Dead, keeping a vigil above Baltasar's grave. I knew exactly what he meant, for in the end, each of us must face evil and the great neverness alone. And so I allowed this noble man to draw his sword and walk into the dark woods outside our camp.

The sky was clear that night, and many stars burned down through the blackness above us. The village a few miles away scented the air with the smells of woodsmoke and roasting meats; I listened to some dogs barking and the rushing of a nearby stream. It was good to sit with Master Juwain, Maram, Atara, Liljana and Kane, as we had so many times on our quest. We all missed Ymiru's great, brooding presence, but Daj's lively company made up for his absence, a little. At the last moment, Estrella joined us, too. It raised my spirits to be surrounded by my old friends, even if it did seem to me that the world had come to an end.

I had many questions for Kane, and he answered many – but many more of them he did not, for that was his way. This gruff, growling wolf of a man had long since abandoned any niceties or etiquette that did not suit him. If he chose not to respond to a query, he would neither evade nor apologize but simply glare at one as if in warning. So it was that he would not tell us of his hunt for the two Skakamen, Elman and Urman, that he had tracked down and killed. Nor would he tell us how he had discovered that Morjin had unleashed them upon Ea. His reticence, in this matter, rankled Maram. He kept sipping from his cup of brandy, and he finally looked at Kane and muttered, 'Ah, but you keep too many secrets.'

'That I do,' Kane said, sipping from his own mug. 'There's much that you don't need to know.'

'Don't need to know!' Maram cried out. 'That skulking Noman nearly killed us all! You say that Morjin summoned the Skakamen from Khutar. What if he summons more of them?'

'*That* is unlikely,' Kane said, gazing up at the sky. He stabbed his thick finger toward the Bear constellation and added, 'Earlier this year, there was an alignment of the planets and stars. This created a door that Morjin was able to open. So, the next such alignment of Ea and Khutar won't occur for another five hundred and twenty-three years.'

At this mention of stellar alignments, Master Juwain turned his good ear toward Kane in hope that he might say more about this art of descrying earthly events in the movements of the stars. But Kane had no mind for such arcane talk. He leaned over and squeezed Maram's knee as he said, 'Will you sleep better tonight knowing that Noman was after Val and not you?'

'No,' Maram said, 'I won't. 'It was all too close – too, too close.'

'That it was.'

'Even your arrival in King Kiritan's hall – I dread what might have happened if you hadn't unmasked Noman, so to speak. How did you recognize him?'

Kane's harsh, handsome face pulled into a scowl as he said, 'How does one wolf recognize another in the middle of a pack of dogs?'

So bright did his eyes flare just then that it was hard to look at him.

'But if you *could* recognize Noman,' Maram persisted, 'if this Skakaman *knew* this, then I don't understand why he hadn't issued orders to King Kiritan's guards to bar you from the hall?'

'Let's just say,' Kane growled out, 'that Noman had good reason to think that I was dead.'

Then he smiled at the sky, showing his long, white teeth to the glittering heavens as he called out, 'Ha, but I'm not dead, am I? It's Noman who is dead, thanks to Valashu Elahad.'

He turned to look at me. I touched the hilt of my sword, and I told him, 'Twice he nearly killed me. And then, in King Kiritan's hall . . .'

I fell silent as I listened to the crickets chirping in the grass and gazed into Kane's blazing eyes. And he said to me, 'So, I sent the letter to Liljana to warn you. And I killed two horses riding straight through to Tria. Elman was to have mimed and murdered King Kiritan. If I had known that *Noman* would find a way to contrive such a foul crime at the last moment, I'd have warned Atara, too – and King Kiritan.'

The fire's flames seemed to dance in the white cloth covering Atara's face. I could tell that she struggled to keep her jaw from trembling. It tormented her that she had not even been able to stand over her father's grave.

To Kane, she said, 'If I couldn't see the danger, there's really no reason that you should have.'

'Well, I *should* have,' Kane said. 'If one plays chess with the Red Dragon, it's perilous to overlook any possible move.'

'What *I* don't understand,' Maram said, 'is how Noman could have foreseen so much? All right, all right, so he found a way to get close to King Kiritan, to stick a knife in his back and bury the body in the gardens somewhere outside the palace – ah, excuse me, Atara, for speaking so bluntly. But how could he know that Master Juwain would challenge his reading of that old chronicle? And summon that ghost out of his crystal and condemn Val for all to hear? Master Juwain didn't know it himself!'

It saddened me to see Master Juwain take out the shards of his akashic crystal and sit holding them piled up in his rough hands.

With the breaking of this wondrous gelstei, all its colors had died, and each individual shard glowed dully like a chunk of gray glass.

'So, Noman could *not* have foreseen this,' Kane said. 'The Skakamen are clever – but not *that* clever. First of all, I doubt that Balakin ever wrote any such chronicle and left if for the Narmadas to collect. Likely Noman had a book of genealogies or some such and was only pretending to read from it. He needed only to challenge Val's claim.

Ha, it's strange, isn't it, that he was able to do this by twisting the truth to his purpose?'

Although it was a cool night for midsummer, I was sweating beneath my diamond armor. I wiped my forehead as I shifted about on my cloak, but I said nothing.

'As for Master Juwain's crystal,' Kane continued, 'Noman had some good luck and some bad. The ghost's reciting of the verses played right into Noman's strategy. But in any case, he certainly meant to challenge Val as he did – and to incite the Valari kings into drawing their swords. That was to be an excuse for seizing Val, and the Lightstone. Likely Val would have been put to the sword in some foul dungeon, or even there in the hall. There might have been war between the Nine Kingdoms and Alonia. Morjin's disciple would have sat upon Alonia's throne, unknown to all. And Morjin would have regained the Lightstone.'

At the mention of this little cup that had caused so much trouble, I drew it forth and sat staring into its golden hollows.

'The Beast meant to destroy you, Val,' Kane said to me. 'And not just your life but your honor – the legend that has grown around you.'

'Well,' I said, squeezing the Lightstone's hard gelstei, 'at least my life still remains. And this.'

But my self-pity seemed only to anger Kane. If I expected him to tell me, as Sajagax had, that I shouldn't blame myself for what had happened, then I would have been a fool. As a volcano trembles with fire, Kane fairly seethed with blame for me – and for himself.

'*What* in all the blazes of heaven were you thinking?' he suddenly shouted at me. So violent was the pent-up passion that erupted from him that two of the Guardians at the edge of the camp turned to regard him in alarm. But Kane ignored them; he sat facing me as his black eyes glistered with a barely-controlled fury. 'Valashu Elahad, the great Shining One – the Maitreya! Ha! *You* were supposed to guard the Lightstone *for* him! It was this realization, wasn't it, that rendered the Lightstone visible to you in the first place? How could you have been so wrong?'

As he continued glaring at me, Master Juwain rattled the ragged bones of his ruined crystal in his hands, and he said, 'I'm afraid that I encouraged Val to believe that he was the Maitreya. You see, there were so many signs: Aos and Niran at the midheaven, conjuncting the sun. Siraj in the Ram constellation, the stars . . .'

His voice died into the crackling of the fire and into Kane's thunderous silence. And then Liljana leaned forward and shook her finger at Kane. 'Don't you speak that way to Val! If you knew that he couldn't have been the Maitreya, why didn't *you* warn him?'

With Kane fixing his bright, black eyes upon me as a tiger might stare down another of his kind, it seemed that he had heard nothing of what our friends had said. He seemed to be asking me, in a howl of outrage, again and again: how could I have been so wrong? And so I finally held the Lightstone out toward the Hill of the Dead as I told him, 'I wanted to end war. The suffering . . . of everyone. Even death.'

Kane's breath suddenly burst from him as if a sword had pierced his lungs. His face softened, and so did the light in his eyes.

'Yes, of course you would have wanted that,' he said at last. 'I should have known you would. I should have spoken of this before. Perhaps Maram is right that I *do* keep too many secrets.'

He took a sip of brandy and held it in his mouth a moment before swallowing. I could almost feel the dark liquor burning all the way down his throat. And then he said, 'That ghost told truly. Ghost, ha! He is one of the Urudjin who dwell in the realm of the Alama Almithral. They are the keepers of memory and time. So, there is a story that comes out of the beginning of time. An old, old story that goes back to the Ardun Satra before the mountains were born. There was a world, it's said. Erathe was its name. And there the Lightstone was sent and came to Ashvar, who was the first Maitreya. He used it to raise up Erathe's people to the order of the Valari. The greatest of these, their king, was named Adar. And it was he who became the Lightstone's first guardian.'

He took another sip of brandy as he stared at the golden cup that I held. 'Adar was the first man to walk the stars. Man, ha! You Valari have always been something more. So. So. After Ashvar finished his work on Erathe, Adar led a host of Valari knights to other worlds – and they brought the Lightstone with them. Theirs it was to find other Maitreyas and set it into their hands. And so they did. Adar finally died, as men do, but the guardianship of the Lightstone passed to his firstborn, Shakhad, then to *his* son, on and on, through the great ages and the small, as the Elijin were raised up from the Valari and the Galadin from them. And always the Lightstone passed to one of Adar's descendants – as *guardians*, never Maitreyas. His line has never failed. Elahad was of it. And so are you, Valashu.'

The little cup in my hand suddenly seemed as heavy as the moon. I could hardly believe what Kane had told me. And so I said to him, 'All those millennia of millennia, father to son, son to grandson – it seems impossible.'

'We're all miracles of creation,' Kane said, sweeping his blunt hand around the circle. 'Each of us was born of a mother and grandmother,

431

going back in an unbroken line to the first days when the Ardun arose from Eluru's many earths.'

'Yes, it must be so,' I said, thinking of *my* mother and grandmother. 'But you must be wrong that the Lightstone passed always to one of Adar's descendants. There was Angra Mainyu. There was Morjin.'

'*Must* I be wrong?' Kane said to me as dark lights flashed inside him. 'So. So. You must be told. Mainyu, too, was of the line of Adar.'

I drew in a sharp, quick breath. In King Kiritan's hall, Ashtoreth's messenger had said this to me: *Angra Mainyu once held the same dream as do you. He, too, wanted to end death, suffering itself. He deceived himself, as have you, Valashu.*

'No, no,' I murmured. 'It's not possible. Angra Mainyu was the greatest of the Galadin.'

'So he was before he fell. But before that, long, long ago, he was of the Elijin. And before *that* he was born of the Valari, even as you were.'

'But he *stole* the Lightstone – so you told me!'

'That he did.' Kane eyed the gleaming golden cup that I held. 'You see, he gave up any claim to its guardianship when he became an Elijin. So it must be. The highest orders are not permitted to use the Lightstone, nor even to touch it.'

I noticed that the fingers of both his hands had drawn into fists. I could feel the muscles trembling in his arms up through his tense shoulders and quick, savage body.

'But *you* have touched the Lightstone yourself,' I whispered to him. 'More than once!'

'Yes, I have.'

'But you are yourself of the Elijin! Your true name is –'

'Be quiet now!' he snarled, cutting me off. He glanced over his shoulder at the knights keeping watch on the Hill of the Dead. 'We will not speak that name – so you promised me!'

'My apologies,' I said, looking at him. The veins along his muscular neck stood out as if they could not bear the pressure of the blood beating through them. I wanted to take away the torment of his fierce, pounding heart. 'But the ghost – he of the Urudjin – he told us of the Battle of Tharharra. It was you, wasn't it, who defeated Angra Mainyu? And then took the Lightstone from Marsul?'

I looked into Kane's black, unfathomable eyes. As the light of the crackling fire played in their liquid centers, his gaze fell cold and strange. I felt inside him a vast distance, like the ocean of space between the earth and the stars.

'*Was* it I?' he said in a low, mournful voice. He opened his hands and stared down into them. 'Was it truly I? It was so long ago, you

432

can't imagine, the years, working at him as wind and water do the face of a mountain. What remains of the child you once were, Valashu? What was the shape of *your* face before you were born? I have a memory of the one you speak of, I think. A memory of a memory. He was one of the great ones, once. He dwelled on other worlds, beyond the stars.'

Kane sighed as he clapped his hands to his face and rubbed his eyes. Then he brought out the dark, oval stone that he had cut from the forehead of the leader of the Grays who had once pursued us through the nearby country. And he told us, 'I didn't defeat Angra Mainyu. He is not defeated. I used a black gelstei similar to this one to suck the life from him, for a moment only, while Manwe and others bound him on Damoom.'

I tapped my fingernail against the rim of the Lightstone, and I said, 'But in the end, you *did* surrender this to Valakand?'

'Yes,' he said, gazing at the golden cup.

'And on the first Quest, in the Age of Swords, you regained this for one of Elahad's descendants to guard?'

'Yes.'

'And In Argattha, you might have claimed this for yourself, yet you gave it back to me?'

'So. So I did,' he murmured, looking at me. 'You are its rightful guardian.'

'No,' I said, shaking my head. 'I should give this to my father for safe-keeping. Or perhaps Asaru – one of my brothers.'

Kane edged between Maram and the fire, and knelt before me. He grasped my wrist then. His hand bruised me like iron, like some evil device that one might find in a dungeon. And he told me, 'I won't hear such talk from you! Do you understand? This is no time for that!'

He sighed again as he let go of me. And then he said, 'Do you remember the story of the eagle and the sun?'

'No,' I said, 'that story is not told in Mesh.'

He returned to his place between Maram and Master Juwain, and retrieved his cup of brandy. He took a sip from it. And then he drew in a deep breath and said, 'Once there was an eagle, one of the sky lords of the Crescent Mountains, whose gift it was to fly higher than any of his kind. He hated night, as all eagles do, for then he could not hunt or even see to fly. And so one day he set forth to soar up to the sun, to sink his talons into the golden orb and bring it back to earth so that there would never be night again. But the sun set his feathers on fire. And like a shooting star, he fell burning back to earth.'

He took another drink of brandy, and then continued the story: 'As fate would have it, he fell in with a flock of ducks. His shame was so

433

great that he did not want even to look toward the sky. And so he resolved to learn to swim like a duck. He waddled like a duck; he quacked like a duck. Even after his feathers grew back, he flew like a duck, low over lakes and marshes.'

Kane stopped speaking suddenly as his bright eyes blazed into mine.

'And is that the end of the story?' I asked.

'No, it is not – you know it is not. You see, the eagle was *not* a duck, and never could be. One day he woke up and heard the far-off cry of his kind, and he remembered who he really was. And he flew back to the mountains to take his place in the aeryies there, among the rocks shining in the sun.'

He paused to pick up the bottle of brandy and refill his mug. And then he gazed at me.

'Ah,' Maram said, holding out his own mug, 'I suppose the moral of the story is that if we're not careful, we'll all wind up as dead ducks.'

'Fat fool!' Kane said, grinning savagely. Then he looked at me and said, 'In the end, it doesn't matter how far we fall – only how high we rise again.'

I thought about this for a moment, then said to him, 'Are you speaking of me or yourself?'

'Perhaps both of us,' he admitted. He looked at me so intently that I could hardly hold his gaze. 'So, you must decide if you are an eagle or a duck. And you must decide soon. I've news for you that you won't want to hear.'

'What news, then?' I asked him.

'I learned this only last week: on the 11th of Marud, an army bearing the standards of the Red Dragon marched east out of Argattha.'

'East!' I cried out. 'East! But we had thought that Morjin would strike out *west*, against the Ymanir!'

'So we did. But that was before you set out to Tria to claim the Lightstone.'

'But Morjin couldn't have hoped to intercept me on the Wendrush!'

'No, he was too late for that, and his army is mostly foot. They could never have caught you.'

'Then why march at all? What is his objective?'

'So, east of Sakai is the land of the Niuriu. They've opposed Morjin for many years. If he could defeat them, he could move against the main Urtuk clans, and the whole center of the Wendrush might collapse.'

My eyes tore into him as I said, 'You do not believe that Morjin has led an army east at this time solely to attack the Niuriu.'

'No, not solely,' he told me. 'East of the Niuriuland lies Mesh.'

My heart beat inside me like one of the great war kettles that my kingdom's drummers struck when marching into battle. 'How many are his men?'

'That is uncertain. Perhaps twenty-five thousand.'

'Twenty-five thousand,' I repeated. 'And is it certain that Morjin leads them?'

'No, that also is unknown.'

'He could not defeat my people with such an army,' I said. 'Not *Valari*.'

'Perhaps not, but he could slay many.'

'But he would risk losing everything. Would he do that, truly?'

'He might if one of the slain was Valashu Elahad.'

As Kane caught me with a blazing look, I listened to the wood hissing and popping in the fire.

'Think of this as a game of chess,' he said to me. 'Morjin could not have known what would happen in Kiritan's hall.'

'No,' I said, thinking of Ravik Kirriland and Baltasar. 'What if Noman had failed to murder King Kiritan and I *had* claimed the Lightstone? What if the kings had pledged themselves to the Alliance?'

'In that case,' Kane said, 'Morjin would have done well to spend an army in order to weaken what would have been the core of the forces arrayed against him. And in order to unsettle you.'

'Then that,' I said, 'only betrays his desperation.'

'So, desperate the Dragon has been ever since you nearly killed him and made off with that little trinket you're holding.'

I looked down at the golden cup that it seemed I could not let go.

'But he's something more than desperate,' Kane went on. 'Or something less. It was always likely that the Alliance would fail. What if it did?'

'Then,' Maram said, stating the obvious, 'it would be as it is now.'

'Just so,' Kane said, looking at me. 'The question is, what should be our next move in this little game we've been playing with Morjin?'

I wrapped my hands tightly around the Lightstone, and I said, 'Everything depends upon this "trinket". We must hurry back to Mesh and keep it safe there.'

At this, Maram's face blanched as if a demon had drained him of blood. 'Go back to Mesh? Ride right into the jaws of the Dragon? Are you mad?'

'My home stands to be invaded, Maram. My duty lies there.'

'Your duty,' he said to me, 'is first as Lord Guardian of the Lightstone. Take it to some safe place!'

Liljana looked up from a tunic that she was embroidering, and she

435

said, 'And where would this safe place be? We've traveled from one end of Ea to the other, and were nearly killed at every mile along the way.'

'Even the Nine Kingdoms will be dangerous for us,' Master Juwain said. 'King Hadaru will certainly challenge Val's right as Lord Guardian, now. And let us not forget that the Red Dragon has offered a million-weight of gold to anyone who will deliver the Lightstone to him. Such a sum would tempt anyone to betray us.'

Maram took a huge gulp of brandy, then blurted out, 'It would not tempt the Lokilani! What of the Vild? The wood of Pualani and Danali – and Iolana – lies not far from here. We could hide there for years!'

'So,' Kane said, 'we *could* hide there – if we could find it. But we could not hide forever. Eventually, Morjin would deduce where we had disappeared to. After he'd conquered Alonia, he'd burn her forests to the ground to uncover the Lokilani's wood and take back the Lightstone.'

As Maram muttered a profanity into his cup, I grasped his arm and said, 'Take heart, my friend. We're not under Morjin's spears yet. His army set out only twenty days ago. It's unlikely that they could make much more than fifteen miles per day, especially if they bear siege-craft in their baggage train. Their march might have taken them as far as the Niuriuland. They'll have to fight Vishakan's warriors to get through it. And after that, it's another two hundred and fifty miles to Mesh – and more for them to fight their way through the passes and push through to the Valley of the Swans. All right then. We have time to return home, if we ride quickly. No army has ever successfully invaded Mesh. And my father's castle has never been taken. The Lightstone will be safe there – as safe as any place on Ea.'

'Ah, so you say,' Maram muttered as he looked at me. 'But has it occurred to you that Morjin will expect you to reason precisely as you have? Kane speaks of a game of chess! Well, what moves does Morjin plan that you haven't foreseen? What if he's suborned another of Alonia's damned dukes? Do we know we won't have to fight another army along the Nar Road? And what if he sets the Stonefaces upon us again or some other evil creatures? And what if –'

'We've taken worse chances than this before,' I said, cutting him of before he terrified himself to death. 'The Lightstone *will* be safe inside my father's castle. We could withstand a siege there for years.'

'You think so?' Maram said, shaking off my hand. He reached into the pocket of his cloak and removed his ruined firestone. 'And what if the Dragon bears one of *these* with which to burn down your castle's walls?'

'*That*,' Kane said, pointing at Maram's cracked, red crystal, 'was the last remaining firestone on Ea.'

'Are you sure?'

Kane paused to take a drink of brandy and then said, 'Reasonably sure.'

After that, for the next hour or so, we debated what we should do. We finally decided that my first impulse would be the best: we would ride like the wind back to Mesh and deliver the Lightstone to my father's hall. The Guardians would stand around it, a diamond wall of the finest Valari knights surrounded by the great, impregnable walls of the Elahad castle. I would send out a call to all the Nine Kingdoms to send other knights to join us. Morjin's army, fighting so far from its base on sacred Meshian soil, would be defeated. And as in ancient times, the Lightstone would blaze like a beacon of hope for all of Ea's peoples.

'If it was my fate not to be the Maitreya,' I said, holding up the golden cup, 'then surely it is upon me to see that this calls forth the Maitreya.'

After that, for a long time, I sat by the fire thinking about the days to come. I played over and over in my mind all of Morjin's possible moves, determining to make no blunder in my own moves. I *must* not lose this game, I told myself. I could not believe that the future was set like words chiseled into stone. It was possible, I thought, that the Valari kingdoms would send aid to Mesh – and then there would no battle. Even so, as I stared into the fire's red flames, I felt fate hammering at my soul, trying to beat into me an acceptance of that which must be.

30

We broke camp early the next day before first light. We rode, if not quite as quickly as the wind, quick enough to feel the morning mist whipping back our hair and moistening our eyelashes. In truth, we could not keep up such a punishing pace for long without ruining our horses. As it was our beasts were already thin from our journey, and we had scant fodder for them and few enough rations for ourselves. When we came to Suma around midafternoon the day following that, we stopped in this ancient city to replenish both. I purchased two stout wagons and filled them with bags of oats, wheels of cheese, dried apples, rye flour and other foods we would need to fuel our flight from Alonia. Not even Maram suggested trying to find an inn for the night. We took to the road again as soon as we could. When darkness came, we camped in a great clearing beneath a starry sky. The forest before us stretched on to the south and east for hundreds of miles.

And in the days that dawned after that, with each mile that we trod, as the iron wheels of the wagons ground against the paving stones and our horses' hooves beat against the road, I tried to sense in wind, earth and aether any sign that we were being followed. In four hard days of travel from Tria, we put some hundred and thirty miles behind us. We passed from Old Alonia into that wild country of forest and hills claimed by no duke, baron or other lord. I felt sure that no battalion of knights or marauders pursued us. And yet something did. Baltasar's death hung heavy upon my soul like an iron shroud that had not been buried with him. So did that of Ravik Kirriland. The dying shrieks of many others, from the past and future, filled the air whenever I listened deeply enough or drew my sword. Each morning we rode east into the sun, and this fiery orb cast a long shadow behind me. The faster I rode, the faster it moved after me, like my black cloak with its swan and stars billowing out behind me. Could any man, I wondered, ever escape his fate? With the earth spinning beneath me and turning day into night, and night into day, I felt myself only hurrying toward mine.

On the sixth of Soal, we found ourselves winding through the misty tors where Atara and I had once fought off the fierce hill men trying to rob and ravish her. Perhaps the memory of the violence that we had visited upon those barbaric men stirred Atara to memories of the future – or visions of faraway things. For just as we were passing a bald prominence above the swathe of oaks to the south of us, Atara froze in her saddle and faced in that direction. I drew in beside her, and the columns of knights behind us came to a halt. And Atara clapped her hand to her blindfold and cried out, 'Oh, Val, there's been a battle! There *is* a battle, it's being fought now, or soon will be. On the Wendrush. Just east of the Red Hills, between the Two Rivers. The Niuriu warriors, the arrow storm, so many dead, so many dying. Morjin! I see him! He *does* lead his army. On a great white stallion. I count nearly thirty thousand spears behind him. And the Urtuk ride with them! I count seven standards: bear, hawk, badger, lion, wolf, otter and eagle. Seven clans of the eastern Urtuk! Damn them! Damn them for going over to Morjin!'

As quickly as it had come, her vision seemed to leave her. She slumped in her saddle and seemed to collapse like a bellows emptied of air. And she murmured, 'The victory is to the Dragon! The way to Mesh stands open before him.'

I reached out my hand to grasp hers and squeeze some courage into her. But I had little to spare. I hated the brittleness in my voice as I said, 'Will the Urtuk ride with Morjin to Mesh? *Are* they riding with him?'

'I don't know,' she told me. 'I can't see that. I can't . . . see.'

With the sudden failing of her second sight, the panic that always accompanied her helplessness seeped into me. Dread filled all my limbs like cold, stagnant water. That evening, when we made camp in the tall trees off the side of the road, Estrella helped Atara hunt in the underbrush for some madder. They found a few of these plants growing beside a stream, and dug them out of the ground. With Liljana's help, Atara boiled their roots in an iron kettle and rendered out of them a dark, red dye. She then rubbed this foul-smelling liquid over the shafts, feathers and points of two of her arrows. And when she had finished staining them, as with blood, she held up one in either hand and said, 'This is for Morjin's right eye. And this is for his left.'

The day after that we passed through the gap in Morning Mountains, and for the next four days we rode through a wild country of tangled forest that had long ago been emptied of people. Nothing, it seemed, could halt our charge homeward or even impede us. In several places, great trees had fallen across the road; we brought out axes and chopped through them. For three days straight, it rained driving sheets of water from dark clouds blown in from the Alonian Sea to the east. We rode straight through this cold, shivering misery. When we came to the lowlands near the border of Anjo and the road flooded out, we abandoned the wagons and forced our way around the flood through the dense forest.

On the 12th of Soal we crossed the Santosh River into Anjo. I had worried that some of my Anjori knights, upon seeing their home again, might wish to abjure their vows and remain in this land of rolling plains, pastures and green hills leading up into the snowy heights of the Morning Mountains. But no one did. These men who had ridden with me for so many miles and had stood by me as we fought our enemies together sensed that something was troubling me. How could they not when my heart leaked my dread as if pierced with spears? When we made camp that night in an abandoned field in the domain of Yarvanu, ruled by Count Rodru, Sar Valkald came up to me and told me, 'It's good to walk this soil again, and it would be even better to see my father and mother, too. But they are of Daksh, and we will not be passing their way. No matter. My vows were made gladly, and will gladly be kept – all the way to Mesh, or anywhere the Lightstone goes.'

Sunjay Naviru, upon overhearing Sar Valkald's pledge, took me aside and reassured me: 'All the Guardians feel as he does, Val. No one blames you for what happened in Tria.'

'Do they not hate me for striking down Lord Ravik?'

'Hate you? It is just the opposite. They are sad that you slew an innocent man, it is true. But that is war. They grieve your loss of glory. In the end, though, it doesn't matter to them if you are the Maitreya. They know who you really are.'

As I looked into Sunjay's face, so faithful and bright, I gave thanks for having such a good friend, and I missed Baltasar all the more. And I wanted to reassure Sunjay as he had me. But how could I? What could I say to this sweet, vital man who seemed marked out for suffering and death? What could I say to anyone?

Although Master Juwain had warned against bringing the Lightstone into any of the Nine Kingdoms, we had no difficulty passing through Anjo. We had ridden ahead of King Danashu, King Hadaru and the other kings, and so we preceded the news of the debacle in King Kiritan's hall. We told little of this to any of the travelers that we

440

encountered on our way, nor even to a company of Count Rodru's knights whose task it was to patrol the road. I said only that the Red Dragon threatened invasion and that my father had called me home to Mesh. I asked for aid, and I received it: in oats for our horses and supplies for my men, if not in stout-hearted knights girded for war. So it was when we passed into Vishal, ruled by Baron Yashur, and in Onkar whose lord was Count Atanu. If either of these great nobles had been tempted by Morjin's million-weight of gold, they did not betray themselves – or me. Perhaps they simply did not have time to summon a force great enough to wrest the Lightstone from my knights. In any case, we came to the juncture of the Nar Road and the North Road without incident. There we turned toward King Danashu's domain of Jathay. It took us two and a half days to put the rest of Anjo behind us. Late in the morning of the 16th of Soal, we crossed the Aru-Adar bridge into Ishka.

Ninety miles as the raven flies it was across this beautiful land to the border of Mesh and more for us because the road bent far to the east toward Loviisa. After passing through a hilly country between Lake Osh and a spur of mountains to our left, and then through some rich farmland glowing green in the strong Soal sun, we came to Ishka's greatest city two days later. Sar Jarlath galloped ahead of us to ask for supplies and tell of our need for haste. Prince Issur, whom King Hadaru had appointed as regent, rode out with Lord Mestivan and ten knights to meet us. We held quick counsel on horseback by a clear stream running down to the Tushur River. We told Prince Issur that Morjin and his army were likely marching upon Mesh even as we spoke. This was news to him. As he told us, none of the sentries who kept watch over the Wendrush had sighted any armies, be they Sarni or of Sakai.

'If you're right about the Red Dragon,' Prince Issur said to me, 'then please excuse my abruptness, but there's much to be done. Messengers need to be sent to the fortresses, and our battle lords must be alerted and knights called up. Morjin might just as easily be marching on Ishka.'

'That is unlikely,' I said. 'His quarrel, for the present, is with Mesh.'

'Yes, but what if Mesh is defeated?' he said. He rubbed between his large nose and his eyes, which were as black as coal.

'Mesh would be less likely to be defeated,' I told him, 'if you have battalions to spare reinforcing us. Do you?'

The suggestion that Ishka might ride to Mesh's aid seemed to astonish Prince Issur. His eyes widened, and he looked at me as if to make sure that my adventures in strange lands hadn't whittled away my good sense. Then he told me, 'Even if we did have such forces, it is not upon me to commit them. My father, you say, still remains in Tria?'

'He was there when we departed,' I said. 'It may be that he is returning home.'

I began to tell him of the conclave's evil happenings, but it seemed that Sar Jarlath already had. Prince Issur cast me a cold, penetrating look as if he had never really believed that I could be the Maitreya. 'It is upon me to prepare Ishka for the worst. That cannot include weakening our forces. My father, I believe, would want things so.'

'Your father,' Lord Mestivan said to him, 'would want the Lightstone to remain here, where it would be safe.'

Then Lord Mestivan turned to stare at me. His hand, I saw, hovered almost casually near the hilt of his sword. So did Sar Jarlath's hand and Sar Ianashu's and those of the other Ishkans who had taken vows as Guardians. But it was toward Lord Mestivan and the ten knights with him that they directed their ire. It brought tears to my eyes to think that they might be willing to fight their own countrymen in the Lightstone's defense – and in mine.

'Sometimes it's hard to know my father's wishes,' Prince Issur said to Lord Mestivan. 'Certainly if the Lightstone remained here, it might tempt the Red Dragon to turn north. Therefore let Lord Valashu take it to the Elahad castle as quickly as he can.'

Prince Issur and many of the Ishkans, I thought, would not be sorry to see Mesh humbled or even beaten in battle. And as for me, they seemed secretly glad that the disaster in Tria had brought me down from the heavenly heights into the realm where mere mortals were forced to live.

We hurried on our way then. From Loviisa, the road wound west through some more farmland and then turned south toward the mountains separating Ishka and Mesh. We pressed our horses all the harder now, for I felt time pressing at me like a great, lead weight. I led my friends and the Guardians, in their three sparkling columns, pounding down the road. On the 20th of Soal we began the steep climb up toward the pass between Raaskel and Korukel. The forest about us gradually changed from oak and elm to towering spruce trees pointed like great, green spears up toward the sky. When I saw that we could not make it through the pass by dusk, I called for a halt. We made camp just below treeline between two rocky ridges. There a swift, clear stream ran over rounded stones. As my men set to pitching the tents and making the fortifications, I took a few moments to sit alone beside the stream. I stared up through the trees at the pass: a great cleft cut through solid rock. It was thus that Kane found me, with my sword drawn and pointing toward it.

'May I join you?' he said as he sat on a large boulder across from me. He followed my gaze, and said, 'You're wondering what you'll find on the other side, eh?'

I nodded my head as my sword flared brighter.

'So, you'll find what you'll find,' he said to me. 'And then you'll do what you must do.'

'Yes, but what is that? As you said, I've been so wrong. I don't ever want to be wrong again.'

'Then guard the Lightstone for the Maitreya. That will be enough.'

'All right, but *who* is he, then? How will we ever find him?'

'By three things,' he told me, 'the Maitreya is known: steady abidance in the One; looking upon all with an equal eye. And unshakable courage at all times.'

I smiled sadly and shook my head as I murmured, 'Courage.'

He reached out to grasp my shoulder. 'Don't let yours fail you now.'

I smiled again as I tapped my sword's hilt against my chest and said, 'I'm afraid it already has. Something flutters inside here now, and it's not an eagle.'

'Be strong,' he told me as he looked at me.

'Be strong,' I repeated, 'and protect the weak – you should have seen Sajagax's face the first time he heard the whole of the Law.'

'That is *not* the whole of it,' he said. Although it was falling dark, his eyes began to brighten. '"Be strong and protect the weak – and help them to become strong."'

Even as he said this, his hand grew tighter around my shoulder.

'Strength, yes,' I said, shaking off his hand. I picked up a pebble and cast it against a nearby tree. It hit the rough bark with a little 'tonk,' then bounced off it and plopped into the stream. 'But even the strongest tree will fall to fire.'

Kane's eyes grew hot and pained as he watched me, waiting for me to say more.

'It's my fate,' I finally told him.

'*What* is your fate?'

'That's just it – I don't know.' I gazed at my sword's silustria, gleaming in the day's last light. 'Alkaladur is named the Sword of Fate. The Sword of Sight. That is the power of the silver gelstei, yes? *Not* to enable one to descry events as a scryer does, but to see if one's life is in accord with a higher will.'

'Ananke, this is called,' Kane told me. 'The universal fate to which

443

all must submit – even the Galadin and the Ieldra. Perhaps even the One.'

'Yes,' I said, 'but I looked away from it. This was *my* will. When I found the Lightstone, I saw my fate, so bright – like the sun rising to touch all the world. Then everyone started calling me the Maitreya, and I believed this. I *wanted* to believe. But now . . .'

'Go on,' he told me.

'Now I feel my fate as fire. Do you remember the story of the robe of fire?'

He slowly nodded his head as he stared at me. It was said that once a time, in the Lost Ages, a great hero named Arshan had slain a dragon who terrorized the land, rending and destroying in the service of Angra Mainyu. And Angra Mainyu, from far away on Damoom, had caused one of his priests in secret to dip a robe of white lamb's wool into the dragon's blood. The priest then presented the red robe to Arshan to wear as a sign of his great deed. But the moment that Arshan donned this bright garment, it burst into flame. It welded to his skin and burnt down to his bones, driving him mad before he killed himself in agony.

'It's that way for me now,' I said to Kane. 'Everything burns. It's as if I've fashioned my own robe of fire, with the blood of Baltasar, Ravik Kirriland – even Morjin.'

I went on to say that I felt the flames enveloping me, consuming me, and sweeping forth in an irresistible holocaust to burn everything away.

'So,' Kane told me as his black eyes caught up the brightness of my sword, 'there is the fire that torments and kills. But there is also the refining fire, the angel fire that burns the world clean and makes new all things to bring in a new age.'

'A new age,' I said, shaking my head. 'I must know what awaits me tomorrow, or next week. The *not* knowing is driving me mad.'

'But we can never know our fate,' he told me. 'All we can do is to accept it when it comes.'

'Must we accept all that is hateful and dark then?'

'Listen to me, Valashu, and listen well.' He took my hand in his and squeezed it as if greeting me for the first time. 'Each man has but one fate. You must love yours as you do life itself. You must greet it every morning, and every moment, with all your heart. You must clasp it to you, fiercely, with joy, and never let go. You must keep faith with it and cherish it so completely that you would wish it to come again and again, a million times a million times, through the fires of eternity and all the cycles of creation.'

I pulled my hand away from his and sat looking at it in the waning light. It seemed that there was neither blood nor bones inside, but only a cold, red jelly that quivered with every thought of the future. I said to Kane, 'Yes, perhaps I should do as you say. But who has the strength for that?'

'Strength is given to each of us equal to what we must bear. That is the design of the One.'

I looked with awe upon this fearsome man who had once been crucified to the naked rock of Skartaru, there to endure the torture of Morjin tearing at his insides every day for ten years.

'Perhaps,' I said, wiping away the cold, slick of sweat on my hand. 'But surely the One looked away from me when I thought to claim the Lightstone for myself. And when I killed Ravik.'

'So, you don't want to be overlooked, do you?' he growled out as he gazed at me. 'Then have faith! When we have faith, we become more visible to the One.'

So saying, he grasped the mandolet that he had slung on his back. He tapped his finger against its polished wood and plucked its strings, tuning it. I was glad that he had taken this lovely instrument, after Alphanderry had died.

For a while, as the campfires below us sent plumes of smoke into the air and night darkened the woods, he played an old song that was one of Alphanderry's favorites. It had no words that I knew, but each of the notes that Kane called forth was as clear and full of meaning as an entire poem. There was mourning in the music that he made, and yet great praise and exaltation, too. It rang out with an immense will simply to be. The sweet, sad melody breathed new life into me and raised up my spirits toward the sky's shimmering stars.

Kane's eyes shone like stars themselves. The fierceness of his face gradually fell away from him. His whole being seemed to open like a great, golden flower with infinitely many layers of petals. There was a part of him at its center, a precious jewel, that he kept always to himself. And within this secret heart gathered a song that was all beauty, fire and grace.

I gasped in wonder when Flick suddenly appeared above the stream and took on Alphanderry's form. I saw Kane smiling as this luminous Alphanderry began singing to the music in a voice so beautiful that I could hardly bear it. It seemed that the constellations above us and all the earth were singing along with him, in fire and in joy, giving answer to the essential anguish of life.

And then Kane finished his song, and Alphanderry vanished back into neverness. And Kane murmured, 'My friend, my little friend.'

'What was it he said?' I asked him. 'This language of the angels – I'm still not able to understand it.'

'Nor I,' Kane told me, staring off at the stars.

'What?' I said. 'But you are –'

'I am who I am,' he told me. 'And I have forgotten this language. Or been denied it. In the end, it amounts to the same thing.'

I listened to the tinkling stream as it rushed over the moon-silvered rocks. I said, 'But how? How is this possible?'

He gazed at me as a sad smile played upon his lips. And then he told me, 'It is strange. The One looks out from my eyes, and yours – and so with a squirrel and a butterfly and all things that see. The One feels the earth through my fingers and yours, the rain upon the face of a child, the wind through an oak tree's leaves. All things have just one taste and blaze with a single flame, infinite and inextinguishable, that is their source and true being. And yet, I forget. So, I forget who I really am, and that's the hell of it – I forget, and then all that is lovely and light falls ugly and dark.'

From somewhere in the mountains around us, a wolf called in his immense loneliness to the moon. I thought I heard an eagle cry out, too, but that seemed impossible since eagles do not fly at night.

Kane strapped the mandolet back over his shoulder, then said to me, 'You must take to heart what I'll tell you now: the One moves all things for a purpose, even if we do not see it. And so *we* must move, ourselves, with this purpose, even if it brings our doom.'

I knew that what he had told me was true. And yet I also believed what my grandfather had once told me: that some men are born to make their own fate. Hope blazed inside me then. I looked toward the dark mountains looming on the horizon like great, humped monsters. Would I find Morjin on the other side of them? I vowed that if I did, this time I would close with him in battle and kill him, even if it killed me, too, as Atara had once warned. How else to deal with this Great Beast who had finally overreached himself? How could I turn away from such a fate?

'Thank you for the song,' I said to Kane, bowing my head to him. I lifted Alkaladur up toward the sky and added, 'Thank you for the sword, too.'

He bowed back to me, then smiled his savage smile. He sniffed the air, which was smoky with the smell of roasting meat. 'So, then, let's go and eat some of that lamb that Liljana is cooking us and replenish our strength, eh? I'm fairly starved.'

He stood up and held out his hand to pull me up to my feet. We walked back to our camp together. After we had our feast, I retired to my pavilion and lay awake almost all night trying to descry the pattern and purpose of the stars.

The next morning I led my columns of knights through the pass and down into Mesh.

31

I t was two days later when we finally turned off the North Road and wound our way up the steep hill to my father's castle. I looked upon its stark granite walls with a new eye, for I saw in its towers and battlements not just a cold, enclosing hardness but the strength to protect people and things that were dear to me. Carts full of grain and shepherds driving flocks of baahing sheep impeded our way up to the north gate, for Morjin's army had been sighted approaching Mesh only two days before, and already the castle was laying in extra stores against invasion. On our ride down from Ishka, we had heard talk of little else. The call to arms had gone out to all men of the kingdom able to wield a sword. From the Culhadosh River to the kel keeps in the west, from Ki in the north to Godhra in the south, farmers were setting down their hoes, and blacksmiths their hammers, and strapping on their kalamas instead. The first of these warriors, in their tens and twenties, were arriving in Silvassu from across the Valley of the Swans. The castle could not shelter them all, and so the army gathered in the fields along the Kurash River, below the city. Some of the knights called up, however, had business at the castle, and these, too, crowded the road ahead of us. Maram insisted that they should make way for the Lightstone's Guardians, but I counseled patience. During the days to come, I thought, all of Mesh would need the patience of the mountains.

Our entrance to the castle was heralded by the blowing of horns and shouts of gladness. As we drew up in the north ward, packed with creaking carts, squawking chickens and dogs barking and darting about, young squires went running to summon my father and brothers. Three of these – Yarashan, Mandru and Ravar – were gone for the day, but Jonathay and Karshur came hurrying out of the gateway leading to the middle ward. 'Val, you've come home!' Jonathay called out to me. I dismounted and gave Altaru over to one of squires who gathered around our horses. I clasped Jonathay's wiry body to me, and then Karshur's blockier form. Then Asaru came into the ward, too, and strode up me. After embracing me and kissing my forehead, he stood back to regard me with his warm, dark eyes.

'It's good to see you,' he said, smiling at me. 'But you look tired.'

'And you look . . . well,' I told him. I laid my hand on him and asked, 'How is your shoulder?'

'Healed but still sore. But it's not so bad that I can't grip a lance. As it seems that every knight in Mesh must soon do. Have you heard the news?'

'There's been little else *to* hear all the way down the North Road.'

I did not tell him of Atara's vision or of Kane's warning me of Morjin's march. Too many people were standing about, and it was not the time to hold council.

Just as I was presenting Atara and my other companions to my brothers, my father walked into the ward. He was tall and grave in his long black tunic, embroidered with the swan and stars of the Elahads. He wore on his thick, black belt the sword that my grandfather had given him. Although he was strong and graceful in all his motions, as always, there was about him a heaviness, as if he wore a suit of mail made of lead. He came up to me and embraced me. And then he said, 'Valashu, welcome. It's good chance that has brought you home at this time – good chance for us, thought perhaps not for you.'

'It wasn't really chance at all, sir,' I told him. 'Perhaps we could speak of this in private, with my friends.'

My father looked at Atara, standing next to me, and at Kane. Then his bright gaze took in the Guardians behind us. I could feel his surprise at seeing so many knights from the other Nine Kingdoms in our company. I was sure as well that he noticed Baltasar's absence and descried the grief written across Lansar Raasharu's face.

'Very well,' he said to me. 'Go and get yourself something to eat. Wash the dust from your face. Then let's meet, in an hour, in the library.'

We did as he had commanded us. I led everyone into the middle ward, and then into the great hall. There we were served a hastily prepared feast of ham and eggs, wheat bread with butter and jellies, quince pies, strawberries, blackberries, peaches and plums. It was good to tuck in so much delicious food. I wondered how much longer such meals would be forthcoming. After we could eat no more, I set the Lightstone back on its stand on the dais beneath the black banner and the portraits of my ancestors. I gave the quartering and command of the Guardians over to Sunjay Naviru. Daj and Estrella were set free to explore the castle. Then I walked with Atara and Liljana down the corridor connecting the great hall to the keep. Kane, Maram and Master Juwain, with Lansar Raasharu, followed behind us.

We made our way past the kitchens and the empty infirmary to the library where my father sometimes held council. My father and Asaru were waiting for us there. So were my mother and grandmother. The moment that we entered this rectangular room, lined on each of its four walls with shelves of books, my mother came up and kissed me, and then so did my grandmother. Nona, I thought, seemed even older and frailer than when I had left for the Tournament at Nar. But her whole being was somehow brighter, as if she were gathering into herself stores of hope and courage that might be needed in the days to come. My mother, too, was in brave spirits. In truth, I had never seen her look so radiant and beautiful. In her bearing was an assurance that she, and everyone around her, would find the will needed to face even the darkest of times. But then she was the daughter of a strong king and the queen of an even stronger one.

We all sat around a large table in the center of the room, my father at one end and Asaru at the other. The dark cherrywood, smelling of rosemary and beeswax, was covered with books. Fresh quills and sheets of paper, along with inkpots, had been set out for the writing of letters. One might have expected to see maps of Mesh spread out across the table's gleaming surface, but my father disdained such when it came to planning the movements of armies. Reliance on maps, he claimed, weakened the mind and made less clear the image of terrain that a good commander should always hold inside his head.

'It's good to meet the rest of Valashu's companions,' he said to Atara, Liljana and Kane. 'One of the measures of a man is his friends. And by that ruler, my son stands tall, indeed.'

Coming from another, this might have seemed flattery, but my father never said anything that he didn't mean.

'Now then,' he went on in a strong, clear voice, 'let us hear what has happened, and we will discuss what must be done.'

For a few moments I gazed around the room at the stands of candles casting their soft light on the many books stacked from the floor to the ceiling. I breathed in the smells of old leather and new ink. And then I told of all that had happened since I had parted company with Asaru and Yarashan after the Tournament. My father's eyes widened slightly at the story of the misty island in the middle of the Wendrush and the single-horned asherahs that wandered its magical woods. He smiled as I recounted Maram's feat in drinking down the mighty

450

Braggod; I sensed his approval – and surprise – of my friendship with Sajagax. But when I turned to telling of the Skakaman who had nearly murdered me, and *my* murdering of Ravik Kirriland and ruin of the conclave, his face fell grim. At the news of King Kiritan's death, he shook his head and said to Atara, 'It's a terrible thing when one king connives to assassinate another – and leaves nothing of him even to bury. But then Morjin, although he claims the sovereignty of Sakai and much else, is no true king.'

He sat gazing at Atara, and there was kindness and compassion in his eyes. In all his life, I thought, he had never looked upon one of the Sarni so closely, except in battle. And never a Sarni woman. Her golden hair seemed to hold great wonder for him, as it did for my mother. That Atara was blind and yet somehow could still see amazed him even more.

Then my father nodded at Lansar Raasharu. 'All of Mesh will grieve for Baltasar. It seems like only yesterday when he played along the battlements with Ravar and Val. He'll be missed, as would one of my own sons.'

Pain welled in Lansar's eyes as he clamped his jaws shut. Then he grabbed at his sword and said, 'Thank you, my lord. There's no help for grief, but there is the cold solace of revenge. It may be the worst of things for Mesh that Morjin has marched upon us, but it is not bad tidings for me.'

My father sat regarding him calmly, but with great perceptivity, as if he could look into his heart and soul – even as he often looked at me. I felt the weight of my father's concern for him as he said, 'Peace, Lansar. Peace to you, and to Mesh if we can find the way to it.'

Now he turned to me and said, 'Even before your last journey, you'd had adventures enough for three lifetimes. And now. A first in the sword and a second in the long lance. Champion. Victor of two battles. Vanquisher of this evil thing called a Skakaman.'

'And slayer of an innocent man!' I cried out. 'I brought ruin upon the conclave – and perhaps upon Mesh!'

'You judge yourself more harshly than Count Dario did – or any man should,' my father told me. 'Ruin, you say, you brought to the conclave. But it was you who brought the Valari kings there in the first place, to sit at one table together, and this is a great thing.'

'Surely they sit there no more,' I said. 'You should have seen their faces when they learned that I was not the Maitreya.'

'*That* is still not proven!' Lansar Raasharu called out, slamming his hand down on the table. 'All we've had are some old verses out of an old gelstei that is now in pieces. Who knows if they really told true?

Val must have faith! Perhaps he'll regain it after we've smashed the Dragon.'

My father looked down the table at Lansar, and then at me. Many things stirred inside him: sorrow, pride, doubt, love. The light of his eyes filled my own like fire. And then he said, 'We must assume that Val is *not* the Maitreya, unless by some miracle it is proven otherwise. Certainly few now will perceive him as such. Certainly the Valari kings do not.'

He paused to take a breath, then asked me, 'You say that King Hadaru and the others have left Tria?'

'They must have,' I said. 'But we rode ahead of them, so it is hard to be sure.'

My father ran his finger along his jaw, and then said, 'It may be, then, that they have already reached their domains, or soon will. Very well. It was not known how things would go in Tria, and so messengers have already been sent to them, requesting aid. It will take some days for them to return with their answers.'

'It would be folly,' I said to him, and to myself, 'to place too great a hope on what these answers will be.'

'Perhaps,' he told me. 'But it would equally be folly to place too little. You say that the Valari kings are cold toward you now. But things build inside men like layers of snow. And even a whisper, at the right moment, can set off an avalanche. Maitreya or no, Valashu, who knows what you've set to whispering in others' hearts?'

Kane, sitting next to Asaru at the other end of the table, kneaded his hands together as if they ached to grip a sword. Then he growled out, 'So, even if Ishka or Kaash *do* march to aid Mesh, they might march too late. What if Morjin moves first?'

Asaru eyed Kane as if he didn't quite like his look. 'The Sakayans sit on the steppe, at the mouth of the Eshur Pass. We've counted seven of the Urtuk clans waiting with them. We don't know what they are waiting for.'

At the mention of the Urtuk clans, Kane, Maram and I all looked at Atara. It finally came time for her to tell of the battle that she had seen from afar, and this she did.

'It may be,' she said, 'that Morjin pauses to care for his wounded – the Niuriu's arrows struck down many.'

'We've had no news of this battle,' my father said. He regarded Atara with that kind of creeping dread that people often feel toward scryers.

'It may also be,' she said, 'that Morjin awaits reinforcement from the Adirii clans.'

'That would be bad news, indeed,' my father said. 'We've counted

452

twenty-five thousand Sakayans under Morjin's command, and two thousand Urtuk.'

'And how many can we field?' I asked.

'We're hoping that sixteen thousand will answer the call. Perhaps seventeen.'

At this, Maram began drumming his fingers on the table as he said, 'Then even if Morjin is not reinforced, he would still outnumber us nearly two to one.'

'*One* Valari,' Asaru said to him, pointing at Maram's ring, 'is the equal of any two Sakayans who ever lived. Don't forget that *you* are a Valari knight, now.'

'In spirit, ah, yes I am,' Maram said. 'And it's to be hoped that the Valari fighting spirit will hold off the Red Dragon and *keep* him from fighting. Why else would he wait before the gateway to Mesh?'

'We cannot overlook the possibility,' Master Juwain said, 'that he awaits the right moment. Surely *he* would look to the heavens before so great an undertaking. With Argald conjuncting Siraj in only another ten days, and the Wolf on the ascendent, then . . .'

For a while, he went on to speak of omens and stellar configurations. And then my mother, who was always practical in a way that reminded me of Liljana, brought matters back to earth 'Perhaps he only waits to bring up more rations and arms. He must be at the end of a very vulnerable and long line of his supplies.'

My mother, I thought, a woman given by nature to love poetry, music and meditation, had spent too much of her life in the company of warriors and kings.

My father sighed as he steepled his fingers beneath his chin. Then he told us, 'Any or all of what has been said are good enough reasons. But we must also consider the letter that Morjin sent to my son. He threatened to destroy Mesh if the Lightstone was not returned to him. Well, the Lightstone has now returned to *Mesh*. Perhaps Morjin had news of this – or deduced this, and has only been awaiting his chance.'

'But what sort of chance is this?' Asaru said. 'We're agreed that he cannot defeat us.'

'Are we?' my father said to him. 'Your confidence and courage befit a king, and yet a king should never forget the uncertainty of battle.'

'Morjin faces the same uncertainty. Perhaps now that he has come this far, he hesitates to come the final miles. Perhaps he hopes that showing us his army will make us give him what he wants.'

'Now, it seems, we come closer to the truth of things,' my father said. 'Morjin made a threat to us, and may have made it known to others. He may have marched, in part, to keep true to his word.'

At this, Kane threw back his head and let loose a howl of laughter so loud that not even the books along the walls could soften the savage sound of it: 'Morjin, a man of his word – ha! The Lord of Lies, he is. So. So. King Shamesh. You know that Morjin hates the truth as the night does the sun. But you are right that he wants to be *seen* as keeping his word. A dragon that threatens a village with fire is scorned if he fails to burn it.'

My father studied Kane for a few moments, and then said, 'You seem to know a lot about the *Red* Dragon.'

'That I do. I've fought him in Yarkona and in Argattha. And in other places.'

'And what places would those be?'

'Faraway places,' Kane said. 'Dark places.'

Kane, I thought, was an even greater mystery to my father than he was to me. At Kane's request, I had said nothing of his origins to my family, or to anyone. My father knew of him only as a matchless old warrior who had fought with me side by side in Argattha, cutting and slaying without mercy to face down Morjin and seek his revenge.

'Very well,' my father said to Kane, and to everyone. 'The Red Dragon has made his threats. Asaru is right that his marching on us may only be another. Therefore it follows that he may send envoys demanding the Lightstone's return.'

'But you can't gamble on that!' Kane snarled out. 'You can't wait upon these envoys and leave your realm open to invasion!'

My father cast Kane a cold, hard look. He did not tolerate presumption, and Kane could be the most presumptuous of men.

'No one is suggesting that we do,' my father told him. 'The kel keep at Eshur Pass has already been reinforced from the garrison at Lashku. They could hold back Morjin's army for a day, possibly two. As soon as my warriors and knights are assembled, we'll make forced march to the pass. And there intercept Morjin's envoys – or his army.'

Neither Asaru, Lord Raasharu or I could fault my father's plan. But Atara sat in silence, twisting her scryer's sphere around and around in her long hands. And Kane glared at a brazier full of coals near his corner of the table. His black eyes seemed as hot as coals as his jaw muscles worked beneath his taut skin.

'Do you have an objection to make?' my father asked him.

'So, there's something here that we do not see.'

'And what is that, then?'

'How should *I* know? How can anyone see . . . what he cannot see?'

'But you have a sense of things, yes?'

'So, a sense. I smell a trap. The Red Dragon has set many such before.'

My father sat drawing in deep breaths of air, and then releasing them slowly. He finally said, 'If you perceive the nature of this trap, please inform me. But until then, there's much to be done. Now, if no one has anything to add, let us all go about our duties.'

After we left the library, I took Maram aside and told him, 'I'm sorry I led you to this. You might have returned home to marry Behira instead of making war.'

And he told me: 'Ah, well, don't distress yourself, my friend. It's sad, in a way, that the events in Tria have postponed my plans. And now this. But the truth is, I'm still not fit to be anyone's husband. If you had claimed the Lightstone and learned to wield it, I had hoped . . . ah, that things might have been different. And some day they *might* be. But until then, I'll need to claim my own sword and wield it more wisely, if you know what I mean.'

Maram seemed almost relieved that the urgency of the situation might occupy his other talents and keep him out of trouble. For my father had been right in what he had told us: thousands of tasks must be accomplished, and soon, to make the castle and kingdom ready for war. My mother took charge of the castle's domestic affairs, finding rooms or sleeping space for the many new people taking shelter there. Asaru rode off to see to the assembly of the army. His would be the critical command of the right wing of heavy cavalry, if my father kept to the usual order of battle. Lansar Raasharu, as my father's seneschal, would act as his closest counselor in all matters of strategy as well as logistics. Since Kane, Atara, Master Juwain and Liljana were guests of Mesh, my father required nothing of them. But he expected a great deal. They did not disappoint him. Master Juwain went to work with the other healers to prepare the army's field infirmary to care for the wounded. As at Khaisham, Liljana would assist him, along with Behira and others. Kane, prowling the castle like a caged tiger, threw himself into whatever work came to hand: drawing water, helping the black-smiths pound hot iron into extra shoes for the horses, giving newly arrived knights lessons with the sword. My father asked me, and Maram, to make sure that the castle was ready to withstand siege. We were to report on how many hundreds of bushels of wheat had been added to the already considerable stores of food in the great vaults beneath the keep. And more importantly: how many sheaves of arrows had the fletchers sent up from Silvassu and how many barrels of oil ready to be heated to boiling and poured down upon any poor Sakayans assaulting the castle's walls? As for these great sweeps of

455

granite, I was to walk along every inch of the battlements, testing mortar and stone, making sure that the archers knew their places and the warriors stood ready to repel ladders or fight off the enemy's siege towers.

For three days we thus busied ourselves. Each night at the end of our work, I climbed the Swan Tower and looked out to the south of the city where the army gathered along the river. Their cooking fires grew night by night from hundreds into thousands of flickering orange lights. On the morning of the fourth day since my return home, my father announced that sixteen thousand warriors had answered his call to battle, with more trickling in from the faroff mountain fastnesses. He strapped on his armor, and prepared to ride down from the castle to join them. But then, toward noon, there came a commotion from the West Gate. Ten knights rode into the west ward escorting two Sarni warriors under heavy guard. The knights' captain, Sar Barshan of Lashku, asked to speak with my father. After my father was summoned and heard what Sar Barshan had to say, he called for an immediate council in his library.

When I entered the library, I was amazed to see Atara standing and talking familiarly with the two Sarni warriors. For she knew them well, as did I. They were Aieela and Sonjah, two of the Manslayers of the Urtuk who had aided us in crossing the Wendrush the year before. It was they, with their sister warriors, who had made Atara's lionskin cloak. Accoutered in their studded leather armor and golden torques, with their quick blue eyes looking wildly about the library at the books and chairs and other objects that they had never seen before, they seemed agitated and out of place. My father did not ease their disquiet. He presented them with cold formality to Asaru and Lord Raasharu. And then he left them standing next to Sar Barshan as he invited everyone else to sit at the table.

'Sar Barshan,' my father announced, nodding at this grim, young knight guarding the Manslayers, 'has hurried here at Lord Manthanu's command. Three days ago, these women presented themselves at his keep with tidings that we all should hear.'

So saying, he nodded at Sonjah, who was the taller and older of the two women. She had an air of gravity, which was enhanced by her considerable substance: heavy arms and jowls and great, wide hips that a Sarni pony might have had troubling holding up. Her voice was heavy, too, with anger, as she looked at my father and said, 'We'll tell our tidings, King Shamesh, for Atara's sake, if not yours. But it is hard to speak in the face of so little hospitality.'

'Forgive me,' my father said, swallowing the anger in his own voice.

456

'But when I was a boy, my brother, Ramshan, was sent to the Urtuks on a mission of peace. Your people showed their hospitality by sending back his head.'

'That was not the doing of the Manslayers or of *my* clan,' Sonjah said. 'It was the Yarkuts who did this. Always they have shamed themselves, even as they do now.'

Lansar Raasharu slapped his hand on the table and broke in: 'Why should we believe anything these women say? They are *Sarni*.'

'You may believe what you wish to believe,' Sonjah said. 'Men always do. I care not. I've come here to speak with the *imaklan*, Atara.'

'How did you know that she had come among us?' Lansar asked her.

In answer, Sonjah gave back his dark gaze with an evil look of her own.

'Let her speak,' my father said to Lansar. 'Then we will judge and decide what must be done.'

Again, he nodded at Sonjah. She gripped her unstrung bow and said to Atara: 'Our Kurmak sisters have sent word that there is war between the Marituk and the Kurmak. They told us, too, that we would find you in Mesh. You are needed, Atara. All the Manslayers, from all the tribes, are uniting against Morjin – and against any tribe or clan that would ally with him. You are called to speak at council. Many speak of *you* as Chiefess of all the Manslayers.'

I had never heard that the Manslayers had ever had a single chiefess before. Neither, it seemed, had Atara. She sat facing across the room toward Sonjah and Aieela as she said, 'It would be a great thing for the Manslayers to unite this way, and those are truly great tidings. But that is not why Lord Manthanu has sent you here under guard, nor why King Shamesh has called this meeting, is it?'

'No, it is not,' Sonjah said as she looked from Atara to my father.

'Then,' Atara said, 'why don't you tell us the rest of your news?'

Sonjah stared straight at my father, and then with the savagery for which the Sarni are famous, she fired these words like flaming arrows at him: 'A Galdan army marches upon Mesh. They are commanded by one of Morjin's priests, a man named Radomil Makan. In five or six more days, they will be upon you.'

'The Galdans!' Asaru cried out. 'Here, in Mesh? Impossible!'

In truth, what Sonjah had told us *did* seem impossible. Galda was still in chaos after the wars fought to otherthrow her king. And it was nearly four hundred miles from Ar to Mesh, with the most impassable terrain of the Morning Mountains to cross. And half of those miles lay in the sere, cruel country of the Mansurii, who would kill

457

Galdans as gladly as they would Meshians or Kaashans or any other peoples.

When Atara questioned Sonjah about this, Sonjah shrugged her shoulders and said, 'The Red Dragon has sent chests of gold to the Mansurii. He has bought safe passage for the Galdans.'

'But he has not bought the Mansurii's bows and arrows?'

'Not as far as we've heard.'

'How many are the Galdans, then?'

'Forty thousand, it's said.'

'Forty thousand!' Maram cried out. 'Oh, my lord – it will be like Khaisham!'

My father sat regarding Sonjah and Aieela. His face seemed to have taken on the color of the old, leatherbound books all around him.

'If *true*,' Lansar Raasharu said, 'this will be very bad. But why should we believe it *is* true? Why should these women risk so much to aid their enemy?'

Sonjah brushed back her thick, blonde hair and said, 'We care not what befalls Mesh. We came here to warn Atara and take her away from what will surely be slaughter.'

I rubbed the seven diamonds set into the black jade of the hilt of my sword. I said, 'Slaughter is *not* certain. You speak of the Manslayers uniting against the Red Dragon. Why not ask your sisters to fight with us?'

'Ally with *men*?' Sonjah said to me. 'We *slay* men.'

'But the Manslayers rode with us against the Adirii clans, who were bought by the Red Dragon.'

'True, but we are Urtuk, not Kurmak. We are too few, and we will not waste ourselves in a hopeless battle – not to aid *Valari*.'

'But all of the Manslayers,' I persisted, 'would *not* be too few.'

Sonjah shrugged her shoulders again. 'Even if the Manslayers will unite, it would take a month to gather all of us together.'

'Too late to be of any help to us,' Lansar said.

Sonjah smiled at him, and her eyes were as sharp as knife points. '*You* will help *us*. You Valari will not die cheaply, this we know. You will weaken the Red Dragon. And then we will harry him along his retreat to the Black Mountain. Perhaps we will slay him, and burn his liver in memory of you.'

Kane glared at her and snapped out, 'Fool! If you think you can so easily outmaneuver Morjin, then you're a fool.'

Sonjah tried to ignore him, but that was something like ignoring a mountain of fire about to erupt. Finally, she managed to turn toward Atara. 'Will you come with us, my *imakla* one?'

'No,' Atara said without hesitation. 'Not now. I will fight along with Val, and his people.'

Sonjah looked at me sadly and said, 'You are the one Valari I *would* ride with. Perhaps another time.'

Lansar glowered at her as he fingered the hilt of his sword. Then he said to us, 'At best, this woman hopes to slay Morjin and claim the Lightstone for herself – after he has plundered it from us. At worst, she is a spy. She is Urtuk, and we have seen the Urtuk clans gathering to Morjin's standard.'

'True,' Asaru said, 'but we haven't seen the Manslayers.'

Lansar waved his hand toward Asaru as if sweeping away the voice of reason. 'Even if the Manslayers haven't been bought by Morjin's gold, these women might have been. Or bought by pain: what if Morjin holds hostage their families and threatens them with torture?'

'Toward what end?' Asaru asked.

'Toward deceiving us about the Galdans. If we believe that they are marching against Mesh, then we might be led to fear taking the field against Morjin.'

'Our Mansurii sisters told us of the Galdans!' Sonjah called out, shaking her bow at Lansar. 'Do you call everyone a liar?'

'The truth is sometimes hard to bring forth,' he said. 'Perhaps a heated iron, held to your face, would help sort the truth from the lies.'

For as long as it took for my heart to beat five times, no one said anything. Master Juwain touched his ruined ear; Atara readjusted her blindfold. The rest of us all looked at Lansar in horror.

And then my father called out, 'Lansar! You forget yourself!'

Lansar's face filled with blood, and he rubbed his eyes. He bowed his head and stared at the edge of the table. Then he looked at my father and said, 'Forgive me, my lord, but since Baltasar died, by another of Morjin's deceptions . . . you see, how can we let such things happen again? And now, not just *my* son but all the sons of Mesh, our daughters, too – it would be madness to trust the word of these manslaying women.'

Sonjah clasped her hand to her cheek as if Lansar's words, if not a hot iron, had burned her. Then she looked at Aieela and said, 'Come, my sister, it's time we went home. Unless King Shamesh would shackle us and keep us in his dungeons.'

In truth, my father's castle held neither shackles nor dungeons. Freely these women had come to us, and freely they would be allowed to leave. My father said to Sar Barshan, 'See that they are well cared for, and escort them from Mesh.'

After Sar Barshan and the two Manslayers had left us, my father turned to Atara and said, 'What do you make of their tidings?'

Atara pulled her black-maned cloak more tightly around her shoulders. Then she said, 'Sonjah tells truly.'

'Are you speaking as a scryer or as a Sarni who knows these people?'

'I'm speaking as Val's friend,' Atara said to him. Some of the room's coldness seemed to have seeped into her voice. 'And as yours.'

'Much may depend upon whether or not we believe them.'

'You *must* believe them,' Atara told him. Her words, even to my ears, seemed less an affirmation than a demand.

My father stared at her and said, '*Must* the fate of Mesh turn on the word of outlanders, and Sarni at that? Are you a truthsayer, then?'

At this, my mother grasped his arm, and leaned closer to him as she whispered something in his ear.

'Forgive me,' my father said to Atara. He let loose a long sigh. 'These are bad times, but that is no cause for unkindness. And Elianora reminds me that she, too, was once a stranger in this land.'

Liljana brought out her little blue gelstei and said, '*I am* a truthsayer, my lord. At least, this stone often gives me to hear truth or lies in what others say. And I agree with Atara: the Manslayer told truly.'

Lansar shook his head as he called out to my father, 'You cannot rely on this!'

'Perhaps not,' my father said. 'But the Manslayer's tidings cannot be ignored, either. If we march to the pass and engage Morjin in battle, the Galdans might fall upon our rear and destroy us.'

Who, I wondered, would ever wish to be a king? Terrible it is to have to make decisions, based on incomplete knowledge, that will determine the life or death of one's people.

'I doubt,' Lansar said, 'that there are any Galdans within a hundred leagues of Mesh.'

'We shall see,' my father said to him. 'We shall send out riders, into the Wendrush.'

'But, my lord, it will take them days to return – if they *do* return. What if this is a ruse, as I believe, and Morjin moves first?'

My father closed his eyes as he breathed in deeply. Then he looked at Lansar and spoke words that gave him much pain: 'From the Eshur Pass, it's hardly two days' march to the Lake Country. We might have to abandon it. Send word that my people are to take refuge in Lashku or flee to the mountain fastnesses.'

'Very well, my lord. But what if the Red Dragon ravages up and down the Sawash Valley?'

'He won't,' my father said. 'But if he does disperse his army, then we *will* march – and destroy *him*.'

That was the end of our council. Lansar Raasharu hurried off to carry out my father's commands. The rest of us tried to go about our business without letting the terror of this new threat undo us.

Later that afternoon, I walked with Atara in my father's garden, which adjoined his rooms to the west of the keep. Walls surrounded us on all sides, giving us a space of quiet and privacy. We paused beneath a cherry tree, and I said to her, 'Perhaps you should leave Mesh, while you still can.'

'Leave for where?' she asked me.

'To the gathering of the Manslayers. To be chosen Chiefess – that would be a great thing.'

'It would,' Atara agreed. 'But the time for that is not now.'

'Then perhaps you should return home. If there is war between the Marituk and Kurmak . . .'

'Are you concerned for my safety?'

'Yes, of course.'

'Then you think to send me into the face of another war?'

I bit my lip as I looked at the butterflies flitting among the honeysuckle that grew over the garden's walls.

'It's all right,' Atara said, squeezing my hand as she smiled at me. 'I *would* be safer there. Likely the war would be over by the time I crossed the Snake. And even if it wasn't, we Sarni rarely war to the death of any tribe.'

The pressure of her fingers against mine told me that we both knew that in the coming war with Morjin, there would be neither quarter nor mercy.

'But the Kurmak,' I said to her, 'are your people.'

'Yes, they are. But so are the Alonians. Your mother and brothers, even your father, and everyone else in Mesh – *everyone*, don't you see? All of Ea's peoples are mine, now.'

'Even the Galdans? Even they of Sakai?'

'Yes, Val, even they. We must set them free.' So saying, she brought out a doeskin and unwrapped her two red arrows. She held them pointing west, toward the Wendrush where Morjin was encamped. 'Here is where the critical battle will be.'

In the days after that, I thought about what she told me. It was a dark time for all of us, and although we tried to keep busy, our work could not distract us from our dread. As promised, my father sent riders into the country of the Mansurii: seven knights, on the swiftest horses. Waiting for their return was a torment. So was life inside the

461

castle. As each day passed, Meshians fleeing their homes poured into it. I gave up my room to old Lord Rathald and his family, and moved in with Yarashan. Jonathay and Ravar likewise surrendered their quarters to other families and joined us in spreading our mats and sleeping furs on Yarashan's floor. But our accommodations remained luxurious compared with that of the sea of women and children who filled the castle's wards. It got so crowded that it was nearly impossible to cross from the Great Hall to the Swan Tower without trampling the sleeping mat or possessions of some poor farmer's wife cooking porridge over a little woodfire. It seemed that the castle could hold no more, but my mother couldn't bear to turn anyone away.

And then on the last day of Soal, one of the riders returned to tell the worst of tidings: an army of Galdans was indeed nearing the mountains of Mesh. He placed their numbers at forty-one thousand. They were making toward the very wide Sky Pass, he said, and should be encamped at its mouth within two days.

I was with my father, in the armory, when he learned of this. I felt the doubt that tore through him like a knife ripping open his belly. After the knight had gone, he stood beneath the racks of spears and swords lining the room's walls, and he told me, 'In what I said after you read Morjin's letter in my rooms, I was both right and wrong. I did not think that he could move in full force so soon. And these two armies are *not* his full force. But they might prove great enough to defeat Mesh.'

Even as he spoke, however, his face hardened with resolve and a fierceness lit up his eyes. And he said to me, 'No, Valashu, we mustn't let that be. There *is* a way to defeat the Dragon. There is always a way.'

My father did not believe in needlessly alarming people. But neither would he keep from them the terrible truth that they all must face. He announced the coming of the Galdan army that evening in his hall. Some of Mesh's greatest lords – Lord Tanu, Lord Tomavar and Lansar Raasharu – favored sending a force against both the passes and trying to keep the enemy's armies from invading Mesh. But my father would not divide *his* army. As he said, 'If either half were defeated, the other half would face annihilation from an attack against their rear.'

He said that Morjin's main objective was surely the recapture of the Lightstone. In order to besiege the Elahad castle, Morjin would first have to destroy Mesh's army. Therefore my father determined to maneuver for good ground on which intercept both of Morjin's armies, and there give battle.

The first of Ioj dawned clear and warm. By noon, the sun was like a glowing coal in the sky. The castle's wards heated up like ovens; thousands of boots and horses' hooves pulverized the dried-out ground and sent up choking clouds of dust. I could scarcely breathe. Although the time hadn't quite come to don my battle armor and ride forth to face Morjin, my long tunic, emblazoned with swan and stars, was hot enough. And the robe of fire pulled ever tighter around me, crushing my limbs and burning through my flesh into my blood.

For the next two days, we all prayed for rain. But the sky remained as clear as a sheet of blue steel. And then, on the third of Ioj, storm clouds moved in from the west: in the form of Morjin's envoys pounding up to the castle on their large, lathered horses. Their leader was the Red Priest who called himself Igasho. But I still called him by his given name, Salmelu, and I could not believe that this murderer of old women and young girls had dared to show his face once again in Mesh.

When my father learned of his arrival, he called for him to be brought to the Great Hall. I stood next to my father beneath the dais, with my brothers and friends. Lansar Raasharu came hurrying into the room, along with Lord Harsha and Lord Tanu. Even my mother and grand-mother came to hear what Salmelu would say.

The company of knights that had escorted him and the other Red Priests across Mesh brought him into the room. According to my father's orders, Salmelu's hands had been bound behind his back. A length of rope had been tied around his neck. One of the knights pulled at it, as on a dog's lead, practically dragging him before my father.

'King Shamesh!' Salmelu choked out, 'is this how you treat Lord Morjin's emissary!'

Salmelu's ugly face was beet-red, whether from the constriction of the rope or his rage, it was hard to tell. The rutilant color nearly obscured the scarlet dragon tattooed onto his forehead. He wore his yellow priest's robe, emblazoned with a much larger dragon. His eyes were small, black marbles, sheeny with hate, and they rolled first toward my father and then toward me.

'You,' my father said, pointing at him, 'are no emissary and have not been accepted as such into Mesh.'

'I *am* Lord Morjin's emissary!' Salmelu said again. 'I speak for the King of Sakai!'

'You may be Morjin's mouth – and eyes – but that is all you are.'

'Remove these ropes, King Shamesh!'

My father pointed at the braided hemp tied around Salmelu's wrists, and he said, 'Thus do we bind condemned men in Mesh.'

463

'Condemned! For what crime?'

'For the murder of the scryer named Kasandra and your own servants.'

Salmelu smiled then, first at my father, and then at Atara. 'Was it a crime to put an old woman who had seen too much out of her misery? And as for the girls, they were slaves, mine to do with as I wished.'

I looked around the hall, with its many empty tables, and I was glad that Estrella wasn't present to hear such lies.

'You brought blood into my house,' my father told him. 'Your death shall wash it clean.'

'You wouldn't dare to harm me!'

In answer, my father whipped out his sword and took a step toward Salmelu. It seemed that he might behead him then and there.

'Slay *me*,' Salmelu cried out, 'and when Lord Morjin has defeated *you*, all your warriors will themselves be slain!'

My father froze, with his gleaming kalama held back behind his head.

'Put *me* to the sword, and all your people shall be put to the sword,' Salmelu added. Against the pull of the rope, he turned his head to stare straight at my mother. 'Those of you, that is, who aren't put upon crosses of wood.'

At this, the swords of my brothers flew out of their sheaths. So did mine. But my father lowered his kalama, and held out his hand to stay us. To Salmelu, he said, 'Speak your master's demands.'

Again, Salmelu smiled. He looked up at the dais where Sunjay Naviru and Lord Noldru and fifty other Guardians stood ringed around the stand holding up the Lightstone.

'My *king*'s demands are simple,' he said, pointing past Sunjay. 'Surrender the golden bowl that your son stole from Lord Morjin, and he shall withdraw from Mesh – the Galdans, too. Between our realms, there shall be peace.'

My father stood tall and straight, and so bright did his eyes blaze then that the two priests to either side of Salmelu cringed and looked away from him.

'Go,' my father said to Salmelu, pointing toward the door. 'Go tell your master that the sons of Elahad will surrender the Lightstone to the Maitreya and no other. If it is war he wants, war he shall have.'

'War is it? You are outnumbered more than four to one!'

'That is true,' my father said to him. I felt him struggling to control his rising wrath. 'But you forget one thing.'

'And what is that?'

The look of scorn on my father's face would have wilted a brass flower. And then he told Salmelu: '*We* are Valari.'

464

And with that he turned his back on Salmelu, and did not look at him again. But Samelu looked at *me*, turning his spite on me as his small eyes promised me torment and death. He said, 'I do not see your reckless friend here. Please give Baltasar my regards when you see him again . . . soon.'

At this, I had to grab Lansar Raasharu's arm to keep him from drawing his sword and killing Salmelu. Then the knight holding fast to Salmelu's rope pulled on it and dragged him from the room.

After the Red Priests had gone, we all stood in silence considering Salmelu's words. Old Lord Tanu, whose family had taken refuge in the keep, gazed upon the Lightstone, and there was great doubt in him. He said to my father, 'It will take at least two days for the priests to return to Morjin, and more for Morjin to march upon us. Kaash and Ishka, at least, might march to our aid first.'

His was a hope that we all shared; but later that afternoon, one of the messengers that my father had sent out came galloping up to the castle with more bad news. King Talanu Solaru, my mother's own father, could not send even a company of knights to aid us. It seemed that King Sandarkan had indeed returned from Tria, and threatened Kaash with war over the Arjan land.

The next day –the fourth of Ioj – more messengers returned to the castle and gave my father their tidings. After my father had heard them out, he sent word that Kane, Maram, Atara and I should meet with him and Lansar Raasharu in the library.

Despite the heat outside, it was cool in that quiet space of flaming candles and musty books. My father bade us all to sit at the table. Then, without wasting a moment, he told us: 'There will be no help from any of the Nine Kingdoms.'

I stared down at a copy of the *Saganom Elu* lying on the table as my heart drummed inside my chest. Then Maram, next to me, said, 'No help even from Ishka?'

'No,' my father said. 'King Hadaru tells me that Ishka must move to punish King Waray for conspiring against him. He has already sent emissaries to Taron to arrange a time and place for battle.'

'Fools!' Kane snarled out. 'They fight over honor at a time where the only honor lies in fighting the Red Dragon!'

'And what of Athar, then?' Maram asked. 'And Lagash?'

'The messengers sent there have not returned,' my father said. 'But it's told in Ishka that on the road home from Tria, King Mohan and King Kurshan drew on each other. It's likely that they will carry their dispute back to their realms and arrange for battle, too.'

'And if they don't?'

465

'Even so, there is no more time. Morjin will probably march tomorrow or the day after. Likewise the Galdans.'

So, I thought, that was that. Mesh would battle alone against two armies, and the Sarni clans, with a combined strength of nearly seventy thousand men.

'Later today,' my father said to me, 'your brothers will ride down with me and join the army. You will remain here and take charge of the castle's defenses.'

'No!' I cried out. 'My place is with them, and with you!'

'Your place,' my father told me, 'is here, guarding the Lightstone. You are Lord Guardian, and it is upon you to command the knights who have sworn to protect it.'

'But Sunjay Naviru could command them equally well! Besides, we all know that there will be no assault upon the castle. You'll need my sword, when it comes to battle.'

So saying, I stood up and drew Alkaladur. Its long blade filled the library with a fierce brightness.

'Sit down,' my father said to me.

'But Morjin will take the battlefield!' I called out to him. 'What he did to Atara, what he did to me . . . you cannot know! He and I – it must be this way, don't you see?'

'Enough!' he shouted at me. His black eyes burned into mine. Then he looked down the table at Atara, and his voice grew more gentle. 'I am not just your father but your king, and so it is upon me to see to Mesh's needs and not your own. There is more to be protected here than just a little golden cup: the wives of Mesh's greatest lords, as well as the children of simple warriors. Your own mother and grandmother. And you have had experience, at Khaisham, in repelling a siege.'

He turned to regard Maram, Atara and Kane. 'All of you – you fought off the Dragon's army under Count Ulanu, and so that is why you will remain here to guard the castle.'

'No, I won't,' Kane growled out, grasping the hilt of his kalama.

'What?' my father said to him.

'I won't remain behind these walls while Morjin finally comes out of that dungheap of a city of his and exposes himself to my sword.'

'As long as you are in my service, you'll do as you're ordered!'

'But I am not in your service, King Shamesh. Freely I've ridden here, and freely I'll ride into battle.'

'Under whose command?'

'Under my own. Where the fighting is thickest, where Morjin stands, there I shall be.'

'And if my knights keep you from this revenge?'

'Then you shall lose both my sword *and* your knights.'

My father and Kane stared at each other with equal savagery. Finally my father said, 'And what if Morjin has a firestone? It's told that you possess one of the black gelstei. With it, you could keep Morjin from burning the castle's walls.'

Kane took out his dark crystal, which looked like a teardrop of obsidian. He squeezed it in his fist and said, 'Morjin does not have a firestone. But even if he did, it would take him a day to burn through the castle's walls. First he would turn its flame upon your army, that none would be left to stop him. And so you would do better to let me take the field, with my gelstei as well as my sword.'

My father nodded his head to Kane, bowing to his logic, no less his fierce will. Then Atara unwrapped her two red arrows and said to my father, 'I, too, shall ride to the battle with Kane.'

'Very well,' my father sighed out. Then he turned to Maram. 'You, at least, *are* under my command. And so you'll remain here, with Val.'

It surprised no one at the table when Maram fought off a smile of relief and gladly assented to what my father had said: 'You wish me to stay by Val's side? I shall! I shall! We'll keep the castle safe!'

After that, my father dismissed everyone except me. He rose from his chair and laid his hand on my shoulder, saying, 'Let's take a walk outside the walls, shall we?'

I followed him out of the keep and then through the throngs of people in the west ward as he made his way to the castle's gates. The great iron doors were still open, and we went outside and stood upon the band of ground between the castle and the drawbridge spanning the Kurash River. In the event of an assault, the bridge's entire end section could be pulled up to cover the castle's gates and break the bridge in two.

'Have you seen that the chains have been oiled?' he said, pointing at the black links of iron that worked the bridge.

'You asked me to, didn't you?'

'Good,' he told me.

He took me by the arm and led me along the narrow ground above the river. We had to step carefully lest we stumble into its churning waters. We rounded the great gate tower and came out on the castle's southern side. A steep, rocky slope led down toward the houses of Silvassu below. It would be impossible, I knew, for any siege tower to be rolled up it to assault the walls – and difficult unto the death for warriors to bring up ladders or grappling hooks. I set my hand upon the warm granite of the wall, looking up at the overhanging parapets high above. I could almost feel burning oil raining down upon me and sizzling into my flesh. Not even a monkey, I thought, could find a handhold in the wall's smooth stone.

'The masonry looks sound,' he said, craning his neck as he looked up.

'It is,' I said. 'Every inch of it.'

'Good. Our ancestors built it well. And we've kept it well.' He rapped his knuckles against the white granite and smiled. 'Even with all our guests, we've food enough to last two years. And the wells will never run dry. Our castle will never be taken.'

'No,' I promised him, 'it won't be.'

'So many Elahads have lived here,' he said to me. 'Going back to the first Shavashar, and Elkasar, for whom your grandfather was named.'

My father must have forgotten that he had told me this before, more than once. His thoughts seemed to be far away, dwelling with the dead.

'A great battle we'll fight soon,' he said to me. 'The greatest ever fought in Mesh.'

As he gazed off at Silvassu and the Valley of the Swans below, glowing a deep green in the late sun, he shifted his weight suddenly and had to fight to keep from plunging down the slope. I clasped onto his arm to steady him.

'Are you all right, sir?'

'I nearly fell,' he said, gripping my hand. And then his eyes darkened as with storm clouds as he told me, 'If I should fall in battle, Asaru will make a fine king. You must help him, Val. You, of all your brothers, he trusts the most.'

'You *won't* fall, sir. This battle can be won – you said so yourself.'

But he seemed not to be listening to me. His eyes grew bright and clear as he gazed out upon Mount Eluru shining white with snow across the valley.

'All of my sons,' he said, 'would make good kings. Even Yarashan.'

'You think so?' I said to him.

'Yes, even he. He is full of vainglory. But in the end, he would overcome it and find his greatness in his love of his people instead of himself. After you won the championship, do you know what he said to me?'

'No, what?'

'He said: "Better Val than me."'

'*Yarashan* said that?'

'Truly, he did. He loves you, you know.'

'Yes,' I told him, 'I know.'

'And Karshur. My second son is so strong, if not possessing the

468

quickest of minds. But he is wise enough to call upon the counsel of others – if he were king, he would need to call upon you.'

'Do not speak so,' I said, gripping his hand.

But he didn't listen to me. He smiled to himself as he affirmed the various virtues of my brothers. Jonathay, he said, seemed too full of whimsy to be a king, and yet he had a way of bringing his dreams down to earth and inspiriting people. Mandru was as fierce as a wolverine, and difficult – and in this very irritation at others, he often found the will to be gentle toward them and protect them. As he had protected me from Yarashan's bullying when I was a boy.

'All of my sons,' he said again. 'It's our weaknesses that make us strong – the way we overcome them. The way we overcome ourselves.'

He turned toward me then, and eyes were like two stars shining with a deep light.

'But you have no weaknesses!' I said to him.

'You think not?' he said, smiling at me.

'Not as a king. No king has ever given more of himself to his people. You cannot know how they love you. All your warriors – they would die for you.'

'And I would die for them,' he said. 'And I love them as I love the mountains and rivers of my home. And yet . . .'

'Yes?'

He gripped my hand so hard that it hurt, and I could hardly bear the way that he looked at me.

'And yet,' he told me, resting his other hand against the castle's great walls, 'if my whole army were lost, it would not be as dear to me as what I know will remain safe inside here.'

'But my brothers,' I said, swallowing back the pain in my throat, 'if they were lost too, then . . .'

My father gazed at me for what seemed a thousand years as my heart pounded inside me. And he said to me, 'As long as one of us lives, Valashu, we all live.'

We went back inside the castle after that. An hour later, my father called for his warhorse, Karkhad, to be brought into the west ward. The crowds of women and children there moved aside to make way for this great, snorting beast. Karkhad's face, neck and chest, as well as his hindquarters, had been fitted with curving sweeps of steel plate. And so it was with the mounts of my brothers, for they gathered there, too. They wore their diamond battle armor and black surcoats emblazoned with the silver swan and the stars of the Elahads. Their shields showed identical charges, except that each one bore a distinguishing mark of cadence on its point. Ravar's was a sunburst, and he was the

469

first of my brothers to embrace me and bid me farewell. Then Jonathay laughed as he embraced me to assure me that we would meet again, and soon. Next I said goodbye to Mandru, and then Karshur, who nearly squeezed me in half with his thick, hard arms. Yarashan, resplendent in all his polished diamonds and steel, stepped up to me and said, 'It would have been a great contest, wouldn't it, to see who could slay more of the enemy? Well, perhaps in another battle.' Asaru took his leave of me in silence. The hope in his eyes, no less his concern for me, was so strong and bright it made me weep.

For a while, the six of them stood there on the hardpacked dirt saying farewell to my mother and grandmother. Lansar Raasharu and a company of knights assembled behind them, back near the Adami Tower. So did Kane and Atara. Then my father pulled on his helm, crested by a white swan plume, and it was time to go. They all mounted their horses. And my father led them pounding through the gateway, and they rode out to war.

32

Morjin's army invaded Mesh on the sixth of Ioj. The Galdans, under the Saroch, Radomil Makan, as the high priests of the Kallimun were called, moved a day later, on the seventh. Messengers brought us word of this desecration of our sacred soil. My father saw no point in wasting warriors at the passes, and so he had ordered the garrisons there to remain within the kel keeps, behind their walls. This presented Morjin with a difficult choice: he could lose part of his army besieging the keep, which might take a month, or simply march around it. But if he did that, then his line of supplies would likely be cut, and his army would be forced to live off whatever they could take from Mesh's countryside. And more, in the event of his defeat, his retreat from Mesh might be hindered. So it was with Radomil and the Galdans. It encouraged no one when Morjin decided to march straight down the road to Lashku and across the Lake County. He paused only to ravage the abandoned farms there, and he bypassed Lashku altogether, leaving that walled city inviolate behind him. He clearly desired a showdown with our army as quickly as possible. It seemed that he did not fear defeat.

The Galdans, however, gave sign that they were at least as interested in plundering Mesh's mineral wealth as they were in giving battle. Reports came that the Galdans laid siege to Godhra for half a day before they broke off and resumed their march north. Morjin must have commanded them to leave its despoliation until their return, after our army was destroyed. As it was, the Galdans raided several armories outside Godhra's walls, and made off with many bushels of diamonds. And worse, they slew half a dozen swordmakers and their families, and others.

Most of my people, however, at least for the time, found safety behind thick stone walls or in the fastnesses deep within mountains. They made sure that there was little to feed these two great armies,

471

taking with them as many cattle, sheep and sacks of grain as they could. In revenge, Morjin ordered the burning of their fields. A line of flaming wheat and barley followed the line of his march like the track of a fire-breathing dragon.

On Ioj the twelfth, the Sakayans and Galdans met up outside Hardu, and my father finally marched south. There followed a series of threats and maneuvers as my father strove to destroy or at least decimate Morjin's combined forces as they crossed the Arashar River. A small battle was fought at Kinshan Bridge, and the Meshians had much the better of the day, killing some three hundred Galdans and even more of Morjin's mercenaries. But Morjin was a skilled and hardened warlord, and he seemed not to mind spending the lives of his men to achieve his objectives. He used this sacrifice at the bridge to move the main body of his army across the river lower down, toward Lake Waskaw where it was shallow enough in this dry season for his baggage train to cross without being swept away.

My father was forced then to order a retreat back north, for he would not give battle in the mostly flat and open country between Lake Waskaw and Silvassu. There it would be too easy for the Sarni to harry his warriors or even ride around them and attack his army from the rear. And in a pitched battle, it would be too easy for Morjin's men, with their much greater numbers, to swarm like ants around our army's flanks and push their spears into our backs.

It wasn't hard for my father to outmaneuver this unruly and motley mass of men. Three armies Morjin had to co-ordinate, counting the Sarni, and his problem in this regard was even worse than it seemed, for the Sakayan force was itself composed of disparate elements: nine thousand heavy infantry out of Argattha; three thousand Blues from the mountains of western Sakai; seventeen thousand mercenaries from Hesperu, Karabuk and other realms of Ea; a thousand Ikurian horse and five thousand of Morjin's famed Dragon Guard, decked out in steel armor that had been tinctured bright red. The Galdans, though all of the same realm, did not all appear to be of the same quality. Twenty thousand heavy infantry formed their core, supported by as many light infantry and eight hundred light cavalry. These, it was thought, could not hold up to the deadly strokes of Valari kalamas. The two hundred Galdan heavy horse were too few to withstand the charge of our knights, and the Galdans were weak in archers, as well. No doubt Morjin counted on the Sarni's arrows to rain down death upon us from afar.

I spent those days of waiting in prowling about the castle and discussing the enemy's strengths and weaknesses with Sunjay Naviru and the Guardians, as well as with Sar Vikan, Sar Araj, Sar Jovan and the other captains in charge of the castle's defenses. Five companies of knights and warriors my father had left behind to man the battlements. Some thought that these were too many, that my father could have made better use of them on the field facing the Sakayans spear to spear and shield to shield. Others argued that they were too few. Whenever I walked through the wards and beheld the mothers reassuring their children that everything would be all right, it seemed that ten thousand warriors lined up along the walls could not be enough to protect Mesh's greatest treasure.

On the evening of the fourteenth, I took my dinner in the great hall with my mother and grandmother, and with Lord Rathald and his family, who shared our table. Lord Tomavar's young wife, Vareva, joined us, too. We had fresh lamb that night, all bloody and red the way we Meshians liked it. There were peas and mashed potatoes, as well, and blueberries with cream. It seemed that it might be the last such feast we would have, for everyone was saying that the battle would begin the next day. But Vareva hardly touched her meal. She was only twenty-three and beautiful, even for a Valari, with shiny, sable hair, ivory skin and eyes so large and full of light that people would find excuses to engage her in conversation just so that they might look upon her. It was something of a scandal that Lord Tomavar had married such a young woman after Vareva's husband had fallen at the battle of the Red Mountain. But it seemed that both of them had married for love. Lord Tomavar, more than once, had endured the laughter of his former rivals when they had caught him picking wildflowers for Vareva to put in her hair. And Vareva, more than once, had been heard to say: 'What do I care if my husband is older than I when he has the hands of a sculptor and the soul of an angel?' It was Vareva who helped me understand how hard it was on the women left behind when their men went off to battle.

When I told her that she should try to eat and gather her strength, she pressed her palm into her belly and said to me, 'Lord Valashu, you were gone on your first journey for how long? Half a year?'

'Yes,' I told her, 'that's right.'

'And on how many of those days were you close to death? Thirty? Sixty?'

'Perhaps,' I said.

Vareva looked down the table at my mother, who had paused between bites of blueberries. And she told me, 'Your mother died, a little, every day that you were gone. And a thousand times every night.'

That night I could not sleep for worrying what the next day might bring to my brothers and countrymen. A messenger from my father had informed me earlier that our army had set up on good ground below the Kurash River, near the village of Balvalam only five miles from the castle. There, on the morrow, on the Culhadosh Commons where only a week before many sheep had grazed on its acres of grass, the warriors of Mesh would stand and bleed the ground red with the blood of our enemies – either that or die themselves.

The ides of Ioj dawned clear and bright with the last of summer's warmth. I was up early, and I put on my battle armor in the quiet of Yarashan's room. As the roosters in their coops gave call, I mounted the stairs to the Swan Tower and stood in the crenel between two thick merlons gazing out at the countryside beyond Silvassu. The warriors stationed there did not speak to me. I shielded my eyes against the sun's fiery glister as it rose over the mountains to the east. The fields and forests below the Kurash were shrouded in haze and seemed as peaceful as a meadowlark singing its morning song. But I knew that only five miles away, obscured by green hills and a swathe of woods, my father's army would be marching out of its camp and lining up to face the hordes of men that Morjin had summoned out of Galda and Argattha.

I listened for the booming of the great kettle drums, but Culhadosh Commons was too far away, and the pounding of blood in my ears was too loud. The streets and yards of Silvassu below were quiet, and so were the houses, for my people had deserted the city to take refuge in the castle or in the mountains to the west. I listened for the sound of silver bells fastened to the ankles of my father's warriors and jangling out into the stillness of the morning. But all I could hear was the squealing of a pig being slaughtered, the sawing of wood, and hammers beating against ringing iron in the shops off the middle ward as the castle awakened and people went about their business. The glowing charcoal of their cooking fires sent plumes of dark smoke into the air. Along the battlements, my warriors stood ready to light fires of their own, beneath cauldrons of oil or sand, should the enemy appear and attack the castle. I leaned out over the crenel and breathed in deeply; my nostrils and throat burned as I recalled the smell of a battlefield's blood that could drive both men and beasts mad. I kept gazing off toward the Culhadosh Commons. The land grew greener and brighter as the sun rose higher in the sky. The air began to heat up; so did the steel plates reinforcing the shoulders of my armor. Sweat slicked my skin down my sides and stung my eyes.

And then, out of the east, a rider appeared. I squinted, trying to make out the details of his tiny form as he made his way up the River

Road toward the castle. He drew closer. Just as he entered Silvassu and the houses blocked my line of sight, I caught a glimpse of his colors: a great, blue rose shining out from a gold field. Now that Baltasar was dead, this could only be the charge of Lord Lansar Raasharu.

I nearly flew down the Swan Tower's long spiral of stairs in my haste to know why he had returned to the castle. I ran across the middle ward, dodging around pots of bubbling porridge and boys playing with wooden swords. Maram happened to be taking breakfast there with a woman named Ursa. He followed me as I crossed the west ward and then shouted out for the guards in the gate tower to open the sally port set into the locked gates. This they did. I greeted Lansar as his horse galloped across the bridge over the Kurash River.

'Lansar!' I called out as he came to a halt. 'What is it?'

I looked closely at him, to make sure that it really *was* Lansar, that some enemy knight hadn't stripped the surcoat from his dead body and donned it to deceive us. But the same homely and noble face that I had known all of my life looked out from beneath his helm. His dark eyes burned with pain; the gold of his surcoat, I saw, was soaked with blood.

'You're wounded!' I cried out.

'Yes, a Sarni arrow,' he called back. 'But never mind that now. You must be told: your father has fallen.'

As the guards from the gate tower came out and gathered next to Maram behind me, I stood there on the bridge above the river. I could not breathe; I could not move against the agony of the terrible spear that Lansar had thrust into my heart.

'My father is dead,' I whispered. 'My father is dead.'

The rushing of the river swept my words away, but not before one of the guards behind me cried out: 'The king is dead!'

From within the gate tower, I heard this dreaded phrase echoing from the stones there, and then I heard shouts from the west ward and deeper inside the castle: 'The king is dead! The king is dead!'

'How?' I asked Lansar. I stood there shaking my head. His sorrowful face was a blur in front of my eyes. 'How . . . did he fall?'

'In a charge against the Galdan knights.'

'And the battle?'

'Nearly lost. Asaru is king, now. He sent me to tell you this: you are to ride to the battle, as quickly as you can. Your sword is needed, now.'

I drew Alkaladur and pointed it toward the southeast. Its long blade blazed like a streak of molten silver. My eyes burned as the features of the world seemed to form up into a face that I both loathed and longed to behold: the proud, gloating face of Morjin.

'If Asaru needs my sword,' I said, 'he shall have that, and more.'

Lansar forced his lips into a grim smile. 'It will be as it was when you were boys. How often did you play that game where the two of you held the Telemesh Gate alone against a whole battalion of Ishkans?'

I tried to smiled, too, but I could not. I told him, 'You remember things that I had forgotten.'

'I remember the story of how you and a few friends slew nearly a hundred men in Argattha.' Here he looked at Maram. 'Asaru remembers this, too. He has asked that you and Maram join him on the field – with a company of knights.'

I nodded my head, and hurried back into the castle. I called out to a squire to summon Sar Vikan, and to another to prepare Altaru for battle. I raced across the middle ward and into the great hall. Lansar and Maram followed me. Fifty of the Guardians stood on the dais speaking in hushed tones as I cried out, 'Sunjay Naviru! My father is slain, and Asaru is now king! I must go to him immediately! You will take charge of the Guardians!'

Sunjay bowed his head to me, and there was no pride in his new command, only acceptance. 'Who will take charge of the castle?' he asked.

I looked at Lansar, standing tall and grave next to the great pillars that held up the roof. My father, I thought, had trusted no man more. And so I said, 'Lord Raasharu, if he is able.'

Lansar rubbed his bloody side and said, 'I'll have to be.'

I turned to say goodbye to Skyshan of Ki, and I grasped hands with Sar Jarlath. Then I stepped over to the Lightstone. I took the golden cup in my hands and pressed my face against it. I set it back on its stand. Its radiance seared my lips as if I had kissed the sun.

Sar Vikan hurried into the room then. He was a compact, energetic man who was an excellent horseman and quick with his sword. I explained to him what must be. As he went off to assemble the company of knights who would ride with us down to the battlefield, I turned to Maram. He neither protested this dreaded new duty nor bemoaned his fate. He just looked at me with his sorrowful eyes as if it were *his* father who had died. I never loved him so much as I did then.

At last my mother came into the room, leading Nona by the arm. I hugged them both to me. My grandmother stood there in silence stroking my fevered hand. My mother, whose insides had just been ripped out, held herself tall and straight like the queen she was. Her eyes held back a whole ocean of tears. She looked at me as if seeing me for the last time.

476

'Asaru needs me,' I said to her. 'You know how it has always been between us.'

She bowed her head and pressed her lips to my hand. She clasped it in hers so tightly that the force of her long fingers squeezed mine together, bruising the bones against the silver and diamonds of my ring.

'Please, Mother, don't worry. After the battle is won, I will return to you. I promise.'

'Go then, if you must,' she finally choked out. For a moment, I thought that she wanted to tell me that war was stupid, ugly and evil, and that I shouldn't throw my life away against the enemy's swords. But in the end she was Talanu Solaru's daughter and Shavashar Elahad's wife – and a Valari warrior down to her bones. And so she told me, 'Go and slay Morjin, if you can. Avenge your father's death.'

I let go of her hand and rushed out into the middle ward, where Sar Vikan sat on top of his armored warhorse, with a hundred and fifty other knights and their mounts. The women and children there made room for us; the news of my father's death quieted even the most boisterous of boys, who stood in silence gripping their wooden swords as they gazed at me. Squires brought out Maram's horse and Altaru, my huge black stallion, jacketed in steel and digging his great hoof into the ground. I climbed upon him. I checked to make sure that my long lance was secure in its holster. Then I led forth into the west ward, and the castle's gates were thrown open. We pounded across the bridge in a single column of glittering diamonds and heaving horseflesh. So loud was the beat of iron against wood and paving stones that it almost drowned out the clanging of the gates being slammed shut behind us.

Good roads led down from Silvassu to the village of Balvalam. We were to follow them almost the whole way to the battlefield. I had to restrain Altaru from winding himself in a gallop. He must have felt my blood lashing at my veins, for his surging body seemed driven by my terrible urge for haste. Battles could be won or lost in minutes, and this one had been raging for at least an hour. It took us only part of an hour to leave Silvassu's houses far behind us and race through the woods south of the farms along the Kurash. We rode mostly downhill, and that gave us more speed. The trees to the left and right seemed to fly past us. The sky's bright blueness beckoned ahead like the end of a dark tunnel – or rather like a doorway into fire, agony and death.

Fire consumed me now. The robe of fire that I called my fate blazed around all my limbs and burned me down to the bone. It maddened me with grief and a raging desire for revenge. My hatred of Morjin, like the kirax in my blood, drove me on and on, whether toward triumph or doom, I almost didn't care.

'Morjin,' I whispered to myself, again and again. 'Morjin, Morjin.'

About a mile from Balvalam, we turned off to our left down a path through the woods, for the reports told that the deserted village was held by the enemy. Now we had to make our way more slowly through the oaks that grew across the low hills, and that was a torment. But this shortcut was the only way to reach the Culhadosh Commons quickly. We heard the clamor of the battle a mile away, through the trees. The blaring of horns, the clash of steel against steel, men and horses screaming – it all seemed to merge into a single, terrible sound that shook the very earth.

We came out of the woods just to the north of Balvalam Hill. Some called it the Mare's Hill – no one knew why. Culhadosh Commons spread out east of this grassy prominence, two and a half miles of green pasture ending at another great wall of woods. Masses of men thrusting spears and swords at each other covered much of it. I had some good height above the clashing armies, and I could see much of the battlefield. Asaru's knights, just below Balvalam Hill, drove against the more numerous Ikurian horse: a great melee of maces beating against shields, shivered lances and flashing swords that fell against both men and beast. To their left, a slender strand of diamond-clad warriors extended east almost all the way to the woods. These eight battalions of Meshian foot, led by Lord Tanu, were stretched very thin, into only three ranks. They faced much deeper blocks of the enemy all across this long front: ten thousand Galdan heavy infantry trying to break the joint between Asaru's knights and the Meshian line; eight thousand mercenaries to the east of them using their ten ranks of spears to beat against my people's shields; a great swarm of naked Blues ululating their hideous war cries as they swung their axes against steel and flesh. In the very middle of the field, two thousand of the Dragon Guard worked furiously to cut a hole through our center. They were supported to the left by more mercenaries and another great mass of Galdan foot soldiers. On the far left of the field, nearest the woods, the Galdan heavy horse fell against the rest of the Meshian knights. They would have been cut to pieces but for the support of the Sarni warriors, firing arrows point blank into the faces of my countrymen, meeting our terrible kalamas with their sabers and dying themselves. Somewhere in this haze of glittering diamonds, steel and brightly colored blazons, my father had fallen. Lord Avijan would be leading our knights now, or perhaps Lord Harsha, if they hadn't fallen, too.

'Father,' I whispered, gazing out at all this carnage. 'Father.'

Sar Vikan and Maram came up to me as our company of knights drew up behind us. We held quick council, deciding what we should do.

'The center is hard-pressed,' Sar Vikan called out, pointing at the Meshian line, which was beginning to bow back toward us under the great weight of men massed in front of it.

'Yes,' I called back, 'but there is still a reserve.'

I drew Sar Vikan's attention to the single battalion of warriors two thousand yards to our left and standing a few hundred yards behind our lines. They were under Lord Eldru's command. I thought I could make out the red and white of his charge gleaming in the sun.

'It seems,' Sar Vikan said, holding up his hand to shield his eyes, 'that Radomil Makan holds back the Galdans, too.'

The enemy, I saw, had reserves of their own, at least twenty times more numerous than ours. Culhadosh Commons spread out to the south, too, down a gentle slope toward a little winding water called the Clear Brook, and beyond. Grouped along this stream, half a mile beyond the killing zone, was the greater part of the Galdan light infantry, nearly twenty thousand strong. A thousand archers gathered to the right of them, behind a curve in the stream. And further to the west, just where the stream bent back toward the village of Balvalam, the Galdan light horse assembled in neat lines with a battalion of the light infantry behind them.

'Look!' Maram cried out. 'I do believe they're going to attack!'

Directly in front of them was grouped the very far right of Asaru's knights, pushed up against the lowest part of Balvalam Hill only four hundred yards from us. And farther up its slopes, most of our archers had been stationed. They stood behind a fence of stakes pounded into the ground, with their sharpened ends pointing outward, toward the enemy. The archers wore only light armor and were without shields, and were vulnerable to attack – which is why they had taken a position on ground that would be difficult to attack. But it seemed that the Galdans were going to try.

A horn blared out, and the Galdans began moving forward. How long, I wondered, would it take them to charge across half a mile of clear ground?

'What shall we do, Lord Valashu?' Sar Vikan shouted at me. I could hardly make out his words against the tumult of shields banging at shields, axes splitting steel, and men and horses screaming as they died.

I stared out across the battlefield, west to east, north to south. I looked for a flashing yellow banner, with its great, red dragon, that might tell me where Morjin was. I looked for the red and gold of Morjin's surcoat and his steel armor, said to be stained red like that of his Dragon Guard. Two thousand of these masterful warriors fought on foot, still working furiously at our center, but where were the rest of them? Perhaps, I thought, Morjin was holding them in reserve to the far southeast, where the Clear Brook disappeared into the woods. At any moment a horn might sound, and these men might come crashing out of the trees in a charge that would cave in our army's entire left flank.

'Val, what shall we do?' I heard Maram say.

I looked for Kane, where the fighting was the thickest, but all across the field men were hacking at men with a fury that seemed to grow more desperate with every moment. I looked for Atara, too. Morjin *might* be in hiding, waiting to charge against our left, but our right flank was being attacked even as we stood watching.

'Forward!' I called out, drawing my long lance. 'Half speed, and stay together!'

It wouldn't do to charge recklessly up Balvalam Hill, where its uneven ground could trip a horse and send both horse and rider crashing down with a snap of broken limbs. The Galdans, however, had different considerations. In the face of the arrows that the archers began firing into them, they galloped up the south slope of the hill as quickly as they could. Some of their mounts did stumble and break their legs – and the necks of their riders. More screamed as they fell out of their saddles with arrows sticking out of them. But they were brave men. They kept charging up toward the archers, with the Galdan light infantry running behind them.

In truth, they were no match, man for man, with the Meshian archers, who now laid down their bows and drew their swords. But they were many, and our archers were few. Now the Galdan horse came pouring around the ends of the stake fence, as with a stream splitting in two. The archers met them with flashing kalamas; steel ran red as my countrymen slashed upward at the Galdans who were trying to stick their lances into them. My knights and I pounded closer, up the grassy slope from the north. Both Galdans and Meshians were dying by the tens and twenties – but more Meshians, for the light infantry had finally forced their way through the fence and were falling upon the archers with shield and spear. In front of us loomed a mob of men screaming and shouting out challenges as they hacked and stabbed at each other. Fifty yards only separated us from them. And then suddenly we were upon them, and the world narrowed into a corridor of rearing horses, red lance points and Galdans in their flimsy leather armor throwing themselves at me.

Within the first minute, I lost my lance through the ribs and back-bone of one of these. I drew Alkaladur then, and my sword's silver gelstei gave me the strength to bear the agony that ripped through me. I swung this bright blade, once, twice, thrice – and three Galdans fell dead or dying to the ground. Maram fought to my right, working his lance against two horsemen opposing him. I heard him bellow out: 'Come! Come! Test your lances against Five-Horned Maram!' He stabbed one of his enemies through the face just as the lance of the other took him in the chest. But the point crunched against the diamonds of Maram's armor, and failed to penetrate. Maram pulled his lance out of the first horseman's cheek and thrust it through the other's groin. So it went all around me, with Sar Vikan and our company of knights. Many of these had drawn their kalamas, and they slashed through the Galdan's armor as if it was paper. Founts of blood sprayed out into the air. The ground began to thicken with hacked limbs, torn bodies and men crying out as they held their hands over their necks or bleeding bellies.

Then a horn blared, signaling the Galdans to retreat. Many of them, however, had already broken; they cast aside their shields and ran back down the hill. Some of the archers pursued them and buried their kalamas in their backs. The Galdan horse fled in better order, and more quickly. I was tempted to ride after them, all the way down to the village and around the wing of Morjin's entire army. But the captain of the archers called for a halt, just as I became aware of a new crisis in the middle of the battlefield.

'Lord Valashu!' the captain cried out. He was a tall man with a sharp nose and chin like the crags of a mountain. He stood grasping his dripping sword as he said to me, 'Where did *you* come from?'

All around us the surviving archers were sheathing their swords and taking up their bows again. Sar Vikan and Maram, with our knights, formed up on the side of the hill behind me.

'You seemed hard-pressed,' I said to the captain. I did not want to tell him or his archers that their king had been slain.

'Hard-pressed and worse,' he said. He wore in his silver ring the three diamonds of a master knight, and I suddenly remembered that his name was Sar Yulmar. 'We might have died to a man keeping the Galdans from coming behind your brother's knights.'

At the base of the hill only twenty five yards away, the knights at the very edge of Asaru's command were battling against the Ikurians:

481

a broad-faced, thickset people from the central plateau of Sakai. Farther down the line of this mass of snorting horses and shouting men, two hundred yards to the east, I caught sight of a swan and stars blazing bright silver in the fierce morning light. Asaru sat on top of his gray stallion slashing his sword against two enemy knights in front of him. He, too, was hard-pressed, as were his hundreds of knights. I wanted desperately to ride down to them, to find Yarashan and join him in fighting to Asaru's side so that we might turn back the flood of these skilled and relentless Ikurians. But then Sar Vikan called to me, and pointed farther east, at the center of the Meshian line.

'Lord Valashu!' he said. 'They're about to break!'

The massed ranks of the Dragon Guard and the Blues, I saw, with phalanxes of mercenaries to either side of them, had pushed deeply into Lord Tanu's and Lord Tomavar's battalions. Our whole line, from Lord Avijan's command in the east to Asaru's knights, had now bent so far backward that it was near to buckling. It was like a long, curved wall of diamonds holding back a flood of steel. In several places only a single rank of warriors kept the enemy from breaking through.

I glanced behind me, taking the measure of the knights in our company. Maybe seven of a hundred and fifty had fallen. I looked back toward the center of our line. Somewhere, in all this fury of swords hacking apart shields and men dying, Mandru led a company of warriors in Lord Tomavar's battalion, as did Jonathay in Lord Tanu's.

'Back!' I shouted to Sar Vikan and the knights behind me. 'Back to the center!'

We rode down the hill too quickly and then burst into a full gallop as we pounded across a mile and a quarter of grass. We came up behind the center of the Meshian line just as Lord Eldru's reserve battalion came forward. But Lord Eldru no longer commanded it. He had finally weakened and fallen from an arrow that had pierced his neck in the first minutes of the battle. Sar Jessu had replaced him. He was a thickset, serious, master knight whose bushy black eyebrows were set with determination.

'Hold, Sar Jessu!' I called to him.

'Hold?' he called back. He stood facing me at the front of twelve hundred men formed up into three neat ranks.

'Wait!' I called to him.

'Wait?' he shouted. 'Our line is about to break!'

Ahead of us the Meshian line was like a bow bending nearly double under the pressure of attack. And as it bent, the Meshian warriors worked quickly to extend the line, and thin it, to two ranks and then only one.

'Lord Eldru ordered us forward!' Sar Jessu shouted.

'And I'm ordering you to hold!'

Horns sounded from hundreds of yards away, back toward the Clear Brook. We still had enough height above the two armies to see the entire reserve of Galdan light infantry, in their thousands, pouring across the stream and marching forward toward the battlefront at double-pace.

'The enemy are too many!' Sar Jessu shouted. 'Don't you see! Don't you see!'

I saw the Dragon Guard, like a great red hammer, pounding at our very center. Next to them stood the hideous Blues, whose naked bodies had been stained with the juice of the kirque plant from head to toe. They howled and cursed as they swung their axes through our shields and chopped down our warriors by the dozen. To their sides, the mercenaries and Galdan heavy infantry, sensing victory, threw themselves forward against our bowing line, which forced them up against the Dragon Guard. Behind them, the Galdan light infantry had abandoned all sense and good order in their lust to rush forward and take part in the kill.

Where was Morjin? I wondered.

'Lord Valashu!'

I stared out at the diamond warriors in our line, which now looked more like a gigantic V than a line. I saw, in my mind's-eye, the funnel-shaped walls of the escarpment at Shurkar's Notch where my knights and I had fought Duke Malatam. I gripped my sword as my heart beat like an axe against my breastbone.

'When the line breaks,' I said to Sar Jessu, 'then we shall go forward!'

Now the Galdan light infantry came up behind the Dragon Guard and the mercenaries, and pressed their backs. The Guard fought furiously to cut down the thin wall of warriors who stood before them. Then the Meshian line, at the joint of the V between Lord Tanu's and Lord Tomavar's battalions, suddenly broke. The Dragon Guard, with the frenzied Blues, screamed out in bloodlust as they smelled victory. The whole center of Morjin's army fell mad with a rage to rush through this hole and destroy us. They threw themselves forward, no longer ranks of well-drilled warriors, but a great mob of murderous men.

'Sar Jessu!' I cried out. 'Forward to fill up the break!'

I turned to Sar Vikan and shouted to him and our knights: 'Cut down anyone coming behind our lines! Now! Attack!'

With Maram and Sar Vikan beside me, I galloped forward. The Meshian warriors at the mouth of the break were fighting with the last of their strength to keep the Dragon Guard and the Blues from streaming through and falling upon their rear. One of these warriors was Mandru. His shield, it seemed, had long since been hacked apart or riddled with spears and cast away. I watched in horror as he thrust his kalama through the throat of a red-armored warrior at the same moment that a great, squat Blue came up behind him with his bloody axe. He swung it down upon Mandru's helm, splitting apart steel, bone and brains. And so the fiercest of my brothers died before he could even open his mouth to scream.

'Mandru!'

I urged Altaru forward, straight toward two Blues working their way behind Lord Tomavar's battalion. My sword took off the head of the first, and then I chopped down at the second, cleaving him from his neck through his thick body and out the opposite side. Other Blues came at me; one tried to vault off the ground and knock me from my horse. I killed them all. I turned to look for more victims for my sword. The enemy were all around me.

How easily a man is made into meat! With every stroke of my sword, it seemed, I cut someone else into pieces. Blood soaked the grass beneath me; it sprayed over me, reddening my hands, chest and face, and ran in rivulets from the grooves in Altaru's steel armor. I kept cutting and thrusting until my arm burned like a knot of fire, like the valarda burning inside me. And still men came at me trying to kill me.

And then a terrible scream split the air, and I looked through a mass of the Dragon Guards toward the frantically struggling warriors in Lord Tanu's battalion. Jonathay stood there. One of the Guards had thrust his spear through Jonathay's armpit and deep into his body. It drove all the sweetness from his face so that only agony remained. He fell beneath the boots of the Dragon Guard, and I did not see him rise again.

'Jonathay!'

Blood filled my eyes, and I pushed Altaru forward into the Dragon Guards. My sword cleaved the steel of their armor; I killed several of them. A spear rammed into my back, nearly knocking me out of my saddle. A sword slashed open the underside of my jaw. One of the Guard hammered his shield against my leg in a rage to break it. Altaru, in a rage of his own, let loose a great whinny as he wheeled and kicked out with his great hoof. He pulped the Guardsman's face and snapped back his head with a 'crack' loud enough to be heard above the great noise of the battle. Then he drove forward into another Guardsman and trampled him to death beneath his savage hooves.

Thus we fought for many minutes. Sar Vikan and the knights fought near me, too. None of them wielded lance or sword so well as Maram, who rode down at least five of the Dragon Guards before they could turn against the warriors in the broken Meshian line. Sar Jessu's reserve companies finally worked their way forward to fill up the gap between Lord Tanu's and Lord Tomavar's battalions. They drove their spears and shields against the enemy still trying to pour through. And suddenly, there was no one nearby left to slay.

'To me!' I called out. 'Sar Vikan! Maram! Knights, to me!'

Sar Vikan's company gathered to me. Twenty of them lay among the many hundreds of dead carpeting the grass. As many bore serious wounds. These, if they could ride, I sent off to the field infirmary a mile to the north, at the Meshian encampment behind the battlefield. Those who couldn't ride, I could do nothing for.

'Look!' Maram called to me. 'The line holds!'

The line of my countrymen fighting on foot in front of us, I saw, *was* holding – and more. Now nearly the whole of the Galdan and Sakayan armies had forced themselves as down into a funnel, as with Duke Malatam's knights at Shurkar's Notch. But there were a hundred times as many of *this* enemy, and the walls of the funnel were not immobile rock, but matchless Meshian warriors thrusting swords and spears as they pressed forward. The Galdan heavy infantry was packed together so closely with the mercenaries, with the Dragon Guard and the Blues, that they could hardly move. They could not lift their shields to protect their bodies against our long, sharp spear points; they could not raise their swords to parry our murderous kalamas. The two wings of the V of the Meshian line began closing upon them like jaws of diamond and steel.

'Your stratagem is working!' Maram said to me. 'I've never seen men fight so!'

In truth, the Meshians were now fighting like the well-drilled warriors they were – and with a fury that struck terror into Morjin's men. They locked their long, rectangular shields together like a wall and pushed at the enemy even as they pierced them with their spears or drew their tharams and stabbed these vicious short swords into their faces. Many of my countrymen had cast down both shields and spears; these fought with their long kalamas, which left hideous gaping wounds in the bodies of men wherever they fell. Those of Sakai who tried to push forward in desperation and break through our line, thin though it was, were cut to pieces. Our enemy could do little more than stand and die.

'Father,' I whispered. 'Mandru. Jonathay.'

Horns sounded from behind the mass of men in front of us, and I knew that someone had ordered a retreat. The Galdan light infantry, I sensed, would be turning to withdraw, or panicking altogether, casting

485

down their weapons and running. And the rest of the two armies caught in the funnel of death would *want* to run. But so many thousands caught like fish in a net could not so quickly break away.

'This is our chance!' I said to Maram. 'Do you see?'

Just then, I caught a flash of gray and red to my left, and I turned to see Kane and Atara galloping behind our lines straight toward us. Kane's mail, from neck to knee, was spattered with blood. But I saw that Atara's quiver was still full of arrows. She rode trusting to the sureness of Fire's quick stride, and I swallowed back a surge of fear to see her so helpless and blind.

'Val, why are you here?' Kane called out to me.

He reined in his horse and drew up in front of me. Somehow, Atara found her way to me, too.

'Asaru sent for me,' I told him. 'My father is dead.'

'So, I saw him fall, but I did not know that he walked the stars.'

Atara turned her beautiful face toward me. Her white blindfold showed splotches of red. She said to me, 'You shouldn't have come – why have you come?'

'I came to kill Morjin!' I shouted, shaking my sword at the sky.

'Ha, Morjin!' Kane growled out. 'We've sought him, too, for an hour, all across the left flank.'

'Who leads our knights there now?' I asked him.

'Lord Avijan.'

'And my brothers? What of Karshur? Have you seen Ravar?'

Kane's blazing eyes softened with sadness as he told me about them.

This is how Karshur died: Just as he pushed his lance through the chest of an Urtuk warrior, another close by fired an arrow into his horse's side, causing this great beast to rear up in screaming agony. And in that moment, a charging Galdan knight collided with them. Karshur crashed to the ground, and his huge warhorse, Jurgarth, fell on top of him, crushing him to death.

This is how Ravar died: Just as he cast his throwing lance through the eye of an Urtuk captain, one of the captain's men fired an arrow through Ravar's forehead, killing him instantly.

Upon hearing this, I stared out at the armies battling in front of me. The din of clanging steel faded to a hiss. And I opened my mouth to cry out a single name in a shout that seemed to shake the world: MORJIN!

In that moment, Atara sat up straighter on her horse, and I knew that she had regained her second sight.

'There's a great chance here,' Kane said to me. He pointed toward Balvalam Hill, where Asaru's knights were slowly pushing back the massed Ikurian horse. 'Do you see? If we could break them, we could encircle the rest of the army. And kill Morjin, if he is there.'

'Let's ride then,' I said. I nodded at Maram, who nodded back. So did Sar Vikan and several of his knights. 'Let's finish this, if we can.'

I nudged Altaru's sides, and my great-hearted horse fairly leapt into a gallop. Everyone followed me. We rode west behind our lines, turning toward the north as we neared Balvalam hill. We made our way straight into the snarl of knights and screaming horses there. The clash between Asaru's knights and the black-bearded Ikurians had degenerated into hundreds of individual battles, as knight fell against knight in a frenzy of stabbing lances and scything swords. Hundreds of men lay dead or dying on the bloodstained grass. Riderless horses wandered about looking for a way to escape the carnage all around them. We rode through this shrieking chaos seeking out Morjin or the lord and captains of the Ikurians – or anyone else we could find to cut down with our swords.

In the first minutes of this new battle, I killed two of the Ikurian knights, stabbing one through his mail and cleaving the other's fur-trimmed helm. I looked for Asaru in the throngs of heaving horses and panting men around me. I looked for Yarashan, too. And then, from forty yards away across the pasture, my brother called out to me. Yarashan, who had somehow lost his helm, raised up his bloody lance as he shouted, 'Valashu!' He took great courage from my gladness to see him. He smiled to see the new knights that I had led onto the field. I felt in him my own burning desire to end this battle, now, in one blaze of violence that would sweep the field clean. I felt in him as well a deep urge to inspirit others by showing brave. And so he bowed his head to me, and then turned his horse toward two Ikurians thirty yards from him. And he let out a shout of challenge as he lowered his lance and charged straight toward them.

'Yarashan!'

My brother's aim was true, and he speared the first Ikurian knight through the throat. He held up his shield to cover himself from the second knight's revenge, even as he freed his lance and wheeled about. But this second knight had great skill at arms. He knocked his own shield into Yarashan's, and then slammed his mace into the side of Yarashan's head. My brother died as he would have wanted to, with the eyes of many Meshian knights witnessing his valor.

Then I charged upon this proud Ikurian, and my sword chopped through his upraised arm and then cut the mail covering his neck. I heard Kane, somewhere behind me, let loose a great cheer to see me kill the knight who had killed Yarashan.

But the Ikurians on their stamping horses nearby did not celebrate my feat. One of them cried out that their captain had been slain. Then two others cried out their rage, and the three knights charged me from three different directions. I cut through the lance of one of these, but the steel point of his friend's lance slammed into my back and propelled me from my saddle. I hit the ground with a crushing force that drove the breath from me.

'Yarashan!' a voice called as if from far away. And then, louder, now, 'Valashu!'

I tried to rise from the ground, but I could not. My fierce black stallion stood above me, frantically kicking his hooves at the two knights trying to stick their lances down into me. Then three other Ikurians whipped their horses to a gallop and bore down upon me to take part in the kill.

'Valashu!'

I looked up to see Asaru appear like an angel from out of the hundreds of knights spread across the field. He rode in a full-out fury to intercept the three charging Ikurians. I saw that he had already fought too hard that day. Mace blows had knocked loose diamonds from his chest and back, and he had lost his shield. A sword or lance had cut his cheek to the bone. I could feel the stabbing pain in his shoulder that hadn't quite healed. He was exhausted, anguished, bloody – but he had eyes and heart for only one thing.

'Valashu!'

Just before he closed with the Ikurians, he looked at me. There was death in his bright, black eyes, and something more. What is it to love one's brother? Only this: that you would die for him so that he might live.

'Asaru!'

He stabbed his lance through the face of the first knight even as the lance of the second knight split open a bare patch of his armor and drove clean through his body and out through his back. I would never know how Asaru managed to keep his saddle with this great shaft of wood transfixing him. Or how he drew his sword and killed first the knight who had killed him, and then kept the third knight away from me long enough for Maram to come forward and deal him a death blow with his mace. The last wild surge of his heart ripped through me with an unbearable pain, and I cried out in astonishment as he died in utter gladness.

ASARUUU!

I pushed myself up to one knee; just then my faithful warhorse kicked out yet again and struck down one of the knights still trying to spear me. Then Kane rode up and killed the other knight. He reached down, grasped my hand, and pulled me to my feet. I climbed on top of my horse. I stared at Kane. There was death in his eyes, too, and something more: a terrible joy in the wrath he saw building inside me.

Atara and Maram rode up then. My best friend seemed sick with what he had seen. He could hardly bear to look at me. And I could hardly bear myself. The robe of fire had burned me so completely that nothing remained except the fire.

'To me!' a deep voice boomed out from across the field. 'To me!'

Eighty yards away, a score of Ikurian knights gathered around a large, thick-bearded man with ostrakat plumes sticking out of his golden helm. The red dragon leaping out from his golden surcoat was larger than those of any of the knights or captains around us. I took him to be the Ikurians' lord. I hated him upon sight. Although he was not Morjin, in his person, he was all of the Dragon's evil, visited upon my people of his own twisted will.

I touched Altaru with my own flaming will to destroy, and my stallion surged forward into a gallop. Maram, Atara and Kane followed closely behind me. Atara's bow cracked twice as she sent arrows burning into the bodies of two of the enemy knights. And then we were upon them.

Next to me, Kane's sword struck out like the head of a cobra, and one of Ikurians grabbed at his throat and tried to scream. Kane slashed out to the side, cutting through the body of another knight with such savagery that he nearly cleaved him in two. He growled like a great, killing cat as he thrust and parried and lay about him with his long sword. Blood sprayed his wild face; he licked his lips and screamed out all of his old joy in rending and slaying. The ancient Elijin warlord out of legend, in all his wrath, rode upon the reddened field, and he was terrible to behold.

And I, too, that day was an angel – an angel of death. For this, I feared, was also part of the One's design. Altaru bore me into the mass of our enemies, and I whirled about on top of him, left and right, swinging my bright sword in a blaze of death. With every knight that I maimed or killed in vengeance for my father and brothers, I seemed to desire only more killing. My sword flared like pure flame then, and I could hardly hold onto it. It seemed to have a life of its own. And yet I knew that its life was only my life, swelling like the sun, growing stronger and more brilliant every moment as my fury to destroy swept me away. Men screamed before me. I cut them down. Men screamed out my name all around me and from farther across the field. They shielded their eyes as from a lightning bolt. The whole world seemed to cry out in agony.

And then, for the moment, there was no one left to kill. I sat on Altaru's back gasping for air. Dead knights lay on the grass all around me. It seemed that I had slain the Ikurian lord, for his great body had been cleaved in half, from neck to groin. Or perhaps Kane had sent him on to the stars, for my terrible friend sat perched on his horse, looking wildly about him as he held up his dripping sword. Maram and Atara pressed close to me on my other side. I couldn't guess how many men Maram had dispatched or Atara had added to her count.

A great fear struck into the Ikurian knights who had witnessed this terror. It passed like a sick heat into the bellies and limbs of their brethren all across the field. Without a word being spoken, ten knights turned their horses to gallop back toward the village and across the Clear Brook. And then twenty more broke, and then a hundred, and suddenly the entire mass of Ikurian knights lost their will to battle and fled the field in a panic to save their lives. A few score of our knights galloped after them. But then I called out to Sar Vikan, and to the other captains and all the rest of the knights of Mesh: 'Hold! Help our line! Take the enemy from behind!'

Where was Morjin?

To our left, the two wings of our line had now closed in even more tightly upon the elements of the two armies caught between them. Many men, however, were fleeing from this death trap. To the far left, two thousand yards across the once-green pasture near the woods, the Urtuk warriors had given up the battle as lost. They simply rode off the field, and would keep on riding, as I later learned, clear across the Lake Country and through the southern passes out of Mesh. The Galdan heavy horse, those still alive, fled ahead of almost the whole of the Galdan light infantry. But the others could not retreat quickly enough.

Lord Avijan led the charge around the enemy from the left, and I led Asaru's knights against the enemy's rear from the right. We charged around and forward, meeting up with Lord Avijan's companies, and we thrust our lances through the backs of many Galdans and Sakayans. A few of them managed to turn toward us, and these died facing the terrible weapons that laid them under. Only a few battalions of the Galdan heavy infantry had escaped the enclosing Meshian line, and almost none of the mercenaries, Blues or the Dragon Guard. These were caught in a ring of steel a mile wide; they were packed together like cattle. They moaned and screamed like cattle, too, as the ring drew tighter and tighter and we killed them without pause or mercy.

What followed then was sheer butchery. I had no care to stop it,

490

nor did Lord Avijan, nor Lord Tanu, nor any of the other Meshian knights or warriors who had lost friends, brothers or sons there that day. We kept striking our swords into the enemy until our arms grew so tired that we had to rest and let our companions next to us deal out this unrelenting death. The ground beneath us grew soggy, like a bog. Blood overflowed the close-cropped grass, and ran in little, snaking rivulets down to the Clear Brook, turning it red. Hours it took to slay all of our enemy, down to the last man. When the battle was finally over, the sun was an unbearable smear of red raining down fire from the sky.

I wandered for a long time among the heaps and twists of bodies. Later there would be a count of them, but all I knew was that there were too many thousands of them. In truth, even one man killed this way was too many – unless he was Morjin. I looked for him everywhere. Had he somehow escaped this dreadful battlefield? I looked across the Culhadosh Commons, from one end to the other. Nearby a young man lay moaning as he clapped his hands to his belly, trying to keep his insides from spilling out. Farther away, the horses of the enemy were grazing peacefully where they could find a clear patch of grass. Lord Tanu and other lords were calling out to reform their battalions, trying to bring order, if not sense, to the madness that had befallen here.

Then a rider picked his way among the dead and found me where I stood above Asaru's body. He said to me, 'Lord Valashu, King Shamesh calls for you.'

I stared at him as if he had spoken words to me out of a cruel dream. I told him, 'My father is dead.'

'No, his wounds are mortal, but he still lives,' the messenger informed me. He pointed toward the woods to the east of the battlefield. 'I am to take you to him.'

I shook my head in amazement. Hadn't Lansar Raasharu *seen* my father die? Perhaps he had only assumed the worst. And reported this to Asaru, and me. Such mistakes were often the result of the fog of battle.

I mounted my horse then, and followed the messenger across the field. We came to a place next to the woods ringed by many lords and knights. And at the center of this ring, my father sat back against a tree. Someone had removed his helm. His long black and silver hair, tied with many battle ribbons, spilled across his shoulders. His eyes were closed as he coughed up blood and gasped for breath. A bright red froth bubbled from the great hole in his armor over his chest. He held his long, bloody sword across his knees.

I dismounted, and the knights made way for me as I walked forward and knelt by my father's side. He opened his eyes and looked at me. It seemed to take a great effort for him to speak my name: 'Valashu.'

Lord Harsha stepped up to me and laid his hand on my shoulder. His cheek was bleeding where a saber had nearly taken out his remaining eye. He pointed at my father's chest and said simply, 'A Galdan lance.'

'But we've got to get him to Master Juwain!' I said. 'He's healed such wounds before!'

'Your father wouldn't allow it,' Lord Harsha told me, shaking his head. 'Not while the battle was still being fought.'

My father reached out and grasped my hand. He said to me, 'I told you not to come.'

'But I thought you'd been slain! Lord Raasharu told me that Asaru was king and had sent for me!'

A spasm tore through my father's body as he worked to breathe. Then he gasped out, 'Lord Raasharu . . . was not himself.'

His eyes cleared and touched mine. And suddenly I knew. I saw the evil tapestry that Morjin had woven for me, all of a piece.

'Asaru is dead,' my father said to me. 'All of my sons, gone . . . except you.'

He let go of his sword as he smiled at me. With all the strength left in him, he pulled off his ring, with its five bright diamonds. He pressed it into my hand and said, 'Now you must be king.'

I squeezed this heavy circlet of silver in my fist. I shook my head. 'No, there is still time!'

'No, there is no time.'

I held his hand as his breath sucked in and out, in and out, growing weaker and weaker. Then he raised his finger to point over my shoulder, west, toward Telshar, Arakel and the other mountains. And he said to me, 'You should never have left the castle.'

He coughed, once, very hard, and his whole body shuddered. He gripped his sword with one hand and my hand with his other. For a moment, his eyes grew incredibly bright, like stars. He gazed at me as if he had finally come home. And then he died.

I kissed his hand and laid it upon his sword. I kissed his lips. I stood up slowly. I pulled off my surcoat and laid it over him. I could not weep for him, not yet. I could not grieve for Asaru, or Yarashan or any other warrior of Mesh who had fallen here today. For the battle was not yet over. In truth, it was only beginning. I turned to look up the grassy slope of Culhadosh Commons, where the hills beyond blocked a clear line of sight of my father's castle high above

Silvassu. It was *my* castle now, I told myself, what was left of it. I stared up at the great plume of smoke that my father had pointed out to the west, and I watched it rise like the souls of the dead into the sky.

33

In my flight back toward Silvassu, with the smoke billows above the castle looking ever larger, I paused only long enough to remove the heaving moldings of armor that were hampering Altaru's motions. Even lightened this way, he had a hard time of it, for the going was mostly uphill, and he was already tired. I pressed him hard, even so. By the time we pounded up to the castle's south gate, he was nearly lathered. I, myself, could hardly breathe when I saw that the drawbridge was down and the iron gates hung open.

We had to pick our way across the bridge, for much of it was char and other parts were still burning. I gagged on the smell of oil with which its stout timbers had been soaked. As we entered the castle, I gagged on the smell of death. Just inside the gates lay the bodies of a dozen Meshian warriors. All of them, it seemed, had been killed by slashes to their throats. In the west ward, the dead were everywhere. Many of these were of the Dragon Guard, whose red armor had been cut open by dreadful kalama strokes. I noticed with grim satisfaction that these ravagers outnumbered the dead Meshians who had fought them here. But I could do nothing except rage helplessly at the sight of all the women, children and old men who had been slaughtered like animals. Hundreds of them lay in pools of blood near the garden wall's gate leading into the middle ward. It seemed that they had been cut down trying to flee toward the safety of the keep.

The much larger middle ward held even more bodies. The garments of some of these had been doused in oil and set aflame. I was not sure that all of them had been dead when Morjin's men immolated them. Carts and wagons were smoldering, too, and bales of straw, barrels, heaps of spears and wooden swords, the timbers in the black-smith's shop – any and all things that could be set on fire.

The gates to the keep had been battered into splinters and also put to the torch. Many knights had died trying to defend it. I dismounted

494

Altaru and made my way inside. It was a charnel house. The stones in the halls were soaked with the blood of the many dead who had fallen there. More of my countrymen lay in bloody heaps in the various rooms. In the armory, swords and spears had been snapped into pieces and cast upon a pile of corpses. The treasury was empty. In my room across the hall, I found Lord Rathald and his family. Lord Rathald, it seemed, had been killed trying to protect his daughter and his grand-children, who were gathered in the corner behind his cold form. He still gripped his bloody kalama. I did not know why the Dragon Guard who had killed him left it in his hand.

Now I could bear my dread no longer, and I burst out into the hallway. I stumbled over a long line of bodies as I ran toward my parent's rooms crying out as loud as I could: 'Mother! Nona! Mother!'

But the rooms were empty. I searched as well in the adjoining servants' quarters, and in the library and the kitchens. I called out for my mother and grandmother, many times. And then I swallowed my gorge and went into the great hall.

And there I found them. Two of the great, long tables had been shorn of their legs, and then upended and bound with ropes against the stone pillars holding up the roof. And my mother and grand-mother had been fixed to these tables with nails. My mother was dead. Her tunic was torn with many bloody gashes; to either side of her, the table's wood was riven with deep slits. It seemed that the Dragon Guard, after they had crucified her, had used her for target practice with their spears.

But they had shown no such mercy to my grandmother. I saw to my amazement that she still lived. Blood oozed from her palms and bare feet; her breath barely filled her frail, old body as she struggled to speak to me.

'Valashu!' she gasped out.

I came up to her and kissed her feet. Great spikes of iron had been pounded through flesh and bones, deep into the table's wood.

'We've got to get you down from there!' I called to her. Her head had dropped upon her chest, and I looked up into her milky, blind eyes.

'Please, help me,' she said to me.

I drew my sword and cut the ropes holding fast the table. With a great heaving that nearly broke my back, I eased this great slab of wood onto the floor, between the bodies that lay there. I knelt beside my grandmother. I touched her quavering arms, her bloody hands. I could think of no easy way to pull her off the bent-over nails without further tearing her flesh.

'Who did this to you?' I cried out.

She gathered in a deep breath and murmured, 'It was . . . Morjin. He said that he wanted you to know this. The traitor, Samelu – he held my wrists. And Morjin pounded in the nails.'

'Damn them!' I shouted. I shook my sword at the stones of the ceiling high above. 'Damn them to death!'

'Valashu –'

'Damn them! Damn them! Damn them!'

'Valashu, listen to me!' she pleaded. 'You must help me, please.'

I gripped my sword as I used my other hand to brush back the sodden white hair from her forehead.

'Help me to die in peace.'

I looked down through the blur of water in my eyes at my grandmother's beautiful face. In the soft, anguished lines, I saw to my wonder that there was no hate there. There was no resentment, either, nor anger at her fate – only a warm and overwhelming concern for me. For she, too, was a Valari warrior in her fierce, sweet spirit. And so she said to me, 'Promise me you won't waste your life in seeking vengeance.'

'But how can I not?' I shouted. My fury struck her like a blow, and I bit my lip to see her wince in pain. I lowered my voice and gasped out, 'How can I not slay Morjin?'

'Slay him if you must,' she said to me. 'But do it only because you *must* . . . for Ea's sake, not out of vengeance. Do not let the burning for his death destroy you.'

'But I –'

'Please, Valashu. Don't let him kill you this way.'

She fell still then, and I thought she had died. But I felt her heart beating, weakly, somewhere inside her.

Just then footsteps sounded along the hallway leading into the keep. Then Kane, Maram and Atara came hurrying into the room. 'Oh, my lord!' I heard Maram cry out. 'Oh, my lord!' It seemed that someone had told them of my father's death, and they had followed me up from the battlefield.

'We've got to get her off of here!' I said, laying my hand on my grandmother's wrist. 'Help me.'

Atara descried a great, iron maul cast onto the floor near the body of a little boy whose brains had been bashed out. She went over and picked it up, and wiped the gore on the surcoat of one of the Dragon Guard, adding another stain of red to the bright yellow cloth. She brought the maul over to me.

'Why don't we try pounding out the spikes from the other side?' she said, tapping the maul against the table.

Kane, Maram and I made ready to lift the table off the ground, but

496

just then, my grandmother opened her eyes. I knew that, somehow, she could see the only part of me that really mattered. And she whispered to me, 'Promise me – please promise me.'

'All right,' I told her. 'I will.'

'Good,' she said. And then she died, too, joining my mother, father and brothers in that icy, black emptiness from which there is no return.

After that, we took down both my grandmother and mother from their mounts of wood. We laid them on the cold floorstones. I pulled the great black and silver swan banner off the wall, and covered them as with a shroud.

Then there came the sound of horses and men entering the middle ward outside. Kane told me that Sar Vikan and his knights had ridden up to the castle, too.

'Keep them out of here!' I said.

My grim-faced friend went out of the hall's southern doors for a few moments to confer with Sar Vikan, and then returned, shutting the doors behind him.

I began walking slowly around my slain people, toward the dais at the end of the hall. As I neared it, I had to step over a small wall of Morjin's knights and the Guardians who had fought them. Sunjay Naviru, in death, looked younger and smaller than I had remembered. Skyshan of Ki had fallen next to him, and Sar Kimball, Lord Noldru and many others. I climbed up the dais, where there were more of the enemy; a ring of dead Guardians fairly surrounded the white granite stand.

The Lightstone no longer rested upon it. In its place had been set a square of paper, topped by a piece of gold. I grasped both in my hand and tucked them down into my armor.

Maram came up to me and said, 'Maybe one of our knights secreted the cup on his person. Or had time to hide it, somewhere.'

I swept my sword down toward my dead knights. It glowed only dully. I pointed Alkaladur south, in the direction that Morjin would have ridden with the thousands of his Dragon Guard in order to escape from Mesh with the Lightstone. And its blade flared a bright silver.

'No, it is gone,' I said.

A shudder ripped through me as I tried not to fall writhing to the floor. It was as if one of Morjin's knights had chopped my legs out from under me and then gutted me with his sword.

Kane came over and placed his hand on my shoulder. 'So, then, we'll take it back! We'll ride after them and kill the Dragon!'

Atara shook her head at this. 'No, that's impossible, now.'

'*You* say that?' he growled out.

'Yes, I do. This was well-planned. Morjin is hours gone from here. We will never overtake him.'

'We *must* overtake him.'

'He will have had fresh horses stationed in relays all along his way,' Atara said, holding her hand against her blindfold. 'Our horses are all exhausted and would have trouble galloping a mile.'

'But Lord Avijan still commands a battalion of knights!'

'Half a battalion, now,' Atara said. 'And they, too, are exhausted. I doubt if they have the will to pursue Morjin.'

I wrapped my hand tightly around my sword as I struggled to find the will to keep standing. I stared at the stand's bare granite where once the Lightstone had shone so splendidly. Then I cried out, 'But why did this have to happen!'

The echo of my words off the hall's cold stones, falling like thunder upon the dead, was my only answer.

Kane stepped over to the dais and rolled over one of the bodies there. I ground my teeth together as I stared at the face of Lansar Raasharu.

'It was he who did this,' I said to Kane. 'Somehow, he killed the guards at the gates, and opened them to Morjin.'

'So,' Kane said. 'So.'

'He was a ghul,' I murmured. '*He* was the one that Kasandra warned of.'

'No,' Maram forced out, shaking his head, 'not Lansar – it can't be.'

'He always hated Morjin,' I said. 'Too much, for too long. And then, when I struck down Ravik and Noman killed Baltasar, the hate, too terrible – like a robe of fire, you see. It maddened his soul. And then Morjin seized him.'

Kane slowly nodded his head. His black eyes searched for something in mine. 'Yes, it would be like that.'

'And I made it worse,' I said. 'I encouraged Lansar to believe that I was the Maitreya. And so he had already surrendered part of his will to me.'

'So, it was *his* will to do this,' Kane told me.

'Why didn't I see it?' I said, looking at the wounds in Lansar's body where Morjin must have stabbed him with his own sword.

'Please, don't blame yourself,' Atara said, moving over to my side.

'Why didn't I see *any* of it?' I said, looking at my sword.

There came a knocking at the door leading into the keep, and I shouted for whoever it was to go away. And I heard Master Juwain's voice call back to me, 'Val, open the door!'

I sent Maram to open it. I turned to see Master Juwain and Liljana walk into the room. Their robes showed almost as much blood as the garments of the dead.

'Why are you here, sir?' I said to Master Juwain. I gazed at Liljana. 'There must be wounded from the battle to attend to. Thousands of them.'

'I'm afraid there are,' Master Juwain said. 'But there are other healers. We heard that the castle had been overrun. And so we came here to attend to the women and children.'

I stared at the black banner covering my mother and grandmother. 'Then you've come in vain. They're all dead.'

But in this, I was wrong. Again, someone knocked at the door, and again Maram went to open it. And Daj and Estrella ran into the room.

'What?' I cried out.

Estrella hurried up to Atara and buried her face against her leather armor as she burst out weeping. Daj clasped my hand in his, and his eyes filled with a wild light.

'We hid beneath the wine cellars,' he explained to me. 'In the chambers there.'

'But there are no chambers beneath the wine cellars!' I said.

But it seemed that there were: secret chambers, as Daj told me, built long ago. Somehow, Estrella had discovered them. Like a rat, Daj had once survived in the dark, tunneled earth beneath Argattha. And now he and Estrella had miraculously survived again.

'At first we tried hiding in the granary, with the others,' Daj told me. 'But then, when Lord Morjin's men started killing everyone and taking slaves, we had to find a better place.'

'He took *slaves*?' I said to him.

Daj nodded his head. 'Dasha. Priara. Lord Tomavar's wife. Other women.'

'Dasha Ambar?' Maram cried out. Tears sprang into his eyes. 'Then I'll never go riding with her again! Ah, too bad, too bad. But at least she was spared. These beautiful, beautiful women, still alive.'

'No,' I said to him, clenching my fist, 'they're worse than dead.'

I looked out into the hall, at the still and silent people lying there. The faces of all those I had seen fall that day on the Culhadosh Commons burned like writhing flames in my mind.

'So many dead,' I murmured. I thought of all the women and children taking refuge in Lashku and Godhra and in Mesh's other cities and towns. I thought of all those in the other cities and realms of Ea, and I said, 'So many waiting to die.'

Atara slid her hand over mine and said, 'Val, you –'

'I killed them all!' I shouted.

'No, you mustn't blame –'

'It is upon me!' I said, pulling my hand away from hers. 'If I hadn't gone to Tria, and killed Ravik Kirriland there, the Valari kings would have sent help to Mesh. Morjin would never have dared to invade us.'

'But you can't know that!'

I was hardly listening to her. I said. 'I was warned of a ghul. I thought it was me. But it was I who *made* Lansar into what he became.'

'No, no.'

'My father was right: I should never have left the castle.'

Any why *did* I leave? Because I thought that Asaru had called for me? Or because I was all too glad to have a chance to ride out and kill Morjin?

'So many dead,' I whispered, looking about the hall.

And suddenly, their souls called to me from that dark and dreadful place that I had always turned away from, and I wanted to join them. Asaru's dying breath burned from my lips. So did that of Mandru and Yarashan, and all my brothers. My mother cried out my name as spears pierced her limbs and belly. And my father. The son of Elkasar Elahad and all of my ancestors, even *the* Elahad, himself – calling, calling like wolves lost in an endless night. Surely the moment had finally come to end their proud and ancient line that went back to Adar in the mists of the beginning of time?

So much death, I thought as I gazed at the black shroud covering my grandmother. *So much evil.*

I hated this dark twisting of the soul as I hated Morjin – as I hated myself. I, freely, of my own will, had chosen to believe that I was the Maitreya. And death had descended upon this wrong as surely as night follows day.

'I knew,' I whispered. 'I always knew.'

Smoke wafted into the room, and I could hardly breathe. I choked on the stench of blood and charred flesh. The end of the world, in a hellish conflagration hotter than the sun, seemed to hang in the air. Cold knives pierced my belly, groin and throat – every part of me. My heart was a swollen sack of poison ready to burst open. There was too much pain. I had brought much of it into the world. I was a murderer, truly, and the punishment for murder was death.

I walked away from my friends, looking for a crack in the floor-stones. I never again wanted to see a child hacked into pieces with a sword. Never to see the terror in a man's eyes when I fell upon him with *my* sword, never to smell his fear or to hear his shrieks: all that I desired was to join my brother Guardians in peace, quiet and nothingness.

500

'No, Val, no!' Atara cried out.

I finally found a good place to wedge the hilt of my sword so that I could fall upon it. I moved to do so. But Kane was too quick for me. He leapt across the room like a tiger and grabbed me from behind. He was strong, like a beast, like an angel, so unbelievably strong. His arms encircled me like iron bands.

Maram and Liljana came forward to help hold me, too. Master Juwain pried my fingers open while Atara took hold of my sword. After Kane had let go of me, she gave it to him. He stood holding the bright blade that he had forged long ago.

'So, Val,' he murmured as he stared at me.

'I have another sword,' I told him. 'With it, I killed Ravik Kirriland.'

The hate built inside me, hotter and hotter, deeper and deeper. It was like a fire out of the heart of the stars that nothing, least of all I, could resist.

Then Daj stepped closer, and the shackle marks on his wrists reminded me that many had suffered more than I. In the blaze of Kane's bright, black eyes was the assurance that there was no pain so great that a man could not bear it. Maram, I knew, wanted to tell me that we still had many a glass of beer to drink together. Atara touched my hand in love. It was with love and gratitude for her life that Estrella looked at me – and with something more. For she was truly the mirror of my soul. And in this magical child I saw myself, for all my failings: wild, noble and free. Master Juwain and Liljana, too, came up to me, and they rested their hands over my heart. Then Flick appeared out of nothingness, and Alphanderry's bright face shimmered in the air. My friends all surrounded me like a ring of angels. And then they took away my other sword.

'Live,' Kane said to me. 'Promise me that you'll live.'

I felt within my hands and heart the life that the One had given me, still pouring through me like a glorious flame. Who was I to put it out?

'All right,' I told him. 'I promise.'

Kane's hand smacked into mine, and then squeezed me, hard, as if testing my resolve. He pulled me up so close to him that I could feel his eyes burning into mine. And he murmured, 'So, Val, so.'

A moment later, he broke away from me. 'Ha!' he cried out. Then he gave me back Alkaladur.

In its silvery substance I saw his savage, smiling face – and my own. I said to him, 'You would have killed me with this, wouldn't you?'

And he growled out, 'Yes, I would have. As it was for Lansar, so it is for you. If you have given up, if you had despaired, utterly – Morjin

501

would have made a ghul of you. Can you not feel his presence in this room?'

I looked from one end of the hall to the other, and I nodded.

'Now that he holds the Lightstone,' he said, 'his power will be even greater. We must all watch for each other and guard our souls.'

I walked back over to the dais where the Guardians had given their lives, if not their souls, in defense of that which I had forsaken. I laid my hand on Sunjay's forehead. I said, 'I have done such a great wrong.'

'Yes,' Kane told me, 'you have. And your punishment is to live.'

I bowed my head in acceptance of this judgment. Once, I had tried to defy the will of the One in trying to rid the world of suffering. Now I would no longer try to flee from my own.

I gazed deep into the silustria of my sword, and I saw a terrible thing: that it was not only my own wrongs for which I must atone, but those of all people who had come before me, on this world and others, back through the ages great and small to the first Ardun who had come forth into being. For my life had been forged in fires that were ignited millennia, even millions of years, before. I had not made the world; I had only tried to live in it. This was not my fate alone. This was the tragedy and glory of life, that all people touched upon each other in their deeds and must suffer the agonies and joys of each other.

Kane came over to me and said, 'We should go, now. There's much to be done.'

'No, I'll never leave this place,' I told him.

I looked about the quiet hall. In the hundreds of bodies of the Guardians near the stand on the dais, I saw my own crumpled form where I should have joined them. A part of me, I knew, would always remain with them. But the part of me that still lived had duties to perform. It came to me then that the dead cannot weep for the dead – only the living can. And with this thought, all that I had been holding inside broke me open. I sheathed my sword, then fell against Kane's chest and began sobbing like a little boy.

'Val,' he said to me. 'Val.'

My other friends moved over to help hold me up. And that was a true miracle. For as Atara's hand found mine and Maram's great arm pressed into my back, my friends all surrounded me, and they fell against each other sobbing, too.

After a while, I stood back and looked at Kane. With his fierce, beautiful face, softened with his regard for me, he reminded me of my grandfather. And Master Juwain was like unto my father, as Liljana was my mother, and Estrella and Daj were the little sister and brother that I would never have now. In Maram I must find all of Asaru's faithfulness, Karshur's strength, Jonathay's laughter, Yarashan's bravura and even his blessed vainglory. And Atara. Her long, gentle hand held all my hope for the future and the new family we might call forth upon the earth.

'We should go,' Kane said to me again. 'Go out and rejoin the army.'

'Yes,' I said. 'Perhaps we *might* still overtake Morjin.'

'You must be king now, Val.'

I brought out the ring that my father had given me. I shook my head. 'No, I cannot be king.'

'You *must* be. You must take the throne.'

'No, I've brought only destruction upon Mesh. And death.'

'And now you must bring new life.'

'No – I'll renounce the kingship.'

Atara squeezed my hand and said to me, 'Is this, too, how you think to punish yourself?'

I drew in a deep breath as I stood gazing at the cloth binding her face.

'Don't you dare punish your *people* this way!' Liljana scolded me. 'What do you think your father would say?'

Master Juwain smiled at me and bowed his bald head. 'I'm afraid Liljana is right. If you refuse the throne, you'll only bring chaos upon Mesh.'

Maram smiled at me, too, and said, 'Ah, King Valamesh – that's what they'll call you, isn't it? It has a nice ring to it, don't you think?'

Daj told me that he wanted some day to enlist in my service as a knight, and without words, Estrella told me much the same thing.

And then Kane said to me, 'Only you can be king, Val.'

I bowed my head to the inevitable. 'All right then, if this is what must be, I will.'

I put my father's ring on my finger. It fit me well.

It pained me to walk with my friends out of the hall, leaving my grandmother and mother unattended – and everyone else. But we had already spent too much time letting Morjin get away. We gathered our horses in the middle ward and met up with Sar Vikan, who informed me that everyone who had taken shelter on the upper floors of the keep, and elsewhere in castle, had been put to the sword. For the moment, it seemed, there was nothing to do except rejoin the army, as Kane had said. And so we mounted our horses, and I led the way out of the west gate and across the charred bridge, back down to the Culhadosh Commons where I would stand before the warriors of Mesh to be acclaimed as king.

* * *

It was late in the afternoon when we reached the battlefield. The sun was dropping toward the mountains, but its heat still seared the thousands of men laying upon the grass. Those who had survived the battle worked quickly to prepare the dead for burial. In the sky, the carrion birds gathered and flew in slow, lazy circles.

Lord Tanu had taken command of the army. I found him at the center of the field conferring with Lord Tomavar, Lord Avijan, Lord Harsha and Lord Sharad, who now led the knights of Asaru's battalion. We rode straight up to them past the blood-spattered warriors and knights of Mesh.

'Lord Tanu!' I called out as we drew up before them. 'Lord Avijan! We must mount a pursuit before it is too late.'

Lord Tanu's crabby face tightened into a frown. Despite the tiredness of his old body, he pulled back his shoulders and stood up straight, which made him seem almost like a tall man.

'Lord Valashu,' he said, 'we've decided that there will be no pursuit. It will soon be dark, and our warriors have no will for it.'

The faces of those about me, I saw, were haggard and haunted. As they went about their business of wrapping the dead in shrouds, their limbs trembled with exhaustion. Their every motion seemed a burden and a pain.

'But how can we just let the enemy get away?' Lord Harsha put in. It seemed that he had been making this argument for hours. 'They will be as tired as we are!'

Lord Tanu shook his head at him, then turned toward me to recount the logic of his decision. He said that the remnants of the enemy were mostly Galdans and Sarni. The Sarni we would never catch, and as for the Galdans, why should we waste the life of even one more warrior hunting them down?

'They will certainly flee Mesh now,' he said, 'and return to Galda, if they can. Their army is broken, and pose us no threat.'

'But what of Morjin?' I said. 'And the Dragon Guard?'

Sar Vikan had already sent word to Lord Tanu of the ravaging of the castle. And so he had learned that Dashira, his faithful wife who had believed that I must be the Maitreya, had been butchered. Lord Tanu's old face screwed up with hate as he said, 'We would ride after them, if we could. But we've had reports that they had remounts stationed along the South Road. There isn't a horse within five miles of here who has the strength to catch up with them.'

Some men find in the murder of their loved ones a terrible rage for vengeance; others wish only for an end to their anguish. I knew that Lord Tanu's sons rode with Lord Avijan. Perhaps he could not

504

suffer them to risk their lives a second time this day.

'But we must try!' I said. 'Morjin has carried off the Lightstone!'

Lord Tanu trembled with a barely contained fury as he pointed first at the dead spread out across the field and then back toward the smoking castle. And he snarled out, 'The Lightstone? The Lightstone? That cursed thing has brought only ruin upon our land!'

'No, you're wrong,' I said to him. I turned to look at Lord Avijan, whose strong, youthful face burned with a desire for revenge. I said to him, 'Do *your* knights lack the will to pursue Morjin?'

'Not those who saw your father slain,' he told me. 'We would ride with you, if we could.'

I nodded at Lord Sharad, a tall, spare man whose gray hair was caked with blood. 'And you, Lord Knight?'

'After what we saw when you slew the Ikurians after they killed your brother? We would ride with you to the end of the earth.'

'Very well,' I said, to him and to Lord Avijan. 'Then us make ready.'

'Hold!' Lord Tanu said, sticking his palm straight out. 'It has been decided that we will not pursue the enemy – and this includes Morjin.'

'And whose decision was this?'

'Mine.'

'Very well. But a new decision has been made.'

'No, Lord Valashu, it has not.'

'No?' I said, holding up my hand to show him my five-diamonded ring. 'Who is in command here?'

'As long as the warriors haven't acclaimed you, I am.'

The light sparking from the white stones in my ring stabbed into my eyes, and I called out, 'Assemble the warriors, then.'

It was a bad time to dispense with formalities, but the ancient laws must be obeyed. And so Lord Tanu gave the order for the army to come together upon the northern section of the pasture, which the battle had left almost untouched. It took quite a while to call the warriors from across the two miles of devastation, and to form up fifty deep in their companies and battalions. Despite their weariness, they held themselves straight as trees, covered in diamonds and blood. I dismounted and stood before the whole army. Behind me, also on foot, were Kane, Atara and my other friends. Between me and my men, Lord Tanu and the other Lords of Mesh gathered close by, facing me along with nearly a hundred master knights who captained the army's companies. Seventeen thousand men had marched to battle here earlier in the morning, and it broke my heart to see many fewer of them still standing here now.

Then Lord Tanu stepped forward and shouted out, 'Who will speak in favor of Lord Valashu Elahad becoming King of Mesh?'

'I will!' Lord Harsha shouted back. His single eye sent out sparks of its own as he limped forward and held out his hand toward me. 'We all know Lord Valashu's character. We all know his deeds. They are greater than those of any of Mesh's kings, not discounting even Telemesh and Aramesh. What more is there to say?'

'Only this!' a sturdy master knight called out. It was Sar Jessu, who had led the reserve battalion to fill up the break in the Meshian line. 'Lord Valashu commanded us to hold back until the enemy lost their senses. It was this tactic that won the battle and gave Mesh our greatest victory since the Sarburn. What more is there to say?'

'Only this!' Lord Sharad shouted. 'Lord Valashu charged twenty of the enemy, and with his own sword, slew eight of them. And then led the attack against the enemy's rear. It was this tactic as well that gave us victory. Forty thousand of the enemy have died here today against four thousand fallen of Mesh. The enemy outnumbered us four to one, and we have slain them ten to one! What more is there to say?'

'Only this!' Lord Avijan called back. 'The sons of Elahad have always been kings of Mesh. Never has their line been broken. It would wrong to break it now. What more is there to say?'

So it went for quite some time as the sun pushed down upon the snow-covered peaks to the west. Some of the warriors to the far right and left, and in the ranks farthest bank, had trouble hearing what was said. Like ripples upon the sea, in a murmur of voices, their fellow warriors passed these words back to them.

'Very well,' Lord Tanu called out at last. 'Who will speak against Lord Valashu becoming king of Mesh?'

For a moment, no one moved. It seemed that thirteen thousand warriors held their breath. Then Lord Ramjay, a grizzled veteran of many campaigns, stepped forward.

'I will!' he cried out. 'We all *do* know Lord Valashu's deeds. At the Battle of Red Mountain, he hesitated in slaying the enemy. And in Tria, it is said, he slew one who was *not* the enemy, a great lord of Alonia. He struck down an innocent man in a fit of wrath, with this cursed power of his. And so ruined our chances to make an alliance against the Red Dragon. What more is there to say?'

'Only this!' Sar Jalval shouted. He had commanded one of Lord Tomavar's companies and was nearly as strong as Karshur had been, with great, long arms and a great nose once cleft by a sword. 'Lord Valashu's recklessness in holding back the reserve almost destroyed us. It caused the deaths of his own brothers, Sar Jonathay and Sar Mandru, and many others. It nearly brought upon us our greatest defeat since the Battle of Tarshid in the Age of Law. Four thousand of us have fallen today, and how can we count that a victory? We shall be a generation replacing such losses. If indeed our sons still left to us ever grow to manhood now. What more is there to say?'

'Only this!' Lord Tomavar shouted. He turned his long, horsey face toward me, and in his tormented eyes there was great anger. 'Four thousand warriors have fallen here – and how many of our kin who took shelter in the castle? Two of my own grandsons and four grand-daughters were slaughtered like pigs! My daughter, my . . . young wife. It is said that Vareva has been carried off into foul slavery, as have others! Who standing here has also lost sons, daughters and wives today? And why? Because Lord Valashu wantonly deserted his post for the glory of battle. And so the castle was taken through sorcery, and the Lightstone was stolen, and our families were slain. What more is there to say?'

It seemed, for the moment, that there was nothing more to say. No other lords or master knights came forward to testify against me. The thousands of warriors lined up before me gazed upon me with their dark eyes as a great lamentation of doubt broke through their ranks.

And then Lord Tanu said to me: 'What words will Lord Valashu speak for or against those spoken here?'

I looked down at the last of the sun's rays caught up in the bright-ness of the five diamonds of my ring. I looked at Lord Tanu and at Lord Tomavar, tall and grave and waiting upon my words. I looked out at the thousands of warriors of Mesh. What could I say to them? How could I dispute their interpretation of my actions when I condemned them myself? In one matter, however, they were wrong. And so I drew in a breath of air because the truth must be told.

'The castle was taken through *treachery*,' I said to Lord Tomavar. 'It was Lansar Raasharu who betrayed us in becoming a ghul.'

I told him what I knew of ghuls: that a man's soul could not be seized against his will but only surrendered.

'All men, when put to the fire, will break in the end,' I said. 'And so Lord Raasharu deserves our pity more than our blame. But this great man was reduced to being Morjin's eyes, hands and mouthpiece. It was Morjin's words that Lord Raasharu spoke to me, not Asaru's. Lies, they were. And so believing that my brother was king, what else was there to do but to obey his command?'

'You should have obeyed your *father's* command,' Lord Tomavar said. 'You were to remain and guard the castle – and with good reason it was you he chose for this charge. For the castle was surely taken through Morjin's sorcery. The gates must have been thrown open by guards maddened by Morjin's illusions. But it is known that Valashu Elahad has gained the power to defeat such illusions. If you hadn't abandoned your post, then Morjin never would have ravaged as he did. The only treachery I see here is *yours* in putting glory before duty.'

My face was beginning to burn, but not from the heat of the long day's sun. I said to Lord Tomavar, 'You have suffered terrible loss today, as have many of us. Who could think clearly after the maddening things that we have seen? But I ask you to think of this: why would Lord Raasharu have left the battle if not to deceive as he did?'

Lord Tomavar summoned forward one of the master knights behind him. This was a stolid man with a square jaw and sad, dark eyes full of death. I remembered that his name was Sar Aldelad.

'Tell us,' Lord Tomavar said to him, 'what Lord Raasharu told you.'

Sar Aldelad bowed his head to him and addressed the nearby lords and knights: 'As Lord Raasharu was riding off the field, he told me that King Shamesh had sent him back to the castle to request that Lord Valashu send a company of knights to aid us.'

'Another lie!' I said. 'Lord Raasharu lied to Sar Aldelad, as he lied to me.'

'Is it indeed a lie?' Lord Tomavar said to me. 'That word falls too easily off your tongue.'

'My father would never have sent away his greatest lord in the middle of a battle!'

'He might have,' Lord Tomavar said, 'if he needed to choose someone whom you would trust absolutely. And you did trust him, didn't you? And then betrayed that trust by deciding to lead the company of knights yourself?'

'No, it was not so!' I cried out. 'I *did* trust Lord Raasharu, but he betrayed me, as he did everyone standing here and all of Mesh!'

Lord Tomavar shook his long head back and forth. The ribbons tied to his long hair rustled against each other. Then he gathered in all the scorn in his powerful voice as he called out: 'You should be ashamed to slander such a great man who was so faithful to your father – and to you. Lord Raasharu is dead, in defense of *your* castle, and so he cannot defend himself against your wanton accusations.'

'All that I have told here today is true!'

'*Is* it? And who is left alive to confirm your story?'

As it happened, neither Sar Vikan nor any of the knights in his company had heard Lansar Raasharu request my presence on the battle-field. But one man had.

'All that Lord Valashu said *is* true!' a great voice boomed out. Maram strode forward like a great bear and stood in front of Lord Tomavar.

'I was present at the gate with him and Lord Raasharu.'

Lord Tomavar nodded his head to him. 'Everyone knows what a faithful friend you have been to Lord Valashu. Perhaps *too* faithful.'

'Are you calling me a liar?' Maram bellowed out.

His face flushed deep red and seemed to burn through the brown curls of his beard. His hand fell upon the hilt of his sword. He would have to be mad to draw upon Lord Tomavar. But it seemed that he might, for the hellish furnace of war had forged him into more of a Valari knight than even he suspected.

'No, I would never call *you* a liar,' Lord Tomavar said. 'But in the heat of the moment, with the news of the battle, you might easily have misheard Lord Raasharu's words. And so there is no dishonor in that.'

'I did *not* mishear him!' Maram called out. 'As for my own honor, I'm not concerned. But you should not stain the honor of my friend. Val has told you nothing but the truth! He's the most truthful man I know – sometimes *too* damn truthful! He would never lie!'

Lord Tomavar stood very still as he glared at me. With his diamond armor and face all smeared with blood, as he gathered in all his wrath, he was terrible to behold. And then, like a crack of thunder, he cried out: 'In Tria, when Lord Valashu was asked if he was the Maitreya, he affirmed that he was. Thus his honor is already stained with the shame of this lie if no other.'

After that Lord Tomavar fell quiet, and so did Maram – and everyone else assembled there. Now there was truly nothing more to say.

The sun finally disappeared behind the mountains, and a shadow fell upon the field. I felt the eyes of thirteen thousand warriors burning into me. I could not move; I did not want to breathe. I stood ensnared in a web of evil, lies and great blame.

Then Lord Tanu, true to the ancient forms, called out: 'Who will draw his sword to Lord Valashu as King?'

As with a single motion, with the ringing of steel like the rush of a cold wind, five thousand knights and warriors drew their swords to me. They held their bright kalamas pointing at me like so many rays of light. But eight thousand men did not draw their swords. And so I could not be King of Mesh.

I tried to keep my face as stern as those of the lords and master knights standing near me. I slipped the great ring from my finger, and for a moment held it tight inside my fist. And then I cast it down into the grass. I turned about so that no one could see the shame burning my face and the tears in my eyes. I began walking north, toward the woods that edged the Culhadosh Commons. I was only faintly aware of Altaru nickering as he followed after me, and my friends and their horses as well. I moved without purpose or destination. I wanted only to keep on walking, through the Valley of the Swans and out of Mesh, until I walked right off the edge of the world.

34

After the burials, we took shelter on Lord Harsha's farm eight miles farther up the valley. Forest surrounded his fields on three sides, affording us a sense of isolation. Atara, Liljana and Estrella settled into one room of Lord Harsha's stout, stone house, while Maram, Kane, Master Juwain, and Daj shared two others. I spread out my cloak on some clean straw in the barn, next to the stalls of Lord Harsha's gray mare and his other horses. Behira, having finished with her duties with the wounded from the battle, prepared us meals of good, solid Meshian fare: bacon, eggs and hotcakes in the morning; beef and barley soup for lunch; lamb roasts with herbs and potatoes for supper. I could hardly eat any of it. Liljana, who helped with the cooking, kept urging upon me these tasty viands; she told me that I must at least try to strengthen my body for what was to come.

'It's an old saying of our Sisterhood,' she told me. 'Nourish the body, and the spirit will flourish.'

And I told her: 'We of Mesh say that the spirit alone gives the body life.'

I thought of my grandmother's fierce will to speak with me before she died, and I knew this was true.

For most of five days, I lay as one dead in the half-darkness of the barn, listening to the chickens squawk, breathing in the scent of straw, manure and old wood. I watched a spider weave an elaborate web between the rafters above me. I tried not to think of what I had seen in the ruins of my family's burnt-out castle. I dwelled on all the deeds of my life. My friends, in their wisdom, left me alone.

And then, on a cloudy day with the first chill of autumn in the air, I roused myself and went to work. I saw to Altaru's shoeing and changed the poultice where a sword had scored his flank during the battle. I began gathering in stores: dried beef and dried plums; cheeses as yellow as old paper; year-old hickory nuts; and battle-biscuits almost hard enough to drive nails. My friends watched in silence as I made these preparations. And then, when Maram could bear it no longer, he caught me out behind the barn oiling my old suit of mail that I had retrieved from my rooms in the castle.

'What are you doing?' he asked me.

'What does it look like I'm doing?' I said. Heavy rings of steel jangled in my hands as I examined them for any broken or weak links. 'I cannot remain in Mesh.'

Maram, too, had put aside his diamond armor; he stood before me wearing a plain half-tunic and trousers, topped with a leather hunting jacket. He looked every inch a Valari knight at his leisure.

'But where are you going?' he asked me.

And I told him: 'To Argattha.'

He shook his head as he looked out to the west and watched the clouds in the sky building thicker and darker. 'Ah, Val, Val, it's a bad season to be setting out on *any* journey. But *this* – surely you know this is madness?'

'I don't care.'

'But I *do* care,' he told me. 'You promised Kane to stay alive.'

'No, the spirit of the promise was that I would not kill myself. And I won't.'

'But you're throwing your life away!'

'Am I? Are you a scryer then, that you can see the future?'

'But you'll never even get past the guards at Argattha's gates! They'll shackle you in chains and drag you before Morjin. And before you die, he'll –'

'I'm not afraid any more, Maram.'

He slapped his fist into his hand as his fat cheeks puffed out. 'No? No? Are you *proud* of that? To be without fear is to be without hope.'

'Hope,' I murmured, shaking my head.

'I know, I know,' he told me. 'But what else can we do but try to find a good outcome to all the horrible things that have happened?'

'Life isn't a story,' I said to him. 'It doesn't have a happy ending.'

'Don't say that, Val. We're all involved in a great story, as old as time, whose ending hasn't yet been written.'

I looked down at the rings of oily steel in my hands, and I said, 'Perhaps it hasn't. But it's not hard to see what that ending now must be.'

'Are *you* a scryer?' he said to me. Then he grasped my arm and told me, '*I* am afraid enough for both of us. And so I won't let you go.'

'How will you stop me?'

'I won't let you go . . . alone.'

512

His courage caused me to gasp against the shock of pain that stabbed through my chest. I gazed into his eyes, all soft and brown and shining with his regard for me.

'No, you can't come with me,' I told him. 'It would be your death.'

'And how will you stop *me*, my friend?'

He smiled at me, and for a few moments, we stood there taking each other's measure. Then a gray, cold drizzle began sifting down from the sky; I covered my suit of armor with my cloak and told him, 'I *won't* let you go to Argattha.'

Later that day, as I walked through the woods beyond the stone wall at the edge of Lord Harsha's fields, I came upon a great, old elm tree that had once been felled by lightning. I sat upon its moss-covered trunk. Rain pattered against leaves and soaked into my cloak. Atara found me there, staring at the dark trees all about me as I rubbed the scar on my forehead.

'Maram told me I might find you here,' Atara said to me. 'He told me where you're thinking of going.'

She pulled her lionskin cloak more tightly around her shoulders as she sat down beside me. I said to her, 'If he tires of being a Valari knight, he can always find work as a spy.'

She smiled at this, then took my hand. 'It's cold, here, Val. Why don't you come in out of the rain and sit by the fire?'

I shook my head as I pointed at the mat of dripping ferns spread across the ground. 'This is the spot where the bear nearly killed me. He nearly killed Asaru, too. All my life, Asaru told everyone that I'd saved *his* life.'

She said nothing as she oriented her head facing the place that I had pointed out. I wondered if she could 'see' me as a young boy plunging my knife into the huge, brown bear's back in a frantic effort to keep the beast from mauling Asaru.

'When the Ikurians were upon me,' I said to her, 'he gave me back my life. But not in repayment. Only . . . in love. You should have seen the look in his eyes, just before he died. He didn't care that he would have made a better king than I.'

Her hand tightened around mine, and its warmth flowed into me.

'I can't believe I'll never talk to him again,' I said. 'My mother, my father, all of them – I can't believe they're really gone.'

Atara's blindfold, I saw, was wet with rain, if not tears. I thought it cruel that she could never weep again, just as Liljana could not laugh.

'What was the *point* of us going to Argattha,' I asked her, 'if it all came to this?

'I don't know, Val.'

'But you're suppose to see everything.'

'I wish I could.'

'So many dead,' I murmured. 'And in the end, we only succeeded in giving the Lightstone back to Morjin. *I* did.'

'You mustn't blame yourself.'

'Who should I blame then? Kane, for not seeing all of Morjin's plots and perfidies? You? The One for creating the world?'

'Please, do – blame us, if that would be easier for you.'

I squeezed her hand, and pressed it to my forehead. 'I'm sorry,' I told her.

'And I'm sorry, too,' she said. 'But not even a scryer can make out all ends. Something good may yet come of what has happened in a way that we can't see.'

'Something good,' I said, shaking my head. 'I should have done better to have claimed the Lightstone from the very beginning.'

'Please, don't say that.'

'Why not? If I had come forth as the Maitreya, that day with Baltasar in my father's hall, I might have united the Valari without even going to Tria. Morjin would never have attacked Mesh, and the Lightstone would be mine.'

'And what then?' she asked me. 'You know the prophecy. Would they come to call you the Great Silver Swan? Would you have that name become a curse, like the Red Dragon?'

'At least,' I told her, 'my people would still be alive.'

'There are some things more terrible than death,' she said, rubbing at her blindfold. 'Do you doubt that you could become as Morjin – or worse?'

I recalled the look on Ravik Kirriland's face as I had struck him down. I sat there in silence, listening to the rain.

'You would have brought great evil to the world,' she said to me. 'Great destruction and death.'

'Could the suffering that entailed have been any worse?'

'I don't know. I don't know how to measure such a thing. Do you?'

I pressed my fingers against her wrist, where I could feel her heart sending out pulses of blood like an anguished and savage thing. I said, 'There's no end to suffering.'

'No, perhaps not,' she said. 'But I must believe it has a purpose.'

I smiled grimly as I recalled Morjin's letter, and said, 'To torment us into hating the One so that we might become as angels?'

She smiled, too, as she shook her head. 'No, Val. But there is something strange about suffering. It carves the soul, hollows it out – and in the end leaves room for it to hold more joy.'

514

'*You* say that?'

I stared at her blindfold, and I wondered what the hollows beneath it held inside their scoops of darkness?

'I *do* say that,' she told me. 'I have to make myself believe that there is still hope for all of us.'

'Have you been talking to Maram, then?'

She let go of my hand and brought out her scryer's sphere. Drops of rain broke against the white gelstei, and ran in streaks down the curves of the crystal.

'Have you seen these joys with which you hope we'll be blessed?' I asked her.

She smiled as she shivered against the cold of the rain. And then she told me, 'Many believe that the kristei was forged to show visions of the future. But its true power is to create it.'

That was all she said to me, then. She stood up to make the short journey back to Lord Harsha's house. She left me sitting on my soggy log; she left me to wonder how a little ball of clear crystal – no less a man – could create anything good at all.

The next day the rain deepened, and I spent most of it in the barn, hunched beneath my cloak and brooding upon things to come. Late in the afternoon, the peace of Lord Harsha's farm was broken when a rider dressed all in black came galloping up the road. I hurried out of the barn to see Kane emerge from the house and walk up to confer with this stranger. That he was no Valari I could tell immediately: he was rather short and thick, and his broad face and dense black beard reminded me of the Ikurians. But his eyes were bright blue, and his skin was fair, and I could not guess what land he called home. An air of danger and darkness surrounded him. I was sure that he was a master of the mysterious Black Brotherhood.

Kane, however, did not present this man to me – or to any of us. The tension in Kane's brutal body and flashing black eyes warned us away. The rider did not remain to partake of Lord Harsha's hospitality. As soon as he had finished his business, without a word of greeting to any us, he pulled his horse about and rode off again into the rain.

That evening, like a king issuing a summons, Kane insisted that I come inside the house to take dinner with everyone else. My curiosity overcame my moroseness. I sat at Lord Harsha's long table with my friends, and feasted on roasted pork, peas and potatoes. I forced myself to eat the apple pie and cheese that Behira served for desert. Then, when we were all full, Lord Harsha called us into his great room to sit by the fire. On the andirons were piled several logs throwing out flames and a comforting heat; above the fire, many cups rested on the cracked oak of the mantle. Lord Harsha informed us that his wife, Sarai, had made them from good Meshian clay. He invited us to sit on the floor, which was covered with bearskins and cushions. His eye gleamed as he began filling the cups from a bottle of old brandy. Two cups, of course, would have been enough for him and Behira, but once his house had held many more: his three sons, killed in various battles, a daughter taken by a fever before her fifth birthday, and another daughter who had died with Sarai in childbirth. Lord Harsha's mother and aunt, too, were long gone, but he took pride in displaying on the walls the bright tapestries they had once woven from the wool of the sheep that he kept on his north pasture. He was a prideful man, and the toast that he proposed as we all raised our cups was both a proud and a poignant one: 'May our land always be blessed with sons as valorous as those who fought and fell at the Culhadosh Commons, and with daughters strong and wise enough in spirit to raise up true Valari warriors.'

He sighed and sipped his brandy as he patted Behira's hand. Then he looked across the bearskins at Maram and said, 'Ioj is gone and Valte is racing by. The months pass almost as quickly as the years. And still we're no nearer to setting a date for the wedding, are we?'

'Ah, no, sir, I have to say we're not,' Maram choked out. He nodded at Behira as he smiled his most sheepish smile. 'And now, with all that's happened . . . well, you see, I couldn't take vows with the whole world turned upside down.'

'There you're wrong, lad,' Lord Harsha said to him. 'There will be many marriages this season, as sad as it is. Too many widows will need husbands now, and too many widowers will need new wives.'

In his farmer's way, he spoke of life always engendering more life, of apple trees bearing fruit and new shoots of barley growing out of winter's dead fields. I couldn't blame him for wanting to bring more children into his land – and into his house.

'Then it wouldn't do to make Behira a widow so soon,' Maram told him. 'The wedding will have to wait until I return – if I do.'

He told everyone then that I was setting out for Argattha, and that he would follow me to the end.

At this, Lord Harsha fixed me with his bright eye and asked, 'Then you really do intend to go back to that evil place?'

'Yes,' I told him. 'I do.'

'My daughter and I accompanied you to Tria, but this is no journey for us.' He turned back to Maram and said, 'There are crops to be raised here, and a land to be healed. We'll be waiting for you when you *do* return.'

516

He might have added that there was a new king to be chosen and a kingdom to protect, but he would not speak of such things in front of me.

'Now that we've dispensed with that,' he said sadly, 'it's time that Lord Kane gave us the news he's been waiting to tell us.'

Kane peered out over the edge of his cup, gazing first at Estrella, who edged up close to my side, and then at me. Daj was to my right, and then Liljana, Maram and the others. We all sat in a circle, holding council as we had many times during the quest.

'There's news from Alonia,' Kane said. 'There's been war between Tarlan and the Aquantir, and Baron Monteer has declared Iviendenhall an independent domain. And Count Dario leads the Narmadas in fighting the Hastars and the Marshans for the throne.'

Atara, sitting between Maram and Master Juwain, faced the fire without a word, and I watched the light of its orange flames play across her impassive face.

'And I've learned the truth about Ravik Kirriland,' he said, looking at me. 'An innocent, you called him, Val. Ha! He was a Kallimun priest, as I suspected from the first. In the middle of the melee, he was to have plunged a poisoned needle into Atara's neck to murder her so that she could not give Noman away. So, your instincts were right. And so you did *not* slay an innocent man.'

I stared at the scar on my hand that my teeth had torn in my anguish over Ravik. I felt my heart beating with new life. Kane's words were like a magic incantation that lifted away a great stone crushing my chest.

'Are you sure?' I asked him. I did not want to know how his black knight had come by this knowledge, but I needed to be certain it was true.

'So, I *am* sure,' he told me. '*You* were the innocent one.'

I smiled sadly as I shook my head. Other stones still pressed down upon me with the weight of worlds, and I would never be innocent again.

'So, Val, so.'

His eyes flashed with a knowing light, and I marveled that he could tell me so much with three simple words with a single, luminous look.

'This changes nothing,' I said to him. 'I'm still going to Argattha.'

'You're determined, eh? Well, I've also had news about *that* hell-hole. Morjin has hung new gates, of iron and thicker by thrice, over the entranceways. Packs of dogs he has posted there. And squadrons of knights now patrol every approach to the black mountain.'

517

I looked at my scabbarded sword, which I had set down upon the bearskin beside me. I said, 'Morjin anticipates me. From the beginning, he has outthought me – and outfought me.'

'What if he has? He has great cunning and even greater power: Skakamen and whole armies at his command.' Kane paused to take a drink of brandy, then continued, 'So, we lost *this* battle, but we nearly killed him in Argattha, didn't we? There will be other battles to come.'

'And that,' I said, 'is why I'm going back to Argattha.'

'*That*,' he said, 'is precisely why you mustn't. Morjin has seen into your mind, Val. Don't you think it's time you tried seeing into his?'

At this, Liljana shook her head with so much force that her gray hair whipped the side of Maram's face. And she said to me, 'Look into his mind? Don't you dare try! There's nothing there but snakes, hissing, rats disappearing down holes and dark, twisted things.'

The look of kindness that came into Kane's eyes then surprised me, as it did when he spoke to Liljana with a rare gentleness: 'You were warned against using your gelstei to enter Morjin's mind. And it nearly destroyed you, I know. But we're all warriors, eh? Val proposes to fight Morjin. So, the first rule of war is to know your enemy.'

He turned to me and said, 'Don't you think it's time you read his letter?'

'But how did you know he left me a letter?'

'I saw you put it inside your armor.'

'How do you know I *haven't* read it?'

'*Have* you?' he asked, staring at me.

I noticed Lord Harsha and Master Juwain, and everyone else, staring at me, too. And so I shrugged my shoulders and pulled Morjin's letter out of the pocket of my cloak. The memory of finding it in the Lightstone's place on the stand still scorched my mind. As before, with Morjin's first letter, in my parents' chambers, Master Juwain advised me not to open it. But at last I gathered in my courage, and used my knife to break the red seal. I slid out the square of paper inside, unfolded it, and began reading its neatly penned lines out loud:

My Dearest Valashu,

Forgive the brevity of this note, but I write in haste, and there is still much to be done in this little castle of yours. I'm sure you understand.

As I promised, I have taken back the cup you stole from me. If you can be true to the logic of the beliefs you profess, you will rejoice that this is so. You have sought to place the Lightstone in the hands of the Maitreya, and that you have done.

518

You will have ascertained that you are not and could never be this Lord of Light. If you had believed me when I advised you of this some time ago, you might have avoided the ugly events of the past month. The death of an innocent man is upon you, as is the defeat of your army and the destruction of all who sought refuge in your castle.

Your mother, you will want to know, died well. After my knights had finished with her, when it came time to put her on the wood, she told me that she would never give me the satisfaction of making her cry for mercy – or even cry out at all. In all my years, which have been many, I've seen few go beneath the nails in silence. Your mother, though, was true to her word. You Valari are strong, and the Elahads the strongest of all.

And you, dear Valashu, if you choose to live, will be a very volcano of strength. I predict that you will so choose. Hate will drive you deeper into life. I do not expect that you will come to thank me for this. Nor thank me for impelling you to find the fire to slay Lord Ravik and all the others that you will want to dispatch with a great, if fearsome, joy. You are who you are. And so I also predict that you will return to Argattha. I shall be waiting for you. Towards this end, I have taken leave to appropriate several of your garments, that my hounds might become acquainted with your scent. I will leave with this letter a piece of gold in repayment for them. After all, I am not a thief.

You will also have ascertained that I keep my promises. Do you remember what I wrote to you previously about the Maitreya's obligation to show the world the terrible truth of things? That truth, I'm afraid, in the event of your incredible presumption in claiming the Lightstone for yourself, has become even more terrible. You have tempted many to speak against me and to make treason against their lord. They shall all be crushed. So shall the evil that you have engendered. Think of this when you behold the forests of crosses that spring up from the soil of Mesh, Ishka, Taron and the other Valari kingdoms. That is, you may dwell upon the suffering you have brought the world, if you live long enough, which I suspect you will not. That is too bad. I would have liked for you to have sired children out of the beautiful Atara so that you might some day know the agony I endured after you murdered my beloved son, Meliadus. But sons and daughters you will have none.

You have scorned all my offers of peace, aid and recompense for the service you owe me. There will be no more. Your life is now forfeit. The million-weight of gold that I promised for the return of the Lightstone shall now be paid to anyone who brings me your head. Of course, I would rather mount the whole of you upon a cross in the hall that you defiled. We've much still to discuss, and I would like to thank you face to face for

519

inspiring me to visit this pretty land of yours. If only you'd allow me that opportunity, I shall be forever grateful.

Faithfully, Morjin, King of Sakai and Lord of Ea

After I had finished reading, I leaned over past Estrella and cast the letter into the fire. I watched the writhing orange flames devour it. I listened to the hissing of the logs and to my own ragged breath. Then my senses died into a screaming light that threw out sparks like hot, hammered iron. In the deeps of my mind, I shouted the name of my tormenter with all the hate inside me: **MORJIN!**

When I could see again, when the sound of Atara weeping softly and the sight of Maram choking on his brandy broke upon my ears and eyes, I pressed my fists to the sides of my face and cried out: 'I . . . am sorry! But sometimes, the fury, almost like a madness – there's no controlling it.'

Liljana, who was weeping, too, as she pulled Daj against her bosom, wiped her eyes and said to me: 'Well, you'd *better* learn to control it. Else you'll kill us all, if don't kill yourself first.'

Everyone in the circle except Kane was reeling from the terrible thing that had torn me open. But even as the black stone that he bore could absorb the fire of the red gelstei, his blazing black eyes seemed to drink in all my hatred for Morjin.

'I'm sorry,' I said again. 'But that is another reason I must go to Argattha . . . alone.'

'No, Val,' Kane said to me, 'you mustn't go at all.'

'But you said yourself that I should try to see into his mind. I think I have. And more, I've *felt* what is in his heart. He fears me.'

His eyes flicked toward my sword as he said, 'I'm sure he does. You're a fearsome man, eh? But that won't stop him from capturing and crucifying you.'

'I'm not afraid of that,' I told him.

His dark eyes, and all the tension in his great body which had once been nailed to Skartaru's black rock, told me that I *should* be afraid of such torture.

Master Juwain rubbed at his ruined ear, and he sat studying me as he might a puzzle. And he said to me, 'The Red Dragon still lies to you. And why? So that hatred will continue to blind you.'

'There is no getting past that now, sir,' I said to him. 'I will hate him, always, no matter what he says or doesn't say.'

'But can't you see that is what he wants? He's woven a web for you, and invites you to your doom.'

520

'Everyone dies,' I said. 'And doom is upon us all.'

I went on to say that with Morjin's recapture of the Lightstone, it would be only a matter of time before he summoned Angra Mainyu from Damoom and unleashed an unstoppable evil that would destroy the world.

'My killing Morjin,' I said, 'might be the slimmest of chances. But it is our *only* chance.'

'No, Val,' Master Juwain said to me. 'There is one other.'

I looked into his gray eyes, waiting for him to say more.

'Before the akashic stone was broken,' he told me, 'I learned *this* about the Maitreya: that he might possibly be able to wield the Lightstone from afar.'

'Go on,' I said, nodding my head to him.

'If *we* could find him, and bring him to one of the Brotherhood's sanctuaries, we might forestall the Dragon from using the Lightstone.'

'That . . . does not seem possible.'

'It *must* be possible. We know the Maitreya has been born, somewhere on Ea. I was wrong, so terribly wrong, to convince us both that he must be you. But it would be even more wrong, now, if we didn't try to seek out this man.'

I looked around the circle at the faces of my friends. I knew that none of them, not even Kane, favored a mission to murder Morjin.

'I'm sorry,' I said to them, 'but I've lost faith in this Shining One. And so I still must go to Argattha.'

'Then,' Master Juwain told me with a sigh, 'if that is what you truly decide, I will go with you.'

'And I, as well,' Liljana said. 'As it was before, your chances will be greater with all of us behind you.'

Maram, I saw, was sweating now, even though he sat farthest from the fire. But his jaw was set with resolve, and he fought to keep the terror from his eyes. He reassured me that he would stand by my side. Atara told me much the same thing. And Kane's lips pulled back into a savage smile, and he said, 'So, Val, so.'

Then Daj, upon exchanging looks with Estrella, traced his finger along the swan-carved hilt of my sword. And he told me, 'We're coming with you, too.'

'Who is?' I asked him in astonishment.

'Estrella and I.'

'No, you can't – you're both too young.'

Daj regarded me with his sad, dark eyes, which had seen sights that would have wilted most grown men. 'We're not too young for Lord Morjin to kill, are we? No one is. We were supposed to be safe in the

521

castle. But no place is safe now – you said so yourself.'

Estrella's face fairly danced with lively expressions as Daj nodded his head. Then he said to me, 'I know the tunnels on Argattha's lower levels, and Estrella might be able to find another entrance that Lord Morjin doesn't know about. It's our *only* chance, Val.'

I slowly shook my head, marveling at the courage of this boy.

Then Estrella smiled at me, and I could not bear the brightness of it. Her trust in me was like a lump of pain in my throat that all my swallowing could not dislodge. She pressed into my side, and grabbed my arm as if she would never let go.

And Daj said to me, 'We both feel safest with you.'

I wiped my stinging eyes; it felt as if hot cinders from the fire had gotten into them.

'No, I'm sorry,' I said, 'but I *can't* let you come with me.'

I turned to look at Liljana, Maram, Atara, Master Juwain and Kane. 'I'm sorry, but there are already too many deaths upon me, and so I must go alone.'

I stood up and bade everyone goodnight. Then I walked out into cold rain to return to my bed of straw in the barn.

A few days later, when the weather had cleared, I finished the last of my preparations. One task remained to be completed. And so I filled a rucksack with some rations and personal things. In the crispness of an autumn morning at dawn, I set out to climb Mount Telshar. Kane caught me coming out of the barn, and I saw that he had a rucksack of his own – and a large coil of rope. And he said to me, 'If I can't come with you to Argattha, at least I can see that you get up and down *this* mountain without breaking your neck.'

For a long time I looked through the half-light at this deep and powerful man before nodding my head and saying, 'All right.'

We spent most of the morning crossing the valley's forests and farms. The chittering of many birds greeted the rising sun. The leaves of the trees showed bright colors: oranges and yellows and vivid reds. In the fields, cattle lowed and golden barley waited to be cut.

We paused by a stream to eat a lunch of cheese, scallions and fresh bread that Behira had baked for me. Then we made our way up through the forest that blanketed Telshar's lower slopes. We followed the tinkling stream higher and higher, through crunching leaves and clear air that smelled sweet and clean. The walking was mostly easy, though the path steepened toward the end of the day. When dusk touched the trees with the first shades of darkness, we were glad to come across the first of the stone huts built into Telshar's flank. We mounded leaves inside, and spread our cloaks on top of them. For dinner that night, we had ham sandwiches and apples. We slept to the sound of the wind shushing through the trees and the wolves howling somewhere below us.

Early the next morning we set out through a frost that sparkled the forest's fallen leaves. Just before breaking out of the treeline, we gathered some wood, and slung these cumbersome bundles on our backs. I put a few stones in my rucksack as well. Half a mile farther on we came out upon naked rock, cold wind and brilliant sunshine. We climbed all that day, past the second hut, into air that grew thinner and thinner, and here we worked very hard, sweating in the sun and gasping for breath. Our route up the mountain's rocky slope was long but not particularly dangerous, and so we did not make much use of Kane's rope. When we found the third and last hut, rising up from the snowfields of Telshar's upper reaches, we unburdened ourselves of the wood and lightened our rucksacks of almost everything except a few apples and shelled nuts, and the six flat stones I carried. The weather held true, with clear skies and little bitterness to the air, and that was good, for already our feet were cold inside our stiff leather boots from crunching through old crusts of snow. And so we decided to finish our ascent in what remained of the afternoon.

I reached the summit first, with Kane only a few steps behind me. I unroped and stood staring at the beautiful thing that my people had built there. On Telshar's very highest point, many stones had been piled into a cairn, nearly half again my height and shaped like a pyramid. And on each stone rested a silver ring. Into many of them was set a single diamond; other bands showed two or three of these sparkling gems, and a few gleamed with the four diamonds of a lord. The rays of the setting sun fell upon this cairn so that the whole of it shimmered like a small mountain of brilliant lights.

I edged up close to it, blinking my eyes against the diamonds' fire. I opened my rucksack and took out the six stones. Careful not to dislodge any of those already piled there, I reached high above my head and set them in place at the top of the cairn. Then I brought out my brothers' rings. Ravar's and Mandru's I set on two of the stones, and so with those of Jonathay, Yarashan and Karshur. I rested Asaru's ring, with its four shining diamonds, on the highest stone at the top of the cairn. From mountains these slips of silver and gems had been mined, and to the sacred mountain we called Telshar they had returned.

'You Valari,' Kane said, gazing at the cairn, 'are a strange people. And a beautiful one.'

We laid our rucksacks on the snow, and sat down on them to eat some apples and nuts and take a little rest. After a while, I brought out the silken bag of astor seeds that Ninana had given me. Would the time ever come, I wondered, to plant them? I shook my head, and gave the seeds into Kane's hand for safekeeping.

He clenched the bag in his fist. Then he sniffed at the air and said, 'We'd better not linger. If a storm comes up, it would go badly for us.'

Soon enough, I thought, winter's storms would sweep down from the north and heap snow upon Telshar's summit, and bury the diamond-encrusted cairn, until spring uncovered it again. But now, here, at the top of the world, the sky was perfectly clear in every direction. Although it wasn't yet dark enough for the stars to come out, already in the east, above the mountains along the Culhadosh River, a great and glowing moon rose into the immense blue dome of the sky. To the south, far beyond Silvassu and the shining white granite of the castle, the verdant Lake Country opened up toward the Shoshan range, which curved fifty miles west and north around Lake Marash, forming a purple and white wall against the sweeps of the grassland beyond lost into the haze of the darkening distances. It seemed that from this great height, I could look down upon all of Mesh. The beauty of my land made we want to weep. Great swathes of color burst across the hills and valleys below: bands of yellow where the aspen trees edged up the mountains, and blazes of red, orange and green lower down. Scarely a stone's throw from Telshar, the deep cut in the earth of the Gorgeland showed the Arashar River's silvery sheen. I couldn't help wondering if I was seeing it for the last time.

'It's all so lovely,' Kane said, looking out toward the west. 'All of Ea, so lovely.'

I munched on an apple as I followed the line of his gaze. Beyond the mountains of my home, the Wendrush reached out into that part of the world where it seemed it was always night. For beyond the grasslands, nearly six hundred miles away, rose the Black Mountain called Skartaru.

'Some places on Ea,' I said to him, 'are less lovely than others.'

He smiled, showing his long, white teeth. Then he said, 'Surely you know that you haven't even a slim chance of slaying Morjin?'

'I know,' I told him. 'But before I die, I want him to feel what is inside me.'

'Then you hate him that much, eh?'

'Yes – don't you?'

'Hate him?' he cried out. He made a fist around a handful of snow, and his eyes burned like coals. 'So, I hate him as fire does wood, as steel does flesh. If I could, I'd cut off his head and crush it between stones like grain beneath a gristmill – then put a torch to the wound so that he couldn't grow another. I'd cut his body into pieces and feed them to the rats that infest his foul hole in the earth. I'd burn every book that mentions his name. No man deserves death more than he. And yet. And yet. He is a *man*, even as you are. He has hopes and dreams and a sense of how he might have been good, and might still be. You cannot defeat him if you can't understand this.'

I sat upon my lumpy rucksack as I dug my heels into the snow of Telshar's summit and listened to the wind. It was an incredible thing for him to tell me.

'Defeat him?' I said as I looked at him. 'I just want to fight him.'

'So, Val – so do I. To fight him and win.'

'But there is no winning,' I said. 'Once I thought there was, but I was wrong.'

'Were you? You nearly killed Morjin in his hall, and the day may come when you have that chance again.'

'No, he is too powerful now. And soon Angra Mainyu will stand beside him. No, there is no winning, not that way.'

'Then why fight at all?' he asked me.

'Because in just fighting,' I said, 'we win *something*. There's never a final victory, only the struggle to attain it. And *that* is the only virtue. It's the only way in which good can triumph.'

Kane lifted back his head and looked up at the night's first stars. A sudden coldness fell over him, and I felt his whole being trembling with longing for distant lights that would always remain just out of his reach.

'I believe,' he said to me in a strange, deep voice, 'in a victory so final and complete that even the stones buried miles down in the muck of the earth will sing with joy and light.'

I shook my head at this, not quite wanting to credit what I had just heard. And I blurted out: 'But evil can't be defeated!'

And he smiled and told me, 'Neither can good.'

Far below us, as night stole the light from the world and darkness crept across Mesh, the houses of Silvassu were beginning to glow a soft orange from candles and fires lit within. All across my beautiful land, mothers would be serving meals and weeping at the absence of their sons, and fathers would be raging at the fate of daughters carried away to Argattha.

'Morjin,' I said to Kane, 'is so evil.'

Again he surprised me, saying in a soft voice, 'But there are no evil men, Val. Only evil deeds.'

'Truly,' I said, 'but some men choose, again and again, to do the worst of deeds.'

'So – just so. And that is why we must strive, again and again, every moment, to do good.'

I looked past the castle and then toward the south at the darkening green of the Culhadosh Commons. I said, 'I've failed, too often.'

'So have I,' he told me.

'In Tria, I wanted so terribly to defeat him. And so I lied.'

'Morjin's whole life is a lie.'

'Yes,' I said. 'But we can't fight lies with lies, or hate with hate. Not unless we are to become like Morjin. And that is why he'll win.'

'No, he won't. He mustn't. Don't give up.'

'Sometimes,' I said, 'I don't care. I think of my grandmother and my mother, Estrella, too. And Atara – Atara. Suffering *is*. It's way the world will always be. And in the end, we all lose . . . everything. And so why should I care if I lie to gain advantage over our enemies or stab them in the back with a poisoned knife? Or torture them as they have me? Why should I care about anything at all?'

'Because if you don't,' he said, looking at me, 'you'll lose your soul.'

'Sometimes, I'm not sure I care about that, either.'

'So,' he told me. 'So it was with Morjin – and Angra Mainyu, too.'

I thought of Morjin as he once had been and perhaps still imagined himself to be: a man with golden eyes and a smile like the sun, beautiful in form and face. And now he was little more than sack of sickly flesh surrounding a core of corruption, foul dreams and a will to destroy his enemies that took its power from his terrible hate. The waste of it all made me want to weep. The anguish of his life built inside my chest with a sharp, pulsing pain that would not go away. And I hated myself for pitying, even for a moment, this dreadful man.

'I've been so close,' I said to Kane, 'too often, so terribly close.'

'So have I,' he told me.

'Why?' I said to him. 'Why do we choose what we choose?'

Although it was falling colder, with many stars now stabbing their bright, twinkling swords through the sky's blackness, he plunged his fingers down through the crusty old snow and seized a handful of it to hold it against his forehead. Then he stared down into the Valley of the Swans as if listening to all the sounds of the world.

And he said to me, 'Two wolves fight within your heart now. One wolf is vengeful and howls with hate. The other wolf is compassionate and wise.'

'Yes, that is true,' I said, pressing my palm against my chest. 'But which wolf will win the fight?'

'The one you feed.'

I, too, gazed down into the valley that had given me birth. The light of the stars and the rising moon showed a gentle and peaceful land of farm houses, fields and silent forests.

'So many dead,' I murmured, repeating these words like a chant. 'So many dead.'

Kane looked back at me and said, 'Sometimes the worst defeats open the door to the greatest victories.'

I rubbed the scar on my forehead against the hot, angry pain that burned into me there. 'You can say that because it wasn't *your* family that was lost.'

'All people are my family, Val.' Starlight rained down upon him, and his face seemed as sad and distant as the moon. 'And I've lost them a thousand times a thousand generations.'

His dark eyes drank me in, and I gasped to behold the unfathomable depths inside him. Everything was there: whirling constellations and blazing suns and worlds without end. The growling of a lion devouring his prey half-alive and the scream of a woman giving birth to her son. The song of a child singing to a butterfly. He grabbed my hand of a sudden, hard, and smiled as he held on to me with all his might. Something passed into me then. Not his unquenchable will to life, but a calling and quickening of my own.

I did not know if suffering could truly leave the soul open to more joy. But, like fire, it could burn away all of a man's conceits, desires and delusions so that only a greater and deeper will remained. Somewhere, in the charred ruins inside me, in the deepest chamber of my heart, there was a light. It blazed with all my will toward the beautiful, the good, the true. And, unless I let it, it could never go out.

'So many stars,' I said, looking up at the sky.

Their soft radiance bathed the cairn and all its rings in a silvery shimmer. Light poured down upon the mountain and touched its luminous fingers to the white granite of the Elahad castle and the white stones marking the place along the Kurash River where we had put my mother and grandmother, and everyone else Morjin had slaughtered, into the earth.

'So many stars.'

If I *did* feed the compassionate wolf, I wondered, what would it be? Only love.

'Father,' I whispered. 'Mother.'

As softly as I could, I spoke the names of Nona, Karshur, Yarashan, Jonathay, Mandru and Ravar. And Asaru. I listened for their voices in the rising wind.

And then, far below, a wolf called out its strange and beautiful song, and all my hatred left me.

I drew my sword then, and held it up toward the sky. It came alive with a light of its own, and it seemed both to feed the fire in the diamonds of the thousands of rings and to gather it back into itself. Alkaladur, the Sword of Sight, suddenly blazed as bright as the moon, the snow and the stars. And I saw, clearly, the whole design of my life, what I should have seen all along: tomorrow or the day following that, I would leave the Morning Mountains to seek the one they called the Lord of Light. My friends would come with me – all of them. As Kasandra had foretold, Estrella would show this Shining One to me, wherever he was. And then, some day, somehow, I would win back the Lightstone and place it in his hands.

We know, I thought, *we always know.*

And that was the great mystery of it all, that no matter our confusions and the lies we told ourselves, we always knew good from evil, right actions from wrong. And if only we had the courage to listen and follow our hearts, we might suffer or die, but we would never betray the great promise of life.

When I told this to Kane, he let loose a great howl of laughter and pressed the bag of astor seeds back into my hand. He leapt up, pulling me to my feet along with him. And he pointed above his head and told me, 'An eagle flies only as high as the sky. But a silver swan, reborn from its funeral pyre, flies to the stars.'

I could not share his joy at my decision. Tomorrow, I knew, or soon, in the days that were to come, I would hate again. I would kill, in fury, with my sacred sword. I would weep and rage and gnash my teeth at the terrible pain that would never go away. For that, too, was the mystery of life. But now I stood in the cold snow on top of a mountain in the deep of night. I felt the sighing of the fir trees below me and the very breath of the world rise in both mourning and exaltation. And then, for a moment, the souls of the dead bore me up like a great and beautiful swan toward the stars, and that was enough.

'Come,' Kane said to me, pulling at my hand. 'It's late and it's cold, and we've half a mile of a mountain to get down in the dark – it will go badly for us if we get lost.'

It was hardly dark, I thought. The moon illuminated Telshar's upper reaches and showed the track back down to our hut.

'We won't get lost,' I told him.

I bent to pick up the rope and tie it around my waist again. Then I turned to walk back down the mountain. I would wander my mother earth, always seeking my master, my brother, my other self who could hold the secret light in his hands. I would wander for a year or all the days of my life, never lost, knowing that the fiery and brilliant stars would always point the way.

APPENDICES

HERALDRY

THE NINE KINGDOMS

The shield and surcoat arms of the warriors of the Nine Kingdoms differ from those of the other lands in two respects. First, they tend to be simpler, with a single, bold charge emblazoned on a field of a single color. Second, every fighting man, from the simple warrior up through the ranks of knight, master and lord to the king himself, is entitled to bear the arms of his line.

There is no mark or insignia of service to any lord save the king. Loyalty to one's ruling king is displayed on shield borders as a field matching the color of the king's field, and a repeating motif of the king's charge. Thus, for instance, every fighting man of Ishka, from warrior to lord, will display a red shield border with white bears surrounding whatever arms have been passed down to him. With the exception of the lords of Anjo, only the kings and the royal families of the Nine Kingdoms bear unbordered shields and surcoats.

In Anjo, although a king in name still rules in Jathay, the lords of the other regions have broken away from his rule to assert their own sovereignty. Thus, for instance, Baron Yashur of Vishal bears a shield of simple green emblazoned with a white crescent moon without bordure as if he were already a king or aspiring to be one.

Once there was a time when all Valari kings bore the seven stars of the Swan Constellation on their shields as a reminder of the Elijin and Galadin to whom they owed allegiance. But by the time of the Second Lightstone Quest, only the House of Elahad has as part of its emblem the seven silver stars.

In the heraldry of the Nine Kingdoms, white and silver are used interchangeably as are silver and gold. Marks of cadence – those smaller charges that distinguish individual members of a line, house or family – are usually placed at the point of the shield.

Mesh

House of Elahad – a black field; a silver-white swan with spread wings
    gazes upon the seven silver-white stars of the Swan constellation
Lord Harsha – a blue field; gold lion rampant filling nearly all of it
Lord Tomavar – white field; black tower
Lord Tanu – white field; black, double-headed eagle
Lord Raasharu – gold field; blue rose
Lord Navaru – blue field; gold sunburst
Lord Juluval – gold field; three red roses
Lord Durrivar – red field; white bull
Lord Arshan – white field; three blue stars

Ishka

King Hadaru Aradar – red field; great white bear
Lord Mestivan – gold field; black dragon
Lord Nadhru – green field; three white swords, points touching upwards
Lord Solhtar – red field; gold sunburst

Athar

King Mohan – gold field; blue horse

Lagash

King Kurshan – blue field; white Tree of Life

Waas

King Sandarkan – black field; two crossed silver swords

Taron

King Waray – red field; white winged horse

Kaash

King Talanu Solaru – blue field; white snow tiger

Anjo

King Danashu – blue field; gold dragon
Duke Gorador Shurvar of Daksh – white field; red heart
Duke Rezu of Rajak – white field; green falcon
Duke Barwan of Adar – blue field; white candle
Baron Yashur of Vishal – green field; white crescent moon
Count Rodru Narvu of Yarvanu – white field; two green lions rampant

534

Count Atanu Tuval of Onkar – white field; red maple leaf
Baron Yuval of Natesh – black field; golden flute

FREE KINGDOMS

As in the Nine Kingdoms, the bordure pattern is that of the field and charge of the ruling king. But in the Free Kingdoms, only nobles and knights are permitted to display arms on their shields and surcoats. Common soldiers wear two badges: the first, usually on their right arm, displaying the emblems of their kings, and the second, worn on their left arm, displaying those of whatever baron, duke or knight to whom they have sworn allegiance.

In the houses of Free Kingdoms, excepting the ancient Five Families of Tria from whom Alonia has drawn most of her kings, the heraldry tends toward more complicated and geometric patterns than in the Nine Kingdoms.

Alonia

House of Narmada – blue field; gold caduceus
House of Eriades – Field divided per bend; blue upper, white lower; white star on blue, blue star on white
House of Kirriland – White field; black raven
House of Hastar – Black field; two gold lions rampant
House of Marshan – white field; red star inside black circle
Baron Narcavage of Arngin – white field; red bend; black oak lower; black eagle upper
Baron Maruth of Aquantir – green field; gold cross; two gold arrows on each quadrant
Duke Ashvar of Raanan – gold field; repeating pattern of black swords
Baron Monteer of Iviendenhall – white and black checkered shield
Count Muar of Iviunn – black field; white cross of Ashtoreth
Duke Malatam of Tarlan – white field; black saltire; repeating red roses on white quadrants

Eanna

King Hanniban Dujar – gold field; red cross; blue lions rampant on each gold quadrant

Surrapan

King Kaiman – red field; white saltire; blue star at center

Thalu

King Aryaman – Black and white gyronny; white swords on four black sectors

Delu

King Santoval Marshayk – green field; two gold lions rampant facing each other

The Elyssu

King Theodor Jordan – blue field; repeating breaching silver dolphins

Nedu

King Tal – blue field; gold cross; gold eagle volant on each blue quadrant

THE DRAGON KINGDOMS

With one exception, in these lands, only Morjin himself bears his own arms: a great, red dragon on a gold field. Kings who have sworn fealty to him – King Orunjan, King Arsu – have been forced to surrender their ancient arms and display a somewhat smaller red dragon on their shields and surcoats. Kallimun priests who have been appointed to kingship or who have conquered realms in Morjin's name – King Mansul, King Yarkul, Count Ulanu – also display this emblem but are proud to do so.

Nobles serving these kings bear slightly smaller dragons, and the knights serving them bear yet smaller ones. Common soldiers wear a yellow livery displaying a repeating pattern of very small red dragons. King Angand of Sunguru, as an ally of Morjin, bears his family's arms as does any free king.

The kings of Hesperu and Uskudar have been allowed to retain their family crests as a mark of their kingship, though they have surrendered their arms.

Sunguru

King Angand – blue field; white heart with wings

Uskudar

King Orunjan – gold field; $^3/_4$ red dragon

Karabuk
King Mansul – gold field; $^3/_4$ red dragon

Hesperu
King Arsu – gold field; $^3/_4$ red dragon

Galda
King Yarkul – gold field; $^3/_4$ red dragon

Yarkona
Count Ulanu – gold field; $^1/_2$ red dragon

THE GELSTEI

THE GOLD

The history of the gold gelstei, called the Lightstone, is shrouded in mystery. Most people believe the legend of Elahad: that this Valari king of the Star People made the Lightstone and brought it to earth. Some of the Brotherhoods, however, teach that the Elijin or the Galadin made the Lightstone. Some teach that the mythical Ieldra, who are like gods, made the Lightstone millions of years earlier. A few hold that the Lightstone may be a transcendental, increate object from before the beginning of time, and as such, much as the One or the universe itself, has always existed and always will. Also, there are people who believe that this golden cup, the greatest of the gelstei, was made in Ea during the great Age of Law.

The Lightstone is the image of solar light, the sun, and hence of divine intelligence. It is made into the shape of a plain golden cup because 'it holds the whole universe inside'. Upon being activated by a powerful enough being, the gold begins to turn clear like a crystal and to radiate light like the sun. As it connects with the infinite power of the universe, the One, it radiates light like that of ten thousand suns. Ultimately, its light is pure, clear and infinite – the light of pure consciousness. The light inside light, the light inside all things that *is* all things. The Lightstone quickens consciousness in itself, the power of consciousness to enfold itself and form up as matter and thus evolve into infinite possibilities. It enables certain human beings to channel and magnify this power. Its power is infinitely greater than that of the red gelstei, the firestones. Indeed, the Lightstone gives power over the other gelstei, the green, purple, blue and white, the black and perhaps the silver – and potentially over all matter, energy, space and time. The final secret of the Lightstone is that, as the very consciousness and substance of the universe itself, it is found within each human being,

538

interwoven and interfused with each separate soul. To quote from the *Saganom Elu*, it is 'the perfect jewel within the lotus found inside the human heart'.

The Lightstone has many specific powers, and each person finds in it a reflection of himself. Those seeking healing are healed. In some, it recalls their true nature and origins as Star People; others, in their lust for immortality, find only the hell of endless life. Some – such as Morjin or Angra Mainyu – it blinds with its terrible and beautiful light. Its potential to be misused by such maddened beings is vast: ultimately it has the power to blow up the sun and destroy the stars, perhaps the whole universe itself.

Used properly, the Lightstone can quicken the evolution of all beings. In its light, Star People may transcend to their higher angelic natures while angels evolve into archangels. And the Galadin themselves, in the act of creation only, may use the Lightstone to create whole new universes.

The Lightstone is activated at once by individual consciousness, the collective unconscious and the energies of the stars. It also becomes somewhat active at certain key times, such as when the Seven Sisters are rising in the sky. Its most transcendental powers manifest when it is in the presence of an enlightened being and/or when the earth enters the Golden Band.

It is not known if there are many Lightstones throughout the universe, or only one that somehow appears at the same time in different places. One of the greatest mysteries of the Lightstone is that on Ea, only a human man, woman or child can use it for its best and highest purpose: to bring the sacred light to others and awaken each being to his angelic nature. Neither the Elijin nor the Galadin, the archangels, possess this special resonance. And only a very few of the Star People do.

These rare beings are the Maitreyas who come forth every few millennia or so to share their enlightenment with the world. They have cast off all illusion and apprehend the One in all things and all things as manifestations of the One. Thus they are the deadly enemies of Morjin and the Dark Angel, and other Lords of the Lie.

THE GREATER GELSTEI

THE SILVER

The silver gelstei is made of a marvelous substance called silustria. The crystal resembles pure silver, but is brighter, reflecting even more light. Depending on how forged, the silver gelstei can be much harder than diamond.

The silver gelstei is the stone of reflection, and thus of the soul, for the soul is that part of man that reflects the light of the universe. The silver reflects and magnifies the powers of the soul, including, in its lower emanations, those of mind: logic, deduction, calculation, awareness, ordinary memory, judgment and insight. It can confer upon those who wield it holistic vision: the ability to see whole patterns and reach astonishing conclusions from only a few details or clues. Its higher emanations allow one to see how the individual soul must align itself with the universal soul to achieve the unfolding of fate.

In its reflective qualities, the silver gelstei may be used as a shield against various energies: vital, mental, or physical. In other ages, it has been shaped into arms and armor, such as swords, mail shirts and actual shields. Although not giving power *over* another, in body or in mind, the silver can be used to quicken the working of another's mind, and is thus a great pedagogical tool leading to knowledge and laying bare truth. A sword made of silver gelstei can cut through all things physical as the mind cuts through ignorance and darkness.

In its fundamental composition, the silver is very much like the gold gelstei, and is one of the two noble stones.

THE WHITE

These stones are called the white, but in appearance are usually clear, like diamonds. During the Age of Law, many of them were cast into the form of crystal balls to be used by scryers, and are thus often called 'scryers' spheres'.

These are the stones of far-seeing: of perceiving events distant in either space or time. They are sometimes used by remembrancers to uncover the secrets of the past. The kristei, as they are called, have helped the master healers of the Brotherhoods read the auras of the sick that they might be brought back to strength and health.

THE BLUE

The blue gelstei, or blestei, have been fabricated on Ea at least as far back as the Age of the Mother. These crystals range in color from a deep cobalt to a bright, lapis blue. They have been cast into many forms: amulets, cups, figurines, rings and others.

The blue gelstei quicken and deepen all kinds of knowing and communication. They are an aid to mindspeakers and truthsayers, and confer a greater sensitivity to music, poetry, painting, languages and dreams.

THE GREEN

Other than the Lightstone itself, these are the oldest of the gelstei. Many books of the *Saganom Elu* tell of how the Star People brought twelve of the green stones with them to Ea. The varistei look like beautiful emeralds; they are usually cast – or grown – in the shape of baguettes or astragals, and range in size from that of a pin or bead to great jewels nearly a foot in length.

The green gelstei resonate with the vital fires of plants and animals, and of the earth. They are the stones of healing and can be used to quicken and strengthen life and lengthen its span. As the purple gelstei can be used to mold crystals and other inanimate substances into new shapes, the green gelstei have powers over the forms of living things. In the Lost Ages, it was said that masters of the varistei used them to create new races of man (and sometimes monsters) but this art is thought to be long since lost.

These crystals confer great vitality on those who use them in

541

harmony with nature; they can open the body's chakras and awaken the kundalini fire so the whole body and soul vibrate at a higher level of being.

THE RED

The red gelstei – also called tuaoi stones or firestones – are blood-red crystals like rubies in appearance and color. They are often cast into baguettes at least a foot in length, though during the Age of Law much larger ones were made. The greatest ever fabricated was the hundred-foot Eluli's Spire, mounted on top of the Tower of the Sun. It was said to cast its fiery light up into the heavens as a beacon calling out to the Star People to return to earth.

The firestones quicken, channel and control the physical energies. They draw upon the sun's rays, as well as the earth's magnetic and telluric currents, to generate beams of light, lightning, heat or fire. They are thought to be the most dangerous of the gelstei; it is said that a great pyramid of red gelstei unleashed a terrible lightning that split asunder the world of Iviunn and destroyed its star.

THE BLACK

The black gelstei, or baalstei, are black crystals like obsidian. Many are cast into the shape of eyes, either flattened or rounded like large marbles. They devour light and are the stones of negation.

Many believe them to be evil stones, but they were created for a great good purpose: to control the awesome lightning of the firestones. Theirs is the power to damp the fires of material things, both living and living crystals such as the gelstei. Used properly, they can negate the working of all the other kinds of gelstei except the silver and the gold, over which they have no power.

Their power over living things *is* most often put to evil purpose. The Kallimun priests and other servants of Morjin such as the Grays have wielded them as weapons to attack people physically, mentally and spiritually, literally sucking away their vital energies and will. Thus the black stones can be used to cause disease, degeneration and death.

It is believed that that baalstei might be potentially more dangerous than even the firestones. For in the *Beginnings* is told of an utterly black place that is at once the negation of all things and paradoxically also their source. Out of this place may come the fire and light of the universe itself. It is said that the Baaloch, Angra Mainyu, before he was imprisoned on the world of Damoom, used a great black gelstei to destroy whole suns in his war of rebellion against the Galadin and the rule of the Ieldra.

THE PURPLE

The lilastei are the stones of shaping and making. They are a bright violet in hue, and are cast into crystals of a great variety of shapes and sizes. Their power is unlocking the light locked up in matter so that matter might be changed, molded and transformed. Thus the lilastei are sometimes called the alchemists' stones, according to the alchemists' age-old dream of transmuting baser matter into true gold, and casting true gold into a new Lightstone.

The purple gelstei's greatest effects are on crystals of all sorts: but mostly those in metal and rocks. It can unlock the crystals in these substances so that they might be more easily worked. Or they can be used to grow crystals of great size and beauty; they are the stone shapers and stone growers spoken of in legend. It is said that Kalkamesh used a lilastei in forging the silustria of the Bright Sword, Alkaladur.

Some believe the potential power of the purple gelstei to be very great and perhaps very perilous. Lilastei have been known to 'freeze' water into an alternate crystal called shatar, which is clear and as hard as quartz. Some fear that these gelstei might be used thus to crystallize the water in the sea and so destroy all life on earth. The stone masters of old, who probed the mysteries of the lilastei too deeply, are said to have accidentally turned themselves *into* stone, but most believe this to be only a cautionary tale out of legend.

THE SEVEN OPENERS

If man's purpose is seen as in progressing to the orders of the Star People, Elijin and Galadin, then the seven stones known as the openers might fairly be called greater gelstei. Indeed, there are those of the Great White Brotherhood and the Green Brotherhood who revered them in this way. For, with much study and work, the openers each activate one of the body's chakras: the energy centers known as wheels of light. As the chakras are opened, from the base of the spine to the crown of the head, so is opened a pathway for the fires of life to reconnect to the heavens in a great burst of lightning called the angel's fire.

Only then can a man or a woman undertake the advanced work necessary for advancement to the higher orders.

The openers are each small, clear stones the color of their respective chakras. They are easily mistaken for gemstones.

THE FIRST (also called bloodstones)

These are a clear, deep red in color, like rubies. The first stones open the chakra of the physical body and activate the vital energies.

THE SECOND (also called passion stones or old gold)

These gelstei are gold-orange in color and are sometimes mistaken for amber. The second stones open the chakra of the emotional body and activate the currents of sensation and feeling.

THE THIRD (also called sun stones)

The third stones are clear and bright yellow, like citrine; they open the third chakra of the mental body and activate the mind.

THE FOURTH (also called dream stones or heart stones)

These beautiful stones – clear and pure green in color like emeralds – open the heart chakra. Thus they open one's second feeling, a truer and deeper sense than the emotions of the second chakra. The fourth stones work upon the astral body and activate the dreamer.

THE FIFTH (also called soul stones)

Bright blue in color like sapphires, the fifth stones open the chakra of the etheric body and activate the intuitive knower, or the soul.

THE SIXTH (also called angel eyes)

The sixth stones are bright purple like amethyst. They open the chakra of the celestial body located just above and between the eyes. Thus their more common name: theirs is the power of activating one's second sight. Indeed, these gelstei activate the seer in the realm of light, and open one to the powers of scrying, visualization and deep insight.

THE SEVENTH (also called clear crowns or true diamonds)

One of the rarest of the gelstei, the seventh stones are clear and bright as diamonds. Indeed, some say they are nothing more than perfect diamonds, without flaw or taint of color. These stones open the chakra of the ketheric body and free the spirit for reunion with the One.

THE LESSER GELSTEI

During the Age of Law, hundreds of kinds of gelstei were made for purposes ranging from the commonplace to the sublime. Few of these have survived the passage of the centuries. Some of those that have are:

GLOWSTONES

Also called glowglobes, these stones are cast into solid, round shapes resembling opals of various sizes – some quite huge. They give a soft and beautiful light. Those of lesser quality must be frequently refired beneath the sun, while those of the highest quality drink in even the faintest candlelight, hold it and give back in a steady illumination.

SLEEP STONES

A gelstei of many shifting and swirling colors, the sleep stones have a calming effect on the human nervous system. They look something like agates.

WARDERS

Usually blood-red in color and opaque, like carnelians, these stones deflect or 'ward-off' psychic energies directed at a person. This includes thoughts, emotions, curses – and even the debilitating energy drain of the black gelstei. One who wears a warder can be rendered invisible to scryers and opaque to mindspeakers.

LOVE STONES

Often called true amber and sometimes mistaken for the second stones of the openers, these gelstei partake of some of their properties. They are specific to arousing feelings of infatuation and love; sometimes love stones are ground into a powder and made into potions to achieve the same end. They are soft stones and look much like amber.

WISH STONES

These little stones – they look something like white pearls – help the wearer remember his dreams and visions of the future; they activate the will to manifest these visualizations.

DRAGON BONES

Of a translucent, old ivory in color, the dragon bones strengthen the life fires and quicken one's courage – and all too often one's wrath.

HOT SLATE

A dark, gray, opaque stone of considerable size – hot slate is usually cast into yard-long bricks – this gelstei is related in powers and purpose, if not form, to the glowstones. It absorbs heat directly from the air and radiates it back over a period of hours or days.

MUSIC MARBLES

Often called song stones, these gelstei of variegated, swirling hues record and play music, both of the human voice and all instruments. They are very rare.

TOUCH STONES

These are related to the song stones and have a similar appearance. However, they record and play emotions and tactile sensations instead of music. A man or a woman, upon touching one of these gelstei, will leave a trace of emotions that a sensitive can read from contact with the stone.

THOUGHT STONES

This is the third stone in this family and is almost indistinguishable from the others. It absorbs and holds one's thoughts as a cotton garment might retain the smell of perfume or sweat. The ability to read back these thoughts from touching this gelstei is not nearly so rare as that of mindspeaking itself.

BOOKS OF THE SAGANOM ELU

Beginnings	Mendelin
Sources	Ananke
Chronicles	Commentaries
Journeys	Book of Stars
Book of Stones	Book of Ages
Book of Water	Peoples
Book of Wind	Healings
Book of Fire	Laws
Tragedies	Battles
Book of Remembrance	Progressions
Sarojin	Book of Dreams
Baladin	Idylls
Averin	Visions
Souls	Valkariad
Songs	Trian Prophecies
Meditations	The Eschaton

THE AGES OF EA

The Lost Ages (18,000 – 12,000 years ago)
The Age of the Mother (12,000 – 9,000 years ago)
The Age of the Sword (9,000 – 6,000 years ago)
The Age of Law (6,000 – 3,000 years ago)
The Age of the Dragon (3,000 years ago to the present)

THE MONTHS OF THE YEAR

Yaradar	Marud
Viradar	Soal
Triolet	Ioj
Gliss	Valte
Ashte	Ashvar
Soldru	Segadar